Praise for Ma

THE *Stone* THAT TF

"Extraordinary. . . . Exhilarating. . . . Bell's supple, exact prose . . . [has] hallucinatory force. . . . Almost every moment is full, like some great narrative painting, alive with the detail that puts you on the road or in the house where some murder or meeting is about to take place. . . . These books do what novels are meant to do: they propose their own vivid and inexorable history."
—*The New York Times Book Review*

"A towering work. . . . Bell has emerged as one of the most brilliant, artistic and daring historical novelists of our time, creating a vividly imagined, nearly week-by-week fictionalization of the bloody birth of a nation, synthesizing and transforming an enormous amount of research into tales that are extraordinarily empathetic and rich in emotions that range from hatred, fury, terror and bloodlust to humor, joy, ecstasy and love. He has brought messianic Toussaint L'Ouverture—a courageous warrior, master strategist and heroic champion of human rights—to vital and poignant life as no one has ever done before. . . . In sum, Bell has created that rarest of works, a masterpiece." —*Chicago Tribune*

"Bell uses fiction to take us where history books cannot go—into the thoughts and fears of the revolutionaries and plantation owners and those in between who got caught up in the riots and bloodshed. . . . These three novels succeed in redefining American cultural history in powerful and profound ways."
—*San Francisco Chronicle*

"Epic. . . . Heartbreaking. . . . Absorbing. . . . Strikingly rich detail. . . . Riveting and immensely satisfying. . . . A masterly piece of work." —*Fort Worth Star-Telegram*

"Astonishing. . . . Bell's immersion in the world he creates [is] so complete that . . . [it] has an osmotic effect. . . . It's hard to imagine that anyone could have chronicled Haiti and the travails of Toussaint with an eye more unblinking or with a hand so steady."
—*The Washington Post Book World*

"Breathtaking. . . . Bell has crafted such a profound page-turner, full of action and high drama. . . . A spectacular achievement."
—*The Miami Herald*

"Remarkable. . . . Bell is a gifted craftsman. . . . He's the sort of writer one can always turn to on faith; he seems incapable of writing an inelegant phrase. He captures the flavor of the island with depth and obvious love, including enough French and Creole for linguistic flavor, and interweaving English translations for clarity. The balance is close to perfect."
—*The Seattle Times*

"Dazzling. . . . With assiduousness that does not flag even through the most detailed of battle scenes, Bell has taken this shadowy historical figure and revealed what is essential, heroic and lasting in his legacy. . . . A masterpiece."
—*The Boston Globe*

"Powerful. . . . Bell manages both to render a readable narrative . . . and to use language with skill and beauty. . . . It's hard to say anyone is writing better."
—*Houston Chronicle*

"[Bell] has proved himself to be a master of historical fiction. . . . There is no question that this trilogy will make an indelible mark on literary history—one worthy of occupying the same shelf as Tolstoy's *War and Peace*. . . . No matter what readers take away from it . . . Bell has triumphed."
—*The Baltimore Sun*

"Breathtakingly successful on so many levels. . . . One wonders how the events of today will be drawn in two hundred years, if a writer should exist of Mr. Bell's masterful abilities."
—*New York Post*

"Riveting. . . . Bell's formidable achievement not only makes impressive literature, but he has managed to turn military, political and colonial history into such delicious reading that I found myself still going at 4 AM, unwilling to put sleep before pleasure."
—Annie Dawid, *The Oregonian*

"Triumphant. . . . By turns powerful and appalling. . . . Bell does a superb job with an incredible mass of material, but he never lets the material overwhelm the story. . . . [He] has created an amazing work of historical fiction."
—*The Tennessean*

Madison Smartt Bell

THE *Stone* THAT THE *Builder Refused*

Madison Smartt Bell is the author of fourteen works of fiction, including *Master of the Crossroads*; *All Souls' Rising*; *Save Me, Joe Louis*; *Doctor Sleep*; *Soldier's Joy*; and *Ten Indians*. He lives in Baltimore, Maryland, with his family and teaches at Goucher College.

Also by Madison Smartt Bell

THE *Stone* THAT THE
Builder Refused

To Mark Binky

Madison Smartt Bell

Vintage Books
A Division of Random House, Inc.
New York

FIRST VINTAGE BOOKS EDITION, FEBRUARY 2006

Copyright © 2004 by Madison Smartt Bell

All rights reserved. Published in the United States by Vintage Books,
a division of Random House, Inc., New York, and in Canada by Random House
of Canada Limited, Toronto. Originally published in hardcover in the
United States by Pantheon Books, a division of
Random House, Inc., New York, in 2004.

Vintage and colophon are registered trademarks of Random House, Inc.

Portions have previously appeared in the following publications:
Calabash, *Callaloo*, *Chattahoochee Review*, *Conjunctions*, *Five Points*,
Ginkgo Tree Review, *Idaho Review*, and *Virginia Quarterly Review*.

Permissions acknowledgments appear at the end of the book.

The Library of Congress has cataloged the Pantheon edition as follows:
Bell, Madison Smartt.
The stone that the builder refused / Madison Smartt Bell.
p.   cm.
1. Haiti—History—Revolution, 1791–1804—Fiction. 2. Toussaint Louverture,
1743?–1803—Fiction. 3. Slave insurrections—Fiction.
4. Revolutionaries—Fiction. 5. Generals—Fiction. I. Title.
PS3552.E517S69 2004
813'.54—dc22   2004040027

Vintage ISBN-10: 1-4000-7618-8
Vintage ISBN-13: 978-1-4000-7618-5

Map by Jeffrey L. Ward

www.vintagebooks.com

Printed in the United States of America
10 9 8 7 6 5 4 3 2 1

Moyse Dézo
Prann sa pou prinsip-O
M'ap poté dlo par kiyè pou plen kanari mwen

FOR ALL WHO WALK WITH THE SPIRIT OF TOUSSAINT
LOUVERTURE IN THE FIGHT FOR HAITI'S FREEDOM,
THEN AND NOW

The stone
that the builder refused
will always be
the head cornerstone.

—Bob Marley

Thanks to David Baker for patient, painstaking, and skillful work on these long and sometimes trilingual manuscripts.

Without Dan Frank, Jane Gelfman, Altie Karper, Suzanne Williams, and Sonny Mehta, I'd never have rolled this stone to the top of the hill.

To those who've helped me on my ways in and out of Haiti—Rolph Trouillot, Jean de la Fontaine, Gesner Pierre, Faubert Pierre, Lóló Beaubrun, Manzè Beaubrun, Guidel Présumé, Alex Roshuk, Handy Laporte, Robert Stone, Lyonel Trouillot, Michelle Karshan, Patrick Delatour, Eddy Lubin, Rachel Beauvoir, Nicolas Bussenius, Uriode Orelien, Abraham Joanis, Evelyne Trouillot, Rodney Saint Eloi, Georges Castera, Père Max Dominique, Père William Smarth, Marie-Claudette Edoissaint, Laetitia Schutt, Gerard Barthelmy, Richard Morse, Anne-Carinne Trouillot, Max Beauvoir, Bob Shacochis, Myrieme Millot-Colas, Ephèle Milcé, Tequila Minsky, Bob Corbett *ak tout moun nan Corbettland, tout moun nan Morne Calvaire, tout moun nan Lakou Jisou—m'ap di gran mèsi.*

To the spirit of Père Antoine Adrien, who put every day of his life on the line for Haiti's history and Haiti's future, *benediksyon pou moun k'ap goumen pou la jistis.*

CONTENTS

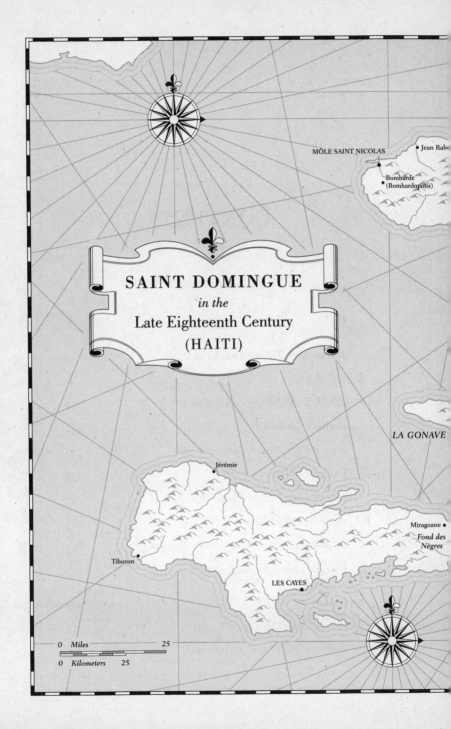

SAINT DOMINGUE
in the
Late Eighteenth Century
(HAITI)

MÔLE SAINT NICOLAS • Jean Rabe

Bombarde
(Bombardopolis)

LA GONAVE

Jérémie

Miragoane •
*Fond des
Nègres*

Tiburon

LES CAYES

0   Miles   25
0   Kilometers   25

PREFACE

In 1776 the American Revolution began in the guise of a tax revolt, while proclaiming self-evident natural rights to life, liberty, and the pursuit of happiness. In 1789 the French Revolution began as a violent class struggle, declaring an ideology of liberty, equality, and brotherhood among all men. That all *white* men were intended went without saying.

In 1791 what would become known as the Haitian Revolution began as a rebellion of African slaves against their white masters in the French colony of Saint Domingue. Ripples expanding from the French Revolution had begun reaching Saint Domingue two years before. The whites of the colony, who numbered some forty thousand, were bitterly divided between Jacobin Revolutionaries of the lower economic classes and the large property holders, who were more likely to be royalists and who hoped to make Saint Domingue a refuge for the *ancien régime*. These two classes agreed only on the absolute necessity of denying political rights to the people of mixed European and African blood who inhabited the colony. Many of these *gens de couleur*, as they were called, had been educated in Europe; many owned property and slaves themselves. Recognized as a third race under the French slave system, this group had begun, on the eve of the French Revolution, to agitate for political privileges to match its already considerable economic power. Repression from the whites (who had fathered this third race) was extraordinarily vicious. The first genocidal pogroms in Saint Domingue were conducted by whites against mulattoes in the mid-1780s. In 1790 a final mulatto uprising ended with the ringleaders, Ogé and Chavannes, being tortured to death in a public square in the town of Cap Français.

In 1791 there were about twenty-eight thousand free persons of color in Saint Domingue, or a little less than the number of whites. Both groups depended for their prosperity—in what had become France's richest colony and the source for much of Europe's sugar and coffee—on the labor of at least seven hundred thousand black slaves, of whom over half had been born in Africa. The conditions of slavery in Saint Domingue were so atrocious that the slave population did not reproduce itself—an importation of more than twenty thousand per year was necessary to maintain a stable work force. The fighting of the white slave masters among themselves and against the mulattoes took place within their view, while the revolutionary events in France and Europe were discussed within their hearing. The carelessness of the whites in this hazardous situation can only be explained by their belief that their slaves were something other and less than human.

The slaves set out to prove them wrong. By the autumn of 1791 most of the colony's vast sugar plantations had been destroyed by fire, a great many white colonists had been massacred, and many more had fled. Those who held on were isolated in the cities of the coast; the interior had become an anarchy traveled by roaming bands of rebel slaves. Over the next several years the situation of Saint Domingue degenerated into a three-way genocidal race war in which each race did everything in its power to exterminate the other two. Meanwhile the European powers—England, Spain, and France—circled the perimeter, hoping to regain a foothold.

On August 29, 1793, the same day that the French Revolutionary Commissioner Léger Félicité Sonthonax proclaimed the abolition of slavery in Cap Français, another proclamation issued from the camps of the rebel slaves in the mountains: "Brothers and Friends, I am Toussaint Louverture. My name is perhaps not unknown to you. I have undertaken to avenge you. I want liberty and equality to reign throughout Saint Domingue. I am working toward that end. Come and join me, brothers, and fight by our side for the same cause."

Since the fall of 1791, the man formerly known as Toussaint Bréda had been among the armed bands of rebel slaves in the interior—bands that were nominally in the service of the Spanish government in the eastern half of the island, though not under much actual Spanish control. Toussaint was over fifty years old when the first uprisings broke out. Born in slavery, he could read and write, had served as an overseer on Bréda plantation, and had some knowledge of both native and European medicine. He served the rebel leaders as a doctor first, then began to assemble his own fighting force—small at first, but unusually well trained and well disciplined. When he learned that the French National Assembly had abolished slavery, he turned on the other black leaders who were still in the service of royalist Spain, drove them over the border, and made himself master of the chain of mountain forts called the Cordon de l'Ouest, which controlled the passages between the Northern and Western Departments of Saint Domingue. That much accomplished, he offered his services to General Etienne Laveaux, who commanded for Revolutionary France in the colony.

Toussaint's *volte-face* turned what had seemed inevitable defeat for the French in Saint Domingue into victory. Acting as Laveaux's second-in-command, Toussaint repelled both Spanish and British invasions from the colony between 1794 and 1798. Laveaux hailed him as "the Black Spartacus," and made him Lieutenant Governor of Saint Domingue. Meanwhile, Toussaint proved himself to be as adept in politics as on the battlefield. Outmaneuvered by the black leader, Commissioner Sonthonax returned to France in 1797; Laveaux followed him not long after. A new commission headed by General Thomas Hédouville, sent to reassert the authority of the French government, succeeded only in fomenting a bloody civil war between the blacks led by Toussaint and the mulatto faction.

When Toussaint's forces had won this struggle, Toussaint stood unchallenged as the de facto ruler of Saint Domingue. He seems never to have intended to make the colony independent (when offered a British alliance if he would crown himself king, he refused it), but rather to govern it as a French protectorate. By 1801 he had done much to stabilize the war-ravaged territory and had made real progress in restoring the economy, inviting the exiled white planters, whose expertise was needed, to return and manage their properties with free labor. The foundation of a society based on liberty and on genuine equality and brotherhood among Saint Domingue's three races appeared to be in place. Toussaint consolidated these gains by creating a constitution for the colony which, among other things, appointed him governor for life, with the right to choose his own successor.

France, meanwhile, had passed through the Terror into reaction. When Toussaint sent his constitution to the capital for ratification, Napoleon Bonaparte, though not yet Emperor, ruled under the title of First Consul. The story that Toussaint began his letter to Napoleon with the phrase "from the first of the blacks to the first of the whites" is apocryphal, though inspired by real similarities between these two extraordinary self-made men, who each had risen to power through the military. Napoleon would certainly have recognized their likeness, though perhaps he was mistaken to measure Toussaint's ambition by his own. The strongest ideological objections to slavery had been swept away with the Terror, and Napoleon was under serious pressure to restore the slave system in the French colonies, from factions of dispossessed Caribbean planters who included his own consort, Josephine. No doubt his vanity was pricked by the temerity of Toussaint's constitution, which could easily have appeared to be a declaration of independence in all but name. But Napoleon was very much a pragmatist, and he saw the attraction of accepting Toussaint's cooperation so as to use his forces and the base of Saint Domingue not only to threaten the English in the Caribbean but also to secure or even expand the French presence on the North American continent, via Louisiana, then still a French possession. So the decision would not have been an obvious one for him.

THE *Stone* THAT THE

Builder Refused

Fort de Joux, France

October 1802

Toussaint sat hunched forward, consumed by his shadow, which the fire-light threw huge and dark and shuddering behind him on the glistening wall. He was cold, mortally cold, with his ague. Drawing closer about his shoulders the ratty wool blanket he'd taken from his cot, he thought of adding to the fire one of the three or four chunks of wood that remained in the cell. But his trembling would not permit this action. His teeth chattered with the vibration of his chill, so that the bad teeth in his injured jawbone shot a bolt of pain to the very top of his skull. The white flash seared away everything. He gripped the blanket closer to his throat and dug the fingertips of his free hand around the swelling of his jaw, containing the pain, compressing it.

His trembling stopped. So, apparently, did the cold. He felt a moment of equilibrium. The blanket slipped down on his shoulders. Experimentally he spread both arms. The shadow loomed, and startled him; he tilted slightly in his chair.

Baron de la Croix. Lord of the Cemetery . . . In a voice not his own he seemed to hear the whispered phrase *If it's not your time, Ghede won't take you.*

He gathered his feet beneath him, feeling capable now of a balanced movement, but before he could rise, the fever swelled into the space the chill had vacated. The blanket slithered down around his waist. He heard his voice, harsh and distant: *Tuez les responsables!* A log broke in the fireplace, gnawed to a spindle by the small blue flames, and red coals scattered on the hearth. Kill everyone responsible! His order had not been respected. He had lost the strength that would have carried him far enough to add a piece of wood to the fire. In any case the fever warmed him now. Sweat poured from his every crevice, pooling in the hollow of his throat. His firewood would not be resupplied till morning. He seemed to see the damp and anxious face of Baille, commandant of the Fort de Joux and Toussaint's jailer, muttering uneasy complaints about his use of firewood, sugar . . . The face dissolved into the fever and the long-winged shadow hovering on the seeping wall.

It was late morning when he woke, as he knew by the color of the light leaking in through the half-inch mesh of the grating; high under the vault at one end of the cell, it supplied his only traces of the light of day. The usual draught sucked through the space, flirting from the grating to the narrow crack beneath the door. He had slept considerably later than was his custom. While he was unconscious, they had come to bring more firewood and replenish his small store of food and water.

He got up slowly, bare toes freezing against the flagstones. The cold contact shocked him into brighter consciousness; he welcomed it for that. His joints ached, but for the moment he felt neither chill nor fever. That was well, though he knew that as the day wore on his symptoms might renew themselves.

He knelt on the hearth stones, uncovered the fading coals from the ash, and breathed on them till their life returned, then fed them with splinters till stronger flames began to rise. In one of his small, sporadic kindnesses, Baille had furnished a bag of cornmeal, knowing that Toussaint preferred this to oats. Boiling water in a small iron kettle, he made an adequate serving of mush. *Maïs moulin* . . .[1] there were no beans, and no hot peppers. Scarcely sugar or salt enough to give it any flavor at all. He ate dutifully, for the sake of his strength, his lucidity, and cleaned the bowl with a scrap of ship's biscuit, which was itself too hard for his shattered teeth to break. He held it in his mouth a long time while he thought.

A bell tolled in some distant tower of the Fort de Joux, and as if in answer a current of cold air swam through the cell. The beads of water on the inner wall, raw stone of the mountain, had taken on a pearly luminescence. It was months since Toussaint had left his cell, but the wind and the cold without had struck him when he'd first been brought here, though that was a milder season. Here in the Jura Mountains the peaks were snow-capped all summer long, and the wind cut and whistled like a whip.

---

[1] A glossary of French and Creole words begins on page 703.

He had marked the stones to count the days of his confinement; his mental calendar was clear. Twelve days since Bonaparte's agent, Caffarelli, had departed, bearing Toussaint's own memorandum to the First Consul. For the past four days, Toussaint had felt his anticipation of response spreading like an itch on saddle-chafed skin. As a general in the French army, he merited a reply from his ultimate superior. He was due his trial, his day in court; in justice he must pass before a tribunal. In the memorandum he had sent, the case was thoroughly presented. Blame for the war still rumbling in Saint Domingue, while Toussaint sat in this freezing cell, was shifted to Napoleon's brother-in-law, the Captain-General Leclerc, whom Bonaparte had sent to attack him without cause. Yes, without the least legitimate reason, when Toussaint Louverture had never faltered in his loyalty to France—and was recognized too, as Governor-General of the colony. If Leclerc had presented himself in a friendly fashion, instead of forcing his entry everywhere with cannon and sword, much bloodshed would certainly have been avoided.

At last the hardtack gave way and crumbled on his tongue. He swallowed, took a sip of water. The fire returned a faint warmth to the arches of his outstretched bare feet. With his thumb, he checked the corners of the three letters sewn into the lining of his coat. He'd asked Baille for a needle and thread to refasten some loose buttons. The jailer had consented, more than a little nervously, insisting on the return of the needle as if it might be used for a weapon or an instrument of escape. Here Toussaint had managed a small moral victory, transforming Baille's anxiety into humiliation and shame. Baille was not well fitted to the role assigned him; he had no natural strain of cruelty. An invisible chain bound him together with Toussaint, like two slaves in a coffle.

And still, Toussaint considered, more shame was due the men who had betrayed him . . . of the three letters snug in his coat lining, one, from Chief of Battalion Pesquidoux, was of small consequence. He had simply happened to receive it the same day as the other two . . . that last day.

The first from Leclerc—and this, after all difficulty had been smoothed between them. Toussaint had at last acknowledged the authority of the Captain-General, had formally retired both from the Governor-Generalship and the French army, and withdrawn with his family to his plantations surrounding Ennery. And yet the oily words of Leclerc still pursued him there: *Since you persist in thinking that the large number of troops now found at Plaisance are frightening the cultivators there, I have charged General Brunet to arrange the placement of a part of those troops with you . . .*[2]

This letter enclosed in another from Brunet:

---

[2] Source documents appear in the original language beginning on page 735.

Here is the moment, Citizen General, to make it known in an indis-
putable manner to the General in Chief that those who may have been
able to deceive him on the subject of your good faith are nothing
but miserable slanderers, and that your own sentiments have no
tendency but to restore order and tranquillity to the area where you
live. It is essential that you support me in this matter. We have, my
dear general, some arrangements to make together which cannot be
dealt with by letter, but which a conference of one hour would com-
plete. Were I not overcome by work and troublesome details, I'd be
today the bearer of my own response, but as I am unable to leave
these days, come to me yourself, and if you are recovered from your
indisposition, let it be tomorrow. One must never delay when it is
a question of doing good. You will not find, at my country planta-
tion, all the amenities I would wish to organize for your reception,
but you will find there the frankness of a gallant man who has no
other wish but for the prosperity of the colony and your own personal
happiness . . .

La bonne foi, indeed. Toussaint sniffed and leaned sideways to spit
through the gap in his front teeth onto the ashes in the hearth. Good
faith . . . that Brunet and Leclerc should soil that phrase with their
duplicitous tongues. Or Napoleon Bonaparte himself, for that matter. To
whom Toussaint had appealed, most recently, for not only justice but
mercy.

He stretched his hands toward the fire, palms down, seeking what
heat still rose from the fading embers. A glance at the woodpile, so mea-
gerly replenished, let him know that he must not build it higher, since
this small store must be eked out for all of the day and the evening. But
more than the cold, it was the constant damp which troubled him. He
released a wet cough from the ache in his chest, and glanced over his
shoulder at the pearlescent, oozing wall. It seemed to him that his left
hand grew slightly warmer than his right. With an effort of his will, he
stopped both hands from trembling.

His memorandum, that legal résumé of his self-justification and
self-defense, had been penned to his dictation by a secretary procured by Baille. At the last minute, after the secretary had departed,
Toussaint had added a final note in his own hand, his own uncertain orthography, before finally presenting the packet to Caffarelli for
delivery:

Premier Consul, Père de toutes les militre. De fanseur des inno-
sant, juige integre, prononcé dont sure un homme quie plus malheure
que couppable. Gairice mes plai, illé tre profonde, vous seul pour-
ret poeter les remede, saluter et lan pé ché de ne jamai ouver, vous
sete medecien, ma position et mes service mérite toute votre a tan-

tion et je conte an tierment sur votre justice et votre balance. Salut et respec.[3]

Toussaint Louverture

As he ran over those words in his mind, it seemed to him that his wounds must all reopen. To dwell upon thoughts such as these was to call the spirit of Ezili Jé Rouge, enraged with the bitterness of her losses and the terrible betrayals she had suffered. With her nails and her teeth she would tear at her clothing and the ground where she crouched, lay open her own cheeks in bloody furrows, and otherwise rend the flesh of the postulants she possessed.

But Toussaint never walked with Ezili Jé Rouge. Ezili Fréda he had sometimes known, the sponsor of love, who bore the great wound in her heart with patience and devotion. If he trusted Caffarelli in little else, Toussaint did trust him to deliver the letter he had written to Suzanne. Which by this time he must have done, so that even now it might be in her hands.

Ma cher Epouse,

Je profite l'occasions dunt bon général pour vous donné mé nouvel. J'ai été malade an narrivant ici, mais le commandant de cet place qui et un homme umain ma porté toute les cecours possible; grâce à Dieu, sa va beaucoup mieu; vous savé mon namitier pour ma famille et mon nattachement pour une femme que je chéris, pour quoi mavé vous pas donné de vos nouvel.

Bon jour à toute pour moi. Je les pryer d'être bien comporté, beacoup de sageste, et la vertus. Je vous sé déjà dire que vous sète responsable de lheure conduite devant Dieu et à votre maris, mandé moi ci Placide et tavec vous.

Je vous sanbras tout tandrement. Je suis pour la vis votre fidèle époux.[4]

Toussaint Louverture

[3] First Consul, Father of all soldiers. Defender of the innocent, honest judge, pronounce on the case of a man who is more unfortunate than guilty. Heal my wounds, it is very deep, you alone can bring remedies, heal and prevent them from ever opening, you are the doctor, my position and my service deserve all your attention and I depend entirely on your justice and your measure. Salutations and respect.

[4] My Dear Wife,

I profit from the occasion of the good general to give you my news. I was sick when I arrived here, but the commander of this place, who is a humane person, has brought me all possible aid; thanks be to God I'm doing much better; you know my friendship for my family and my attachment to the woman I love, why have you not given me your news.

Then it seemed that Suzanne was near him for a moment, without the bars and the frozen stone walls and the free-falling descents from the cliffs of these Jura Mountains. He calmed, and a generous glow of warmth spread below his breast bone. The dangerous spirit of self-destruction had withdrawn. Without emotion, he recalled Blanc Casse-nave, who'd died in the jail where Toussaint had sent him, so furious at the injustice he felt he'd received that his heart had exploded in his chest. But it was he himself, and not Toussaint, who'd broken faith and turned to treachery—Blanc Cassenave died by the work of his own hands.

The warmth enclosed him now, embraced the surface of his skin. His arms sank down, hands dangling from the wooden arms of his chair. Though the pressure grew uncomfortable on his upper arms, he was not inspired to alter his position. Again he felt Suzanne's near presence, stirring *soupe giraumon* in the dooryard of the little house they'd shared at Bréda long ago. He smelled the soup and heard the little cocks so proudly crowing on the slopes of Morne du Cap, and he could hear his three sons breathing near him in the darkness before dawn.

His head snapped back. Before him on the wall appeared the face of a black man, a strong face struggling under terrible duress, cords in his neck stretched to the limit and the eyes and teeth a white rictus of tor-ment and pain. Dieudonné. This was Dieudonné, he knew, though he had never seen his face. His undoing had been accomplished through intermediaries, and at a distance of many miles (though not so long as the distance between Saint Domingue and France). Dieudonné would have taken the ten thousand men he led to join the English invaders at Port-au-Prince (such had been the appearance of the thing), but instead he was betrayed by one of his own seconds and delivered to the mulatto general Rigaud in the south, then locked in a prison where, the story had come back long afterward, he suffocated slowly beneath a weight of chains.

All this was only fever dream. Carefully, Toussaint brought his aching head upright. The tortured face had faded from the wall, and if its glistening surface now resembled the mirrored face of a calm sea, that too was an illusion of his fever.

Receding now, though the pain in his head was worse. The castle bell had been tolling but he had not counted the strokes. The clock on the shelf, notoriously unreliable, read half-past four.

And if the spirit of Dieudonné had risen from beneath the waters to confront him, then? Dieudonné had been free to choose. The choice had been laid plain before him by a letter from Toussaint. *Quand il s'agit*

Hello to everyone from me. I beg them all to behave themselves, lots of prudence and the virtues. I have already told you that you are responsible for their conduct before God and your husband, let me know if Placide is with you.

I kiss you with all tenderness. I am for life your faithful husband.

de faire le bien on ne doit jamais retarder. If he had not hesitated, all might have come out otherwise. And Dieudonné was not alone. There were others, many others: Rigaud himself, Joseph Flaville, Toussaint's adopted nephew Moyse in all his terrible particulars. Each and every one of them the author of his own doom.

Toussaint had reached an islet of stability somewhere amid the ocean of his fever. He crouched and blew the dormant coals to life and built the fire to a considerable brightness. There was now just a little fuel to spare, since during his delirium he'd used none.

However, he must make good use of the present interval of lucidity. He warmed his hands till they flexed easily, then pushed himself upright and went to the small square table. The writing implements were still at hand, though the secretary had long since departed. He arranged the pen, the ink, the paper, and sat for a moment looking down on them.

He would not allow the spirit of embitterment to devour him. Between betrayer and betrayed it was equal in the end, when they should come together beneath the *mapou* tree, or when the crossroads sprang upright before their faces, for their judgment . . . The truth was that Toussaint had known, when he kept his rendezvous with Brunet, what would follow. Or it seemed to him now that he had known then, just as, when he first saw Leclerc's great fleet assembling off Point Samana, he had known the secret orders of the First Consul which it bore—orders to which only Leclerc and a very few of his entourage had been privy. As he knew also, certainly enough, the outcome of his present situation.

In the end it was all one. And now there was one more letter to write. He lit the stub of candle affixed to the table top by its own melted wax, dipped the pen in the ink and began.

Au Cachot du Fort de Joux, ce 17 Vendémiaire

Je vous pri au nom de Dieu au nom de l'humanité de jai té un cou deuille favorable sur ma réclamation, sur ma position et ma famille, employé votre Grand Génie sur ma conduite, sur la mannière que je servis ma patris, sur toutes les dangés que je courir an faisant ma devoire, j'ai servis ma patrie avec fidelité et probité jai les servis avec zèlle et courage, et jai été devoué à mon gouvernement. J'ai sacrifié mon sant et emporté ce que je pocede pour la servire et malgré mes séfort tous mé travaux a été envin, vous me permettrai premiere consul de vous dire avec tout les respec et las soumition que je vous doit: le Gouvernement a été tromppé entièrement sur le conte de Toussaint Louverture, sur une de cé plus zellé et couragé serviteurs à Saint Domingue. J'ai travaillé depuis lontans pour aquiérire l'honneur et la gloire de mon gouvernement et atire lestime de mes concitoien, et je suis aujourd'hui couronné des sépines et lingratitude le plus marqué pour recompence, et je ne desavoue pas les fautes que je pourais faire et je vous sant fait mé excuse, mais ce parti ne vaut les care de la punition que je reçu ni les traitement que jai essuies: premier Consul, il est mal heureux pour moi, denet pasconnus de vous, ci vous mavé connus au fon pendant que jai été à Saint Domingue, vous ceré tranquil sur mon conte et me rendré plus de justice, mon interrieur est Bon.[5]

And here he faltered. It seemed to him that if only his accuser, judge, could see him face-to-face and know him to the core, then the future would be redeemed. This thought was the very truth, he felt, and at the same time illusion of his fever. The words were squirming on the page like knots of insect larvae, the whole room rocked to the rhythm of the wooden ship that had conveyed him into this cold land. Carefully he laid the pen aside, so as not to blot his paper, leaned back and let the fever take him.

[5] From the Dungeon of the Fort de Joux
October 8,
I beg you in the name of God in the name of humanity to cast a favorable glance on my claim, on my position and my family, apply your Great Genius to my conduct, to the manner in which I have served my country, to all the risks I have run in doing my duty, I have served my country with faithfulness and honesty, I have served them with zeal and courage, and I have been devoted to my government. I have sacrificed my health and spent all I possessed to serve it and in spite of my efforts all my works have been in vain, you will allow me first consul to tell you with all the respect and submission that I owe you: the Government is entirely mistaken on the subject of Toussaint Louverture, on one of the most zealous and courageous servants of Saint Domingue. I have worked for a long time to win honor and glory for my government and to attract the esteem of my fellow citizens, and today I am crowned with thorns and the most marked ingratitude for my compensation, and I don't deny the mistakes I may have made and I make my excuses to you for them, but that part doesn't deserve the [severity] of the punishment I have received or the treatment which I suffer: first Consul, it is unfortunate for me that I am not personally known to you, if you had known me to the depths while I was in Saint Domingue, you would be at peace on my account and would render me more justice; my interior is Good.

Part One

DEBAKMEN

December 1801–February 1802

J'ai à me reprocher une tentative sur cette colonie, lors du consulat; c'était une grande faute que de vouloir la soumettre par la force; je devais me contenter de la gouverner par l'intermédiaire de Toussaint.

—Napoleon Bonaparte,
Mémorial de Saint-Hélène

I have to reproach myself for an attempt on that colony during the Consulate; it was a big mistake to want to subdue it by force; I ought to have contented myself with governing it through the intermediary of Toussaint.

I

James Howarth, captain of the *Merry Bell*, rolled sideways to the edge of his hospital cot and heaved black bile into the gourd *coui* which Zabeth held trembling beneath his wide-strained jaws. Doctor Hébert leaned forward to steady her, a hand on her spine. When Captain Howarth had done vomiting and collapsed onto the cot, the doctor took the stinking gourd from her hands.

"Give him the tea," he told her, leaning to wipe a thread of the bloody vomit from the patient's chin. Zabeth rose, her head lowered, and walked out into the hospital courtyard, where the infusion simmered over a charcoal brazier. The doctor watched her with a mild dissatisfaction. Her legs moved jerkily, stiff from fear. Zabeth was an excellent nurse for almost any illness, but not for *mal de Siam*, the yellow fever.

He carried the gourd out of the hospital enclosure and emptied it into the ravine behind the wall. Used for the dumping of various ordures, the ravine was slightly fetid, especially in this season, when rainfall was thin. Bad air. It was a fault in the location of the hospital, though otherwise the place was good, high on a generally windswept slope at the upper edge of the town of Cap Français. In this still weather, though, the ravine bred mosquitoes. Irritably the doctor pinched one from the hollow of his throat, rubbing his thumb and forefinger together till the blood splotch came away in brownish crumbs.

When he returned to the hospital gate, he saw with relief that Guiaou was just coming in, accompanied by the three women he'd brought to help him through the night. Guiaou had lately been promoted corporal in the honor guard of Governor-General Toussaint Louverture, but he was willing to spend many of his off-duty hours tending the hospital in order to earn something extra for his family. Doctor Hébert had trained him as an assistant on various battlefields of the recent wars and had a perfect confidence in him. There was no disease that gave him pause; Guiaou feared nothing except water.

The doctor glanced once more into the dormitory. Captain Howarth lay quiescent, flanked by three of his crewmen and the second officer of the *Merry Bell*. They'd all fallen ill the day after the trading packet moored in Le Cap harbor, following a zigzag voyage up the Windward Islands from the South American continent and the Orinoco River. Two of the crew were barely breathing; the doctor doubted they would last the night.

He beckoned to Zabeth and led her from the hospital. Guiaou appeared to bolt the gate behind them. The doctor reached through the bars and touched the back of Guiaou's hand; the two of them exchanged a glance and a nod. It was not the first death watch he'd shared with Guiaou, but somehow he was particularly grateful to be relieved of this one.

He walked down the sloping street from the hospital, stealing the odd glance at Zabeth, who came a pace or two behind. *Don't be afraid*, he wanted to tell her. He had already told her that. About ten years earlier, when still in her teens, Zabeth had survived a bout of yellow fever, the same that had killed among others the doctor's brother-in-law Martin Thibodet. Zabeth had nearly died herself—as had the doctor when his turn to take the fever came a couple of years later. But those few who lived would not fall prey to the same disease again; it was not like malaria, which revisited its sufferers often enough. The doctor was sure of that and that alone. It was almost all he understood of *la fièvre jaune*, but his own experience proved it well enough. He had announced the point to Zabeth several times and explained that her survival and immunity was the exact reason he had chosen her to nurse these men.

The explanation had not reassured her. However, the farther they got from the hospital, the more her hips and back and shoulders relaxed, until she had resumed that smoothly flowing, floating gait, so beautiful in the black and colored women of the colony. Glancing back at her, the doctor thought with a slight pang of his own wife. But he had sent her with the children over the mountains to Ennery, the moment he'd recognized these sailors' fever for what it was.

"*M'ap rantré*," Zabeth said. I'm going in. She paused on the corner of the street which led in the direction of the house the doctor was currently sharing with his sister, Elise.

"Tell my sister I will be there within the hour," Doctor Hébert said. Picking up his pace, he went on down the hill, turning his face into the breeze that blew back from the harbor. He emerged on the waterfront near the customs house, which was just shutting its doors for the night. Beyond the shelter of the buildings the wind was stiff indeed; he took off his hat and held it fluttering in his hand as he walked into the wind down toward the battery of the Carénage. The wind whipped his few remaining strands of hair around his bare sun-freckled crown, and stuffed wisps of his beard, which wanted trimming, into the corners of his mouth. He continued until he came to the fountain at the end of the esplanade, then stopped and turned to face the wide oblong of the harbor.

Black mouths of cannon poked from the embrasures of the Carénage battery, aimed fanwise across the water. The *Merry Bell* was moored far out, beyond the reef, the colors of the North American Republic just discernible to the naked eye. She had already exchanged her cargo, but would not put to sea without her captain. Doctor Hébert had ordered the ship quarantined as soon as he'd remarked the yellow fever. His close relationship to Toussaint Louverture gave him the power to enforce such measures, though he had no official function in the port.

By irony, the *Merry Bell* had brought him out of South America a substantial shipment of cinchona bark. At first the doctor had taken it for Providence, when the men from the ship began to fall ill, and had so informed James Howarth. The bitter brew of cinchona bark was almost magically effective against malaria in the early stage. He'd begun the treatment straight away, but a day or so later, when his patients suddenly turned yellow, he'd known it to be useless. Therefore he had substituted *herbe à pique,* an herb he'd learned long ago from Toussaint to be effective in many fevers. It too was useless against *la fièvre jaune* but could be harvested locally, unlike the precious cinchona. It was necessary to give the sick men something to shield them from despair.

Then the black vomiting had begun. Such was always the course of the yellow fever. A man would reduce his bulk by half before he died, in three days or two or sometimes one. Or if he lived. The difference lay in the will to live and the grace of God.

Above Fort Picolet, a great frigate bird was wheeling against the rapidly paling sky. The doctor's spirits lifted when he saw it. It was rare to see one of these huge birds so close to land, and somehow it felt to him like a good omen. Then a huge wave slapped against the pilings, showering him with spray, and he let the dousing chase his frustration with the fever from his mind. Turning his back to the wind, he walked back in the direction he had come, whitecaps hurrying behind him over the water.

When he reached the townhouse he shared with his sister, he found her in the company of her bosom friend, Isabelle Cigny. No surprise, for her own house was just around the corner. Till recently, both he and

Elise had used the Cigny residence as their base when in Le Cap. But two months ago, Elise, who enjoyed a considerable inheritance from her late husband Thibodet, had purchased the present house at a very advantageous price; it had been left vacant by the demise of one of the colored gentlemen who had for a season ruled the town, but had then been so unwise as to mount a rebellion against Toussaint Louverture and his overwhelming black armies.

Isabelle turned her bright black eyes on the doctor the moment he walked in. "What news?" she cried, flirting her skirts around her hips as she rose and resettled herself. The doctor smiled on her; he and Isabelle had been friends for most of a decade, but her coquetry was automatic.

"The men from the *Merry Bell* are like to die, I think, by morning," he advised her, dropping his weight into a wooden chair in a corner of the half-furnished room. "Except the captain—he may live. I hope so, for I rather liked him."

"I share your wish, of course," said Isabelle, and tapped her slippered foot in token of impatience. "But what interests me more is news of the port."

"Ah," said the doctor, turning toward Zabeth, who had just entered the room with a tray bearing a concoction of rum, lime juice, and sugar, and a letter from his son Paul at Ennery. He took the drink and smoothed the letter on his knee.

"No news," he said. "You must not worry."

"It has been weeks!" Isabelle protested.

"Yes," Elise put in. "But you know Xavier. His routes are ever indirect." It was the sort of thing she would normally say with fondness, but tonight there seemed a bitter flavor to it. Isabelle had noticed it too, the doctor thought, for at once she dropped her own subject and began to chatter of fabric for curtains and the possibility of imported paper for the walls.

It was the new prosperity—new security really—that had moved Isabelle to send for her children, who had these last few years been sheltered from the turbulence of Saint Domingue in a boarding school at Philadelphia. But Isabelle's husband was not free to fetch them, and for some reason she had not elected to make the voyage herself. Xavier Tocquet, who was Elise's current husband, had volunteered to escort the children. It appeared that he had some business with certain Philadelphia factors, whose nature was not yet precisely known.

The doctor took a long pull at his rum, then broke the seal of his letter and unfolded it. His eldest, Paul, was eight years old. His formal education had been scattershot thus far. Sessions with the village priest at Ennery. There was a regular school here in Le Cap, but his attendance was sporadic since he was often absent in the country. The doctor supervised him intermittently, as he had time. His mother, Nanon, could read reasonably well but her writing ability was negligible. However, it had been her idea that Paul must write and send a weekly letter to his father whenever they were parted.

The boy's penmanship was passable, his spelling insecure. He conveyed the news in a sufficiently engaging manner. Their trip over the mountains had passed easily. They'd arrived at Ennery with a great supply of cassava and fruit collected along the way. Paul had reconnected with his great friend Caco, a black boy a couple of years older who lived on the plantation at Ennery. But Caco, because of the new work codes lately issued by Toussaint, was obliged to devote part of his time to either the cane fields or the coffee. Paul had followed him for a day or so. He found both occupations disagreeable, the coffee somewhat less so. There was to be a *bamboche* on Saturday, with pigs killed for the *boucan*. Paul's younger twin siblings were well. Likewise his mother and his cousin Sophie, Elise's child. Paul sent his kisses to his honorable father . . .

"A good report of the twins," the doctor said, passing the letter to Isabelle, "if not especially detailed."

Isabelle snapped the letter open on her crossed knee and scanned it rapidly for the mention of François and Gabriel, relaxing perceptibly when she had found their names. Elise cocked an eyebrow at her, but she did not seem to notice. The doctor sipped his rum. When Isabelle had read the whole letter through, she leaned to give it back to him.

"He writes appealingly, your boy."

The doctor nodded as he swallowed. "And never mind the spelling."

Zabeth came in, bearing Elise's year-old baby, asleep on her full bosom. She passed the infant Mireille to her mother, who accepted the bundle absently. Zabeth turned toward the doctor's empty glass.

"I'll just come with you," he said, standing up to follow her from the room.

Zabeth's own infant slept in a basket in the pantry at the rear of the house. While Zabeth prepared his second drink, the doctor stooped to peer at him. The child was vigorously healthy, substantially bigger and more robust than his nursing partner. The father was dead, executed by Toussaint the previous fall for some military infraction. Because the two babies were roughly of an age, Elise had turned her own over to Zabeth to wet-nurse. By virtue of Zabeth's excursions to the hospital, the babies were beginning to be weaned.

"What time is supper?" he inquired, rising to accept the freshened glass.

"Oh, I don't know," Zabeth said, mildly flustered. "Madame said she will go out, and perhaps you with her? But I will speak to the cook, what will you take? There is either fish or chicken."

"Chicken," the doctor said. When he returned to the parlor, Isabelle

was standing to make her farewells. She teased the baby's chin with a fingernail, exchanged a maternal glance with Elise, kissed the doctor on
both cheeks, and then went out.

"Now then," Elise said, giving him a measuring glance. "Your beard is
a bit bedraggled, sir."

The doctor took a great gulp of his drink. "It's hardly worth troubling
a barber with the few hairs which remain on my head," he said.

"Perhaps you're right," his sister returned. "But just you come with
me."

In her boudoir, Elise laid the baby on the bed and hemmed her in with
cushions. Mireille mewed and smacked her lips, but did not wake. Elise
motioned the doctor to a chair by the french doors onto the balcony—
there was still enough light in the sky to see clearly there.

"Now then." She extracted a small pair of scissors from an enameled
necessary box. "Be still." For a moment she clipped in silence. Then—"I
wish you would excuse Zabeth from the hospital."

"Well, if you—"

"*Don't* talk—I'll nick you if you wag your jaw." She flashed the scis-
sors. "Mireille is restless in the daytime when Zabeth is gone. And
Zabeth is so fearful of the fever, no matter what you say. You know it
upset her terribly when Toussaint ordered Bouquart to shoot himself.
Here, turn your head this way. *This* way . . . Perhaps they ought to go to
Ennery with the other children."

"Oh indeed, if you think it best . . ." the doctor began. This had been
his own original suggestion, when the yellow fever first appeared among
the crew of the *Merry Bell*, but Elise had not wanted to be parted from
Mireille. "And would you go with them, then?"

Elise drew back to study him, scissors poised. "You are presentable,"
she declared. She put the scissors away in the box, and went to her dressing table to light the two candles either side of the mirror, for the room
was rapidly growing dim.

"No, I don't think I will go to Ennery just now," she said. "Not when I
expect my husband hourly into port." The wry expression accompanying
those last words brought out faint wrinkles at the corners of her mouth,
which the doctor could see in the reflection. Elise must have noticed
them too. She brushed at them with powder.

"You're going out, I gather." The doctor touched a fingertip to the
shortened hairs of his beard.

"The *soirée* at Government House," Elise said, catching his eye in the
mirror. "Will you come?"

"No, I think not, not tonight. It has been a weary day at the hospital.
They are already stewing me a chicken here."

Elise had stopped listening. She adjusted her *décolletage* in the mirror,
then returned her attention to her face. Though the flush of her youth
was gone, she was certainly still a handsome woman, her natural graces

now requiring just the slightest, most subtle assistance of art. The doctor was reluctant to disrupt her concentration. Much as he tried not to think about it, he knew very well she had recently taken a lover.

"*Madame ma sœur,*" he said hesitantly. "It strikes me that you have chosen a very dangerous *divertissement* . . . and for so many reasons."

"Reasons for the danger, you mean?" Elise made another minute adjustment to her bosom before rotating on her stool to face him. It was to preserve that asset that she'd elected not to nurse her second child herself. "Or the reasons for my choice of diversion?"

The doctor, who felt he had already overspoken, said nothing more.

"Well then," Elise said, snuffing the candles decisively as she rose to leave the room, "don't let us dwell on it."

As was his habit on any ordinary day in town, the doctor rose just at first light, took nothing but coffee as his morning refreshment. He'd arrived at the hospital gate by the time the sun began to spread fingers of light down the sloping street from the mountain above. Two corpses lay on planks under the tall palms of the enclosure, covered with a single sheet of sailcloth.

"I will send for the cart from La Fossette as I go down," Guiaou told him.

The doctor inclined his head, and touched the black man on the shoulder as he went out the gate. As the hoofbeats of Guiaou's horse receded over the paving stones, he lifted the canvas from the stiffened visages of the two dead crewmen, then let it fall.

In the dormitory the ship's second officer still tossed in delirium. One of the night-shift women stayed by him. Captain Howarth and the surviving crewman slept calmly. The doctor touched Howarth's head and hands, then took his pulse, which had slowed remarkably. The night-shift woman watched the procedure, her eyes grave below the crisp line of her white headcloth. The doctor nodded to her and let out a sigh that almost amounted to relief.

When he heard the creaking wheels of the cemetery cart, he went out to supervise the loading of the bodies. He directed that they should be buried deep—futile instruction for La Fossette, a swampland where the single length of a shovel blade was likely to strike water.

Captain Howarth sat propped on a bolster when the doctor returned to the dormitory, sipping from a cup of tea his own hands now had strength to hold. His eyes were very weary, ringed with shadow, but looked clear.

"I think you've saved my life," he said, and raised his cup a quarter inch in token of a toast.

"Not so," the doctor said. "You must give thanks to God, and the strength of your own constitution."

Captain Howarth looked at him narrowly. "Are you a religious man?"

"Sometimes," the doctor said, inclining his head toward the sunlight that now streamed over the doorsill. "When I see miracles."

In the following days, both Captain Howarth and the third crewman rallied rather quickly, while the second officer passed through the crisis of the fever and looked likely to recover altogether. Doctor Hébert took private note that this rate of recovery was quite unusual for the disease in question, and that he had no idea what had brought it about. Mid-week, Captain Howarth had himself rowed out to the *Merry Bell*, where he learned that all surviving members of his crew were sound. Unlikely there would be an epidemic in the town. Lifting the quarantine, the doctor breathed out the last vapor of his relieved sigh.

By Friday, he pronounced Captain Howarth fit to attend one of the evenings at Government House, about which the American had expressed great curiosity. At this good news Isabelle Cigny claimed Howarth as her escort, since her husband would give little time to such social exercises, and in any case was absent from the town, tending his plantation on the Northern Plain. Accordingly, the four of them descended on the palace together, Isabelle on Howarth's arm, and Elise on the doctor's.

The doors were swung open for them by Guiaou and Riau, the latter a black captain of the Second Colonial Demibrigade. The doctor clapped his hand on the shoulder of Riau, who had often served as orderly in the hospital or on the battlefield, and who now returned his smile. Within the main reception hall, several dozen people were circulating: the principal white men and women of Le Cap, along with some visitors from other regions or abroad; a sprinkling of the colored men still trusted by Toussaint, some accompanied by their wives or daughters; and numerous of the senior black officers, looking a little stiff in their dress uniforms. At the rear of the room, a small musical ensemble was tuning up—a flute, a pair of trumpets, a violin, and an African drum. There was a long table of refreshments, and servants roamed the room with silver trays. The doctor accepted a glass of red wine, wet his tongue in it, and stood holding the glass in his hands. When he glanced around for Isabelle, he found her congratulating their mutual friend Maillart on his recent promotion to the rank of major.

"Well, let me see you." The doctor embraced Maillart, then held him at arm's length to admire the new insignia. "Why, yes, the change becomes you."

"And leaves my accomplishments much as they were," said Maillart with a wink. He'd languished so long in the colonial service without promotion, through the period when the black officer corps was rocketing higher and higher in rank, that the matter had become almost indifferent to him.

"What news have you?" said the doctor. Because of the fever outbreak he had not seen Maillart for nearly two weeks. The major rolled his eyes and caught him by the sleeve.

"Vincent has been exiled to Elba."

"What?"

The doctor contained his response to a hiss, and yet he felt it had been too loud. Isabelle and Elise were taken up in an exchange of compliments with Colonel Sans-Souci and a couple of other black officers, but Captain Howarth, unattached for the moment, seemed to be looking at them curiously.

Maillart pulled the doctor a step further away and stooped to mutter in his ear. "I had a letter sent direct to me, or rather it had been smuggled out, I—"

The sounding of a trumpet stopped the conversation. All around the room people left off their chatter and turned to face the entrance, where Guiaou was just lowering the horn from his lips. Those who had been seated got quickly to their feet. The doors swung wide for the entrance of Governor-General Toussaint Louverture.

The doctor stole a glance at Captain Howarth to measure his reaction. The *Merry Bell* put out of Charleston, South Carolina, where slavery was quite vigorously in force, and before he fell ill Howarth had passed a couple of remarks about the oddity of finding himself landed in a "nigger republic." Might Toussaint cut a comic figure in his eyes? The black general was slight in stature, with a jockey's build and the slightly bowed legs to go with it. When he was dismounted, his head, with its long heavily underslung jaw, looked ill-balanced and distinctly too large for his body. General Henri Christophe, commander of the Second Colonial Demibrigade, seemed to tower over Toussaint as he walked beside him, stooping to catch his murmured words.

Tonight Toussaint wore a small tricorne hat, adorned with black and white plumes, and a single red one. Aside from that his dress was simple: trousers and jacket of an extremely fine white linen. As he began his circuit of the room, conversation resumed, though in lower tones. Riau and Guiaou walked just at his back, sometimes pausing a moment to converse with a group from which the Governor had just detached.

As Toussaint drew nearer to their own cluster, Doctor Hébert shot an alarmed glance at the two women in his charge. Although Toussaint encouraged white ladies at these gatherings, he had a prudish dislike of the fashionably exposed bosom, so that most of the local belles presented themselves dressed as if for church, demurely buttoned right up to their chins. Absentminded as he was in such matters, the doctor seemed to recall that Elise's toilette fell rather short of the requisite standard. But when he looked now, he saw that she had cunningly tucked a handkerchief into her bodice, folded and teased into a ruffle which successfully camouflaged the vista of ripe flesh that he'd remembered . . . Toussaint was bowing, murmuring over her hand, then Isabelle's.

Madame Cigny, the doctor took in, had deployed a similar device over her own bodice.

The doctor presented Captain Howarth, "lately recovered from *mal de Siam.*"

"So?" Toussaint pulled himself straighter and raised his head, looking from Howarth to the doctor. "It is not the fever season."

"Apparently shipborne," the doctor muttered. "At any rate it has not spread into the town. Since Wednesday the quarantine is lifted from his vessel."

"Excellent," said Toussaint. "We are favored by Providence."

"In addition to which," Captain Howarth put in, "I credit this gentleman with my survival."

Toussaint smiled and in the same movement masked his bad teeth with one hand. The other he laid on the doctor's shoulder. The two of them were roughly the same height, Doctor Hébert perhaps an inch or so taller, but Toussaint had a knack of projecting some force outward from himself, which made him seem much larger than he really was, when one was near him.

"The first among my men of medicine," Toussaint said. He squeezed the doctor's shoulder and let it go.

"You give me too much credit," the doctor said, genuinely embarrassed. He knew that Toussaint knew how very slight was his knowledge of the yellow fever.

Toussaint nodded to Howarth's bow, then continued his perambulation. Christophe had lingered to speak to Isabelle. Riau brushed the doctor's hand in passing. Howarth turned to say something to Isabelle, for Christophe's attention seemed to vex him a little. The burr of conversation grew generally louder. Maillart caught the doctor's eye, cleared his throat, and then shook his head.

"No, no, of course," the doctor said. "I'll find you later."

He walked to the refreshment table and found himself some cold meat and cheese. After all, he did not much enjoy these occasions . . . It took Toussaint almost an hour to complete his circuit of the room. Toward the end of his tour, the musicians struck up a country minuet. In the arms of Colonel Sans-Souci, Elise came smoothly gliding onto the dance floor. The doctor felt his pulse leap upward. Toussaint, who was himself no dancer, watched the couple with an indecipherable expression, one hand at the white neckcloth which swathed his throat. Presently a few other dancers joined the first couple, and Toussaint turned away.

As the Governor withdrew in the direction of his offices, Riau and Guiaou made discreet signals to certain members of the company. Isabelle, the doctor, and Captain Howarth were elected. Elise, still on the dance floor, was not.

It was not quite the inner sanctum, but the outer office, which Doctor Hébert knew well, and which could comfortably seat some twenty people. Included this evening were Christophe; Borghella, an important merchant visiting from Port-au-Prince; a couple of other members of Toussaint's constitutional assembly; the priest Anthéaume; Julien Raymond, a mulatto who'd served on the last commission sent out by the French government; Pascal, a Frenchman who now served as one of Toussaint's principal secretaries and who also happened to be Raymond's son-in-law; and a few others, besides the doctor's party, of similar status or interest in the colony. Toussaint presided, sitting in a carved wooden armchair facing the outer door from a corner. He had taken off his hat, beneath which he wore, as almost always, a yellow madras cloth bound tightly over his brow and knotted at the back. He addressed himself first to Isabelle Cigny.

"What news have you of your children, Madame?"

"None at all for some weeks now," Isabelle said, with a petulant moue. "I expect them hourly in the port." She laid her cheek aslant on her wrapped hands and looked charmingly wistful.

"Ah, they are returning? That is good," Toussaint said. "What age have they?"

"Robert is twelve," Isabelle said. "And Héloïse—my baby!—is now ten."

"So the eldest is of an age to have been confirmed in the faith."

At this the priest roused himself to a greater display of attention. Isabelle lifted her head from her hands and sat primly upright.

"As to that, there has been some delay, but I and his father intend to accomplish his First Communion once he is safely arrived here."

Toussaint nodded. "So he, and the younger girl also, must be well instructed in their catechism."

"So I must presume. They have been installed in a convent school in Philadelphia—it is all quite correct." Isabelle hesitated, as if aware of the stiffness that had come into her voice. "You understand, it has been some years since it has been possible for me to examine them in person."

"*Sa bay tristesse,*" Toussaint said. That gives sadness.

"So it does," Isabelle said, and the expression she'd artfully put on dissolved into a look that seemed sincere.

During this parley, glasses had been handed round, and now a servant appeared with two bottles of wine. Toussaint studied them with some care, giving more attention to the seals than to the labels, then nodded that the corks should be drawn.

"You put out from Charleston, Captain," he said to Howarth. "So I am told."

"It is so, Governor," Howarth replied. The doctor studied his profile. Howarth had a square, bony face, and wore the sort of sailor's beard which sketched a line from one ear to the other along the outer edge of his jaw.

Toussaint made inquiry into certain particulars of his voyage and the trading he had done along the way, especially at Martinique, where the *ancien régime,* including slavery, persisted, and nearby Guadeloupe, where the slaves had freed themselves through revolution, as at Saint Domingue. Howarth made his answers with an air of unconscious frankness, but the doctor, as he nursed the wine which had been served him, thought he must be aware that a net was being subtly arranged around him.

"Governor," he said at last. "I would not venture to make a comparison of those two places. That is a political question with which I do not engage. I am only grateful for my right of entry to those ports—at Martinique and Guadeloupe, and here."

Toussaint nodded. "You know very well the port of Charleston, I imagine. There is a great importation of slaves there still, is there not? Tell me, how many?"

"What?" said Howarth. "By month, by year? How do you mean?"

"Let us say by year."

Howarth thought for a moment, frowning, then produced a number.

"And the cost of a slave?"

"On the block at Charleston? But that depends on many things."

"Let us say a young and healthy, able-bodied male."

Howarth frowned. "Still it depends, on the sagacity of the buyer and the cunning of the seller. Such sales are made at auction as you may know. But . . ." After a moment he produced another figure.

"And in Africa?" Toussaint said.

"In *Africa?*" Howarth was now genuinely perplexed. "Truly I don't know—five sticks of tobacco and an iron axe head? If you mean to suggest that the profit margin is very great, it certainly is so, but—"

"You yourself have never undertaken such a voyage?"

Captain Howarth put aside his half-drunk glass of wine and drew himself ramrod straight on the edge of his chair. "I have not, sir, and I would not."

Toussaint leaned forward. "Tell me your reasons."

Howarth seemed to relax, just slightly, just visibly, though he remained at the edge of his seat. "I have seen those ships discharge their loads." He stroked a hand backward over his head. "I have even visited their holds. Well, once—it was sufficient. The conditions there are much worse than for animals. There is much loss of life on that passage. And it is human life."

He paused. It was now so quiet in the room that the doctor could hear his neighbors breathing. Through the closed door came dampened strains of the country dance tunes.

"I abhor it," Captain Howarth said finally. "Oh, I don't judge the other captains who pursue it. They are my friends, some of them, even my partners on occasion, but in other enterprises. I will carry any cargo but not that one. I abhor the slave trade for myself."

Toussaint folded his arms across his narrow, wiry chest and looked very piercingly at Captain Howarth. A ring of white appeared around his eyes. For perhaps a whole minute the two men's gazes were locked. Then Toussaint breathed out, nodded, and turned to ask Borghella some unrelated question.

At that, the mood in the room relaxed, and the conversation became somewhat more general, though subdued. The session continued about an hour more. Then Toussaint rose and beckoned Pascal and one of the other secretaries. Bidding his company good night, he led his scribes into the inner office and shut the door.

"A cat may look at a king, they say," Howarth muttered to the doctor as they shuffled out. "He asks the hard questions, your Governor."

What do you think of a nigger republic now? the doctor thought, but it would have been spiteful to say it aloud. It was not the first time he'd witnessed such conversions. People under Toussaint's scrutiny would blurt out things about themselves they didn't know they knew.

"I thought he'd drill me through the wall with that examination on the slave trade."

"He wanted to know the prices, I think," Doctor Hébert said. "There is a clause in his constitution which authorizes the importation of slaves."

"You're joking."

"Oh no," said the doctor. "The object is to reinforce the army, I believe. It is not yet much practiced so far as I know, but there it is written in plain black and white—I have copied out those lines myself."

In the large reception hall the musicians went on playing merrily. Isabelle inserted herself into the doctor's arms and waltzed him away from Captain Howarth's astonished face. He was an indifferent dancer as a rule, but Isabelle had skill and verve enough for both of them. She led him so easily that the doctor forgot to worry about his feet and began to enjoy the music, which was very accomplished, despite the odd combination of instruments. Sometimes the Government House evenings were attended by a more orthodox orchestra, drawn from the military bands, but this evening's troubadours, as they were styled, were making the most of their occasion. The violinist shot an occasional glance of resentment at the two trumpeters, though both had their instruments muted with rags.

The doctor glanced about the room for his acquaintances as he danced. Most were still present, but Guiaou and Riau, he noticed, were no longer to be seen. On a violin crescendo, he saw his sister drop backward almost as if fainting, giving the full weight of her shoulders to Colonel Sans-Souci's crooked arm. She had undone the handkerchief from her bodice (probably as soon as Toussaint had retreated with his inner circle of the evening) and it now trailed from her right wrist, a flag, a signal, sweeping the dance floor at the end of her limp arm as her body turned with Sans-Souci's expert pirouette, the white of his grin turning on the same axis above her upturned face. With her head thrown back and her free arm trailing, the blue veins beneath her jaw and on the pale underside of her free arm were brought helplessly near to the skin. The doctor was struck by that effect, in the moment before Sans-Souci's tightening spin brought her upright again, into his embrace, flushed and excited and laughing . . . Others, too, observed them from the edges of the dance floor, General Christophe slowly stroking his chin as he studied the steps of Sans-Souci.

"There has been a letter from the First Consul, I have heard," Isabelle whispered discreetly in his ear.

"Oh indeed." Doctor Hébert returned his attention to his partner. One source of trepidation intruded on the other. Elise had been dancing only with Sans-Souci for more than an hour, or so it appeared. It amounted to making a public declaration. That was not the first time Elise had made some stroke of scandalous boldness. Nor was she the only white woman to consort with the black officers in these latter days. Yet with Tocquet expected any moment now, it was a little unnerving. One did not trifle with Xavier Tocquet, in any matter serious to him.

"But you are distracted," Isabelle breathed in his ear.

The doctor returned to the moment: her small, light, bird-boned body, the steely strength he knew it hid. She laid her dark head on his collarbone.

"There is to be an expedition," she murmured. "He sends his sister, that famous belle, Pauline."

"In command of the expedition?"

Isabelle laughed and rapped a finger on his forearm as they waltzed around. "Oh no, of course not, but her husband . . . I forget his name."

"And in what force?" the doctor said. At once he remembered what Maillart had begun to tell him earlier, about Vincent.

"I don't know. You might ask Pascal—he must have seen the letter. I thought you might have seen it yourself." Isabelle looked at him sharply to see if perhaps he actually had. "The letter is reported to say that enough troops will be sent to ensure that French sovereignty is respected."

And just how many would that be? The doctor felt the bottom of his stomach drop. Following Isabelle's expert lead, he spun and caught a glimpse of Maillart, beckoning to him as he moved toward the outer door. By good luck Captain Howarth, on the other side of the ballroom, was signaling his interest in a dance with Isabelle. Doctor Hébert surrendered his partner with a smile and followed the major onto the steps outside.

It was calm and cool outdoors beneath the crescent moon, and a breeze was shivering the leaves of the tall palms. A few other men stood smoking, talking quietly lower on the steps. Farther in the courtyard or beyond the gate, some of the guests had brought their ladies to still more private colloquies. Maillart offered his flask and the doctor took it gratefully and drank. The burn of new white rum spread through him. He was humid from the effort of his dancing, but now he felt a little cooler from the breeze.

"Vincent," he said. "Elba—what does it mean?"

"As you may imagine," said the major, "Toussaint's constitution, which Vincent was charged to present to the First Consul, was no better received than he had predicted before he left here."

"I can imagine all too well." The doctor returned the flask to Maillart, who nursed at it contemplatively.

"Yes," he said. "In such cases the messenger sometimes must suffer, as everyone knows. But Vincent, despite being so compromised, was recalled more recently to give his opinion on the advisability of sending an expedition in full force."

" 'To ensure that French sovereignty is respected,' " Doctor Hébert quoted. "And Vincent's opinion?"

"Against," said Maillart, as he capped the flask and slipped it into the pocket of his coat. "By his own account, Vincent advised the First Consul simply to reject the constitution. That he send a token force escorting a new governor. Toussaint would then be left the choice of submission or open rebellion against France."

"I do not think he would openly rebel," the doctor said.

"Perhaps you are right," said Maillart. "Do you think he would submit to a new governor? When the constitution which you yourself have copied out names him Governor for life?"

The doctor exhaled, with a noisy flutter of his lips.

"So," Maillart went on, "when pressed on the point of a military excursion, Vincent advised that it would be most unlikely to succeed, since there are forty thousand natives under arms in some fashion or other, which a force of twenty thousand French soldiers could not—in his opinion, mind you!—reduce. The native troops, who can live on nothing, would hold out in the mountains, beyond pursuit, harrying the European soldiers who would be rapidly dying of fever, the climate, their inevitable privations . . . along with casualties inflicted by a numerically superior force."

"An uninviting prospect," said the doctor.

"Yes," Maillart said. "Of course, one does not safely suggest to Bonaparte that his arms could ever fail. For that reason, we may presume, our friend Vincent now finds himself addressing his correspondence from Elba."

In the ensuing silence, Pascal emerged onto the steps, biting at his thumbnail.

"I thought you were in for a night of it," said the doctor, who himself served often enough as one of Toussaint's many scribes. Toussaint required no more than a couple of hours' sleep out of twenty-four, and would often drive his secretaries until dawn.

"No," said Pascal. "The Governor has left the town."

"Where was he bound?" Maillart inquired.

"Fort Liberté was what he said."

"So he may be going anywhere but there," the major muttered. He displayed his flask and Pascal reached for it eagerly.

"There's rumor of an expedition," the doctor said. In the back of his mind he was recalling the disappearance of Riau and Guiaou. Toussaint was famous for his sudden, secret, rapid journeys, escorted only by a couple of his finest riders, whose horses could keep pace with his own extraordinary mount.

"Of course there are always such rumors," Pascal said.

"I wonder," said the doctor, "if you may have seen that letter from the First Consul which figures in the latest gossip."

"You will recall that the last time the First Consul announced an expedition to Saint Domingue, it was only a ruse to outwit the English," Pascal said. "The fleet was actually dispatched to Egypt, then."

"But now there is peace with the English," Maillart put in. "No risk of a naval blockade here."

Silence, and the wind rushed through the leaves. The flask was making another round when a lean figure wearing a broad-brimmed hat walked in at the lower gate. The doctor choked on his liquor.

"Xavier," he coughed. "Is it you? You're back."

"So I am," said Xavier Tocquet, removing his hat as he came up the steps and embraced the doctor. He was still sticky with salt from the sea. For a moment he and the doctor held each other at arm's length. Tocquet flashed his crooked, toothy grin. His long, salt-stiffened hair hung down his back, gathered in a leather thong.

"Well, the old pirate." Maillart held out the flask. "Was it a profitable voyage?"

"Isabelle is most anxious for her children," the doctor said.

"They are safe and well," said Tocquet and drank, his Adam's apple pulsing. "Along with a hold full of muskets warm from the Pennsylvania foundries. Is the Governor at home?"

"You've missed him by half an hour," Pascal said. "He has just ridden out of town."

"Then he must wait for the good news of his shipment." Tocquet looked again at the doctor. "The children are installed *chez* Cigny, and as I found no one but the servants at either house, I came here to bring their news." He smiled again. "And also, of course, to embrace my wife."

"They are both inside." The doctor turned his face to the shadow, meaning to hide his qualms.

Tocquet climbed past him; the doctor followed him into the great hall. There had been a pause in the music, so the babble of talk seemed louder. Isabelle was first to spot the newcomer. She rushed toward him, then checked herself, to give the wife her precedence.

By great good luck, the doctor noted with an inward sigh, Elise had separated from Sans-Souci, who stood at the opposite end of the room from her, chatting with his brother officers by the refreshment table and the punch bowls. His back was toward her, even though he turned his head a moment to observe. Elise was still flushed, a movement visible on her bosom, her blond hair slightly loosened from its coiffure by her dancing. She walked toward her husband with a measured step, her arms just slightly raised to join his. Her face still shone with passion, the doctor saw, but in these circumstances, Tocquet might well assume it was all for him.

2

At evening the clouds were scraped in thin mare's tails around the setting sun, and the sea, flowing smoothly from the west beneath the hulls of the French ships, was burnished copper. Placide Louverture stood in the bow of *La Sirène*, rocking with the easy swells, watching the red sky in the west toward which they sailed, watching for birds. There were no birds. They were three weeks out from Brest, somewhere in the Atlantic Ocean. Sixty ships of the great fleet strung out as far as the eye could see, as far as the curved knife-edge of the horizon.

Placide's hands just grazed the railing; knees slightly flexed, he held himself balanced on the smoothly shifting deck. Now and then he tasted a burst of spray as the ship plowed forward. The army captain, Cyprien, stood a few yards back of him, propped against a mast; Placide was aware of his presence but paid it no heed. Presently his younger brother, Isaac, came out to join him, walking a little unsteadily and clutching the rail as he went. On their first voyage, from Saint Domingue to France, they both had suffered considerably from seasickness. That had been six years ago. Since then, Placide had made another voyage, intended to go all the way to Egypt, but Isaac had not accompanied him then.

The nausea scarcely troubled Placide this time out, not after the first day. Isaac was making a slower adjustment, though he looked a little better now than the day before, favoring Placide with a weak smile as he stopped beside him.

"*Ki jan ou yé?*" Placide asked him, "*W byen?*"

"*Pa pi mal.*" Isaac drew himself a little straighter. "*M'ap kenbe.*" He rocked back on his heels, catching his weight against his handgrip on the rail. No worse; I'm hanging on . . . During their years in France they'd spoken Creole seldom, even among themselves. The *patois* was frowned upon at the Collège de la Marche, though many of the other students had it as their mother tongue.

A flying fish came out of a billow, whirred toward them, then drilled into another wave. Isaac's breath caught, and Placide turned to smile at him again. Ill below decks for so many days, Isaac had till now missed most of the wonders the sea had to display.

The first fish was followed by another, and another; then dozens all at once were in the air, glittering, wet, and iridescent red in the light of the setting sun. Placide wondered what the appearance of the fish might augur. This thought too had the taste of home, where every natural manifestation had its meaning if one could know it. He and Isaac had been children when they left Saint Domingue. Now they had the age of men. When he'd summoned them to that audience before their departure, the First Consul had presented them each a splendid uniform, a brace of pistols, and a sword. But they had little knowledge of the use of these arms.

Nor did they know what awaited them in Saint Domingue. Placide's memories of that land were fractured; his brother's still less clear. Placide had been tantalized with the prospect once before, for when that other fleet had sailed to Egypt, Saint Domingue had been the declared destination—his own presence meant only to lend credence to that deception. When the real mission was revealed to him (at the same time as to most of the rest of the passengers), Placide had soothed his disappointment with the thought that he might look upon the Pyramids, and especially the Great Sphinx, which he had seen in pictures. But the English navy, undeceived by the ruse, had intercepted them and turned them back to a French port.

Monsieur Coisnon, their tutor, now appeared beside Isaac, the skirt of his dark cassock snapping in the wind. The flying fish were still exploding from the waves, and Coisnon began to speak of them in terms of natural history. Placide's mind drifted. He recalled that, on his return from that aborted voyage to Egypt, Monsieur Coisnon had told him how in reality the Great Sphinx was somewhat diminished from what he'd seen in the engravings, the vast sad features of her face blown to flinders by Bonaparte's artillerymen, practicing their aim. Coisnon had meant that tale for consolation, Placide thought, but he had not been much consoled.

Amidships, a brass bell clanged.

"Mess call," Coisnon said. Isaac and Placide looked at each other grimly. Coisnon shaded his eyes to peer up at the sky.

"You will remember," he said, "that when Columbus first undertook this voyage, his men thought to mutiny when he would not turn back, sick as they were of salt meat spoiled in the cask, and fearful they'd sail off the edge of the world altogether. It was the birds' flying out from the islands that saved him then, restoring the confidence of the crew. As the dove saved Noah from the failing faith of his companions, returning with the olive branch."

Placide followed his tutor's expansive gesture. For a moment it seemed to him he caught the scent of flowers. He looked again; there were no birds.

"Come," said Monsieur Coisnon. "Let us to table."

Isaac gulped. They did not eat as poorly as Columbus's men in the last days of that first voyage, and there was plenty of fresh water for them still. But after these few weeks at sea the last of any fresh food had been exhausted. Each meal was labor more than pleasure, and the tot of rum served out beforehand seemed meant to give one courage to face it.

Placide, then Isaac, clumped down to the officers' mess, Monsieur Coisnon bringing up their rear. They found their places at the table. Certainly there was no one aboard enjoying better victuals. They ate not at the first table, with the ship's captain and his mates, but at the second, in the company of four young army officers and a lone naval ensign whom everyone seemed to ignore. The army captains were Cyprien, Paltre, Daspir, and Guizot. No one seemed to be able to recall the ensign's name, not even Monsieur Coisnon, who was armed with tricks for memorizing his ever-changing pupils.

"Thanks be to God," Coisnon muttered, and inhaled a blast of rum from his cup. Placide and Isaac bowed their heads momentarily; the army captains avoided each other's eyes. Tonight it was salt cod, as opposed to salt beef.

"One might try a hand at fishing," Captain Guizot proposed.

"If one had line and a hook," said Paltre.

Daspir lifted his plank of salt cod and held it dangling. He squinted at it comically. It was an unappealing ochre shade, with a rank smell that struck at a distance. The shifting light of the swinging lantern made its surface seem to crawl.

Placide looked away. He chewed mechanically, ignoring the sour flavor. There was a mess of boiled beans and meal to complement the fish. Isaac nibbled at the corner of the chunk of hardtack he'd tried to soften in his rum. Placide nudged him to encourage him to eat; the younger boy dutifully poked a spoonful of the bean mash into his mouth and struggled to swallow it down.

"Now, what shall we find delectable in Saint Domingue?" Daspir inquired.

Both Placide and Isaac looked up. Conversation at these meals was restricted to this sort of innocuous question. Or else there might be disquisitions from Coisnon on topics which had suggested themselves to

him during the day. The army men were hard put to conceal their bore-
dom with his lectures; yet their talk among themselves was constrained
by the presence of the boys and their tutor. Placide remembered something of the same sort from his Egyptian voyage, the same hesitancy,
same sense of withholding.

"*Maïs moulin,*" he said. It was the bean mash that prompted him.
Maïs moulin stood in the relation of pure Platonic form to the sludge
they were trying to eat now.

"*C'est quoi ça?*" Daspir said. What's that? He was a plump young man,
with round cheeks and shining olive skin; he loved good food and felt
privation more keenly than the others. Placide described: stewed cornmeal mixed with highly seasoned beans, with onions, peppers, perhaps a
dash of syrup whose sweetness worked against the spice.

"What else?" Daspir's eyes were shining. "What for meat?"

Placide shrugged. "Goat. Fresh pork. Roasted on the *boucan* it is very
good. There are many kinds of fish."

"*Lambi,*" Isaac put in. "*Lambi* with green cashew sauce." With a rapture rising to Daspir's own, he told how the meat of the conch was tenderized with papaya juice, served with a sauce of tomatoes and fresh
cashews, the soft consistency of mushrooms. Then to follow there might
be fruit: oranges certainly, guava, mango, soursop, several different
kinds of banana—*banane figue, banane loup-garou,* and Isaac's own
favorite, the tiny sweet *banane Ti-Malice.*

Inspired by these recollections, Isaac managed to empty most of his
plate, as Placide noticed with some relief; his brother had not succeeded
in taking much nourishment since he had been laid low by *mal de mer.*
And thus another dinner hour had passed more agreeably than some.
With Coisnon, the two boys climbed up to take their evening constitutional on the deck. There was no moon, and the night was marvelously
clear, starlight blazing down on them from a black velvet sky. The swell
seemed just a little stronger than before.

Raising his arm to the constellations, Coisnon began to recount the
myths of Cepheus and Cassiopeia. But he had to interrupt himself when
Isaac, without warning, doubled over the rail and spewed his recent
meal into the sea. Placide steadied his head while he retched and
coughed; Coisnon anchored him with a hand's grip in his waistband.

"Excuse me," Isaac said, when he'd regained that much control. "I am
very sorry."

"It's nothing, dear boy," Coisnon told him. "I'll take you down to your
berth. No, no," he said, as Placide moved to assist. "You should stay here,
and profit from the air."

Placide remained, turning again to face the ocean. At the Collège de la
Marche he'd had the reputation of a solitary, especially when compared
to the much more gregarious Isaac, and he was glad of a taste of solitude
now. Even a partial taste. From the corner of his eye he could see the

faces of Cyprien and Guizot by the hatchway, lit by the intermittent red glow of their cheroots. Somehow or other at least one of these officers was always nearby. Placide understood that the four of them were assigned to him and his brother as guardians, if not guards, though he had not discussed it with Isaac.

He raised his head to find the Northern Cross, and near it, picked out in dimmer stars, the compact form of the Dolphin. The stars went dark where the water met the sky, but the running lights of the French ships came stringing back to where he stood in the bow of *La Sirène*. One of those other vessels (Placide was not sure which) carried a flock of his father's most significant surviving enemies, notably the mulatto rebels: Villatte, Pétion, Rigaud. The thought made him uncomfortable. He felt eyes burning at his back and turned to face them. Cyprien and Guizot looked away from him, stepped out of his path as he entered the hatchway and went below to find his berth.

Since their embarkation, the four officers detailed to the sons of Toussaint Louverture had run a nightly game of *vingt-et-un*, and when Cyprien and Guizot had finished their smoke they went below to join this night's session. They'd set up a packing case for a card table in the officers' quarters, in the bow a deck below the captain's cabin. A thin partition divided the card parlor from the four berths in the narrowest part of the bow, which were occupied by Placide, Isaac, their tutor, and the young ensign whose name no one could recall.

Daspir, who was rich, served as the bank. Night after night, the bank was irritatingly prosperous. Cyprien and Paltre, who were marginally more seasoned soldiers than the other two, had at first assumed they'd fleece him easily. But Daspir played with a quiet acuity belied by his fatuous manner. Or else, as Cyprien sometimes bitterly put to himself or to Paltre, he was just damned lucky.

Daspir was shuffling now, smiling at the other three. Above the packing case an oil lamp swung on its chain with the steady movement of the waves. Daspir's smile evaporated as he dealt the cards. His own hand showed a ten face-up. Cyprien glanced at his hole card and folded. Paltre did the same, but Guizot drew to a six, then groaned.

Expressionless now, Daspir raked in the money and dealt again. Nine up. Cyprien checked his hole card and tossed in his hand. Daspir covered bets from Paltre and Guizot and then took both their money.

When he had won a few more hands, Daspir squared the deck and rose from his seat, leaving the cards on the table, then crossed to his bunk and stooped to drag his chest from beneath it. After shifting the contents around for a minute or two, he produced a bottle of very decent brandy. It was not the first he had discovered during the voyage, though now he squinted at the level through the glass, as if to suggest that his supply was not completely inexhaustible.

"Permettez-moi," he said, smiling again as he came back to the packing case. Allow me. Despite the roll of the ship his step was steady and his hand too as he poured—he smiled with his mouth but his eyes remained cool. Again, Cyprien thought that the man was not the idle voluptuary he might seem. He pushed his cup forward for the splash of brandy, grunted his thanks.

Daspir sat down and dealt the cards. Cyprien and Paltre folded three times in succession, while Guizot bet heavily and lost. Guizot said nothing, but Cyprien could sense his rising anger; he had a weak head for liquor as well as for cards. Perhaps Daspir was aware of the strained mood also, for he squared the deck again and poured another dose of brandy all around.

"Your health, gentlemen," he said, and when they'd drunk, "How long do you suppose we'll be about this business?"

"Judging by tonight's progress," Paltre said, "you'll have parted us from the remains of our substance in another week's time."

"In Saint Domingue, I mean," said Daspir, with one of his fey giggles.

"Oh," Paltre said, raising eyebrows in mock surprise. "In *Saint Domingue.*"

"How long can it possibly take to put down a nigger insurrection?" Guizot burst out. But Daspir kept looking quietly at Cyprien, who picked up his cup of brandy and drank. Guizot was already drunk, that was plain, and angry over his losses at the table.

"One rag-headed monkey at the head of a band of brigands," Guizot grumbled. "Why, the four of us might go out and arrest him and put an end to the whole affair in a week."

"Quiet," Cyprien snapped, glancing pointedly at the partition in the bow. "You know that we have no such orders."

"Nonsense." Guizot belched. "They are sleeping. And if they heard, what would they understand . . ."

Daspir had begun to shuffle the cards again. His soft olive hands, with the neatly trimmed fingernails, moved smoothly over the deck. Cyprien exchanged a glance with Paltre. This *nigger insurrection* had been going on for ten years, though the two of them had thought no more of it on their first trip out than Guizot did now. During that earlier mission there had been some idle chatter of the same sort: a mere handful of men might arrest Toussaint, and never mind all Hédouville's tedious temporizing. A couple of those chatterers, young officers with whom Cyprien and Paltre had struck up a short-term friendship, had been found dead on the road outside Gonaives, victims of an ambush which had never been explained or punished.

"Ours is a peaceful mission," Cyprien said, reciting the official line. "As Toussaint Louverture professes loyalty to France, he must certainly bow to the authority of the Captain-General Leclerc."

"Oh, to be sure," Guizot snorted. "And for that one requires twenty-five thousand troops of the line. No, you speak of Hédouville and *his* style of diplomacy—and Hédouville ran home with his tail between his legs."

Cyprien flattened his hands on the splintery surface of the packing case. For a long moment there was no sound audible above the ocean's rhythm except the fluttering of the cards. A ship's rat ran along the groove of the wall and deck and squeezed through a crack in the bow partition.

"I am sure you do not mean to insult me," Cyprien said.

"Certainly not." Daspir had spoken; he put down the cards. "Nor you nor Captain Paltre, I am sure." Daspir looked at Guizot, his eyes grown chill.

"Not in the least, my friends." Guizot, who was seated between Paltre and Cyprien, looked quickly from one to the other. "No, you are both men of courage and honor." He hiccuped. "Enough word-mincing, is all I mean to say. Are we to be outfaced by some gilt nigger in a general's suit? Are we not soldiers?"

Guizot reached for Cyprien's and Paltre's hands. Cyprien let his own be taken. At once he felt a surge of confused emotion, as if Guizot had communicated it with his touch. Daspir joined hands with them to close the circle.

"Come, shall we make a pact?" Guizot said. This time it was he who gave a meaning look at the bow partition. "We may be placed to have some special opportunity—and there'd be glory in it. Let it be the four of us who bring the rebel in."

Cyprien thought of his comrades dead by the roadside, of Hédouville's abrupt departure, which did have the taste of ignominy. For a second he caught Paltre's eye. Shadows stroked across their faces with the swinging of the lamp. After all, there was something here to be avenged.

"So be it, then," he said. "I'll drink to that."

There was a squeeze of all their hands, and all at once they cheered. Then Daspir broke the circled handclasp, reaching one more time for his brandy bottle.

Placide woke with such a start he knocked his head against the wall. It was a minute or two before the movement of the sea reminded him where he was. There was that, and Coisnon's snoring, and the muttering of that young ensign, who often talked unhappily in his sleep. A ship's rat scuttled in the bilges beneath his plank berth. Through the partition he could hear the muffled, unintelligible voices of the four army officers at their cards and liquor.

What had he dreamed? Billows, above which were billows, rolling one into the next like ocean waves, but these were waves of sand. A searing light over golden dunes, and then rising from the sand the august scarred face of the Sphinx, looming over him with her wounds, the weight of all that stone—it was then that he'd begun to be afraid (his heart still thumping even now) under the weight, fear of the Sphinx and her terrible stony voice, but then it was night, the sand was sea, and there in the place of the Sphinx (but still enormous) was the mermaid spirit Lasirène, glowing blue-green like phosphorescence or like stars, the dark pull of her gravity bearing Placide down beneath the waters.

He put his hand against the curving boards, feeling the pulse of the ocean. The rush of the water outside helped to calm him. He listened to the breathing of the other three in his compartment, to the persistent scrabbling of the rat. What was it they were sailing toward this time?

He needed to relieve himself, but he did not want to walk out to the jakes abovedecks; he didn't care for the way the four captains looked at him, so late, when they'd been drinking—nor the way they avoided looking at him, sometimes. He found a bottle he'd laid by for such situations, unstopped it, and directed his stream so that it ran soundlessly against the glass wall. When he was done he corked the bottle and wedged it back in the same place. Isaac coughed and shifted in his sleep, and Placide stepped across the narrow space and leaned over him, listening, till his younger brother's breath grew regular. Then he lay down again on the hard boards of his bunk.

Drowsiness carried him back toward the fearful immanence of the great *loa*. Lasirène, Erzulie of the waters! Placide had been a long time out of his own country; he had remembered the beauty of this mystery, but not her weight. Coisnon had taught them of Odysseus, how he stopped his crewmen's ears and ordered himself bound to the mast, that he might hear the siren song without being carried down by it to his own drowning. But that was only an old Greek story.

Placide worked his shoulders against the plank bed. This berth was a privilege of a sort, and yet he would have slept more easily in a hammock such as the ordinary sailors used. But in his discomfort he had pulled away from the dream vortex and the fish-tailed goddess waiting at the bottom. He was thinking with his mind. Surely it must be no accident that this ship itself was called *La Sirène*. No accident either that she had not yet sailed ahead of the main fleet.

"Your father," the First Consul had told them when he summoned them to his cabinet at the Tuileries, *"is a great man; he has rendered eminent services to France. You will tell him that I, the first magistrate of the French people, I promise him protection, glory, and honor. Do not suppose that France has any intention to bring war to Saint Domingue: the army which she sends there is not intended to fight the troops of the country but to augment their force. Here is General Leclerc, my brother-in-law, whom I have named Captain-General, and who will command this army. Orders are given such that you will be fifteen days ahead in Saint Domingue, to announce to your father the coming of the expedition."*

Following this reassuring address, Placide and Isaac had been guests of honor at a grand dinner, attended by the Captain-General Leclerc himself, with his seductive wife Pauline, sister of the First Consul. Also the Vice-Admiral Bougainville was there, with state counselors and many other persons of distinction, even Vincent, the colonel of engineers, whom Placide knew to be a close and trusted friend of his father. Yet Vincent had seemed unusually silent and withdrawn that evening, though he was always friendly to the boys. The two of them appeared in the gorgeous dress uniforms they had just been given, and Pauline Leclerc, world-famous for her coquetry as much as for her beauty, made much of Isaac's fine appearance, while her husband (himself only twenty-nine years of age) pretended to growl at the flirtation.

In the event, however, their ship had remained moored for a very long time at Brest, while soldiers and supplies were assembled and embarked. *La Sirène* had put out in the midst of the entire fleet. For many days, Placide and Isaac believed that somewhere in the mid-Atlantic their ship would simply put on more sail and speed out ahead of the others, bearing the two of them, and the First Consul's letter, to their father. Isaac, at least, had believed wholeheartedly that such a thing must happen, while Placide, experienced in voyages of disguised destination and in being used himself as a decoy, had privately been a little doubtful from the start. And now they must be less than fifteen days from their landfall in Saint Domingue. What if a different ship had sailed ahead—the one that carried Rigaud and his cohorts, or some other?

It might be for that that Lasirène seemed angry: she had been deceived, ill served. *Mais ce n'est pas de ma faute!* Placide cried mentally, I couldn't help it! A spirit might pardon your failure if it was plain you could not have prevented it. Placide thought he remembered that much, though Toussaint had been very firm in directing his sons away from the *hounfors* and into the Catholic Church. Still, with his father's long campaigns and frequent absences, there were times when both he and Isaac had followed the drums. Placide had seen the gods come down, seen the people who bore them totter with the shock of their descent.

This was the mystery into which he sailed, and he was helpless to change his course. Let it be, then. Let it come to him, to them all. He closed his eyes and made his breathing slow and even, though he no longer had the least desire to sleep.

3

"You were uneasy in the night," Michel Arnaud remarked to his wife.

"Oh?" said Claudine Arnaud, pausing with her coffee cup in mid-air. "I regret to have disturbed your rest."

"It is nothing," Arnaud said. He looked at her sidelong. The suspended coffee cup showed no hint of a tremor. In fact, Claudine had appeared to gain strength these last few months. She was lean, certainly, but no longer looked frail. Her face, once pallid, had broken out in freckles, since lately she took no care against the sun. She sipped from her cup and set it down precisely in the saucer, then reached across the table to curl her fingers over his wrist.

"Don't concern yourself," Claudine said with a transparent smile. "I have no trouble." Behind her chair, the mulattress Cléo shifted her feet, staring mistrustfully down at Arnaud, who raised his eyes to meet hers briefly.

"Encore du café, s'il vous plaît."

Cléo moved around the table, lifted the pot, and poured. The pot was silver, newly acquired—lately they'd begun to replace some of the amenities lost or destroyed when the rebel slaves burned this plantation in 1791. Household service was improving too, though it came wrapped in what Arnaud was wont to regard as an excess of mutual politeness. And Cléo's attachment to his wife was a strange thing!—though he got an indirect benefit from it. In the old days, when Cléo had been his mistress as well as his housekeeper, the two women had hated each other cordially.

He turned his palm up to give his wife's fingers a little squeeze, then disengaged his hand and stirred sugar into his coffee. White sugar, of his own manufacture. There was that additional sweetness—very few cane planters on the Northern Plain had recovered their operations to the point of producing white sugar rather than the less laborious brown.

Marie-Noelle came out onto the long porch to serve a platter of bananas and fried eggs. Arnaud helped himself generously, and covertly studied the black girl's hips, moving deliciously under the thin cotton of her gown as she walked away. In the old days, he'd have had her before breakfast, and never mind who heard or knew. But now—he felt Cléo's eyes were drilling him and looked away, from everyone; he hardly knew where to rest his gaze.

Down below the low hill where the big house stood, the small cabins and *ajoupas* of the field hands he'd been able to regather spread out around the tiny chapel Claudine had insisted that he build. The blacks were now taking their own morning nourishment and marshaling themselves for a day in the cane plantings or at the mill; soon the iron bell would be rung. Claudine and Arnaud were breakfasting on the porch, for the hypothetical cool, but there was none. The air was heavy, oppressively damp; drifts of soggy blue cloud cut off the sun.

Arnaud looked at his wife again, more carefully. It was true that she appeared quite well. There was no palsy, no mad glitter in her eye. Last night they had made love, an uncommon thing for them, and it had been uncommonly successful. They fell away from each other into deep black slumber, but sometime later in the night Arnaud had been roused by her spasmodic kicking. She thrashed her head in a tangle of hair and out of her mouth rose a long, high, silvery ululation. Then her voice broke and went deep and rasping, as her whole body became rigid, trembling as she uttered the words in Creole: *Aba blan! Tuyé moun-yo!* Then she'd convulsed, knees drawing to her chest, the cords of her neck all standing out taut as speechlessly she strangled. Arnaud had been ready to run for help, but then Claudine relaxed, went limp, and presently began to snore.

He himself had slept but lightly for what remained of the night. And now he thought that Cléo, who slept in the next room, beyond the flimsiest possible partition, must have heard it all. Down with the whites. Kill those people!

Down below the iron bell clanged, releasing him. Arnaud pushed back his chair and stood. When he bent down to peck at his wife's cheek, Claudine turned her face upward so that he received her lips instead.

· · ·

A hummingbird whirred before a hyacinth bloom, and Claudine felt her mind go out of her body, into the invisible blur of those wings. She had gone down the steps from the porch to watch her husband descend the trail to his day's work. Behind her she heard Cléo and Marie-Noelle muttering as they cleared the table.

"Té gegne lespri nan têt li, wi . . ."

True for them, and Claudine felt no resentment of the comment. There was a spirit in her head . . . She was so visited sometimes when she slept, as well as when the drums beat in the *hounfor*. To others, a spirit might bring counsel, knowledge of the future even, but Claudine never remembered anything at all. Unless someone perhaps could tell her what words had been uttered through her lips—but she would not ask Arnaud. Afterward she normally felt clean and free, but today she was only more agitated. Perhaps it was the heavy weather. Her hands opened and closed at her hips. She could not tell which way to turn.

At this hour she might normally have convened the little school she operated for the smaller children of the plantation (though Arnaud thought it a frivolity and would have stopped it if he could). But in the heavy atmosphere today the children would be indisposed. And though her teaching often soothed her own disquiet, she thought today that it would not. She turned from the descending path and walked around the back of the house, swinging her arms lightly to dry the dampness of her palms.

Here another trail went zigzag up the cliff, and Claudine grew more damp and clammy as she climbed. A turn of the trail brought her to a flat pocket, partly sheltered by a great boulder the height of her own shoulders. The trail ended in this spot. She stopped to breathe. This lassitude! She was weary from whatever had passed in the night, the thing that she could not recall. She waited till her breath was even, till her pulse no longer throbbed, then, standing tiptoe, reached across the boulder to wet her fingers in the trickle of spring water that ran down the wrinkles of the black rock. The water was sharply cold, a grateful shock. She sipped a mouthful from the leaking cup of her hand, then pressed her dampened fingertips against her throat and temples.

"M'ap bay w dlo," a child's voice called from behind and above her. *"Kite'm fé sa!"*

Claudine settled back on her heels. In fact the runnel of the spring was just barely within her longest reach. Etienne, a black child probably five years old, bare-legged and clothed only in the ragged remnant of a cotton shirt, scampered down toward her, his whole face alight. I'll give you water—let me do it. There was no trail where he descended, and the slope was just a few degrees off the vertical, but a few spotted goats were grazing the scrub there among the rocks and Etienne moved as easily as they. He bounced down onto the level ground beside her, and immediately turned to fish out a gourd cup that lay atop a barrel of meal in a crevice of the cliff—Arnaud having furnished this spot as an emergency retreat. Grinning, Etienne scrambled to the top of the boulder and stretched the gourd out toward the spring, careless of the sixty-foot drop on which he teetered.

Claudine gasped. *"Attention, chéri."* She took hold of his shirttail. But Etienne's balance was flawless; he put no weight against her grip. In a moment he had slipped down to the boulder and was raising the brimming gourd to her.

"W'ap bwe sa, wi," he said. You'll drink this.

"Yes," Claudine said, accepting the gourd with a certain ceremony. The water was very cool and sweet. She swallowed and returned the gourd to him half full and when he'd drunk his share, she curtsied with a smile. Etienne giggled. Claudine smoothed her skirts and sat down on a stone, looking out.

Below, the cabins of the field hands fanned out randomly from the little whitewashed chapel. They'd overbuilt the site of the old *grand'case* which had been burned in the risings of 1791—the house that had been the theater of her misery when Arnaud first brought her out to Saint Domingue from France. More distant, two dark threads of smoke were rising from the cane mill and distillery, and further still, two teams of men with ox-drawn wagons were cutting and loading cane from the wide *carrés* marked out by citrus hedges.

The higher ground where Arnaud had built the new *grand'case* was a better spot, less plagued by insects, more secure. On any height, however modest, one had a better chance to catch a breeze. Claudine realized she had hoped for a breath of wind when she climbed here, but there was none, only the heavy air and the lowering sky, the dull weight of anticipation. Something was coming—she didn't know what. She might, perhaps, ask Cléo what she had shouted in her sleep . . .

A cold touch startled her. She turned her head; the smiling Etienne was dabbing water around the neck line of her dress. After the first jolt the sensation was pleasant. She felt a drop purl down the joints of her spine.

"Ou pa apprann nou jodi-a," he said. You are not teaching us today. A statement, not a question.

"Non," said Claudine. And as she thought, "It is Saturday."

Etienne leaned against her back, draping an arm across her shoulder. His slack hand lay at the top of her breast, his cheek against her hair. In the heat his warm weight might have been disagreeable, but she felt herself wonderfully comforted.

Idly her gaze drifted toward the west. Along the *allée* which ran to the main road, about two-thirds of the royal palms still stood. The rest had been destroyed in the insurrection, so that the whole looked like a row of broken teeth. It seemed that the high palms shivered slightly, though where she sat Claudine could feel no breeze. Beyond, the green plain curved toward the horizon and the blue haze above the sea. A point of dust moved spiderlike in her direction.

She shifted her position when she noticed this, and felt that Etienne's attention had focused too, though neither of them spoke. They watched the dot of dust until it grew into a plume, pushing its way toward them through the silence. Then Claudine saw the silver flashing of the white horse in full gallop, and the small, tight-knit figure of the leading rider. The men of his escort carried pennants on long staves.

"Come!" she said, jumping up from her stone. "We must go down quickly."

It seemed unlikely that Etienne would have recognized the horseman, but he ran down the path ahead of her in a state of high excitement, his velocity attracting other small children into his wake. Claudine went more slowly, careful of the grade. As she passed the house, Cléo came out onto the long porch, shading her eyes to look into the west, and Marie-Noelle joined her, wiping her hands on her apron.

Claudine stopped at the edge of the compound, looking down the long *allée* to the point where Arnaud had recently hung a wooden gate to the stone posts from which the original ironwork had been torn. She watched; for a time there was no movement. Nearby a green shoot had sprung four feet high from the trunk of a severed palm, and a blue butterfly hovered over its new fronds. Etienne and the playmates he'd gathered went hurtling down the *allée*, scattering a couple of goats that had wandered there. The children braked to a sudden halt at the skirl of a *lambi* shell. Immediately the wooden gates swung inward. Flanked by the pennants of his escort, Toussaint Louverture rode toward her at a brisk trot, astride his great white charger, Bel Argent.

Claudine drew herself a little straighter and crossed her hands below her waistline. She was conscious of how she must appear, fixed in the long perspective of the green *allée*. There was a hollow under her heels where once had been a gallows post. She took a step forward onto surer ground, and recomposed herself for the reception.

Spooked by the advancing horsemen, the children turned tail and came running back toward her. Etienne and Marie-Noelle's oldest boy, Dieufait, took hold of her skirts on either side and peeped out from behind her. Toussaint had slowed his horse to a walk several yards short of her, so as not to coat her with his dust. He slipped down from the saddle and walked toward her, leading Bel Argent by the reins. As always, she was a little surprised to see that he was no taller than she was herself once he had dismounted. Shaking the children free of her skirt, she curtsied to his bow.

"You are welcome, General," she said, "to Habitation Arnaud."

"*Merci.*" Toussaint took her hand in his oddly pressureless grip and bowed his head over it. Claudine felt a tingle that sprang upward from the arches of her feet—when she'd thought herself long immune to such a blush. There was a pack of rumors lately, that Toussaint received the *amours* of many white women of the highest standing, attracted by the thrill of his power if they were not simply angling for gain. He did not kiss her hand, however, but only breathed upon her knuckles, and now he raised his eyes to meet her own. His hat was in his other hand, his head bound up in a yellow madras cloth. The gaze was assaying, some-how. Toussaint broke it with a click of his tongue, as if he'd seen what he'd been looking for.

"You'll stay the night," Claudine said. "I trust—I hope."

"Oh no, Madame," Toussaint told her, and covered his mouth with his long fingers, as if it pained him to disappoint her. "Your pardon, but we are pressed—we stop for water only, for our horses and ourselves."

Behind him, Guiaou and Riau had ridden up, Guiaou still brandish-ing the rosy conch shell he'd used to trumpet their arrival. Claudine pressed her hand to the flat bone between her breasts.

"But—tomorrow we will celebrate the Mass."

"Is it so?" said Toussaint, smiling slightly, with the same automatic movement to cover his mouth. "Well then. Of course."

Claudine fluttered at the little boys who still stood round-eyed at her back. "Did you not hear?" she hissed at them. "Go find something for these men to drink—and take their horses to water."

Michel Arnaud received the news of Toussaint's arrival with mixed emotions. The word that horsemen were on the way came to him shouted from man to man across the cane fields, and by the time he stepped to the door of the mill he had the comical view of tiny Dieufait leading the huge white warhorse toward the water trough. Toussaint was here, Arnaud thought, in part to reassure himself—to touch the proofs that his government had restored conditions wherein a planter might refine white sugar. For sugar was money, and money was guns . . . Arnaud chopped off that sequence of ideas. Also of course there was the issue of inspection, and enforcement of the new and strict labor code for the free blacks. Arnaud had benefited from these rules, although his workers found them very harsh. But at any rate it was better to be inspected by Toussaint than Dessalines. The whip had long since been abandoned, but if Dessalines got hold of a laggard or a truant, he might order the culprit flogged with a bundle of thorny vines, which tore the skin and laid the flesh open to infection, so that the man might afterward die. It was true that the others would work that much harder, for a few days at least after Dessalines had passed. Toussaint had a different style—if he had not been terribly provoked, he punished only with a glare, whereupon the suspect would apply himself to his cane knife or hoe with tripled diligence, pursued by his own imagination of what might follow if he did not.

But somehow Arnaud was not eager for this meeting. Let Claudine play hostess if she would; he knew she'd press Toussaint and his men to dine with them that night. If he accepted, they'd be in for a display of his famous piety on the morrow morn . . . He pulled down the brim of the wide straw hat he wore against the sun, and walked behind the mill down the crooked path which led through the bush to his distillery. Arnaud did not drink strong spirits as carelessly as he once had, but it seemed to him now advisable to test the quality of the morning run.

There, about twenty minutes later, Toussaint came down with his companions: Captain Riau of the Second Demibrigade and Guiaou, a cavalryman from Toussaint's honor guard. At once Arnaud, bowing and smiling, proffered a sample of his first-run rum, but the Governor-General refused it, though he saw it dripped directly from the coil. Riau and Guiaou accepted their measure, and drank with evident enthusiasm.

"What news have you from the Collège de la Marche?" Toussaint inquired.

"I beg your pardon?" Arnaud stuttered.

Toussaint did not bother to repeat the question. Arnaud's brain ratcheted backward. A couple of Cléo's sons, whom he had fathered, had indeed been recently shipped off to that same school in France where Toussaint's brats were stabled. They were actually Arnaud's only sons so far as he knew, as Claudine was barren, but he had never meant to acknowledge them. He had sold all Cléo's children off the plantation when they were quite small, but a couple of them had reappeared, a little after Cléo did. Faced with Cléo's importuning, Arnaud had seen the wisdom of sending those boys overseas to school—which got them off the property at least. In his present situation he was not able to pay the whole of their expenses, but it seemed that Cléo had a brother who'd prospered quite wonderfully under the new regime . . .

How the devil had Toussaint known about it? He made it his business to know many unlikely things. At least he had not put the question in Claudine's presence; there was that to be grateful for.

"No, no, we have heard nothing yet," he said, with rather a sickly smile. "The boys are remiss!—they do not write their mother."

There the subject rested. The four of them set out on the obligatory tour: cane fields, provision grounds, the cane mill and refinery . . . At the end, Toussaint intruded into Arnaud's books, pursing his lips or raising his eyebrows over the figures of his exports and his income.

Claudine, with the aid of Marie-Noelle and Cléo, had organized a midday meal featuring grilled freshwater fish, with a sauce of hot peppers, tomato, and onion. Toussaint took none of this, but only a piece of bread, a glass of water, and an uncut mango. Arnaud knew or at least suspected that his well-known abstemiousness was rooted in a fear of poison. But Riau and Guiaou ate heartily, and Riau, the more articulate of the pair, was ready enough with his compliments. Then, finally, at the peak of the afternoon's heat, it was time for the siesta.

. . .

The mattress was soggy under her back. Claudine could feel sweat pooling before the padding could absorb it. She could not sleep, could hardly rest, tired as she felt from the night before. The heat was still more smothering than it had been this morning. Toussaint's arrival partly explained her mood, she thought; it was the thing she had felt coming, but it was not yet complete, and so her restlessness was not assuaged. Through the slats of the jalousies she could hear Cléo's murmuring voice as she gossiped with one of Toussaint's men on the porch.

At her side, Arnaud released a snore. Claudine felt a flash of resentment, that he could rest when she could not. But he'd taken a strong measure of rum with his lunch, which was no longer his usual practice. When he lay down, Arnaud had taken her left hand in his and dozed off caressing, with the ball of his thumb, the wrinkled stump of the finger where she'd once worn her wedding ring. He did this often, almost always, but there was nothing erotic in it, and hardly any tenderness; it was more like the superstitious fondling of a fetish. Now she carefully disengaged her hand, slid quietly to the edge of the bed, and stood.

Cléo sat on the edge of a stool, in a pose which showed the graceful line of her back as she bent her attention on Captain Riau, who stood below the porch railing, looking up at her. "Where are you going with Papa Toussaint?" she asked him. Claudine heard a flirtatious lilt in her voice.

"To Santo Domingo," Riau said. "Across the border, at Ouanaminthe—" It seemed as if he would have continued, but he saw Claudine in the doorway and stopped.

"*Bonsoir, Madame,*" he said, lowering his head. "Good evening." His military coat was very correct, despite the suffocating heat—brass buttons all done up in a row. As soon as he'd spoken, he turned away and began striding down the path toward the lower ground. There was room in the *grand'case* only for Toussaint himself, so Marie-Noelle had found pallets for his men in the compound below.

Cléo turned toward Claudine, her face a mask. That same face with its long oval shape and its smooth olive tone, which Claudine had once hated so desperately. The years between had left some lighter lines around Cléo's eyes and at the corners of her mouth, but she was still supple, still attractive, though Arnaud no longer went to her bed. In her frustration, Claudine stretched out her hands to her.

"What was that shout in my sleep last night?" she said.

Cléo's face became a degree more closed.

"*M pa konnen,*" she said. I don't know.

Claudine felt a stronger pulse of the old jealous rage. The one face before her became all the faces closed against her, yellow or black, withholding the secrets so vital to her life. In those old days she could not visit her anger directly upon Cléo (Arnaud had protected the housekeeper from that), so she had worked it out on others in her vicinity. She took a step forward with her hands still outstretched.

"*Di mwen,*" she said. Tell me.

Cléo's expression broke into an awful sadness.

"*Fok w blié sa,*" she said, but tenderly. You must forget it. She took Claudine's two hands in hers and pressed them. Claudine felt her anger fade, her frustration melt into a simpler pain, more pure. It was too hot for an embrace, but she lowered her hot forehead to touch Cléo's cooler one, then let the colored woman go and walked down the steps.

In the compound below, Claudine drifted toward her schoolhouse, no more than a frame of sticks roofed over with palm leaves, which the children would replace as needed. There were some solidly made peg benches, and a rough lectern Arnaud had ordered built as a gift to her. This afternoon, four of the benches had been shoved together to make room for two mats on the dirt floor. Guiaou lay on one of these, breathing heavily in sleep, and Riau on the other, his uniform coat neatly folded on the bench beside him. His eyes were lidded but Claudine did not think he was really asleep; she thought he was aware of her presence, though he did not show it. She could see her own spare reflection warped in the curve of the silver helmet he'd set underneath the bench.

Pursued by Etienne, Dieufait ran by outside, rolling a wooden hoop with a stick. The two children disappeared among the clay-walled *cases*. Grazing her fingertips over the lectern, Claudine left the shade of the school roof and walked toward the chapel. En route she passed the little *case* inhabited by Moustique and Marie-Noelle. The cloth that closed the doorway was gathered with a string, and glancing past its edges, Claudine saw Moustique's ivory feet hanging off the edge of the mat where he lay. Marie-Noelle was on her side, turned toward him, and between them their new baby lay curled and quietly sleeping.

Envy pricked at Claudine again as she went into the chapel. There was no door, properly speaking, but close-hung bead strings in place of one whole wall, which could be pulled back to open a view of the altar to the compound outside. The interior space was very small, built on the same plan as a dog shed that had once stood there. The walls were whitewashed, and eight pegged benches like those in the school were arranged in a double row. Claudine sat down on the farthest bench from the altar—no more than an ordinary wooden table. Above it hung a crucifix carved in mahogany from the fevered imagination of one of the Africans of the plantation—or maybe it was drawn from life, for certainly there had been horrors enough, in the last ten years of war, to inspire such a grotesquerie as he had made.

Claudine sat still, her back rigorously straight, hands folded in her lap. The bead curtain hung motionless behind her, and on the roof the heat bore down. She could not pray or think or breathe. That drumbeat she almost thought she heard was only the pulse in the back of her neck, a headache rising; it would not move the spirit through her.

After a long time, the bead curtains rustled and Toussaint Louverture walked into the chapel. Claudine registered his presence without quite turning her head. Reciprocally, Toussaint displayed no consciousness of her. He walked slowly between the two rows of benches, stopped before the altar, and stood looking up at Christ's carved wounds. After some time he crossed himself and sat down on the first bench, to the left of the cross. Reaching both hands to the back of his head, he undid the knot of his yellow madras, which he spent some time folding into a small triangular packet. Claudine had not seen him completely uncovered before. The dome of his head was high and long, the black skin gleaming on the crown. He gave his folded headcloth a couple of firm pats with his right palm, as if he meant to secure it to the bench, then joined his hands and bowed his head to pray.

As time passed the light seemed to grow dimmer. Claudine did not know if the clouds were thickening outside or if it were only an effect of her own fatigue. She watched Toussaint, whose right hand slowly clicked through the beads of a curiously carved wooden rosary. A movement of the damp air stirred the strings of the curtain behind her, and she felt a current lifting toward the roof, where the eaves had been left open for ventilation.

Finally Toussaint had concluded his prayer. He stood up, gathering his folded headcloth in the hand that held the rosary. When he turned toward Claudine, he enacted a startle of surprise.

"O," he said. "Madame Arnaud."

"Monsieur le général." She made a slight movement as if she would rise. A gesture of Toussaint's palm restored her to her seat. She watched him walking slowly toward her. His head was outsized for the wiry, jockey's body—the great orb of his skull counterbalanced by the long, jutting lower jaw. The body, whose meagerness was accentuated by the tight riding breeches he wore, carried its burden of head with a concentrated grace that rid Toussaint's whole aspect of any comical quality. He took a seat across the dirt-floored aisle from her, swinging a leg across the bench to straddle it like a saddle.

"It is good to see our Catholic religion so well observed here," he said, "when so often it is neglected elsewhere, among the plantations."

Claudine inclined her head without speaking.

"I have catechised some of the children walking the grounds this afternoon," he told her. "I find them to be well instructed. The boy Dieufait, for example, recites the entire Apostolic Creed with perfect confidence."

"As well might be expected of the son of a priest." Claudine attempted an ambiguous smile, in case Toussaint were moved to find irony in what she had said.

"They say that you give them other instruction too," Toussaint said. "That you teach them their letters as well as their catechism. This afternoon I passed by your school—of which one hears talk as far away as Le Cap, if not farther."

"Is it so?"

"Why, yes," Toussaint said. "You are notorious."

Claudine felt a bump of her heart. Behind her the strings of the curtain shivered; outside a wind was rising. She was notorious for a great deal more than her little school, and Toussaint must know something of that, though she wasn't sure how much.

"You rather alarm me," she said.

"There is no need, Madame," Toussaint said. "Of course not every comment is favorable, as there are always some who believe that the children of Guinée must be held in the ignorance of oxen and mules."

Claudine lowered her head above her lap. One of her feet had risen to the ball, and the whole leg was shaking; she couldn't seem to make it stop.

"Yes," Toussaint said. "My *parrain*, Jean-Baptiste, taught me my letters when I was a child on the lands of the Comte de Noé."

Claudine raised her head to look at him. He was telling her the true version of the story, she thought, which was unusual. Of late he had been circulating a tale that he had learned to read and write just before the first rebellion, when he was already past his fiftieth year.

"If not for that," Toussaint said, "I should have remained in slavery."

"And many others also," Claudine said.

"It is so." Toussaint squeezed the bench with his thighs, as if it really were a horse he meant to urge on. "But your husband, Madame. What view does he take of your teaching?"

"He indulges it." Claudine lowered her head.

"Does he not find himself well placed today, Monsieur Arnaud?" Toussaint seemed to be asking the question of a larger audience than was actually present; his voice had become a little louder. "With the restoration of his goods, the men back working in the fields. Why, a field hand may learn to read a book and be no less faithful to his hoe. Does he not find it to be true?"

"I hope so," Claudine said. "I believe so . . . yes, I mostly do."

"You may not be aware that your husband conspired long ago in a royalist plot against the Revolutionary government here," Toussaint said. "Or then again, perhaps you know it. Those men engaged to start a false rising of the slaves in ninety-one—thinking to frighten the Jacobins with a spectacle of the likely outcome of their own beliefs. They thought they could control a slave rising, those conspirators, but as you see they were quite wrong. He was one of them, Michel Arnaud, with the Sieur de Maltrot, and Bayon de Libertat my former master, and Governor Blanchelande himself, who later lost his head for it, to the guillotine in France."

"As did so many others," Claudine murmured. As she spoke, her eye fell on the rosary, which Toussaint held in one hand against the yellow headcloth, and she saw for the first time that each of the small wooden beads was an intricately rendered human skull.

"What an extraordinary article," she said. It seemed to her that each carved skull was just a little different from all the others.

"It came to me as a spoil of war," Toussaint said and put the rosary into his pocket, without telling her what other thing it might have come to mean to him now.

Outside she heard voices, the clucking of chickens as they scuttled for shelter. The wind rose further, as the air grew chill with the coming rain.

"Ah well," said Toussaint. "We have our dead."

All at once Claudine's leg stopped trembling and her raised foot relaxed against the floor. How intimately she had her dead! She wondered if Toussaint was similarly placed, sometimes, or always. It was certain that he'd caused the deaths of many more than the considerable number he'd ushered out of the world with his own hands.

"Yes," she burst out. "My husband killed many before the risings—he killed the children of Guinée with no more regard than for ants or for flies, and with torture sometimes, as bad as that—" She flung out her arm toward the crucifix. "Yes, this morning you rode your horse through the place where there once stood a pole, and to that pole my husband used to nail his victims, to die slowly as they hung—like that—" Her rigid fingers thrust toward the cross again. "And there was worse, still worse than that. No doubt you know it—he was famous for it all." Her whole arm dropped, and she felt her face twisting, that alien sensation as she moved a step farther away from her body. The blood beat heavy in her temples, and she heard the other voice beginning to come out from behind her head. *Four hundred years of abominations—four hundred years for all to endure, and his no larger than a grain among them—*"

She stopped the voice, and came back to herself—she wanted now to remain herself. Toussaint had leaned back a little away from her and regarded her with his chin cupped in one hand.

"During the risings my husband suffered very much," Claudine said. "For a time he was made clean by suffering, as fire will burn corruption from the bone. Oh, he has still cruelty in his nature, and avarice, and too much pride, with contempt for others, white or black, but now he fights against it. I see him fight it every day."

Her voice cracked from hoarseness; her throat felt very dry.

"And yourself, Madame?"

She took it for an answer to the prayer she could not voice. With a lurch she dropped to her knees on the space of packed dirt between them, embraced his legs, and pushed her face into his lap.

"Hear my confession," she said, but her voice was too muffled to be understood. Toussaint was pushing her back by the shoulders.

"Madame, Madame," he said. "Control your feeling."

"No," Claudine said. "No—I want to touch you not in the flesh but in the spirit." But she had grasped his wrists now, to hold his hands firm against her collarbones.

"Hear my confession," she said, clearly now.

"I am no priest," Toussaint informed her. He twisted his hands free and drew them back. "You have your own priest here, who must confess you."

Claudine's arms dropped slack to her sides. To her surprise, he reached for her again, wrapping both hands around her head, balancing it on the point where his fingertips joined in the deepest hollow at the back of her neck.

"It is not easy to enter the spiritual world," he said. From the soft and absent tone of his voice, he might have been talking to himself. But he was looking into her head as if it were transparent to him.

"So you have been walking to the drum, my child," he said. "Sometimes there is a spirit who dances in your head."

The release of his hands let go a flash of light behind her eyes. The wind had blown the bead strings apart and was stirring the dust under the benches around them.

Toussaint cocked his head. *"Lapli k'ap vini,"* he said. The rain is coming.

"Yes, you are right," Claudine murmured. "We must go up before we are caught here."

Outside, the sky bulged purple over them, and above the mountains a wire of silent lightning glowed and vanished. Toussaint turned his head to the wind, letting his yellow madras flag out from his hand, then caught it up and bound it over his forehead and temples and knotted it carefully at the back before he followed Claudine, hastening to the *grand'case*, reaching the shelter of the porch's overhang in the seconds before the deluge came down.

Because Toussaint had stated, over dinner, his need for an early departure, the Mass commenced exactly at first light. The hour was painfully early for some, and fewer of the plantation's inhabitants turned out for it than might have otherwise, but still there was a respectable crowd for Moustique to part when, with a slow and solemn step, he carried the wooden processional cross into the little chapel. Behind him the children of Claudine's school marched, singing, *Wi, wi, wi, nou sé Legliz, Legliz sé nou* . . . Claudine took her seat in the front row, next to the yawning Arnaud, irritable with his too-early rising. Yes, yes, yes, the Church is us, we are the Church . . . Toussaint, the guest of honor, sat at Arnaud's right hand, while Riau and Guiaou shared the opposite bench with Cléo and Marie-Noelle. The other benches were filled with *commandeurs* and skilled men from the cane mill or distillery and other persons of a similar importance. The bead curtain had been tied up above the eaves, so the whole wall was open to the larger congregation outside, whose members sat cross-legged on the ground as soon as the signal was given.

Claudine paid small attention to the words of Moustique's sermon; her mind was utterly fixed on the cross. *Ah well*, she thought, *we have our dead* . . . As she stared, she perceived that it was the vertical bar of the cross which pierced the membrane between the world of the living and the world of the dead, and allowed the spirits to rise.

Now Moustique was chanting the Sanctus in Latin, his voice high and whining. Above the altar, the dark crucifix ran and blurred before Claudine's weary eyes, till it became another image. She saw the body of her *bossale* maid Mouche, who'd been lashed quite near to that very same spot in the days when a dog shed stood on the chapel's site, and saw again the flash of the razor in her own hand as it slashed out the child Arnaud had planted in Mouche's womb and let the fetus spill on the dirt of the floor, then cut so viciously at the black girl's throat that it uncorked her blood like a fountain. And now, as Moustique presented the host, the children sang, *"Sé Jezi Kri ki limyè ki klere kè nou tout. Li disparèt fènwa pou'l mete klète . . ."*

The chapel was opened to the east, so that when the rising sun cleared the mountains it struck the whole interior with such force that everything before Claudine's eyes was obliterated in the blaze. But the bread had been torn, the wine consecrated. She groped her way forward and knelt to receive.

It is Jesus Christ who is the light that illuminates all our hearts. He drives out the darkness to put light in its place . . .

A fringe of cloud drifted over the sun, dimming the interior enough for Claudine to see more plainly. Toussaint, hands clasped before him, opened his mouth for the descending Host as meekly as a baby bird. Claudine's turn followed. Moustique served Arnaud, Riau, and Guiaou and the other two women, then began his second circuit with the chalice made from a carefully trained and hollowed gourd. Claudine held the body of Christ on her tongue. She had confessed her crime many times and to more than one priest, but still the chalice, when raised to her lips, returned to her the salt taste of blood.

4

On the thirty-first day of their voyage, the troopship *Jean-Jacques* drew within range of *La Sirène* and lowered a boat which labored slowly toward them over the deep swells. The passenger in the bow was an ensign who carried a letter addressed to Placide and his brother. Admiral Latouche-Treville presented his compliments and desired the sons of Toussaint Louverture to transfer themselves and their effects to the *Jean-Jacques*.

Within half an hour they had loaded their belongings onto the same boat that had brought the message. Isaac's face looked pale to Placide, who sat facing him, opposite the oarsmen, but this was from excitement now, not nausea. He had got over the last of his seasickness weeks ago. Today was a clear morning, with the wind freshening in the east. The boat tossed like a chip among the billows. The troughs were deep enough that at moments they could not see either ship. Monsieur Coisnon crouched, clutching the gunwales, but Placide felt lighthearted, and Isaac went so far as to drop an arm and trail his fingers through the sea-green water. Coisnon shook his head tightly and mouthed the word *shark*. Isaac, grinning cheerfully, raised his dripping hand and kissed his salty fingers toward the tutor.

Arrived, the boys climbed a swinging ladder to the deck of the *Jean-Jacques*. While Coisnon went immediately below to claim space for themselves and their trunks, the boys remained topside, flush with the excitement of the change and the activity. For some reason the two ships still held a tight parallel course, and the boat shoved off again toward *La Sirène*. Placide looked toward the western horizon, nudged Isaac when he saw the black curve of a dorsal fin break water.

For twenty minutes the porpoises swam and leapt around the *Jean-Jacques* and *La Sirène*, circling the ships with their flat tails flogging the water, jumping so high sometimes that their whole bodies left the waves to be outlined against the sky. Monsieur Coisnon, looking much more confident now that the broad deck of the larger ship was under his feet, reappeared to tell them how Dionysus, Greek god of wine, had turned the pirates who would kidnap him into dolphins. It was a bright moment for the three of them, but a few minutes after the porpoises dove without resurfacing, Placide noticed the boat returning from *La Sirène*, loaded down this time with Guizot, Cyprien, Paltre, and Daspir.

His heart regained its weary weight. Till this moment he had not realized how much it had relieved him to think they were quit of the four army officers. For the last couple of weeks it had seemed they had got up some conspiracy or scheme among themselves. They were forever whispering and sneaking sly glances at Isaac and Placide or, still worse, looks of pity.

Now Placide would not meet Isaac's eyes. One after another the four officers came grunting and clambering over the railing . . . Though they'd said nothing to one another, Placide and Isaac had both hoped this transfer meant they would now speed ahead of the rest of the fleet on this new vessel, as the First Consul had assured them, to bring word of this expedition to their father. But in the event it was *La Sirène* that put on sail and left them behind, hastening to Guadeloupe, as they were told, with orders of the government.

One day after another slipped down behind the stern of the *Jean-Jacques*. Since putting out from Brest, the fleet had been scattered by some bouts of heavy weather. It was after the last of these storms that Isaac had made his complete recovery from *mal de mer*. But also the last storm had blown several of the squadrons out of touch with one another. Placide did not know if they were ahead or behind the main body of the fleet, but he was aware that he was no longer anxious for the voyage to end.

There was no special accommodation for them on the *Jean-Jacques*, the officers' quarters and cabins of choice having already been claimed by others. Placide and Isaac swung in hammocks with the ordinary seamen, and slept the better for it. The food was vile, but no worse than aboard *La Sirène*. The army officers grew edgier by the day, however, as Daspir's private stock of brandy dwindled down toward nothing.

One pearlescent dawn Placide happened to be standing by when a sailor fishing off the leeward side of the ship snagged a waterlogged branch, from whose crotch there flowed a trailing orchid, waxen yellow bulbs sealed and pickled in the salt. The army officers appeared and passed the flower from hand to hand, admiring it, nosing it for scent, which it had none. But afterward, as the sun broke water to the east, Daspir remained standing near Placide at the rail, tilting his face to the warmth and flaring his nostrils in the western breeze.

"I have heard that the rum of Saint Domingue is very wonderful," he said.

"It has been so long," Placide said, somewhat coldly. "I don't remember." In fact he had been forbidden to drink rum by his father, though once he had made himself drunk and ill on *tafia* stolen by older boys. At the recollection, he felt again the sick dizziness and the prickling numbness of his face.

Daspir did not seem to be put off. He rolled his soft shoulders forward and back under his military coat, pressed up on the rail to stretch his spine. "There's a change in the air," he said. "Do you not think—" He broke off and raised his arm to point. "Look, look there."

Placide squinted but there was nothing to see on the western horizon but a low bank of cloud.

"Birds," Daspir breathed out, as if in rapture. Then Placide saw something swirling up from the cloud bank, a smoke-like current of vaguely moving specks. Someone else had shouted indistinctly from the bow.

"Land birds, they are," Daspir said, and turned on Placide a glowing smile. "I'm certain of it—and the land cannot be far."

In the early afternoon Major Maillart, riding in the midst of a squad of Toussaint's honor guard, reached the crossing of the roads to Ouanaminthe and Fort Liberté. Here an ancient woman sat beneath a rickety shelter made of crooked sticks and broad flat leaves, with rows of green coconuts and bananas spread on the ground before her. These comestibles must have been carried some distance, since an almost treeless plain expanded all around the crossroads as far as the eye could see, to the ocean in one direction and the mountains in the other.

Couachy, who led the squad, called a halt and purchased six green coconuts. With short chopping blows of his saber he opened each one and handed it around. The men shared the thin sweet liquor before breaking the shells apart for the white meat.

Maillart bought a stalk of *bananes Ti-Malice* and immediately broke off four of them for the two small boys who were crawling around the old woman's low stool. The children sat up and stared at him, too shy to peel their fruit. Maillart ate a couple of the bananas himself—each about the size of his thumb—and offered them to the other men, but still two-thirds of the stalk was left for him to tie at his saddlebow before remounting.

They rode in the direction of Ouanaminthe, maintaining a gentle trot.

Toussaint had outfitted the two thousand men of his personal guard with the best horses on the island; they ate up the ground relentlessly. The road was pinkish dust and the plain surrounding it almost featureless except for a few longhorned cattle grazing over the pasture. *Bœuf marron,* Couachy muttered, whenever he saw one of these, wild beef. His eyes lit up with appetite.

Maillart was adrift in his own restless humor. He carried a note from Tocquet to Toussaint, announcing the arrival of the muskets, but this was a matter of no great urgency—boatloads of guns hove into the Le Cap harbor almost every day, it seemed. The truth was, he'd wanted to get out of town. The arrival of Isabelle's children had disrupted his *amours,* though of course it was only natural for her to dote upon them after such a terribly long separation. The children, who might have half-forgotten her during their long absence, were rather cool to her at first. She won back Héloïse, the younger, easily enough, but Robert remained aloof. It was absurd to be jealous of a twelve-year-old boy! . . . and yet Maillart had felt that sting.

The worst was that Isabelle wasn't doing it to torment him, as in her sometime dalliances with other swains. No, this time she was not thinking about Maillart at all. Possibly there'd be no coals to discover under the ashes this time around, supposing her attention ever returned. After all, Isabelle was far from her first youth, he reflected, and there was always the modestly inconvenient matter of her husband. Maillart might have sought the affections of another . . . however, it was surprising how many of the attractive white women of the town were receptive to the addresses of the black officers, the most enterprising of whom were advancing in wealth as well as in power, as Toussaint put the plantations back to work.

Therefore Maillart had tried to distract himself in a thirty-six-hour fling with a colored courtesan of his acquaintance. This woman, though beautiful and exquisitely skilled in her profession, had finally left him a feeling of shame. And it was generally uneasy around the town, with the constant rumors of an expedition coming from France. A turn in the countryside, Maillart had thought, might do him some good.

For the last hour the grade of plain had been gradually mounting, and the afternoon light reddened on their backs. A final twist of the road spilled them onto the main street of Ouanaminthe. All of a sudden they had an escort of barking dogs and scattering goats and small children running alongside the horses shouting "Toussaint! Toussaint! Papa Toussaint!" They'd recognized the fine horses and tall riders, the plumes and silver helmets each with the motto *"Qui pourra en venir à bout?"* But Toussaint was wont to send detachments of his guard hither and yon, to distract inquiring eyes from his own actual whereabouts.

Maillart was saddle-weary by now, and thirsty too, his throat caked with dust. But they did not stop in Ouanaminthe. Couachy led them straight to the Massacre River, where they forded, the horses going down to their withers, the setting sun blood-red on the calm water as it curved away to the west. They rode up a ravine on the other side and entered the Spanish town of Dajabón.

Toussaint was not here either, it turned out, but they found meager accommodations for themselves at an inn. The men stacked up, triple and quadruple and some sleeping on the floor. Thanks to his status as Toussaint's aide-de-camp, Maillart had to share his room with only Couachy. A barrel of rum was quickly discovered, and some chickens commandeered for their supper. Maillart turned in and slept without dreams. At dawn they were riding again through a low pass eastward toward the Saint Yago River.

By midmorning they had reached the river valley and were riding eastward along the low bank. The mountains rose towering on either side, dark verdant peaks thrusting into the clouds. There were few signs of cultivation or even of habitation, except every so often a thread of smoke from a charcoal fire hidden on a jungled slope. Once, when they rounded a bend of the river onto a wide flat shoal of gravel, they came upon a dozen black women washing clothes. The laundresses must have come out from some maroon settlement nearby—there had been movement over the border, since Toussaint had claimed the Spanish side of the island for France. The women straightened from their work and stared after the riders, in a grave silence, without a smile or a wave. They and their families would be fugitives, Maillart thought, from Toussaint's labor laws.

In the late afternoon their party was startled by a runaway horse rushing down the river toward them, on the opposite bank. The shoreline was too high and rocky to cross in this place, so there was nothing they could do but pull up and watch the spectacle. It was a splendid animal, however wild, a magnificent blue roan. The horse came down the far bank full tilt, punctuating its gallop with episodes of explosive bucking. Through it all the rider was fixed in the saddle, as tight as a barnacle—no daylight to find between his rump and the leather. He was in shirtsleeves, a white shirt open to the breastbone. When he came nearer, Maillart saw the yellow madras headcloth.

"My Christ," he said, with a glance at Couachy. "It's the Governor-General."

Toussaint and his furious mount shot past them by a hundred yards or more. Then at last the run petered out and the exhausted roan collapsed into a walk. No choice now but to accept the rider. Toussaint turned the roan and brought it back up the bank on a fairly short rein. Now Riau and Guiaou had appeared on their horses, riding toward Toussaint at an easy canter. Riau held a braided lariat coiled in his right hand, but Toussaint waved it away—no need.

Couachy called across the river to Guiaou, who beckoned them to follow. They went at a walk, since Toussaint's horse was blown. The roan had run something more than a mile downriver, Maillart realized. It was at least that far when they reached a ford, and above it on the farther shore was a long oval corral which penned about thirty more as-yet-unbroken horses.

Maillart had heard from Tocquet and others that Toussaint maintained a *hatte* like this, somewhere across the Spanish border. Apparently Tocquet had once been charged to herd a string of these horses down across the Central Plateau to Gonaives. Maillart splashed across the ford and raised his hand to salute the others. Riau returned the salute smartly. Toussaint, smiling more openly than was usual for him, was buttoning his shirt with his free hand. Soaked with sweat, the white cloth clung transparently to the ribbed muscle of his torso. Only a tuft of grizzled hair at the throat betrayed his age.

"Mon général," Maillart said. "When you risk yourself so, you risk the colony."

Toussaint wiped away his smile with a hand and looked at Maillart closely. In truth it had been a heart-stopping moment for the major. As in the case of many French officers in a similar position, Maillart felt a strictly personal loyalty to Toussaint: the prospect of any of his black subordinates succeeding him was enough to give one an uneasy pause.

"Oh," said Toussaint, "if I make a brief return to the work of my youth, it is only for a moment's refreshment." The smile flashed again, then disappeared. By then they had come to the edge of the corral. Toussaint dismounted, stroked the neck of the gentled horse, clucked his tongue reprovingly when the roan tossed its head at his touch. He passed the reins to a bare-chested groom who'd appeared, smiling, beside him, nodded to Maillart and the others, and walked up the slope toward the cluster of low buildings above the corral.

A couple of hours of daylight remained, and Maillart spent them watching the horse-breaking. He was offered a try at the game himself, but declined it. He might have ridden one of these animals to submission in an enclosure, but that mad dash downriver was not for him. The method certainly did work, however, and no one seemed to get killed in the process, though one man was thrown to the grassy verge, and some time was spent recapturing the horse with the lariat. Riau, who'd worked under Toussaint long ago as a slave on Bréda plantation, took a horse out and brought it back tamed. Guiaou was offered the same opportunity, but only ducked his head, teeth tight in a grin, and slid down the fence rail closer to Maillart.

They dined rather splendidly that evening, though in the open air. Chairs and tables were set out on the grass, and platters brought from the kitchen fires. In that cool altitude there were no insects to annoy them and they had a fine view of the evening settling on the mountains across the river. Wild pig had been roasted on the *boucan*, garnished with baked fruit and supplemented by rice and brown beans and a rich *callaloo*. Maillart fell on the food with enthusiasm, ravenous after the long day's ride. All thought of Le Cap and the people who lived there was now far from his mind. Toussaint, he noticed, ate less sparingly than usual, taking a fair portion of meat and a bowlful of *callaloo*, along with his usual bread and whole fruits. He must have one of the old women he trusted to cook for him tucked away nearby. But when the rum went round he let it pass, drinking only cool water drawn from a spring above the *hatte*.

At the end of the meal, Maillart presented Tocquet's note, and as Toussaint cut the seal with his thumbnail, he went to fetch the musket from the shipment he'd brought along to show. The demonstration struck him as a little excessive (and the extra weight had been irksome), but Tocquet must be feeling some immediate need to remind Toussaint of his usefulness . . . Nodding, Toussaint slipped the letter into his coat and stood up to receive the musket. Taking a step away from the table, he turned the weapon this way and that in the fading light, then pulled back the hammer to test the spring.

"It is not new," he said. "French—the M-seventeen-sixty-three. But the condition is good." He whistled sharply at one of the barefoot men who had served the tables, and when he raised his head, Toussaint tossed him the musket. Maillart's eyes tracked its flight. The barefoot man caught the musket in both hands.

"*Ki jan ou relé?*" Toussaint said. What is your name?

"*Guerrier, parrain,*" said the barefoot man with a broad smile. "*Guerrier, sé mwen-mêm.*" Maillart realized he was, most likely, witnessing a promotion from worker to soldier—all the more enviable just now when for the first time in ten years they were not actually at war. He noticed too how naturally the man had addressed Toussaint as *godfather*.

"*Lè ou wé envahissè, ki sa w'ap fé?*" Toussaint inquired. What will you do when you see the invader?

"*Tiré, tuyé.*" Guerrier had brought the musket to his shoulder with an air of sufficient competence and was sighting down at the shoals of the river. Shoot to kill.

"*Byen, kenbe'l,*" Toussaint said. Good, keep it. Then, almost as an afterthought, he told Guerrier to report to Riau for an assignment and a horse.

Next morning Guerrier rode out among Toussaint's guard, well mounted though without the silver helmet. He wore a ragged pair of Revolutionary trousers with the horizontal stripes, which was his only sign of a uniform. But he was a horseman, Maillart took note, his carriage in the saddle as presentable as anyone's. Toussaint rode third in their single file, with Couachy and Guiaou in the lead. As usual in the field he wore a simple blue uniform coat without epaulettes, and today he had put aside his general's bicorne for a round hat, a plume fixed to it with the tricolor Revolutionary rosette. The change of headgear altered his appearance considerably, though of course Bel Argent was almost as recognizable nowadays as his rider.

By the end of that day they'd reached the town of Santiago, occupied by the mulatto general Clervaux and garrisoned by about half of the four thousand black troops posted this side of the border—the rest were in the hands of Toussaint's brother Paul, in Santo Domingo City to the south. At Santiago there was no feast to mark their arrival—Maillart and the guardsmen were left to forage, which they accomplished with a fair success. Toussaint was closeted with Clervaux for a long time, their candles burning deep into the night, with no one else invited to their council, white or black. Next morning they were off at dawn, riding eastward along the River Cayman into the wide expanses of the Consilanza Valley. The area was sparsely populated with Spanish cattlemen and their few black retainers, who were nothing so numerous as on the French side of the island. The Spanish herdsmen stood in their doorways or turned in their saddles to stare at the passage of Toussaint's guard, with never a hail or a greeting. Black rule was not popular in these parts, though it hardly seemed to have had much effect on those who lived here. Maillart had never been so deep into Spanish Santo Domingo, and the vast plain struck him as desolate, though the grass was lush and green, seedheads flowing knee-high on men well mounted as they were.

They sought no civilized shelter that night, but camped out in the open, beating down the grass to spread their bed rolls and hobbling the horses, that they would not founder on the unusually rich pasture here. To Couachy's great delight he was given leave to fell and butcher one of the half-wild grazing steers; there was *bœuf marron* that night to everyone's content. Toussaint scrupulously sent a gold portugaise to the nearest *hatte*, in payment for this meat they'd requisitioned. Next morning they rode out as the first mist was rising from the dew-bowed grass, swinging down toward the pass through the mountains which would bring them through to Santo Domingo City on the south coast. But before they had begun the ascent, a rider bore down on them from one of the northern observation posts. He was breathless, with his horse in a lather, and before he was well within earshot he began to shout that many, many ships were gathering at the mouth of Samana Bay.

It was then that Maillart had it confirmed how much more a horse could count than its rider. Not that he would belittle Toussaint's abilities in the saddle. But at his urging, Bel Argent swung out into a gait so swift and smooth that the white horse seemed a different order of being from the other horses expected to follow him. Maillart was proud enough of his own horsemanship and also thought well of his mount, a strong bay gelding he'd named Eclair as much for its speed as for the lightning blaze in the center of its forehead. But the best he could manage was to hold his pace a length or two behind Riau's mount—that same blue roan that Toussaint had broken just three days before.

Toussaint and the white warhorse had been out of sight for half an hour by the time Maillart and Riau rode onto the peninsula above Samana Bay. His round hat with its plume and cockade lay on the ground, and Bel Argent stood by him, reins slipped under stirrup, huffing and flanks heaving with the strain. Riau slipped down and went at once to Bel Argent and began to walk the big horse in a long looping circuit to cool him down. It was utterly unlike Toussaint to leave an overheated horse standing. Maillart began to walk Eclair, with Riau's mount on the other side, which was awkward since the blue roan kept trying to reach across his chest to bite the bay. Meanwhile the rest of the honor guard gradually grew from dots in the middle distance; at last they came trotting out onto the point. The men dismounted, muttering to each other and their horses. No one dared to approach Toussaint, who stood at the cliff's edge, observing the mouth of Samana Bay with a folding brass spyglass. Every so often he lowered the instrument and polished the lenses on the tail of his coat, then raised it to his eye again with a disbelieving shrug.

Maillart passed Eclair's reins to Guiaou, and led the blue roan toward Riau, who stood still holding Bel Argent, a respectful ten paces in back of Toussaint. The white stallion snorted, shook off a fly. Its breathing had calmed considerably. Toussaint turned his back to the sea.

"Get ready to die," he said. His face was gray. "All France has come against me." He passed one hand across his mouth and added, in a steadier voice, "They have come to enslave the blacks."

Maillart lifted the glass from Toussaint's slack fingers and pulled the telescoping joints to their full extension. The messenger had not been quite accurate in what he said, for the ships had not actually entered the bay, but stood a good distance off the point. At that distance it was hard to ascertain their number; Maillart kept losing count, but he thought there must be between thirty and forty.

He folded the spyglass and held it toward Toussaint, but the black general seemed blind to the offer. He had taken his sheathed sword from his belt and stood leaning on it as if it were a cane. His face remained bloodless; he seemed to shrink inside his clothes. For the first time Maillart saw the man's age visible upon him.

Finally Toussaint did reach for the spyglass. Unconsciously he dropped it into a coat pocket, then walked haltingly to a boulder at the cliff's edge and sat down, balancing the sheathed sword across his knees. At a little distance, Guiaou and Couachy and the others of the guard stood by their horses, staring at the fleet with an impassivity they could barely maintain. It was not the number of the ships that frightened them, Maillart realized, but that their commander had been so obviously shaken.

But how could Toussaint have known the magnitude of France? The black general had made himself so absolutely master of the island that Maillart had forgotten that he had never been anywhere else—that he was born in Saint Domingue and had never left its shores. As for himself, he had been twelve years in the colony, and France, the motherland, might just as well have been a fancy, or a dream.

A smaller frigate had detached from the fleet and was sailing northeast around the peninsula. They would be landing a small party, Maillart supposed, to get the news and maybe look for pilots. Toussaint seemed indifferent to the movement, if he had noticed it at all, and presently the ship had disappeared around the headland. Maillart remembered what he'd said two nights before, when he'd tossed the musket to Guerrier. But why must this advent be taken for invasion, why not the simple arrival of a friendly force? After all, Toussaint had always professed his loyalty to France and almost always seemed to act on it. Could not this point be put forward? Maillart took a step and cleared his throat, but Toussaint had already spoken.

"Riau." Now the voice was crisp and clear, though not too loud. *"Vin'pal'ou."* That radical compression in the Creole phrase, Come here to me so I can talk to you. Riau lowered his head to Toussaint's lips, then dashed to Bel Argent's saddlebags, took out a folding writing desk, and returned to sit cross-legged below the boulder where Toussaint was stationed.

Maillart remained where he was. He felt—no, he knew himself to be held at exactly this distance, just a few paces from Toussaint and his scribe, but, with the noise of the waves slamming into the rocks below, completely out of earshot. Toussaint was on his feet now, pacing, gesticulating, while Riau bent over the desktop on his knees, pen point grooving the parchment. Now and then Toussaint paused, weighing one phrase against another, and once he even glanced at Maillart, but did not ask his opinion. He had not yet recovered his fallen hat, and the yellow madras seemed to throb with the heat of his concentration.

Maillart wondered if someone might have turned a spyglass on him from the fleet, an admiral, perhaps Bonaparte's brother-in-law Leclerc, who was rumored to command the military force. What would it matter if they were watching? he thought. They won't know what they're looking at.

Riau was melting wax in a small flame; Toussaint ground his ring down on the seals.

"Guiaou, Couachy," he called sharply. Then, after a pause, "Guerrier." The three men jogged to him.

"Take these messages," Toussaint said. He had two letters in his hand. "Go to my brother, the General Paul, at Santo Domingo City . . ." He lowered his voice and turned his back so that Maillart could no longer hear him, but he saw that while Couachy had put one of the letters into his outer coat pocket, he'd shoved the other down inside his waistband, and was adjusting the tuck of his shirt to conceal it.

"Maillart!" The major trotted over and threw up a sharp salute. The party for Santo Domingo was already swinging into the saddle, moving out. Toussaint extended a single letter. Maillart grazed the seal with his thumb, warm and still a little malleable.

"Go with Riau," Toussaint said. "Take the rest of these men and bring my messages to the General Dessalines—he should be at Port-au-Prince, but wherever he is you must reach him."

For a moment Maillart's eyes locked with Riau's. Well, he thought, have I got the real dispatch or the decoy? He had already dropped the letter into an inside pocket. He had been through a number of battles with Riau, and trusted him as much as any man of any color.

"But yourself, sir?" Maillart said. Toussaint had left himself no escort with these orders, not even a pair of heralds.

Toussaint had picked up his round hat and jammed it back on his head. He folded his arms across his chest, took one deep breath, and exhaled through his nostrils so forcefully that Maillart expected to see dust stir on the ground between his feet. He strode to Bel Argent, dropped the folded desk into one of the saddlebags, and from the other pulled out a fat feather pillow sheathed in rose-colored silk. Because of his short legs, his head barely reached the horse's shoulder, but a one-handed vault put him into the saddle. He stood high in the stirrups, adjusting the pillow beneath him, then settled down upon it.

Maillart caught himself breathing through an open mouth. He had seen Toussaint take out the feather pillow only once or twice before; in rides of normal duration he didn't bother with the cushion. What it implied was that he meant to remain in the saddle for several days straight.

"*N'alé!*" he said. A short sharp bark: Let's go. And now, with a twirl of his left hand and squeeze of his heels, he was already gone.

5

Only two days since they'd made their first landfall, but each so wearily the same. As if in doldrums, the *Jean-Jacques* lay at anchor among the other ships of the French fleet, off the rocks of Point Samana. Captain Guizot climbed out of the forward hatchway to greet the same brilliant tropical dawn, a land breeze wafting toward him a scent of green jungle. On a coil of rope by the forward mast, that unfortunate sailor sat, staring morosely at the brown-stained bandage wrapping the stump of his left wrist. The day before, he and one of his fellows had conceived the idea to lower a small boat beside the ship and wash the maggots off the most fetid pieces of salt meat left in the bottoms of the barrels. But when he dipped the first piece in the water, his arm came back without the hand. His astonished shout brought half the crew of the *Jean-Jacques* gaping to the rails. His companion in the boat had saved his life by slapping on a rag tourniquet which stopped the spurting blood until the surgeon could reach him.

Well, it was quite possible the man would still die. Such grave wounds festered easily in the tropics—so at least Guizot had been told. The truth was that he had no experience of any real campaign before this one. He and Daspir were both comparatively recent recruits, and though they could hold their own in gambling and whoring, drinking and boasting, they knew little more of a soldier's life than that. Guizot looked the other way as he passed the handless sailor. But Placide Louverture was standing nearer to the bow, gazing calmly out toward the surf beating on the shoreline, and Guizot did not wish to approach him either. He stopped and looked down at the water, its opaque surface glinting with the progress of the sun. Somewhere invisibly below, the same shark must be turning, in its belly the lost hand of the sailor clenching and loosening like seaweed as the flesh was loosened from the bones.

Presently Daspir came to join Guizot where he stood, yawning and stretching and scratching his untidy hair. Then he turned his nose to the wind and pointed, trembling, almost like a hunting dog.

"Oranges," he said, and faced Guizot. "Do you not smell oranges?".

"No," Guizot said, ignoring Daspir's hopeful half-smile. "No, I smell nothing." Although there certainly was some tantalizing odor on the breeze. But Guizot was weary and anxious and bored. So was Daspir, so were they all. It was the tiresomeness of waiting for action or even the news that there would be none. What they really seemed to be waiting for was the regathering of the scattered ships of the fleet; the squadron including the vessel of Captain-General Leclerc had arrived off Point Samana just yesterday. Leclerc had sent one small boat into shore; it brought back the rumor that Toussaint Louverture was supposed to be in Spanish Santo Domingo—perhaps very near, then, to this point where the *Jean-Jacques* rode at anchor.

"We might execute our pact, no?" Daspir turned to Guizot once again, the smile ingratiating. "If only we could get on shore."

"Well, yes," Guizot said, struggling for a more amiable tone. "I know I'm ready for it." As he spoke, he did feel some returning flutter of the spirit that had moved him to propose that the four of them ought to be force enough to arrest the rebel Toussaint, though at this hour of the morning there was no rum or brandy in him to give it fire.

Daspir looked dreamily toward the shoreline, his soft lips working—sucking the pith of a fantasy orange. A sailor dumped a bucket of slops off the stern and at once all the gulls appeared out of nowhere, circling and shrieking and diving for scraps. Guizot scanned the water for shark fins and saw nothing. He glanced at the bow; Isaac had come up to join his brother. Both boys had certainly heard the news of Toussaint's proximity yesterday; Guizot thought they must surely be more restless than he.

A rowboat bumped the hull on the starboard side, below where he stood; and a sailor ran over to lower a rope ladder for the messenger to climb: a youth of sixteen with a pimpled nose, the collar of his uniform coat rucked sideways. "New orders!" he piped, as he reached the deck. He shook out the scrolled paper in his left hand and looked down at it. "For the captains Guizot and Paltre. You are to rejoin your regiments."

"Now?" Guizot said stupidly, with a thrill and a wobble in his belly.

"The boat is waiting," the courier squeaked.

Guizot exchanged a quick glance with Daspir, then made for the hatchway. "Paltre!" he called into the dim, as he thumped his way down the ladder. "We've orders!"

Without a question, and in no particular haste, Paltre commenced gathering his belongings from his berth. Guizot began to stuff his own things into his pack. When he realized his hands were slightly trembling, he stopped and forced himself to breathe more deeply till they stilled. He resumed his packing more slowly, making sure of all his things. When he climbed back toward the deck, with Paltre and Cyprien following, he was outwardly calm, though the flutter in his stomach persisted.

Somehow he'd expected to enter the colony in the company of the more seasoned soldiers, Paltre and Cyprien. But now he'd be separated even from Paltre, who belonged to the command of General Boudet, while Guizot himself was billeted to General Rochambeau. They'd both been plucked from their ordinary postings to this duty of escorting Toussaint's sons.

"Wait!" Daspir called to Paltre, who'd already swung a leg over the rail to the rope ladder. Daspir's face had paled a little, Guizot saw; he too was startled by the change. Daspir beckoned the others in toward him. "Give me your hands."

Paltre's boot heel hit the deck, retracted from the ladder. At Daspir's urging the four of them stacked their hands. The pimpled courier looked on curiously, while at a longer distance Placide and Isaac seemed also to have turned their way.

"We'll keep our compact, gentlemen," Daspir said excitedly, "though we be separated." Daspir's palm spread dampness over the top of Guizot's knuckles. With relief he felt that his own palm was dry. It irritated him a little that he'd not thought of this reaffirmation.

"We'll keep it still," Daspir said and lowered his voice slightly. "It shall be *one* of us four who brings the old raghead in."

Guizot restrained himself from looking toward Isaac and Placide, somewhere behind him.

"Well enough," Paltre said. He seemed impatient with the exercise, which did indeed seem a little foolish, now it was not fortified by rum.

"And the winner shall have . . ." But Daspir seemed not to have thought this sentence through to a conclusion.

"His life," Cyprien muttered.

"Hurrah!" Daspir shouted, tossing all their hands into the air with his own. A strange retort to Cyprien's grim remark, but it did produce a surge of conviviality—all four of them pounding each other on the back and making loud promises of reunion.

Then they were over the side, descending. A deep roll of the *Jean-Jacques* sent Guizot in a sick swoop over open water, his pack and his heavy sword dragging him out toward a free fall, then slapped him back against the hull. His knuckles were bruised on the cords of the ladder, but he kept his grip, and a moment later had safely dropped beside Paltre, onto the boards of the gently rocking rowboat.

Vice-Admiral Magon sailed his squadron westward out of Samana Bay. The larger portion of the fleet, commanded by Admiral Villaret-Joyeuse, made for the open ocean, and soon its sails were lost to the sight of Magon's ships, which hugged the northern coast. Guizot, with nothing else to do, remained on deck, watching the shoreline slip by. Long gray-green flats were interspersed with heavily wooded collines, and in the farther distance a range of high mountains stood sharp against the clear sky. As they sailed on, that mountain range verged slowly nearer to the shore, until its backbone bound itself to the cliffs immediately above the waterline.

At evening, when the setting sun had cast a copper gleam across the ocean, they sailed round the point of Monte Christe and into the Baie de Mancenille. The spot was named, Guizot had heard, for a poisonous tree frequent on the shore, with a caustic sap which burned and blistered skin at the least touch. In the bay they saw for the first time a number of dug-out canoes and slightly larger wooden boats, some of the latter fitted out with trapezoidal sails, angled in the manner of Chinese junks. These must be fishermen out of Fort Liberté; of course they might also function as spies. But darkness covered them absolutely, almost the instant the last burning curve of the sun had dropped below the horizon, leaving only a flicker of firelight from one of the forts which covered the passage into the harbor of the town.

The ships swung at their anchors, moored well out from the shore. Guizot lay quietly in his hammock, his mind turning and turning in empty speculation as to what the next day would bring. He'd had little conversation with anyone during the day, for he was in the company of veterans now, not only his fellow officers but even the men directly under his command, and he felt that silence must be the best cover for his own innocence of war. He listened, but there had not been much to overhear; the soldiers were taciturn, looking to their equipment. In theory there was no battle to expect—in theory theirs was a peaceful mission, and yet the general assumption was that Toussaint Louverture was in rebellion and would be likely to oppose their landing. Of course there was no telling where Toussaint himself might be, behind the cliffs and heavy jungles that barred the coast.

Guizot had glimpsed a naval chart which showed the harbor: the shape of a broad-based wine decanter, with a short, narrow neck. The town itself, with its principal fort, lay at the bottom of this jug, while two others, Fort Labouque and the Fort de l'Anse, covered the narrow passage from opposite sides . . . Guizot lay in his hammock, listening to the snoring, inhaling the fog of human odor in the close space around him. Was that splash the sound of a paddle, or only a fish or a dolphin leaping? He was still thinking he would never sleep that night when the harsh clang of a bell awoke him.

At dawn the ships were sailing in close formation toward the harbor's mouth. Guizot stood nervously on deck, without a function; he had nothing to do but keep out of the way. The artillerymen stood by their cannons, fuses already alight. Guizot's jitters increased when he noticed that.

Some unintelligible shout came from the wall of Fort Labouque as soon as the squadron drew within hailing distance. General Rochambeau stood in the bow of the ship immediately to port of Guizot's, and the captain could plainly hear his bellow: *We are the Army of the French Republic! Make way for our landing!*

Guizot had barely time to think that this was not the most temporizing greeting imaginable. Now he could understand the retort from the fort—*Pas de blancs! Pas de servitude!*—together with a puff of smoke, and an instant later the explosion and the splash, in the water before them, of an undershot cannonball. No whites! No slavery! The cannon nearest Guizot recoiled; he had not seen the gunner lower the fuse to the touch-hole. The explosion saturated him in a hot gunpowder smell, and all at once his fear dissipated (he could call it fear now it was gone) and was replaced with a quivering excitement like that of a pointing dog. One of his sergeants, who stood nearby, turned the ghost of a smile toward him, as if he'd somehow smelled his change of state.

Guizot wanted to act, but in the absence of action he found that he could observe, and with a reasonably clear head. In any case, his own ship was sailing away from this first engagement, following Rochambeau's vessel into the mouth of the passage, leaving a couple of other ships to continue the bombardment of Fort Labouque. It was not clear to Guizot if the first shot had been fired from the fort or one of the ships of his squadron, but certainly the engagement became general without much in the way of a parley beforehand. He watched the naval gunners, smooth in the rhythm of their work. The artillerymen of the fort did their best to keep up a constant fire, but the mobility of the shipboard guns was too much for them, and within the hour the cannon of the fort had gone silent.

A landing commenced beside the smoking wreckage of the Fort de l'Anse. Guizot, half-deafened by the cannonade, responded to the gestures of Rochambeau's aide-de-camp, a youth whom he knew to be a son of the Duc de Châtre, though at this moment, in the surge of excitement, he could not recall his name. He was able to marshal his men behind him in sufficiently good order once they were out of the boats. Another platoon was routing the surviving defenders out of the Fort de l'Anse, and lining them up against one of the broken walls. *Aba blan!* some of the blacks went on shouting. *Aba lesklavaj!* At thirty yards distance, Captain Guizot looked at them curiously. It was not often he had seen

Africans before. Though the walls that covered them had been shattered, these men had never lowered their flag. *Down with whites! Down with slavery!* Under the leveled muskets, the chant continued.

Through his ringing ears, Guizot heard the order to move out. He about-faced his men as sharply as he might. It appeared that Rochambeau himself would lead this maneuver; a short and rather stubby figure, he wore on the battlefield a tall black shako, with a single plume pinned to the front. Guizot's men fell into formation with the others as the column began to move eastward around the edge of the harbor. On the other side, the guns of Fort Liberté proper hurled shot that fell harmlessly short in the water.

Aba blan! Aba lesklavaj! Behind the marching troops there sounded a patter of musket fire, and the chanting voices stopped. In the farther distance, Guizot could still hear the barrage around Fort Labouque. But now the ships that had shattered the Fort de l'Anse were bearing down swiftly upon the fort at the bottom of the harbor.

Guizot realized he had been under fire for the last couple of hours, though hardly in any real danger, and now the cannons of the fort were diverted by the rapid attack of the naval squadron. Now Rochambeau's aide-de-camp grunted an order back down the line, flinging an arm up to gesture across the harbor. Reflexively Guizot turned to repeat the order; the pace of the march went double-quick. Behind the fort, a great black wing of smoke was spreading out above the town.

To reach the fort and the town by land was triple the distance as by water, around the long curve of the wine-decanter bay. The French column snapped along the shoreline at a pace just short of a jog, men stumbling over the rough ground and catching their woolen trouser legs on the low thorny scrub. It was midday and the sun was broiling; never in his whole life had Guizot known such heat. He had neglected to fill a canteen, and his dusty tongue clove to the roof of his mouth as they plunged forward, his sweat-soaked uniform also caking with dust, like the clothes of all the men around him.

Smoke was boiling everywhere as they entered the first streets of the town, and out of the smoke came several shots. Guizot saw Rochambeau's aide-de-camp take a step backward, dropping his sword and gathering both hands gently over his belly. He swayed, then moved cautiously to the side of the street and sat down on a doorsill. For a moment, Guizot stared, transfixed, at the blood leaking out through his laced fingers. Then he stooped and picked up the sword the other man had let drop and swung it in flourish round his head. The son of the Duc de Châtre—hard as he tried, Guizot still could not recollect his proper name.

"Forward!"

That was his own hoarse voice. Away he sprang at the head of his troops; the men charging with him, bayonets fixed. But the smoke cloud at the end of the block contained no adversaries. The few shots still falling among them seemed to come from the rooftops—but what kind of fighter would hold out in a burning house?

No bullet struck Captain Guizot. At the first contact his heart, already pounding from mere physical effort, had made a swelling lunge into his throat, but now it beat more steadily, pumping his body through the necessary paces. He had only to lead, gesturing with the sword he had recovered (his own hung a dead weight at his side), propelling his men from one block to the next. At the third intersection they met an enemy skirmish line, and Guizot stepped aside as the sergeant formed the musketeers.

Ready. Aim. Fire!

At the second volley the skirmish line scattered and Guizot's men advanced through their own powder fumes, mingled with the smoke of burning buildings. All at once they had broken through into the central square. No serious resistance continued here or in the adjoining streets, though there was still fighting at the fort. Guizot received the order to turn his men to douse the fires. With the help of the sergeant (what was the man's name?) he organized a bucket brigade. As the vessels passed in the line he scooped a palmful of water to ease his throat. The partisans who'd set the fires had fled the town, and the several squads of impromptu firefighters were able to bring the flames under control before too many buildings were destroyed. At the end of this labor Guizot was exhausted, charcoal-stained, his throat raw from shouting and inhaling smoke, but the order came down for him to re-form his men and proceed on the double to Fort Labouque.

Again the rapid march around the contour of the bay. Guizot lurched forward as if in a dull dream. The sword of the fallen aide-de-camp still swung in his hand, for he had nowhere to sheathe it. Somehow the whole day had passed in this action; sunset stained the water of the harbor. They were bringing up the rear of the French column now, and by the time they reached Fort Labouque a white flag dangled from the battlement. The victory had not been without cost, for a good many corpses of French grenadiers were scattered around the outer wall.

As Guizot led his troop into the fort, Rochambeau was just receiving the sheathed sword from the surrendering black commander, Charles Barthelmy. Rochambeau drew the weapon from the scabbard, glanced for an instant at the polished blade, and then with a quick jerk broke it over his knee and tossed the clanging pieces aside.

Barthelmy's nostrils flared slightly; that was his sole response. About thirty of the captured defenders stood with him, already disarmed, their backs to the fort's central blockhouse. They were standing in another kill zone, Guizot realized, where the first of his comrades to storm the outer wall had been caught in fire from loopholes from the central redoubt. Some death detail had already dragged their bodies into rows beneath the shadow of the battlement behind them.

Rochambeau rounded on Guizot. "Captain," he said, "you bring me fresh troops."

"*Oui, mon général.*" Guizot drew himself to rigid attention, thinking uneasily that neither his men nor their officer was anything like fresh. Rochambeau's small, dark eyes lazed over him. Guizot was acutely conscious of his soot-streaked face and grubby uniform. But it was the extra sword that puzzled the general. Rochambeau took it from Guizot's hand, looked at the fancy chasing of the hilt, and raised it closer to his face to study an inscription engraved on the blade.

"I have lost too many men to these rebellious brutes," Rochambeau said. "And not only the son of the Duc de Châtre." He aimed the sword's point at Barthelmy and his men. "Don't waste your powder on them, Captain." Rochambeau returned Guizot's salute and stalked out of the enclosure.

Guizot's heart bulged and his breath went short. He looked at the master sergeant. What was his name? It was an order Rochambeau had given; certainly it amounted to an order and its purport was sufficiently clear. Guizot's mind scurried. There was no evading the order. No matter where his thoughts went scrambling, there was no way out. It would be necessary to set the example for his men.

Guizot reached for the sergeant's musket; for a moment their eyes met. Aloyse, that was the man's name. Sergeant Aloyse. Guizot felt a pulse of affection for him. The sergeant had been at his elbow all that day, ready to support him if he hesitated. But Guizot had not faltered. He had done every necessary thing.

There was a shuffle of boots on stone as Guizot's men moved up, a pace behind him. One step more would bring him into contact with Barthelmy. Guizot held the sergeant's musket, bayonet fixed, low by his hip. He caught the acrid, slightly foreign odor of the black commander's sweat. Behind him, the row of loopholes in the blockhouse wall stared like empty sockets. Barthelmy stood in a correct posture, erect though not stiff, his hands apparently relaxed at his sides, though the skin of his face looked tight on the bone. A handsome face, in its alien way: strong jaw under a day's growth of beard, mouth set firm, eyes deep-set and intelligent, the whites of them vivid against the dark skin. He must not look at the man's face, Guizot realized, and shifted his focus to the spot below the breastbone. The bayonet's point shuddered at his side.

"*Aba blan,*" Barthelmy pronounced. Guizot didn't know if he was shouting or whispering.

Aba lesklavaj!

Guizot stepped forward, twisting his hips into the hooking upward thrust, a movement he had practiced many times before on bales of straw.

· · ·

At dawn of the next day, Guizot joined a burial detail, digging shallow graves for the grenadiers who'd fallen outside the walls of Fort Labouque. Or rather he helped to supervise the digging, for although he would have liked to occupy himself by throwing his strength against the handle of a spade, it was no work for an officer of his rank. The graves were shallow of necessity, since the ground on the promontory by the fort was rocky and hard. The ordinary soldiers covered the bodies of their dead fellows as best they might, and at Guizot's suggestion piled cairns of stones to mark each spot. As for the bodies of Barthelmy and his men, they had been tumbled into the harbor the day before, a feast for the sharks or for crabs.

Guizot watched the awkward heaping of the stones. His head ached and his tongue was thickly swollen in his head. Great stores of colonial rum had been tapped after yesterday's fighting. Guizot had swallowed his ration and more. While thoroughly drunk, he'd done his best to wash his uniform in the mouth of a creek that ran into the harbor. The effort had not been wholly successful—today the bloodstains on his tight white trousers persisted as blurry streaks of brown.

Crouched barelegged by the bivouac fire, Guizot had drunk a great deal more rum, listening to stories of other battles told by the veterans and the sergeant while he waited for his trousers to dry. Despite the ugliness of those tales, they were only strings of words and served well enough to distract him from the actual events of his day, until at last he'd had rum enough to suck him down into a dense unconsciousness.

The ornamented sword of Rochambeau's aide-de-camp stuck out of the cairn of stones that marked his grave. The general himself had thrust it there, nodding to Guizot as he did so. A gesture of approval, Guizot supposed. He might have made progress in his commander's favor, though this thought seemed distant from him now, masked in the fog of his hangover.

How quickly the light came up in this tropical place! As they turned from the grave site it was already blazing day. Already it was growing very hot.

There was much work to be done in the town. The fortifications they'd done their best to shatter yesterday must be slapped back together somehow today. The fire-damaged roofs must be patched sufficiently to protect the stores laid by beneath them. Guizot, however, was ordered to lead his men to reconnoiter outside the town. It was a privilege to be sent on this mission, rather than be reduced to manual labor as most other soldiers would be. Guizot saw that notion reflected in the expression of Sergeant Aloyse when he relayed the order. And yet Guizot would rather have been rebuilding a wall or something of that sort; mere marching left him too freely at large in his own thoughts.

The civil authorities of Fort Liberté had received Rochambeau's division willingly. Today they went on cooperating, doing all they might to preserve their property. The fire damage, overall, was rather less than one might have expected. The partisans who'd fought the French troops street to street had evacuated the town when the battle turned against them, taking with them a good number of white hostages inland toward the Rivière Massacre. Guizot's small detail went on their trail, following the road toward Ouanaminthe and the Spanish border.

Guizot marched in a rum-sodden daze at the head of his men. The heat increased his feeling of oppression. He thought of his brother novice, Captain Daspir, wondering what had come to him in the twenty-four hours since they'd parted. Had Daspir found the tasty food he always craved? had he caught so much as a glimpse of the general Toussaint Louverture? had he received his own baptism in the bloody art of war? When Guizot reached for the sense of competition he'd felt when he'd clasped hands with the other three captains at their parting the day before, he could find no trace of it. Then Sergeant Aloyse jogged his elbow and pointed, west of the road, to where the V-shaped forms of carrion birds were circling around a thread of smoke.

It had been a coffee plantation, and though the enemy in retreat had tried to fire the groves, the trees were green and had not burnt—some few were smoldering, but most would survive. Likewise the citrus hedges that lined the approach to the main compound. The plantation's *grand'case* was burned to the ground; here the ashes were still hot, and the smoke still rising.

The house had been built on a low hill which afforded Guizot his first broad view of the surrounding country since they'd left Fort Liberté that morning. Eastward, the path of the enemy's retreat was evident in more smoke fingers smudging the sky, receding toward the mountains. Unless, perhaps, they'd gone the opposite direction after all, or both at once. To the northwest, across the great Northern Plain toward Le Cap and the blue curve of the ocean, there were further blots of smoke scattered above what must be burning cane fields.

The vultures were making a tight spiral behind the smoking ruin of the *grand'case*. At Sergeant Aloyse's nudging, Guizot moved in that direction and discovered the bodies of two white men spreadeagled on a hedge. The proprietors of this place, he supposed, or managers of someone else's good. It was thus that shrikes, in European fields, would pin their kill to thorns. But there was something more, a sign.

Aba blan. Aba lesklavaj.

The scavengers had already picked the eye jelly from those two bloodless heads. As Guizot turned his face from the dead men, the image came to him unbidden: Charles Barthelmy spewing blood from his mouth as he doubled over the upthrust bayonet, the blood-slick on the surface of the harbor, under the hot sunset light, and bodies turning, thumped by the hungry sharks . . . In another flash he saw the stump of that unlucky sailor's hand. An instant more and all those pictures disappeared, into the oubliette where Guizot wished with all his power to consign them. He shaded his eyes and looked away at the blotches of smoke on the sky above the distant plain.

The sun was directly overhead by now, and Guizot's skin was burning. His thighs were chafed and burning also—there'd been too much salt in the water in which he'd tried to wash his trousers. He saw relief in the eyes of the men when he announced their return to Fort Liberté, and even in the expression of Sergeant Aloyse. There'd be nothing to find if they went forward, he was sure enough, except for more of the same.

Guizot made his report to Rochambeau, then went to his meal and his ration of rum. He did not drink as much as the night before. Bone-weariness was sufficient now to send him into the dreamless sleep he coveted.

At dawn the next day he was back on the march. Leaving just enough of a garrison to secure the town, Rochambeau formed a column of most of the eighteen hundred men he'd arrived with, and set out briskly, urgently, into the Northern Plain.

6

At the close of the intermission, Doctor Hébert took note that his sister had not returned to her seat. Isabelle Cigny was still chattering with an acquaintance to her right when the house lights were snuffed, but Elise was nowhere to be found. Someone shushed Isabelle as the curtain was raised. The doctor shifted restlessly, rearranged his legs; there was a cramp in the left one, most likely from nerves. He had been cajoled, not to say coerced, to attend the theater with his sister and her friend—the lone male escort available to them. Monsieur Cigny was absent on his plantation; Major Maillart away on some military mission to the eastern part of the island. Xavier Tocquet had, with small ceremony, declined the evening's program of entertainment. The doctor thought there was more to his aloofness than his usual lack of interest in such pastimes. In the weeks since his return from the North American Republic, a chill seemed to have settled over Tocquet's relations with Elise.

The doctor's eyes swam as he looked at the stage, a blur of cheap, bright-colored fabric, the glitter of costume jewelry streaming in his tears of ennui. He could make no sense of what the players were saying to each other. Fatigue and distraction—he might have dozed off, but he knew that Isabelle's sharp elbow would rouse him. The empty seat on his other side oppressed him. He understood now that Elise would not return; the whole excursion was no more than a ruse, to which he'd been made an unwitting accomplice. That afternoon he had picked up from Pascal that Colonel Sans-Souci was making one of his flying visits to Le Cap from his post at Grande Rivière . . . visits whose frequency had by no means decreased since Xavier Tocquet's return to his household.

When the performance had finally ended, he remarked on Elise's disappearance as he left the theater with Isabelle depending lightly on his arm.

"O," said Isabelle. "She complained of a headache." Her eyes held the doctor's eyes quite as steadily as if she believed she was telling the truth. "I'm certain she has gone home to her bed."

Or to someone's bed somewhere, the doctor thought, but he held the retort behind his teeth. They descended into the Rue Espagnole, where Isabelle's carriage waited.

During the short ride to the Cigny house, they did not converse, though now and then Isabelle leaned out to wave at some passing acquaintance. The carriage was a recent purchase, thanks to the renewed prosperity of the plantations under Toussaint's regime. Its excellent springs made the ride silky smooth, and Isabelle snuggled into the cushioned seat with all the delight of a child.

At the Cigny house the doctor got out to help Isabelle down. A black footman waited in the open doorway, candles aglow in the room behind him.

"Do come in," Isabelle said. "Perhaps a brandy?"

"No, I think not," the doctor said. She laid a hand on his sleeve as if she would stay him.

"Never fear," he snapped. "I mean to take a very long walk—I will not risk returning to my sister's house before her."

"O, don't be cross," said Isabelle.

"Pardon," said the doctor, stifling his annoyance. "But let us have an end to this dissimulation, at least between you and me."

"Why, what can you mean?" she said, her tone still light.

The doctor glanced at the impassive face of the servant within the doorway. "It is foolish, never mind the rest of it, for Elise to deceive Xavier—or to think that he is likely to remain deceived for long. And if I cannot influence her otherwise, at least you two must not make me a party to it."

Isabelle's upturned face went serious. "Perhaps it is I who should ask your pardon," she said. "I . . . I had not thought that you . . ."

"You hadn't thought I noticed anything? Well, often enough I don't. But something of this magnitude is hard for anyone to overlook. One might argue that a dalliance with a black officer is folly enough, but to carry it on under the eyes of the husband, and such a man as Xavier Tocquet—"

"What is folly is to stand discussing such a matter in the street," Isabelle said. "Come in, and I will hear you out at leisure."

"But no," the doctor said. He took her hands. "I don't mean to quarrel with you, yet I am weary and my temper is short—let us leave it for another day."

"As you prefer." Isabelle stood tiptoe to kiss his cheeks, then loosed his hands and went inside.

Doctor Hébert walked two blocks down the slope to the harbor—a maneuver which took him well clear of Elise's new house—and turned into the Rue Royale. A reception was under way, with a great many people coming and going, at the house of General Henri Christophe. Military commander of the town and its surrounds, Christophe had built a mansion of the most spectacular opulence—the *fêtes* he held there were second only to those put on by Toussaint himself in the Government House. Someone hailed the doctor as he passed, beckoning him into the torch-lit court behind the gate, but with a wave of his hand and some muttered reply he walked on, without quite recognizing who it was who'd invited him.

Gaiety still surrounded him for the next couple of blocks. Le Cap night life had resumed in force, propelled by the recent surge of prosperity. It was nearly ten years, the doctor reflected, since the whole town had been burned to the ground, but now it was rebuilt to an even higher standard of luxury (not to say ostentation) than before. Save for the scorch marks clinging to some foundations (though tonight he could not even see those, in the dim), no visible trace remained of that old conflagration. The doctor did not know just why his thoughts had turned in such a direction. Perhaps it was an overflow of his apprehension about Elise and Xavier Tocquet. Ahead there were torches blazing in the Place Clugny, but they were there to furnish light rather than destruction.

A chorus of deep-voiced drumming grew stronger as he entered the square, slipping around the edges, away from the light. White faces had disappeared from the pedestrian traffic in the last couple of blocks he had walked. What he approached was an almost purely African festival. He kept to the shadows, where no one seemed to notice him or pay him any mind. Three drums were beating, west of the carved stone fountain with its Latin inscription. It was unusual for drums to emerge in the center of town, but the Place Clugny was the site of the Negro Market, and sometime theater of popular entertainments for the blacks. Here too a guillotine had once been erected, when the French Jacobin Commissioner Sonthonax had ruled the region. But after a single beheading, the blacks who witnessed it had torn down the machine, all in one spurt of spontaneous rage—too appalled by its mechanical cruelty to let it stand.

How darkly his thoughts were running tonight! The doctor gave his head a brisk shake, and then the drumming filled it. An old woman in a blue headcloth and a long striped skirt was dancing before the drums, pirouetting with the light grace of a girl. There were other dancers, a few men and women dressed all in white, dancing less with one another than with their own shadows, the unseen patterns of the drums . . . beating, beating with the pulse at the back of his head. Relaxing, the doctor let himself be drawn toward it further, further down into the throb of it. After a time it was the sustained overtone, a great hollow drone, that one heard and attended to, above and beyond the percussive strokes of palm or stick. He thought of Claudine Arnaud, well known to participate in such dances to the full. But he would remain observing from the outskirts, like those black men in uniform who watched from the opposite side, still without being rigid.

The tone of the drumming went harsh and dry, as the tempo picked up speed; the doctor seemed to feel it fluttering in his throat. His attention was drawn to a tall man who stood behind the drums, clashing two pieces of iron together with a fierce, piercing sound. A rusted rivet, and yes, a curved piece of a broken manacle, which he tossed in his hand to make it ring. The sound of the irons was like the crack at the end of a whip's uncoiling. The people pressed in, knotting more tightly around the drums and dancers, singing now:

Kalfou, sé Kalfou ou yé
Maît Kalfou, sé lwa . . .
Sé Kalfou ki vini nou
Kalfou k'ap pase baryè-a . . .

And with those verses a small figure burst into the circle with arms stretched wide. The upper part of his face was hidden by a fringe of hanging leaves bound to his forehead by the edge of the blood-red headcloth he wore. His movement drove the other dancers backward, like magnets repelling yet at the same time attracted. A small, knotty figure, dancing and turning with slightly bowed legs, arms rigidly outstretched, like wings of a gliding hawk. The arms were trembling, they were held so taut. The doctor watched, fascinated. Under the leaf-mask the jaw was heavy and underslung, the mouth a grinning rictus, the head overall too large for the body. The arms trembled with their tension as the dancer turned his back—the doctor could see the small muscles along his shoulders twitching.

Kalfou, it's Kalfou you are
The Master of the Crossroads is a god . . .
It's Kalfou who comes among us
The Master of the Crossroads is passing through the gate . . .

The old black dame in the striped skirt passed by the doctor, a sweep of her hem inviting him into her movement. *Ou vlé viré?* she said as she twirled again toward the drums, Do you want to dance? But the doctor only took another step back, raising his eyes away from her. Kalfou was standing stock still now, his back to the doctor, the knot of his headcloth tight as a bloodclot to the base of his skull, his arms pressed hard against some invisible containment like the arms of Samson brought to bear on the pillars of the temple. The clash of the irons at the end of each drum phrase was like a slap in the doctor's face. On the opposite side of the circle, one of the men in uniform was positioned so as to see Kalfou's face, and there seemed to be something there he recognized, though with an expression of disbelief. That onlooker wore an officer's epaulettes, and all at once the doctor realized it was Colonel Sans-Souci.

Next morning he woke just before dawn, despite the restless night he'd passed. The sight of Sans-Souci in the Place Clugny had freed him to go home at a relatively reasonable hour (for even if Elise had not yet returned, at least he knew she was not in assignation with the black colonel). In the event, Elise and Tocquet were closeted in their boudoir by the time the doctor climbed the stairs, and when he went to his own room in the back of the house he could still hear the querulous tones of their voices, jerking along with the same uneasy rhythm as those drums.

Zabeth, who knew his habits well, had brewed coffee. He stirred in sugar and drained his cup in a couple of gulps, put on his broad-brimmed straw hat, and went out. Elise was still abed, no doubt, and where Tocquet might be was anybody's guess. At this hour the doctor was alone on the street but for soot-stained charcoal burners down from the hills, their donkeys loaded with their product, drifting ghost-like from one kitchen to the next.

There was no crisis at the hospital today, nor had there been one since Captain Howarth had put to sea with the *Merry Bell* just a few days before. The yellow fever, by the grace of God, had not spread beyond the victims in Howarth's crew. All the same, the doctor had yielded to Elise's importuning and released Zabeth from hospital duty. He needed skilled nursing less urgently now. There were just two cases of malaria, recovering well enough, and three of dysentery, which clean water and a sound diet should soon cure, and finally an exceptionally careless cane-cutter from Habitation Héricourt, who'd severed the toes of his left foot with an unlucky stroke of his own *coutelas*.

Once the other patients had been seen to, Doctor Hébert spent some careful time unpeeling the dressing from this wound, soaking in well-boiled water steeped with antiseptic herbs. Thus far there was no sign of gangrene, and with sufficient attention the foot might be saved. Héricourt had recently become Toussaint's headquarters on the Northern Plain, as well as an important source of his personal income, and the doctor was sure that Toussaint had numbered each hair on the head of every worker there . . .

By the time he'd put a fresh bandage on the de-toed foot, one of his women nurses was spooning out the noontime meal: boiled rice, with a serving of spicy black beans for those whose stomachs could digest it. Plain rice, the doctor had learned, was most salubrious in cases of dysentery. He took a spoonful of beans with his own helping, and ate it slowly, seated on a stack of bricks that had been delivered for repairs to a crumbling interior wall. A parrot chattered in the crown of the tall palm tree against his back. There was some commotion on the heights above the hospital, northward in the direction of Fort Picolet—a musket fired from a signal post, and voices shouting down into the town. The doctor paid it little mind. He'd slept so poorly the night before that food in his belly made him groggy. When he had finished the meal, he returned his *coui* to the cook and climbed into a sailor's hammock strung between the palm trunk and one of the gateposts, meaning to doze through the heaviest heat of the day.

As soon as his eyes closed, he seemed to tumble into the confusion of last night's dream, or was it the reality? Again the unsettling rattle of the drums, dizzying spin of the dancers, the black soldiers watching from the far edge of the circle, their fixed eyes glittering in the thrusting red flames of the torches . . . The figure of Kalfou with its arms stretched out as if by an invisible rack—what could that apparition portend? Riau or Guiaou might have given him some hint, if he'd known how to put the question with sufficient tact, but neither one of them had been seen in the town since they last rode away with Toussaint. Kalfou revolved in the direction of the doctor, tilting the stiffened wingspread of his arms, his long jaw loosening below the veil of leaves. As the mouth opened there was a rattling of iron and the voice was the voice of a woman, rimmed with hysteria—

Doktè! Doktè!

He sat up so suddenly the hammock dumped him in the dirt below the palm tree. Zabeth, disheveled and all in a lather from running across half the town, kept calling out his title, her head tossing as she shook the bars of the gate. The doctor got up and dusted the seat of his trousers and unbolted the gate for her.

"Madanm mandé w tounen lakay tout suite!" Zabeth babbled as she stumbled into the enclosure. Madame wants you to come back to the house right away. A full circle of white went round her brown irises. The doctor gave her a shake, then pressed down on her shoulders to anchor her in place while he dipped a gourd of cool water from the pail beside the ashes of the cook fire. He splashed a handful into his own face, then pressed his dampened fingers to Zabeth's temples and the insides of her wrists.

"Calm yourself," he said. "What is it?"

"Ships." Zabeth flailed an arm in the direction of the sea. *"Gegnen bato anpil anpil anba—gwo batiment yo!"* Big French warships in the harbor. Many, many . . ."

The doctor stepped out through the gateway and shaded his eyes to look, but the section of the harbor he could see from this angle was empty except for the usual sprinkling of small fishing craft. All the same there might well be a French fleet of any size beyond the harbor mouth to the north. He could hear trumpets sounding in the *casernes*, just a couple of blocks away.

"It was Madame Elise who asked for me?" he said, glancing at Zabeth for confirmation. "And Monsieur Xavier?"

"Pa konnen, pa we'l," Zabeth said. I haven't seen him, I don't know.

"Dousman," the doctor said, unconsciously quoting one of Toussaint's favorite admonitions. Easy. "We'll go back."

He swung the heavy gate shut behind them and they set off across the Rue St. Avnie, but almost at once their way was blocked by a column of infantry streaming from the gates of the *casernes* down toward the harbor. The doctor and Zabeth went zigzagging down the slope, but the troops reached every corner ahead of them, and finally they stood waiting in the Rue Royale. When all the troops had finally gone by, the doctor took Zabeth by the wrist so as not to lose her as he weaseled his way through the crowd of excited onlookers across the intersection. Two blocks further on, they saw General Christophe's coach bearing down on them at a great rate. The doctor climbed a curbstone to let it pass, but the coach halted just where he had stopped, and the door slapped open.

"Climb in, sir, I want you." It was Christophe who spoke, and the doctor saw there was no refusing. He let go Zabeth's arm and got in.

Zabeth stood on the curbstone, the fingers of one hand spread over her throat, pulsing with the rhythm of the hoofbeats as General Christophe's coach went jolting and creaking down the Rue Royale. When the coach had turned the corner, she smoothed her hand down over her bodice and turned to go, more slowly now, toward the house of Madame Elise. Her unsuccess in retrieving the doctor weighed down on the top of her head, in the same spot where the midday sun was beating. With her two thumbs she wiped back buds of sweat from her temples, along the trim line of her tight white headcloth. The new carriage of Madame Isabelle, she saw, was standing by the door of Madame Elise.

"W pa join'l?" the porter said as he opened the arch-topped wooden door for her. You didn't find him?

"M pa kenbe'l," she said. I couldn't hold on to him, smiling ambiguously as she passed into cooler, dim interior, her hips seeming to swing themselves, as if they were independently aware of the porter's attention. He was a new man in the house and Zabeth knew he admired her, but she had not yet even learned his name. Madame was with her friend, she thought, so she need not go to her at once; she walked to the small bedroom in the back of the house, where the two children were sleeping—

Mireille in her white lacy bassinet, and her own Bibiane, the child of Bouquart, on a pile of clean rags beside it. Mireille murmured and snuffled, her soft mouth opening against the pillowslip, and Zabeth felt her milk start, seeping against the pads of folded cloth arranged over the nipples, under her chemise—she waited, but neither child awoke, and after a moment she slipped out, softly shutting the door behind her.

The door to the second-floor parlor was just ajar, and Zabeth had raised her hand to knock, but the voice of Madame Isabelle came faintly leaking through the crack, and Zabeth let her hand float to her waist. Madame Elise was with her friend, there was no need to interrupt her . . . she might have forgotten that she had sent for her brother, or she might be angry, or distressed, that he did not appear. The mood of Madame Elise was very changeable these last weeks. She had given Mireille to Zabeth to nurse, and for that Zabeth was calmer than her mistress, or at least she felt so now. The agitated spirit of Elise had driven Zabeth frantically through the streets to the hospital in quest of the doctor and on the return she had felt just as perturbed by the uneasy excitement of all the people milling in the streets around her as the soldiers passed, but now, in the quiet of the house, she was still and heavy again, a little sleepy too.

On the landing two steps below the parlor door was a basket of sewing on a short-legged, rough-carved chair. Zabeth sat down and lifted a piece of work from the basket—a soft white cotton gown, trimmed with red ribbon, for Mireille. There was another identical to it in the basket, meant for Bibiane; it was a fancy of Madame Elise to dress the two children alike. Both garments wanted hemming. Zabeth squinted to thread her needle, then began the quick small stitches as Elise had taught her long ago, half attending to the voices of the white women that came curling around the door.

"O," said Isabelle, turning before the open doorway to the balcony above the Rue Royale, "I do feel *oppressed*."

"It is the heat," Elise said, automatically. She felt it too—the heat was inescapable at this hour, and on an ordinary day she would have passed the time in her bedroom, sleeping, or trying or pretending to.

"It is *ennui*," Isabelle said.

"Today?" Elise said quizzically, but even the effort of arching her eyebrows seemed too much; she lolled back on the rolled arm of the divan where she sat. "Why, we have had our share of stimulation, with the news of the fleet—and more to come before the day is out."

"I daresay," Isabelle said, still pacing along the three doorways letting onto the balcony. "O, I don't know, I cannot settle."

"You miss your captain, maybe?" Elise said. "Major, rather."

"We shall see officers aplenty once they've landed," said Isabelle. "A dozen regiments, according to the rumor. And Pauline Bonaparte, the

First Consul's sister, is supposed to have come out with her husband. I shall be curious to see her—she is said to be a very great beauty."

"And also a very great flirt," Elise yawned. "Do sit down—you are making me restless."

But Isabelle continued to walk, twirling just enough to make a slight flare in her skirt with each turn. "The streets were almost impassable on my way here," she said. "A movement of troops from the *casernes*."

"Troops? Where were they going?"

"Down toward the Batterie Circulaire."

Elise sat up. "You don't imagine they mean to oppose the landing."

"O surely not—it would be such folly. I suppose it was only a parade."

A breath of heavy, humid air moved through the open archways, bare hint of a breeze that soon faded. Elise felt a return of the turmoil she'd experienced when the news of the fleet had first been shouted down the block.

"It is to be Héloïse's First Communion soon, is it not?" she said, for a distraction.

"Yes," Isabelle said, looking out through the archways, setting a fingernail to her lower lip. "I ought to have taken her back to the dressmaker this morning. But she is willful—she does not like to go."

Then Isabelle swung suddenly toward Elise. "My dear, your brother is concerned for you."

"And I for him," Elise said. "Well, I'd sent for him before you came— and why has he not come?" She made as if to rise, but Isabelle advanced upon the divan, took her hands, and settled her back down.

"If the landing *should* be opposed?" Elise said. "Where *is* Antoine?"

"Then there will be a great deal of trouble." Isabelle held Elise's hand in her own, stroking the small bones of the back of it with her fingertips. "But if you are frightened, I wonder that you have not sent for your husband."

"I should not know where to send," Elise sniffed. "His movements are a mystery to me." The contact of their palms was sweaty, and Elise pulled her hand away, irritated by the dampness. "I thought that man would set me free," she said. "But now . . ."

Isabelle had drawn back a little and was adjusting her skirt over her knees, as Elise stared at the lines on the palm of her hand. "It seems to me," Isabelle said, "that you have exercised quite a considerable freedom, during Monsieur Tocquet's voyage to the North American Republic."

"If so," Elise said, "was it not wrong of him to leave me too much to my own devices?"

"My dear," Isabelle said. "It is difficult to imagine a more dangerous lover than Xavier Tocquet. And yet I believe you have contrived to find one."

Elise stared at her. "But you encouraged me with Xavier, from the beginning."

"Yes, because I could not bear to see you wither in the clutch of your first husband," Isabelle said. "And at that time, it appeared that Xavier did set you free."

"I won't deny it." Elise looked away. Through the arched doorways the slate-colored line of the horizon appeared, beyond the red-tiled roofs descending the slope to the harbor front. "But now . . ."

Isabelle resumed smoothing her skirt. "Of course I cannot say from my own experience what it might be like to marry one's lover . . ."

"You who are so well versed in *ennui*?" Elise said, and then, at once, "Oh, do forgive me that."

"Consider it forgotten." Isabelle allowed Elise to take her hands and search her eyes. "It's not *ennui* I see in you," she said. "That is not a feeling that our Monsieur Tocquet would be likely to inspire. No, I think it is resentment—that you feel yourself neglected."

Elise had the impulse to pull away again; to contradict it she squeezed Isabelle's hands and brought her face in closer. A dozen years since they'd first met—Elise brought out from France as the bride of the planter Thibodet, and Isabelle the Creole *demoiselle*, born and raised and married in the colony; she'd seemed to know everything Elise had yet to learn. From the first they had *looked* well together. Isabelle's smallness, with her dark eyes and black hair and her ice-white skin, had set off Elise's blond hair and high coloring and her willowy height. If their different beauties had not been so complementary, perhaps they might never have become friends at all.

Elise leaned in to kiss Isabelle's cheek, then observed her from the nearer range. Isabelle took great good care of herself, and yet when one looked so very closely there were crows' feet faintly fanning from the corners of her eyes, and other pale lines lay across her throat.

"Would you have married Maillart if you could?"

Isabelle laughed merrily. "Not him, not O'Farrel, nor any of those. Well." She let go of Elise and put her hand to her bosom, covering a pendant that lumped beneath the cloth. Elise looked at her curiously.

"In a different world, I might have married Joseph Flaville."

Elise felt her mouth plop open. And yet, somehow she had always known it—only now it had been voiced, she could recognize what she knew.

"Do I shock you?" Isabelle said. "Of late, my dear, you have equaled me even in that adventure, or almost, and yet the world as it is constrains us still. If your brother—"

"That my brother should remind me of the proprieties," Elise said sourly. "When he himself has actually married a mulattress."

"I meant to say that an indiscretion must be very flagrant to be noticed at all by your brother," Isabelle told her. "He who has no eye nor ear for such things. If he is troubled, you must see that you really have gone very far. Yet I think what troubles him is not propriety, but that you may provoke Xavier too much."

"Xavier has a sense of justice."

"So he does," said Isabelle. "Are you certain you know exactly how it operates?"

The thump of a distant cannon brought them to their feet. In an instant they were both craning out over the filigreed iron railing of the balcony. But the harbor was calm and quiet as it had been before, all the way to the cliffs on the promontory that hid Fort Picolet from their view.

"It is nothing," Isabelle said finally. "A salute, a signal shot . . . but I must go—I don't like to be so long away from Robert and Héloïse, until it has all passed over."

"Of course it *will* pass over," Elise said. They kissed at the parlor door, then Elise drew it open, starting to see Zabeth at her sewing on the landing.

"How long have you been here?" she said, more sharply than she'd meant, and then, "Have you brought Doctor Hébert?"

Zabeth stood up, the baby dress trailing from one hand by its half-finished hem. *"Oui, madanm,"* she said. "But General Christophe took him into his carriage. Just there—" She pointed, through the house walls, in the direction of the Rue Royale.

"Took him where?"

Letting the dress fall in the basket, Zabeth turned up her empty palms. *"Pa konnen, madanm.* I don't know. They were going toward the harbor."

Isabelle and Elise exchanged a glance. "He will have all the news, Antoine, when you have found him," Isabelle said. "You must send a note—or come to us this evening."

"Yes, of course," Elise said. Isabelle blew her a final kiss and turned to descend the stairs. Elise kept looking at Zabeth as if she might say something more, but instead she withdrew, closing the parlor door behind her, taking care that it shut completely.

Zabeth sat down and resumed her sewing. The image of Madame Isabelle's trim straight back receding into the stairwell persisted in her head. She had learned little from overhearing their conversation she had not already known. Bouquart had brought to her the rumor of what had passed between Captain Flaville and the white lady, and the result of it. That was before Bouquart had to go beneath the waters because he'd rebelled against Papa Toussaint. Afterward other voices had brought Zabeth the story of how Madame Isabelle had fainted dead away, here in the Place d'Armes of Le Cap, when she saw Flaville shot to death by cannonloads of grapeshot, for the same crime.

From the direction of the Place d'Armes, Christophe's carriage crossed the Rue Neuve and passed along the outer wall of the waterfront *casernes.* Another turn brought them again in view of the port. To the right, the wall of the artillery emplacement which covered the harbor curved toward them. The air of urgency among the cannoneers manning the post made the doctor's stomach tumble for a moment. The carriage turned northward, onto the Quai d'Argout.

"What do you suppose to be the meaning of this expedition?" Christophe said.

"Pardon?" said Doctor Hébert. "The expedition?"

"The forces of the French army—if that indeed is what they are— contained in the fleet which has just appeared in the harbor's mouth," Christophe said. "That expedition."

"Eh . . . ," the doctor breathed. "Possibly it is meant for a reinforcement of the corps of Governor-General Toussaint?" He looked out the window to avoid Christophe's gaze. The harbor was calm and quiet and more vacant than usual, except, he now noticed, for a number of canoes that were taking up the buoys which marked the channels where a deep-draught ship might enter.

Christophe exhaled with a flutter of his lips. "Or perhaps they have come to reduce us to submission, Doctor?"

"I . . . they have not offered any hostilities, I suppose?"

"Why, Doctor." Christophe smiled with his lips. "That is just what we are now on our way to discover."

The doctor made himself meet Christophe's eyes. The black general was an imposing figure, his strong chest swelling his uniform coat, the large head carried proudly above the stiff collar. On an ordinary day, the doctor would have felt as easy in his company as with any of Toussaint's senior officers, and more so than with most of them. Since 1791 he'd risen rapidly in the black officer cadre, and generally appeared to be a model of military orthodoxy. Christophe was a person of high intelligence and some sophistication. He had been to sea as a cabin boy on an English vessel, and he spoke English as well as French, and some Spanish too. While still a boy he had gone with the soldiers of the Comte d'Estaing to assist the North American revolutionaries in the siege of Savannah; it was rumored that this action had won him his freedom. In the years that followed he'd emerged as manager of the Hôtel de la Couronne here at Le Cap, a position which put him in touch with all the international news and gossip. Undoubtedly he'd known how to make use of what he heard. Christophe was not such a one as Toussaint, who could ferret out one's secret thought almost without one's knowing it, and yet the doctor knew that Christophe meant to sound him for the feeling of the white community here.

What did he really know on that subject, and how much would he be willing to say? Before he had formulated any response, Christophe broke their gaze himself and fell to looking out the opposite window.

Soon enough the pavement ended, and the coach jounced onto a trail running up and down the hills of the shoreline. At last it descended onto a small pebbled beach, enclosed by cliffs on every side. From this point forward, the way to Fort Picolet was a footpath. A number of wagons had already reached the beach and a file of porters carried loads around the point: sacks of coal and grilles of iron which would be used, the doctor realized with another tremor, in the preparation of red-hot shot to fire upon the ships.

From the battlements of Fort Picolet the view of the sea was much broader, and indeed there were a great many ships standing off the coast—the doctor could make out at least twenty. Immediately below the walls of the fort, a small cutter was just mooring, and the doctor recognized the port captain, Sangros, as he disembarked in the company of a French naval officer. The silence was perfect as these two men climbed toward where he and General Christophe stood, except for the rush of water and the rising wind and the clatter of metal as the men set up braziers for heating *boulets rouges*.

If the naval officer was impressed by this preparation, he did not show it. His manner was haughty, though his voice was high and a little shrill. He presented himself as one Ensign Lebrun, aide-de-camp of the Admiral Villaret-Joyeuse.

"How is it, General," he said to Christophe, "that you refuse to admit French ships to the port?"

Christophe extended a hand toward Sangros, who passed him a brass spyglass. Christophe did not bring it to his eye, but simply held it across his breast as he spoke. "I see twenty-three warships there, and some of them show foreign colors. On what authority do they come? I have no order from the Governor of this colony to admit them."

"Sir, the Governor of Saint Domingue is *there*," said Lebrun, turning to point toward the harbor mouth. "He is the Captain-General Leclerc, and his are the orders you are charged to obey."

"General Toussaint Louverture is Governor of the colony," Christophe returned. "I admit no warship to the harbor without his order."

"Well, and where is he to be found?" Lebrun sniffed. "Your General Toussaint Louverture."

Christophe said nothing. The wind was rising; the doctor anchored his hat with one hand. After a moment, Lebrun extracted an elaborately sealed letter from a large stack of documents he held under his elbow. Christophe returned the spyglass to Sangros before accepting it. He broke the seal with his thumb and, upon a first glance at the contents, gestured at the men to be quiet. The iron clatter stopped, and Christophe read in a voice loud enough to be heard by all present.

I learn with indignation, Citizen General, that you refuse to receive the fleet and the French army which I command, on the pretext that you have no order from General Toussaint. France has made peace with England, and the government now sends forces to Saint Domingue which are capable to subdue rebels, if one must still find them in Saint Domingue. As for yourself, Citizen General, I admit that it would cost me a great deal to count you among the rebels. I warn you that if today you have not turned over to me Forts Picolet and Belair and all the other batteries of the coast, tomorrow, at daybreak, fifteen thousand men will be landed. Four thousand are landing this moment at Fort Liberté; eight thousand at Port-au-Prince; you will find attached my proclamation; it expresses the intentions of the French government, but recall that whatever personal esteem which your conduct in the colony has inspired in me, I hold you responsible for whatever may occur.

General in chief of the Army of Saint Domingue, and Captain-General of the Colony.

Signed: LECLERC

Christophe refolded the letter. "Well," he said. "It is all very complimentary. Let me see this proclamation of which the letter speaks."

"I am instructed to give it to none but the General Toussaint Louverture," Lebrun said, with a certain smugness in the rejoinder.

"As you prefer," Christophe said. Seeming not to know what to do with the letter addressed to himself, he turned it this way and that, then handed it back to Lebrun, who took it with an air of puzzlement.

"Come with me," Christophe said shortly, and beckoned Lebrun through the portal onto the steps which ran down to the narrow beach. The wind came up in a sudden tugging spiral, loosening the doctor's hat, which he'd left off holding in place. He caught it just as it lifted off, and held it crushed against his hip. A great dark cloud was gathering over Morne du Cap, beyond the town.

"Those ships will have to stand further off the coast," Sangros muttered in his ear, "if they do not come into the harbor immediately."

The doctor felt unreasonably relieved by this prediction. Before he could answer, Christophe's voice came booming from outside the gate.

"*Vini moi, m'sieu l'docteu!*—come with me!"

The carriage had vanished from the beach, but three saddle horses waited in its place. Christophe mounted without a backward glance. Lebrun followed suit and the doctor brought up the rear. Unfamiliar to him, his horse was more skittish than he liked, tended to shy at every fragment of windblown debris that the wind carried past, and even at the whitecaps foaming on the sea below the narrow trail. The wind was beating in their faces, and sometimes came the odd raindrop, almost with the velocity of a bullet. As they rode into the edge of town, papers began to pull free from the packet Lebrun carried, whipped away by the wind. The doctor did not know if he ought to say anything about it. When one of the sheets plastered itself across his chest, he stuffed it into his shirt without looking at it.

Great trees of the lightning writhed in the cloud above the mountain by the time they reached the Place d'Armes, but the wide square was still fairly busy, with *marchandes* packing up their stalls, their customers just beginning to scurry for shelter. As the three horsemen crossed, a great chunk of the papers detached itself from Lebrun's bundle and scattered away over the steps of the church. Lebrun seemed to smirk when the doctor's eye caught his, and this time Christophe had noticed too—his face contracted to a fist, but he said nothing.

Within the courtyard of the Government House the raindrops were beginning to slap down with greater frequency, raising puffs of dust. Quickly they handed off their horses to a groom who waited under the tall palms, and climbed the steps at as fast a gait as might preserve their dignity. When they had passed under the doorsill, Lebrun turned back to look at the rain, which just that suddenly had begun pouring down in sheets.

"Comme c'est impressionnante!" he said, his face shining with humidity and the exertion of their dash up the stairs. How impressive it is!

The doctor merely nodded; the roar of the rain was quite deafening. Christophe looked at Lebrun impassively, then led their way along the corridor. As they passed, the doctor thought he saw Pascal, slipping discreetly into a side door.

Christophe brought them to the anteroom where Toussaint was accustomed to receive his *petits cercles* during Government House balls. No further, though there were only the three of them, and the door of the inner cabinet stood ajar.

"Do sit down," Christophe told them. As the doctor and Lebrun obeyed him, Pascal put his head in the door to ask if they would take coffee, and then went out again.

"Well then," Christophe said to Lebrun. "You may now give to me the papers addressed to Toussaint Louverture."

Lebrun cupped an ear and returned an inquiring look. Christophe went to close the casements to mute the roaring of the rain. Beyond the glass, everything had turned a greenish black. Christophe repeated the statement as he resumed his seat. The doctor, feeling the corners of the paper prick the skin beneath his shirt, wondered if the documents Christophe was requesting had been scattered during their ride.

"By my orders they must be confided to no one but himself," Lebrun said. "And the issue is not the documents, sir, but the prompt admission of the fleet into the harbor." He hesitated, looked at the doctor, and went on. "You must know that the Captain-General Leclerc intends to show you every favor, if only you cooperate with him."

"For the moment, it is impossible for the ships to enter," Christophe said, "owing to the violence of the wind, and the unquiet sea. You must accept our hospitality until tomorrow. In the meantime—"

A woman came in with a tray of coffee, Pascal following. There was a brief bustle of pouring, stirring in of sugar. The woman went out, leaving the tray; Pascal remained. The rattle of the rain on the window grew and subsided with the shifting wind.

"The coffee is excellent," Lebrun said stiffly.

"You are kind to say so," Christophe told him. "If you do not give me those papers directed to the Governor-General, it will be impossible for me to hear you any further."

Lebrun glanced at the doctor, then at Pascal, but found no help in either of their faces.

"Very well," he said, half rising to offer the documents. "As you are so extremely insistent . . ."

"Thank you," Christophe said as he accepted the papers.

He went into the adjacent cabinet and shut the door. At this, Lebrun raised his eyebrows, but both the doctor and Pascal avoided his glance; the former looking out the window into the pounding rain, while the latter gazed up into a high corner of the ceiling. After a few awkward minutes, Pascal tried a couple of conversational sallies—the weather during Lebrun's crossing, the state of the theater in France—but none of these tendrils took any root, and soon the silence resumed. Minutes crawled by with a terrible lethargy, approaching the sum of an hour. The rain abated, and the last glimmer of daylight shone beyond the windows when Christophe emerged from the cabinet. This time he left the door half open, though at such an angle that the interior was completely obscured from view.

"The Governor is on the Spanish side of the island," he announced. "Without his order, I cannot permit myself to receive the fleet or the troops it carries." When he began, his voice seemed loud enough to be heard in the street outside, and he raised it still higher as he went on. "The proclamations which you bring exhale despotism and tyranny—I will have my soldiers swear the oath to uphold liberty, be it at the cost of their lives."

Christophe slammed his hands down on the table. An orderly appeared at the outer door, as if it were a signal.

"As the fleet has raised anchor and is no longer in sight," Christophe said, lowering his voice just slightly from before, "you will remain with us tonight and rejoin your countrymen tomorrow. Your meal has been ordered, you may go with this man."

Christophe nodded in the direction of the orderly. Lebrun opened his mouth, then closed it again. With a slight inclination of his head, he stood and followed the orderly out of the room.

"And you, Doctor Hébert," Christophe said. "Thank you for your presence here today."

"It is nothing," said the doctor, feeling that in truth he had not done anything at all.

But Christophe had already turned to Pascal. "Stay a moment, will . . ."

Understanding himself to be dismissed, the doctor bowed out and walked down the corridor. A fragrance of highly seasoned goat stew caused him to glance into the formal dining room as he passed its open door. Ensign Lebrun sat at the head of an otherwise empty table, a service of gold plate laid out before him. A servant stood behind his chair, and half a dozen others manned the sideboard, each assigned to a covered dish or carafe of wine. The candles were lit from one end of the long table to the other. Unnerved by this spectacle of solitary splendor (as Lebrun's expression showed him to be also), the doctor hurried past.

People were coming out onto the rain-washed streets again, voices ringing through the damp air as they called to one another. Someone hailed the doctor from behind, but he only returned the greeting over his shoulder, without slackening his pace as he went toward his sister's house.

"A glass of rum," he said to Zabeth in the foyer. "A large one, if you please."

"Yes, Doctor," she told him. "With lime? or water?"

"Just bring the bottle," the doctor said.

Elise was already calling him from the upper story, an impatient edge in her voice, and the doctor could tell from other sounds that there must be some company there. Nonetheless he waited—it seemed to take Zabeth a very long time to arrange a bottle and glass on a tray. When at last she returned, he poured two fingers of rum and drank it off, then climbed the stairs with the glass in one hand and the bottle in the other.

"Where have you been all the day?" Elise said, and then, when she saw what he was carrying, "As bad as that?"

"I don't know how bad it is," said the doctor. He refilled his glass and set the bottle on a small mahogany table. "What news do our friends bring?" He saw Michel Arnaud at the rear of the room. Isabelle, somewhat uncharacteristically, was in the company of her husband, Bertrand Cigny.

"French ships were sighted outside the Baie d'Acul," Arnaud said. "Such is the rumor—I did not see them. There is no news of a landing. But there is some tale of trouble at Sainte Suzanne."

"I heard the same, Monsieur," Cigny added. "A man passed me on the road, coming down from Haut Limbé. From the height, he told me, one can see smoke over Grande Rivière."

"But you must know much more than we," Isabelle said. "If you have been with General Christophe until now."

"I'm not sure what there is to know." The doctor sank into a chair. Fortifying himself with another warm swallow of rum, he began to recount the events of his day.

"I can't make out why he wanted me there," he said as he concluded. "There was nothing at all for me to do, neither at the fort nor at Government House."

"Except to witness his loyalty to Toussaint—" Isabelle blurted.

"I thought of that," the doctor said, "but . . ." He had not mentioned the curious business of Christophe's long retreat to the inner cabinet. He hesitated now, looking at Elise, who sat with one hand covering her mouth, her face turned to the shadows that edged the room beyond the candlelight. If there was fighting at Grande Rivière, the doctor realized, Sans-Souci would probably be in the thick of it. The strange scene before the drums in the Place Clugny returned to his mind's eye, though it seemed the intervening time had been a year.

"And where *is* Toussaint?" Isabelle was saying.

"In Santo Domingo," the doctor muttered. "According to report."

"But such reports mean nothing," Isabelle snapped, with an impatient flourish of her hand when Monsieur Cigny murmured to quiet her. "Can Toussaint mean to resist a French landing? He is loyal to France to the marrow of his bones—or so he has always claimed."

"*Doucement,*" the doctor said, though for the moment he was losing faith in the magical efficacy of this word.

"*Doucement?*" Isabelle snorted. "If fifteen thousand men should fight their way to shore tomorrow, how sweet and gentle will that be?"

"Oh, I don't think—" the doctor began, but a commotion below made him stop. Certainly that was the creak of the house door opening, and he could hear the voices of Gros-Jean and Bazau, two black men who went almost everywhere with Xavier Tocquet, like his twinned shadow.

"I don't think it will come to that . . ." The doctor let the sentence trail away; the stairs were creaking and all eyes were on the door. He picked up his glass of rum and drained it. Then the door opened and Tocquet walked in, Zabeth's unreadable face just visible in the shadows behind him. He had been caught in the rain somewhere, for the film of dust on his clothing was dampened to a film of clay. Above a line of crusted grime, the pallor of his forehead showed where his hat had covered it.

"What news, Xavier?" Isabelle was on her feet and staring.

Tocquet appraised the anxious faces in the room, then raised one finger, signaling for patience. He picked up the doctor's glass and poured himself a mighty dose.

"Your health," he said to all in general, and raised the glass and drank. "Rochambeau has landed at Fort Liberté. There has been a full day's fighting, but Rochambeau is master of all the forts and the town itself, and he has put the defenders to the sword."

The ripple that ran around the room set Isabelle swaying from her ankles. But she was not the fainting kind, and before Arnaud could reach her side she was already motioning him away.

Tocquet unfastened the leather thong that bound his long queue in the back. He pulled the rope of his hair forward and began combing water out of it with his fingers onto the floor. Elise stifled a sigh as she watched him. Finished, Tocquet shook his hair loose over his back, refilled the glass he'd appropriated, and strolled toward the doors which opened on the balcony.

"Zabeth," the doctor said, for the girl still stood by the door she'd opened for Tocquet. "If you please, bring us more glasses."

"Aye," Tocquet grunted, settling into a chair near the balcony. "I had more trouble coming this way from Ouanaminthe than I have seen for a good many years. All the field hands have thrown down their hoes and are shouting *Aba blan! Aba lesklavaj!*—though they've burnt only a few fields yet . . ."

"Claudine." Arnaud was on his feet and making for the door.

"Don't be a—" Tocquet cut himself off, as he pushed up to his feet also. "Pardon, but it would be folly to leave the town tonight. If your wife is at Habitation Arnaud—she has such credit with the blacks, she will be safer there than you. Think of it. In any case there is no word as yet of trouble in Acul." He put one hand on Arnaud's shoulder, and with the other produced two lumpy black cheroots from the inside of his canvas shirt. Arnaud accepted one of these and moved away from the door.

"But can they really mean to restore slavery here?" said Isabelle.

Tocquet had returned to the balcony doors to light his smoke. "You know it hardly matters what their intentions are," he said, exhaling a thin blue wreath, "but what they are believed to be."

Zabeth came in with a smooth gliding movement, her steadiness betrayed only by the slight clinking of the glasses on the tray she bore. As the doctor reached to take one from her, the paper he'd forgotten rustled in his shirt. He plucked it out.

"Here," he said. "I have one of the papers I saw Lebrun let fall."

There was a general movement to snatch it from his hands. The doctor yielded it to Monsieur Cigny, who, having settled a pince-nez on his nostrils, brought the document near to a candle and began to read in a slow, sermonizing tone.

From the First Consul to the inhabitants of Saint Domingue

Whatever may be your origin or your color, you are all French, you are all free and equal before God and before men.

France has been, like Saint Domingue, preyed upon by factions and shredded by civil war and by foreign wars; but everything has changed: all peoples have embraced the French and have sworn peace and friendship to them; all the French have embraced one another as well, and have sworn always to be brothers and friends; come also yourselves to embrace the French, and rejoice to see once more your friends and brothers from Europe.

The government sends you the Captain-General Leclerc; he brings with him great forces to protect you against your enemies and the enemies of the Republic. If anyone should say to you: These forces are destined to tear your liberty away from you; reply: The Republic will not suffer it to be taken from us.

Rally around the Captain-General; he brings you peace and abundance; rally around him. Whoever may dare to separate himself from the Captain-General will become a traitor to the fatherland, and the wrath of the Republic will devour him like fire devours your dried cane stalks.

Dictated in France, at the palace of the government, 17th Brumaire in Year Ten of the French Republic.

The First Consul
Signed *Bonaparte*

"So," said Isabelle, as her husband passed the paper to Arnaud. "There is nothing in those to cause any disturbance or alarm."

Tocquet snorted. "Would that those words accorded better with the actions. I must point out that Rochambeau, at least, has less the aspect of a friendly force than that of an invading army, as he cuts his way through Grande Rivière."

"Grande Rivière?" Elise said sharply.

Tocquet gave her a narrow look. "I do not know what resistance he may be encountering," he said. "We took care to avoid his line of march. But more than likely he is moving on this town. And what of the fleet here? There was all manner of talk on the street as we came in, but you have told me nothing."

"Christophe has denied them a landing until orders arrive from Toussaint," the doctor said.

"Toussaint is not here?" Tocquet said. "He was seen on the road yesterday, as nearby as Héricourt, and supposed to be riding in this direction."

"There is a man wont to be seen in a great many places where in fact he has not been," Isabelle remarked.

To this the doctor did no more than nod. "In any event," he said finally, "Christophe has taken the markers from the channels. And the fleet has put out to sea again, owing to the storm this afternoon."

"Ah," said Tocquet. "That may gain us at least one day." He stepped out onto the balcony to knock his ashes over the rail.

"Us?" Monsieur Cigny said.

"Then again," Tocquet said as he returned to the room. "It is as likely they may try a landing at the Baie d'Acul, to come upon the town from the landward side, perhaps having joined with Rochambeau—"

"Then there *will* be trouble at Acul." Arnaud was headed for the door again.

"Stay, Michel, it was only a thought!" Tocquet said. "If we go anywhere, let us go tomorrow by the light of day."

"Go where?" Elise said sharply.

"*Ma chère,*" said Tocquet, a little too loudly. "I wish to God that you at least would take Mireille down to Ennery. It will be safer there than anywhere else, for many excellent reasons that you know."

"And leave this house?"

"This house," said Tocquet. "Which you have so recently purchased and repaired and furnished and decorated. My dear, I don't mind speaking honestly before our friends. If all should go well, the house will be intact when you return to it. If all should go ill, the house is not worth your life, nor yet Mireille's."

"As bad as that?" Elise said, her chin held high.

"I mean to take you down to Ennery myself," said Tocquet quietly. "If you do not refuse to go."

"Where you go, there I will follow." Elise bowed her head.

Silence followed, inspired by Elise's unexpectedly submissive attitude, or the darkness of the assumptions which underlay what Tocquet had said, or something of both; the doctor didn't know. Then Zabeth cleared her throat discreetly in the doorway.

"*Messieurs, mesdames,*" she said. "*Le dîner est servi.*"

Elise had been to trouble with this dinner—*porc au pruneaux,* with the prunes expensively imported from France. It might have been so much soggy oatmeal for all the attention paid to it, though all the guests ran heavily on the wine. They fed themselves mechanically as they drank and debated what might possibly be done. In the midst of the conversation a servant came in with a note which had been urgently forwarded from the Cigny house. A deep quiet filled the room as Bertrand Cigny read the missive to himself, the point of his beard twitching as he muttered through the lines.

"Some hope in this, perhaps," he said at last.

"O, let me see it!" Isabelle snatched the paper from his hand.

"Télémaque, at least, has been persuaded by the First Consul's proclamation, it would seem," said Cigny. "So too have most of the civil administration here, be they white or black or colored. Télémaque is getting up a deputation to persuade Christophe that he ought to receive the French fleet peacefully. And he invites us to join them . . ."

"Of course we will go!" Isabelle said, flapping the letter from one hand. "We *must* go—what choice have we?"

Her dark eyes flashed around the table. The doctor looked into the shredded remnants of his pork. He was not certain how much influence Télémaque, the black mayor of the town, would have with Christophe in such circumstances.

"Will you not join us?" Isabelle was addressing Tocquet, who returned her a thin smile.

"No such invitation has been addressed to me," he said. "Perhaps I would not lend credit to the enterprise."

"But what else is there?" Isabelle said. "Are we only to wait for a word from Toussaint? And why does he not come?"

Tocquet took out another cheroot and rolled it in his fingers. "Since Rochambeau has slaughtered the garrison at Fort Liberté, the peaceful reception of his comrades here strikes me as unlikely," he said. "However much it may be wished for, by our honorable mayor or anyone else. As for Toussaint, I have known him longer than the rest of you, I think—I knew him when he broke horses at Bréda, and drove the coach of the Comte de Noé. If he does not show himself in this affair, I think it is no accident."

"Think of our children," Isabelle said.

"Indeed, I do." Tocquet, ignoring Elise's extremely audible sigh, leaned forward to light his cheroot at a candle flame.

"*I* will certainly go with this delegation," Arnaud said, giving Tocquet his haughtiest look.

"And I also," Elise said.

Tocquet leaned back, breathing smoke at the ceiling. Elise turned her face to him.

"But first I will order the servants to pack," she said. "In the worst case, we shall be ready to go to Ennery in the morning. In the meantime, we ought to do whatever we can, that the worst case might be avoided."

"And you?" Isabelle said to Doctor Hébert.

"*Moi?*" the doctor grunted. At the sound of his own voice he realized he knew what he would say. "I shall return to Government House," he told Isabelle. "I am sure General Christophe will receive me, and I may get some news from Pascal, or the others. In case Télémaque's effort proves unpersuasive, we will then have some footing, at least, in the other camp." He felt Tocquet's approving glance as he pushed back his plate and rose from the table.

Arnaud and the Cignys stayed to wait for Elise, while she searched out her trunks and valises and gave Zabeth her many directions, so the doctor was the first one down to the street. The night was clear, with a half-moon risen, the air cool and fresh after the evening storm. He was grateful to be alone on the street and to occupy himself with walking. There was some commotion in front of Christophe's mansion in the Rue Royale—a wagon and a gang of porters working under torchlight. When the doctor came nearer, he saw that a dozen large barrels of tar were being rolled into Christophe's courtyard. He gulped back the sour bubble of wine that swelled unpleasantly into his throat, and hurried up the slope to the Rue Espagnole.

The effort broke out a light sweat on him; the night air was humid as well as cool. In the Place Montarcher, half a dozen men were clustered, braiding rags to the ends of long poles and twirling them in an iron cauldron that reeked of tar. Fire spears, the doctor realized with another jolt—*lances à feu*. A bunch of children loitered at a little distance from the tar pot, giggling and chattering and shoving each other, for all the world as if it were some festival in preparation. Their eyes on the doctor seemed not altogether friendly. He went by quickly; the enclosure of Government House was just across the street.

Those drums in the Place Clugny the night before seemed to beat in his head again; again he saw the stiff masked figure, revolving with its rigid outstretched arms. Instinct told him that Télémaque's mission was not at all likely to succeed, and if it failed—the doctor had been present for the fire that razed Le Cap in ninety-three. He and Nanon and the child they'd made together had just escaped that conflagration with the clothes scorched on their backs. All he had to do tonight was blink his eyes to see it all in flames again.

Within the Government House compound, the silence was complete, funereal. The doctor recognized several faces among the men of the guard, but no one greeted him, nor did they talk among themselves. There was no sound at all except the shivering of the leaves of the tall palms.

Inside the building the formal dining room had been shut up, and the doctor wondered what had become of the envoy, Lebrun. He put this question to Pascal, whom he found waiting in the anteroom, outside the closed door of the inner cabinet.

Pascal shrugged. "He has been sent off to bed, I suppose. And tomorrow he will be returned to his general—weather permitting, of course. With what message, we do not know."

"The weather looks clear," the doctor said aimlessly. "The storm has passed over completely."

"What excellent news," Pascal said, raising his eyebrows. "Then the warships can sail in upon the town with no impediment!—unless there should be firing from the forts. Have you heard the story of Fort Liberté?"

"In general terms," the doctor said, glancing automatically at the cabinet door. As if on a signal, the door popped open and the port captain Sangros whipped through the antechamber and disappeared into the corridor without a backward glance. Christophe stood smoldering on the threshold of the inner room, but his expression softened slightly when the doctor stood to greet him.

"Doctor Hébert, I am glad to see you," he said. "Please stay near me, if you will."

The doctor bowed and straightened. Christophe left the cabinet door wide open as he returned to his desk. From where he stood the doctor could see every corner of the little room; it was plain that Christophe was the only occupant.

There would be no serious conversation in the anteroom while that door stood open. With a sigh, Pascal groped in his coat pocket and pulled out a box of small dominoes carved from bone. He and the doctor played, inattentively, for the better part of two hours. The bells of the church in the Place d'Armes were tolling midnight when an orderly came in to announce that Mayor Télémaque had arrived with a great many people who desired to see General Christophe.

The orderly went into the cabinet and at Christophe's order shut the door behind him. An instant later he burst out again, as if pursued by hornets. Pascal took a deep breath and went in to Christophe. The doctor could just hear his voice murmuring, behind the door, which had been pushed to. Then Christophe shouting, "But I can do nothing for these people now!" Pascal's murmur resumed, persistently.

The cabinet door was jerked inward and Christophe appeared in its frame, his chest swelling, lifting the decorations pinned to his coat, and then collapsing in a sigh. He pulled down his coattails, lowered his head, and marched in the direction of the ballroom. With the briefest of glances exchanged between them, Pascal and the doctor followed.

The petitioners were numerous enough to fill two-thirds of the ballroom. Most of the civil administration was there behind Télémaque, with the bankers, the merchants, and the factors of the port, along with a good many householders. Télémaque had prepared an address in writing, which among much other matter quoted Bonaparte's proclamation of eternal liberty in full, and then presented an argument in favor of its probable sincerity . . .

Christophe heard him out, standing to face the assembly in a posture of parade rest. There were moments when it seemed he would make some movement to stop the flow of Télémaque's discourse, but always he swallowed back whatever interruption he had meant to make, and let the mayor continue. The doctor stood behind him, near Pascal, among Christophe's various aides and adjutants; he had the mildly uncomfortable feeling that he was on the wrong side of the room.

His sister stood with Isabelle Cigny, in the front row of the assembly. The faces of Arnaud and Bertrand Cigny were visible behind them. Isabelle was flanked by her two children. Robert, who would be twelve by now, looked sleepy and a little sullen, but Héloïse, younger by two or three years, was clearly frightened, though it was not likely that she understood what it was all about. And Elise was holding Mireille swaddled at her bosom—what freak of fancy had inspired her to bring the baby out tonight? Mireille began to squirm and mew; Isabelle took her easily from Elise and held her against her own shoulder, patting her back till she calmed. All the while Télémaque droned on, for more than half an hour, his voice cracking occasionally, then slowly recuperating its strength. At the end he recited a long list of signatories, looking around to identify those who were present, making complex apologies for those who were not. Throughout this long conclusion, the doctor could feel Christophe's impatience building, like electricity gathering in a thunder cloud.

"Messieurs, mesdames," he said, when Télémaque had finally ended. "I am aware of all you say. I am awaiting orders from the Governor-General. Without his order, I cannot admit the French fleet to the harbor."

With that, he turned smartly and started for the door, on the wave of a hubbub that broke out among the crowd of people who had spent the whole length of Télémaque's speech shifting their weight quietly from one foot to the other on the polished ballroom floor. Isabelle's voice stood above the rest, high and clear and unignorable.

"General, wait."

Christophe's step locked. Slowly he turned to face her as she advanced a step or two.

"General, it is not quite ten years since all our town was burned to cinders. And now—" Holding the baby with one arm, she made an expansive, swirling gesture with the other. "Do you not see how all of us have labored, shoulder to shoulder and hand in hand, to rebuild it to still a more splendid state than before? With that, we now have peace, prosperity, freedom, and dignity for all. And is all that to be destroyed?"

"Chère madame." Christophe's voice was almost inaudibly soft. "It is not I who come to destroy it." Again he turned as if to depart, but Isabelle's voice held him.

"Think only of your own house, General. The effort that it took to raise it to its present glory. Then multiply that effort by all the houses, and the finest public buildings of our town . . ."

In a flash the doctor pictured the tar barrels he'd seen rolled through the gateway to Christophe's mansion, and wondered if Isabelle might have seen them too. Héloïse was clinging to her mother's skirts with both hands now and hiding her small face in the cloth.

"Can you not think of our children?" Isabelle said, and thrust out Mireille toward Christophe at the length of her two arms. Startled by the brusque movement, the baby began to wail. "My little girl," Isabelle went on. "In three weeks' time she will be carrying her candle to the cathedral—if it has not been wasted by a greater flame."

Héloïse, as if on cue, began to sob into her mother's skirt. Isabelle raised her voice just enough to be heard above their cries. The doctor felt one of his occasional twitches of dislike for her, and yet she was only giving the effort her all. Such an energy was pent in her small body—the concentration a hummingbird must use to hold itself midair, suspended before the blossom which it meant to penetrate.

"Look at her, the innocent, and think of all the others." Mireille's face was glowing angry red as Isabelle talked across her body, which wriggled like a caterpillar. "Will you see them all unhoused, sent begging from the ruin of their homes?"

"Madame! Madame!" Christophe thundered. Then at once he reined his voice back from fire to ice. "I can only await the order of the Governor-

General Toussaint Louverture. Without his order, I cannot and will not admit the fleet." He paused, then shifted into Creole. *"Ou mêt alé,"* he said, You may go, and with that clipped instruction he revolved on his heel and stalked from the room.

It seemed that Isabelle might hurl herself to the floor, to enjoy an hysterical fit of rage and frustration and tears. But as such a demonstration would serve no purpose, she restrained herself from it. The doctor thought that in just half a second, this entire calculation was legible in her face. Isabelle handed Mireille back to Elise, who had stood by her through it all, dazed and expressionless as if in a dream. She took her own children by their hands and led them in the direction of the outer doors.

A few more voices were raised in protest, but they were feeble now, and Christophe was no longer there to hear them. The aides and adjutants were moving forward, encouraging the petitioners out of the ballroom, toward the front steps and the courtyard. The doctor slipped through their ranks and followed Pascal on the trail of Christophe.

The black general was just emerging from the cabinet when they reached the anteroom, paper and a stand with a pair of inkwells and two pens in his hands. He sat down with his back to the cabinet door, and for a moment covered his eyes with his large hands. In that posture he seemed exhausted, past the point of collapse. But when he had lowered his hands from his face, he looked solidly composed.

"Gentlemen," he said, with a nod toward the writing instruments he had brought out. "I shall want two copies of this letter."

Obediently the doctor and Pascal each reached for pen and paper. Christophe spread his fingers and pressed lightly down on them, looking over their heads at the ceiling as he began to speak.

From the headquarters of Le Cap, 13 Pluviôse, Year Ten. Henri Christophe, brigadier general commanding the arrondissement of Le Cap, to General in Chief Leclerc.

Your aide-de-camp, General, has delivered to me your letter of this day. I have the honor to let you know that I cannot deliver to you the forts and other places confided to my command until beforehand I have received the orders of the Governor Toussaint Louverture, my immediate superior, from whom I hold the powers vested in me.

The doctor noticed, as his pen scratched, that Christophe's voice was loud enough to be quite audible through the cracked door of the cabinet behind him . . . but surely he had seen that small space to be empty, not more than an hour ago. And now there was nothing for him to do but concentrate on Christophe's words, though every one of them made his heart sink lower.

I would very much like to believe that I am dealing with the French, and that you are the chief of the army called "expeditionary," but I am waiting for the orders of the Governor, to whom I have dispatched one of my aides-de-camp, to announce to him your arrival and that of the French army; and until his response has reached me, I cannot permit you to debark . . ."

On the deck of the flagship *L'Océan*, Captain-General Leclerc paused in his reading and looked out across the coast. He had walked down from the bow of the vessel for the sake of privacy, though Lebrun and the admiral Villaret-Joyeuse had followed him and stood at a little distance, watching. Leclerc inhaled the many-layered scent of the nearby land. At sunrise they'd sailed closer into shore, and now the fleet stood west of Fort Picolet, well out of the range of cannon. Though certainly he could reduce that place in an hour, if it came to that. The town itself was hidden, behind the point where the fort was placed, sunk in the deepest pocket of the bay.

A gull swooped at the letter, mistaking it for bread. Leclerc tucked the paper to his belly and turned to give the striking bird his shoulder. The gull spiraled up and away from him, shrieking, losing itself among the several others gliding around the masts of the ship like chaff in the updraft of some bonfire. Had his movement seemed a flinch? Leclerc stole a glance at Lebrun and Villaret-Joyeuse, to see if they'd been amused at his expense, but they had turned their faces to the coast. He knew that there were some who mocked him, and because of his small stature called him *the blond Napoleon;* they accused him of aping his brother-in-law.

Leclerc looked up toward the bridge, where Pauline, his lady wife, was holding court. The captain's chair enthroned her. She had got herself up in an exotic motley of kerchiefs, scarves, and bandannas—her fantasy of what a grand Creole dame would wear. The junior naval and military officers were fawning all over her, as usual, as if she were already Queen of Saint Domingue, as she soon expected, in effect, to be. It was this whole extravaganza that had sent Captain-General Leclerc down from the bridge to the spot where he now stood.

Since his marriage to the First Consul's sister, Leclerc had had more than one occasion to reflect that perhaps *husband,* at the end of the day, was not the most enviable relation to enjoy to the most recklessly beautiful woman in Europe. Never had he felt it so keenly as when Bonaparte had ordered his sister to accompany this expedition. At first Pauline herself had howled as if she were being exiled to a prison colony. It was no easy matter to pry her out of Paris—though the First Consul, embarrassed by the scandals in which she constantly entangled herself, was determined to do it one way or another. At length she'd been persuaded by her friends that it would all be a great party of pleasure. How she would reign over Saint Domingue, attended by whole regiments of Nubian slaves, and how well her charming self would appear in the very most daring colonial *déshabillé!*

For Pauline's fancies, all the best cabins of the flagship *L'Océan* had been refitted as boudoirs, parlors, antechambers, and stuffed brimful with musicians, poets, *chefs de cuisine,* dancing masters, lady's maids, mummers and players and jugglers and all the indispensable accoutrements of the court she meant to install as soon as they had occupied Le Cap, renowned as the most beautiful city in any colony of France: the Jewel of the Antilles. It was a great nuisance and distraction to a man in command of a military enterprise.

On the bridge, Pauline was on the point of losing one of the forty-odd kerchiefs which, after all, left her mostly uncovered. The attendant officers blundered into each other in their haste to retrieve the stray rag for her. Despite his irritation, Leclerc did not immediately look away—this tableau held the eye, like the glitter of a diamond or a bit of broken glass.

Were it not for Pauline, he would never think of temporizing now. He did not like to think of it. If Rochambeau had met resistance at Fort Liberté, he would certainly by this time have hammered it to dust . . . and General Boudet would be doing the same at Port-au-Prince, and Kerverseau on the Spanish side of the island, while Captain-General Leclerc had the chore of taking Le Cap undamaged, preserving its most fragile charms for the delectation of his wife.

Leclerc turned in the direction of the sea. He thumped the folded letter against his tightly trousered leg. The day was fine and clear, the air rinsed clean by yesterday's storm. If he decided to force a landing, the weather conditions could be no better . . . as Villaret-Joyeuse had already mentioned this morning.

To his port side the ship *La Vertu* swung at anchor, crammed to the gunwales with all the surviving leaders of the mulatto faction in the colony's recent civil war. Pétion, Rigaud, Villatte, Léveillé, Boyer, and dozens of others all eager to try their swords one more time against Toussaint, who had defeated them and driven them out of the colony. Their knowledge of the place, along with their passion for revenge, might well prove useful if it came to war again and everything had to be done by main force. If the colony could be occupied peacefully, however, Leclerc had orders to ship the mulatto chiefs to Madagascar, never allowing them to set foot in Saint Domingue.

He turned to starboard and studied the *Jean-Jacques,* the vessel which contained Toussaint's two sons—Leclerc's best instruments of diplomacy. To prevent the effusion of blood, and the wrecking of cities, he might send them with their tutor to join their father; they might well persuade Toussaint to cede his command of the colony without a fight. The difficulty was not knowing where to send them. Toussaint was somewhere on the island, presumably, but no one seemed to know just where,

not even the officer he'd left in command of Le Cap. Leclerc shook out
the creases of the letter, and continued, reluctantly, to read.

> . . . *until his response has reached me, I cannot permit you to debark.*
> *If you have the force with which you threaten me, I will offer you all*
> *the resistance proper to a general; and if the issue of arms should be*
> *favorable to you, you will not enter the city of Le Cap before it has*
> *been reduced to ashes—and on those ashes, I will fight you still.*

7

Couachy, to whom Papa Toussaint had given the two letters for Paul
Louverture, led their way south from Point Samana toward Santo
Domingo City. Couachy had been to that place before, not so long ago,
when Papa Toussaint had sent his army to the Spanish side of the island
for the first time, but Guiaou had not. He had not been to Point Samana
either until that day when Papa Toussaint had brought them to look at
the ships of the French. It was the first time he had traveled so far across
the border, but he had known Couachy for a long time and was content
to follow him. Couachy rode in front, then Guerrier who had just been
made a soldier by Papa Toussaint, and Guiaou third. Guiaou had never
seen Guerrier before yesterday when Papa Toussaint tossed him the
musket he carried now across his saddle bow, but he felt a warmth
toward Guerrier because he remembered how, a long time ago, Papa
Toussaint had taken him in when he was nearly naked and had made
him a soldier too by giving him a gun. Guerrier rode well—he must have
spent some time training horses at Toussaint's *hatte* across the border—
but he did not seem to know what to do with the musket. He kept turning it and flourishing it one way and another, and Guiaou's horse
twitched uneasily between his knees whenever the sunlight flashed on
the barrel.

They had to ride someway inland along the north bank of the River

Yuna to find a ford where they could cross. Even there the water was deeper than Guiaou liked, chest-deep on the horses in the middle of the river. It rose to touch Guiaou's boot in the stirrup, cold water seeping through the seams of the uppers. The cold water climbed his shinbone toward his knee, spilling over the boot top. Guiaou closed his eyes and felt his teeth clench tight. He prayed, *Gras lamisérikòd,* loosening the rein and trusting his horse to follow the others without guidance. *Gras lamisérikòd, Papa . . .* The water climbed onto his thigh and he waited for the sick lurch when the horse's hooves would be uprooted from the bottom and the horse would begin to swim. But this did not happen. Instead the water began to sink, finally releasing its grip on his ankle, and Guiaou opened his eyes as the horse came scrambling up the southern bank of the river. He prayed his thanksgiving as he dumped the water from his boots and slung them over his saddle bow. The cloth of his trousers and the skin of his legs dried quickly as they rode east in the afternoon sun, warming against the drying hide of the horse.

On the south side of the bay the trail became narrow, difficult, running steeply up and down the cliffside above the ocean. Far to the east, where the bay's mouth gave onto the open sea, appeared white splotches of bellying sails—ships of the *blancs* sailing toward Cape Engaño.

"Ki moun yo yé?" Guerrier said. Who are they? The voice startled Guiaou, for there had been no word spoken among the three of them since they parted from Papa Toussaint, only the noise of the surf and the cries of the gulls diving down the black walls of the cliffs above the water.

"Moun fransé," Couachy told him. French people.

"Poukisa y'ap vini?" Guerrier asked. What have they come for?

"To make us slaves again," Couachy said shortly. Guerrier looked back over his shoulder, over the black switching tail of his bay horse. His eyes caught Guiaou's for a moment before he faced forward again, but he did not ask another question. They rode on.

The sun turned red and quickly fell behind the mountains to the west. They rode through the brief twilight, and then, for a little while, under the stars. The trail was difficult in the faint light and they went slowly, often dismounting to lead their horses over the tricky ground. A warm, wet wind blew inland from the bay, carrying with it a shelf of cloud. By the time they had made their way down from the cliff trail to lower ground, the stars had all been darkened and they were making their way across a mangrove swamp by touch.

"Nou pa kab vansé konsa!" Couachy announced. We cannot go on like this! He looked around himself—the writhing shadows of the mangroves stretched out in all directions. "We must stop for the night—in the dark we would miss the road."

Guiaou said nothing, though a discontent settled on him—he pictured the *blanc* ships sailing on through the night, around Cape Engaño to the port of Santo Domingo City. But Couachy could not be disputed. It was a lucky thing that a horse had not already twisted a leg among the mangroves. Also it might be a long way before they found another broad dry hummock like this one, where they might stop in comfort. There was even a scraggly coastal pine tree here, whose lower branches might be broken off for firewood.

They tied their horses and built a small fire, though there was nothing to be cooked. Guerrier brought some dried beef out of his bundle—there was much smoking of beef at the *hatte* he had come from. Guiaou had some morsels of cassava bread wrapped in a rag inside his shirt, and Couachy brought out two shriveled, pulpy mangoes. They shared the food and ate it slowly, reserving about half of the dried beef for the next day.

After eating, Couachy and Guiaou reclined on their elbows beside the fire, while Guerrier sat up crosslegged, caressing the barrel of his musket intently, as if it were a cat. The knobs of his knees stuck out from the faded rags of his tricolor trousers. He told them how he had once been a slave on a coffee farm in the hills above Ouanaminthe, how he had run away across the Spanish border and lived for years as a maroon in the mountains near Santiago. When Couachy and Guiaou did not volunteer anything about themselves, Guerrier asked how they had come to know each other.

"Nou tuyé blan ansanm," Couachy grunted, rolling up on one hip to scratch his back. We killed whites together.

"Wi, blan ak milat, nou tuyé yo." The words sounded from his mouth without Guiaou's intention—Yes, whites and mulattoes, we killed them . . . He had first met Couachy during a raid on the English on the outskirts of Saint Marc, a long time ago before Papa Toussaint had chased all the English out of the country. In those days Guiaou had had an especially lively hatred of mixed-blood people—he still did when he thought about it—and that day he and Couachy had been able to kill many of them up close with their knives. That raid was led by Moyse, who was dead now, shot by a firing squad at Port-de-Paix, because he had dared to raise a rebellion against his uncle, Papa Toussaint.

It took Guiaou some time to think all of these thoughts, and during that time no one said anything more. There was no sound except the whine of the mosquitoes, which were plentiful here in the mangrove swamp. Couachy sat up to put a damp, leafy branch onto the fire. The smoke thickened, but it did not discourage the mosquitoes very much. Guerrier coughed and spat to one side.

"Why did the general give you two letters?" he said.

"Let-sa-a bay manti," Couachy answered, pulling out a corner of the letter he carried in his outside pocket. This letter tells lies. He moved his hand to pat the second letter, which he held hidden under his shirt. "This is the letter which tells the truth."

"What does the letter say truly?" Guerrier said. "And what does the letter say which is not true?"

Guiaou felt that Guerrier asked too many questions, and asked them too directly. He would never have asked such questions himself, not even in his thoughts, but Couachy did not seem unwilling to answer and Guiaou found that he himself was curious to know.

Couachy brushed his outer pocket. "This one says that the General Paul must welcome the French as brothers and friends and do all that they say." He smiled and tapped the letter tucked into his waistband. "This one says that he must burn Santo Domingo City, kill the *blancs* and retreat to Saint Raphael."

At that Guerrier only nodded and stretched out on the ground beside his musket. The fire burned down to its last coals. Guiaou lay with his eyes closed, listening to the plop of frogs in the swamp, the horses snuffling at the brackish water along the edge of the mangroves, finally the familiar sound of Couachy's snoring. After a blank period his eyes came open on the mist of a gray dawn. The others slept, but one-eyed Ghede was there, sitting in the shadow of the salt-withered pine tree, greedily scooping up food from a bowl with the fingers of his right hand. His left hand reached out as if to gather and protect another bowl, but Guiaou saw with a pulse of alarm that Ghede's left hand was hovering above the head of sleeping Couachy. It seemed to him then that Ghede wore the face of Moyse, who had lost an eye in battle with the *blancs,* so that the lid sagged wrinkled and gray into the empty socket, but Moyse had gone to be with the dead already—Guiaou rolled awake so quickly that his own horse snorted and jerked at its tether. It was still night, but the clouds had dissipated, and a slender new moon had risen among the stars. In the cold light the path lay palely visible, running from hummock to hummock through the mangroves.

Guiaou walked around the cold feathery ashes of their fire, and stooped to rock Couachy by the shoulder.

"*Ann alé,*" he hissed. Let's go.

Couachy came awake with a grumble. He slapped at a clutch of mosquitoes that battened on his neck and wiped the wreckage of their legs and wings in a blood smear over his collar bone. His eyes came clear enough to take in the new moonlight and the plain lie of the path between the hummocks.

"*Dakò,*" he said. All right.

Guiaou woke Guerrier by tapping the flat of his *coutelas* across the ball of the sleeping man's bare foot. Guerrier came up into consciousness without a whisper. There was no coffee to be brewed so they were on their way at once, going single file among the mangroves. By the time first light had begun to lift the blue herons and white egrets out of the hummocks and into the air, they had come to the edge of the swamp and reached the junction of a broad road which ran south through the lowlands from the edge of the bay.

In this spot they paused for long enough for Guerrier to share out the last of his dried beef. They rode on, at a brisk trot. The road was wide enough for them to ride all three abreast. Guiaou wished for greater speed—he feared ships would be outdistancing them around the cape, and the lingering images of his dream filled his head with chilly fog. One did not meet Ghede in dreams without a reason. But Couachy was the better horseman and more knowledgeable of the country where they were and the distance they had yet to go, and he would not press their pace for fear of overheating the horses. It was true that the heat rose very fast once the sun had cleared the mountains east of the wide savanna where they rode. Guiaou held his morsel of dried beef in his mouth, encouraging it to dissolve slowly with just an occasional pump of his jaw.

By midday the taste of that beef was not even a memory. They came in sight of a small cabin seated some twenty yards from the road. Though they'd passed several small herds of cattle grazing untended, this was the first evidence of human habitation they had met. A small black boy stood at the roadside watching their approach, covered to his knees in a dirt-brown canvas smock.

"*Salwé,*" Couachy said as they drew near, and when the Creole greeting drew no answer, "*Holá.*" The boy turned and ran for the house, dashing in the open door. Two kerchiefed heads of women peeked out the doorway and as quickly withdrew. Then a white man dressed in a pair of loose cotton trousers stepped barefoot into the dooryard and stood yawning and scratching at the hair above his waistband as he inspected them. A young woman came out behind him, carrying a pail. With her free hand she traced a line of string that ran from the house to a small *cocotier* off to the left. Beside the tree she stopped and began drawing water from the well.

The white man left off his scratching and beckoned. Guiaou would have returned to the road. But Couachy clucked to his horse and rode down into the packed earth of the yard, dismounting without waiting for an invitation.

"You come from Toussaint?" By his accent it was plain he was a Spaniard, though he spoke in Creole.

"No," said Couachy. "We come from Clervaux, at Santiago."

It was a good answer, Guiaou thought, a lie well chosen. A dispatch from Clervaux's garrison at Santiago to Paul Louverture would be no more than routine. But he saw the Spaniard's eyes flick from the faded tricolor rosette Couachy wore pinned to the frayed lapel of his short jacket to the guardsman's helmet that crowned Guiaou. Guiaou had been tremendously proud of this helmet ever since Toussaint had elevated him to his honor guard, but now he took it off and tucked it under his arm, wishing very much that he could make it invisible.

"How far is it to Santo Domingo City?" Couachy said.

"Oh," said the Spaniard, "not so far at all. You are quite near. But have something to eat before you go on, and you must fodder your horses, certainly."

"You are kind—" Couachy began, but Guiaou broke in: "Let us go on."

The Spaniard looked sharply into Guiaou's face. "Is your mission so urgent?" His fingers worked the sprigs of hair on his pointed chin; they did not quite amount to a beard. As his gaze lowered from Guiaou, it caught for a moment on the red wax seal of the letter visible in Couachy's pocket.

"Not at all," Couachy said. He turned in Guiaou's direction but without quite meeting his eyes. "Though, after all, we must not stay long."

"Very good," the Spaniard said. The young woman was coming back from the well with her pail slopping onto the dirt, free hand still running over the string. From the fixed regard when she came near, Guiaou guessed she must be blind. She had pleasant features, but these were confused by many dark red blotches on her face, from some disease.

Two larger boys, both of them white, were peeking around the door frame now. "Take these horses to the barn," the Spaniard said. "And bring some eggs to feed our visitors."

Unhappily Guiaou slid down from the saddle; Guerrier followed suit.

"Go in, go in!" The Spaniard gestured to the open door. Guiaou let his horse be taken and led around the corner of the cabin. Clutching his musket to him still, Guerrier followed Couachy into the house. Guiaou looked back and saw that the Spaniard had walked closer to the boys as they led the horses off, to give them some further instruction.

Guiaou stepped over the threshold, cradling his helmet, blinking in the dim interior.

"Sit down." The Spaniard walked inside, waving his arms at a rough-hewn table against the wall. The others were already seated there. Guiaou lowered himself gingerly to a three-legged stool and pushed his helmet under the table, out of sight.

The Spaniard rattled off a phrase of his own tongue to the older woman, the one who was not blind. She grunted something in reply and stooped to lift an iron tripod and a kettle. Guiaou moved to take the tripod, an excuse to follow her out the back door. Another string, he noticed, ran from the door frame to a small barn at the crest of a little rise behind the house. The horses had been taken there, he thought. He did not see the horses, but the figure of one of the white boys flashed for a second across the rise, running down toward a dark tree line beyond it.

Very slowly, the old woman was arranging the tripod, the kettle, the pan below the kettle which would be spooned full of coals, once the fire which had yet to be kindled had produced the coals. It would all take too much time, Guiaou thought. He stepped back into the house. The Spaniard had picked up his helmet and was turning it in his hands, muttering the phrase embossed on the front of it: *Qui pourra en venir à bout?*

Guiaou moved to whisper to Couachy that they must not wait for this promised meal, but the Spaniard seemed to intercept his thought.

"Where are those boys?" he said, his beard wisps lifting in a rubbery smile. "Our hens are all half wild, you see? They hide their eggs, and it takes time to find them."

"I will help them," Guiaou said. Couachy sat looking vacantly out the doorway, eyes half shut. He had put one hand under his shirt tail to warm his belly for the reception of hot food. Guiaou could not get his attention. He reached for the helmet, but the white man's hands stuck to it, his fingertips lingering on the raised motto.

"Who will be able to come through to the end?" he said with the same uneasy smile. "It is a curious phrase."

Guiaou twisted the helmet away from his clinging hands. "I will put eggs in it," he said, to cover the roughness of his action. He jerked his head at Guerrier as he went out the door. The older woman was still puttering over the business of lighting the fire. Guiaou marched quickly up the rise. The Spaniard's voice sounded behind him and he looked back once. The blind girl was following him, but slowly, finger on the string.

The string ran from stall to stall in the lean-to area on the far side of the barn, and stopped at the door of a raised-floor room closed with a wooden latch, where fodder must have been stored. The three horses, tethered by a brace of oxen, were tossing their heads over a small wisp of hay. There was no sign of the two boys, nor any hens or eggs. This, Guiaou had expected. And now there was something like a rumble in the ground. He could not really hear it yet, but felt it in a prickle from his heels through his spine. He stepped clear of the barn and looked down the road they'd been traveling before they'd stopped here.

Nothing at first, then a crawling speck on the road, a dust cloud, horses, many horsemen. Guiaou ran into the barn and began to untie the horses, fumbling in his hurry. He'd put his helmet on, to free his hands. It was awkward leading all three horses at once, and the animals picked up his nervousness. One of them twisted around to bite another on the haunch, and the bitten horse whinnied and made to rear. Before Guiaou came to Toussaint he had been afraid of horses as much as of water, and now it seemed to him that the skill and confidence he'd gained since might drain away and leave him helpless, like the blind girl frozen on her string halfway between the barn and the house. The yard was empty except for her—the older woman must have gone back in. Guiaou remembered the conch shell he carried in a saddlebag. He yanked it out and sounded it. At the harsh tone, Guerrier's horse pulled free. Guiaou could not chase it—he started toward the house leading the two others, and the third horse followed, as he should have known it would do.

He mounted and rode down toward the yard at a trot, trailing the second horse by the reins. Guerrier came dashing out of the house, carrying his musket. The horsemen on the road were near enough to be counted, and there were more than fifty of them, white men all, with the look of

Spanish militia. But one of them wore the blue coat and epaulettes of a French cavalry officer, though it seemed impossible that those ships could have landed anyone this soon.

Now, at last, Couachy came through the door. With a sweep of his head he took in the approaching riders. The Spaniard came scurrying after him, his messy mouth open and his arms spread out in some remonstrance. Couachy pulled out his dragoon's pistol, took time to steady the barrel over his right wrist, and shot the other man in his shirtless chest. The range was so short that the impact sent the Spaniard cartwheeling backward, oversetting the iron kettle and tripod into the fire as he fell. The older woman stood screaming in the door frame.

At the shot, the horse Guiaou was leading reared and broke the reins, but Guerrier ran up on it before it could go far, caught the mane, and vaulted one-handed into the saddle, always clutching the musket with the other. The third horse had bolted all the way to the horizon. Guiaou screamed wordlessly to Couachy, who was taking a slow, deliberate time to charge his pistol. A shot sounded from the approaching riders, and Guerrier fired his musket wild into the sky. Taking a carefully studied aim, Couachy shot one of the militiamen out of the saddle. His fall broke the advance of the others. Their horses milled. Couachy turned and walked toward Guiaou, in no obvious hurry, though he did not stop to reload his pistol now.

The French officer was shouting orders, and the militiamen were regrouping for a charge. Guiaou, who had pushed his horse to a canter, pulled out his own pistol and fired into the cluster without seeing the effect of his shot. Couachy was reaching for his free hand, to pull himself up behind. As their fingers touched, several shots went off and Couachy's hand jerked back as if it had been burned. Guerrier was twisting his musket around helplessly; it was too long for him to reload in the saddle. Couachy pulled his hand away from his shoulder and reached for Guiaou again, but his fingers were all slippery with blood and the shock of the colliding horses separated them.

Guiaou gained a moment by smashing his pistol barrel into the face of the nearest militiaman, feeling the dampened crunch as cartilage gave way. Guerrier had set the stock of his empty musket to his shoulder and galloped in, guiding his horse with only his knees. His bayonet struck another Spaniard and swept him backward over the tail of his own horse. But Guiaou could not find Couachy. He wheeled his horse out of the melee and turned. Now he saw Couachy getting up from the dirt, one arm swinging loose from the bloody shoulder and the other reaching. Guiaou switched his discharged pistol for his *coutelas* and glanced at Guerrier, who rode at the Spanish again with his bayonet fixed as before. Guiaou moved toward Couachy, who made a spring to reach him, but as he jumped there was a whole volley of shots and Couachy's arm was limp, jelly-like when Guiaou's hand grasped at it. The arm ran through his fingers like water and Couachy slipped down under the hooves as the horses shocked together again. Guiaou took a tremendous blow to his helmet, from a saber or gun butt, he didn't know, but it was hard enough to blur his sight. He swung his horse into the clear. There were too many, too many to fight.

His vision resolved and he saw that he was riding on the blind girl now, who still stood paralyzed and mute, the red blots much darker against the sudden pallor of her skin. If one of the boys who'd betrayed them had been standing in her place, Guiaou would have cut him down with joy, but he turned away from the girl at the last moment, slashed her guide string and rode through, with a quick glance over his shoulder to see that Guerrier was following. Further back, the French officer and another militiaman had jumped down to flip over Couachy's body, which lay face down in the dirt, but the rest of the Spaniards were pursuing.

In a flash Guiaou and Guerrier had crossed the tree line. Green branches whipped Guiaou across the face. He plastered his upper body along the horse's neck. There was space enough among the pines for them to hold their pace, and they had the better horses. When they'd lost the Spaniards deep in the pines, they cut back in the direction of the road, halting finally at a point a quarter-mile north of the house. Guiaou took the time to load his pistol. He was still breathless, so he only motioned to Guerrier, who seemed to take his meaning well enough. They rode behind the screen of pines until the barn had lined up with the house, and then came out into the open, urging their horses to the gallop as they crossed the rise. Only two militiamen had stayed by the house, and they did not have time to reach their horses. Guiaou hacked the first one down with his *coutelas* and Guerrier pinned the other to the house wall with the bayonet.

By the overturned kettle the older woman lay across the body of her husband, her shoulders heaving silently. Further off, the blind girl turned in a widening spiral, her arms outstretched, with nothing to grasp. Guerrier covered her with his musket, but Guiaou pushed the barrel aside. He dropped to his knees beside Couachy's body. Couachy's eyes were showing white and his mouth hung slack and there was a paste of blood and dirt on his teeth. Guiaou turned out all his pockets—empty. The true letter was gone from his waistband as well.

Guerrier stood looking unhappily at the twisted bayonet on his musket. He'd broken off the point with the force of his charge against the house wall. Now he picked up the musket of one of the dead militiamen and compared it to his own to see if it would do. Meanwhile Guiaou was searching those bodies as quickly as he could, but the letters were not there. The French officer must have taken them, and he was riding back toward the house now, leading the Spanish horsemen on a wild charge out of the trees.

Guiaou stood up, his head gone red inside from frustration and rage.

He might have shot the blind girl or stabbed the grieving woman in the back. Instead he caught up a brand from the cookfire and set three corners of the house thatch alight. The fire was burning hungrily by the time he got onto his horse, and several of the militiamen had to stop to try to put it out. As for the rest, Guerrier and Guiaou still had the better horses. They rode in a wide curve around their pursuers and lost themselves in the pine forest once more.

All through that afternoon they picked a way through the pine woods, headed generally south, still toward Santo Domingo City, though under the trees one could not reckon by the sun, and they could not be certain that the edge of the forest was parallel to the road they'd been traveling earlier that day. It was Couachy who had known this country. Couachy had fought beside Guiaou more times for more years than could be counted now. They had both been so concentrated on the work of killing white men and mulattoes that their heads were one red blaze together in each fight. Now Couachy was dead, because he had wanted to eat a fresh egg, or because Ghede had been ready to take him this day, down below the mirror of the ocean to the Island Below Sea.

They stopped that night by a pooling stream, still within the shelter of the woods. As Guiaou dipped water to wash himself, he thought of Couachy on the other side, and the cold clasp of the water on his wrist seemed like the handgrip of Baron Cimetière, that same shadow that had drifted through his dream the night before. With a snatch of both arms he swirled away the ghost of his reflection from the surface of the pool and threw water in his face to drown the thought.

Guerrier, who'd submerged himself completely in the pool, watched Guiaou rinse his shoulders and torso with the water he dipped from his kneeling position on the grassy bank. Guiaou knew that Guerrier was looking at his scars and wondering why he did not come all the way into the water himself.

"What happened to you there?" Guerrier said, pointing at the ragged tears that showed stone-white on Guiaou's rib cage and underneath his arm.

"*Reken,*" Guiaou said shortly. Shark. He raised his forearm to a warding position over his head to show how the cut on the inner arm flowed into the deep furrow across his cheek and down his shoulder. "That one was a sword cut from a *blanc.*"

Guerrier nodded and asked no more, turning in the water to face the declining sunlight in the west.

"I thought you were not a soldier before yesterday," Guiaou said, to show he was not offended by the question. "You fought well today. And how well you ride!"

Guerrier smiled up at him from the sunset-reddened water. "I spent much time training horses at the *hatte* of Papa Toussaint." He climbed out of the pool and shook himself briskly, hurling water in all directions, then drew on his trousers and dried his hands on his shirt. Sitting down crosslegged, he drew the musket captured from the Spanish militia onto his knees and began to unfasten its bayonet.

"Why do you not use that musket instead?" Guiaou asked him. "It is newer than the other."

"Is it?" asked Guerrier. He had now undone the broken bayonet from the musket he had started with. "But this one was given me by Papa Toussaint."

Guiaou was silent, considering this. The lock of the first musket given him by Toussaint had broken irreparably long ago, so that weapon had been discarded. But that musket had only been issued to him at Toussaint's order, it had not come direct from Toussaint's hand like Guerrier's. He sat crosslegged opposite Guerrier, fondling his helmet in his lap. There was a deep dent in the front of it, and though Guiaou had something of a headache now, he thought that without the helmet his head would have been split in two.

Now the new bayonet was fixed. Guerrier raised the musket and sighted it across the darkening surface of the pool. With a satisfied grunt he laid the weapon down beside him and felt a pocket of his trousers.

"I have a tinderbox," he said, looking at Guiaou.

"We have no food to cook, after all." Guiaou felt his stomach draw up as he said it. "Better not to show a light."

The horses were tethered away in the pines, and Guiaou walked down and felt in the straw *macoute* strung to his saddle. He took out a brace of pistols and gave them to Guerrier. He'd harvested four pistols in all from the dead men around the cabin that day, and a purse of coins he had not yet examined.

"That is good," Guerrier said. Holding the pistols near him, he lay down on a drift of pine needles where they would both sleep. "What will we do now?" he said.

"We must go to Paul Louverture if we can, and tell him the truth of the true letter face to face," Guiaou said. "Because the French officer will be bringing him the lying letter, that is sure."

In the next days they kept traveling toward the south coast, but indirectly, since they did not know the way, and it seemed safer to go by night, especially after the second day when they found a handbill nailed to a tree by a crossroads they'd come upon. The first glimpse of it made Guiaou cold in the belly because it looked so much like the warnings of runaways that had been posted during slavery time. The pictures at the top might have been any two men, and Guiaou could not read much of the text. Riau had taught him his letters in different camps where they were together, but he could only make out a few words of this, and it hurt his head to do that much. Still, after staring at the paper for a long time he seemed to understand that he and Guerrier were denounced as brigands and murderers, though not by their names, and that his scars were described well enough that he was likely to be recognized.

From then on he went somewhere to hide whenever Guerrier needed to go to ask directions. When he must lie hidden he would close his eyes and listen to the nearby breathing of his horse and picture the blind Spanish girl closing her hands on the empty air, with all her guide strings severed, limp, invisible at her feet. What if Guerrier did not return? But Guerrier did come back each time, though his directions were not usually clear or accurate.

In this way they finally reached the south coast, losing count of the days it had taken them to get there. In the darkness, while Guiaou hid himself, Guerrier approached the gate of one of the forts protecting Santo Domingo City and Ozama Bay. When he called up the name of Toussaint Louverture he was answered by a volley, one musket ball whining past his ear like an angry bee, and he came running back to tell Guiaou that the Spanish *blancs* and *sang-mêlés* had seized the fort and meant to hand it over to a large French army commanded by General Kerverseau.

At that, Guiaou was chilled all over. It plagued him to have abandoned the body of Couachy, though there had been no choice. And why had not Couachy done as Toussaint must have meant for him to do? He might have shown the false letter to the militia when they came and so won a safe passage with the true one. Or maybe it was Guiaou himself, his action, that had put them in the place where they could only run or fight. And maybe the ruse would have failed anyway. But Santo Domingo City would not be burned now. He had no more hope of reaching Paul Louverture if the French were already landing there, and he and Guerrier could not burn it all alone. But they could go back to Saint Raphael, as the true letter ordered Paul Louverture to do.

This journey too was difficult, indirect and slow. They had to steal their food from the fields by night. There were gold coins in the looted purse, but it was too dangerous to spend them. All the country this side of the border seemed to have turned in favor of the French army, and once when Guerrier risked a turn through a village market, he learned that Clervaux, who commanded for Toussaint at Santiago, had been persuaded by the Bishop Malveille to accept the French as friends, and so most of the garrisons from Santiago down to Santo Domingo City had done the same, and Paul Louverture also, it was said.

For that, they turned away from Santiago, and rode across the wide, grassy central plateau toward the French part of the island, but when they came near to Saint Raphael they met streams of people running out of the town with a story that the General Rochambeau was coming with a French army that would make them slaves. Those people were running toward Dondon, or to Grande Rivière where Sans-Souci was fighting. No one knew where Toussaint had gone, or where his other armies were to be found. It was plain enough to Guiaou and Guerrier that they did not want to be caught up in the current of these fugitives, and Guiaou knew another route, through the mountains to Gonaives on the western coast, by way of the steep and narrow Ravine à Couleuvre.

8

Ogûn-O . . . Roi des Anges . . . this was the song that sang in my head as
we rode west from Point Samana, but I, Riau, did not let the words come
aloud out of my mouth. Riau held his mouth closed tight, and rode with
his body springing straight up from the saddle like a palm trunk rooted
in the spine of the horse, eyes fixed straight between the shoulders of
Major Maillart, who was leading our way down to Port-au-Prince. Everything was silence all around us except for birdsong and the insects in the
grass, but the song rang inside my head from one wall to the other.

Ogûn-O . . . Djab-la di l'ap manjé moin, si sa vré . . .

And I, Riau, I knew what the letter riding in Maillart's pocket said,
because Riau's hand had written down the words that Toussaint spoke.
Those words were shaped with a twisted tongue, so that there was nothing in the letter which would make Maillart, a *blanc* and a Frenchman,
unhappy to be carrying it. But Toussaint had put another word directly
into the head of Riau, without any paper to hold it still. Between this
word and the words sealed into the paper Maillart carried in his coat,
there was a crack where the devil came in.

Ogûn-O . . . the devil says he is going to eat me, is it true?

We rode, then, down the Valle de Consilanza, where the road ran south
of the Cibao Mountains. It was Maillart who led our way, though Riau
knew this country just as well. I had come over in the army of Toussaint

to set free slaves of the Spanish *blancs*, and before that, long before, Riau had wandered in these mountains in the time of *marronage*.

Others of Toussaint's guard rode with us, but before the end of the first day's riding they turned from our road to bring Toussaint's message to Clervaux at Santiago. When darkness came it was Maillart who knocked at the door of a Spanish cattle herdsman to ask for food and shelter for us two. Maillart was a tall man with a big mustache and the *blanc* skin of his face all burnt brick color by the sun. He had a voice that was usually loud and sounded happy. People liked him, both *blanc* and *nèg*, and Riau liked him very well too. In the night when we lay near each other on pallets put side by side on the floor, Maillart spoke in a lower voice, which would not wake the Spanish people sleeping in the loft. *You are quiet tonight, Riau, and all day long you have been so quiet, my friend.* I did not give any answer to this, but instead I made my breathing sound like sleep. Maillart had come over to Toussaint a very long time ago, and in the days and years that followed he had taught many black men all he knew about the *blanc* way of soldiering. Riau had learned very much from him. In those first days he was my captain. Yet I thought how easy it would be to shoot him in the spot between the shoulder blades where my eyes stopped when we were riding. It was for that I rode behind, for each mile of that journey.

. . . *Djab-la di l'ap manjé moin* . . .

Next day we rode still further south, around the Lake of Enriquillo. This road took us very near the mountains of Bahoruco, with the signs and the spirits of the old *caciques* all through their hollow caverns. Riau had stayed a long while at Bahoruco in the time of *marronage*, and my spirit turned in that direction when we passed, but I would not go there now, not yet. We passed that lake, and the Etang Saumatre. It was all peaceful in those places, as if there were no *blanc* soldiers coming out of the ships from France, and it was peaceful also in the town of Croix des Bouquets.

The people in Croix des Bouquets said that Dessalines was in the *casernes* of Port-au-Prince, so we rode there, though not so quickly with Maillart leading. I was not sure how quickly Major Maillart wanted to get to Dessalines, who was no friend of any white people whether they served Toussaint or not. It was night when we came to Port-au-Prince, and at the *casernes* they told us that Dessalines was not there. He had gone to Saint Marc, people thought, where he had built a fine house for himself, but no one knew for certain where he was.

In the place of Dessalines a *blanc* called Agé commanded the town, with Lamartinière, a mulatto, as his second. It might be that Dessalines hated colored men even more than he hated the *blancs*, and he had seemed to enjoy killing them very much during the war against Rigaud, but Lamartinière was one of the few he liked and respected for his courage. I, Riau, had not known Lamartinière well before this night, but we had seen each other's faces and knew each other's names, and I went to sit near him when we came into the council room, while Maillart went to the white general Agé.

The ships of the French soldiers had come into the bay of Port-au-Prince already but no one had landed, except for a messenger, Captain Sabès. Another *blanc* named Gimont was with him, but it was Sabès who carried the words. The council room was scattered over with papers this Sabès had brought, each paper saying the same thing, that the French soldiers were not coming to take away our freedom but that they were sworn to protect us and our liberty. I thought that these papers gave nothing but lies, and it seemed to me that Lamartinière did not trust them either. Agé would have sent Sabès back to the ships with a message for friendship, but Lamartinière wanted to hold him there, though without hurting or killing him. There was that difference between Agé and Lamartinière, and though Agé commanded, the men were with Lamartinière.

I learned these things while talking quietly with Lamartinière at one end of the room, while Maillart and Agé had put their heads together in the other. I told Lamartinière that Toussaint had made a lying letter for someone like Agé, telling him to receive the French though not too quickly, but the true word from Toussaint's mouth to Riau's ear was that if French soldiers began to land, Dessalines must burn the town and kill the *blancs* and go into the mountains. Then Lamartinière told me that Dessalines had gone not to Saint Marc but to Léogane. He wanted to know where Toussaint was, but I did not know anything to tell him.

That night a letter was written by Agé which said to the French in the ships that Dessalines had gone away from Port-au-Prince and that they must not land till Dessalines came back, or sent his order. Maillart was given this letter to carry to the ships, and Agé whispered to him to tell the French generals that he, Agé, did not really have any power now to control what happened in the town.

We did not know about this whispering until afterward, but still Lamartinière found a way to send another message to the ships, with someone different than Maillart. His message said that if the French soldiers made any sign that they would come ashore, three cannon shots would be fired from the mountain and at this signal the *blancs* would all be killed and the town set afire. And that was near enough to what Toussaint had wanted.

Maillart went to the French ships then, and Agé stayed with Sabès in the *casernes*, but I, Riau, went into the streets with Lamartinière. Lamartinière wanted to raise the people to defend the town, besides the soldiers of our army who were already there, but not many people came to join him at first. The town was full of *blancs* that Toussaint had protected, and colored people and some blacks too, who had built great houses for themselves and had barns full of sugar and coffee to be sent away on ships for money, and these people did not want any fighting, and they did not want to see the town burned down. So Lamartinière began to say that we would defend the town without burning it. All the time he was getting angrier—Lamartinière was a proud man.

At last we came to the Armory, and there at the door was a *blanc* named Lacombe, who had the keys to the Armory, and he would not give up the keys when Lamartinière asked for them. Lacombe had got a copy of the same paper which Sabès had managed to scatter in the streets on his way to the *casernes*, and he said that because the paper said that the French were coming in friendship, there was not any reason to get weapons out to fight them. Some of the people who had been following us through the streets called out that they agreed with him. Lamartinière did not spend any time arguing with Lacombe, though, but only called him a miserable *colon* and with the same word shot him, so that his brains came out of the back of his head and splashed on the door of the Armory. There was nobody in the crowd who agreed with Lacombe any more after that, and Lamartinière took the keys from his body and opened the door to get out the guns.

No one noticed Riau going away while these things were happening. I had seen how many ships there were at Samana Bay, and I had seen how Toussaint was made weak for a moment when the sight of those ships first struck his eyes. It did not seem to me to be sure at all that Lamartinière could protect the town without burning it, and the people in the town were divided, too. I walked back to the *casernes* and got my horse without saying anything to anyone and rode out the south gate toward Léogane.

It was just dawn when I started from Port-au-Prince, and by the time I came to Léogane it was full day and the heat was rising. Dessalines was not at Léogane. I lost much time looking for him in one place and another, because I was suddenly afraid of what would happen, and I could not believe that Dessalines could not be found when he was needed. Everyone at Léogane told me now that Dessalines was at Saint Marc, but I did not know if I believed that I would find him there either. While I was looking for him, there came word to Léogane that *blanc* soldiers had landed at Lamentin and they were coming up the road.

I went then to the fort of the Piémont, which covered the road from Léogane to Port-au-Prince. Soldiers of the Sixty-eighth were in this fort, though Dessalines was not, but Lamartinière came there soon after I did. Then the French soldiers came in sight around a bend of the road below the fort, which was a half-circle earthwork with six big cannons. One of the *blanc* officers came out in front of all the rest. He came near enough that a musket shot could have reached him easily, but no one fired at him. Everyone waited, and the officer called in a loud voice—*We have not come to fight you—you are French! you are our brothers!*

Saying these words, he took his sword out of the sheath and threw it away to the side of the road. He shouted that he wanted to come into the fort alone to parley with us. But at that his own soldiers began to argue with him and at the same time some of the officers in the fort began to argue with Magny, who was the *chef de bataillon* there. Some of them wanted to let the French come up and believed that we should not fight them after all.

Lamartinière stood apart from this talk. He was light-skinned enough that Riau could see how all the blood had washed out of his face. His head was turned to one side, listening. He was waiting to hear the cannons at Fort Bizoton, but they did not fire.

In back of the French soldiers I could see that there were some officers much bigger than the one who had come forward. Generals of brigade were there, and one general of division. I knew to recognize them now by their epaulettes and the markings of their coats. All at once I saw that Maillart was among them. He was far off, but I could see it was Maillart, and it seemed that I could even see his mustache moving as he turned to say something to one of the generals of brigade.

Then someone shouted from the top of the fort, *Come up! Advance! We have the order to receive you!*

I had not heard any order like that. But the French soldiers all began to walk forward when they heard this cry. Lamartinière stood very still. He did not look like he knew what was happening there in front of him. I wondered what spirit might be standing in his head. It was very quiet, and we could all hear the feet of the French soldiers shuffling on the road.

Then came three cannon shots from the mountain above Port-au-Prince. Lamartinière trembled, from his feet to his head. A wave went through his body and his right arm swept down. *Fire!* he said, and Magny gave the same order, *Feu! Feu!* Then the muskets and the cannons all shot together and a great many of the French soldiers fell down all at once, hundreds of them, as if a broom had swept them down. But behind them more were coming.

I did not know if Maillart had been shot down or not, though I had seen him moving forward with the others. There was a lot of noise where we were, but I could also hear cannons firing in the bay of Port-au-Prince. I got my horse then and rode around behind the fort and down to the road to the north. The soldiers in the fight were too busy to notice me, and I wanted to see what was happening on the bay. I looked back once as I rode toward the water. The French soldiers were still marching on the fort. They did not stop to reload at all, but kept coming with their bayonets, steadily and keeping close together. They did not seem to care how many of them were shot down. I saw them go over the lip of the earthwork like ants going into a sugar jar.

When those three cannon shots were fired, they did begin killing the *blancs* in Port-au-Prince, as Lamartinière had promised. Many *blancs* were taken down to the Savane Valembrun where they were shot, but I did not know that until later. I rode to the waterside where I could see the bay and the town harbor. Fort Bizoton was quiet because the French soldiers coming over the land had taken it already, but the other forts were fighting the ships on the bay. It seemed that I could not stop watching this, though it was terrible to see. The ships moved too quickly and the guns of the forts could not follow them. The firing from the ships was very strong and they kept firing till the guns of the forts stopped talking back, and then the forts themselves were blown in splinters in the air.

In all my life I never saw such power. I thought then that Toussaint must have seen such a picture in the eye of his mind already, when he first looked at those ships in Samana Bay.

Saint Marc was far from where I was, to the north of Port-au-Prince. I could not go there with a battle to pass through, and anyway it was too late for Dessalines to come. I turned from the water and rode into the plain of Léogane. Toussaint had told me to go south once I had given his word to Dessalines. He had a word to send to Laplume, who commanded for him in the Southern Department. Since I had not found Dessalines yet anyway, I was not really sure which way I should go. *Djabla di l'ap manjé moin* . . . I could not think how to get this devil to stop biting me at all. At evening I was riding south away from the fighting, when a big gang of men stopped me on the plain.

They did not seem so friendly when they stopped me. They looked at my uniform with hard eyes. These were maroons, though not all of them had run away from *blanc* masters before the rising. Men still ran from the plantations even now, since Toussaint had ordered that all must work, and set soldiers of the army above the men who must work with their hoes in the cane fields. In this rule there was no man harsher than Dessalines himself. That was why these men were not very happy to see the uniform I wore, I thought. Or maybe they were happy after all, to catch a soldier riding alone as it grew dark. My horse was tired, and I didn't know what was going to happen, but then I saw Jean-Pic among these men, and Jean-Pic smiled to see Riau.

I jumped down from my horse, letting the reins fall so I could wrap my arms around Jean-Pic. He had a beard now, which rubbed against my face. When we let each other go, the other men seemed easier, and I did not worry about them any more. I had not seen Jean-Pic for a long time, since I left him in Bahoruco long ago, when I went back to Toussaint. But I had known Jean-Pic for a long time before that, years and years before the rising. Jean-Pic had been with the maroons in the north when I, Riau, first ran away from Bréda plantation to join them.

Jean-Pic and I walked together to the camp of these maroons, with his hand lying in mine as lightly as a bird. Someone else was leading my horse, because all these men were friendly to me now. That was a big camp they had on the plain, among banana trees and plantain, corn and manioc. Many hundreds of them were there, with children, and women working around the cookfires now that it was night. Jean-Pic had found a woman when he came out of Bahoruco the year before, and there was a baby sleeping in their *ajoupa*, and the woman stirring sweet potatoes in a pot. Some goat meat was cooking too, and *callaloo*.

When we had eaten, Jean-Pic and I told each other our news. I told him about Merbillay and the children I had made with her, because Jean-Pic had known Merbillay from the time before, when we were all maroons together in the north. But I did not tell him anything about Guiaou, and I did not say much about the fights that I had been in, or the army, or Toussaint. It gave me sadness to think that now there were a lot of things I could not easily tell Jean-Pic. Afterward when the fire had died and I lay looking up at the stars and waiting for sleep, this sadness grew larger. I had not felt such a big spreading sadness since I had stopped remembering Guinée, that time before Riau was stolen and sold in chains onto a ship and brought as a *bossale* to Bréda. The sadness I felt was as large as that, though I was happy to find Jean-Pic, and the devil had stopped biting me for a while.

In the morning, Lamour Dérance came. Lamour Dérance was leader of all of these maroons now. He wanted to know what was happening on the coast, because there were rumors about the ships. I told him about the ships with their guns that blew up the forts, and how Lamartinière had looked like he would lose the fight outside Léogane, even though a lot of the French soldiers were killed in the first shooting.

When I had told all I knew, Lamour Dérance asked for my name again, and when he had it, he stood with his arms folded and his eyes very deep. His nose came open and closed as he breathed in and out, as if he wanted to catch the odor of my spirit. I did not flinch when Lamour Dérance looked at me so. I kept straight, like a *blanc* soldier almost, as Maillart had taught me, and I did not let my eyes fall down until Lamour Dérance had stopped looking into them, but I felt shame inside my body. When Lamour Dérance had gone away, I told Jean-Pic that Riau must go also, because we were going to have to fight the *blancs* again.

That was true. But when I had left the camp of the maroons, I did not think of going to Laplume any more, partly because of the way Lamour Dérance had looked at me. I went north again, in the direction of Saint Marc. I had to go around Port-au-Prince on the road past Morne Diable, because the French soldiers had taken the town. As I passed I learned that Lamartinière had got away with most of his men to Croix des Bouquets, but he had not managed to burn Port-au-Prince, so now the white men had it whole. I did not go at once to Dessalines, but kept on north beyond Saint Marc, until I came to Ennery.

I reached Habitation Thibodet after dark, and kept away from the *grand'case* there. I did not even go in by the main gate, but passed through a tear in the lemon hedges and led my horse along the slopes where the small *cases* were scattered among the provision grounds. At different times Riau and Guiaou had made the walls of Merbillay's *case* more strong with clay, and built the floor up high against the rain. Over the door there was now an open shelter roofed with leaves, and Merbillay was sitting there when I came, with some other women, and Quamba was there too, playing a slow music on a flute made out of a bone. It was late and the people had already eaten and the fire had burned down. I sat on the ground near Merbillay and after a moment she reached to touch my hand, her head still turned in the direction of the flute.

My son Caco I did not see. He would be running in the trees with the other big boys, I thought. Yoyo was sleeping, inside the *case*, and Marielle, who had only four years, was walking around the edge of the ash circle where the fire had been, yawning and rubbing her eyes with the back of her wrist. When she saw me she came and wrapped her arms around my leg, then climbed up onto my lap and curled herself against my belly. Very soon she was asleep, before Quamba had finished the music he played on the flute. I thought of my *banza* still hanging from the roof tree inside the *case* behind me. Sometimes I played such music with Quamba, but tonight the weight of sleeping Marielle held me where I was.

I had been thinking of these children ever since I saw the French blow up the forts at Port-au-Prince, Caco whose father was Riau, and Yoyo whose father was Guiaou, and Marielle who had the two of us for fathers. It was a good time for Riau to come to Ennery, since Guiaou had been sent to Santo Domingo by Toussaint. Guiaou and Riau did not fight any more about Merbillay, but we did not stay in the *case* with her at the same time either, so this way it was better.

When Quamba had finished his music, he stood and walked away with only a nod to us before leaving. I carried Marielle inside and laid her on the shucks beside her sister. In the darkness of the *case* I spent some careful time unwinding the cloth which wrapped Merbillay's head and folding it and laying it carefully down on top of a stool, before I laid my hands onto her shoulders. The sweetness was sharp, as always after a time away. It was the time away that made it so. Afterward I thought again how strange it was that there were many women in the country and many of them beautiful and strong, but for Riau and Guiaou there was only this one.

Then Merbillay slept, but Riau did not. I listened to the two girls breathing in the shucks, and the mice walking on the leaves of the *case* roof. After a while Caco came in on very quiet feet and crept to lie down on the other side of the *case* from his sisters. I felt glad then, to be in the same house with all of them together, but still sleep did not come to me. I was thinking how the people at Port-au-Prince had not wanted all they had built there to be torn down again and burned. A lot of them who were *blancs* had since been killed in the Savane Valembrun, so it did not matter any more what they wanted. Riau did not mind the killing of *blancs* at all, and when the red magic flowered in his head he killed *blancs* himself with pleasure. Maybe I did not want the whole country to be torn apart and burned again, but I knew it was going to happen, and not only because of the words which Toussaint had put into my head.

I did not know what it was that I wanted, or which way I should go. Instead of sleep, the sadness of the night before came down on me again. At Bahoruco, as in Guinée, each day unfolded a path before me, one path without any crossroads. Now every step brought Riau to some crossroads and he did not know which way to turn, nor even if he could pass through that *kalfou* at all.

Then I got up from where I lay. Merbillay shifted into the space I opened, but she did not wake. I went out from under the leaf roof over the door and stretched my back. At the top of a round hill to the east I saw the roof of the *hûnfor* with the long cane flagpole reaching very high into the starlit sky. The *hûnfor* was all dark and quiet, no drums, and the *kay mystè* was shut. I climbed up there and stood outside the cactus fence, looking out over the valley.

Word was that the *blanche* Elise had come back to the *grand'case* here, with her youngest child, and Zabeth and her baby. They were going away from some trouble at Le Cap. French ships had come there too, but that was as much as any one I talked to seemed to know about it. From Zabeth my head turned to Bouquart who was the father of her child. Bouquart was dead now, because he had joined in the *soulèvement* with Moyse, and when Toussaint commanded Bouquart to shoot himself, he did not think that he might not do it.

None of this was long ago. It was not yet one year since Moyse had died, shot by a row of muskets at the fort of Port-de-Paix, and Moyse had given the order himself for the men to fire their bullets into him. Riau was witness to that shooting, and maybe he had been part of the cause of it too.

Ogûn-O . . . Djab-la di l'ap manjé moin, si sa vré . . .

Riau had known Moyse for longer still than he had known Jean-Pic. They knew each other from slavery time at Bréda, where each of them had Toussaint for his *parrain*, though Riau ran away into *marronage*, and Moyse stayed. In the days of the first risings Riau and Moyse killed many *blancs* together. When Riau ran away from Toussaint's army into a second *marronage*, it was Moyse who received him back again, and maybe Moyse had saved him from being shot, when Toussaint might have ordered this for Riau's deserting. Now Moyse was dead, but Riau had not served his spirit, and there on the hill at Ennery I felt his spirit at my back, and very near.

This was the shame given to Riau by the eyes of Lamour Dérance.

When Moyse made the *soulèvement* against Toussaint, Riau knew his reasons. I was even in the same spirit with Moyse then, because Toussaint was making the army to be like *commandeurs* for the *blancs* to make people work in the fields with their hoes in a way too much like slavery time had been. I knew the mind of Toussaint also, which was thinking we must make sugar and coffee to turn into money because that money must buy guns to fight the French soldiers if they came again. When they came. But my heart was with Moyse. Still, when I heard that Moyse's people had risen in the north, I sent Guiaou south to warn Toussaint, and I told him to be certain to tell Toussaint it was Riau who sent him. I did this because I saw that Moyse was not going to win this time, and if I followed my heart to Moyse it might be Riau, and not Bouquart, that Toussaint ordered to blow out his own brains.

Lamour Dérance rose in favor of Moyse in the south then. Toussaint was at Verrettes when it all started, and it did not take him long to put it down. But Riau's name, which I had told Guiaou to give Toussaint, must have reached Lamour Dérance also in this business. As for Guiaou, his head was so full of Toussaint that there was no room for anything else and nothing else behind it. Toussaint put Guiaou into his honor guard, later on when the *soulèvement* was broken and everyone he ordered to be shot was dead, and gave Guiaou the silver helmet to wear on his head. That was a great thing for Guiaou, because all the men in the honor guard were tall and handsome, where Guiaou had his face and body spoiled by shark teeth and saber cuts.

Ogûn-O . . . Djab-la di l'ap manjé moin, si sa vré? Men genyen BonDyé O, genyen tou les sen yo . . .

There was the hole where the devil had come in. I saw this now, standing outside the *hûnfor*. And I saw how the devil could be sent away too. *Voyé djab-la alé!*

Quamba stepped up to me then. He had been standing in the shadow by the fence for some little time, I did not know how long. The bone flute was in his hand but he was not playing it. Quamba had become *hûngan* in the place, after the old *hûngan* had died. He had his *case* now on the first flat ground cut out of the hill on the path below the *hûnfor*, and I had passed there as I climbed, though as I told him I had tried to set my feet down softly so I would not wake him or his people.

"It was the singing," Quamba said. I had not known I had been singing this song out loud.

Ogûn-O, that devil says he is going to eat me, is it true? . . . but there is God, there are all the saints . . .

Then Quamba opened the gate for me, and stood aside for me to pass. It was a small enclosure there on the point of the hill, and the *kay mystè* was so small a man must bend double to enter it. I sat crosslegged on the ground outside, with my back to the cross of Baron Cimetière and my face toward the open door of the *kay mystè*.

Ogûn-O . . . Djab-la di l'ap manjé moin, si sa vré? Sé pa vré, ti-moun you, sé pa vré! sa sé jwet, ti-moun-yo, sa sé blag . . .

I was breathing the night air very deep as I sat there, and keeping my eyes half shut, and after some time it seemed my breath was answered out of the mouths of the *govi* and *canari* jars inside the *kay mystè*, as the wind moved in circles round the hilltop.

Ogûn-O . . . That devil says he is going to eat me, is it true? It's not true, my children, it's not true! that is child's play, my children, it is a joke . . .

Quamba was waiting. He did not say anything, but followed me out when I rose from the ground. He pulled the gate shut behind us. I did not speak until the gate was fastened.

"*M dwé fé pou Moyse youn wete mò nanba dlo,*" I told him. I must bring the spirit of Moyse back from beneath the waters.

Quamba nodded, and he said, "I can do that for you when it is time."

"I must do it myself," I said to him.

Quamba looked at me then, but his eyes did not hold much surprise. "For that you must take the *asson,*" he said.

"Yes," I said. "When it is time." I knew it would be so. Quamba did not say anything more after that, but he took hold of my elbow and my arm with both his hands, as if he thought I would need his touch to guide me on the pathway down the hill.

In the *case* of Merbillay I slept soundly then, until the morning sun was full. It was the voice of Caco that woke me. Outside the *case* he was splashing himself with water which the girls had carried and making himself ready to go and work in the coffee. He wanted to see me admire the bigger arms and legs and chest he had got from this work since I had seen him, though he had not yet got all his growth, and this I did. Caco was yet a child, but a man's work made him proud—he did not hate it. I watched him go into the coffee grove, thinking, at least he is not made to work the cane.

It was not such a good thought to have in my head even so. That devil had taken his teeth out of my neck, but I could still feel him waiting near. I knew I could not stay in this place with Merbillay and the children. Toussaint had his wife and youngest son Saint-Jean on a *habitation* just next to this one, and I knew he must be thinking of them now, and if he came to see them, he might even come to Thibodet, because he often visited here. Now the *blanche* Elise was in the *grand'case,* and she could recognize Riau.

I rode down by Gonaives that day, taking care as I passed the town, but there was no word of any French ships yet in the harbor there. From Gonaives I crossed the Savane Désolée, and then the rice country, and came at last to Saint Marc in the evening. Here Dessalines had built for himself a house as fine and grand as the one Christophe had made at Le

Cap, but today the walls were all painted with tar, and men of the Eighth Brigade stood outside with lit torches. In the Place d'Armes and before the church it was the same. The whole town was ready for burning. But there was a lot of commotion in the *casernes*, where all the soldiers were making ready for a movement.

At last I found Dessalines down at the port, walking back and forth along the *embarcadère*. He wore his uniform pinned with many medals and draped with sashes and covered with long golden cords. Dessalines had come to his place as general under Toussaint, the same as had Moyse. But there was room in his head for more than Toussaint, and one could not always know what was behind it. He walked up and down the *embarcadère*, turning his snuffbox in his hands. There were not any French ships on the sea in front of Saint Marc, but I thought Dessalines must know by now what had happened in Port-au-Prince, from Lamartinière or from some other.

"Riau!" he said when he saw me. "Where do you come from!"

"From Toussaint," I said. It was true, even if I had not come in a straight line.

"From Toussaint?" Dessalines said. "I have a dispatch from him already."

"I have no letter," I said. "Only the words which are in my head." Then I told him what they were.

"Ah," said Dessalines. "It is the same." I was glad to see him put his snuffbox into his pocket then. He took out a letter and gave it me. The seal was cut and at the bottom of the paper I saw Toussaint's name in his own writing, though the rest was copied in someone else's hand. Truly these words were much the same as those Toussaint had given me.

> . . . *Do not forget that while waiting for the rainy season, which will relieve us of our enemies, our only recourse is destruction and fire. Remember that the earth we have bathed in our sweat must not furnish the slightest nourishment to our enemies. Cut off the roads, have corpses and dead horses thrown into all the springs, have everything burned and annihilated, so that those who come to put us back into slavery will always find before them the image of the hell which they deserve.*

It was sure that if Dessalines had been at Port-au-Prince, all the town would have been burned before the French could land out of their ships. Now it was too late for that, but this letter had been written since I left Toussaint, and since the French had landed too, and the letter said to Dessalines that he must wait for another chance to burn the town, when some of the French soldiers might stray out of it. For that, Dessalines was getting ready to move his men down to Croix des Bouquets where Lamartinière was. It was not sure if he would burn Saint Marc before he left, though it seemed the letter wished him to. I, Riau, did not wait to see, but rode out before light the next morning and before the men of Dessalines were moving. I did not want to move with this army myself, and I thought too that now I had found Dessalines, I might go again to look for Laplume, to finish the work Toussaint had given me.

9

Elise descended to the kitchen well before her usual hour, in the first cool light of dawn. Zabeth had prepared coffee; without a word, she poured. Cradling the warm cup in her hands, Elise walked out the kitchen door into the small enclosed garden. There were some first flower plantings there, bougainvillea and hibiscus, and the shoot of a yellow coconut palm which would grow in time to shade this spot. Her brother sat with his coffee near the palm shoot, fingering a week-old letter from Paul.

Elise sat down in a wicker chair near his. There was a rustic table for them to set their cups. This little garden was a work in progress. A work interrupted.

"Are you decided to come with us, or stay?"

At her voice the doctor glanced up, blinking. Elise saw him register the man's attire she wore, but he made no comment on it.

"There is that wounded cane-cutter in the hospital, and if I remain for a day or so more, I may see him safe to Héricourt again . . ."

"A cane-cutter?" Elise sniffed her incredulity.

"The Cignys are determined not to leave," the doctor said.

"Will you stay for Isabelle?" Elise dropped a teasing note into the question.

The doctor turned his head from her, his beard jutting up toward the mourning doves which were calling softly from the eaves of the house. Light flashed from the lenses of his spectacles. "When Maillart has gone off who knows where . . ."

"She does, after all, have her husband here."

"Yes," said the doctor. "But she will not have you."

Elise nodded. The doctor's hand lay on Paul's letter; for a moment she covered it with hers. Then she got up and walked out through the garden gate.

At another time of estrangement from Tocquet, she'd worn these clothes as an incognito. They were his: the rough canvas shirt loose on her torso, the extra length of the trousers bloused into high-top riding boots. It was her fancy when she traveled now to wear such garb and ride astride, like a man— the practice brought her a slightly scandalized attention, which she quite enjoyed. But no one paid her any mind this morning. There was next to no one abroad at all so early, only the charcoal burners and the first fruit sellers come in from the mountains, striding with their baskets balanced on their heads. In trousers, she herself moved with a longer, freer stride, and a few minutes' brisk walking brought her into the Place d'Armes.

A smell of hot tar hung over the square. A sexton was sweeping the steps of the church, and opposite the doors from where he worked sat a charcoal burner, a small gnarled man, with his knees drawn up to his heavily underslung jaw. She passed him and went into the church, pausing just over the threshold for her eyes to adjust to the dim. In the motionless air of the interior, the scent of candle wax and stale incense mingled with the tar smell from outside. After a moment she sat down on a bench so far to the rear that she could barely make out the glimmer of the cross on the altar. Lowering her head, she began mechanically to recite the Lord's Prayer. Just why she had come here she did not know. An impulse, to walk in the town before leaving it, concealed in her man's dress. She had a desire to pray for deliverance, but she could not yet name or know the thing from which she needed to be delivered, and because she had no habit of prayer the words were dry and lifeless on her tongue.

A paper scuffed onto the bench beside her, folded and sealed with a glob of red wax. Automatically she whisked it into the belly of her shirt. As she touched the paper, the image of the little charcoal burner flashed behind her eyes. Impossible. He had been soot-stained all over his clothes and headcloth and his hands and face, but she had seen no sack of charcoal near him. She stood up, securing the letter with a hand pressed to her waistband. He was there on the bench behind her, but she did not venture to look at him directly. The sexton had shuffled back into the church and was puttering in the area of the font.

"*W pa konnen'm. Pasé!*" She turned her head just enough to glimpse

the whites of his eyes beneath the soot-stained cloth. You don't know me.
Pass on!

In a moment she was standing on the steps outside the church. At the
sound of his voice she had felt somewhat more sure. They had spoken
Creole to each other that one time, in urgent sibilant whispers. The
slight roughness of his tone was like cat fur. Some white women who
courted him were seeking preferment, but for Elise it had been different.
Tocquet had absented himself to the North American Republic for God
only knew how long, and she had wanted some great powerful secret for
herself. In fact even Isabelle, who usually could divine the little Elise did
not tell her, knew nothing of this interlude.

And must she really go this day? The smell of tar was stronger now, all
over the Place d'Armes. On arriving she had not noticed the little group
of men at the opposite corner of the square, clustered around an iron
cauldron from which the tar smoke rose. Two of them held unlit *lances à
feu* upright before them, like standards.

"*W'alé!*" The grating whisper came from a pace behind her. As if he'd
read the question from her mind. "You are going. Now. Before the fire."

Elise went stumbling, as if the voice had shoved her. Or maybe it was
the boot heels, still slightly unfamiliar to her feet. She hurried, not once
looking back. At the next corner from the Place d'Armes she found in her
pathway a worn-out, broken broom with its two pieces crossed. The
débris in the interstices seemed arranged with some calculation; among
the ordinary litter she picked out a twist of tobacco, an elaborately knotted string, a small, faceless doll sewn in black cloth, and a whole hen's
egg . . . Some nonsense of African superstition. She ought to feel free to
walk right over it, to kick it carelessly out of her way. Instead she turned
into another street, fear clawing in her abdomen and raking down the
muscles of her back. And what if her every crossroad were blocked by
some such *ouanga*? But at the next intersection the road was open all the
way across the Rue Royale, and she could see the horses waiting at her
door.

For the next half-hour she could busy herself with preparations for
the departure (though the real packing had been done the night before).
Tocquet was supervising Gros-Jean and Bazau as they hitched the cart
which would carry their luggage, and in which Zabeth and the two
infants would ride. Yes, it did still amuse Elise to install her maid in such
a vehicle, while she herself went horseback.

The sun had cleared the rooftops and the day's first real heat had
begun to bear down, when Isabelle appeared to see them off. At the sight
of her, twirling a parasol above her small, neat head, Elise felt a deep
misgiving. "Come with us," she murmured as she embraced her friend.
"You must come—now—before they burn it down."

"No, no," said Isabelle, as she pressed her lightly powdered cheek
against Elise's. "I don't believe it will come to that—who stands to gain

from such destruction? And everything will be put right, as soon as Toussaint has come."

Elise drew back to her arm's length, though she still held Isabelle by the shoulders; Isabelle raised her parasol again to shade them both. She was reaching for something in Elise's expression, but there was no way for her to describe her encounter at the church that morning. It would be taken as a freak of deranged fancy, and what if that were really all it had been? Xavier was studying her too, but perhaps only because it amused him to see them so together; in her current dress Elise might be taken for one or another of Isabelle's swains.

"Then send the children," Elise said, turning her head; Robert and Héloïse had come along this morning with their mother. The boy stood flicking his wooden hoop an inch or so this way and that, while his sister gaped at him, stunned by the heat.

Isabelle's features stiffened slightly. "No," she said. "I have been too long apart from them—I will not send them from me now."

"It is your choice," said Elise, and dropped her hands. "Let it be." She forced a lightness into her voice. "But you must come to us as soon as you may. Come to us at Ennery. We shall see each other soon."

"Indeed we shall." Isabelle leaned in to brush her cheek once more, and then Elise turned toward Tocquet, setting her foot in the palm he offered as a stairstep to the saddle of her mare. He gave her knee a solid slap once she was settled, and Elise felt a flush of gratification; there had been few enough such friendly touches between them these last weeks.

So they set out. Elise rode behind Tocquet; Gros-Jean and Bazau brought up the rear behind the cart. She looked back once as they turned the corner. Isabelle still stood with her brother and the children in the street.

On the Rue Espagnole there was some turmoil. A gang of half-grown boys ran alongside the horses for a block or two, calling to them in voices that did not seem altogether friendly. At the corner of the street leading down to the Place Clugny another knot of men was gathered by a tarpot. The batting of their *lances à feu* was well coated with the stuff, and one of them thrust his shaft unpleasantly in their direction as they rode by. Elise felt a clutch, remembering the broken broomstick she'd discovered in her way. Her earlier mixture of feeling was entirely gone, and all she wanted now was to be safely out of the town. Would anyone actually block their passage? In the event the gate was open and they went through it without incident, onto the road toward Morne Rouge and Limbé.

When the dust of his sister's departure had settled on the road, Doctor Hébert bade Isabelle good day and walked across to Government House to see what news might be had there. En route he found various small squads of the Second Demibrigade busy tearing down copies of

Napoleon's proclamation of eternal liberty for the former slaves, which Télémaque had caused to be posted earlier that morning. Inside the building, he found Télémaque himself at the end of a shouting match with General Christophe. He would order out the municipal guard, Télémaque's voice boomed down the corridor, to prevent any such act of barbarity. Fulminating, he stalked past the doctor and disappeared down the hall. The doctor reached the anteroom in time to see Christophe's coattail disappearing into the inner cabinet. The door slammed. Pascal stood facing it, the edge of his thumbnail pinched between his front teeth.

"And what act of barbarity might that be?" the doctor said.

Pascal lowered his hand from his mouth and hid it in his pocket. "The general has ordered the town to be evacuated." He swallowed. "And burned."

"When?"

Pascal shrugged. "At any moment. Or if the fleet attempts a landing . . ."

"And Télémaque?"

"He believes the municipal guard will hold loyal to France," Pascal said. "But of course they cannot hope for much if they have to resist the army."

With one more glance at the closed door to the inner cabinet, the doctor left the room and went back into the street. Slowly he walked in the direction of the hospital. The sun blazed down, and the grade of the ascent was enough to make him sweat. Inside the hospital enclosure he stopped for a moment to rest in the shade, with one hand braced against a palm tree. Further from the gate, the toeless cane-cutter was hobbling slowly across the enclosure with the aid of a peeled stick.

When he had cooled sufficiently to think, the doctor sent out for a cart to convey the cane-cutter back to Habitation Héricourt. Two of his dysentery cases had been let go already, and the third was well enough to travel, along with the two malaria patients. In an hour's time he had got them loaded on the cart with the cane-cutter—they would be dropped off at Haut du Cap, on the way to Héricourt. When the cart had creaked off down the hill, he sent the two *sages-femmes* who served him as nurses home as well. The hospital was closed until further notice.

Most of his medical supplies had been sent down to Ennery with Elise and Tocquet. He was not sure why he had not gone himself. His interest in Isabelle was no more than friendly, and while he would like to see her safe, that was not the only thing that kept him hanging on in the town. It puzzled him, as it had his sister, for he was anxious for Nanon and his own children, to whom he might have gone this morning instead of staying here.

He went into the chamber that served him as office and examining room, and collected a bundle of his most essential herbs and a small surgical kit in a leather case. Since the fleet had appeared at the harbor's mouth, he had been wearing a brace of pistols hidden under his coat, and now he took them both out, checked the priming, and holstered them again. His long gun was at his sister's house in the town.

He had just finished looping a chain through the iron gate that closed the hospital compound when he heard a voice calling to him in the street:

"Doktè Doktè, madanm mandé w tounen lakay . . ."

He turned toward the voice with a sense of *déjà vu*—it was that new porter from Elise's house. Michau was what they called him, he remembered.

Doctor, Doctor, Madame wants you to come back to the house.

"Ki madanm sa yé?" he said, thinking that Elise was gone. What Madame is it? He snapped the padlock on the chain, checked his key, and turned from the gate.

"Madanm Isabelle," Michau panted.

"Dousman," the doctor said. He laid a hand on the black man's shoulder to calm him a little and slow his pace. Michau caught his breath, then reached for the doctor's bundle of herbs. The doctor let him take it as they walked together down past the *casernes*. There was indeed a movement of municipal guard through the streets, as Pascal had predicted. With the help of many ordinary citizens, they were organizing buckets and barrels of water. At the same time the small parties of soldiers grouped around tar pots, their *lances à feu* at the ready, were no less numerous than before.

An officer of the municipal guard was just coming out of the Cigny house as the doctor arrived. Arnaud was waiting on the ground floor, just within the double doors, coatless, with his loose sleeves pushed back past his elbows.

"What news?" the doctor said, glancing at the withdrawing guardsman as he stepped into the shade. Michau remained outdoors, arms folded, his black face slightly glossy with sweat, impassive under the full sun.

"There is to be a bucket brigade," Arnaud said. "In case Christophe does fire the town. Cigny is already gone down to the Fontaine d'Estaing, and I was only waiting for you."

"Yes," said the doctor, raising one finger. "I'll just have a word with Isabelle first." Arnaud nodded and the doctor moved to the stairs.

"Maman," Robert was saying, as the doctor tapped on the frame of the parlor door. Isabelle, distracted, didn't notice his knock.

"Oui, chéri?" she said.

"Will the black soldiers be coming to burn down our house again?"

The doctor was struck by the polite neutrality of the boy's question. But a wave ran over Isabelle's features, before she composed herself to reply.

"Nonsense!" she said. "No such thing—did you not hear the man who has just left? The mayor himself, Monsieur Télémaque, assures us that nothing of the kind will happen—"

With that she saw the doctor and ran tripping across the room to catch his hands and draw him out onto the landing.

"Have you been to Government House?" she said.

"Yes, but I learned nothing there," the doctor said. "I have been shutting up the hospital. I suppose I ought to go with Arnaud, to join your husband. But it may be that you should not be left alone in the house, with all the uncertainty of the day."

"No, no," Isabelle said hurriedly. "You must certainly go and make yourself useful. I have my coachman here, and a footman too—" She glanced back into the parlor, giving his hands a little squeeze. "I do wish you would take Robert with you. If he stays here with nothing to occupy him, he will upset his sister with his fancies."

Fancies? the doctor thought. "You ought to make ready to leave," he told Isabelle. "Just—"

"I won't hear of it," Isabelle snapped, and lowered her voice at once. "Télémaque has assured everyone that nothing will happen."

"As you wish," the doctor said, and beckoned to the boy.

Robert was yet too small to do any heavy lifting, but he made no trouble as the grown men set about the work. He was quiet and seemed abstracted, scanning the harbor's mouth. His company made the doctor wish for Paul. Often enough he followed the direction of Robert's gaze, looking for the sail of a French warship, but for the moment the skyline was vacant, the water calm.

Through the rest of the afternoon they were busy, collecting buckets and barrels and troughs, setting depots of water at the principal corners, and organizing for the passage of water from the Fontaine d'Estaing at the port and from two other fountains higher up in the town. Télémaque appeared briefly at every station, and the men of the municipal guard were industrious, along with all of the white citizens who had not thought it better to depart. All the while small squads of soldiers were also moving through the streets. The soldiers did not interfere with the water haulers, but they were in charge of a parallel movement of tar barrels and *lances à feu*.

By the time the sun had begun to redden and drop toward the heights of Morne du Cap behind the town, a water station had been set up on the corner of the Cignys' block. Accompanied by Michau and Arnaud, the doctor brought Robert back to his mother. Isabelle was preparing a supper of cold chicken and fruit, but the doctor excused himself, saying he would go to secure his sister's house.

With Michau, he set out in that direction. At the opposite end of the Cignys' block, a squad from the Second had installed itself, with a tar barrel and *lances à feu*. A couple of the men were holding lit torches.

Without a word, with their eyes averted, they drew back to let the doctor pass.

Elise's house was vacant now, except for one old woman who cooked. The doctor told her she was free to go; he would be dining *chez* Cigny that night. He went to his bedroom and got his American-made rifle and a small bundle of clothes he'd already made up, and carried these things down to the stable. Two saddle horses remained from the morning's exodus, and one blue mule. The doctor considered for a moment, and reached for the mule saddle.

"You can ride?" he said to Michau as he strapped the rifle scabbard and saddlebags into place. "Excellent. I think I had better shut up the house, but get anything you want from the kitchen. If there is trouble you must bring the horses to Madame Cigny, or if you cannot, take them to the top of La Vigie." He pointed to one of the peaks behind the town.

Michau nodded, and the doctor clapped him on the back. He gave the porter a couple of minutes to clean out the larder, then began closing the double doors and fastening them with the iron padlocks Elise had left with him. The last lock fell against the door with a drum-like thump. The doctor dropped the bunch of keys into his saddlebag and mounted the mule. Touching his hat to Michau, he rode into the street.

More soldiers than usual were stationed outside Christophe's mansion, but no sign of the general himself. The doctor did not see Pascal, or anyone else it seemed wise to hail, as he rode through the area of Government House, perched on the high, narrow ridge of the mule's back. He did not take the road that led to the beach this time. There was a trail that went higher on the hill around the point, a difficult one which was not much used except by charcoal burners. It was for that he had chosen the mule, and the animal went up it nimbly enough.

At the crown of the hill he pulled up and looked back. The sun had dropped behind the mountain, its red glow staining a few feathers of cloud. A couple of denser darker clouds were drifting across the plain from the east, but they were small and widely separated—there wouldn't be much rain tonight. There still was light enough for him to see threads of smoke rising from the fires that warmed the tarpots at the Place d'Armes and the Place Clugny and many intersections in between. Hardly anyone had come out for the evening promenade. The red-tiled roofs and empty streets looked weirdly tranquil.

He clucked to the mule and rode on, turning his face into a freshening wind off the sea. A mild chop and a few whitecaps below. He was overlooking the open ocean now, and the masts of the fleet were plainly visible against the horizon. He started counting, gave it up. His heart sank as he looked at them. Here the trail was level and he could move the mule to a trot. In a couple of minutes he was looking down an abrupt descent onto the battlements of Fort Picolet.

No one thought to glance up in his direction. The men were all concentrating on heating up shot. General Christophe stood at the outer wall among the gunners, erect and uncharacteristically rigid, looking out to sea. The doctor saw a frigate detach itself from the fleet and begin to sail down upon the fort. He took a small brass spyglass from his pocket and pulled it to its full extension. With the help of the lens he could make out the name of the approaching ship, *L'Aiguille*. But his arm was unsteady and the circle of magnification bounced around, beyond his control. He collapsed the spyglass and put it back in his pocket. *L'Aiguille*, the *Needle*, was quite near now. Everything was becoming indistinct in the rapidly lowering dusk. The doctor saw iron shot glowing red on the grills above the coals. He saw Christophe thrust his right arm toward *L'Aiguille* as if he were hurling a javelin.

"*Feu!*"

A single cannon spoke. The hot iron of the ball drew a red line across the water, then fell sizzling, short of the frigate's bow. *L'Aiguille* cut nimbly to the south and returned a broadside on the fort. This time a dozen cannon replied from Picolet. But Christophe had already left the battlement, as if the outcome of this engagement were of no more concern to him. In the thickening darkness the doctor could just make out the general's silhouette hastening down from the fort to the pebbled beach, where an orderly waited, holding his horse.

The doctor's mule had not much reacted to the cannon, only swiveling its long ears in the direction of the noise. He turned the animal's head toward the town and kicked into a risky trot: the white shale of the path was barely visible underfoot. Behind he could hear the firing continue. More ships had sailed in to join the battle, and there was sound of splintering stone and men's voices crying in rage or pain.

On precipitous descent of the hill the mule had to slow and pick its way. Christophe would certainly be making faster progress on the lower road, once he had got off the rocky beach. The doctor had a fine panoramic view of the town, where the *lances à feu* had now been lit; it looked like hundreds of them. He watched the points of light spiraling out of the Place d'Armes and the Place Clugny, spreading out of the *casernes* and along the waterfront. No buildings had yet been set on fire.

When he reached street level, he kicked his mule to the fastest pace it would deliver. The soldiers with their *lances à feu* moved in tight order or stood with a fixed regard. None of them paid him any mind. They did not seem to see him whirling past.

Christophe was just dismounting in front of his own house when the doctor turned into the Rue Royale. The general passed his reins to a soldier in exchange for a burning *lance à feu*. The doctor halted the mule on the opposite side of the street. He opened his mouth but no words came out. A couple of other white men had come over from the water station on the corner, and they seemed to be in a similar state of speechlessness.

Through the arch of the gateway, they watched Christophe stride into his own front door and climb the curving stairway in the foyer. At the top, he turned to face the street, and after a moment's pause on the crux, he tilted his *lance à feu* to touch a wall. Every surface of the interior must have been painted with tar already, for the whole house was instantly ablaze. Framed against the thrusting flames, Christophe descended the stairs at the same slow and stately pace as he had climbed them. When he had emerged across the threshold, he turned and flung his fire spear back into the burning house.

"*Alé!*" he said in a loud harsh voice, as he came out through the archway onto the street. "*Alé, meté feu partout.*" His eyes cut across the cluster of white men. Go, set fire to everything!

As the soldiers with torches began to disperse, the doctor rode for his sister's house. He was thinking of Michau and the horses. But the stable was already afire when he arrived. He pulled up the mule and watched a pair of soldiers use a tar keg to smash in the front door of the house. The rolling keg spread its black ichor in a curve across the floor; then one of the soldiers picked it up and tossed the rest of the contents on the walls. Another man was already thrusting his *lance à feu* into the eaves. The house went up in one great whoosh.

The soldiers were already on to the next building, but the doctor remained, watching with a queer fascination as the fire ate through a tar-coated door. In two minutes the weathered wood was rendered frail and transparent as a strip of muslin, and the fire outlined the hinges and hasp and the padlock the doctor had fastened there that afternoon. As the door collapsed and fell out of the frame, he turned his mule toward the Cigny house.

No sign of Michau or the horses there, but Isabelle stood halfway down her stairs, holding Héloïse in her arms and arguing with a private soldier of the Second.

"I will not have it—not a second time," she cried. She stamped her foot on the wooden riser. "I will not see my home destroyed. I will not!"

"*Madanm, tannpri,*" the soldier said, while another man drizzled tar across the ground-floor carpets. Arnaud stared up at Isabelle, eyes bulging and mouth agape. Cigny, standing with one hand on Robert's shoulder, had simply covered his eyes with the other . . .

"*Madanm, tannpri,*" the soldier repeated. Madame, please. A strange courtesy, the doctor thought. The burning of this town in ninety-three had been a wholesale orgy of murder and rape. To this Isabelle had been witness, had barely escaped being a victim herself. Of course that had been ten thousand savages, by comparison to this quite well-disciplined army.

"*Ma chère,*" he said to her from the doorway. Isabelle's eyes locked onto his. Héloïse turned her sobbing face against her mother's bosom.

"My dear," the doctor said. "It's time to go."

With a swallow, Isabelle came unglued from her post on the stairs.

The soldier who'd been cajoling her sighed as she swept past him. In the foyer she paused to hurl at the man with the tar barrel—"You will be held to account for the cost of those carpets you have spoiled!" But then she let her husband guide her out into the street.

The bucket brigade was not functioning as planned; the doctor had scarcely given it a thought during his hurried ride into town. But now Isabelle thrust Héloïse into her husband's arms—the child howled louder at the unwelcome transfer—and dashed to the water station on the corner. Arnaud and the doctor followed. An old horse trough had been moved to this spot, meant to be replenished by a chain of buckets stretching as far as the fountain on the Place d'Armes, but all the street in that direction was nothing but a tunnel of fire, and half the water in the trough had evaporated in the withering heat. Isabelle seemed unconscious of these aspects of the situation. Mechanically she filled a bucket, passed it to Arnaud, scooped another for the doctor, and led the men back the way they'd come, lugging her own pail.

By then flames were shooting out the windows and roof of the Cigny house. Isabelle tossed her bucket against a burning wall; it disappeared in a hiss of steam. She turned to march back for more water, but now their way was barred by a squad of soldiers, holding their muskets crossways. When Isabelle advanced, unheeding, one of the soldiers hooked her bucket away from her with a bayonet point and flipped it into the nearest fire. The doctor ran up and caught her arm. His own weapons were handy enough, but it would have been folly to produce them. The soldiers marched against him and Isabelle, shoving with their sideways muskets. Isabelle reached out her small hand and pushed one of them in the chest.

"Stop it!" the doctor said. "It is no use." Beyond, he could see that other soldiers had dumped the horse trough over and were staving in the bottom with their gun butts. Isabelle did stop, but not because of what he'd said. A cinder had landed on her cheek, and carelessly she brushed at it, leaving a smear of soot. Her gaze was fixed down the next block, where a great white warhorse emerged through a wreath of fire. Scrambling up onto its back was a small man with a jockey's build, dressed in a charcoal burner's rags, a dull red cloth bound over his head. He gripped the horse's mane with one hand and swept the other forward.

"Alé! Meté feu partout! Boulé tout kay-yo!"

Isabelle did not exactly slump, but the doctor felt the force go out of her. She did not resist now when he turned her away. As they returned toward the others, she staggered and the doctor caught her around the shoulders. Cigny was reaching his free hand toward hers.

The soldiers moved up, pressing on them and their neighbors who'd been driven from their own burning houses. Impelled by thrusts of the crossways muskets, they went up the sloping street, the doctor leading his mule by the reins. Soon they had joined a much larger crowd of refugees being chivvied along the Rue Espagnole by the soldiers. Télémaque was among them, with the municipal guard and the rest of the civil officials of the town. In reasonably good order, never firing a shot or using the point of a bayonet, the soldiers of the Second shepherded them past the *casernes*. They turned onto the road that climbed toward the summit of La Vigie.

Isabelle had begun to stumble. "Let us get her up on the mule," Cigny said. Isabelle objected at first, but it was explained to her that she could then hold Héloïse and try to calm her. The girl, not unreasonably, was howling even louder than before. At that Isabelle consented to mount, and in her mother's arms Héloïse did lower the volume of her wailing. They went on, the doctor still leading the mule, up the steep and twisting ascent. Cigny and Arnaud followed the mule, each holding one of Robert's hands.

On the summit of La Vigie, some hundreds of refugees were clustered. The couple of houses that stood there were already full to bursting with infirm or injured people. The doctor's party settled on the ground. They'd got out with little more than the clothes they were wearing, but Isabelle produced a scrap of sheet for them to sit on.

The doctor went off to tether the mule by a clump of trees where he'd noticed several horses. There he found Michau tending the two saddle horses from Elise's stable. A bit of good fortune he had not expected. He gave Michau a squeeze on the arm and left the mule in his care as well.

The cannons at Fort Picolet were long since silent. There was no more artillery fire at all, though the doctor could hear small arms popping in the burning town, as he made his way back to the Cigny group. From this height the view was panoramic, and he saw the lights of the French ships sailing into the harbor, though none of them approached the burning waterfront. It was for this spectacle he'd stayed, he thought. The town was on fire from one end to the other.

The doctor settled his haunches on the piece of sheet, by Isabelle. Héloïse had now cried herself into collapse and snuffled gently against her mother's blouse. This high on the hill, it was rather chilly at night, though their faces were warmed by the fire below. The doctor watched firelight flickering on Robert's face, wishing again that his son Paul were nearer. Isabelle's boy seemed calm enough, fascinated. And certainly the vision was both awful and grand. The cathedral and the customs house were two great bonfires. The doctor looked toward Government House in time to see the whole of its roof collapsing in the fire. He picked out the enclosure of his hospital, it too engulfed in flames. Then the powder depot of the Batterie Circulaire blew up, blasting the embers of its building into the star-speckled sky. The crowd on the hill responded with an awestruck moan. Isabelle turned her ashen face toward the doctor.

"That was he," she said in a soft voice. "You saw him too—riding Bel Argent. That was Toussaint we saw."

"Yes," said the doctor, thinking that this was another sight he had stayed to behold. "I believe it was." As he spoke, the arsenal of the *caserne* blew up, and another deep moan passed through the crowd like wind.

IO

During those two days when Leclerc's portion of the fleet lay waiting outside the harbor of Le Cap, rumor of Christophe's defiance glided from one vessel to another in the manner of the wandering gulls. On *La Vertu* it was received with hope. The leaders of the mulatto rebellion against Toussaint walked the deck and sniffed the air, as if to test the limits of their prospects. The pink-roofed town was tranquil in the pocket of the bay. Rigaud, Villatte, Boyer, Pétion—these colored gentlemen who'd been defeated and driven into exile by the armies of Toussaint had all got wind of the semi-secret order which Leclerc bore from the First Consul. They knew that if Toussaint resisted, their knowledge of the land and its people would be recognized as of inestimable value—they would certainly be sent into the field and with luck might receive commands of their own. They also had a good idea that if Toussaint were to receive the French fleet peaceably, their presence here would be judged a liability.

Aboard the *Jean-Jacques* the mood was much the opposite. Isaac had no direct memory of Le Cap, since he was too young when he had left it. And neither boy had ever spent much time there before they'd been sent to the Collège de la Marche in France. But Placide remembered enough that he could point out the salient features to Monsieur Coisnon: Fort Picolet, the Batterie Circulaire, the Fontaine d'Estaing, the roof of Government House, and the elevation of the church. And even Isaac had ideas of the town transmitted to him by his elder brother and by other colonial students at the Collège, some vivid enough they'd merged with his own fund of memories. Both boys and their tutor were looking forward to seeing the town at closer range.

During those same two days, Captains Cyprien and Daspir found themselves billeted to the general staff aboard *L'Océan*—which meant, as it turned out, dancing attendance on Madame Pauline Leclerc, to stoop or run to recover her dropped kerchiefs and windblown scarves, and be rewarded with glimpses of her famous alabaster skin. There'd been worse duty in the world, as Cyprien remarked. Their position also put them in the way of news more reliable than the common run of rumor.

Possessed of all the patience of a butterfly, Pauline soon grew petulant at their delay in landing in the town. "But what is this impertinence—to burn the place and fight us on the ashes?" she exclaimed. "The General my husband has only to act swiftly to prevent such a disaster. I do not understand why he is dilatory. After so many weeks penned up on this chip of a boat, I am sure we should all be glad of a chance to stretch our legs on shore." So saying, she extended her own slender leg, which the attending officers could admire through its gossamer skirting as they murmured their assent to her opinion. As for Leclerc himself, Captain Daspir noticed with some interest, he seemed to steer clear of Pauline's daylong levées on deck. Indeed, he gave her a wide berth altogether, except of course at night when the couple retired together into the elaborate boudoir fitted out for them below. Not the most *spartan* exercise of martial virtue, Cyprien quipped, to which Daspir replied that a good general was duty-bound to do his best to prevail and conquer in whatever field he might find laid before him . . . But the sounds that filtered past the bulkheads suggested bickering more often than bliss.

For roughly thirty-six hours Leclerc, no matter Pauline's impatience, seemed willing to temporize with Christophe and await developments, but by February 4 he was persuaded that Christophe meant only to delay, to make time for the resistance to be organized on shore—and organized, perhaps, by his superior in command, for the envoy Lebrun had been sensitive to the half-open door of the inner sanctum, during his interview with Christophe at Government House. Once Leclerc had been so persuaded, he was quick enough to order action. Leaving *L'Océan* with his bride at its mooring, he transferred his command to another vessel, which would sail round the point for a landing at the Baie d'Acul. That area had been reconnoitered early, and was well out of view of the guns of Picolet.

Now Daspir was reassigned to the staff of General Hardy, embarked in the same squadron as Leclerc. "Hard luck," he called to Cyprien, though his stomach fluttered as he climbed down into the boat.

"What do you mean?" Cyprien's face hung moon-like over the rail above.

"Why," said Daspir, "you stand to miss this action."

"There may be action enough here as well." Cyprien smirked. "And I will keep our lady safe, till we are reunited."

"See that you do," Daspir shouted, as the oarsmen pulled his boat away. "And don't forget our wager—we'll bring the raghead in." But Cyprien did not reply to this; perhaps the wind had blown his words away.

It was no great distance that their squadron had to sail, but contrary winds delayed them. Slowly the ships tacked out past the end of the promontory that stretched into the Atlantic beyond Fort Picolet. Curled like a beckoning finger, that last spit of land sheltered an inviting strip of sandy beach inside its curve.

The wind blew full in Daspir's face from the open ocean, and the gulls whirled above them, crying. He stared at the densely jungled shoreline and thought of Pauline's careless words. He was eager enough to set his foot on shore, and readier still for the fresh provender that might be found once they landed. The idea of confronting savage Negro armies gave him a more ambiguous feeling. Perhaps before the end of this day he would be facing enemy fire for the first time. Somehow it did not seem so light a matter now as it had when he and the others had toasted their compact with the excellent brandy he had brought out on this voyage from his father's cellar in France. All gone now, that brandy, squandered, except for half of the very last bottle, wrapped in a shirt in Daspir's pack. But wonderful things were said of Saint Dominican rum . . . If his mind could dwell on such a prospect, Daspir thought, then he must not be afraid—the wobbly sensation in his belly must be no more than excitement. Still, he wished the other three were with him, or even just one of them, whether Guizot, with whom he might have shared his innocence of combat, or one of the other two, who were at least somewhat familiar with this country.

The molten coin of the sun was boring through the flat plane of the ocean by the time the squadron had reached the mouth of the Baie d'Acul. The word went round the ships that they would wait till the next day to effect their landing. Daspir ate his evening ration without much tasting it. He thought wistfully of a dram of brandy, but decided to conserve it for some time of greater need—and he had no acquaintances on this ship he cared to drink with anyway. He found his hammock and lay rocking from the cross timbers of the lower deck, breathing the fetid air as shallowly as he could. There was a throbbing of drums on shore and he wondered if it had a meaning, if perhaps those drums were signals. The next thing he knew, someone was shaking him awake with a hard clasp on his bare ankle and he came bolting up from a host of dreams he could scarcely remember.

He pulled his boots on, collected his arms, and clambered to the upper deck, yawning behind one hand and scratching mosquito bites with the other. The staff officers were clustered around General Hardy, who was studying a map by lamplight, as it was not quite dawn. Daspir joined the edge of this group, just as Hardy raised one hand to point at the surface of the bay, which lay calm and silvery with starlight.

"There," he said, comparing with the legend of his map, "it was just there that Columbus sank one of his first ships, the *Santa María*, and on that shore where he raised the first settlement in this land."

Daspir shivered in the morning chill. The thought of the ancient beams of the *Santa María* dissolving in the silt somewhere below their own vessel rang ominously against something in his unremembered dream. And he had heard how Columbus's first settlement here had been sacked and destroyed by Indians, when the great explorer was voyaging somewhere else . . . But Hardy's forefinger had settled on the map again. Daspir leaned in to peer more closely. A road was marked out from the lower end of the Baie d'Acul, back across the peninsula they'd sailed around the previous day.

"Here there is something of an ascent," Hardy said, tapping the parchment. "Once we have achieved the height, we descend thus—and from that point the road should be open, through Morne Rouge and Haut du Cap to Le Cap itself and the harbor there. Or if it is not, we shall open it."

At first light the boats were plying between the ships and shore, as a cool mist drifted up from the water of the bay. There was the usual splashing of paddles, creaking of oarlocks, grunting and cursing of soldiers and sailors. The troops had formed on shore before the sun had cleared the top of the hills above them. There'd been no opposition to their landing in this place. In fact the whole area was quite eerily empty of any human sign at all—not so much as a fisherman's canoe here on the bay. But when they began to march up the steep road Hardy had indicated, a dry rattle of drumming started off to their left, hidden somewhere in the jungle.

The first rays of sun slanting in through the treetops gave a hint of the blazing heat that would follow. Daspir was sweating in his wool uniform, though as a staff officer he'd been given a horse. Sweat-soaked in half an hour's time, the laboring infantry smelled rather like wet sheep. They went double time up the steep zigzag ascent, which was more of a goat path than the road Hardy's map had suggested. Daspir pressed up on his stirrups, lifting his seat from the saddle and leaning forward to ease the burden on his mount. The men pressed on, wooden faced, their pigtails hanging limp behind them in the moist heat. The air of the woods surrounding the trail had a thick scent of ripeness and rot. Daspir's nose wrinkled. They had reached such a height now that the open stretches of the trail gave them a splendid wide view of the bay where the ships were moored and the ocean bending away beyond.

The drum sound thickened in the jungle, picked up speed. Then from the crook of the trail ahead came the sudden roar of cannon. Daspir was in the van with General Hardy; at the noise his horse spooked and slipped from the trail. The struggle of mastering the panicked animal and bringing it back to level ground helped him control his own impulse to jump down from the saddle and cower on the ground. Another horse had fallen with a shattered leg, pinning the rider half under it. After a moment Daspir dismounted and helped the other man free. The action calmed him. Their forward movement had scarcely been checked. Daspir swung back into the saddle. Someone shot the wounded horse and it lay still. Daspir's mount trembled between his knees but was willing to go on, and Hardy was urging the troops forward with his sword. The cannon fired again and then were silent. Daspir moved up, dimly noticing the bodies of a couple of grenadiers spilled to the side of the trail, passing a wrecked gun carriage flung off the next bend. Then they had burst into a cluster of small clay-daubed houses, just over the crest of the height they'd been climbing. Cannon fired again, from the road below, and women and children and livestock ran scattering in all directions, throwing themselves down the defiles, plunging into cover of the jungle where the hidden drums kept grumbling. The women shrieked in a language that sounded exactly like French, yet Daspir could not find a single intelligible word in it.

At that he stopped short and groped at the back of his head, wondering if he'd taken some unfelt hurt that had knocked the comprehension right out of his brain. But then he realized he still understood Hardy's shouted orders well enough. He choked, coughed, and saw that the roofs of all the little houses had been set afire. No wonder the women were all screaming. He squeezed his horse forward down the slope, behind the front line of infantry. The horse was cooperating with him better now—it was not such a poor horse as he'd at first thought. A row of black soldiers appeared across the road, and Daspir felt his hat go crooked; only as he set it straight did he hear the volley of musketry. The French soldiers moved on unperturbed except for those who had fallen. Enemy cannons spat out fire, and there was another ring of female screeching. Among the black soldiers Daspir picked out a huge white horse with a small black rider, swirling a sword as long as himself through clouds of smoke above his kerchiefed head. Daspir, who prided himself on his own horsemanship, had not seen such a stallion in his whole life. He swallowed and instinctively spurred out ahead of the infantry line.

Alé! Meté feu partout!

Hardy's infantrymen were charging with the bayonet. Now they had the advantage of the downhill grade to add to their momentum. A shock, and the enemy line was dispersed. White horse and dark rider had vanished. The black soldiers were scattering into the trees. Hardy's infantry re-formed and continued marching down the slope. Of a sudden their column was raked by musket fire—not an organized volley, but a series of isolated shots from the cover of the jungle on either side. A few men fell. Daspir picked at his mosquito bites absently as he rode down; the bites were turning to sores where they chafed against his coat collar. He twisted in the saddle and looked back. The blue coats of the infantry flowed down the hill in a steady stream out of the burning village, the white knees of their breeches flashing like scissor blades in the sun.

He felt a flash of exhilaration, without reason, beyond it. Then a tight outward bend of the trail brought him clear of the cover of the trees, and all at once he could see the whole expanse of the great Northern Plain. The land was on fire like a checkerboard: some plantations were ablaze while others remained green and somnolent. Columns of men moved through the fuming landscape like lines of worker ants. At this distance Daspir could not discern what men they were. The humid air was heavy with the smell of scorching sugar.

"Forward!" Hardy ordered. For a moment, the general himself had been staggered by the panorama of the burning plain. But now his men were coming down onto flat and open terrain, with the black soldiers falling back before them. Hardy massed his infantry, signaled a charge—but the blacks would not stand to receive them. They were retreating, in reasonable order, dragging their cannon across a wooden bridge.

Daspir rode up. Without realizing it, he had passed the front line of his own troops to reach the bank of a swift-running brown river. Oxen were laboring on the shoals of the stream bed, hauling on ropes attached to the posts beneath the bridge. There was that small rider on the big white horse, shouting commands to the ox drivers. With a great heave and a groan of ripping wood, the posts gave way, the bridge buckled and collapsed into the water. Scraps of plank and broken joist came eddying out into the spiraling currents of the stream. Daspir watched as the white horse scrambled up the opposite bank; once on level ground, it broke into a canter. A magnificent animal—and the old rag-headed Negro certainly rode with a consummate skill. He moved as fluidly with the horse as if the two were one. By instinct Daspir rode down the bank and scouted the water's edge, but it looked too deep to cross without swimming. When he looked up he saw that the black riding the big stallion had paused in his movement to study him, and felt a thrill at that recognition.

"What are you doing there, Captain—come back!" It was Hardy's voice; the general had just appeared on the bank above. Daspir leaned forward and pushed his horse up to join him; Hardy watched his riding with a grudging respect.

"Look you well," the general said, when Daspir had swung his horse in beside him. "We have the honor to bring the battle to Toussaint Louverture."

Across the river the little man had slipped down from the warhorse and was moving among the gun carriages, nudging, gesturing. Daspir stared at him, only half believing. But it must be. Something whined between him and Hardy. Daspir reached automatically for his mosquito bites, then realized it must have been a musket ball.

"Get out of this," Hardy told him. "Ride to the Captain-General and let him know the bridge is down."

Daspir snapped his fingers to his hat brim and turned his horse to the rear. There was a volley of cannon as he spurred up, and cries as the front rank of Hardy's infantry was torn by grapeshot on the riverbank. Daspir did not look back. The drums from the jungle had gone silent, yet their absence seemed to hum in his head.

"Then we must hurry to find a ford," Leclerc said, when he'd received the message. "I want to enter Le Cap before dark." He stroked his silky blond sidewhiskers absently down toward his chin, and narrowed his eyes at Daspir. "But are you not wounded?"

"No," Daspir said, confused. "I do not think so." Leclerc seemed to be peering at his hat brim. Daspir pulled off the hat and looked at it. Halfway up the crown was a hole big enough to admit his thumb.

"A fine souvenir that will make of this day," Leclerc said with a brilliant smile. "And a fortunate first day of battle for you, Captain."

Daspir flushed with pleasure at the compliment. He saluted Leclerc and rode back toward the riverbank. The cannon barrage Toussaint had organized had now stopped, and the men swarming on the opposite bank were different now. One of Rochambeau's flying columns had appeared to join them and driven the black soldiers out of their position.

Suddenly weary, Daspir slipped down from his horse. His legs went rubbery when they struck the ground and he caught a stirrup leather for support. Unbelievingly, he squinted at the declining angle of the sun. Almost the whole day had passed in this skirmishing, though to him it had seemed no more than an hour.

Leclerc would never reach Le Cap by nightfall, Daspir realized now. He took off his hat, rubbed the felt, and traced the edge of the bullet hole with one finger. The reddening sun was dropping toward the ridge of Morne du Cap, and east of the mountain the smoke that came boiling up from where the town itself must have been was thick and black as tar.

On the deck of *La Vertu* the mulatto leaders pressed against the rail, listening to the cannonade that had begun as soon as *L'Aiguille* was fired on from Fort Picolet. In the space of an hour or even less, all response from the fort had ceased. Rigaud looked to see any sign of a movement of retreat from Picolet, but darkness had settled in to cover everything. An ominous orange glow increased beyond the headland.

The flagship *L'Océan* weighed anchor and sailed for the harbor's mouth; *La Vertu* and the other vessels followed. Their entry was slow; since the channel markers had been taken away the day before, Admiral

Villaret-Joyeuse was obliged to send a small boat out to take soundings in advance of the deep-draught warships. Gradually the men on the deck of *La Vertu* coasted into full view of the burning town.

Villatte, who'd served as commander of Le Cap during the time of greatest mulatto ascendancy there, stared numbly out at the fire. Rigaud studied his face, which seemed bloodless and drawn in the fierce fire-light. He gave Villatte a slap on the shoulder. "Don't trouble yourself," he said. "It has all been burned and rebuilt before. And of a certainty, we shall not be sent to Madagascar now."

Captain Cyprien, meanwhile, was free to pace the deck of *L'Océan*, as the flagship meandered after the sounding boat. He stared moodily out at the conflagration. Madame Leclerc had gone below. The reduction of Fort Picolet had excited her, and even the first sight of the burning town had been something of a thrill at first, but as it sank in that the Jewel of the Antilles would surely be reduced to a heap of cinders before she ever set her satin slipper on the quai, the expression of her small features shifted from amazement to petulance.

Pauline had retired in a very bad humor, and Cyprien felt quite suffi-ciently morose himself. Since he'd come aboard the flagship, the other staff officers had been quizzing him about the pleasures of Le Cap, where he'd been posted . . . years before, during the not especially suc-cessful mission of General Hédouville. Cyprien had had a good deal to report about the voluptuous joys of the town, wine and song and espe-cially women . . . those extraordinarily beautiful and remarkably skilled colored courtesans who'd been so readily available to the officers of Hédouville's suite. But tonight no one approached him. The town was nothing but a bonfire. Even at half a mile's distance it seemed he could feel the heat of the blaze full on his face.

It would be hard duty once they got ashore. That much seemed plain. Clearly, Leclerc's encircling maneuver had fallen well short of its goal. Where was Daspir now, Cyprien wondered, and what might have become of Guizot, with Rochambeau at Fort Liberté?

On shore a powder depot went up like a volcano, hurling chunks of masonry and boulders into the night sky. A sighing moan of awestruck response could be heard all across the decks of *L'Océan* and even, Cyprien thought, from one ship to the next. He turned in the direction of the *Jean-Jacques*. If Placide and Isaac had stayed on deck to see the spec-tacle, what must they be thinking now, and what would they be saying to their tutor?

At dawn the doctor pushed himself upright, creaking and stiff after the scraps of sleep he had snatched, lying on the open ground. All around him he heard people coughing, for the whole hilltop was smoth-ered in smoke, and there was a woman crying somewhere off to the left. Isabelle slept sitting up, her lips slightly parted, propped on the bear-like mound of her husband, who lay snoring on his side. Héloïse lay in her lap and Robert was quietly curled nearby. Arnaud was nowhere to be seen.

The doctor got up and walked through the trees where the horses were tethered till he had found a sufficiently sheltered place to open his flies and relieve himself. As he was refastening his trousers, a lady came bursting out of the bushes and gave him an exasperated look as she shook her skirts down over her legs. She had a fashionable, lofty coiffure, rucked a little to one side, and her face was striped in rice powder and soot. The doctor had seen her at the theater and other such places but could not recall her name, and she had already flounced off toward the clearing before he could formulate a greeting or apology.

He returned to the horses. Michau was sleeping tranquilly on the ground beside them. The doctor gave some of the raw sugar he habitually carried in his jacket pocket to the two mares in turn and then to the mule. The mule's rubbery lips warmed and moistened his palm, searching to capture the last crumbs. The doctor himself did not feel hungry, though his belly was hollow and his head somewhat light.

The wind turned, carrying the smoke and clouds of ash out over the harbor. The doctor stood on the crown of the hill, looking out over the fuming ruin of the town. The devastation seemed to have been quite perfect. Every house and building was a well of coals and ash and not a single roof was left intact, though many walls were still standing, smoke-stained and cracked from the heat. The doctor had missed seeing this aftermath when the town was burned in ninety-three, for he and Nanon had fled the environs while the fires were still raging through the streets.

All those streets were lifeless now, except for smoldering embers. The clouds of smoke obscured the harbor. At the end of the town, near the gateway of the road to Haut du Cap, the Second Demibrigade was massed and waiting.

Something plucked at his trouser leg; he looked down and discovered Héloïse.

"J'ai faim," she said, in a neutral tone. I'm hungry. Reflexively the doctor put a hand into his pocket, but he had already given all the sugar to the horses. He peered at the little girl's smudged face. Her First Communion would be long delayed, he realized, as the cathedral lay in ashes at the bottom of the hill.

"Well, well," he said. "Let us go and find your mother." He led Héloïse back to the spot where the others were still sleeping. To the best of his recollection they'd come away empty-handed the night before, but when he cast about now he came upon a sizable basket, covered with a grease-stained cloth, which proved to contain the cold chicken and fruit from the supper they'd not had leisure to consume the night before. He picked out a whole banana and broke the peel for Héloïse, then hunkered down to watch her eat it. She was rather a striking child, with her mother's coloring and dark hair, and eyes such a very dark blue they were almost purple.

"Save a little something for your brother," he told her, as she tossed away the banana peel and went to forage in the basket.

"*J'ai soif,*" Héloïse replied, pausing to look up at him. I'm thirsty.

The doctor stood up and leaned backward, feeling his vertebrae crack. There was no water. No spring or well nearby. And now, with the sun just rising over the bay, it was already hot. He dug in the basket till he found an orange for Héloïse. As he cut into the peel with his thumbnail, Arnaud came hurrying up, in a sweat from some exertion.

"Ah, my friend," he said. "Your skills are wanted." He pointed toward the two low houses where the more infirm of the refugees had found shelter the night before.

The doctor left Héloïse trying to wake Isabelle and followed Arnaud to survey the sick and wounded. There were the predictable cases of shock and hysteria, a few people ill from want of food or water or both, a couple of incipient cases of fever . . . Several people had been injured by rock flying out from the explosion of the powder magazines. Most of these hurts were fairly slight, but one man had a hand so badly crushed that amputation was the only option.

For the next couple of hours he bandaged and poulticed, muttered and comforted as best he could. He awakened Michau and set him to brewing *tisanes* over a small fire. When it came time for the surgery, Michau and Arnaud were both engaged to hold down the hapless patient. There was no rum or any other liquor to blunt the pain, and the screams of the victim were most distressing to the other sufferers in the vicinity, until, finally, he passed out. By the time the tourniquet had been fixed, the doctor was sweat-stained and trembling and could have done very well with a tot of rum himself, though he didn't think he was likely to get one.

He walked out of the building, swinging his arms to loosen his cramped shoulders. A cluster of people had gathered at the trail head and were watching a dozen soldiers of the Second who were climbing up. Perhaps they meant to bring some succor. But when they'd reached the hilltop, their officer declared that he had orders from Christophe to burn the houses here.

Télémaque, still an imposing figure though the vestments of his office were grubby with soot and torn in the trouser legs from last night's struggle up the hill, drew himself up to protest. "You cannot mean to carry out such an inhuman action," he declaimed. "There are women and children who are sick and hurt, and all of them have lost their homes. You cannot mean to destroy the last meager shelter which is left to them."

"General Christophe suggests that you and your people remove to Haut du Cap," the officer said stolidly, pointing to the town's lower gate where the rest of the troops were still collected. "You will not be harmed. The houses on La Vigie are to be destroyed."

"Impossible," said Télémaque. "We have for example a man who has just lost his arm and he is in no state at all to be—" But the doctor had already turned from the debate and walked inside his makeshift surgery. Save for the amputee, who still lay moaning in a faint, most of the patients could shift at least a short distance under their own power.

"A moment," he said, raising one finger to Christophe's officer, who'd followed him into the building. The doctor knew the man, by sight though not by name; he was an acquaintance of Riau. Grasping his meaning, the officer followed him to the edge of the woods and helped him trim two stout green sticks and set one of his men to help Michau weave strips of torn palm leaf between them.

On this rude stretcher they moved the amputee to the shade where the horses had been tied. The first of the two houses was already being knocked down. The soldiers had not brought tar up the hill (perhaps that substance had been completely expended the night before) and the buildings were sluggish to catch fire. The soldiers fell to knocking them to pieces with blows from their boots and musket stocks. The woman with the cockeyed hairdo, whom the doctor had encountered that morning, ran at them, screeching incoherently. One of the soldiers rounded on her and marched her back to the other onlookers at the point of his bayonet.

They tried setting the rubble afire again before they left; the splintered planks burned fitfully. With the help of Arnaud and Michau, the doctor cleared horse manure from the area where the stretcher had been laid and began to rig up leaf-topped shelters to cover the feeblest of the refugees from the furiously blazing sun.

Perhaps it would have been better to go to Haut du Cap, though the doctor did not much like the thought of lugging the stretcher so far. Hand on his hip, he walked to the edge of the hilltop. Télémaque was debating the alternatives with most of the white women and the other civil functionaries and men of the municipal guard. The doctor took a few steps out of earshot and shaded his eyes. In compact order, the Second Demibrigade was marching through the gateway and onto the road away from the town.

At a nudge to his side he glanced down and saw Isabelle. Though her dress was grimy and limp and her hair bedraggled, her eyes were clear and bright and she did not seem so much the worse for the night spent in the rough.

"Look there," she said. "I believe they are landing."

A shift of the wind was now carrying the smoke over the headland and Fort Picolet, so their view of the harbor was clear. Indeed, several of the ships had sailed up to moorings along the quai, and something was being unloaded on the docks before the Batterie Circulaire. The doctor unfolded his pocket spyglass and set it to one eye.

"Fire pumps," he said. "They are unloading fire pumps there—though they have come a little late for the occasion."

"Give it to me," Isabelle said, and plucked the instrument from his hand. The doctor looked in the direction of her focus. With his naked eye he could see some sparkling commotion on the after deck of the flagship *L'Océan.*

"Why, certainly, that is Pauline Bonaparte!" Isabelle said. "I mean of course Madame Leclerc—and she is preparing to land."

The doctor reclaimed the glass and peered through it. Yes, it did seem that a lady of high station was the center of all the bustle on the deck of *L'Océan.*

"But we must go down to receive her!" Isabelle cried.

"Are you mad, *ma chère?*" It was the same lady with the lopsided hair, who'd pulled away from the discussion around Télémaque, possibly attracted by the spyglass. "How can we appear before such a one, as we are now, my dear?" She spread her stained and tattered skirts to demonstrate her point.

"We'll appear as we must," Isabelle said, turning on the lady with a somewhat cutting smile. "I certainly mean to greet her. You, *ma chère,* may do as you like."

"But no matter what, we can't stay here," the doctor said. He took a step between the two ladies and squinted up at the pale sky. Vultures had been circling La Vigie all through the morning, and were turning closer now and seemed more bold to land. It was plain enough as well that they could not stay where they were, without water, through the broiling heat of the afternoon.

In the end the party of refugees separated. Arnaud led a group which included most of the women and children out in the direction of Haut du Cap, where he hoped among other things to get some intelligence of what might have happened on his plantation at Acul. Télémaque and his retainers, meanwhile, would descend to make contact with the French landing party. Isabelle and her husband elected to go down with Télémaque. She insisted on keeping her children with her, and the doctor decided to stay with them. Arnaud had taken charge of conveying the stretcher with the amputee as far as Haut du Cap.

When they had got down to street level from the trail of La Vigie, the ground underfoot was so very hot it was difficult to walk. Again the doctor felt grateful to Michau for his calm and his loyalty in saving the horses. He got Isabelle up on one of the mares. She took Héloïse on the saddle before her, while Robert scrambled up on the other mare behind Cigny, and the doctor and Michau went double on the mule.

"Let us go home, then," Isabelle said. Télémaque's group had already moved further downhill toward the waterfront.

"My dear—" Cigny started to say, but Isabelle stopped him with a movement of her hand. They rode across the Rue Royale, their mounts uneasy with the smoke and the hot street surface, but manageable all the same. They passed the wreck of Christophe's mansion. Elise's house was utterly destroyed, the small rear garden a waste of cinders, that slim green palm shoot obliterated. The doctor took out the bundle of keys with which he'd locked up the place so carefully the day before and tossed them idly in his hand.

A finger to her lip, Isabelle counted scorched foundations from the corner of her street until she'd found her own. She slipped down from her mule, setting Héloïse onto her feet, and began to kick over the ashes with her slipper, wincing a little for the heat. Héloïse stood mute and still as a doll. Presently Isabelle found a scrap of ironwork, with a twisted remnant of the "C" monogram on their gate. She loosened one of the rods with a slight effort and began to use it as a tool to probe the ruin. Robert slipped down and got his own remnant of iron and began to pick over another area, while Cigny stared down at them, apparently stupefied.

Robert discovered one thing and another and brought them to show to his sister, a broken saucer, a pair of spectacles strangely unbroken, with the lenses just recently smoked, a bit of glassware melted down into a colorful swirl. Watching his excavation, the doctor began to wonder if it might somehow be possible that a whole bottle of rum had survived the holocaust . . . Isabelle stooped to the ashes abruptly and came up holding the lock for her front door. Moved by the same impulse as the doctor, she pulled out her keys from a slit in her skirt and found the right one and tried it till the mechanism turned.

At the Place Montarcher they found the masonry of the fountain shattered and the headless carcass of a goat jammed in the well shaft. The doctor and Michau dragged the bloated goat away, turning their faces aside from the stench. Water pooled out over the pavement once the obstruction was removed. Now the cracked coffee cup which Robert had salvaged from the ruins proved to be very useful indeed, for they could use it to share a drink. Then Isabelle tossed a few cupfuls over his face and hair, which she shook out and tied at the back with a strip of ribbon. She cleaned Héloïse's face and hands with the dampened tail of her skirt, then ordered Robert to wash himself. In the unflatteringly brilliant sunlight her face showed a few lines under a fresh pink sunburn, and yet she looked as vital as the doctor had ever seen her.

"Well," she said, looking around the square as she smoothed her damp hair back from her forehead. "It does not appear that Christophe is offering any great battle for these ashes now."

Remounting, they rode downhill toward the quai. There were some dead goats and dogs and burros in the street, with the carrion birds beginning to settle on them. Whenever a human corpse hove into view, Isabelle covered the eyes of her daughter with both hands so that she would not see.

Presently they emerged onto the waterfront and turned in the direction of the Batterie Circulaire. Here it was sticky underfoot, for the sugar in the warehouses had melted down and run over the roadway. There was now a stiff breeze coming off the ocean, which fortunately discouraged the flies and bore away the smoke; most of the buildings were still smoldering. The wind was pleasantly cool on the doctor's face. The movements of the mule made his belly slosh with all the water he'd gulped down in the Place Montarcher, and he was beginning to feel some trace of an appetite, alongside his craving for rum.

As they approached the shattered walls of the Customs House, they encountered a queer sort of palanquin, improvised from hammocks and pieces of sailcloth. It contained Pauline Leclerc, litter-borne on a tour of the town. Four stout sailors carried her craft, a couple of army officers walked alongside, and there was a gang of disconsolate-looking courtiers in her train.

Isabelle slipped down from her mare and made a graceful curtsey. "Madame Leclerc—it must certainly be you," she said. "Your reputation precedes you, and that of your illustrious husband. Allow me to present myself, Isabelle Cigny—allow me to make you very welcome to our town of Cap Français." She swept her hand toward the slopes of smoking ashes which surrounded them.

"*Enchantée,*" Pauline replied, and extended a languid arm from her litter. Isabelle took her hand and lowered her head over it for a moment. The doctor, meanwhile, recognized Cyprien at the side of the palanquin; the two men exchanged the very slightest of nods.

"Pray excuse the disarray in which we at present find ourselves," Isabelle was saying. "It appears that we have somehow blundered into a state of war. If our hospitality should be somewhat impaired by that condition, all that remains to us to offer is entirely yours."

Isabelle placed her keys into Pauline's hand and, after a moment, produced the battered lock from her front door and laid it into the other. Exhibiting the curve of her famously graceful neck, Pauline inclined her head to study these items. Then she fitted the key to the lock and turned the mechanism as Isabelle had done before, shooting the bolt out, then retracting it, shooting it out a second time. She raised her pretty eyes to meet Isabelle's. The two women held their gaze for just an instant before they were swept off into a wild gale of mutual laughter.

In the midst of plenty, if plenty there was, Daspir got a very poor supper indeed. No more than a square of moldy hardtack, softened from its concrete consistency in gritty river water and slowly worried to pieces by his teeth. In the darkness he consoled himself with surreptitious sips of brandy; there was no friend with whom he wished to share. They'd bivouacked with Rochambeau's men once they'd got across the river, and Daspir slept uneasily on the cold ground—it was quite surprisingly cold at night, after the fierce heat of the day. Whenever he woke he reached for the bottle again.

At reveille he sat up with a headache and all his passages shut with phlegm, looking regretfully at the much diminished brandy bottle in the bottom of his pack. But half an hour's time in the saddle as the troops went swinging down the road cleared his head and warmed his blood and improved his disposition. After all, he'd survived his first day of battle, and not discreditably. After all, they were victorious. And it seemed he had been face-to-face already with Toussaint Louverture.

There was a rumor that Christophe's soldiers were coming out from Haut du Cap to challenge them, but this did not occur. In all this day's march they met no organized resistance though gangs of rioters were setting fire to the plantations all around and there was a good deal of sniping from the hedgerows. They marched on; there was no enemy who would stand and fight. Wherever they found a plantation intact, Leclerc detached a few men to guard it. Rochambeau had done the same as he maneuvered across the plain from Fort Liberté, which explained the patchwork pattern of ash and green which Daspir had observed from the heights above Acul.

The image of that raghead Negro on the warhorse nagged at him. Had he truly been so near to Toussaint Louverture? Hardy's information was not certain after all—it was the women of Limbé who'd claimed that he was there, who'd threatened the French soldiers with his presence even as they ran for cover in the bush. Yet there was the splendid horse, and his riding. And the consensus between Rochambeau's detachment and Leclerc's was that Toussaint must have been the one to order all the burning. If he could be brought to bay, then the destruction would be stopped. As he rode, Daspir began to imagine how he might put it to Cyprien and Paltre and Guizot. *I might have hit him with a stone from across the river—I was that near. If only the bridge had not been down, I should have won our bet.* The bullet hole through his hat would give at least some credence to this claim . . .

Near noon they found themselves marching along an undamaged hedge whose tight-laced branches were heavy with green oranges. Some infantrymen made this discovery, and all at once a part of the column broke up into disorder as the soldiers attacked the hedge. Daspir knew he should be commanding them to cease, but instead he leaned sideways out of the saddle and captured an orange for himself. Under the lumpy green hide the flesh was pale yellow, fragrant, and sweet. Whatever thing he had eaten before under the title of orange bore no comparison to this. He was gnawing the rind when Hardy came up, and at once Daspir began to bellow to the troops to reform, the sweet juice still sticky on his chin.

In the late afternoon they came marching into Le Cap along the Rue Espagnole. Through the smoke, which was heavy still, the sun spread a hellish light on the river where it uncoiled slowly into the bay. In their departure Christophe's men had even tried to set fire to the trees lining the avenue on the approach to the city gate. On the Rue Espagnole they encountered a team of Villaret-Joyeuse's sailors manning a pump, and learned that the admiral had made his landing the day before. The fires had been extinguished or brought under control, but there was no roof nor any shelter left standing anywhere in the town.

Grimly they marched down the slope to the waterfront, where the fresh wind dispersed most of the smoke, and proceeded along the quai. Nothing to see during their descent but cracked fire-blackened walls and foundations. The whole town resembled the crater of a volcano. The admiral's men had dragged the carcasses of dead animals into the public squares and piled them up in preparation for another burning. Leclerc's men marched in a sepulchral silence, their boots whispering over the ash. Now and then a man cursed softly when his foot came down on a hot coal.

L'Océan was moored not far from the smoking shell of the Customs House. Leclerc was quick to hail the first man he saw on the deck. When he was told that Pauline had disembarked the day before, the little general's face seemed to go slightly paler under the film of ash that covered it already—or so Daspir thought, from where he sat his horse. The sailor pointed up the street into the wreckage of the town, and Leclerc and Hardy and their staff set out in that direction.

In two blocks they'd reached the enclosure of the colonial Governor's residence. The outer wall still stood, and some of the stone archways of the destroyed building. An area under these arches had been swept clean and given a tent-roof made of sailcloth furnished with a couple of cots and Indian hassocks arranged on flagstones recently scrubbed clean of soot. A pot steaming over a small brazier gave off a fresh citrus scent that awakened on Daspir's tongue the taste of that green orange. Pauline sat crosslegged on a hassock, next to a dark-haired Creole woman to whom Daspir's eyes were instantly drawn. But everyone else was watching Pauline. She sprang to her feet when she saw Leclerc, and after a nicely balanced pause, rushed up to fling her arms around his neck. A performance—everyone knew that—but it was a spirited one, and Leclerc seemed to appreciate it as much as any of the others standing by.

Fort de Joux, France

October 1802

Toussaint moved with the smoothness of wind or water, or possibly it was the earth that rolled back beneath his planted feet, rushing its features up into his face. With a lifting of his heart, he knew he was again in Saint Domingue: the warmth of the air, heavy before rain; the stirring leaves of the almond trees; somewhere in the background a faint, fruity odor of corruption. A banana grove charged toward him, split to flow around him, the broad flat leaves whipping around his shoulders, skimming over his cheeks. He moved his hands to tighten the reins and check the reckless pace, but there was no horse, no bridle. He was looking up, abashed, into the crown of an enormous *mapou* tree, the dark green leaves all shivering together, and above a little hawk, the *malfini*, circling against the crimson sky. The odor he'd noticed was stronger now, and he swept onward, through undergrowth stunted by the shade of larger trees. Within the stone ring of a scorched foundation, there appeared a dump of mango seeds, banana peels, crushed cane stalks with the juice pressed out of them, some chicken bones and scattered feathers. Hence that fruity smell of ripeness, rot, and ferment. A couple of long-eared black pigs rooted through the garbage mound. One of them raised its head to look at him, its eyes red-rimmed, a wet red glare in the hollow of its nostrils.

The color seemed wrong, as it had in the sky. Toussaint came awake, with a shudder. One hand had trailed from the cot to the floor; the cold of the flagstone cut through the skin of his knuckles into the bone. He raised the hand and cradled it to his chest, pressing with both hands to push down the rising cough. When the moment had passed he relaxed his diaphragm. The vapor of his breath was visible when it emerged, like smoke.

With a painful contraction of his sore belly muscles, he managed to sit up. His stomach ached and his ribs were bruised from coughing. The cell wavered in the currents of his fever. When it came to rest, he crept to the hearth. A few quiescent coals still lurked beneath the whitish layer of ash. On hands and knees, Toussaint blew them to life, fed the nascent flame a handful of splinters, then a larger stick. He sat back on his skinny haunches. The fire was like a picture of a fire, it yielded no more warmth than that. But all his body burned inside with fever. Stiffly he pushed onto his feet, then lowered himself, joint by joint, into the chair beside the hearth. The movement made his head hurt terribly. His head-cloth had come undone while he slept. He shook out the square of madras, lowered his head to refasten it, firmly tightening the knot at the back. The ring of compression around his brow and temples always seemed somewhat to ease the pain.

He relaxed in the chair and began to drift. Swirls of chilly air moved in the cell around him. In the giddiness of fever he felt rather amused by the sight of his breath steam dissipating. When he closed his eyes, the black pig appeared again, thrusting the red holes of its snout. He heard it grunt—but no, that was the turning of the lock. His eyes popped open and he struggled to compose himself. If news had come at last from the First Consul, he must try to rally himself to receive it.

In the open doorway appeared Colomier, standing beside another man whom Toussaint did not recognize. Baille, he remembered now, had gone away on a brief leave, placing this Colomier in temporary command of the Fort de Joux. A certain laxity seemed to have resulted. For example, Baille would not have let the cell door hang open quite so long, so that Toussaint could see a long way down the vaulted corridor, past the two soldiers standing there, old pigtailed veterans both of them, one holding a sputtering torch and the other shuffling his feet on the wet floor.

"The doctor," Colomier said, and the stranger stepped over the threshold with a little birdlike bob of his head.

"Dormoy," Colomier said, apparently by way of introduction. "Toussaint." He swung the door, the lock crunched shut. In a moment Toussaint heard his feet and those of the guards splashing in the second corridor, which had held several inches of water when he was brought through it, however many months before; since then, he had not left this cell. Colomier, unlike Baille, never stayed to listen at the door.

Dormoy was a small man who twittered in his movements. He carried a small leather satchel, which he set upon the table as he sat down. Remaining in his place by the fire, Toussaint merely turned his head to look at him. Even this small shift of position sent a rocket of pain to the top of his skull.

"*Gegne douleu,*" he said, tongue thick in the mouth cavity. "*Têt-moin bay problèm anpil, anpil.*"

"I don't understand," Dormoy said, with a fluttering smile.

I have pain, Toussaint thought. What language had he spoken? My head gives many, many problems . . .

"Take off?" Dormoy said tentatively. He raised both hands and made a queer unfurling gesture in the neighborhood of his ears. "Take off your . . ."

Toussaint touched the knot of his headcloth, let his hand drop away. Dormoy reached into the satchel and pulled out a pair of scrolled brass calipers.

"Your prominences, General," he said, a little shyly. "I should especially like to measure the bump of cunning, and that for ambition— *amour de la gloire,* and of course the bump of sagacity." With a flutter of his right hand the caliper points clicked together like an insect's mandibles.

"I am not an animal," Toussaint said, concentrating on the crisp isolation of each word. He drew himself up very straight in his chair.

Dormoy blushed and deflated. "No more am I a doctor." He set the calipers on the table and gave them a wistful look.

"Have you news from the First Consul?" Toussaint said.

Dormoy did not appear to hear him. At the sound of the fort's bell tolling nine slow rusty strokes, he raised his head toward the grating at the other end of the low vaulted cell from the door. This grate admitted freezing air in good supply, but only a few weak checks of daylight. If Toussaint stood peering through it for long enough, he might eventually see the bootheels of a sentry in the yard. He felt a kind of weakness at this thought.

"If you are not a doctor," he said, "I am still in need. Can you arrange for a doctor to come?"

"I was a priest once," Dormoy said, turning his watery smile toward Toussaint. "Once, I was mayor of Dijon. But today I am only a schoolmaster."

"If you are a priest," Toussaint said, "have you come to confess me?"

"Oh no!" Dormoy hissed. "You see, I have been—well, I cannot exercise the priestly functions. Today I am only a schoolmaster."

On the red glow of Toussaint's closed eyelids appeared the image of that mad *blanche,* Claudine Arnaud. She had demanded that he confess her, an age ago and an ocean away. How had he answered? *It is not easy to enter the spiritual world.*

He opened his eyes and stared at Dormoy. The window of clarity which by dint of concentration he had opened in his fever was beginning to collapse around the edges. It could not be that this person had appeared for no reason. There must be a message, or a sign.

"Mon père," he began. "Father, I—"

"No, no," Dormoy said, his hands fluttering before him. "It is only, I only—I was one of the Jesuits during my priesthood, and all of my order had the greatest sympathy for the sufferings of the slaves, you see—oh, I was not posted to Saint Domingue! nor to any other such place. You see, I only wanted to look upon the Liberator. See the face of Toussaint L'Ouverture. He who had the audacity to address the First Consul so: *To the first of the whites from the first of the blacks.*

"I never used any such form of address," Toussaint said wearily. "It is another of their lies."

"I only imposed myself as a doctor in coming here," Dormoy went on, heedlessly. "Perhaps I was wrong, but I meant no harm. I meant only to offer you my congratulations—well, my . . . admiration. My best wishes, as it were."

Toussaint regarded him. The man was weak. Sometimes a weak vessel was better than a strong one. A weak man was like a chink in a wall which might be enlarged till the whole wall came down. One might inhabit the weak man altogether, subject his poor will entirely to one's own. But for the moment Toussaint did not have the strength, himself, to set about it.

"It must be dreadful for you here," Dormoy said. "This climate, the cold, for a man from the tropics . . ."

"The First Consul sends me no word," Toussaint said. "I have been waiting for my judgment—I do not know how many months." He paused. "I believe they mean for me to die here."

He felt a tremble rooting in his spine—the chill succeeding fever: ague. With a tremendous effort he clenched it in. He would not allow his teeth to chatter in the face of this lunatic guest. Though it was the first time he had allowed that last sentence to surface even in his thoughts.

Dormoy plucked from his vest pocket a gold pince-nez which he clipped neatly upon the bridge of his nose. "I am a friend of the *sous-préfet* of Pontarlier," he said, pointing a finger at the floor of the cell. "It was so that I was able to arrange my visit." He broke disconcertingly into a high-pitched giggle. "Not so difficult at all, really!" he said. "It is surprising." He glanced at Toussaint, over the lenses of the pince-nez.

Toussaint did not respond. He knew next to nothing of Pontarlier or its subprefect. The place was further down the mountain and he had been brought quickly through it once while being conveyed here.

"Well," said Dormoy, lowering his gaze. "No matter. In connection with your presence here, my friend sometimes receives copies of correspondence addressed to the Consulate, or to the Minister of Marine."

He was unfolding a small square of paper as he spoke. Toussaint's attention bore down on the folded sheet. The aperture in his fever had regained its boundary.

"This from the Captain-General Leclerc," Dormoy said. "It is recent. I find his sentiment quite extraordinary! It struck me so that I copied it out."

"Do let me hear it," Toussaint said.

Dormoy squinted at the paper. *"We must destroy all the mountain Negroes, men and women, sparing only children under twelve years of age. We must destroy half the Negroes of the plains, and not allow in the colony a single man who has ever worn an epaulette. Without these measures, the colony will never be at peace."*

Dormoy folded the paper, pulling the crease between his finger as he glanced up. "Such a carnage!" he said. "Does one suppose he means to undertake it?"

"He may undertake it, if he will," Toussaint said. "To carry it out will not be possible."

"No," said Dormoy. "No, I rather think the same." He put the pince-nez into his pocket. Still, for the first time since he had entered, he looked at Toussaint with a certain gravity. "If you are right, then—"

Before he could complete the sentence, the cell door came flying open. There was Baille, returned, with an unaccustomed number of the guard—half a dozen of them.

"What is the meaning of this?" he shouted. "What do you—" When Baille looked at Dormoy, Toussaint could tell that the two men were acquainted at least to some degree, though Baille was in no mood to acknowledge it now.

"Arrest that man!" he bellowed, thrusting his arm at Dormoy. Two guards descended on Dormoy and, gripping him by the armpits, began to hustle him from the cell. Dormoy's head spun round like an owl's, questing for his satchel and his calipers. "Wait!" he said. "I—My—" A third guard had taken up his effects and was following. "Ow!" Dormoy went on squeaking. "Gently, friend, I am—"

The slam of the corridor door cut off his querulous voice. Baille looked down at Toussaint. "Do you mean to murder me?" he said.

Toussaint raised his hands to massage his aching temples. "That question might be better put by me to you."

Baille colored, coughed, and bowed out of the cell. Snap of the lock, shuffle and splash of boots retreating. Then silence.

The door had never looked so solid. It did not matter. With the force of the fever at his disposal, Toussaint might shrug himself out of his skin and travel anywhere at all, free and fast as a *loup-garou*. Already he could feel the walls dissolving, and as he began to drift, Dormoy's broken sentence mended itself in his mind: *Then they have lost, and you have won.*

Part Two

RAVINE À COULEUVRE

February 1802

Je pensai que la conduite du général Leclerc était bien contraire aux intentions du gouvernement, puisque le premier consul, dans sa lettre, promettait la paix, tandis que lui, il faisait la guerre. Je vis qu'au lieu de chercher à arrêter le mal, il ne faisait que l'augmenter. <<Ne craint-il pas, me disais-je, en tenant une pareille conduite, d'être blâmé de son gouvernement? Peut-il espérer d'être approuvé du premier consul, de ce grand homme, dont l'équité et l'impartialité sont si bien connues, tandis que je serai désapprouvé?>> Je pris donc le parti de me défendre en cas d'attaque, et fis, malgré le peu de troupes que j'avais, mes dispositions en conséquence.

—*Mémoires du Général Toussaint Louverture*

I thought that the conduct of General Leclerc was much contrary to the intentions of the government, since the First Consul, in his letter, promised peace, while he, Leclerc, made war. I saw that instead of seeking to stop the evil, he did nothing but increase it. "In maintaining such a conduct," I said to myself, "Does he not fear to be blamed by his government? Can he hope to be approved by the First Consul—that great man whose impartiality and fairness are so well known—while I will be disapproved?" So I took the part of defending myself in case of attack, and in spite of the small number of troops that I had, made my dispositions accordingly.

II

In the fresh damp cool of morning, Elise walked from the rear of the *grand'case* of Habitation Thibodet, following the shallow canal her brother had designed to the peak of a low rise, then diverging from it, moving downhill again, through the small mud-walled *cases* and their patchy gardens. Her daughter, Sophie, and her brother's wife, Nanon, accompanied her, but they did not converse. Nanon seemed abstracted (perhaps she was merely sleepy) and Sophie was busy running after butterflies, laughing and swinging her empty basket round her head.

Elise watched her, reserving judgment. When they left the house this morning, she'd been unable to influence Sophie to put on shoes. The black women who were just coming out of the little *cases*, waisting the cotton door-curtains with string to admit light and air, smiled at the flashing of the girl's dusty heels, then turned on Elise just slightly more fixed smiles. Even now she must still be the white mistress to them, after so much upheaval and change.

The day seemed ordinary, tranquil as any. If these black women had breathed any rumor of the trouble fermenting at Le Cap, they gave no sign of it . . . and Elise knew them well enough to sense when some such knowledge was quietly shared among them. She herself knew little more than they. No news had come, since their departure, of the impasse between Christophe and the French fleet. No word from the doctor either, and of course Nanon's slight aloofness might be explained by her concern for him. It was like her not to speak of it.

Now they had come to the border of Habitation Thibodet with Habitation Sancey, a citrus hedge on the near side and a cactus fence on the other, punctured by gaps through which spotted goats came wandering. Here was a crossroads, at the meeting of a path which crossed the stream between the two properties with another trail running parallel to the tumbling water. In the dark green shade of an old *manguier* there was a little market; women had come down from the heights of the surrounding *mornes* with baskets of oranges, limes, papaya, and corrosol, stalks of bananas and plantain, bunches of manioc root still crusted with black earth. Today Elise had come for mangoes. There were several different sorts: *mangues fils rouges, mangues baptistes,* and the small sweet rosy mangoes, no bigger than a peach, for which the region of Ennery was known.

Elise negotiated, while Nanon, once a price had been agreed, packed the purchases into one of their baskets. Elise bargained with determination, sometimes miming a flat departure if the price would not come down. She was thinking as she often did that many of these mangoes must have been harvested from her own fruit trees on Habitation Thibodet. In the end the baskets were full and Elise added a couple of avocados and two pineapples to the store. Reaching into the pocket tied below the slit of her skirt, she withdrew a small bag of soft Spanish leather and shook out a few coins to pay.

"Be so good as to carry these baskets back to the house," she said. "I have an errand in this direction." She glanced across the stream toward the gap in the cactus, through which the path wound on through Habitation Sancey.

Nanon simply nodded to this announcement, leaving her eyes lowered, but Sophie shook her head. She could not speak immediately, because one of the market women had given her a *mangue fils rouges* and she was busy sucking the pulpy seed, unconscious as any *bossale* fresh off the coast of Africa.

"I want to go with *you,* Maman."

"You may not," Elise said, and then more mildly, "Not today."

Sophie flung the seed into the stream and stamped her foot. Her full lips parted, but Elise cut in before she could pronounce a word.

"You are impertinent," she said. "If you persist, I may as well send you to Madame Arnaud to be corrected."

Sophie's eyes widened, a flash of white in her olive face. In her complexion she favored Tocquet; moreover she took no care against the sun. Elise did not know if those round eyes were meant to mock her or if Sophie had been genuinely impressed. But all the children of their circle were a little afraid of Madame Arnaud, perhaps with reason, though it had been long since Claudine's madness had bloomed in its full flower.

"*Au revoir, Maman.*" Sophie picked up her basket, docilely enough, and followed Nanon through the wooden gate in the citrus hedge. When she had gone a few paces up the trail on the other side, she swung her basket up to her head and walked on with it balanced there. Elise opened her mouth to reprove her—to carry a burden so, like an African!—but then said nothing. Nanon was managing her load in the same fashion, her empty hands flowing idly in the current of her swinging hips. This exercise trained a grace of movement which no other schooling could imitate. Elise knew that she lacked it herself, though she had other graces.

She watched Sophie away along the trail—the slim straight back, the posture sinuously erect, the buds of her new breasts pushing out her muslin delicately. Thirteen years old . . . Elise ought to have sent her to school in France long since. But she had never had the heart for that. And Tocquet had never shown the least support for such a program. There had been a rumor that Toussaint's two eldest sons had come back with the fleet now standing outside Le Cap, and Elise wondered now if it might be true.

She walked down to a point where the stream widened over a gravel shoal and crossed in the shallows, skipping from stone to stone. A couple of women washing clothes on the shoal grinned up at her as she passed. A little goat bleated and trotted to one side as she came through a hole in the cactus fence. She followed the foot-worn rut on a meander around a field of sprouting corn, then up a slope through coffee trees. A gaggle of children, strangers to her, scattered at her approach and ran laughing over the top of the hill. No chance of arriving unobserved or unreported—not anywhere in this country.

Now it was beginning to grow hot. Elise, who had let herself hurry more than she ought, came to a full stop in the shade of a big coffee tree. She took off her straw hat and remained standing there until the light sweat she'd raised had dried completely on her forehead. Then she tucked up a stray lock of hair, pinned her hat back into place, and went on more deliberately, fingering the edges of the letter she carried through the fabric of her dress.

Crossing the hilltop brought her in sight of the long rectangular *grand'case* of Habitation Sancey. Her approach was from the rear. Some of the women and children stirring between the house and its outbuildings glanced up, startled at the sight of a *blanche* coming from this direction. Outside the doorway of the kitchen a black woman in an ordinary cotton dress was tending an iron pot set on a tripod above a charcoal fire. If she were struck by Elise's arrival, she gave no sign of it. She stirred the pot with a long wooden spoon. A shift in the humid currents of the air brought Elise the scent of simmering goat and plantain.

She circled the *grand'case* to the left, emerging onto the oval drive in front. A long *allée* of royal palms ran down the slope to the main gate.

Elise might have ordered out her coach and driven in from that direction, with all due formality. When she asked herself now why she had not done so, she could form no clear answer.

A pack of noisy little dogs swarmed out the door of the *grand'case*. At the foot of the gallery steps, Elise stood completely motionless. The dogs raced partway down the steps, yapped at her, and retreated. Saint-Jean, who was Toussaint's youngest son, came out the front door and called them back, smiling down at her apologetically.

As Saint-Jean herded the dogs around to the side porch, Suzanne Louverture appeared in the doorway. In her passage through the house she had slipped on shoes and laid aside the spoon with which she'd stirred that cauldron. She stepped onto the tiles of the gallery floor and with a slight smile beckoned Elise to come up.

"Madame Tocquet," she said. "I am surprised."

Elise climbed to her level, and stood a moment to catch her breath. Suzanne waited on her calmly, her eyes serene beneath the forehead knot of her blue *mouchwa têt*. Unlike most prosperous black women, she had put on no great storehouse of fat, though she had thickened somewhat with her years. A curl of hair that escaped the blue headcloth was white, but she still had in her least movement the grace which came from carrying large burdens on one's head.

"Vous avez l'air d'une tête chargée," Suzanne said quietly. You seem to have a heavy-loaded head.

"No, not at all." Elise felt herself verging on a stammer—it was unnerving to have one's thought read in that way, even if it were only by coincidence. Her fund of social banalities seemed to fail her before Suzanne Louverture. Isabelle, she thought fleetingly, would surely have done better in this situation. Suzanne did not go much into society, though she had been sometimes a guest at Habitation Thibodet, when Toussaint happened to be in the neighborhood. But Suzanne seldom attended his larger celebrations at Le Cap or Port-au-Prince, preferring to remain secluded here at Ennery.

"I am charged only with this missive." Elise produced the letter from the folds of her clothing and held it out.

Suzanne looked down to see her own name inscribed—if she could read so much Elise was not certain. Saint-Jean was watching them, from the shadows of the doorway. Suzanne took the letter into her hand and looked from it into Elise's face.

Piqued, Elise took off her hat and shook down her blond hair, which fell below her shoulders. As she tossed her head, she felt herself flushing. Well, even a blush was a white woman's charm, though she must walk closely covered against the sun, to guard the responsiveness of her complexion.

"You must come in," Suzanne was saying. "Take coffee."

"No, no, I cannot stay . . ." Elise set about pinning up her hair again, turning her head to show her neck, a glimpse of her milky shoulder; she was after all a great many years the black woman's junior.

"Let me," Suzanne said and moved behind her to help with the hair. A few light flicks of her cool fingers, and it was arranged.

"Do come in," Suzanne repeated, motioning toward the shade of the doorway, from which Saint-Jean had disappeared.

"Thank you, but no." Elise could speak more easily now. She glanced down at the letter. "I had better leave you to the company of your husband."

To this Suzanne only nodded and held out her hand. Elise clasped it briefly, let go, and turned to the steps.

After all, she did feel somewhat relieved, once she had crested the ridge behind the house and begun her descent through the coffee trees. It was not Suzanne's jealousy that had been in question, but her own—which had obscurely plagued her from the moment she'd seen that the letter Toussaint had passed her at the church in Le Cap was meant for Suzanne, not for herself. And had Suzanne the skill to read it through? Well, Saint-Jean had some instruction, and might read it to her if need be.

The same laundresses smiled up at Elise again as she followed the stepping stones across the stream. Indeed, she thought she recognized some of Tocquet's shirts in the hands of one. Well, perhaps Suzanne had learned to tolerate the wanderings of her husband, as French wives were obliged to do. And Toussaint's dalliance with Elise had been so brief—a single instance—that it was likely Suzanne did not know of it. It was possible that no one did.

For the first time in a long while, Elise thought of her first husband, Thibodet, dead for the last decade, of yellow fever. By the luck of his draw, for he might equally have expired from excess of drink, or been shot dead for a gambling debt, or succumbed to the pox which his lechery had won him, or to the mercury treatments he took for the pox. But Elise had gone off with Xavier Tocquet before Thibodet fell ill with the fever. She had a horror of the pox, and had been lucky enough not to take it. In truth she had never loved Thibodet, though his dash had impressed her when they first met in Lyons, and of course he was reputed wealthy. It was her brother who'd attended his last illness, while Elise was away across the Spanish border with her paramour. And now she herself was two years past the age of Thibodet when he had died . . .

These reflections carried her as far as her own backyard, where a gang of the older children—Paul, Caco, Sophie, Yoyo—were hopping up and down with the excitement of watching a kitchen maid wringing the necks of a brace of ducks. This task completed, she caught their blood in a gourd bowl into which the juice of several lemons had been squeezed. Elise looked on, approving the procedure.

Merbillay came out of the kitchen *case*, took the beheaded ducks, and strung them up by their feet from the low caves of the building. In this climate, a fowl need not be hung for longer than a day. These ducks would be plucked and stewed and served with their garnish of mango this same evening.

Merbillay beckoned Yoyo into the kitchen to help with the peeling and dicing of mangoes. Elise put her head in the door to observe. It was just lately that she had taken account of Merbillay's talent for cooking and incorporated her into the service of the *grand'case*, though the woman had been at Habitation Thibodet for years and often used to cook for the soldiers when they were encamped nearby. Her oldest, Caco, was Paul's great friend. And Sophie often played with Yoyo, though the difference in their ages was greater. But now Sophie, though she was the elder, had run off squealing with the other children, leaving Yoyo to work at her mother's side.

Merbillay gave Elise the ghost of a smile and turned to grinding spices in an old stone mortar. Her elaborately turbaned head lowered over this work. She took some pains with her appearance, was a lover of beads and gold bangles and colorful cloth. Elise did not know her age, but for the several children she had borne she still seemed youthful—her flesh plump and taut and not a line on her full face. Furthermore, she seemed to manage the two men who were her children's fathers with no trouble.

What was the secret to that, Elise wondered, with an admiration which did not quite rise to envy. She walked around the house and up to the gallery of the *grand'case*. Tocquet and Nanon were seated there, drinking coffee. Elise was a little surprised at this, for it was now late morning, and Tocquet would usually be away on his own affairs at this hour. She sat down with them, spreading her skirt, and Zabeth came at once with a fresh cup and saucer and the silver coffeepot.

"Successful in your foraging?" Tocquet said.

"But of course," Elise replied. "I should think Nanon would have showed you our booty."

Nanon smiled, looked here and there, and suddenly caught sight of her one-year-olds, François and Gabriel, tumbling toward the edge of the pool below the gallery.

"Oh," she said. "You will excuse me." She jumped up and ran trippingly down the steps, her skirts caught up and bunched in one hand. Elise watched her rush across the lawn; there was more than mere pretext for her haste. Gabriel, the black one, bolder of the two, was making a long, precarious reach for a violet flower of the *bwa dlo* ornamenting the pool, and if Nanon had not caught him up by the scruff, he would quite likely have fallen in. Though the water was scarcely knee-deep, a child of that age did not need much water to drown.

Elise watched the scene, a little sourly. Gabriel made no sound, but his eye was on the flower and his arms and legs kept churning, without purchase, toward the goal. It was François, the pale one freckled by the sun, who gaped his jaws and began to wail at the sight of his brother's frustration. The two boys were not much alike for twins, and Elise rather doubted that her brother was father to either of them.

But this was a subject not to be explored. She felt Tocquet's eyes on her now, as if he'd press into her thoughts. In truth, Nanon had been the reason of the first rift between them. Not that Tocquet had strayed in her direction, not at all. But Elise had turned her energy toward breaking her brother's liaison with Nanon, after their first child was born—she had disliked the notion that he might *marry* this mulattress. Over this issue she and Tocquet had quarreled, bitterly though not openly, for Tocquet kept his displeasure close to his chest; his way was simply to withdraw from her. And in the end she'd recognized and owned her error. She and Nanon were good friends now, and she and Tocquet had stood together at her brother's wedding.

That breach was healed. But what was this? Elise turned her head to face him.

"My husband," she said. "How have you passed your morning?"

Tocquet breathed in, wrinkling his nostrils. "I went riding up the road a little way toward Marmelade," he said. "To see what I might see . . ."

"And what was that?"

"People are coming down through Dondon," he said. "With their households strapped to their backs, or loaded on their donkeys. They're fleeing the war at Grande Rivière."

"You call it war?"

"It is certainly war that Rochambeau has carried into that region," Tocquet said. "Though they say that Sans-Souci is holding him, for the nonce, in the mountains of Grande Rivière."

He stopped and turned his eyes full on her then. Elise met his gaze without a flinch.

"And no news from Le Cap?" she said.

"Thus far, none."

"But if it is peaceably settled there—"

Tocquet clicked his tongue and looked away across the pool toward the cane mill at the far edge of the yard. "That I think is most unlikely, since the slaying of the garrison at Fort Liberté, and all that Rochambeau has accomplished since."

To this, Elise said nothing. She watched the children on the lawn. Nanon had lured them from the pool's edge: Gabriel was walking with a certain confidence, while François still preferred all-fours.

"You know my mind," Tocquet said. "It would be well to take the children over the border, and even as far as Santo Domingo City, while we may. If Rochambeau breaks out of Grande Rivière, I think the passes toward Saint Raphael will be closed."

"But—it was your own notion that we should be safest here!" Elise burst out. "There's Suzanne Louverture with her youngest son, quite tranquil at Habitation Sancey—I saw her there this very morning. And—

you've said so yourself—Toussaint is bound to protect this whole region, so long as his family is here, so where on the whole island could be better?"

"I don't know that Toussaint is bound to do anything," Tocquet said. "All I know of him for certain is that he has not been in evidence—not here nor anywhere else—since that fleet first appeared on our horizon." He paused. "Also, if I need say it, I would not trust our safety to the force of another."

"But what have we to fear from the French?" Elise flung out. "When after all we are French ourselves."

"Look to yourself then," Tocquet said softly. "You have your freedom." He pushed up from his seat and made for the steps.

"But you are chimerical with me!" Elise said sharply.

Tocquet turned his arched eyebrows toward her for a second, then continued his descent. He bowed in Nanon's direction, then strode across the yard and went into the cane mill.

Elise stared blindly at the brick face of that building. *Why are you chimerical with me?* was the usual form of that reproach. But she had not put it as a question, for fear of the answer she might have.

Freedom. How was it now that all her friends so loved to tax her with that word? Isabelle had been the last, before Tocquet this morning. Yet she wished that Isabelle were here. It seemed peculiar for her to have chosen to stay at Le Cap, amid such pressing dangers. But that had ever been Isabelle's way.

A thread of smoke leaked from the window of the cane mill. Tocquet was smoking in there, of course, and most likely reading a book about chess, maneuvering pieces on a board according to the book's suggestions. The mill machinery was idle—refining sugar was a complicated business and Elise had thought it better to turn their resources to the production of coffee, which was easier to cultivate at Ennery in any case. They did still grow a little cane, for rum. Though Tocquet kept them in money with his smuggling, he had no head for plantation management. Elise had never resented this. His latest sally to Philadelphia had turned a very handsome profit, on that shipload of guns he'd delivered to Toussaint. Though had it not been for his long absence, she would not—

She stopped that thought. Oh, but she did not wish at all to go to Santo Domingo City!—or anywhere else in that dull and primitive Spanish colony. Even in the capital, society was strait and prudish, and Elise had already a reputation there, from her first elopement with Tocquet. In Santo Domingo, she would have small use of her freedom indeed.

That word again. Oppressed, Elise pushed aside her cup and stood up, resting her hands on the railing. Vines of the purple-flowering bougainvillea twirled through the bannisters, briers grazing the heels of her palms. She looked at Nanon, who stood a little apart from the two boys, watching them. In Isabelle's absence, she might have confided her trouble to Nanon, who was certainly discreet enough for that purpose. Yet something held her back from it.

Gabriel and François stood loosely embraced, like waltzing bears, uncertainly balanced on their hind legs. Then François lost his grip and plopped down on his bottom. This time he laughed, instead of wailing. At her remove, Nanon joined in the laughter. Gabriel, meanwhile, remained standing, rocking a little, his balance sure enough. His face was grave, his large head slightly lowered between his heavy shoulders. Already he had the build of a little man, and there was something familiar in that pose. Elise leaned further over the rail to peer more closely: the features of Joseph Flaville came rising to meet her, like the face of a drowned man surfacing from dark water.

Her stomach rolled; she clenched her jaw and forced herself to swallow. No, she would certainly keep this down. They had all kept it dark from her. Joseph Flaville, whom Isabelle would have married, *in a different world*. Perhaps Isabelle *had* been trying to tell her, in her way . . . and long enough after the fact. Well, no white woman had so much freedom as that to exercise. Elise raised her eyes, and Nanon met her gaze. Her melting look of patient resignation—in times gone by, Elise had wished to slap it off her face. She felt nothing of that now, though Nanon must have known from the beginning.

An infant's cry sounded from within the house. Elise turned from the rail and hurried toward it. Her stomach rolled again with the sudden movement; again she swallowed the sour taste. In the nursery she found it was her own child, Mireille, who'd awakened wet and screaming, while Zabeth's Bibiane lay, alert but silent, on her pallet on the floor. Elise took up Mireille and held her to her shoulder, crooning as she patted her back, but the child seemed difficult to calm, and when Zabeth came hurrying in, smelling of milk, Mireille stretched out her arms and cried for her.

Elise sat down, while Zabeth gave Mireille her breast. The nausea subsided, once she was still. Bibiane lay on her back, her brown eyes bright, reflective, watching patiently. Now it was calm. Elise had thought it one of Isabelle's quirks, a whim, to accompany Nanon for her confinement to Vallière—a place so remote that there'd be no witness of any importance to what births might chance to happen there. Clearly it had been no whim at all. And what of her brother—he must have known too, afterward if not before. But he would simply have declined to see it, that was *his* way.

Mireille's lips slackened from the nipple, and she rolled to her back in Zabeth's cradling arm. Zabeth got up and made to change her.

"No, let me," Elise said, rising. "Bibiane must have her share."

Zabeth smiled briefly, brilliantly. She stooped to the pallet, raised Bibiane and gave her suck. At such moments there was always a bloom of warmth in Elise's belly and beneath her breastbone, and she felt she shared it with her maid. She kissed a bubble of milk from Mireille's mouth, then cleaned her bottom and powdered it well. The child was cheerful now, gurgling and smiling up at her. But Elise's fingers froze on the hem of the fresh diaper. There might be something else she had failed to recognize, though all the signs were obviously before her. And possibly Isabelle had meant to warn her of this also, in her elliptical fashion. But what if it already was too late?

12

Dermide, who was the Captain-General's sole heir thus far, was three years old, but large for that age, and heavy to boot, if not overfed. He had the squatty figure of a little troll. What were his mother's marks of beauty had in him gone wrong: the plump lips pursed but seldom smiling, the full cheeks so swollen that they pressed his eyes to slits.

Or maybe it was Isabelle's jaundiced eye. She had brought her own children to play with the little paragon and had undertaken the task of minding them herself, mostly as a matter of policy. She was curious about Pauline, but it took small perspicacity to see that the Captain-General's lady was not naturally fond of other women, especially those attractive enough to draw attention from her own suite of admirers. Therefore Isabelle had dressed for this visit much more severely than was her wont, which was easy enough since most of her town wardrobe had been destroyed in the fire, so that she had been constrained to make over a dress of one of her maids. She watched the children without interfering, though Dermide was a little brute.

In the wreckage of the Governor's residence, Pauline had imagined a sort of Bedouin tent, roofed by sailcloth stretched over the fire-blackened masonry, and furnished quite opulently with the articles brought from her refitted cabins aboard the flagship *L'Océan*. By arrangement of the furniture the space under the canvas had been divided into three distinct areas. Pauline reigned over one, reclining on a divan with her head elegantly propped on an elbow, while the officers of her husband's staff jockeyed to improve their nearness to her, and those who were less successful consoled themselves by slighting the local gentlemen who'd managed to be admitted to her presence. A second area, suggestively curtained in damask, served as the boudoir. Isabelle watched the children in the third.

This latter space was scattered over with all sorts of elaborate toys, none of which seemed to much interest Dermide. Many of them were probably beyond the grasp of a three-year-old's intelligence, to be sure. Robert, nearly ten years older, had fallen upon Dermide's several regiments of toy soldiers and had laid them out in battle array—French opposing the English. He picked them up man by man and studied them lovingly, for the markings of each uniform were painted in the most up to the minute detail.

Dermide, meanwhile, had no thought but to snatch away a little cloth doll Héloïse was cradling—an inconsequential thing but dear to her, since she had carried it on her voyage from the North American Republic. She was a year senior to Dermide, but smaller and more delicate, and so unused to being mistreated that she made no cry or movement when Dermide grabbed the doll, though her mouth popped open in a round of silent surprise. Isabelle watched but took no action. Dermide, smirking, took a few backward steps with his prize, then Robert's foot snaked out to trip him and he fell over backward, a dead weight, slapping the back of his head on a flagstone. After a moment he set up a howl.

"Oh the poor *darling*!" Isabelle cooed, and rushed to pick him up. "Has he hurt his head?" She gave him a quick sharp pinch on the roll of his belly fat least visible to Pauline and the others. Dermide shrieked louder and struggled in her grasp. A couple of the officers had turned their heads at the racket, but Pauline seemed deaf to it—the maternal was not first among her instincts.

Isabelle let Dermide slip down to the floor. Enraged, the boy cut a swath of destruction through the toy soldiers with a great swing of his foot; the vigor of the movement overbalanced him and he fell again, this time on his bottom. Winded, he fell silent instead of crying out. Robert, meanwhile, had removed himself from the scene of his sly crime and stood with his back to the room, turning the crank of some odd mechanism Isabelle had not much noticed before. The air was filled with a high piping music. Héloïse, who'd recovered her doll when Dermide dropped it, skipped toward the sound. Even the conversation on Pauline's side of the room took a pause.

"Oh, it is charming!" Isabelle trilled. "But whatever can it be?"

Pauline rose from her divan, assisted by several eager hands which she shook off once she was balanced on her feet. She crossed toward the children's area in a wave of scent and fluttering scarves. A handful of her courtiers followed in her train, helpless as iron dust swirled by a magnet. Robert turned the crank again and the whistling tune progressed a few more notes.

"It is meant to teach our canary to sing," Pauline said, turning upon Isabelle her bright artificial smile. Dermide attached himself to her leg, snuffling urgently into her flimsy skirt. She gestured then at an empty cage which swung above the crank-turned organ. "But the wretched creature fell down dead in the middle of our passage."

"How dreadful for you," Isabelle said. "We must find you another."

"It is no matter," Pauline said, her interest dimming. She peeled Dermide's fingers from her skirt, sniffing distastefully at the dampness he'd left on the fabric, and ambled lazily back to her couch. Her officers followed, all but one, a young captain with a pleasantly full olive face, who remained at Isabelle's elbow, looking at her with some interest.

"Is it true?" he said.

"What do you mean?" said Isabelle. This officer had been giving her sidelong glances since the previous day, she realized—the only one of them all to have eyes for anything other than Pauline. A presentable youth, some years her junior. Half-consciously she turned her face a little from the light, giving him her fine-cut profile and also perhaps concealing a few faint lines around her mouth and eyes.

"That you might find her another bird?"

"Why yes," said Isabelle. "Of a sort, perhaps." She gave him a brief direct look and as quickly turned away. "I would require some assistance, I think."

"Allow me." The young officer bowed low. "I am Captain Georges Daspir—entirely at your service."

The ruins of Le Cap fumed all around them; in some spots they were still aflame. Latouche-Treville's sailors continued to convey fire pumps among the points of active burning. The few human corpses had by then been collected and carted away to La Fossette, and squads of infantry were now engaged in hauling off dead animals. Isabelle, her skirts hitched up above the ash and her face masked with a handkerchief, led her small group from the Governor's house toward the remnants of her own home. With her free hand she held tight to Héloïse, who was similarly masked against the smoke and dust. Robert walked a pace behind, answering the questions Captain Daspir put him about life in Le Cap before the holocaust. Of course Robert's replies were generously invented, since he had scarcely returned here himself before it was all destroyed one more time.

Well, Isabelle allowed herself to think, perhaps after all they should have gone down to Ennery with Elise and Xavier Tocquet. Certainly they had preserved little enough by remaining here. They turned a corner and hove in view of the ash pit that had been her house. The rafters had burned out from under the roof, sending a cascade of rose-colored tiles down through smoldering holes in the second floor. Some parts of that planking were still intact. Doctor Hébert, Arnaud, Bertrand Cigny, and Michau were all at work shoring up those remnants for a temporary shelter. Sailcloth or canvas of any kind was at such a premium they had not been able to get any, but Michau had negotiated for some bundles of palm leaf from the countryside, which might be used for thatch. In the heat the three white men had stripped to the waist and were so soot-coated as to be indistinguishable from their black companion.

"What news?" the doctor said. He walked toward Isabelle, his eye-glasses glinting from his grimy face.

"Madame Leclerc's canary has perished," Isabelle announced. "We are on a mission to find her another, and didn't you once know—"

Her words were cut off by the collapse of a charred beam, whose fall brought down a quantity of the recently placed thatch. Cigny cursed and wriggled to shrug off scraps of leaf. He stared up through the vestiges of his roof into the cloudless, azure sky, then abruptly rounded on his wife.

"It's not enough for you to complete your morning calls in the midst of this catastrophe, but now you propose to go galloping off after *canaries?*"

"What would you have me do?" Isabelle inclined slightly, spreading her empty hands. "I can be of no great use here. It was not I, after all, who incinerated the town."

"No, but you might have got yourself out of it, and taken the children to some place of security—as indeed you were urged to do."

"If I ought to have done so, that cannot be helped now," Isabelle said. "And the children are better to go with me than to stay here in the ash and smoke. Now I shall want you," she said, turning to the doctor. "And I think I might take Michau as well—"

"Off hunting canaries?" Cigny shouted. "In this midday sun—have you gone *quite* mad?" He was taking in breath for a louder protest when Arnaud stepped across and laid a hand on his arm.

"Let her go," Arnaud murmured, too softly to be heard by any but Cigny. "If it seems frivolous, you must consider that the favor of the Captain-General may mean a great deal to all of us now, and they say his wife has larger influence with him than any man."

Cigny clicked his tongue but said no more; he let Arnaud guide him back to the thatching.

"I may as well accompany you," the doctor said. "My handiness at this work is not such that I will be much missed—but you must leave Michau, for he is truly wanted here."

Captain Daspir went along with this new procession: Isabelle, Doctor Antoine Hébert, Robert, and Héloïse astride one of the two little donkeys Michau had been able to commandeer. The excursion looked a more

cheerful pastime than any other open to him now, and he'd decided that
Pauline's dismissive nod must be sufficient to release him from any other
duties of the day. Yesterday all had moved efficiently enough, when there
was fighting to be done, but now that the army was regathered on this
ruin it had conquered, it seemed that half its members were disoriented,
stumbling through their shock. The night before, Cyprien had conducted
Daspir through the blasted streets to a bawdy house he had frequented
during his earlier visit here—where he had known pleasures of wine and
gambling and especially the favors of many gorgeous colored women, so
delicately shaded one could scarce tell them from white . . . Now there
was nothing left of this establishment but a smoking hole in the ground.
Or possibly, Cyprien muttered, it had been in some other street. Daspir
had forborne to point out that all the streets were in a similar state of
utter devastation.

Now they passed along the blackened wall of what the doctor told
him had yesterday been his hospital. At the end of the block the road
curved into the jungle and went winding up into the hills. Soon it had
narrowed to a trail. This was farther than the fire had reached, and the
air, filtered through dense foliage, was moist and fresh. Though the heat
and the sharp grade of the ascent had Daspir sweating in his wool uniform, he felt encouraged by the change of scene. His head was light and
his stomach shrunken (he'd had nothing to eat since the orange he'd
plucked from the hedge yesterday but a scrap of rock-like, moldy hardtack for his supper, and a cup of very weak tea this morning *chez*
Pauline), but he did his best to keep up some conversation with Isabelle.
As the climb did not seem to wind her, Daspir struggled to cover his own
breathlessness, though he had to keep his ripostes short. But this was a
lady who in her person and her personality did live up to the vaunted
charms of Saint Domingue. He had been struck by her at first sight and
found that he admired her more the steeper the path grew. He cocked
his hat in her direction, hoping she might notice the bullet hole in the
crown.

At last they came around the brow of a hill, where the path leveled out
above the sea. Daspir saw that they had maneuvered outside the deep
pocket of Le Cap's harbor; what lay below them now was open ocean.
Here there was a pleasantly cool breeze, and he opened his coat and
loosened his collar the better to profit from it. His sweat turned chill as it
dried on him. They were descending now, picking away down the zigzag
path. Immediately before them a village unfolded in terraces cut into the
cliff wall: little clay houses fenced in by cactus and surrounded by a few
cornstalks or vines of potatoes or beans.

A small dog rushed to the cactus fence. Doctor Hébert shouted over
the noise of its yapping, in that language which sounded to Daspir like
French, though he could not comprehend a word of it. The dog circled
and dashed at its boundary. Presently the door of the little *case* sagged

open on its leather hinges and a white-haired old man came stooping out onto the packed earth of the yard, leaning on a crooked stick.

"*Konpè mwen*," the doctor called cheerfully. "*Ki zwazo ou gegne jodi-a?*"

"*Gegne zwazo, wi*," the old man croaked. "*Gegne zwazo anpil, anpil. M'ap montré'w tout zwazo sa yo.*" He limped forward on his stick and unfastened a string across a gap in the cactus, which symbolized a gate. "*Vini, vini.*" He beckoned, leading them farther on the trail, where it wound into a crevice better protected from the sea wind. Here the plantation was more considerable, and there were more of the little *cases* running backward toward a freshwater stream that trickled down the rock. A gaggle of mostly naked small children had joined their rear, silent and awestruck by the presence of strange whites.

The old man led them to another enclosure, without a house or a dog, but more tightly fenced than the others and overarched with trees like a bower. Within, a number of wing-plucked crows and parrots hopped on the ground, and some smaller birds were shut in cages made of bamboo splints, which hung from the branches overhead.

"How does he get them?" Daspir said at large.

"With snares," the doctor turned his head to say. "For the smaller ones he makes a kind of bird lime."

The old man raised a crow on his forefinger, and showed how it could curse in both French and Spanish. Isabelle made a moue of mock distaste. The children who waited outside the fence poked each other and giggled at the bird's coarse talk, all but one little girl who was staring mutely at pale Héloïse. The old man lifted one bird after another; all could pronounce a phrase or two, but there was no great difference of vocabulary. Daspir cast his eye over the cages; there were pigeons, doves, a lurid green-and-orange parakeet, but nothing resembling a canary.

"Have you no birds that sing?" Isabelle said finally.

"Madame, these are birds who *speak*," the old man said. "Any bird of the forest may sing."

Isabelle peered through the bamboo at the little parakeet. Seeing her interest, the old man opened the cage door and laid a finger behind its claws. Reflexively the bird stepped backward onto the new perch, and the old man drew it out through the opening. The parakeet revolved its head to look at Isabelle with one eye and then the other.

"*Comme tu es belle*," it suddenly squawked. How beautiful you are!

"Oh," said Isabelle, coloring slightly as she pressed her fingertips against her lower lip. She turned to Daspir. "What do you think?"

"Madame Leclerc cannot fail to be charmed by such a sentiment," Daspir said. "Though it is more properly due to yourself."

They made their way back by the same path, the parakeet's cage strung to the wooden cross of a donkey saddle. Héloïse tried to engage the bird on several topics, but all it would do was assure her of her beauty. In this direction the harbor mouth was more obvious and Daspir saw two craft of the French fleet negotiating the outer reefs, though he didn't know from what direction they'd come, nor what news they might bring.

The doctor caught his eye and pointed directly down the cliffside from the bend in the trail they were turning. "Picolet," he said briefly. Daspir peered over the edge and saw the abandoned harbor fort, much of its masonry shattered by the cannonade of four days before. No more than a couple of French sentries were posted there now, for Christophe's men had spiked the guns before their retreat, and tumbled them down from their carriages. And Leclerc had no reason, at this time, to prepare for any attack by sea.

At the point where the trail widened into a road, a trio of wizened old black women had appeared to spread over the ground wares to make Daspir's mouth water: stalks of bananas and baskets of mango and avocado and more of the large green oranges. There were several live chickens trussed up, *boucan*-dried pork, and even a couple of ducks. Now Daspir understood the reason for the second donkey, for Isabelle bought enough to load the animal down. As they departed, Daspir fished in his purse—he meant to buy a single banana, but once the old woman had bitten the coin he offered, she grinned and gave him the whole stalk. Daspir broke open one of the fruits and gulped it so quickly he nearly choked—when he was done he remembered to share more of the bananas around the company, and chose a second one to eat more slowly.

They had been two hours on this expedition, and the sun was just past its meridian when they came again in view of the town. From the height they had a panoramic view of the fire-blackened ruin, with squads of soldiers worming through the streets like maggots at work on a rotting carcass. And they themselves had nowhere else to go . . . A gloom settled on them as they went down, and there was no more talk, not even from the parakeet.

Isabelle's cook had stayed with the family, though all other servants but Michau had followed the army out of town. She had salvaged some of her iron pots from the wreckage, and when they returned to the shell of the Cigny house, she was stirring a big kettle over a fire, which proved to contain a stew of cornmeal and beans.

"*Maïs moulin,*" she explained to Daspir, with slightly forced good cheer. "It is popular among the people here. Well, we have brought a thing or two to increase the savor . . . You will dine with us, of course."

"With pleasure," Daspir was quick to say. In fact the smell from the kettle was very appealing, and it improved once Isabelle had diced in some tomatoes and peppers she'd bought on the way back, and added a ration of shredded dry pork. The men had swept clean the floor of what had been the downstairs parlor, and thatched over enough of the area to provide some shade. They ate sitting cross-legged on the stained tile, using banana leaves for plates. When they were done, with only the slightest tick of hesitation, Daspir brought out the last of his brandy and shared it round the group. When it was gone they curled up in the shade of the thatch and slept.

It was still full day when Daspir woke, with sweat pooling under his clothing on the tile.

"Come," Isabelle said. It was she who had roused him. "We are going to bring our gift to Madame Leclerc."

Daspir got up, aching in his hips and shoulders from having lain on the hard tile. The doctor was polishing his glasses on the tail of his soot-streaked shirt, while Cigny used his fingers to comb flakes of ash from his beard. Isabelle studied herself in a shard of mirror that Michau had fished out of the wreckage.

"Well, let us go," she finally said.

Daspir had the honor of carrying the birdcage, while Cigny bore a basket of fruit Isabelle had selected from her purchases earlier in the day. They left the children in the care of Michau and the cook, but the doctor and Arnaud accompanied them. The fruit basket attracted some envious glances along the way toward the Governor's house, since provisions were now very scarce in the town.

Captain-General Leclerc himself was there beneath the canopy, and in consequence Pauline's entourage of admirers was somewhat reduced, though Cyprien was waiting in a corner; Daspir exchanged a covert nod with him. The lady herself looked bored and petulant, but she practically sprang to her feet when she saw Isabelle come in.

"Oh," she said, "what have you there?"

Leclerc cleared his throat, a little cross at the interruption. Pauline ignored him, and Isabelle followed suit.

"The merest token," she said. "We do not know if it can be schooled to sing . . ." She opened the cage door and coaxed the bird onto her finger. The parakeet gave Pauline the benefit of both its profiles.

"Comme tu es belle," it said.

". . . but as you see, it has some power of discernment," Isabelle concluded.

"I love it," Pauline said decidedly, stretching out her hands. "Give it me."

Isabelle transferred the parakeet to Pauline's forefinger, while Cigny, with an unaccustomed courtliness, bowed to lay the fruit basket at her feet. Leclerc was tapping the toe of his boot meanwhile. As Pauline did not notice him, he turned to Daspir.

"Sir, where have you been all the day? Out hunting birds?"

Daspir lowered his eyes. *"Mon général,* the wish of Madame Leclerc was my command."

Leclerc's lips tightened, then relaxed. "So be it then," he said and stroked his long blond sidewhiskers with his thumb. "But now I shall return you to your charges." He gestured toward the corner where Cyprien lurked, and now for the first time Daspir remarked that Placide and Isaac sat in the shadows, immobile in their stiff new uniforms, with Monsieur Coisnon, near invisible in the black robe of his office.

"The sons of Toussaint Louverture," Leclerc said, raising his voice considerably. "I would send them to parley with their father. But one is not certain where he may be found. There is a rumor he has stopped on a plantation on the road from Haut du Cap . . ."

At that, Isabelle nudged the doctor, and when he found nothing to say, she glared at Arnaud.

"That would be Habitation Héricourt," Arnaud said hurriedly. "Toussaint holds it in *fermage* from the Comte de Noé."

"Ah," said Leclerc. "You are familiar with the place."

"Entirely," Isabelle cut in. "And we might happily guide your people there, if you have need."

Leclerc considered her, stroking his sidewhiskers down toward the jutting tip of his collar. Isabelle gave Arnaud a surreptitious poke.

"If Toussaint is not at Héricourt," Arnaud blurted, "he has another substantial holding near Ennery—we could convey you there as easily, though the distance is greater."

"Supposing the way to Ennery is safe," the doctor said.

"Have no fear for your security," Leclerc said. "The French army has the situation well in hand. But tell me, how great are these distances?"

"One might still reach Héricourt before nightfall—it is not far," the doctor said. "Ennery is a matter of another day's travel."

"Assuming there is no impediment on the road," Cigny said.

"You will be provided with sufficient force to sweep away any impediment," Leclerc said. "So help me, I am grateful for your offer."

"But do you mean to leave me?" Pauline said plaintively from the divan where she now posed with her bird. "Who shall come to amuse me then?"

Isabelle crossed the room and knelt down at her side. "I'm sure you will not want for company. And we will return as soon as may be. Why, I will surely take you on a tour of the countryside, if you wish it, as soon as things are . . . calm."

Pauline stretched up to kiss her cheek, then returned her attention to the parakeet. Isabelle rose and took a step toward Isaac and Placide.

"I met you both when you were boys," she said. "Though you will not remember."

Placide got up to meet her. "Who could forget Madame Cigny?" He lowered his head over the hand she offered.

"You are men now," Isabelle said. "Your father will be proud to see you so."

"Let us hope he is as proud to see them in their country's uniform," Leclerc said pointedly.

Isabelle turned to face him. "It is arranged, then," she said. "Only leave us one hour to make ready. My house, or rather the spot where it formerly stood, is on the way to the city gate, and I believe your excellent Captain Daspir knows the way."

In fact it took Isabelle considerably less than an hour to prepare to travel, for the few things she had preserved were already packed in the small leather portmanteau they'd hauled up and down the slope of La Vigie. The balance of the time allowed she divided between finishing a particular bit of needlework and debating with her husband.

"Yes, I *know* it was I who insisted on staying here," she said. "Call me inconstant if you must. I will even admit that I was wrong! We have succeeded to save nothing out of it all."

Cigny grumbled. "They say the plantations on the plain have all been burned as well."

"I'll promise you that Héricourt is intact, if Toussaint is in residence there," she said. "We would find a better shelter for ourselves, and for the children." She touched her hair and then looked critically at her fingers. "There might even be the chance of a bath."

"And if Toussaint is not at Héricourt?"

"Then on to Ennery and Habitation Thibodet." Isabelle smoothed the calico she was sewing over her knees.

"The mountain passes will not be secure, after everything that has just happened," Cigny said. "No matter what General Leclerc may say."

"But at the least we are promised a strong escort. I see no better chance to make the journey."

"I don't know that I see the point of this journey."

"Thibodet is so hemmed round with Toussaint's properties, I do not think that he will let it burn."

Cigny stood up and kicked a chunk of cracked masonry off the swept tiles into the ash pit. "No more did you think he would let Le Cap burn," he snapped. "Are you so eager to trust in his protection now?"

With a snap of her teeth, Isabelle bit off her thread. "You do wrong to mock me, though I was mistaken once." She lowered her voice, which had grown shrill. "We must seek our shelter where we may find it. And I see little enough here."

"I would go with you, Bertrand," the doctor said mildly. "As far as Ennery, if it proves possible. I should like to know that Nanon and the children are safe, not to mention my sister and her family."

"And I also," Arnaud said. "As far as Acul."

"My God," said Isabelle. "To think that we had forgotten Claudine."

Arnaud's mouth tightened. "Well," he said. "She has come through the wars before this one."

"As we all know," Isabelle said. "God grant she has saved herself as well this time." She made the sign of the cross and turned away.

Because he knew something of the terrain, Cyprien was given command of the expedition, with Daspir seconded to him. The escort in sum had a strength of twenty-two. They found the Cigny group prepared when they arrived; the adults all furnished with some sort of mount, a couple of them with mules. The two children doubled on one of the donkeys they had used that morning. Cyprien protested, in Daspir's ear, that he had not expected to be saddled with these brats, nor yet with so many extraneous adults, when Arnaud alone would have sufficed as a guide. But Daspir told him that the children could hardly be left to their own devices here, when only Michau and the cook were remaining to supervise the shell of the Cigny establishment, and when Isabelle appeared, Cyprien let the subject drop. She had cut and resewn the skirt of her maid's dress to contrive a costume that let her bestride her mare, and even in this getup she managed to cut an exotically elegant figure.

"So you have fallen in with this crew," Cyprien said musingly, one eye appreciating Isabelle's trim figure in the saddle. He and Daspir rode several places back in the group, behind the Cigny party and directly following Placide and Isaac. Their whole column was led by a wedge of five hussars, one of whom carried the flag of France before them.

"You seem to hold some reservation," Daspir said. "Were you acquainted with them before?"

"That I was," said Cyprien.

"I have happened to meet them at an inopportune moment—for them, at least," Daspir said. "Yet I confess to find them very amiable, especially Madame Cigny."

"Yes, she can be . . . ingratiating," Cyprien said. "She held quite a court in that house we just left, during the mission of Hédouville. No sign of any children in those days. She must have sent them away from the island, for their safety."

"Then they have had an unlucky hour for their return." Daspir felt a real twinge at this thought; he had a half sister in France about the age of Héloïse.

"They say she's had more lovers than hairs on her head," Cyprien went on, still gazing at Isabelle's supple back.

"I take it you were not among them?" Daspir divined from the other's tone that if he'd applied, he'd been rejected.

Cyprien coughed and cleared his throat. "Maybe not all of them were white men either. Toussaint's black so-called officers were frequent enough in her parlor at that time, if not in some chamber closer to her . . . well. The husband is a cipher, turns a blind eye to it all. Was mostly absent in the countryside—they have a plantation near Haut de Trou."

"Scandalous," Daspir said. His voice emerged ironic, though what he felt was simple curiosity.

Cyprien shot him a critical glance. "As for your Michel Arnaud, he was renowned for torturing his slaves to death, before the insurrection, and how he escaped being murdered by them afterward is a great mystery. They say his wife chopped off her own finger and gave it to the brigands—"

"What, in exchange for his life?"

"Who knows?" Cyprien said. "They say she participates in their savage rites. A madwoman."

"These are interesting people indeed," Daspir said. "And what do you know of Doctor Hébert?"

"The good doctor? He has a skill in native remedies, along with his European education. I'm told he's saved a great many limbs that another sawbones might have hacked off and thrown to the dogs. His sister ran off with a notorious gunrunner, while her legal husband was still groaning on his deathbed, and since then they've been playing both sides of the game."

"And the doctor?"

"Certainly he has been *very* thick with Toussaint," Cyprien said. "Beyond that, I can tell you that he is not entirely what he seems to be—"

At that, almost as if he'd overheard, the doctor twisted in the saddle and looked back at them, lowering a hand to balance his long gun across the pommel of his saddle. He did no more than give them a wide smile, whose mood was unintelligible because the reddening sunlight flashed from his spectacles and hid his eyes.

Cyprien fell silent. They rode on. Long since they'd passed the city gate. On either side of the road they traveled, an expanse of devastation continued to unfurl. The air was heavy with the scent of scorched sugar. No human activity was anywhere to be seen; the charred landscape was utterly still except for occasional swirls of smoke, and carrion birds wheeling above certain points on the plain. Daspir glanced at the red orb of the sun, which was dropping rapidly toward the ridge line of the mountains to the west. He wondered how far it might be to their destination, but did not like to ask.

For distraction, he turned his attention to Placide and Isaac, who rode on either side of their tutor. Now and again one of them pointed out some feature they were passing to Monsieur Coisnon, though how they could identify anything from what now remained of it, Daspir could not imagine. But both the youths looked more impressive horseback than shipboard. They were both good riders, erect in the saddle, holding their heads high. Isaac had perhaps the firmer seat, and certainly held a tighter rein, whereas Placide seemed to proceed from a natural sympathy with the animal.

Now they were passing along a citrus hedge which did not seem to have been scorched at all. And then, between two grand gateposts, appeared a glimpse of tall cane trembling in the evening breeze. Placide reached between the horses to tap Isaac on the shoulder.

"Bréda," he said, and pointed to the gate.

Isaac turned his head to look. To Daspir the unfamiliar word seemed fraught with some significance. Was this the hedge from which he'd plucked his orange yesterday? Or had that been nearer to Limbé? He could not tell, but would have gladly had another.

The doctor reined up his horse and dropped back in the line to ride beside Daspir. "Habitation Bréda is also a property of the Comte de Noé," he said. "Toussaint was coachman there, and *commandeur*, before he rose to his present estate. They called him Toussaint Bréda in those days. And of course the boys spent their early childhood there."

"Is it so?" Cyprien said carelessly.

The doctor shrugged. "That Bréda has been preserved from the burning bodes well for our intention, I believe." He gave his horse a flick of his heel and rode forward to rejoin Placide and Isaac.

The sun was lost behind the mountains by the time they had reached the next intact citrus hedge, this one on the opposite side of the road from Bréda. A scrolled iron gate was closed between the posts. Cyprien rode up and rang the bars with the pommel of his saber.

"We bring dispatches from the Captain-General Leclerc to Toussaint Louverture!"

At that, two men clothed in a green livery appeared from behind the gateposts. Neither spoke, but one of them unlocked the gate with an enormous key, and together they dragged its two halves open. Cyprien sheathed his blade and led the party through.

The long drive ran between cane fields on either side. These were lowlands, the most fertile part of the Northern Plain, and Daspir thought he could smell the rich loam beneath the green scent of the cane, which stood dense and well above man height. There was not the slightest hint of smoke.

The drive was surfaced with a gravel so tightly compact that the horseshoes clacked as if on cobblestone. Their flag hung limp against its staff in the damp air. As they rode through the rapidly thickening twilight, Daspir became aware that large numbers of barefoot, bare-chested black men were filtering silently through the cane fields on either side of the drive, shadowing the movement of the riders. There seemed to be some hundreds of them, though it was difficult to estimate their numbers as they slipped in and out of the cane, and every man of them carried a long *coutelas*. Of course it was merely an implement of their work—these must be field hands, coming in from an ordinary day in the cane, and yet their silence was eerie. Daspir glanced over his shoulder and saw that the gate behind them was shut.

The driveway terminated in a flat oval below the gallery of the Héricourt *grand'case.* The horsemen circled counterclockwise and, with a jingle of harness, halted below the steps. Though there was still a fair amount of light in the sky, servants were lighting the lamps on the gallery, whose rail was twined with purple bougainvillea. An amazingly tall and spindly black man appeared at the head of the stairs. The doctor hailed him.

"*Monchè Mars Plaisir!*" he said. "We are looking for the Governor-General Toussaint."

The tall man spread his spidery hands. "*L'ap soti,*" he said.

The doctor slipped down from his horse.

"Who is that fellow?" Cyprien said, looking down on him.

"Mars Plaisir? He is Toussaint's personal valet."

"What does he say? Is Toussaint here?"

" 'He has gone out,' " the doctor quoted. "That's what he said."

"That's useful," said Cyprien.

The doctor shrugged. "With time and patience we may learn more," he said. "We'll stop the night here, in any case."

Indeed, Mars Plaisir was already leading Placide and Isaac into the house, a long arm draped over each of their shoulders. Isabelle followed them, with her children, through the front door of the house. Daspir dismounted. Several grooms had appeared to take charge of the horses.

"Come," said the doctor. "Let us go into the garden."

Both Daspir and Cyprien followed him around the corner of the house. A flagstone path wound through a great luxuriance of closely planted trees and flowers, many of which Daspir did not recognize. He could pick out banana stalks, young coconut palms, some almond trees . . . The path had a number of forks, but the doctor seemed sure of his way. He led them to a corner of the wall where water trickled from a spout into a pool. A clay jug and a cup stood on a stone. The doctor poured water over his wrists and splashed his face, then filled the cup and drank. He passed the jug and cup to Daspir and, without a word, vanished around a turn of the garden path.

Daspir drank and gave the cup to Cyprien. The water went on whispering from the spout into the pool.

"I saw him," Daspir said abruptly.

"Saw whom?" said Cyprien.

"General Toussaint," Daspir said. "Toussaint Louverture. He met us in the battle by Limbé. He was riding a tremendous white horse . . ." The image flashed behind Daspir's eyes. Had it been yesterday? the day before? a year?

"I wonder that you did not bring him in on a string," Cyprien said.

"Ah," said Daspir, attempting a light tone. "There was a river between us."

"Do let me know if you see him again," Cyprien said and abruptly started—a small winged thing had flickered between them.

"It's only a bat," said the doctor's voice. "It will not harm you."

Cyprien sniffed and turned away, heading for the lights of an open arcade that ran along the side of the house. An agreeable smell of cooking came from that direction. Daspir swallowed, ran his tongue around his hollow mouth. White petals from a tree he did not recognize came drifting down over the path that Cyprien had followed.

Daspir reversed himself and stood beside the doctor, looking into the heart of the garden. There were still some dusty rose reflections from the clouds above the wall. The sound of water murmured, at their left. He wondered where Guizot was at this moment, if he were still alive and unhurt. Then for some reason his mind returned to the black men with their long knives, drifting dark as ghosts through the cane.

"The field hands here have just recently been mustered out of the army," the doctor said. "It's Toussaint's system. You may be sure they have their firearms near at hand."

Daspir glanced at him, then looked back into the leaves. There was a movement of the air, stirring the feathery shoots of the *cocotiers*, shivering the round leaves of the almonds. All the garden seemed to contract with an inhalation. Then release.

"He has been here, has he not?" Daspir said. "Not long ago."

"Yes," said the doctor. "I think he has."

"But how can you know?"

"*Sa nou pa wé yo,*" the doctor said. "In this country, your knowledge comes to you out of the invisible. Or at least at this hour, when all of the garden breathes at one time, what you don't see means more than what you do."

In the quiet that ensued, Daspir felt the garden draw in its breath once more and let it go. The doctor touched him very lightly on his sleeve.

"Come," he said. "Let us go in."

13

From the clifftop retreat Arnaud had prepared, Claudine could still sense the curve of the earth below, though most of the horizon was blotted out by smoke. She sat on a stone with her ankles crossed, looking out beyond the gate of Habitation Arnaud, over the charcoal expanse of the Plaine du Nord. The light sound of water running from the spring purled on, behind and to her left. The crossing of her ankles brought her lean shanks wide, stretching the fabric of her skirt and framing the lower loop of a long chain of blue beads, which wrapped twice around her neck before releasing its last length to her kneecaps. The beads were a deep, dense blue, and very shiny and hard, like polished stone, or pottery fiercely fired and glazed; she did not know which.

She shuttled them across her lap with her fingers, one by one, with little clicks. *Hail Mary, full of grace, the Lord is with thee. Blessèd art thou among women . . .* And there she stuck, her mind refusing to advance the words of the prayer. She did not know where the beads had come from, or knew it only by hearsay. By hearsay and by her fatigue and the marks on her body she knew that two days before, when the fighting began on the road from Limbé, a spirit had mounted into her head and ridden her down to the front gate of Habitation Arnaud. In the open gateway she had danced and shouted and gibbered and torn great chunks of earth from the ground to smear into the scratches she'd clawed on her cheeks.

Then the *serviteurs* must have brought the beads, to adorn the spirit manifest in her.

She had been hard ridden that day, she thought. For a night and a day and another night, she'd lain abed, entranced at first, and later sleeping from exhaustion. This morning before dawn she'd risen, herself again, and slipped from the house to climb the cliff wall, still attired as she had been two days before and wearing the beads to complement that clothing.

Through the smoke, the rising sun appeared like an egg yolk scorching in a neglected skillet. Since yesterday the fires had died, but the smoke still roiled. Yet Habitation Arnaud remained green to the gateway where she had stood, and the gate itself, though built of wood, was still intact. The soldiers' fight had rolled away down the road toward Le Cap, never entering here, and the revolting field hands who were burning all the cane had stopped at the hedges that marked Arnaud's borders.

Hail Mary, full of grace, the Lord is with thee. Blessèd art thou among women . . .

Claudine stood up and moved toward the path, the longest loop of the bead chain swinging low to knock against her shins. As she began her descent, the boys Etienne and Dieufait appeared, fore and aft of her. Etienne led a little brown kid on a string behind him, and Dieufait skipped backward ahead of her, smiling, beckoning, gesturing toward various rocks and roots that might have tripped her as she went down.

As she emerged on the level ground behind the *grand'case,* she caught sight of Cléo, who had just finished sweeping out the back gallery and was throwing out some grain to the hens that had gathered expectantly on the packed dirt. Cléo noticed her too and called out that coffee was served on the front gallery and that Claudine must come and take some nourishment, but Claudine simply shook her head and walked around the house. She glanced back once and saw Fontelle's face above the gallery rail and felt just slightly disconcerted; when had Fontelle come?

In the dooryard of the little *case* beside the chapel, Marie-Noelle was stirring up small sweet potatoes in a *chaudière* above a small charcoal fire, the baby gurgling, propped on a board by the doorsill. The curtain was tied back from the door, so that Claudine could see that Moustique was not inside. Briefly she returned Marie-Noelle's smile and went on, around toward the rear of the chapel. Etienne and Dieufait were capering more widely around her now that they had more room. Etienne's kid got away from him, but he pursued and arrested it by stamping his bare foot on the trailing string.

In former times the central compound here had been clear and bare to the hedges, but since it had first been laid to waste in ninety-one, a growth of bamboo had encroached along the path of a shallow ditch toward the back side of the chapel, and Claudine had prevailed upon

Arnaud to let it stand. Now the tall stalks of bamboo had been bowed and bound to form a *tonnelle*, a greenly arbored passageway of such a height that Claudine scarcely had to lower her head to enter it. The little boys stopped outside; they were shy of this place, on ordinary days, when the drums did not invite all comers inside it. Distantly Claudine heard the voice of Marie-Noelle calling Dieufait to come back to the cookfire. She went on, deeper into the green shade.

After a dozen yards, the arboreal space widened, like a bulb, and in its center opened to the sky. A little cairn of stones stood by the entrance. Round the edges were hung gourds and bottles and bundles of herbs, and several thatched shelters covered small shrines containing vases and bowls or small plaster figures of saints or, in one, a playing card pinned to a tree.

Moustique was here, moving with quiet delicacy in the shadows, serving one altar and another with flowers, crushing sweet herbs into a bowl of water. Claudine passed him, without speaking, and went directly to a niche devoted to the Mater Dolorosa, roughly painted on a scrap of board. For a moment she hesitated, regarding the sorrowful blue madonna, whose weak hand clasped the blade of an enormous sword blade, the point driven deep into her open heart. Then she unwound the beads from her neck and carefully coiled them around a white candle, affixed by its own wax to a flat rock before the icon.

"That necklace was offered to Erzulie Jé Rouge." Moustique had slipped up silently behind her, near enough she thought she felt his warm breath on her neck.

"So it may have been," Claudine said. "But it is I who give it to Erzulie Fréda."

She turned to face him. Moustique was the taller—still a tall and gangly youth, who bent on her a child's expression of puzzlement.

"Was it Erzulie Jé Rouge who turned the war from our gate?" she asked him.

"It was she who danced in your head that day, Madame," Moustique said.

"Yes," said Claudine. "But in the spirit of peace and harmony, I offer the beads to Fréda now."

She trailed her fingers through the bowl of water, and let a few drops fall on the cairn as she went out. A few steps into the *tonnelle*, she turned.

"Your mother is here, this morning."

"Yes," Moustique said. From his face Claudine could see that this was no news to him. Fontelle must have been here for a day or more, then. The force of Claudine's possession had done away with her memory of that arrival.

The Lord is with thee. Blessèd art thou among women, and blessèd is the fruit of thy womb, Jesus. Holy Mary, Mother of God, pray for us . . .

At the outer mouth of the *tonnelle* she stopped. A black bore hole of pain had opened in the spot between her navel and her pubes. She waited, swallowing spasmodically, until it passed, and then stepped out into the light. Dieufait and Etienne were waiting for her there, each chewing a small, round sweet potato in its skin.

"*N'alé lekol,*" Dieufait said. We are going to school.

"We are," Claudine said, and led them to the arbor by the church.

Near two dozen children waited for her in that shade, most too small for field work, with a few older ones for whom Claudine had obtained special dispensation, because of their aptitude for learning. She had devised a reading and writing lesson based on the first few verses of the twentieth chapter of John, where Mary Magdalen discovers the stone rolled away and the cave empty where the body of Jesus had lain. She had meant to push her students forward to the moment of joy, but the children's reading went haltingly and their writing wanted more correction than ever, so that at the end of their time Claudine was left stranded with the Magdalen, weeping over the empty sepulcher, and lost to herself at that moment. When she raised her head, she saw the children looking at her kindly. They felt her pain, though without understanding it; could they know how the one hollow echoed the other?

The noon bell tolled. The children scattered to their houses. Claudine went to the well and filled two large buckets and raised them on a pole across her shoulders. Shuddering a little under the weight, she began to trudge toward the cane fields. From the pole of the sky, the sun weighed down on her like hot iron.

Presently most of the children rejoined her. They were bringing food to their fathers and brothers in the field, and some of them also carried water. Etienne and Dieufait flanked Claudine; each of them caught hold of a bucket handle and took a little of the weight from her load. In the past she had chased them away when they tried to do it, but Moustique had told her that the boys were moved by their own spirits to this action, and that the value of her penance was not diminished by their taking a small share of the burden.

They followed the carter's path cut through the cane till they came to a place where a wagon stood half loaded with fresh stalks. Claudine served out the water as the men received their food. The full two hours of mid-day repose would now be observed, as mandated by the old *Code Noir,* but most of the men did not return to their houses, remaining here instead, in the shade of the fruit trees bordering the *carrés* of cane. They ate, then dozed or played with their children. Claudine thought that they seemed happy and at peace.

All was in equally good order at the mill when she passed that way with her empty buckets. The chief refiner brought her some clear syrup in a white saucer, and she shrugged off her yoke and stuck a finger in to taste it. The stuff was sweet, certainly; she knew little of the process.

"It is good," she said.

"Yes, Madame," said the refiner. Then, with a slight frown of concern, "Have you news of Monsieur?"

"No," said Claudine. She'd had no news of Arnaud for many days. In fact she had scarcely thought of him.

"What news have you?" she said.

The refiner looked at her uncertainly. Claudine gestured at the haze of smoke that hovered on their borders.

"Ah," he said. "The French have landed soldiers, to make us slaves again. That is what they say." Then, inexplicably, his glossy black face split into a brilliant smile.

Raising her buckets, Claudine stepped out of the mill and looked down the trail which led to the patch of shrubbery where Arnaud's distillery was concealed. In the ordinary course of things she did not visit any works except the cane fields, but today she felt the impulse to see over everything and verify that all was well. Yet it was ten years now since she had tasted rum, or any liquor. She'd leave the distillery to itself.

Leaving her buckets at the well, she walked up the slope to the *grand'case*, her legs rubbery beneath her. Cléo received her on the gallery and pressed to her temples a cool damp cloth, then touched it to the base of her skull and the pulse points on her wrists. The table was laid for the midday meal, Fontelle already seated there. Grilled fish, a plate of rice cooked with chopped carrots, a bowl full of fresh peas. Claudine picked at her food and quizzed Fontelle on her recent doings: she had come down from Le Cap a week ago, to visit her new grandson. She had seen Arnaud at the Cigny house there. A French fleet stood outside the harbor, but Fontelle had left before its mission was made known. She had meant to go on to visit her daughter at Ennery before now, but with all the unrest in the region, she did not know . . .

Claudine assured her she was welcome to remain at Habitation Arnaud for as long as she liked, or needed to. She could tell that Fontelle had responded to her questions before, but she did not seem to object to repeating the answers. Coffee was served, but Claudine declined it. Cléo came with her to the bedroom and helped her to loosen her clothes and let down her hair.

"Why are you kind to me?" Claudine said and thrashed her head against the pillow, the unbound hair spreading out its faded color and the strands of white. Cléo looked at her with a grave reserve, as she always did when this question was put. Then, to Claudine's surprise, she sat down on a stool beside the bed and took her hand, the one that lacked a finger.

"I was in the camps at Grande Rivière," she said. "When I left this place, in the time of the first rising."

"In ninety-one," Claudine said.

"Yes, in ninety-one." Cléo stroked the top of her hand absently. "There were many white prisoners there. I took a young *blanche* to be my servant. Each day I sent her to the river to wash my clothes, scrub them and beat them and dry them on the stones. She had pretty hands when she began, small and fine. They were bleeding the first day. Of course she had never done such work. She'd had a slave to brush her hair and another to put on her shoes. I slapped and beat her for every fault. One would not use a dog so, nor a mule."

"Yes," said Claudine, who was familiar with such abuses from her own practice of them in the past. "And then?"

"Biassou took her for his whore," Cléo said, with a distant smile. "One of the many he took so. Day by day and week by week. Her hands were ruined by that time, but Biassou was not looking at her hands. I never saw her again after that."

"What was her name?"

"I have forgotten, if I ever knew," Cléo said. "But in my heart I called her by your name, Madame."

Gently she laid Claudine's hand on the sheet and stood. "You must not torment yourself," she said. "Rest now."

When Cléo had shut the door behind her, Claudine got up and knelt at her bedside and pressed her forehead against the mattress.

Hail Mary, full of grace, the Lord is with thee. Blessèd art thou among women, and blessèd is the fruit of thy womb, Jesus. Holy Mary, Mother of God, pray for us sinners now and at the hour of our death . . .

This time the prayer completed itself without a pang. She stretched out on the bed again. In her mind's eye, before she slept, she thought she saw the comforting face of the Père Bonne-chance.

The air had changed when she awoke; a breeze was blowing, cool and moist. She got up and dressed herself and pinned up her hair, a little awkwardly. When she met Cléo in the hall, she asked for Fontelle and was told that she had gone down to Moustique's house to see the baby. Claudine walked in that direction. The burning smell of that morning was much fainter. The breeze came scudding low across the yard and a bank of purple clouds was building to the north.

She found Fontelle seated on a low chair beneath a young lime tree, holding the baby on her lap. Marie-Noelle was sweeping the dooryard with a broom of split palm leaves. Claudine sat down on a cloth spread on the ground by Fontelle's chair.

"Oh, he is thriving, is he not?" she said.

Fontelle simply smiled down on the baby.

"Do you not think he resembles his grandfather?" Claudine said.

"Oh no," Fontelle said. "He is very dark." She shot a glance at Marie-Noelle, who was of the purest African stock.

"But look here." Claudine reached for the baby, who accepted the change without protest at first. "Look at the nose, and the shape of the eyes . . . I do wish that the Père Bonne-chance could be here to see him."

"Perhaps he has some way to see him all the same." Fontelle crossed herself and lowered her head. The baby mewed and kicked against the front of Claudine's dress. Marie-Noelle propped her broom against the house wall and came to take him up. She knelt on the cloth and undid his swaddling and prodded his soft belly till he gurgled and smiled. As she withdrew her hand, his little penis rose enough to send out a bright jet of urine that arced to the cloth between his legs.

At this the three women shared a laugh, and Marie-Noelle moved him away from the damp spot and began to rub him down. But Claudine was distracted by Etienne and little Dieufait, who came running in a flurry of excitement, calling, "Madame, Madame, come quickly, there is someone at the gate."

The party escorting the sons of Toussaint Louverture had left Héricourt in good time that morning. As no one had been able to obtain any exact information about the Governor-General's whereabouts, they were on their way to Ennery, as previously planned. French soldiers had secured the main road, as Leclerc had claimed, though Christophe and the Second Demibrigade had left a wake of ruin in their retreat, and whatever force had opposed Leclerc's and Hardy's advance from the Baie d'Acul had left behind another trail of ash.

Arnaud's heart sank as he rode through it all. He'd seen his own holdings laid to waste before. In ninety-one it had all been burned—not a stick left standing and scarcely one stone still mortared to another. He'd found a scrap of mirror in that bowl of cinders and not been able to know his own face.

Now he rode in tandem with Bertrand Cigny. They did not speak—there was little conversation that morning among anyone in the group. Arnaud and Cigny had never been close. Cigny was generally tight-lipped and irritable. His wife deceived him so prolifically that he found no friends among other men. Yet today Arnaud felt a certain sympathy for him. They would soon be parting ways—Cigny had determined to investigate the state of his own plantation at Haut de Trou. Somewhat grudgingly, the young Captain Cyprien had agreed to detach two hussars to see him that far. Arnaud himself, who had the shorter distance to go, would travel alone once he diverged from the main road. For his security he had two colossal cavalry pistols, a short sword, and the speed of his horse, which was a good one.

At the riverside before Limbé, he bade good-bye to his companions and urged them brusquely on. A gang of French infantry were still repairing the bridge that had been pulled down during the engagement here a few days before, and those who were going on were obliged to ride along the bank for a few hundred yards to find a place to ford. Arnaud watched till they'd crossed the stream, then turned his horse into the lane beside it.

Much burning here, either side of the way. Arnaud's tongue thickened in his throat. It was possible that Claudine had survived, even if the plantation had been sacked. She might even have gone off with the rebels, as all Arnaud's retainers had done the other time.

The bole of a fallen palm tree barred his way, and Arnaud got down to shift it. It was green wood and heavy, difficult to budge. He was puffing and sweaty when he scrambled back onto his horse. Around the next bend of the road was another. Arnaud dismounted, cursing aloud; the sound of his own voice rather startled him. This time he noticed the fresh ax marks on the stump of the felled tree.

Ambush. A bird shot twittering over the road. Arnaud looked back, and out of his fear there came a gang of blacks advancing on foot along the line of his retreat. He did not stop to number them, but gained the saddle with a vault, not troubling with a stirrup. His horse cleared the tree trunk with an excellent jump. Arnaud pressed into a gallop. There was another tree; they jumped that too. The ash-strewn fields went whizzing by. Arnaud felt a rush of sporting excitement. Around the next bend of the lane was a still more complicated barricade; tree trunks laid in a crisscross pattern, branches sticking up like spikes. With his eyes streaming from the wind, Arnaud could not clearly make it out. But his horse was refusing it. Too late to stop. Arnaud felt the hindquarters bunch beneath him. Then they were sliding, going down, then a flood of the dark.

An explosion roused him and he jerked his eyes open to see his horse's ears twitching against the bark of a fallen tree. Blood was pouring out of the animal's shattered skull. A skinny old black man stood by, blowing smoke from the barrel of his ancient musket.

"*Li pa bon,*" he said, referring apparently to the horse. He's no good. He sat down on one of the trees of the barricade and began painstakingly to reload his weapon.

Arnaud struggled to rise and found his left leg pinned beneath the horse's body. His hands went scrambling; one of them found a pistol which he drew and leveled at the old man, whose white eyes widened. He did not relinquish his musket, but he left off trying to load it. After a moment he stood up and shrugged and backed off, trailing the musket by the barrel, to join the others who were with him. There were about a dozen of them, all old men or boys, mostly armed only with *coutelas*, but some with other antique firearms bound together with bits of wire and string. One had a musket of more recent vintage, from Sonthonax's arms distributions, Arnaud guessed. They all looked at him with neutral eyes, and then as if their minds were one they slipped quickly away through the trees that lined this section of the lane.

Arnaud felt safe enough to lay aside the pistol now. By pushing with both arms he was able to dislodge his left leg from beneath the saddle. At first he thought he was only bruised, but when he put weight on his left foot, a bolt of pain shot to the top of his head, and he sat down abruptly on a log of the barricade.

When he looked at his horse he wanted to weep. The waste of it—and good horses would be hard to come by now. Any kind of horses. Whatever the rebel blacks did not steal would certainly be requisitioned by the French army.

Now he saw that the horse's right foreleg had been shattered. There had been nothing to do but shoot it, after all. Perhaps those men had only meant to help him. Certainly they might have killed him, without much trouble or risk to themselves.

With his penknife he hacked off one of his shirt sleeves and used it to bind up his swollen ankle. He could not get his boot back on when he was done, but the bare foot took his weight with a pain that was just bearable. He was horribly thirsty when he stood up. He'd been carrying some water in a skin bag, but the fall had burst the vessel and the water had run out to mingle with the blood and horse piss soaking the ground. His walking stick, a novelty made of a twisted and dried bull's pizzle, was whole, still strapped to the back of his saddle. He cut it free and went limping down the lane, depending heavily on the stick, his pistol dragging down his other hand.

It was not far, it could not be, but the distance was difficult to cover. Arnaud limped around one bend, then two. There before him appeared the wavering hallucination of a young black woman in a tight red dress, her head bound up in a shimmering blue cloth. She sat on a boulder amid the ashes just off the roadside. On the rock beside her was a tin tray with a white pitcher and a metal cup. Arnaud staggered toward the apparition. To his surprise, she did not vanish in the heat glaze when he came near.

"Ba'm dlo," he croaked. Give me water. The woman only gazed at him, without expression. She was plump, no, ripe to bursting, straining every red seam of her dress. In another time he'd have lusted for her mightily. She poured a cup and set it on the tray. Arnaud pinned the pistol under the arm that held the stick, and painfully stretched down to take the cup. He poured the water down his swollen throat. A little ran out the corner of his mouth and he chased those drops with the tip of his tongue.

"Merci," he said, and fumbled a coin from his breeches pocket to offer her. The woman only looked at him impassively. Arnaud let the coin clang down on the tray. He limped ahead, along the lane.

It was growing cooler now, and breezy, wind running ahead of the rain from the north. If he didn't come to shelter soon, he'd have no water that he could use. Now to the left of the road, nothing was burned, and he could see the leaves of tall green cane, trembling in the wind above the citrus hedges. And this was his own property, if not another chimera. But that woman's water had tasted real enough.

The wooden gate was still there, tended by a toothless crone who garbled something he couldn't make out as Arnaud stumbled through. Two little boys went flying up the long *allée* ahead of him. He crept on, leaning on the stick. There was singing in the cane on either side of him, beyond the surviving palm trees and the stumps with their new shoots. He looked one way and the other but saw no one. The men were hidden in the cane, singing their way out of the fields before the rain.

Presently the figure of Claudine appeared before him, framed in the top of the *allée* like an object seen backward in a telescope. Once something else had stood in that same place, but Arnaud's mind refused it now, like his horse had refused that last jump.

At the time of their marriage he'd felt small love for her, and in their first years together in the colony he'd come to positively dislike her. The prize he'd supposed he'd brought home from France was barren. Afterward, he'd returned to her from a sense of duty, the same motive that made her carry buckets to the cane fields. But he felt very glad to see her now. Why did she not come out to meet him? Perhaps he was already dead, and so invisible to her.

Yet when he had finally reached her, he drew himself up and felt a little stronger.

"Michel," she said. There was just a touch of the alien glitter in her eyes. At least she knew him. "You have come home."

"I see I have still a home to come to," he replied, looking beyond her— it was all there, the rebuilt house and outbuildings all intact. "A miracle."

"If it is a miracle, it must be from God," she said.

"But you are hurt," said Arnaud, and reached out to touch the two scabbed vertical scratches on her right cheek.

"It's nothing," Claudine said. She unfolded his hand from her face and kissed the palm. Then she seemed to take in for the first time his sun-blistered, sleeveless arm, the stick, the melon-sized ankle and the bare foot battered by the road.

"Cléo," she called. "Moustique! Come quickly." Then Arnaud finally felt his legs grow weak.

Placide found that he was easier in his mind once Arnaud had left their party. When Cigny also turned away, a little later, flanked by the two hussars assigned to him, Placide felt better still. Now there were no *colons* among them anymore, except for the woman, Isabelle Cigny. Placide did not consider the doctor to be a *colon*. As for Cyprien and Daspir, he was used to them, which did not mean he liked them, but they were merely strangers in his land, like all the other French soldiers. No matter what he might do or what happened to him, a *colon* could not lose the memory nor the habit of having owned black men and women to use as beasts of burden. Placide had been a small child when Arnaud and his kind had tortured their slaves through the doors of death, but he had heard the stories.

He glanced at Isaac, wondering if he felt the same; they could not speak freely, since Coisnon rode within earshot. Last night at Héricourt, Coisnon had slept in the same room. He was a good preceptor to them, and Placide knew he cared for them profoundly, and yet there could not be the frankness among them here that there had been in France.

Isaac's horse stumbled over a stone, and Isaac clucked his tongue and tightened the reins sharply. "Come up," he hissed, as though it were the horse's fault. Placide turned his eyes to the road ahead.

In some way Coisnon had shared in the shock of their return. Their disappointment. They'd had several days to contemplate the burned shell of Le Cap from the deck of the *Jean-Jacques*, once that ship had entered the harbor and moored. After all they'd told Coisnon of its beauties and joys, their tongues were frozen in their heads. They'd spent their passage to Héricourt in a similar silence, turning their heads around like owls, toward wasteland that stretched to all horizons.

But now Placide's mood, at least, was changing. Now they had passed Haut Limbé and were mounting the steep and winding ascent to Plaisance, jungled mountains towering over them, with plots of corn or groves of bananas terraced into the cliff sides, by the little houses that clung there. *I lift up my eyes unto the hills, whence cometh my hope.* Placide's father had catechized him with this line long ago, though now he could not number the chapter or the verse. Yet he felt now how powerfully Toussaint had attached his hope to the hills, and to these *mornes* in particular; the range of peaks called the Cordon de l'Ouest, running back through the interior to Dondon and the Spanish border.

There were no French troops on this road through the mountains, except for those of their own escort, and there was no sign of war. The market women at the crossroads shouted out their excitement at their appearance, and packs of small children, dogs, and goats, came scampering after them on their way out of Plaisance, until they fell back, breathless, no longer able to keep pace with the horses.

The horses were beginning to be winded too, with the increasing altitude and steady climbing. The way between Plaisance and Morne Pilboreau looked almost flat, but still their mounts had to take it slowly. From the roadside a cliff fell giddily away into the Plaisance river valley. All seemed tranquil, at peace there, along the serpentine turns of the slow stream, except for the vertigo that seemed to pull them toward the brink. Placide realized he was looking down upon the backs of flying hawks which hovered over that deep space.

They rode on. The peak of Pilboreau was sheathed in cloud—a sudden chill as they rode into it, cool droplets condensing on the hairs of their eyebrows and forearms. A great market was here at the crossroads for Marmelade, and all the *marchandes* came rushing to them, out of the floating tendrils of cool mist.

"*Sé fils Papa Toussaint ou yé!*" they cried. You are the sons of Papa Toussaint! Placide could not imagine how they had known it, yet they did know. The crowd pressed tight around the horses, dividing the riders from each other. Placide could see from their pale drawn faces that Cyprien and Daspir were uneasy in the crush, and the French cavalry-men looked positively afraid, but neither of the officers gave any order. There was no order to be given; this riot was peaceful, no weapon in sight. Among the whites, only the doctor seemed at ease, and Isabelle, but the crowd did not press on her so closely, still somewhat in awe of a white woman.

They swarmed around Placide's and Isaac's horses, grasping their stir-rups, the flaps of their saddles, stroking their trouser legs and reaching up to touch their hands and feel the fabric of their shirt cuffs and coat sleeves. Other hands came stretching up to present bunches of bananas and baskets of limes and lemons and oranges and avocados, none offered for sale but all in gift. The chill of the mountain mist was gone, and not only because rays of the westering sun had begun to cut through the cloud, but that the compression of so many bodies and beings around them created a warmth that was almost suffocating. Placide was a little alarmed himself at first, if only at the unidentifiable wave of feel-ing that built in him. Then whatever held it back gave way and the feel-ing poured out of him to flow into the being of all those others who were other no more.

"*Nou la!*" Placide said in his strongest voice. His face was wet with the push and pull of the internal tide. "*Nou la,*" the shining faces upturned to him replied. The words meant simply *We are here*, but also, *We are here and you are here with us* and *We have survived to arrive here in this place where we are meant to be together.*

Placide looked to Isaac and saw to his sadness that his brother under-stood nothing of what he felt and knew. In truth, Isaac's French was more perfect than Placide's, since Isaac had been younger when they were sent from home to the Collège de la Marche. But for the same rea-son the nuances of their Creole mother tongue, which had been rushing back to Placide since they landed, did not return so readily to Isaac. Indeed, the tightness of his face was something like the tension Placide saw in the French officers. He watched Isaac, saying nothing. Isaac reined up his horse so tight that it began to crab sideways, shunting away the people that surrounded him, creating a space in which he was alone.

Some of the hussars had laid hands to their saber hilts. Placide could see they were ready to draw and begin swatting people away from them with the flats of the blades. Captain Daspir must have seen this too, for he called out, "Leave that! Let no man touch a weapon!"

"*Avancez!*" Cyprien said crisply. Move on! Their column re-formed and Placide was closed within it, cut off from the people of the market. Then they had crossed the crest of the mountain and were going down under the red sun that shone on the scrubby cliff walls of this drier face.

Placide twisted in the saddle to look back once, but he could not see the people any more, only the face of the doctor smiling back at him from his place in the line, and dark thunderheads piling up above Pilboreau. He faced forward, looking down the hairpin turns that lined the edges of the gorge below them, believing they'd reach Ennery before the rain.

14

I left Dessalines at Saint Marc then, standing among the burning torches and the tar barrels that had been gathered for the burning of that town. I rode for the south as fast as I could go, which was not so very fast since my horse was tired from the many days of long riding that had come before. In Arcahaye the people ran after me asking for news, catching at the leather skirts of my saddle and my boot heels and even the tail of the horse, but I, Riau, I did not stop for them. I did not know any news to tell them, because I did not know if Dessalines had yet dropped a torch into one of those tar barrels or not, and it seemed to me that was the only news that mattered.

There was no news of Port-au-Prince either, or none that came to the ears of Riau. None that I could trust. Because I wanted to take the long way around Port-au-Prince, I rode my horse to Croix des Bouquets, but this way was not long enough. I ought to have gone further into the plain of Cul de Sac, and passed around Croix des Bouquets in the open country, instead of trying to ride through the town, though that way was a little shorter. There were men of the Third Demibrigade who stopped me in the square. I told them I was carrying messages for Toussaint, but I did not have any letter to show them by that time, only the words that Toussaint had stored in my head.

Now my intention was to try again to carry those words to Laplume in the south, because it seemed to me that maybe I had been wrong not to have done it sooner. These men of the Third did not arrest me, but they would not let me pass, or not until I had come before their commander. They were tired and dirty and stained with mud and sweat, and one of them had brown bloodstains splattered on his shirt, so I thought they must have been in some fighting not long ago.

It was as well to rest my horse, I thought, since it did not seem I could do anything different at that time, and find him some water and some grain. While I was doing these things I thought about the *hatte* which Toussaint kept across the border, where we had been not long ago. So many fine horses were raised and trained there, but it seemed a long way off to Riau now. I knew I would have to make this horse last. In the days to come I would not be able to get another, unless I had the luck to capture a horse in the fighting.

The commander they brought me to was Lamartinière, of course, and it was well that he knew Riau. He called me to eat with him at his officers' table, because it was night by the time they brought me to him. Lamartinière wanted to know everywhere I had been since I left him last, and especially if I had seen Toussaint in any of those places. I told him only that I had been to Dessalines at Saint Marc, and that I did not yet know what Dessalines was going to do. I did not tell him anything more than that, but Lamartinière seemed satisfied with my answer.

Lamartinière was angry and ashamed that night, and I think that maybe he was a little afraid too. The General Boudet had beaten him at the Fort Piémont, as I had thought was going to happen, and driven him out of Port-au-Prince later that same day, as far as Croix des Bouquets where I found him. So he had not been able to defend Port-au-Prince as he'd sworn he would, and he had not burned it either. The French *blancs* had it now, with its roofs and its stores. Lamartinière was not afraid of French *blanc* soldiers or their general. He was ready to fight them again as soon as he might. I believed he would have fought ten thousand Frenchmen himself all alone sooner than he would face Toussaint, when he had not done the thing Toussaint had ordered.

It seemed to me from what Lamartinière said that the French soldiers had not left any strength at Léogane, since they were all busy running up the road to Port-au-Prince from where I had last seen them. I thought that I could go on my way the next morning, and pass through the mountains above Léogane by paths that the *blanc* soldiers would not know, and so go on to the south to find Laplume, or maybe I would meet Jean-Pic again, with the bands of Lamour Dérance. That was the thought I took into my sleep that night, and when I woke at dawn I was ready to ride, but the sound that woke me was Dessalines coming into Croix des Bouquets with all his division and more men besides.

I think Lamartinière was not ready to see Dessalines so soon, after what Riau had said the night before. But many, even those who know him well, could be surprised by Dessalines's speed in moving his men, when they were many and on foot, and often bringing cannon. Dessalines and Lamartinière were alone in a room for a little time, and their faces looked swollen when they came out, so I thought that Dessalines must be angry that Port-au-Prince had not been burned.

Maybe he was carrying that anger from Toussaint, because half of Toussaint's honor guard was with Dessalines that day, and those men had not been there when I left Saint Marc the day before. Almost a thousand men of the guard were there, though not Guiaou or Couachy, or a few others that I knew. Riau knew the commander, Morisset, and we spoke a little together while Lamartinière was alone with Dessalines. Morisset had seen Toussaint at Gonaives, and thought that he might now be in Ennery, though he could not be certain. He knew that Dessalines had come with Toussaint's order, to see if there might still be a way to destroy Port-au-Prince.

I stayed with Morisset when Lamartinière came out of the room with Dessalines. There were some other officers there too, and the camp women brought us coffee and some bananas for us to eat. The officers were all talking about what it would be best to do; only I, Riau, kept silent, only listening. While all this talk was happening, a messenger came to say that General Boudet had come out of Port-au-Prince with a lot of soldiers to attack us here at Croix des Bouquets. He was not very far away at all, so he might reach us in one hour.

Lamartinière's head grew very hot then. He wanted to go out at once and meet Boudet on the road. It seemed to me that his idea had reason, even if it came out of the heat of his head, because I thought Boudet might not know that Dessalines had come with all his men, and that would be a surprise to him, and one that he would not like very much.

But Dessalines said no. It was the order of Toussaint, he said, not to meet the French *blanc* soldiers in the open country. We must not give them a battle on the plain.

At this, Lamartinière grew even hotter. "Maybe Old Toussaint has lived too long," he said. "Maybe his blood is thin, and he gives this counsel out of fear."

At that, Dessalines stroked his snuffbox and smiled in the way I never liked to see. "I wonder if you would be speaking so if 'Old Toussaint' was near enough to hear you." Dessalines looked at Morisset when he said this, and Lamartinière lost a little of the color from his face. I knew that Morisset would not carry any such tale back to Toussaint, but maybe Lamartinière was not certain of it.

Dessalines turned his snuffbox over and looked at something on the bottom of it. "Toussaint has not grown old for nothing," he said. "Toussaint has outlived many of his enemies." He clicked the snuffbox down on the table top. "It is not counsel that Toussaint gives," he said, and made his voice a little stronger. "It is an order."

I was thinking of the letter Dessalines had shown me in Saint Marc before, and I thought that Toussaint had not written this letter in weakness or fear. I thought too from what I had seen already that it was better not to fight these French *blanc* soldiers as they would choose to fight, and I thought Lamartinière ought to know this too, from the beating he had taken from them in their meetings so far. But I did not say anything about it then.

We moved quickly out of Croix des Bouquets and set the buildings of the town on fire as we were going, though it was not much more than a crossroads then. Dessalines's men, and Toussaint's guard, had been traveling fast through much of the night, and they had not rested for more than an hour at Croix des Bouquets, but they went quickly just the same. All that day we burned our path across the plain of Cul de Sac, which was rich country, setting afire the fields and houses. Riau felt pleasure in burning the cane and the big houses of the *grand blancs* that Toussaint had brought back to the country to work their land for him. But Dessalines also took care to burn the little houses of the field workers, those men who were made to work with the hoe. He did this so that they would have to follow him, with their women and children and whatever of their goods they might save. They would not have followed Dessalines for love.

The French *blanc* soldiers were coming on our trail the whole time, as fast as they could follow through the fire and smoke, through country they did not know well, though it was open country and simple enough. Lamartinière kept to the rear with men with long guns who fired on the *blanc* soldiers from a distance and then fell back. This shooting slowed the French down only a little, since our men were commanded not to stand and fight. When the *blanc* soldiers saw they were not going to get any battle, they turned their hands to putting out the fires. Some of the field hands saw them doing this, and they went back to join them. That looked bad to me when I saw it. I thought from the first that Dessalines was wrong to burn their houses, and that his action might cost more than it won.

All the *blancs* from the plantations on that plain we rounded up like they were cattle, and made them hurry along with us toward the mountains in the east. Dessalines did not kill any of them at first, but only took them prisoner. It was hard marching for them that day. There were some hundreds of them, and none had time to get anything to carry with them except whatever was near their hands when they were taken. There were women and children too, of course, and no food or water for them that day. In the heat of the afternoon some of them began to fall down on the ground, crying that they could not go any farther, but when Dessalines ordered these to be shot, the rest of them went on somehow.

When we had reached the shadow of Morne Cabrit, Dessalines gave all these prisoners to Morisset and Toussaint's guard, to take them over the mountains and hold them at Mirebalais, until Toussaint would say what to do with them. At the foot of the mountain he left Lamartinière with the men of the Third on the Habitation Jonc, which he had not burned, telling him he could stand to fight the French *blanc* soldiers as long as he wanted to if they came there.

Then Dessalines took the rest of his men, and Riau also, across the pass at Morne Lacoupe. He meant to cross the Rivière Froide and get onto the low road between Port-au-Prince and Léogane, but the General Boudet had seen ahead of this plan, so that we found French *blanc* soldiers waiting for us on the other bank of the river, many—we had not known there were so many *blanc* soldiers in all the world. Also, a lot of the field hands had joined the soldiers, because Dessalines had been driving them so hard in that part of the country that they thought the French *blancs* could not be any worse, and maybe they would be better.

Dessalines was so angry at this that his two jaws ground his teeth together and bubbles came out the corners of his mouth. But the day was not done yet. We left the bank of the Rivière Froide and went into the mountains again. The French *blanc* soldiers did not try to follow, because the night was coming. They stayed on their side of the river. Still Dessalines kept moving, by trails so narrow and so steep the riders must get down and pull their horses from the front and push them from behind. There was no place for all the foot soldiers on these trails, so they crossed by climbing vines that hung down the cliff walls, with their cartridge boxes and their guns swinging from their backs.

That was the way that I, Riau, had meant to go alone, but Dessalines crossed it with all his army in the dark. At dawn we came into Léogane and found there were not any French *blanc* soldiers waiting for us there at all.

It was the same at Léogane as it had been at Port-au-Prince before, between the white general Agé and Lamartinière. There was a white commander at Léogane who wanted to let the French *blanc* soldiers into the town at once, but his second, who was named Pierre Louis Diane, had said that they must wait until an order came from Dessalines. When Diane met us he smiled and laughed, but his voice shook a little, and his hands too. He had not really believed any order would come, but here was Dessalines himself.

Dessalines sent twenty-five horsemen out the road to Port-au-Prince, to see if that way was open now, and I, Riau, went with them to see what they would learn. By this time I thought I had seen the idea behind Dessalines's head. He had drawn Boudet, with many of his men, to the north of Port-au-Prince into the plain of Cul de Sac. If Boudet was still there, trying to learn the passes to Mirebalais where the *blanc* prisoners had been taken, or maybe fighting Lamartinière at Habitation Jonc, then maybe Dessalines could get into Port-au-Prince from the south, where no one would expect him to be, and burn the town at last as Toussaint had ordered, while the French *blanc* soldiers left it unguarded.

But there were still more French *blanc* soldiers on the road—many dragoons, fresh and well mounted, with red feathers in their helmets that swam in the air like flames. They were riding down toward Léogane as if they would attack us there. When Dessalines had got this news, he was even angrier than he had been the day before on the banks of Rivière Froide. Still, the day was not done yet. Dessalines had his men take all the cannons of Léogane, and all the powder and shot from the magazine, and any other stores they could carry, and bring them to the mountains of Cabaret Quart.

At the same time Dessalines went, with the help of Pierre Louis Diane, from one house to another through all the town, and swept all the *blancs* who lived there into the square of Léogane, which was a quiet place shaded by many tall old trees. When they were all brought there, one of the *blancs* stepped out from the others and began to read the proclamation of Napoleon Bonaparte, which said that the free black men of Saint Domingue were never to be made slaves any more, but he had not read more than the first words before Dessalines changed his snuffbox from one hand to the other, and the *blanc* was shot.

I wondered what Dessalines meant to do with all these people. There were four hundred of them nearly, and he could not take them back across the mountains the way we had come.

There was one man among them all, Fossin, who knew me well enough to catch my eyes, with his own eyes pleading, though he did not dare to speak, after the shooting of that other *blanc*. I knew him because he was one of the *blancs* who spied for Toussaint on the others, and sometimes I had received his messages. Also his wife was a *blanche* thought beautiful by many, and one of those who came in secret to Toussaint's bed, to get some advantage for their families, or because they were drawn to his power. She was not there at Léogane that day, which was a lucky thing for her.

I took Fossin away from the others and brought him before Dessalines, and I explained that Toussaint would not want this one *blanc* to be mistreated. Dessalines looked at him for a long time, his fingers turning the snuffbox around and around, but in the end he said that Fossin was free to leave Léogane and go out and meet the soldiers on the road, if that would be his choice. Out of four hundred *blancs* that day in Léogane, he was the only one to go free.

The drum rolled then, and we began marching the crowd of *blancs* out of the square and through the streets and finally into the wide bed of the river. Our men were close around them with their bayonets for all that way, though it was not long, and the little snare drum kept rolling. At the place where we stopped the riverbed was a shoal of dry stones, because there had been no rain in this part of the country. There was no shade either, except along one bank where a little trickle of water still ran in a deeper part of the streambed. But we had stopped the prisoners in the full sun, and it was so hot I could feel the river stones burning through the soles of my boots.

Our men began to go among the prisoners and take whatever they had that was valuable. Of course they were not so willing to give up their goods, and many had hidden things in their clothing, so that the men went groping all over them for lumps that might be watches or coins or jewelry. Then, when some of the women's clothes were torn, and their pink skin bare, and they were screaming, some of our men wanted to take pleasure from them. But Dessalines shook his head, only a little. Then Pierre Louis Diane caught one of the women by her hair and pulled her head back to cut her throat, and I, Riau, did the same with another, spinning her quickly down on the stones so her blood would not spatter on my clothes.

I did not kill anyone else after that, but stood apart and watched the killing. I did not really want to watch, but Dessalines would have not liked for anyone to turn his face away. It was all done with bayonets and knives, to save powder and shot, so it was a slow and ugly thing.

Now, long before this time, Riau had done such killings too, and delighted to paint himself in the blood of *blancs*, or to use their women and kill them after. But in that time, all *blancs* appeared as monsters to me. They were nothing like me or other children of Guinée. They were only *loup-garou* sent to torture us out of the life of our bodies. Also, on those days of blood long before, I often had my spirit in my head, so it was not I, Riau, who killed, or if it was, I killed to feed the *lwa*. And afterward, what I remembered of what Riau had done would be like a story told about the doings of another.

Those times seemed a long way off, almost as far as Guinée itself, which Riau could hardly remember. Since then I had come to know a few *blancs*, like the doctor, and even his friend the Captain Maillart, and some few others, who did not seem to be monsters out of another world, but persons like myself. Among the hundreds screaming in their blood there in the riverbed, I thought there must be at least a few like that. And my spirit was very far away!—so far I could not recall it. I was alone in my head as I watched the killing, with my two eyes drying up as I forced them to stay open, wondering if Ogûn would ever dance in my head again. It seemed I was alone more and more in this way, and I wondered what was to blame for it. I thought of the service I owed to the spirit of Moyse, and of all the things Quamba said that I must do, but it seemed evil to think of those things in that place, as if I had no right any more even to touch them with my thoughts.

When the killing was finished, a horn was blown and our men began to form up slowly, to march out of the riverbed. Some of the men were in blood frenzy, with spirits mounted in their heads, and these walked as in a dream, with their bloody knives hanging down from their hands. The rest of the men could not meet each other's eyes. They were all very tired from the work they had done, and I was tired too, though I had only been watching. I thought I had come a long way out of the good road, and all my turnings had been wrong.

As we were leaving, some bony yellow dogs came from the other bank down into the riverbed and lowered their heads shyly to begin licking the blood that still smoked on the stones. I looked back over my shoulder once and saw that some long-eared black pigs had joined them, grunting as they rooted among the bodies and turned the soft parts upward with their snouts. Then I wished that a flood would come, and wash it all away into the ocean. It was for that the work had been done in the riverbed, but there would be no rain today—the sky above us was empty.

Dessalines set fire to Léogane before we left it. He had saved enough powder to blow up the magazine. He was taking his army to Cabaret Quart. Some men had deserted during the hard march the day before, and others would slip away today, but not Riau. Dessalines knew me too well—I would be missed. I went to him then and said again how Toussaint had given me words for Laplume, and that I would not get a better chance than I had now to go to the south to find him. Dessalines was ready to let me go, and he told me I should bring him word of Laplume's reply, if it was possible, because he had already heard a rumor that Laplume might be meaning to sell himself to the French.

I went more slowly now, to spare my horse. To the south of Léogane there was no fighting, and none of the French *blanc* soldiers had come there yet. People had heard something of the fighting at Port-au-Prince, and they wanted to get news from me when they saw my captain's uniform. At the end of that day, I got for myself a plate of rice and beans and boiled plantain, and a bed for that night in a clay *case,* by telling the people of that *lakou* part of what I knew. I told them Dessalines had destroyed Léogane, and that Papa Toussaint would be coming soon to drive all the *blanc* soldiers into the sea, but I did not say anything about the killing of the four hundred *blancs* in the riverbed.

In the light of morning I saw that my boot soles were sticky with the blood from the killing the day before. The blood was coated with dust from the roads, so it was not very plain what it was, but I knew. At the first stream I crossed that day, I got down and washed my boots until there was nothing left of that old blood, and went on with the leather damp against my feet. In the afternoon I found the camp of Lamour Dérance, which had moved from the place it had been before, but not too far. Lamour Dérance himself had gone away, maybe to parley with Lafortune, who had another band of maroons not too far off, or to see Laplume himself, or maybe he had even gone to Port-au-Prince, Jean-Pic said to me.

This I was surprised to hear, with all the French *blanc* soldiers there, and after all the fighting I had seen. But Jean-Pic told me then that the French general Boudet had stopped asking for the passports. That news surprised me even more, and made me wonder, and I saw it had done the same to Jean-Pic and all his people.

Since Toussaint had bound the men who were not soldiers to work on the plantations with the hoe, he had also ordered that any man must have a paper if he would leave his plantation to travel on the road, and especially to enter a big town like Port-au-Prince, each man must have such a passport paper to show. It had been the same in slavery time. No slave could travel without some piece of writing from his master, but in those days the rule was not very much respected. Under Toussaint it was much more strict, and truly it was hard for a man to go anywhere at all without a passport paper, unless he had a soldier's uniform like Riau, or ran away to be with the maroons as Jean-Pic had done. It was such strictness that had made Moyse rise up, with a great many people pushing him from below. For a French general to do away with those passports was surprising, and I thought it might be some kind of trick. But Jean-Pic said one might go in and out of Port-au-Prince very freely now. He had not been there himself, but he knew some who had.

Next day I rode still further to the south, until I found Laplume at last, where he had stopped near Miragoâne. He did not have all his troops with him, only a few horsemen from the Twelfth Brigade, and he was coming out of Port-au-Prince himself. I was careful in my first words to him, because I knew he must have had some parley with the French. But I did let him know that I was carrying a message from Toussaint.

"Well, Captain Riau," Laplume said. "It is not the first time you have come to us with something from Toussaint." He folded his arms and looked at me then, and not in the friendliest way. But I did not have any great reason to lower my eyes before Laplume.

I had known Laplume from a long time before, when he was second in Dieudonné's band, and before that too, when the three of us had all been in the band of Halalou. Later on, when I was with Toussaint again, and the English had taken Port-au-Prince and meant to take the rest of the country, Toussaint began to worry that Dieudonné might sell himself to the English. Then Toussaint sent both Riau and Guiaou to Dieudonné, with a letter which argued that he ought to come over to Toussaint instead of going to the English. But before Dieudonné could decide what to do, Laplume had made a plot against him. Laplume's men jumped on Dieudonné while he was sleeping, and they chained him up as a prisoner, so it was Laplume who brought his band to Toussaint, but Dieudonné died soon after, wrapped up in his chains.

These things were true, but in all that history there was no more shame for Riau than for Laplume. In the end Laplume was the first to lower his eyes. He played with the braid on the cuff of his uniform coat, then moved his hand to cover the round Commissioner's medal which once belonged to the *blanc* Sonthonax, who gave it to Laplume just before he left our country.

"Look well, Riau," he said. "You see that we are both officers in the French army, do you not?"

"It is so," I said. Though Laplume was a General of Brigade, and Riau only a captain.

"These new soldiers who have come out from France respect our ranks," Laplume said. "Both mine and yours. If Toussaint fights them, it shows that Toussaint is trying to keep power for himself. Look around you—it is peaceful here, but in Le Cap, I hear, everything has been burned again, because Toussaint would not accept the French . . ."

"And at Léogane, too," I said.

Laplume looked at me sharply then, and I guessed he had not yet known about Léogane.

"Burned for nothing," Laplume said finally. "Nothing but the ambition of Toussaint. And his rule has been harder upon us than what the French would bring. They have not come to bring back slavery—I have this promise from themselves."

"So it is done, then," I said.

"Yes," said Laplume. "It is done."

I saw it would be a great blow to Toussaint, that Laplume was already sold to the French. Laplume had commanded more than three thousand men at Les Cayes, and he controlled the way into all of the Grande Anse, which was almost a third of the country. That was the old country of Rigaud. The French would have the use of that land now, with the seaports and all the goods, except maybe for Jérémie, where Dommage was for Toussaint.

"You see, I am now speaking for the French," Laplume said. "It is no different than before, only that I accept the authority of the Captain-General Leclerc. Have I done you any harm, Riau? You may come along to Les Cayes with me, or go to Port-au-Prince to see for yourself."

I chose to go to Port-au-Prince then, but after all I was not so sure that my uniform would be a good passport there. At a crossroads south of the town, I bought two of the big woven panniers the *marchandes* use to carry their goods on their donkeys—big enough to hide the leather saddle on my horse. I put my uniform coat and shirt and boots and my weapons and even the bridle of the horse into these panniers, and covered them up with green oranges. Only my pistols were just at the top, where I could reach them quickly. I went into Port-au-Prince on foot, leading the horse by a rope halter, as if I were going to market. There were French *blanc* soldiers at the gates, but no one asked for a passport paper or paid me any attention at all.

I walked around the town then, leading my horse. It had not been very much damaged in the fighting of a few days before, and everything seemed peaceful, as Laplume had said. I wondered if it was true that Le Cap was burned again. I felt lighter and cooler without my uniform coat to wear, and it was good to have my feet free of the pinch of those boots for a little while. Also, I sold some of my oranges for more than I had given for them, in a market under some trees in a corner of the Place Royale, not far from the government buildings. All those trees had nailed to them a proclamation of Napoleon Bonaparte. It was addressed to all the people of Saint Domingue, no matter what their color was, and it began by saying that all of us were equal before men and before God. This was the same paper the *blanc* had tried to read in the square of Léogane before he was shot.

I felt eyes on my back while I was reading this paper, and when I looked across the panniers, I saw the Captain Maillart, drinking with some other French officer at a table outside a tavern door. I stood mostly hidden from his view, but Maillart knew something about horses, and he must have seen that mine was not really a packhorse. He got up then and came toward me, and said in a booming voice: "How much do you want for half a dozen of those oranges?"

He was a little drunk already, and I smelled the rum on him when he came around to my side of the horse, but he was still in his senses.

"What are you playing at, Riau?" he said to me more quietly. "I didn't know what had happened to you. What is this masquerade?"

Maillart put his hand on my bare shoulder in a friendly way, but I did not know how to answer him.

"You see everything is all right," he said and turned his eyes for a moment to the proclamation nailed to the tree. "Now get yourself dressed properly and come and have a drink with us." Then he took the oranges he had asked for, and went back to the table with the others.

It was not so much trouble to get back into my coat and my boots. Those other French officers had never looked my way. Before I went to their table, I looked back once more at the paper on the tree.

IF ANYONE TELLS YOU, "THESE FORCES HAVE COME TO TEAR AWAY OUR LIBERTY," REPLY, "THE REPUBLIC WILL NOT SUFFER THAT IT SHOULD BE TAKEN FROM US."

It seemed to me that Maillart believed these words, and I began to ask myself if Toussaint really disbelieved them.

15

"Uncle! Uncle! Tonton Antoine!" Sophie's was the first voice the doctor heard, as she came rushing toward them from the steps of the Thibodet *grand'case* with her heavy dark hair flying out behind her. She slammed into him as he swung down from the saddle, with nearly enough force to knock him from his feet. How she had grown! And she got her height from her father, so she was already almost as tall as he. The Thibodet enclosure was all confusion with the arrival of so many riders. Paul stood at a little distance, with his black friend Caco, and when Sophie had released the doctor he came up more shyly to greet his father. The doctor kissed him on both cheeks. Then Elise had appeared at the gallery railing, calling out, "Antoine! Isabelle! oh, thank God you are safe . . ."

Isabelle dismounted, sagging for a moment against the flank of her mare, then tottered toward the steps on her numb legs, as Elise came tripping down to embrace her. The wind was skirling around the ground, and a rogue gust peeled away the doctor's straw hat. Sophie ran after it and brought it back to him, laughing.

"All very touching, I am sure," said Cyprien, who remained in his saddle. "But where is Toussaint Louverture?"

The doctor squinted up at him through his dust-coated glasses. He ran the brim of his hat through his fingers. "I can't say for certain where he is himself," he said. "His house is a little way further on."

"Then we can't stop here," Cyprien said, glancing at Isaac and Placide, who sat their horses quietly.

"Oh, but you will," said the doctor, "if you don't want to drown."

Indeed the wind was bringing heavy clouds in quickly from the east, and the first fat drops were slamming down, raising little puffs of dust. One splashed into the bald center of the doctor's head. He remembered Cyprien vaguely from the Hédouville mission, and there'd been something about the captain then that he hadn't liked. Certainly he didn't much like the way Cyprien was looking at Sophie now. Nevertheless he stretched out his hand to him.

"Don't be hasty," he said. "Once the deluge starts, you won't be able to see as far as the end of your nose. If you wait out the rain here, we may still bring you to Sancey before dark."

Cyprien hesitated a moment more, then slid down from his horse, though without accepting the doctor's proffered hand. Isaac and Placide exchanged a quick glance, and then they too dismounted. Grooms were already coming out from the stables to take their horses from them.

"Then there will be peace after all," Elise was saying from her place at the foot of the gallery table. "In spite of everything."

The tale of Le Cap's burning seemed to have shaken her only slightly. Indeed her composure was such that the doctor wondered if she'd properly understood the news.

"Our mission is to achieve a peace, Madame," Placide said courteously. "And our resolve."

"Oh, I do not see how you can fail," Elise said, with a meaning look at her husband. Tocquet sat with his back to the railing, his eyes remote, rolling an unlit cheroot between his fingers. Behind him, a wall of rain came down.

"How well you have grown," Elise said, returning to Isaac and Placide. "I would hardly have known you—you are such young men now."

Placide smiled easily and replied with some nicely turned compliment. The doctor studied them, not much attending to what they said. Nanon sat by him, leaning just slightly against his shoulder, her hand warm in his beneath the table.

The sheen of the boys' dress uniforms had been a little blunted by the dust of the road. Isaac was the darker, shorter, and thicker; Placide a head taller, distinctly more slender, his tone a rich coppery red. One might not have taken them for brothers at all, and it had long been rumored that Placide, born before his mother's legal marriage to Toussaint, had been fathered by another, possibly even by a white man. But the doctor thought he saw resemblances now, in the long oval of Placide's face, the shape of his long-fingered hands, even the habit of floating a palm across his mouth between his phrases, as if to hide a smile. And Toussaint had always given him a first-born's preference.

All around them the rain came rushing down, pouring over the gallery steps like a waterfall. The doctor stretched his neck to look over the railing; below, the lily pool he'd designed and dug was overflowing its border of stones, drenching the turf around it. Captain Daspir, munching contently on a concoction of desalted cod Elise had cunningly expanded for the unexpected number, asked him some question about the flowers. The doctor scarcely paid attention to his own reply.

Five years since he had seen these boys, and they'd been as long apart from their mother and father. The invitation to send them to school in France was one which could not be refused. In effect, the boys had been given up as hostages. The doctor was one of the party that conveyed them from Ennery to Le Cap, where then-Commissioner Sonthonax had embarked them for the fatherland and the Collège de la Marche. Toussaint had seemed willing, even pleased to send them, then. Such an education was a privilege, after all, and one that opened the way to many advancements once the graduate returned to the colony. And in those days Toussaint had freely professed that the more French his sons should become, the better. Though later on, the doctor knew, he'd launched a couple of unsuccessful plots to get them back.

Now here they were. What would Toussaint think of them? Bedizened in their military ornaments, as yet unearned. Certainly he could retain them permanently now, if he chose—if in fact he was here at Ennery. If he was not, his order would suffice. Ennery was Toussaint's personal redoubt—though they'd seen no military movement as they came through the narrow passes to this place, no one could come or go from here against his wish.

The doctor wondered if the young French captains knew as much, or if Leclerc had realized it—in their brief encounters, the Captain-General had struck him as a little ill-informed. A crash from inside the house, followed by Zabeth's voice sharply raised, cut off his train of thought. The older children, shut up by the rain, had been chasing each other around the inside of the house for the last hour. Isabelle jumped up hurriedly and went to see what was the matter. Nanon made to rise as well, but the doctor gave her fingers a surreptitious squeeze to keep her by him. Soon enough the giggling indoors was stifled. Weary from the long ride and groggy from the meal that followed, the doctor sank deeper in his chair and dozed.

The night was clear after the rain, clean and sweet-smelling as fresh laundry. Saddlesore as they were, the party that had come down from Le Cap continued toward Sancey on foot. All but a couple of their cavalry escort were left behind, snoring on cots or pallets made up for them in the cane mill. Elise had convinced the French captains that there was nothing to fear between Thibodet and Sancey. The older children had been allowed to come along and were making a festival of it. Paul

and Robert and Sophie, with Caco and Yoyo too, were racing and tagging each other in circles around the path, shrieking when they surprised each other from the shadows.

In the light of the oblong moon, Isaac and Placide watched their play.
The doctor thought that Isaac, especially, might have liked to join in the
game. But he was on his dignity now and kept to the path, which was a
little slippery from the rain, hitching up his belt to keep the tip of his
ceremonial sword from dragging in the mud.

They came to the crossroads beneath the mango trees and, with some
splashing and tittering from the children, picked their way across the
stream. As they passed through the hedge onto Sancey lands, the doctor
noticed a couple of shadows slipping away from them, over the hill.
Their incursion would not go unreported. But no one waited for them
behind the Sancey *grand'case* except an old woman dozing on a woven
stool, her feet stretched toward the dying coals of a cook fire. She
jumped up, stared at Isaac and Placide in the moonlight, then clapped a
hand over her mouth and ran for the *grand'case* as fast as her legs would
take her.

The front approach to the Sancey *grand'case* was considerably more
impressive than the jumble of outbuildings and shanties to the rear. The
house loomed over them in the moonlight. Even Cyprien seemed a little
abashed as he stood below the portico, clearing his throat to announce
their visit. But before he had pronounced a word, the front door popped
open and Suzanne Louverture appeared, flanked by two servants holding tall candlesticks. The boys met her halfway up the stairs; the three of
them clumped together in a tight embrace.

Coisnon, who carried a small valise, put his foot on the first step and
turned an inquiring look on the two French captains.

"Go up," said Cyprien. "We'll wait where we are."

Suzanne was already leading the boys toward her lighted doorway,
her arms around their waists, and theirs across her shoulders. Like soldiers supporting a wounded comrade, Daspir thought, except it seemed
more that she was supporting them. Then they had passed through the
door, and Coisnon with them. The candle flames glowed inside the
jalousies of a room just off the entryway.

"But Toussaint," Cyprien said. "Is he here? Or why does he not show
himself?"

The doctor only shrugged in the darkness, and no one else had any
answer. Then a girl's wailing erupted in the shrubbery at the side of the
house, and Sophie flung out of the bushes to bury her face in her
mother's bodice.

"Now then, what can this be?" Elise cupped her head with one hand.

"Oh, see how late it is," said Isabelle. "We ought to get these children
home to bed."

With that, the women began to collect their flock for the return to Thibodet. Only Cigny and Daspir lingered behind, below the portico of the *grand'case*. The two cavalrymen of their escort stood at a polite distance from them.

"Ah," said Cyprien at length. "We may as well go back with the others. Find ourselves some place to sleep."

"Ought we to let them slip from our charge so easily?" Daspir asked.

"This is an effort of diplomacy," Cyprien said in the tone of one reciting orders. "The sons of Toussaint are to be treated with all consideration—not as prisoners, nor as hostages. It is hoped that through their persuasive influence and the power of their sentiments, their father's loyalty may be bound to France." Cyprien smiled as he turned to go. "Coisnon is with them, in any case, and he has been schooled to the task."

"Wait," Daspir hissed.

A lamp came alight in another room, throwing a shadow on the blinded window. Daspir touched Cyprien's hand and pointed. It looked as though a shadow hand removed the shadow of a bicorne hat, leaving a bare-headed profile to waver on the slats of the jalousies: heavy underslung jaw and high sloping forehead.

"Do you see that?" Daspir hissed.

"Are you so sure?" But Cyprien was whispering too. They went on watching. With the light breeze that rose behind them, the shadow image rippled in the window frame.

"If you *are* certain," Cyprien said, forcing his more supercilious tone, "then now is your chance to collect on our bet."

"No," said Daspir. As he spoke the shadow image dissolved into a blur. Then nothing, as the lamp was snuffed. Had he really seen anything at all? But the wet and heavy darkness all around him seemed suffused with invisible presences. Daspir recalled what the doctor had said, in the garden of Habitation Héricourt. *What you don't see means more than what you do.* The doctor was well away down the path already, with the others, and Daspir felt an urgency to overtake them.

When Sophie's most violent crying had subsided, Elise drew her a little way from the others on the path, to ask her privately what was the matter. But the girl only stiffened and pulled away from her; she would not give up the source of her distress.

"I think you're only tired," Elise said.

"*I'm not at all tired!*" Sophie shook her hair forward to hide her face and went stalking ahead of them all on the path.

Elise kept her distance from her daughter, resisting the sourness that spread over her own mood. These tempests of unreasoning emotion had come more frequently, the last few months. Let it go—it was too lovely a night to spoil. She wished Tocquet were with her, but he'd chosen to remain at home, aloof.

By the time Elise had reached the hallway of the Thibodet *grand'case*,

Sophie had already slammed into her bedroom, forgetting that she shared it, for tonight, with Héloïse. Isabelle stood hesitating, just outside the door.

"Best leave her to it," said Elise. "She's in some pet."

"I wonder if Robert has been teasing her too much," Isabelle said, looking toward the room where Paul and Robert were meant to sleep.

"I'll just look in." Elise cracked open Sophie's door, just wide enough to slip inside, then pulled it to behind her. Sophie was rigid on her bed, feigning sleep, though not convincingly. But at least she had not wakened Héloïse, who slept peacefully with her round face turned to the stripes of moonlight spilling through the jalousies.

She looked for Isabelle in Paul's room, but only the two boys were there, scuffling and muttering in muffled voices as they jokingly disputed the space in the bed they were to share. Elise ordered them to quiet down, then withdrew. Isabelle had gone to the room of Nanon's twins, and was kneeling at Gabriel's bedside, her finger clasped in his sleeping fist. Elise moved toward her in the striped moonlight. She wanted to let Isabelle know she understood—though she did not understand, entirely. But as she floated across the floor, she saw Nanon waiting quietly in a corner, out of the light, and was repelled by a flash of jealousy. These two now kept a secret deeper than any Elise had ever shared with Isabelle, and they had been keeping it close for quite some time.

"I'm sorry," Elise said, too loudly and rather coldly, and turned to leave the room. But Isabelle overtook her in the hall and caught hold of her hand. Elise relaxed, then returned the pressure. She thought she'd try some other subject.

"Is it *really* all destroyed?" she said. "Your house and mine?"

"With all Le Cap, from one end to the other."

"Ah," said Elise. "We had it such a little time."

Isabelle pulled her toward the front doorway. "It's only buildings," she said, swinging her hands toward the moonlight beyond the gallery. "And those can be rebuilt as well as burned."

Tonight Coisnon did not share quarters with Placide and Isaac, though Placide could still hear his stentorian snoring from the room next door. Their tutor was exhausted, from the arduousness of their travel and the unfamiliarity of everything they'd encountered on their way. Isaac was in the same state, though his sleeping breath was quiet, just barely audible through Coisnon's wall-muffled snoring and the ticking of the clock on the mantel.

Placide himself lay calm but wakeful, though he had every right to be weary himself. They'd spent some joyful hours with their mother, who'd insisted on serving them a second supper. Afterward she'd taken pleasure in showing them over the house, which was much more elaborately furnished than any residence Placide had known in the colony. He could remember when the five of them had shared a one-room *case* at Habitation Bréda (though Isaac had probably forgotten those days), and their lodgings around Saint Michel and Saint Raphael, where Toussaint had sent them for shelter from the first months of the fighting, had not been much better. Perhaps Isaac was not so much impressed—the *grand'case* of Sancey was no palace in comparison to the Tuileries—but everything here spoke to Placide of his father's sagacity and power.

Beside the clock on the mantel (the mantel itself no more than an ornamental shelf, as there was no need for a bedroom fireplace in this climate) there stood among other smaller *bibelots* a gray-and-green vase decorated with images of certain battle triumphs of Toussaint Louverture—victories over the Spanish and the English, rendered in the classically heroic manner. This article had been commissioned and presented to him as a compliment by some French general. Isaac had been fascinated with the vase, earlier that night, and had taken it to turn in his hands and study very closely.

Placide would have liked a closer look now, but fatigue and a growing somnolence held him in his bed. The clock ticked to the swing of its pendulum. Above the face it had a dial on which revolved a painted sun, smiling down on scenes of a European landscape. Then it seemed to be beating faster, faster, triple time—

Placide snapped upright in the bed, realizing that what he heard was the beat of shod hooves in the drive outside. He jumped into his trousers and in a flash was out the front door—his mother only a pace or two behind him. A squadron of cavalry had pulled up in the oval drive below the gallery, and the men were just beginning to get down from their horses, their figures dark and crisp in a wide spill of moonlight. There was his father, his silhouette plainly recognizable, between two banners hanging slack against their poles, sitting a horse Placide did not recognize.

"But where is Bel Argent?" Placide blurted. It seemed an idiotic question, but in his mental image of this moment, he must have placed his father astride the great white stallion.

Toussaint did not answer, or even appear to have heard. When they wrapped their arms around each other, Placide realized he was much the taller. How long could that have been so? Then Isaac rushed to join them with an impact that rocked them on their feet.

Awkwardly they climbed the stairs, loath to let each other go. They'd just begun to settle in the parlor opposite the entrance way, when Coisnon appeared in the doorframe, the remains of his gray hair sticking up around his bald spot like a tonsure. The white nightshirt fluttering around his shins was the reverse image of the black cassock he ordinarily wore by day.

"Father, it is Monsieur Coisnon, our preceptor." Isaac's voice creaked like a rusty gate, and when he turned toward Toussaint, it stopped altogether. But Coisnon stretched his arms theatrically wide.

"Is it Toussaint, the servant and faithful friend of France, who holds out his arms to me?"

"Could you ever doubt it?" Toussaint folded Coisnon into an embrace fully as powerful as the one he'd given his sons. Then he held the Frenchman at arm's length.

"So it is you who has schooled my boys," he said. "They have learned Latin. Mathematics." Toussaint's eyes narrowed slightly. "Engineering, perhaps, and something of the science of fortification."

"Indeed they have learned many things." Coisnon held his wide smile fixed. "But you shall hear all from themselves—they come to you now as faithful interpreters of the First Consul and the Captain-General Leclerc. Believe in their innocence and the purity of their sentiments—every word they say to you will be the truth."

As Coisnon was speaking, Placide noticed that, while several of Toussaint's staff officers were filtering in to stand in grave silence around the walls of the room, Isaac had slipped out. It was not long, however, before he returned, fully dressed now in the elegant uniform Napoleon had given him at the Tuileries, complete with pistols and sword. His entrance produced a little murmur, and Placide was aware for the first time of his own appearance: his nightshirt loose at the throat with its tail half in and half out of his crookedly buttoned trousers. He felt his mother draw in her breath and shift her weight on the sofa beside him, and he reached to take her hand.

Isaac stopped before Toussaint, and with a half-bow presented a small gold box in his two hands.

"*Mon père,* I am charged by the First Consul of France to bring this token to you."

Toussaint took the box onto his knee. He unfastened the catch and pushed up the lid, then unfurled a square of tricolor silk to reveal a letter. He ran his thumb under the fold to break the seal. After scanning a line or two, he refolded the paper and looked, smiling openly, up at Isaac.

"Come, sit by me, my son, and let me hear it from your lips."

With his left hand he drew Isaac down to the sofa beside him, and at the same time he took Placide's hand in his right. Isaac looked quickly around the room, and as Coisnon smiled and nodded, he spread the letter on his knee and began to read.

To Citizen Toussaint Louverture, General in Chief of the Army of Saint Domingue

Citizen General,
    The peace with England and all the other European powers which has just seated the Republic in the first place of power and grandeur, allows at the same time for the government to occupy itself with the colony of Saint Domingue. We send to you the citizen-general Leclerc,

our brother-in-law, in the capacity of Captain-General as well as First Magistrate of the colony. He is accompanied by a force suitable to assure that the sovereignty of the French people is respected. It is in these circumstances that we are pleased to hope that you are going to prove to us, and to all of France, the sincerity of the sentiments that you have constantly expressed in all the letters which you have written to us. We have conceived an esteem for you, and we are pleased to recognize and to proclaim the great services which you have rendered to the French people; if her flag flies over Saint Domingue, it is to you and the brave blacks that it is owed.

As he moved into this section of the letter, Isaac's voice grew warmer and stronger. Unconsciously he detached his hand from Toussaint's and began using it to make oratorical gestures.

Summoned by your talent and the force of circumstances to the highest command, you have done away with the civil war, put a brake on the persecution of various ferocious men, returned honor to religion and the cult of God, from whom everything emanates.

The constitution which you have made, while including many good things, also contains some which are contrary to the sovereignty of the French people, of which Saint Domingue forms a portion. The circumstances in which you have found yourself, surrounded by enemies on all sides, without the Metropole being able to help you or supply you, once rendered legitimate the articles of that constitution which otherwise might not have been; but today when circumstances are so happily changed, you will be the first to render homage to the sovereignty of the nation which counts you among the number of its most illustrious citizens, for the services you have rendered it, and for the talents and the force of character with which nature has gifted you.

Isaac coughed lightly, and cleared his throat. He read with an air of puzzlement now, his voice softer and less assured. His free hand settled on the couch, and Toussaint covered it lightly with his own. Now he seemed to be listening more attentively than before. In Placide's eyes, the whole room seemed to warp and bend toward Isaac's face and hands and the paper that they held.

Any different conduct would be irreconcilable with the idea we have formed of you. It would cause you to lose your numerous rights to the gratitude of the republic, and would dig beneath you an abyss which, in swallowing you up, might also contribute to the misfortune of those brave blacks, whose courage we love, and whom it would pain us to be obliged to punish for rebellion. We have made known to your children and to their preceptor the sentiments by which we are animated, and we are sending them back to you. Assist the Captain-General with your counsel, your influence, and your talents. What is it that you can desire? The liberty of the blacks! You know that in all the countries where we have been, we have given that to those people who did not already have it. Recognition, honor, and fortune! After the services which you have rendered, which you will still render in this circumstance, together with the particular sentiments which we have for you, you must not be uncertain of your recognition, your fortune, and the honors which await you.

Make it known to the people of Saint Domingue that the solicitude which France has always held for their happiness has often been powerless because of the imperious circumstances of war, that the men come from the Continent to agitate and nourish factions were the product of factions which themselves were then tearing up the fatherland; that henceforward peace and the force of the government will assure their prosperity and liberty. Say that, if for them liberty is the first of all goods, they cannot enjoy it except with the title of French citizens, and that any act contrary to the obedience which they owe to the fatherland, and to the Captain-General who is its delegate, would be a crime against the national sovereignty which would eclipse their services and would render Saint Domingue into the theater of an unfortunate war where fathers and children would tear out each other's throats. And you, General, reflect that if you are the first of your color who has arrived at such a great power, and if you are distinguished by your color's bravery and military talents, you are also, before God and ourselves, the first responsible for the conduct of your people.

If there have been illwishers who said to the individuals who played the first role in the troubles of Saint Domingue that we have come to look into what they have done during the times of anarchy, assure them that we will not inform ourselves of anything but their conduct during this final circumstance, and that we will not explore the past except to familiarize ourselves with the traits which distinguished them in the war which they maintained against the Spanish and the English who have been our enemies.

Count without reserve upon our esteem, and conduct yourself as one of the first citizens of the greatest nation in the world ought to do.

Paris, Brumaire 27, Year Ten [November 18, 1801]
The First Consul (signed) BONAPARTE

Isaac folded the letter and extended it to his father. Toussaint accepted it and shuffled the leaves, leaning his head back so that he seemed to squint at the paper from the bottoms of his eye sockets.

"But this letter is dated four months ago," he said suddenly. "The Captain-General Leclerc has been very dilatory in bringing it to me."

"There are of course the weeks of the sea passage," Coisnon said, with a downward turn of his palms. "And as you've heard, the First Consul would extend to you every friendship."

"Yes, while his representative, his *brother-in-law*, enters the country with fire and sword," Toussaint said shortly, "—and sends me no word of his own."

Coisnon opened his mouth, but seemed to think better of whatever he had thought to say. Toussaint, meanwhile, had laid the letter aside and picked up the box, which he opened and shut, examining its hinges and fastening. He wrapped the letter in the tricolor cloth, replaced it in the box, and snapped shut the catch. The small click echoed from the walls.

"Your voyage cannot account for so long a delay," he said, "nor even for half of it, as you must know. Have the sentiments of the First Consul changed since it was written? I cannot help but think so, given what I see—the actions of his subordinate who introduces fire and ruin here wherever his men go. And why does not the Captain-General write to me himself? Perhaps he has no explanation for his conduct."

Coisnon made to speak again, but Isaac was on his feet, gesticulating.

"*Mon père*, I can assure you that the regard of the First Consul for you—for us all!—is warm and sincere. His commitment to the liberty of our race is absolute. It is the pledge of all France. Has not liberty for us and for our people forever been the first and last of your intentions?"

Toussaint cocked back his head and caged his fingertips together. "You speak compellingly," he said. "But how are you so sure of this commitment?"

"Why—we have heard it made ourselves, out of his own lips. And . . . he bade us to dine with himself and his family, the Captain-General Leclerc, who is married to his own sister. Papa, she is known now as the greatest beauty in all France! Colonel Vincent was there as well, and others you have always trusted. And also . . ." Isaac looked down on his gaudy uniform, the wide polished belt with its ornate weapons, ". . . the First Consul presented us these arms with his own hands."

Somehow the sword and the chased pistols did not have the same glow they'd had at the Tuileries—though they were still brilliant, their radiance was overshadowed by the dimness of the candlelit room. Now Isaac looked to Placide for help, but Placide could say nothing. A weight lay on his lips. What unease had he felt that evening, during the grand dinner with Bonaparte and his connections? It must have been a premonition of how brittle all that show would seem, before his father.

"Well spoken." Now Toussaint was standing on the carpet, turning to include Placide at the same moment he brushed Isaac's epaulette. "But now you must go to your rest, my boys, for your journey has been long." He touched Isaac's cheek and turned from him, to raise Placide from the sofa with both hands. Stooping, Placide laid his face for a moment against his father's collarbone, and felt the quick, hard pulse of Toussaint's hands in the center of his back. Then he disengaged and, his eyes a little blurry, followed his brother out of the room. Suzanne, her face a mask, went after them.

On an inlaid chess table near the sofa stood a small bronze orary, designed to show the phases of the moon. The clockwork was oiled and the metal polished to a high shine, though Coisnon noticed that the arrangement of the spheres bore no relationship to this month's almanac.

Toussaint pushed at the gears so that the bronze balls moved a few inches on their levers. He looked cannily at Coisnon.

"Perhaps my sons now have a knowledge of such instruments."

"A little," Coisnon said. It was Placide who'd taken an independent interest in astronomy.

"General Louverture," Coisnon said. "Though the Captain-General Leclerc has not committed it to writing, I can tell you assuredly that he invites you to become his second in command. Go to him now! I *know* that you will understand each other." He paused. "I will remain here myself, if you accept it, as a guarantee of your security, and of the honesty of what I say."

"Monsieur." Toussaint's long fingers passed across his mouth, to flick away the shadow of a smile. "For the care you have given to my sons, I offer you all gratitude and my highest regard. And for your offer too, which is brave as it is generous. But it is now too late for what you propose. The war has already begun."

Coisnon said nothing, for he felt certain that these would be Toussaint's last words. The hand passed over the mouth again, and this time it seemed more like it was pressing down a pain. Toussaint had moved to leave the room, but he stopped and turned in the doorway.

"The people are possessed by a spirit of destruction," he said. "Do you know?—when such a spirit has been called, it will not depart before it has eaten its fill. My officers have already begun to sack and burn everything. But if Leclerc will stop his hostilities, I will do the same on my side."

Placide slept in a blank oblivion, as if he were hiding from fear. At the end of an hour he woke like a shot and rushed in his nightshirt to the window. Outside there was no alarming sound, only muttering and the chink of harness rings as Toussaint's escort remounted their horses. The standards wavered on their rods. His father was leaving then, already, and Placide felt riven by abandonment; after the years of separation, Toussaint had seen them no more than one hour. In the hollow of his father's collarbone, he had caught Toussaint's familiar scent, submerged but unforgotten during all their time in France—an odor of oiled leather and horsehair, and beneath these a faint musk all Toussaint's own.

His father was in the saddle now, supple and straight and ready to ride, revealed in a generous spill of moonlight. He turned to salute Placide with a sweep of his hat, and the release of one of his rare uncon- cealed smiles . . . as if he'd known Placide would be there at the window to watch him go, as if they shared a secret understanding.

Soon after first light, before the heat had risen, Elise and Isabelle, with Doctor Hébert and Captain Daspir, set out from Ennery toward Gonaives, on a mission to buy saltwater fish. Or it was this aspect of their journey which most intrigued Captain Daspir, who rode between the ladies, prattling of the fine points of cuisine. The doctor scarcely lis- tened to their talk. He was still stunned by yesterday's journey, but remained watchful as they rode now, though the way was quiet, out of the cleft in the green hills from Ennery onto the wider, tree-shaded road that ran to the south. From the mango sellers on the crossroads, he learned that Papa Toussaint had also come and gone from Ennery dur- ing the night just past.

A pale wisp of moon hung in the cloudless sky as they came onto the white dusty plain that, below Gonaives, rolled on into the Savane Désolée. They overtook files of market women, singing and moving with dancers' rhythm as they balanced their baskets toward the markets of the town. There was no sign of any alarm or disturbance on the road or in the square of Gonaives. Perhaps the black soldiers bunched on the street corners looked a little more edgy than usual, that was all.

Isabelle was hailed by an acquaintance, a refugee from Le Cap like herself, who'd seen Toussaint at mass that morning. Indeed, she said, he had only just left the church and sealed himself up in the head- quarters building on the next street, with a gang of secretaries, to draft his correspondence. There'd been a great scouring of the town for well-lettered folk, she said, with several hauled from their beds before dawn. Meanwhile, Toussaint had communed with his usual devotion, as Isabelle's ladyfriend hissed in a piercing whisper, "—the hypocrite, and when he went to the confessional, did he admit he is the author of our ruin?"

But Isabelle hushed her quickly, and the doctor moved a little away from these two as their voices fell, wondering why he had not been called to Toussaint's escritoire himself, where he often did assist in the black general's minute phrasing and rephrasing of the many, many let- ters he drafted and only sometimes sent. Maybe Toussaint had not known the doctor was at Ennery, or maybe he would not trust a white man with the correspondence of this moment. The doctor knew that Toussaint rarely missed a morning mass any day of the week, and that his faithful attendance was worthless to predict his actions for the rest of the day.

They rode on to the waterfront, where Elise and Isabelle bargained with the fishermen who'd come in with their dug-out canoes and little sailboats, for a supply of shrimp and sole and little Caribbean lobsters to be cooked for a banquet at Thibodet that night. With their purchase wrapped in layers of damp leaves to preserve its freshness, they started back the same way they had come. Two blocks past the pale brick headquarters building, they were overtaken by four of Toussaint's silver-helmed honor guard, escorting Monsieur Granville, who was the tutor of Toussaint's youngest son, Saint-Jean. Though Granville was also bound for Ennery, he was close-mouthed about his errand, tight and drawn about the lips. The doctor guessed that he must have served as Toussaint's scribe that morning, as he was sometimes pressed to do, and that the slightly eerie quietude of Gonaives had found its mirror in his mood.

When Captain Cyprien learned from Granville that the latter was charged with a letter from Toussaint to Leclerc, he said that they must set out at once.

"But the lobsters!" Daspir burst out, his stomach fisting at the news.

"Lobsters!" Cyprien said. "You may dream of lobsters on the road. No, don't trouble to dismount, we are leaving as soon as our own horses are brought up—now where are Toussaint's elder sons?"

Though Daspir did doze in the saddle through the afternoon and night as they rode through the mountain passes, no lobsters were featured in his dreams, though their imagined aroma did torment his waking thoughts. They did not stop for any meal at all, but ate dry, slightly molded ship's biscuit found in one of their saddlebags. There was little talk along the way, only Granville muttering that the citizens of Gonaives were all inspired with a terrible fear for their lives and property, by the news from the Le Cap refugees who'd begun to flood the town, in combination with Toussaint's inscrutable aspect when he'd passed rapidly, briefly among them on his way from headquarters to the church and back. Placide and Isaac said nothing at all. They were both bedraggled from exhaustion, and Daspir thought that nervousness had drained the blood from their dark faces.

The waxing moon lit their way from Limbé down to Le Cap. In the small hours of the morning they roused Leclerc from his camp in the scorched shell of the Governor's residence (where some reconstruction had already begun, Daspir noted). The Captain-General patted down his hair with one hand, smoothed back his silky blond sidewhiskers. He broke the seal on the letter and read Toussaint's reproaches—that Leclerc had come to replace him with cannon fire, and failed to deliver the letter of the First Consul until it was months out of date—these actions made doubtful, Toussaint complained, both his own services and the rights of his color.

Those rights impose upon me duties higher than those of nature; I am prepared to sacrifice my children to my color; I send them back to you in order that you will not believe that I am bound by their presence. Should they remain among the French, that will not hinder me from acting in the best interests of the inhabitants of Saint Domingue. It will require some time to decide which course I am to take; meanwhile I beg you—stop the march of your troops, that we may spare the effusion of blood, of which too much has already been spilled.

Leclerc crumpled the paper and threw it from him. He began to shout and stamp his foot, though his bare heel made no sound on the stone floor.

"This is nothing but a mask for outright rebellion—Toussaint is the most false and deceiving man who has ever lived on the earth. Does he not know that the south has submitted, and the northwest peninsula must soon yield to our attack? My General Boudet is on the march from Port-au-Prince and will not stop till he has reached the banks of the Artibonite. And Toussaint would give me his brats again—well, I send them back to him, but let him beware that I will come for them when it pleases me—with God's plenty of cannon fire, indeed. Take them away!"

Then Pauline's voice was heard from behind the curtain. "My dear, can you not speak more softly?—if you must speak at all. Or take your councils elsewhere—at this hour, really. You make it quite impossible for me to rest, and if Dermide wakes he will not sleep again before morning."

Leclerc wilted when he heard this; he looked at Placide and Isaac as if he'd take back a part of what he'd said. But Coisnon and Daspir were already leading them out of the room. Only Cyprien and Granville remained with the Captain-General.

"So," said Leclerc, with a glance toward the curtain. "He asks me for an armistice. Though my orders forbid me to cease any action of war once it has begun, I will allot him four days and no more. Within that time he may yet become my second in command, but if he has not submitted to that role by the fourth day, I will declare him *outlaw*." Gritting his teeth on these last words, Leclerc shot Cyprien a quelling look (though Cyprien was more than a head the taller), then sent the captain to fetch a secretary to copy out the gist of what he'd said.

Now Placide rocked half-dreaming in the saddle—they'd had no more than three hours' sleep before being sent back, with Leclerc's new dispatch, to Ennery. They'd been too exhausted, if not too discouraged, to whisper to each other from their pallets—besides, their guardians were near. Coisnon and Granville had remained at Le Cap, but Cyprien and Daspir were with them still, and always riding close enough to intercept any private contact. Nonetheless Placide knew that his brother was miserable and apprehensive. He himself was a little frightened, a little excited too.

And yet he dozed. He'd learned to ride at his father's hands, and now he'd ride his father's hours. He knew Toussaint's habit of laying a pillow across the saddle of Bel Argent if he meant to remain there for many days. Placide had no pillow, but his knees held him firmly in his seat and his back held straight, though his head rolled from side to side on the short tether of his neck, as he dozed and woke by fits and starts. The day passed flickering through the mountain passes: Haut Limbé, Plaisance, Pilboreau. At the crossroads the people lined the road to watch their passage, but there were no shouts or celebration this time, though the smiles were all as warm as before.

Toussaint was absent when they reached Ennery, but the impatience of Captain Cyprien was nothing to Suzanne. She fed her sons and put them to bed. Placide smiled inwardly at this—he hadn't known such treatment since he was a small boy, down with a summer fever. But fatigue swelled over him as soon as he stretched out, and he did sleep, and Isaac also, without a private word having passed between them.

In some small hour of the morning, Cyprien and Daspir roused them. Quietly, groggily, they remounted and rode out the drive from Sancey. Placide wondered if the French captains meant to elude Suzanne with this departure, but when he looked back over his shoulder he saw his mother standing on the steps, straight and still as a green sapling, holding a white candle in her hands.

The moon, just one day off the full, shone fitfully through hurrying clouds as they rode into Gonaives. At headquarters they learned from the sentries that Toussaint had gone to mass. Cyprien and Daspir rushed the boys to the church. The ceremony was entering its final phase: the priest chanting, elevating the Host. Though this service was wholly open to the public, most citizens of Gonaives preferred to observe at a more comfortable hour, so Toussaint was alone except for Morisset, a couple more officers of his suite, and a few old women shawled in black.

Captain Cyprien looked ready to interrupt, but Daspir drew him off with some murmured caution. Toussaint was kneeling at the altar rail. The Host was lowered to his tongue; meekly he pressed his lips to the chalice rim. While Placide hung back, Isaac crossed himself hastily and moved to kneel at his father's side, but Toussaint stopped him as he rose.

"If you have not made a good confession this day, Isaac," Toussaint said, and masked his smile with his right hand, "it is better that you wait to take the sacraments."

Both boys sat beside the father on the front bench as the service concluded. They left the church with him, following the cross. Cyprien and Daspir flanked them as they walked toward headquarters, but Toussaint stopped them in the building's anteroom.

"Leave us, please."

Cyprien looked as if he would argue; he was beginning to say something about duty and his commission, but Daspir edged him gently away.

"Let them be," Daspir said, as Toussaint and the boys mounted the stairs. "What can half an hour hurt? As you have said, it is a mission of diplomacy. And I hardly think they'll vanish from us now." He glanced around the low-ceilinged room, where members of Toussaint's guard were subtly checking the handles of their weapons.

"Come," Daspir said. "Let us go out—it's stuffy here."

Together the two captains crossed the narrow street and stood under the eave of the house opposite. A smell of roasting coffee through the slatted door behind them set all of Daspir's stomach juices working. The second story of the headquarters building had a little open porch overlooking the street, but from their angle they could see no more than the muted glow of one lone candle there.

"So when will you snatch him by the scruff of his neck and haul him to account before the Captain-General?" Cyprien said.

"If he concedes to come with us now," Daspir said smoothly, "I think we may fairly claim to have won the bet."

Cyprien stared at him for a second, then let out a snort of laughter. "By God! I hadn't looked at it that way," he said. "But I believe you're right."

Toussaint pointed the boys toward two chairs at a round table on the small second-story porch. He settled himself into a third. From an inner pocket he pulled out a stub of candle and struck fire to it. When the flame was warm, he tilted it and let a drop of wax fall on the table and fixed the candle there.

"My sons," he said, as he leaned back. "What news do you bring?"

Placide looked at Isaac, who reached into his inner pocket and drew out Leclerc's letter. Toussaint turned it over once before he broke the seal and spread the paper on the table, below the candle flame. No request that it be read aloud now, and yet he was a long time in the reading. The candle flame guttered, then steadied and bloomed upward; Placide felt that he and his brother had both suspended their breath. The cords of Toussaint's neck stood out, and his eyes glared downward on the paper, so that Placide thought he might burst into a rage. Instead, he relaxed and sat back in his chair, covering the folded letter with his left hand and looking out to the west, where the ocean lay just out of sight beneath the fading disk of moon, where the black of the night sky was just bleeding a trace of blue.

"My children," he said, "I would not blame your attachment to France—to her you owe your education. But between ourselves and France there is our color, and I will not put us at the mercy of an expedition that includes Rigaud, Pétion, Villatte, and others who are all my personal enemies. This order which the Captain-General mentions, not to stop fighting for negotiations, makes me believe that France has put more confidence in her arms than in her rights. It smacks of despotism. And if they will not deal with us while we have still some power, what do you suppose they will do when we have none?"

Placide looked at Isaac in the gaining daylight. Now it seemed to him that if they had never discussed the matter fully, it was not for lack of a private opportunity but because they had both somehow known that something of this sort would have to be said once the subject was opened. Isaac's face was ashen, bloodless and ghostly in the dawning light, and Placide could feel his miserable uncertainty like a sickness, though he did not know yet what he felt himself.

"My children," Toussaint said, even more softly than before. "I declare war upon General Leclerc, but not upon France—I want France to respect the constitution which the people of Saint Domingue have given to themselves. I cannot treat with the First Consul since he has torn up the act which guarantees all our liberties. My children, I would not go against your feelings, and I will use no violence nor trickery to keep you near me. Remorse would follow me all of my life if I were to become the author of your misfortunes. I leave you free to choose between the Captain-General and the liberty of your country."

Between Placide and Isaac, an agonized look arced like a flash of lightning. Toussaint sat straighter in his chair, folded his arms across his chest.

"What?" he said. "You hesitate in your choice? A man of honor must declare himself for one cause, and not try to serve two at the same time."

"Very well," Isaac said quickly, as if stung. "You see in me the faithful servant of France, who can never bear arms against her."

"*Soit*," Toussaint said. So be it. "I will cherish you all the same. You have my blessing, Isaac, wherever the roads of your life may take you." But when he turned his face to Placide it was full of pain.

Placide, unthinking, dropped onto his knees and pressed his face against his father's tightly trousered thigh, snuffling the scent of horse and sweat and leather for a moment. When he raised his face it was wet with tears. "I fear the future," he heard himself say. "I fear slavery even more." He swallowed and got better control of his voice. "I have already forgotten France and all its glory," he said. "If it is God's will, let me live or die by your side."

"Good," Toussaint said. For a moment he cradled the back of Placide's head in both his hands, looking closely into his eyes. "Stand up now," he said and rose himself. As Placide stood, Toussaint took him by the shoulder and turned him to face Morisset and General Vernet, who were standing by the stairwell that went down into the interior of the building.

"This is my son!" Toussaint said. "Now, go to the drummers and tell them to beat the call to arms."

As Morisset and Vernet clattered down the stairs, Toussaint turned toward Isaac again. Up until now they had been speaking in the most formal French, but now he switched to Creole.

"*Ba'm main'ou,*" he said. *Give me your hand.* Isaac put his hand in his.

"You must go to your mother now," Toussaint said. "Go up to Ennery and tell her how you have decided."

Already the drums were rolling, beyond the headquarters building, toward the Place d'Armes. Toussaint dropped Isaac's hand and, guiding Placide by his shoulder, hurried down the stairs. Isaac followed, a pace behind. As they emerged into the street, the two French captains rushed up toward them; the drum roll and stirring of the troops had thrown them into consternation.

"Ah, my friends," Toussaint said. "You have been waiting a long time. I have a mission for you now. You have taken such care of my sons since they returned here—I ask you now to go with my son Isaac to his mother at Ennery."

"But have you no reply for the Captain-General?" Cyprien said, with rather a sickly smile. "One would not wish to disrupt the filial pieties, but our business is too urgent for another such detour."

"The Captain-General has accorded me an armistice of four days, as you probably already know," Toussaint said. "I invite you to remain as my guests at Habitation Sancey during that time. My son will see to your comfort there, and these ten horsemen of my guard will assure your safety on the road."

"Are we your prisoners, then?" said Cyprien.

"By no means." Toussaint covered his mouth with his hand. "But at present it is not convenient that you return to the Captain-General."

On the Place d'Armes the troops were already assembled: Toussaint's personal guard in the strength of a battalion and two squadrons. The light of dawn was coming up quickly now, though still more bluish gray than rose. The tall palms shivered in the corners of the square. Shoulder to shoulder with Placide, Toussaint stood to address the men.

"The Captain-General Leclerc offers us ignominy and shame," he said. "He wants to destroy the constitution, sole guarantee of our liberty—he wants us to abandon ourselves to the discretion of the French government. Are we cowards who'd submit to such caprices? Will we lower our heads again to wear the yoke of slavery?"

"Never!" Morisset led the cry, and led the men in flourishing their swords. "We all stand ready to die for liberty."

"I give you Placide Louverture," Toussaint shouted. "He is ready to die for our cause also. Accept him in the grade of a commander."

Placide stepped forward, or maybe it was Toussaint who stepped back. But in an instant he was covered with shouts of acclaim as Morisset and Vernet wrapped their heavy arms around his shoulders and pulled him into the ranks. Then all the men were touching him, pounding his back, shouting encouragement and praise. It was like it had been when they first crossed the height of Pilboreau, only this reception was fiercer than that one. But for a moment all Placide's fear was pummeled out of him and he felt nothing but a wild joy.

At the *grand'case* of Habitation Thibodet the women and children and all the house were sleeping, except the doctor, who woke at first cock crow, though it was some other sound, he thought, that roused him. He listened for a moment but heard nothing but more of the little cocks calling up and down the coffee terraces and the jungle beyond. A cool breeze shivered the slats of the jalousies. The doctor leaned over and kissed the tendon of Nanon's neck, just below her ear. Her mouth parted to breathe over her pillow; she sighed and curled a little tighter. He was tempted to remain, but his curiosity was stronger.

Bare-chested and barefoot, he shuffled out onto the gallery. A crew of charcoal sellers was just turning the corner of the house toward the kitchen in back; they grinned at him, teeth white in their sooty faces, but this was not what he had heard. His bare toes splaying in the dust, he walked down toward the cane mill and found Bazau and Gros-Jean, Tocquet's oldest retainers, loyal to him since slavery time, strapping pack saddles to a couple of donkeys.

"*S'ak pasé?*" the doctor said. What's happening?

"*N'ap soti,*" Bazau said and took the doctor's hand in a soft loose grip. We're going.

As Bazau released the doctor's hand, Tocquet came out of the cane mill, carrying a canvas duster rolled up under one arm. He gave the doctor a brief nod, then lowered his head to the business of strapping the garment behind the saddle of his horse.

"They say you are leaving us," the doctor said.

"Only to the border, or a little beyond," Tocquet grunted. "There's a market for tobacco in Gonaives, with all the people who've just come down from Le Cap without any—damn it!" He raised his head and stared at the piece of dry-rotted strap in his right hand.

Bazau jogged to the mill to find him another. But Tocquet moved away from his horse and walked with the doctor. They strolled to a stop above the lily pool.

"Oh," said Tocquet. "It's she herself who's sending me away this time."

"I have not reproached you," the doctor said.

"You have not. But I know your mind."

"With what word does she send you now?"

"No words." Tocquet shook his head, running the rotten strap from one hand to the other. "Nor any action one could name. It is her manner."

"That seems rather a slight cause, and at a time of such uncertainty."

"I would have taken her and our daughters to some refuge on the Spanish side," Tocquet said. "Your family also, certainly. Elise will have none of it. I don't know why. There will be trouble here, and soon—do you not feel it closing in?"

"I only think that everything is all unsettled," the doctor said. "I have no notion how it may resolve."

"There was something between us when I returned," Tocquet muttered.

"From the North American Republic?"

"Yes," said Tocquet. "A barrier, a dam. I thought if I went off for a time, it might give way."

"If absence was the cause of it," the doctor said, "it seems strange to think it would be healed by absence."

"Well, she is welcome to go with me!" Tocquet said. "But she will not. Nor will I force her. That is not my way." Abruptly he turned toward the pack donkeys. *"Bazau! Gros-Jean! W met lesé tonbé tout sa! N'ap reté isit jodi-a."* With no sign of surprise the two black men set about undoing the work they'd begun. You can let all that drop! We'll be staying here today.

The doctor smiled and tapped the shoulder of the taller man. Never before had he seen Tocquet hesitate, but he was happy all the same that he would not follow through his morning's plan.

"I don't mean to stay in this snare forever, understand," Tocquet said. "Perhaps you can try some brotherly persuasion. I would see you out of this situation also, Nanon and Isabelle and their children too."

"You don't believe Toussaint will harm us?"

"With his own hands, no. But the bloodiest work is always done by someone among his subordinates. Listen," he said and lowered his voice. "Isabelle and Elise believe that they are safe because Toussaint is here. And that was your own theory, if I remember well— but now the French columns are certainly closing on this place, for the same reason."

"You know this?"

"I have no certain information, but it must be so. What else? Suppose Toussaint is hemmed up here, and has to cut a line of retreat. Toussaint likes us well enough, but then we will be hostages, not friends. And if the retreat is too hard pressed, we'll finish with our throats slit by the side of the road, man, woman, and child alike. You know very well it has happened before."

The doctor felt he'd inhaled a shadow. "But Toussaint is negotiating with Leclerc."

"No doubt," said Tocquet. "The old fox!—but what if he's only playing for time? If you were Toussaint, after all that has passed, would you give yourself up to a French general without a struggle?"

The doctor looked down at the still surface of the water. There was enough light now that he could see his silhouette by Tocquet's, quavering among the floating flowers, their buds still sealed.

"Well, my friend," Tocquet said. "I do not want to leave you in this fish trap, no more than Elise or our daughters. I will stay a few days more, and hope I have not stayed too long. Maybe you can reason with your sister, or have a word with Isabelle."

"I'll try it."

"In spite of her stubbornness, I think she is afraid," Tocquet said. "Elise, I mean. And I have never known her so. I've seen her wild with passion or with grief, and seen her cold and calculating, even cruel. When she abandoned Thibodet to go with me the first time, she threw away everything a white woman has to lose in this country, and yet she showed no fear. But now . . . Now I feel that she is very much afraid of something, but of what? For what there really *is* to fear ought to send her away from this place without delay, instead of keeping her stuck here like a barnacle . . ."

Tocquet drew two cheroots from his shirt pocket and offered one to the doctor, who shook his head. He shifted his feet and looked to the east, where yellow sunlight was just straining through broad leaves of a banana planting on the lower slopes. It surprised him how well Elise had apparently succeeded in keeping her most recent indiscretions from her husband. And yet she *was* afraid of something, though the doctor had no better idea than Tocquet exactly what it was.

Toussaint paced the length of the headquarters porch and stopped at the corner of the rail. From here he could see to every quadrant of the compass. South, the white dust of the Savane Désolée. Westward, the sea. North, the mountains of the Cordon de l'Ouest, running back to the other ranges that closed the Spanish border to the east. The sun had not yet crossed those mountains, but its light washed over all the clouds that domed the sky, in colors of gray and blue and rose. Among them the moon's disk hung, pale and ghostly, still persistent.

The review of his guard on the Place d'Armes was fifteen minutes in the past. Placide had been absorbed into that body, loyal son that he'd proved to be. Isaac, the weaker reed, would be well on his way to his mother at Ennery by now, with the two French captains whom Toussaint would hold for the duration of the armistice Leclerc had offered. Now, and for the next few minutes, Toussaint was entirely alone.

All his orders had been sent. Let them be delivered safely! Let them be obeyed! He stepped back from the balcony rail, closed his eyes, and closed his arms across his chest. By reflex he sank slightly in the knees, as though he were still astride a horse. His nostrils flared.

In the northwest, at Port-de-Paix, Maurepas and the Ninth Demibrigade would be resisting mightily. If Maurepas could not hold out, he would burn the town and retreat into the mountains. Just to the south, Dessalines would surely be trying still to surprise and destroy Port-au-Prince. As certainly, Dessalines would leave Saint Marc a smudge of ash before he'd let the French enjoy it.

Just to the north, Christophe was fighting a French column, in the mountains around Marmelade, while Sans-Souci held off another, in the mountains of Grande Rivière. Across the Spanish border, the distance was greater and there was no news, but if all had gone according to intention, Clervaux and Paul Louverture would have destroyed the towns they commanded, Santiago and Santo Domingo City, and would be moving toward a junction on the Central Plateau near Saint Raphael without risking any engagement in the open field. Still further to the south, Toussaint had instructed Laplume to burn Les Cayes and the surrounding towns, and retreat into the interior. Laplume could not be fully trusted, but at Jérémie, on the Grande Anse beyond Les Cayes, Dommage commanded, whose loyalty and tenacity were strong.

His eyes still lidded, Toussaint allowed himself a half-smile, remembering the long-ago battle when, having heard that the other was wounded, he cried out, *"Ah, c'est dommage!"* His hearers had taken this French idiom as a proper name, which had stuck to Dommage from then until now. Dommage ought by now to have enacted the order Toussaint had sent him days before: *The whites of France and of the colony have joined to take away our freedom. Mistrust the whites—they will betray you if they can. Their manifest desire is the return of slavery . . .* and so by now all the towns and the plains of the Grande Anse must be ablaze.

So the spirit of war flew everywhere, with hot, dank wings and a breath of fire. Let everything on the coast and plains be razed to the bare stones. Leclerc and the invaders would be defeated by the barren land itself, if Toussaint's men did not destroy them in the mountains.

16

Some years before, Doctor Hébert had given Maillart a bundle of herbs and advised him to carry it with him on every campaign, and on every journey which might present a risk of injury to himself, which included almost any journey at all in this country. Maillart had done as he was told, leaving the packet deep in his saddlebag, forgotten for the most part. By great good luck he had not suffered a serious wound for some years, though not for want of danger. Sometimes, with his loud bluff laugh, the major would joke that the efficacy of the packet must be magical, like the magic bags and amulets many of the black soldiers wore around their necks or wrists—a *ouanga*, a *garde-corps*. But the doctor replaced the herbs from time to time, whenever he remembered and thought that they'd gone stale enough to lose their virtue. They were fresh enough now to have a bright, slightly sweet scent, leaking out from the folds of the yellow paper packet tied up, like a small roast, with string.

Now Maillart presented the herbs to General Pamphile de Lacroix, who had been wounded during the engagement on the road from Léogane, at Fort Piémont, when the black garrison first claimed to have orders to receive the French, then opened fire on them as they advanced unguardedly. This treachery, if treachery it had been, had cost a hundred grenadiers slain in the opening volley, and twice as many wounded, though it was not sufficient to defend Port-au-Prince, nor to allow the black troops time to burn the city as they had threatened to do.

Pamphile de Lacroix had been hurt in that first volley, while Maillart was standing near. At the time he'd seen the general do no more than stumble, grimace, then move vigorously forward, encouraging his troops over the redoubt wall. Afterward, when his trouser leg was cut away, Lacroix scoffed at the wound, which indeed was not deep, though it looked rather complicated; grapeshot had torn the lower muscles of his thigh. At any rate Maillart had heard the doctor make such deductions when he examined similar wounds from other battles. Over the protests of Lacroix, Maillart got out his packet of herbs, and found a knowledgeable black woman to prepare a proper poultice. When Lacroix objected, Maillart gave him a few choice examples of how quickly even so light a wound could corrupt and putrefy in this climate, and reminded him that an amputation—the best treatment a French surgeon could offer—would be above the knee.

At that, Lacroix accepted the poultice and soon found an improvement. He had never been really completely off his feet, but once he was more mobile, Maillart encouraged him to a program of sea bathing. Here Lacroix's resistance was stouter at first, for he'd heard tales (true enough probably) of sharks carrying off a few sailors in this harbor. Also he did not know how to swim. But Maillart convinced him that he could see any menace approaching him through the clear blue water much sooner than it would be able to reach him, and that he need stand just a little more than knee deep to get the benefit of the healing salt. Soon Lacroix grew comfortable enough splashing in the shallows, while Maillart took more ambitious swims, finning along on his back and blowing great water spouts like a whale, and letting his arms and legs and chest turn the same brick color as his face.

In this way Major Maillart developed an easy fellowship with his superior out from France. Lacroix was an amiable man, friendly and frank in his manner, though certainly keen witted, and apt with a turn of phrase. He had a brotherly regard for the men in his command. Maillart was impressed by his courage, which carried with it no braggadocio. Lacroix seemed almost indifferent to pain, though not to the point of stupidity.

"Where did you learn this leaf craft?" Lacroix asked him, when it became clear that Maillart's regime was having a real effect.

"I know little enough of it myself," Maillart said. "It is all the advice of my friend, Doctor Antoine Hébert."

"He is a Frenchman, your doctor, then?"

"Yes," said Maillart. "But he has been ten years in the colony, and learned the arts of a *doktè-fey* at the hands of Toussaint during that time."

"Toussaint Louverture!" Lacroix clicked his cup down on the table.

They were drinking in the garden of a small tavern at the edge of the Place du Gouvernement.

"Yes," said Maillart. This story was so long familiar it no longer struck him as extraordinary. "Toussaint has a great skill with leaf medicine, it is said, and I have seen the evidence. He was doctor to the black troops before he rose to command. And in slavery time he was a veterinarian too, when he kept horses for the Comte de Noé."

"And so, your doctor knows him well."

"My friend was made prisoner, during the risings on the Northern Plain in ninety-one," Maillart said, mindful that collaboration might become an issue in the future, despite the reassuring proclamations now being bruited about. "He was held for some weeks, with many other captives, in different camps around Grande Rivière. At that time, Toussaint used his influence, which was not then so great as now, to keep the blacks from slaughtering them all."

"Ah," said Lacroix. "But where is he now, your friend the doctor?"

"Would that I knew," Maillart said. "I left him last at Le Cap, and you know . . ."

"Don't trouble yourself so much," Lacroix said. "By all accounts the inhabitants came through with their lives intact, though they have lost much property to the fire."

"So let us hope."

Lacroix smiled. "But I think the worst you have to fear is that I have depleted your store of these excellent herbs." He nudged the packet, which was now quite flat, it was so nearly empty.

Riau, who shared the table, unfolded one corner of the paper and shook out a few leaves to examine them. He crushed one into his palm and raised it to his face and inhaled the fading dusty scent.

"*Guérir-trop-vite*," he said. "*Gros piment*—I can find these for you, not far off."

Lacroix's eyes cut to Riau. "You also learned this art at Toussaint's knee?"

"Perhaps as much from my friend Hébert," Maillart said quickly. "Riau has assisted him on many of our battlefields. I'll wager he's nursed more than he's slain."

Lacroix raised a forefinger and looked as if he'd ask some other question, but just then Captain Paltre appeared, hurrying across the Place du Gouvernement and seeming to lean toward them as he walked.

"Gentlemen," he said. "You are wanted by General Boudet."

"What is it?" Lacroix said, already rising.

"I am not certain," said Paltre. "He has found something. A box, a coffer."

Maillart, who had hung back to leave a coin on the table, shot a quick glance at Lacroix. One of the successes of the French debarcation here had been to secure the treasury. Whether because they were intent on defending the town, or through sheer disorganization, the black troops had not removed the funds. Though it was at the treasury that they'd made their first real stand since being routed on the road from Léogane, soon enough they had been driven off, and Boudet's men had taken charge of a sum in the neighborhood of two and a half million francs.

Perhaps the mysterious box was some other treasure chest that had been found elsewhere? Lacroix ventured no more than an arched eyebrow. Riau walked at Maillart's other side, his face calm and expressionless.

General Boudet awaited them in an inner office of the Government, drumming his fingers on the lid of a sizable mahogany letter box. The junior officers filed in, Riau last of the four. Boudet looked for a moment as if he would object to his remaining, but after a glance at Maillart and Lacroix he seemed to swallow whatever he had meant to say.

"Are you familiar with this coffer?" he inquired.

"Somewhat," Maillart answered. Boudet was often putting him such questions, since he'd served in the colony for so long. "Toussaint uses it for his correspondence, I believe, when he is in Port-au-Prince."

"So much we know," said Boudet, gesturing toward a fan of letters on the table beside the box. "This is certainly his hand?"

Maillart glanced at the signature, with the underswept loop of the final *e* enclosing the customary three dots. "It is," he said, and squinted more closely. "These letters are copies, I suppose."

"And of no great moment now," said Boudet. "They are well out of date, along with those that he has received—well, there is this one, from an American merchant, which seems to treat of a purchase of guns?" Boudet raised inquiring eyes to Maillart.

"I have not been privy to such transactions, *mon général*," Maillart said.

"Well, that is not why I sent for you." Boudet stood over the empty box. "Look here." He flattened one palm on the velvet lining of the interior and the other on the table top beside it. "There is a false bottom, do you see?"

"Yes, it is so," Lacroix said. There was a three- or four-inch space quite evident between the levels of Boudet's two hands.

"Try as I may, I cannot divine the method of its opening." Boudet straightened and flexed his fingertips together. "And it is a well-made article; one does not like to spoil it. I thought perhaps you might know its secret."

"Oh," said Maillart, turning his shoulder to include Riau, who stood in the open doorway. "You might do better to ask Captain Riau, who has often assisted Toussaint in writing his letters."

Riau saluted, smartly enough, and remained silent where he stood. After a moment, Maillart stepped up to the table and ran his fingers around the edges of the lining. He could feel no catch or any other clue to its opening.

"We will have to force it then," Boudet sighed.

Maillart brushed back the flap of his jacket and drew from his belt a short, broad-blade knife he found expedient to carry. He drove the point into a corner of the false bottom, twisted and pried. The panel of wood split along its grain and slipped out of the grooves that held it fixed. Maillart lifted it out, the two pieces hinged together by the velvet.

"Look," he said. "It is not so much damaged after all."

But Boudet and Lacroix had put their heads together to peer inside. A musty scent of stale perfume diffused from the hidden compartment. Maillart leaned in. The bottom of the box was stuffed with rings, chains, brooches, little golden hearts pierced with gilded arrows, scented notes in various feminine hands, ribboned locks of plaited hair—blond seeming to be the preference. A whole array of sentimental keepsakes. Boudet picked up one of the notes, then dropped it as quickly as if it had burned his fingers.

"Captain Riau," he said and paused as he pushed himself away from the table. "*And* Captain Paltre, you will leave us, please. Close the door on your way out."

Riau saluted, expressionless still, and moved out of the doorframe. Paltre seemed to hesitate a moment, his lips pinched tight. Maillart saw how deeply he disliked to be grouped with the black man, officer or no. Of a sudden he realized why Paltre had seemed familiar; he'd been one of those upstart, insolent young officers who came out with the Hédouville mission, and had paid court to Isabelle Cigny while stationed in Le Cap. Maillart could enjoy his humiliation, then—if Paltre chose to find the order humiliating. In the end he obeyed it, docilely too, taking care not to let the door slam when he shut it.

Boudet blinked into the bottom of the box. A tittering laugh escaped him. "My Christ, I would not have believed it," he said. "And they say the man is ugly as a monkey! into the bargain with being black."

"But look at his conquests," Lacroix said. "If I don't mistake myself, they are skimmed from the cream of this society."

"A cream polluted with his tar," Boudet said.

"No doubt you've heard the axiom," said Lacroix with a twisted smile. "*We would deify the plague, if the plague gave out preferments.*"

Maillart was not entirely listening. He had taken up a thumb-sized pendant, strung to a fine gold chain. The little disk of china was painted in astonishingly fine detail: the face of a blushing nymph, whose ringlets of dark hair fell loose on her bare white shoulders. A forefinger was coyly placed to her red lips. Isabelle had once owned this ornament—surely there could not be two alike—but more lately Maillart had seen it adorning the bosom of the doctor's sister, Elise.

Lacroix had unfolded one of the notes and was scanning the lines of fine script, his mouth set in a silent whistle.

"Don't read the names," Boudet said sharply.

Lacroix let the paper flutter down into the box. Maillart caught up the loose chain in his palm and closed his hand over the pendant.

"There is an order which you have not seen," Boudet said. "Though likely you will hear of it, before we have done. *All white women who have prostituted themselves to the Negroes, regardless of their rank and station, are to be deported to France.*"

Lacroix snorted. "As if such prostitutions could have witnesses."

"What we have here would denounce more than a few," Boudet said.

Subtly Maillart turned his hip, to conceal the movement of his hand as it dropped the pendant and chain into his pocket. Boudet drew himself up and looked the others in the eye.

"Gentlemen, we'll look no further," he said. "Take these things away and burn them. The box too."

"Even the box?" Maillart said.

"The trinkets won't burn," Lacroix muttered.

"Then you may throw them into the sea," said Boudet. "Somewhere, anywhere they will not be found."

"As you command, *mon général*," Maillart said. He stretched out both hands toward the box, but Boudet stayed him with a gesture.

"Your Captain Riau," he said. "You mean to say he can read and write?"

"Oh, very adequately," Maillart said.

"And has served Toussaint as a secretary."

"From time to time. Toussaint uses many secretaries, often several for each letter that he writes."

"I have heard that the man cannot even speak real French," Boudet said, "only that bastard *patois* which everyone chatters here."

"That rumor is false," Maillart told him. "Toussaint's French is correct. But his spelling is poor, and his handwriting not very legible." As much could be said for the major's own, though Maillart did not mention it.

"I see," said Boudet. He sat down and rested an elbow on the table. "As for your Captain Riau, how do you estimate his loyalty?"

Maillart moved toward the office's sole small window, twisting an end of his mustache. His angle afforded him a view of a section of the Place du Gouvernement, with the roofs of the town's low buildings receding down the slope toward the harbor. Port-au-Prince was mostly built of wood, and it would have gone up in a flash if the blacks had managed to set it alight—much faster than Le Cap. Maillart pushed down the thought of what it must have been like there.

"Major, you are long in choosing your words."

"Excuse me," Maillart said. "I am considering the question. Is it loyalty to France you mean, or to Toussaint Louverture?"

Boudet turned his head to the side, cupping his chin in one hand. "You may analyze the two."

"Very well," said Maillart, then paused again. Long since, though not without some difficulty, he had accepted the status of the competent black officers of Toussaint's command, and Riau was certainly one of these, if not the most devoted. Maillart had in fact been instrumental in Riau's first training in the European arts of war. Since then, Riau had vanished from Toussaint's ranks from time to time, and had at least once been on the point of being shot for desertion. For himself, he liked the black man well enough and trusted him when he had to. Maillart was no politician, but he understood that Toussaint had sent himself and Riau together on the mission from Samana so that each might serve as a check on the other. Where Riau had been or what he had done since they'd been separated, Maillart was not at all sure. Riau's much stronger friendship was with Doctor Hébert, and for that alone, Maillart wished him well.

"I would say that Captain Riau's attachment to Toussaint is not so strong as to hinder his loyalty to France."

"But how great can that loyalty be among any of them?" Boudet grumbled. "To a country they have never seen."

"Why, I think most of them, if not all, attach their loyalty to the freedom of their kind. So long as they find their liberty best protected under the French flag, that is the flag they follow." Maillart stopped and glanced again out the window. "One might say as much for Toussaint, indeed."

"Then why in God's name is he in rebellion?" Boudet shifted his weight and recrossed his tight-trousered legs from one side to the other. "The First Consul's proclamation of eternal liberty has been tacked to every tree on this wretched island."

To this Maillart made no answer. When he looked at the other two, he seemed to feel some muted tension between Boudet and Pamphile de Lacroix. It was the latter who broke the brief silence.

"Consider the example of Paul Lafrance."

"Well," said Boudet. "The name is evocative."

"You know how unswervingly he came to our side," Lacroix said. "How many services he has rendered us since, and with alacrity and diligence. And I have had it on good authority that, black as he may be, he has acted a hundred times to help and protect our color, since the troubles first began in this colony, and often at the risk of his own life."

"Toussaint has done the same, you know," Maillart put in. "When all the plantations of the north were laid to waste in ninety-one he preserved the lives of the white family of the manager of Bréda, where he'd been a slave, and he has been the savior of many French men and women since—including several of my dearest friends."

"One hears much talk of this," said General Boudet. "But it hardly agrees with his conduct now."

Captain Paltre was no longer on the scene when Maillart and Lacroix emerged from the office (Maillart with the letterbox clutched to his chest), but they found Riau lingering on the steps of the Government. He came along with them as they went to dispose of the mementoes of Toussaint's amours. If Lacroix was uncomfortable with his presence he did not show it, and Maillart was rather inclined to include him, after their conference with Boudet.

Lacroix had proposed going down to the harbor, but Maillart said they needn't go so far; there was an irrigation canal much closer by, which fed the grounds of the hospital from a spring in the hills above the town, and would be sufficient to their purpose. At the canal's edge they kindled a small fire and fed it the letters one by one, along with anything else that would burn, always alert for flying sparks, as the weather was windy and dry. A black family passing with their donkeys approached curiously as the keepsake hair locks crinkled in the fire, then as quickly averted their eyes and moved to the other side of the road. Lacroix stood up and shaded his eyes to look after them.

"They must suppose it is some witchcraft," said Maillart from his place crouched over the fire. When it had burned down, he scraped the ashes into the canal with the side of his boot, then threw in handfuls of the rings and chains and hearts. Riau's eyes were sharp on him as the trinkets turned glittering through the cloudy water and disappeared in the silt of the bottom. Why throw away such articles of value? When they were done, Maillart and Lacroix concluded to give the letterbox to Riau—it was a well-crafted article, after all, and there seemed no urgent reason to destroy it.

Two days later, Maillart attended General Lacroix as he conducted a review of the troops of the Port-au-Prince garrison. Lacroix still moved with a slight hitch in his step from his leg wound, but the crispness of the drill was unmarred. The colonial troops who'd come over to the French at the time of the Port-au-Prince landing had by then been incorporated into Boudet's force, and together they gave a good showing. As the review concluded, Maillart noticed Paul Lafrance standing nearby, with Riau saying something in his ear. The old man was grizzled and a little stooped, but his brigadier's uniform was impeccable.

He seemed to be trying to catch Lacroix's eye, and once Maillart had given him a nudge in the right direction, Lacroix crossed the parade ground and greeted him warmly. Paul Lafrance had brought his wife with him to attend to the review, and also three daughters: Agnès, Marie-Odette, and Célestine. Lacroix bowed deeply over the hand of Madame Lafrance, a jet-black woman of a regal height, then turned his courtesies toward the girls. They were lovely, all three of them, in their early bloom, and dressed as they might be for church. All three were demure, their eyes downcast, but though their parents held themselves as stiffly, formally upright as the soldiers who'd lately stood to attention on the

parade ground, the girls could not help themselves from swaying and
shimmering like flowers in a moist spring breeze. They were as light on
their feet as young deer and . . . a man might be moved to impure
thoughts, but Maillart saw how Lacroix paid his respects in a genuinely
respectful manner, so he followed that example. It was plain that Paul
Lafrance was appreciating this decorum. Riau was easier with the girls,
and perhaps he had known them from before, for he thought of something to whisper to Marie-Odette that made her bridle and swirl away,
the whites of her eyes flashing, the grace of her movement such that
Maillart's breath caught for a moment in his throat.

"Gentlemen, you must come to my house," Paul Lafrance was saying.
"Only for a moment—it is quite near, and there you may escape the heat
and find something to refresh you."

"With pleasure," Lacroix said, and Maillart fell into step with him as
they walked where the old brigadier led them. The house was just a
block away from where they'd stood. Paul Lafrance rattled the bars of
the gate, and a servant came out quickly to unchain it. The small dooryard was choked by two large hibiscus bushes; their lurid blooms
brushed over Maillart's sleeves as they passed through.

Within it seemed quite dark, as the windows were blinded, but cool as
Paul Lafrance had promised. Maillart squinted into the shadows. The
room seemed sparsely furnished: a low carved table, a few wooden
chairs. There was a flash of light as a door opened in the rear, and the
women filed through it, going off to prepare lemonade. Riau trailed
them, still bantering with Marie-Odette; her laugh rang back like silver
through the doorway.

But Paul Lafrance had turned to Lacroix and addressed him with a
trembling intensity. "*Mon général*, honesty and frankness are all you
breathe—tell me, in truth, have you come here to restore slavery?"

Maillart felt his jaw go slack. He had not put himself this question, not
exactly, but here it was, announced. In the light spilling in from the rear
doorway, the amiable face of Pamphile de Lacroix looked rather pale.
Why did he not answer? Maillart pressed his own lips shut. Behind him,
something blocked the light.

"Whatever it should be," the old man said, "old Paul Lafrance will
never harm you. But my daughters! my poor daughters . . . to see them
slaves I should die of grief."

"As I myself should die of shame." Lacroix opened his arms as he
spoke, and Paul Lafrance fell into them. It looked to Maillart that the
two men were so moved that they were shedding tears on each other's
coat collars, but for some reason he looked over his shoulder and saw
Riau's form filling the rear doorway, his face attentive, still. Sometimes
looking at Riau's face was like gazing into the darkness of a midnight
well.

When they had drunk their lemonade and praised it, Maillart and

Lacroix made their farewells and departed, leaving Riau, for the moment, behind. After the dim interior the blaze of sunlight outdoors was almost blinding. Maillart flattened his hand above his eyes.

"A touching scene," he said tentatively.

"Indeed it was." Lacroix's tone was rather dry. "And it only reminds us of the need to drive Dessalines away from this vicinity, for all those rumors of slavery are being put about by him, if not by Toussaint Louverture as well."

"Yes, of course," Maillart said. He motioned Lacroix to the side of the street, where they could walk in the shade of the second-floor balconies.

"It is a fortunate thing that Laplume has rallied to our side," Lacroix went on. "Dessalines would present us a much more serious threat if he had not, but still his proximity is dangerous, for aside from those rumors of slavery, he seems to inspire all these people with a terrible fear."

And not without reason, Maillart was thinking, amid a number of other thoughts which simultaneously surfaced in his mind. If the daughters of Paul Lafrance were in their middle teens, as they appeared to be, then they would hardly have any memory of slavery. Lacroix had not really answered the old man's question either, except by his gesture. Maillart's fingers grazed the pendant that still lay in his coat pocket, beneath a crumpled handkerchief. How many secret orders might there be? But then, Lacroix had seemed surprised himself to hear the order to deport white women who had offered their love to black men . . .

Above all this Maillart saw always hovering the face of Riau, watchful and silent, as it had appeared in Paul Lafrance's rear doorway, absorbing the light. But by the next day all such images were scattered; Maillart was sent out with fourteen hundred men under command of the Adjutant d'Arbois for a day of heavy fighting which ended with the capture of Dessalines's mountain post at Cabaret-Quart. At the same time, and to Maillart's utter astonishment, General Boudet commissioned Riau to go as emissary to the large and thus far uncommitted maroon bands that roamed the region of the Léogane plain, led by Lamour Dérance and Lafortune.

17

Dawn at Thibodet came cool and breezy, fresh from the rain the night before. Elise and Isabelle hovered on the gallery, looking down at a pair of wild ducks that had settled on the lily pool. They paddled among the floating flowers, seeming unaware that they were watched.

"One might contrive to trap them somehow." Elise narrowed her eyes on the little drake. "Clip their wings and keep them here to breed."

"Yes, but how?" said Isabelle.

"I should send for Caco," Elise said. "That boy has a hand for catching birds. Where is Paul?"

"You sent him out to gather eggs," Isabelle reminded her. "With Sophie, and Robert."

"So I did." Elise sighed and settled back in her wicker chair, fingering a loose ribbon of her peignoir. The younger children still lingered abed, as did Nanon and the doctor, who had been separated for some weeks before his arrival here. It made Elise a little irritable to think of their morning languors. Tocquet had been absent when she herself woke; he must have slipped from their boudoir before first light.

Zabeth emerged, tinkling a coffee tray. She laid out cups and a sugar bowl before the two white women. Elise watched absently as she withdrew, then looked down at the pool again. Duck and drake still circled each other, among the violet blooms of *bwa dlo*. Then Sophie and Paul and Robert came galloping up the steps, Sophie cradling a basket of speckled eggs, sprinkled over with curls of down and bits of straw. Pauline followed, more slowly, a step or two behind the others—she was old enough now to consider the impression she made when she walked.

"Look how many!" Sophie said. "Shall we have omelettes? Do let us, please." The two boys pressed on either side of her basket.

"No need for such extravagance on a weekday," Elise said, frowning at Sophie's bare feet and tousled hair.

"But there is company, Maman."

"What?" Elise looked past the children. A group of charcoal sellers had arrived in the yard, leading donkeys loaded with bulging panniers coated with black silt. Behind them was a young black man afoot beside a woman who guided her donkey with a little stick. Elise blinked: it was Suzanne Louverture—with Isaac, whom she'd not recognized at first, for he had changed his dress uniform for a plain white shirt and loose canvas trousers.

Suzanne possessed a coach and team, but seldom used them for short journeys among the plantations and the *bourg* of Ennery. Within that area she preferred to travel in the style of a prosperous *marchande*, seated sideways on a fat, well-curried donkey, her forward knee hitched up, beneath her long skirt, on the roll of a finely woven straw saddle. She took her son's hand now as she stepped down.

"Madame Louverture." Elise's hand groped to close the throat of her peignoir. "Do please come up! You must excuse us . . ."

Suzanne caught up her skirt in one hand as she climbed the steps; the other still held the donkey stick, a peeled switch of a finger's thickness and a little more than a foot long.

"You'll breakfast with us," Elise said. "Perhaps an omelette." She turned to Sophie, who was suppressing a spasm of excitement. "Take those eggs to Merbillay. And comb your hair! and put on shoes."

Automatically Pauline reached to take the eggs, but Sophie twisted away from her. The two girls bumped hips, giggling, then Sophie hurried into the house, the boys tagging after. Elise called Paul back to her. "Go and find Caco, quickly," she said. "I have a task for him."

"But he will be working in the coffee today," Paul said.

"Tell them he is excused from the field." Elise pointed over the gallery railing. "Tell him I want him to trap those two ducks."

"*Oui, ma tante,*" Paul said, and clattered down the steps, breaking into a trot as he reached level ground.

Suzanne had come to the table's edge. She wore a long blue skirt and a pale rose blouse, with a dark blue headcloth dotted with white. "I would not inconvenience you," she said. "I will not stay so long."

"Come, sit down." Elise indicated a third wicker chair. "Zabeth! More coffee." She looked about. "But where has Isaac gone?"

Zabeth had reappeared on the gallery, holding the white infant against her shoulder and balancing the black one on her hip. She slipped Mireille into Elise's lap, and set Bibiane down on the boards of the floor. Mireille had just nursed; a bubble of milk formed on her lips. Elise caught the cloth from Zabeth's shoulder as she turned away and wiped the baby's mouth.

"A fine strong child you have, Madame," Suzanne murmured. "How old is she?"

"Six months," said Elise. "Or no, it is seven." She could feel herself coloring at this confusion.

"The time goes quickly," Suzanne said.

"That it does," Elise said. "But where is your son, who has grown so remarkably?"

"He will profit from the cool of the morning by walking over your beautiful grounds," said Suzanne. "He is a little confused in these days, my boy, having been so long from home. He—" She interrupted herself and turned to Isabelle.

"Madame Cigny," she said. "I am sorry for your misfortune."

"My misfortune," Isabelle repeated blankly.

"I heard that your house at Le Cap was destroyed," Suzanne said.

"Oh yes, it is so." Isabelle's social laugh had rather a metallic ring. "Not for the first time. And indeed I share that misfortune with my hostess, and with every property holder of Le Cap. Even yourself, Madame Louverture," Isabelle concluded, in deference to the fact that Toussaint had erected quite a splendid dwelling for himself at Le Cap, though his wife was seldom in residence there.

"But your plantations," Suzanne said. "I believe that they are near Haut de Trou?"

"Yes," said Isabelle. "My husband has gone to see whether or not they have been preserved. But so far he has sent no word."

Zabeth reappeared with the coffee tray, laid a cup and saucer before Suzanne, and poured. The black stream wavered when Bibiane caught hold of the hem of her skirt and pulled. Zabeth set down the silver pot and, with a self-conscious smile, began to pry off the baby's fingers. Suzanne aligned the donkey stick against her saucer and began putting spoons of sugar into her coffee—one, two, three—and stirred the mixture slowly, counterclockwise.

"One grows accustomed to these catastrophes," Isabelle said. "Raze and rebuild. Burn, and rebuild."

Suzanne sipped her sweetened coffee. "It was peaceful before the fleet arrived," she said. "You must have enjoyed that, *mesdames*." Her brown eyes were level and calm beneath the tight crease of her headcloth. The white dots on the dark blue fabric resembled stars in a night sky.

"At least it is still peaceful here," Elise said.

Mireille mewed and stretched her arms in the air. Then she caught sight of her own hands and fixed her gaze upon them, rapt. Suzanne reached her forefinger across the table and the baby curled her fist over it and smiled.

"It may remain so," Suzanne said.

"So we must hope," Elise returned. She shifted her weight; Mireille let go of Suzanne's finger. Isaac had just reappeared from around the corner of the cane mill, pacing with stiff, agitated strides. Suzanne's donkey followed him, trailing the braided reins. The donkey stretched its neck and reached with its loose, rubbery lips to pull the back of Isaac's shirt loose from the waistband. Isabelle suppressed a giggle as Isaac whirled, a hand upraised; he subsided before he launched the blow.

"He is troubled, my boy," Suzanne said. "His attachment to France is so very strong! But his father does not make war upon France, he assures us. Only upon the General Leclerc."

Behind Elise's eyes, the brightening day lost something of its color. Suzanne had spoken with such calm, Elise was not confident she'd heard her right. She stared out over the yard. Isaac had rearranged his shirt and gone back to his aimless pacing. The donkey still pursued him, but at a safer distance. Now Paul and Caco had come into the yard, on the other side of the pool; Paul nudged Caco and pointed at the ducks. On the gallery it was very quiet, except for Zabeth's murmured remonstrances to Bibiane.

Elise exchanged a glance with Isabelle. "The Governor General will make war upon Leclerc," she said, with a slight shake of her head. "Yet not upon France. I do not wonder that Isaac is confused."

"Do you mean to leave Ennery, Madame Louverture?" Isabelle inquired.

"Not at all," Suzanne said. "I will remain here quietly, with my children at Sancey. All is still peaceful, as you see." She took another sip of coffee. Elise turned her eyes back toward the pool, where Caco was setting up a snare with a bent green stick and a loop of string. Paul moved at a crouch toward the edge of the pool, dribbling a line of white corn kernels.

"So it will still be safe here," Elise said.

"Yes, I am certain—there is no safer place." Suzanne picked up her donkey stick and gave it a couple of light flicks against the pale palm of her left hand. The peeled wood was polished smooth and with a honey-toned patina from much handling.

Now Pauline came onto the gallery, bearing a covered platter which sent out a warm fragrance. Sophie and Robert and Héloïse (who had just awakened) trailed her like a string of hungry chicks. Suzanne tapped her palm once more with the stick, gathered her skirts, and rose.

"But you must—" Elise began.

"No, no," Suzanne said. "I have no appetite this morning. And I would return to Sancey before the heat."

"Well, if we cannot persuade you . . ." Elise got up, absently handing

Mireille over to Isabelle. Bibiane now began to scrabble at Isabelle's chair leg, wanting to climb to join her companion. Zabeth clucked at her as she set down the platter. Elise clasped Suzanne's free hand in both of hers.

"You are kind to bring us the news," she said.

"It is only your kindness I return," Suzanne said. "I have never wished harm to my neighbors." Suzanne's eyes were deep beneath the spangled headcloth; Elise could not read them.

Suzanne withdrew her hand and went briskly down the steps, the stick now flicking against her skirted thigh. Elise stood at the gallery rail, watching Isaac hand his mother up onto her donkey. When she was settled, Suzanne gave the donkey a tap on the flank, then raised the stick to the vertical as the animal broke into a trot. Isaac lengthened his step to catch up with her; soon they had both disappeared behind a screen of avocado trees.

Sophie and Robert and Héloïse were in their places at the table, whetting knives against their forks. Paul stayed down by the pool with Caco, watching the two snares that had now been set and baited, but the ducks were not attracted by the corn; they were diving for something underneath the water. Then the doctor appeared in the doorway, fringes of his rusty hair ruffled up around the bald center of his head. He let go Nanon's hand as he moved toward the table. Elise inspected the two of them a little sourly, as Nanon covered a yawn with her graceful hand; she half wanted to slap them both out of their voluptuous contentment.

"Omelettes!" said the doctor, as he uncovered the platter. "What's the occasion?"

"War," said Elise.

"Ruin," said Isabelle.

"Destruction," said Elise.

The doctor sat down, took off his glasses and polished them on his loose shirt tail, then resettled them on his nose.

"But we're told we shall be quite safe here!" Elise said, full of false brightness.

The doctor thumbed his beard and shrugged. "Then that's a comfort," he said, and reached to slide one of the small omelettes onto his plate.

Daspir would not have thought it possible to have crossed this range of mountains so many times in so few days. They'd waited out the period of armistice at Habitation Sancey, dully enough, though in the company of Isaac and hospitably entertained by his mother. A few other relatives were in residence, so that the dinner table was well attended, but though the food was excellent, Daspir thought wistfully of the two Frenchwomen at Habitation Thibodet, especially the enchanting Isabelle Cigny. Suzanne Louverture had two nieces staying in the Sancey grand'case; both girls were strikingly pretty, but subdued as a pair of nuns.

The two French captains were under no obvious restraint, left at liberty to explore the plantation as they chose. Their horses were well cared for at the Sancey stable. But every stablehand wore a pistol in his waistband, and every man on the property seemed to go armed; even the field workers propped muskets in the hedgerows before they lifted their hoes.

If Isaac took any pleasure in how the tables had been turned on his former guardians, he did little to show it. On the contrary, he seemed to court their favor with more interest than before. He escorted them through the house and grounds, relaying anecdotes he must have picked up recently from his mother or younger brother Saint-Jean—the two captains knew that Isaac had not had much of his raising in the elegant surrounds of Sancey—and regaled them with many accounts of the prodigies his father had performed in defending and conserving the colony for France.

Of Placide they saw comparatively little, for Toussaint seemed to have incorporated the older boy into his staff, and Toussaint was spending most of his time at the headquarters in Gonaives, though sometimes he did appear at Sancey with his entourage, late at night, long after the very quiet suppers the captains took with Madame Louverture, Saint-Jean, Isaac, and the handful of other relatives in residence. Placide had put aside the ornate uniform given to him by the First Consul, and now wore the outfit of Toussaint's honor guard—a used one evidently, for the coat was slightly faded and the cuffs a little frayed. Still it fit him well enough that at passing glance he might be taken for one of Toussaint's guardsmen.

At the end of three slow, chafing days, Toussaint summoned Cyprien and Daspir and gave them another letter full of tortured ambiguities and sent them back to Leclerc at Le Cap, escorted by just five of his guardsmen this time. When they reached the main road from Ennery, they were joined by a deputation of Gonaives merchants, both colored and white, whom Toussaint had given leave to call on Leclerc also, to implore him to hold back the violent advances of his troops for the sake of peace and prosperity in the colony. Combined, their party began the ascent from the Ennery crossroads. Toussaint's guardsmen held such a brisk pace that they had reached the height of Morne Pilboreau before midmorning.

They stopped for a quarter-hour to cool their horses. The *marchandes* of that crossroads swarmed around them, waving their wares, but Daspir slipped away from that group and stood on the edge of the precipice looking over the broad Plaisance river valley and into the mountains beyond, the green, gray, misty blue recession in range upon range to the bow of the horizon.

"*Deyè mòn gegne mòn,*" a low voice said behind him. Daspir turned quickly, a little startled. One of the guardsmen stood behind him, his silver helmet caught under one elbow. Daspir did not know his name.

"Behind mountains," he repeated, "are more mountains."

"Yes," said Daspir. "So it appears." Despite the risk of vertigo he could not take his eyes away from the wild expanse. Because of the vertigo, possibly. He felt with a faint shiver that this sentence meant more than the sum of its words.

Yet after so many rapid transits, the mountain passages were beginning to make some kind of sense to him. He could pick out the key landmarks and the most important crossroads, though he always underestimated the peaks and defiles and swoops and curves between them. For Cyprien it must have been the same, or better, since he had some earlier experience of the country. But he and Daspir did not talk much, between themselves or to the merchants' deputation, since Toussaint's guardsmen were always near, and the one who'd addressed Daspir, at least, spoke some orthodox French as well as the strange patois of all the blacks.

Leclerc made short shrift of the Gonaives merchants when they were admitted to his presence late that afternoon. "You may tell Toussaint," he snapped, "that I will answer him with bayonets." He wheeled on Cyprien and Daspir, rattling the paper of Toussaint's own written response. "And what nonsense have you brought me from his hand? He professes himself ready to obey my orders, but will not accept to be my second in command . . . Advises me to halt the march of my troops, indeed—let him know they will not halt before they have made him prisoner! He will learn the respect due to the brother-in-law of the First Consul!" Leclerc stooped and slapped his boot leather with his palm. "I am entering the campaign *myself*," he shouted, his face reddening. "And I will not take off these boots until I have captured Toussaint Louverture!"

The commander's excitement communicated a tingle to Daspir. It looked likely that the two of them would be in the vanguard of the pursuit so hotly announced, though Daspir did not try to share his thrill with Cyprien, whose expression looked a little cynical as they threaded their way through a gang of workmen who were cleaning and repairing the sooty and cracked façade of the governor's residence.

Outside, Monsieur Granville had turned up to greet his acquaintances just arrived from Gonaives. "Do you think it is true?" one of the latter was saying, "The Captain-General will not take off his boots until he has managed to capture Toussaint?"

"Perhaps that is only poetry," Granville said with a choking effort at a laugh. Then, in a lower, more careful voice, "If he does mean it, someone ought to prepare his lady wife for a pair of very smelly feet."

" '*Le Cap headquarters, 28 Pluviôse, Year Ten,*' " Placide read aloud.

Inhabitants of Saint Domingue: The General Toussaint has sent his children back to me, with a letter in which he assures me that he is ready to obey any order I give him. I have ordered him to report to me; I have given him my word to employ him as my Lieutenant-

*General. He has not replied to this order except with empty phrases;
he is only seeking to gain time. I am entering into campaign and I am
going to teach this rebel what the force of the French government is.
From this moment forward, he must be nothing more, in the eyes of
the good French people who live in Saint Domingue, than an insen-
sate monster.*

*I have promised liberty to the inhabitants of Saint Domingue, and
I will know how to make them enjoy it.*

I command the following:

*Article One: The General Toussaint and the General Christophe are
outlawed; all citizens are ordered to pursue them—*

"Enough." Toussaint made a cutting movement with his hand and
scraped his chair sideways to the table. Placide set down the proclamation paper beside the oil lamp.

"Why is it that he outlaws only you and the General Christophe?"
Placide said. "Why not Dessalines or Maurepas or any of the others?"

In lieu of a response, Toussaint stretched out a hand for the proclamation. The printed paper fluttered in the night wind as Placide passed it
over. They were sitting, alone, on the open porch on the second floor of
the Gonaives headquarters, under a waning moon which poured a
cooler, paler light around the yellow orb of the lamp.

Toussaint angled the paper toward the lamp's glow and scanned it for
a moment, his lips pursed. Then he passed it back to Placide. "Read
here," he said, flicking the paper. "And here."

Placide skimmed the lines Toussaint had indicated:

*Article Three: Cultivators who have been led into error and have taken
up arms will be treated as misguided children and returned to agricul-
tural work.*

*Article Four: Soldiers who abandon Toussaint's army will become
part of the French army . . .*[1]

"Enough," Toussaint said again. "It is Leclerc who is truly the outlaw
and I will declare it so."

"I think I see it," Placide said slowly. "He means to isolate you, if he
can, through these betrayals he invites."

"Exactly," Toussaint said. "You see it very clear."

"But why Christophe?"

"I suppose that the Captain-General is piqued at Christophe, at least
for the moment." Toussaint smoothed away a smile with one hand.
"Since Christophe has left him nothing of Le Cap but a wasteland of cinders on which to pitch his camp."

"And the others?" Placide said. "They will not betray us?"

"Not Dessalines," Toussaint said. "Not Maurepas." He exhaled through his loose front teeth. "It may be that some of the field workers will seek the protection of the Captain-General, if he has occupied their land."

"But your officers," Placide said.

"Let us think carefully," Toussaint said. "We must admit that some of the generals may be tempted to follow the example of your brother. Some may accept the false promises of these French *blancs*, especially those who do not much want to fight anyway, or risk the loss of their comforts and position. Laplume has already sworn his loyalty to General Boudet at Port-au-Prince, I know, but the loyalty of Laplume was never worth much."

Toussaint leaned back, his eyes half closed, and set the tips of his fingers together.

"And the Grande Anse?" Placide said, remembering what Leclerc had rapped out, in front of him and Isaac, about the surrender of the Southern Peninsula. The weak smallness of his voice disgusted him.

"Yes," said Toussaint, without moving or widening his eyes. "That is a real misfortune. I could not have believed that Dommage could ever have betrayed our cause. But he did not receive my letter, I am sure. If only Dessalines had not been absent from Port-au-Prince when the fleet appeared—so much misfortune comes from that."

Placide was silent. He remembered his father's aspect the day previous, when he'd received the certain news that Dommage had yielded Jérémie; Toussaint gave no obvious sign of shock, but stopped completely motionless for a few seconds, arresting all his movement like a startled snake. How that connected to Dessalines he did not understand.

"Lamartinière fought bravely to save Port-au-Prince," Toussaint said. "But since he could not hold it, he was wrong. Dessalines would not have left a wall standing there, if he had been present. Then the *blancs* would not have established themselves so comfortably. Perhaps they would not have intercepted my letter to Dommage, and Laplume might not have dared to change sides either, if the Grand Anse held and Port-au-Prince was burned."

Now Toussaint did open his eyes, and hitched his chair around to face Placide. "*Nou pa dékourajé,*" he said. We are not discouraged.

Why not, Placide thought silently, and waited for the answer. Toussaint was unrolling a map, weighting it on either side with his palms.

"Look here," he said softly. "The Grande Anse will be a boon to the *blancs*, but they can be locked in there easily enough. Rigaud held all that country, in the time of his rebellion, but in the end I pushed him into the sea at Tiburon. If they cannot hold the rest of the land, they cannot last on the Grande Anse either."

Toussaint tapped a different area of the map: Port-de-Paix, on the northwest peninsula. "Here is Maurepas," he said with a clear satisfaction. "He commands the Ninth Demibrigade, and a good number of irregulars too. The French General Humbert has attacked him at Port-de-Paix, but Maurepas destroyed the town before he withdrew, and now he is well placed in the gorges of Trois Pavillons, where he has won every engagement since. Humbert cannot move him, and he must ask Leclerc for reinforcements, and all those are soldiers who cannot be sent to trouble us here. It ought to have been like that at Port-au-Prince. Maybe it yet will be."

"And Dessalines?" Placide leaned over the map. "Where is Dessalines?"

"Ah," Toussaint said and masked his smile. "There is the great danger to our enemy—no one knows where Dessalines is for certain from one moment to the next. You were present when Leclerc threatened us with General Boudet—well, let him march to the Artibonite. I will receive him there, when I am ready. But when Boudet has wandered far enough from Port-au-Prince, Dessalines will fall upon the town and destroy it."

Placide looked down at the squiggling line of the Artibonite River and the hatch marks that stood for mountains. He could see it now, how Dessalines might burst out of the mountains at any point, to sweep down over Port-au-Prince.

"The *blancs* may take our territory," Toussaint said. "They cannot hold it. Not for long. We are strong here, and in the northwest still, at Grande Rivière and in Santo Domingo too, where everything is entrusted to your uncle Paul. The French will find no comfort in our land. I know they mean to bring us some hard battles, but it's we, in the end, who will win the war."

For a moment there was silence under the moon, then it was broken by the sound of horses pulling up below, a sentry's challenge, a bustle as the newcomers were admitted. Toussaint, with his eyes heavy-lidded, showed no sign he noticed the commotion, till there came a noise of boots on the stairs and Morisset walked out onto the porch.

"Governor-General, there is news from the north."

"Di mwen," Toussaint looked up expectantly. Tell me.

"Rochambeau has broken out of Grande Rivière," Morisset said. "They say he has taken Saint Raphael—it is not certain."

"Well, Sans-Souci held him there for many days," Toussaint said. "What more?"

"The *blanc* general Hardy has attacked Christophe and driven him away from Dondon."

Toussaint sat up. "Where is he now, Christophe?"

"At Marmelade," Morisset said. "He means to regroup at Morne à Boispins, but it is not certain—it was not an orderly retreat."

Toussaint glanced at the map. "Well," he said. "If he can stand at Morne à Boispins I am content—that is a strong position."

"Ça," said Morisset, relaxing just slightly from the posture of stiff attention he had held since he'd halted before them. It is so.

There was more noise from below, scuffling, and a voice raised in protest. Morisset moved quickly into the stairwell, but in a moment he came backing out again, and the two men propelling him burst past, both of them looking the worse for long hard traveling. One looked almost comical in the tatters of his horizontally striped trousers, the other more imposing, if only for the ghastly scars down one side of his face. This second man wore a battered uniform of Toussaint's honor guard.

"Pardon, *mon général!*" Morisset said from behind the newcomers. "It is Guiaou, as you can see for yourself, and he insists to bring his message in person."

"Guiaou," Toussaint said slowly, studying the scarred face. "Welcome to Guiaou, and . . . Guerrier."

The man in the striped trousers smiled at the recognition, then made his face grave as he stiffened in his stance. Toussaint leaned forward on his elbows.

"What news of Santo Domingo?"

Guiaou swallowed. "The news is bad, *mon général.* We could not bring your letters to the *général* Paul. Also, Clervaux has welcomed the French soldiers at Santiago—he was charmed by the bishop Malveille, so we have heard." Guiaou swallowed again. The rough channel of his scar glowed white. "Today we met many people running from Rochambeau over the plateau from Saint Raphael, and they say there is no one to fight his men if they come to Saint Michel de l'Attalaye."

"*Aï!*" said Toussaint. "It is bad news you bring. What happened to my letters? Where is Couachy?"

"Dead, *mon général,*" Guiaou said. "We were betrayed to the Spanish militia—there was a French officer with them too."

"They took both letters? The false and the true?"

"It is so, *mon général.*"

"*Aï,*" said Toussaint. "They will have given the false letter to my brother Paul, so he will accept the French, as Clervaux has done already."

"It is so, *mon général.*"

"You have been a long time bringing this news."

Guiaou shuddered through the length of his body, then pulled himself upright and hard. "We were hunted all through the Spanish country, *mon général.* That is why we could not come faster, because we had to hide by day and move by night. Also we did not know the way to the border after Couachy was dead."

"*Eh bien,*" said Toussaint. "I see that you have done as well as you could, Guiaou. How did you come here from the border?"

"By Ravine à Couleuvre," Guiaou said. "Then we came up the road from Lacroix."

"Ravine à Couleuvre!" Toussaint was on his feet. "Has Rochambeau come so far?"

"No, *mon général,* he has not," Guiaou said. "They say there is nothing to prevent him, but he has not yet come there. All was quiet today at Ravine à Couleuvre, the depot safe and the men at their posts."

"Very well." Toussaint laid both hands on Guiaou's shoulders, then patted his unscarred cheek and let him go. "You have done your best, and not too badly."

He turned to Morisset. "Take Guiaou and Guerrier and find them some food, and a place to rest."

Morisset saluted and beckoned the other two toward the stairwell. He stood aside to let them pass, then followed them down. Toussaint had resumed his seat, turning his face away from the lamplight. Presently he reached under the flap of his coat and drew out a loop of the wooden skull rosary which hung from his belt. Placide watched his profile. Toussaint's lips moved just slightly with his prayers, though no word was audible. The skull beads clicked three times along the cord. Then Toussaint let the rosary fall to concealment beneath his coat and pressed his fingertips together. His eyes closed.

Placide looked at the map, which was beginning to curl back into its roll—but he could still find the dots of Saint Raphael and Saint Michel. When he looked at his father's silent profile again, he thought he knew what Toussaint might be thinking. At the time of the first risings ten years before, Toussaint had sent Placide, with his mother and brothers, to Saint Michel, where they would be safely out of the way of the troubles. There would be no such safety in those parts now, and none anywhere on the Spanish side of the island. Placide himself was ready to meet the enemy under arms, or at least he had told himself that he was, but the question of his family remained vivid.

He was surprised to see Toussaint smiling openly when his father turned to face him again.

"*Fé konfyans, fils-moin,*" Toussaint said. Have faith, my son. He touched the back of Placide's hand. "We will win in the end. Even if everyone else should abandon us, there is Konpè Général Lafièvre."

"Pardon?" said Placide.

"Our ally, General Yellow Fever!" Toussaint's smile flashed so wide his eyes were slitted, then as quickly disappeared. He passed a hand across his mouth and leaned back in his chair. "One does not like to depend on him for everything. But he will come, when it is his time—and whether he is called or not."

Elise lay soggy in her bed, alone, but she could hear Tocquet on the gallery beyond the front windows, talking softly to someone; she could hear the clink of a coffee cup, though it was not yet light. The wind combed through the palms around the house, and hushed the murmuring voices. She sat up, reached to the bedpost for her peignoir, and went out, fumbling with its fastenings.

Bazau and Gros-Jean were seated at the table with Tocquet. They both got up when she appeared, looking a little uncomfortable. She held her robe together at her throat.

"*A l'aise*," she said, Relax, but the two black men only lowered their heads before her, turned and went in cat-foot silence down the steps.

"Well," said Elise. "They seem a little shy of me, this morning."

Tocquet glanced over his shoulder, where a little gray light in the sky began to outline the long fronds of the palms. "They are going to bring the horses," he said.

"Perhaps they only take the model of their master," Elise said. She caught her lower lip in her teeth. This was not the tone she'd hoped to strike. She loosened her hand, letting go the robe, and spread her fingers over her bare collarbones. When she glanced down, she saw Tocquet's worn leather saddlebags, plump where they lay by his feet.

"So you mean to travel," she said.

"Yes," said Tocquet. "I will go up to the plateau, if I can, and investigate the trails and passes there. I have some goods from Gonaives, and tobacco could be sold here, if the way is clear to get some."

"It seems a strange time to leave your family," Elise said.

"My family declines to accompany me," Tocquet said shortly. "Unless you will reconsider. As I wish very much that you would."

"Madame Louverture was here only yesterday. As she means to remain here, with her family, I do not see the danger to ours."

"Then you have blinded yourself to it," Tocquet said. "Toussaint has been outlawed. It will certainly come to fighting now. There are at least three columns bearing down on Ennery at this moment. In two days' time, the ground beneath your chair may be a battlefield. I would not underestimate Toussaint, but I don't dare predict the outcome. Nor can I predict what outcome would be favorable to our position here—perhaps neither."

Elise wilted into a chair opposite him. In fact she'd had a similar thought to the last one he had spoken. In the face of her silence, Tocquet took out one of his cheroots, ran it under his nose, then put it back into his pocket. Bazau and Gros-Jean appeared in the growing light in the yard, leading two pack mules and three saddle horses.

"I never cared for being a *master*," Tocquet said. "Not of men, nor of women either. I have never forced a woman to do anything. If you had the good sense to come with me of your own accord, I would bring you gladly, even today. It would not take you long to make ready a few things for yourself and the children. There is money enough that we can supply most of our needs in Santo Domingo City."

In the yard two of the geldings were pulling at their leads; one bit the other's shoulder and the other maneuvered to kick. Bazau hitched the mules to the trunk of a tree and moved quickly to help Gros-Jean separate the saddle horses.

"Come, Madame," said Tocquet. "What will you say?"

"If you would not abandon me, I would not—" Elise cut herself off and set her lips.

"What then?" Tocquet said softly. "What is that you would not do?" He moved to the balls of his feet, and paused. "What is that you would undo?"

Silence followed, decorated by cock crow up the slopes of coffee terraces, and the smaller birds beginning to chitter in the trees around the house. Elise sat rigid, her jaw set tight. At last Tocquet stood up and swung his saddlebags to his shoulder. She would not turn her head to follow him down the steps, though she was very much aware of the creak of leather as he mounted, the light ringing of harness when they all rode out of the yard.

Her stiffness declined into lethargy as light came more strongly through the trees. Even without moving a hair, she felt a little nauseated. She sat gazing at the snares Caco had set behind the pool. The ducks had not been tempted to them, though other yard fowl ate up the grain. Now the pool was empty, except for its floating flowers, while the snares remained there, useless.

She was remembering another time when Tocquet had left her in this house. Thibodet had just fallen ill of the fever. She had declined to go with Xavier when he asked her then, for motives that had nothing to do with her reasons today—and despite the fact that she knew very well that Sophie, then three months old, was Xavier's child, and knew that Thibodet suspected it. Xavier had accepted her refusal, or seemed to, at that time. Yet twenty minutes later when she ran down the lane with nothing but the clothes she had on and the baby cradled against her shoulder, she'd found him waiting for her in the road behind the gate.

Would he wait now? She would not go. Could not. Fixed in her seat, she watched a stupid guinea fowl pick its way through the dusty grass at the pool's edge toward the snare. There was not even any bait, and yet the bird still managed to run its head into the noose and spring it—the green stick snapped upright and the guinea jerked and flapped as it strangled. Two naked black children appeared and stood wide-eyed, watching the struggle. Elise came out of her torpor and dashed down the steps to catch up the guinea and break its neck with an awkward twist, thinking there was nothing else to do, and that she'd rather kill it cleanly than watch it yank itself to death before her eyes. A kick had clawed the inside of her forearm; she felt a little ill at the sight of the bright trail of blood. Here was another day to be got through, and here was the first item on the menu, by whatever chance. Elise let the warm body of the bird swing by her thigh, and walked around the house toward the kitchen, to get Pauline to pluck it.

18

Sergeant Aloyse had a face that reminded Guizot of an ax. His whole head seemed to drive to the edge of his heavy, hatchet-bladed nose. His face was weathered and deeply creased, with eyes recessed under bushy brows, and when Rochambeau's columns were on the march, the lines set grimly around the mouth; but at ease, the eyes had sometimes a fond sparkle and the lines relaxed into an amiable expression. All in all it was a friendly ax. Sergeant Aloyse had a salt-and-pepper mustache, and gray streaks ran through the pigtail that hung rope-like down the center of his back. Some dozen years older than Guizot, he had many tales to tell of the two Italian campaigns of which he was a veteran (he'd been with Bonaparte at Lodi) and he'd fought on the German front as well; yet he declared that he'd never seen as forbidding terrain as the mountains they had to struggle through here—not in the Italian Alps or the German either.

The first days after they'd fought their way on shore at Fort Liberté had not been so very difficult. Though much of the Northern Plain had been put to the torch, there was no other resistance to their progress, and the way was flat, though scorching underfoot sometimes, when they had to cross fields of cinder. But the destruction, though extensive, was not so complete that the men could not find ways to supplement their rations. Sergeant Aloyse proved to be an expert and resourceful forager. It was this, he told Guizot confidentially, that the Little Corporal had understood so well—a soldier on the march prefers to conquer meals than territory. Not to mention the high importance of wine and brandy, durable shoes and dry clothing . . . Guizot listened, rapt and mute, fascinated to be in the presence of someone who still had the temerity to speak of the First Consul, even behind his hand, as the "Little Corporal."

In a few days' time the Northern Plain was brought under a reasonable degree of control, and Rochambeau received new orders: to move his force through the mountains of Grande Rivière and up onto the Central Plateau. Thence they would maneuver to encircle Gonaïves from the east; it was there that Toussaint Louverture was believed to have retreated, after the burning of Le Cap and the battle on the roads of Acul and Limbé. Their maps were accurate enough, but the trouble of getting through Grande Rivière belied the negligible distance noted on the paper.

On the first day they met no enemy, though they felt the enemy must be near. This region was supposed to be occupied by a detachment of the Fifth Colonial Demibrigade under command of one of those African officers, Sans-Souci. But Rochambeau's columns encountered no regular troops as they set out through this country. Nor had the plantations been burned here, as in the lowlands. There were few large plantations in these mountains, mainly small *caféières* and provision grounds—but these latter were denuded of provisions.

They could come near to no one. Rounding a bend of the broad river, they might see in the distance a party of laundresses washing and drying clothes on the gravel shoals, but no sooner had they come within view than the women gathered up their bundles, balanced them improbably on their heads, and faded calmly away from the open banks to vanish in the jungle. Sometimes they might arrive in sight of a country market at the crossing of two trails, with bananas and mangoes and corn laid out for sale, but as the French soldiers picked up their pace, the *marchandes* would quietly pack their wares and recede, mirage-like, among the trees.

The country was all cliffs and gorges—with next to no land that would have been found usable in France, but these Africans had managed to plant almost sheer faces with crazy, spiraling, whorl-shaped gardens, had somehow secured their little huts to outcroppings laddered up the cliffs. But every village was abandoned by the time the soldiers reached it, and every garden was picked bare: the only mangoes left on the trees all green and hard; the corn stalks broken, stripped of ripe ears; and only rows of holes remaining where potatoes had been dug. They met no able-bodied men, not at close range, though sometimes men came out to spy on them from ledges on the opposite side of some deep, verdant chasm.

With all the inhabitants invisible, they could find no reliable guides, and the trails, like the plantings, twisted maze-like up and down the peaks and cliff walls, curving, ascending, never seeming to advance. In the first part of the day a bend in a pathway might sometimes bring them in view of the smoldering plain and the pall of smoke that hung over Le Cap. By afternoon there was nothing behind or before or beside but more mountains, and when they marched through the deep defiles, there was so little horizon one could not calculate direction even by the blazing sun.

By midafternoon the heat was merciless, even at these heights. The men were all wearing standard woolen uniforms, officers too. They sweated under their heavy packs as they struggled up the breathless trails. By evening they smelled like a flock of wet sheep. As soon as the sun set, the air turned sharply chill, and the damp wool uniforms sank clammily against the skin. The men made camp, grumbling—they'd not been able to forage any supplement to the rations they carried. Guizot gnawed his lump of hardtack moodily, washed down the jagged, concrete-textured crumbs with water, remembering the stock of good brandy Daspir had brought onboard the ship.

At least it did not rain that night. The sky was cloudless; Guizot lay wakeful, under the piercing stars. There was drumming in the distance, and a skirling sound, like horns. He was tense in his soggy uniform, shoulders stiff against the damp ground. But though that racket must have come from the enemy, there was no attack. He woke to cock crow, the gray mountain mists, and the sound of men snorting and coughing with colds they'd come down with during the night. That morning his company marched in the vanguard, while the caissons and the mounted officers struggled along behind.

There was beauty in the wild luxuriance of the landscape that surrounded them, now gilded by the rising sun, and Guizot felt his spirits lift as his uniform dried and the effort of climbing dispelled the night's chill. He had not caught cold himself so far, and began to feel a pleasant vigor as he marched. Sergeant Aloyse, at his side, had just begun to whistle some martial air when the first shot cracked. There was a shout, a curse, in the file behind them. Guizot half turned. A grenadier sagged backward, supported by his fellows. A dozen more shots tore off, and more men jerked and fell.

Ambush. A boulder came tumbling through the brush and Guizot dodged it, then craned his neck to see it hurl into the empty air of the gorge. A gang of blacks was firing at them from ledges on the other side, but they were out of effective range; the real danger came from musketeers in the jungle just above the winding trail along which Rochambeau's column was stretched. Sergeant Aloyse quivered and pointed at Guizot's side, impatient for instruction.

"Form a line!" Guizot shouted. He drew his pistol, though he could see no target. "Forward!" Shoulder to shoulder with Aloyse he began scrambling up the slope from the trail. Nothing for it but to sweep the ambushers out of the bush, though there would be some cost. Somewhere below he seemed to hear the whinnying of a wounded horse. A ball whined by his ear, and then he saw one black in ragged trousers, cartridge box across his shoulders. He fired his pistol, did not know if he had hit or missed. A flight of arrows came out of the leaves like a covey of startled quail.

Arrows! Guizot gaped at them. "Fire!" he said. His line let off a reasonably concerted volley. "Bayonets!" Was that his voice or the sergeant's? Aloyse was slipsliding just at his side, bayonet at the ready. Guizot came face to face with a young black woman in a mud-streaked dress, with a great lopsided head of wiry, matted, leaf-strewn hair. As he read her face from the shadows of the leaves, she released her bowstring and retreated. A thump on his upper left arm, like a punch. It took him a moment to realize the arrow had struck him. He could not feel it, but it had pierced his sleeve.

"Avancez!" he cried, dropping his discharged pistol into the holster, drawing out his sword in its place. The woman who'd shot him had disappeared among the broad shiny leaves, but he still seemed to feel the brown heat of her eyes. His men were coming along eagerly enough, but no enemy stood to receive them. Guizot pushed up the slope, his boots slithering over mats of half-rotted leaf and loose soil, flourishing his sword with his right hand, clutching at saplings with his left. The left arm seemed to operate normally; there was no pain. A boulder came hurtling down on them through the brush and he sidestepped and turned to watch it fly out over the gorge. Puffs of smoke were rising from the musket fire along Rochambeau's line, which reached out of sight along the hairpins of the trail, and Guizot got a glimpse of the general himself, a stubby figure under his black shako, picking his way forward and exhorting the men as he passed.

"Avancez," Guizot ordered again. He broke out of the trees onto a shallow terrace of red earth: more broken cornstalks and the branches of uprooted manioc, stripped of its tubers. On the other side of the provision ground, half a dozen men and the woman with the bow were hurrying away, toward a black cliff wall that towered above. There they must certainly be brought to bay. Guizot put on speed, stumbling over the soggy ground. He had outdistanced all his men, except Sergeant Aloyse, never mind the arrow wagging in his arm. Where he'd imagined the ambushers must turn and make a stand, they were going up the cliff wall with scarcely a break in their pace, springing nimbly from foothold to foothold, stone to stone. All were barefoot, though one wore a complete uniform of the Fifth Colonial. In his effort to follow, Guizot had to scramble on hands and knees, sword blade banging over the rocks. The ascent was nearly vertical, and he was winded now, pouring sweat through his wool clothing. He could feel an apoplectic heat in his face. The wagging arrow shaft snagged on a bush and the shock of pain brought him up short.

Sergeant Aloyse braced a hand between his shoulder blades to support him from below. Guizot could hear a whistle in his breathing. The ambushers were going up the cliff wall as easily as spiders, still walking upright over angles that Guizot could not have managed by worming along on his belly. He watched the swing of the woman's mud-clotted skirt as she climbed.

The ambushers were pulling themselves over a horseshoe rim on the cliff top a hundred feet above, into a burst of yellow sunlight among ancient, vine-tangled trees. Guizot stuck his sword into a crack between two rocks and began to recharge his pistol. He took a slow aim, bracing right hand over left, at the man who wore the uniform. Then something oblong blocked the light: a chunk of log dropped toward them. Guizot flinched to avoid it, pressing himself into the stone; the log fell past and splintered on boulders below. He straightened and raised his pistol again. The woman had laid aside her bow to lift a naked infant to her shoulder. Over the child's bare back, she looked down on Guizot. He had a sense of calm appraisal, though she was much too far away for him to see her face. Behind her, one of the men put a conch shell to his lips and sounded it; there was that skirling sound from the night before. Guizot held his fire. Another of the ambushers took hold of the woman's hand and drew her away from the cliff rim, out of sight.

A spill of clear water ran down the black rock. All firing had stopped and in the damp silence Guizot heard the trickle of the spring. A throbbing of drums began, above the cliff wall, answered by others on the far side of the gorge. Vines hung down from the lip of the cliff, their small round leaves dotting the black rock with leaves. A few dozen white butterflies floated up the cliff wall from below, spiraling like smoke in a chimney.

Guizot holstered his pistol and caught hold of his sword hilt, loosening the blade from between the rocks. The sergeant's hand came away from his back, and he turned, awkwardly, making ready to descend. His men were beginning to gather on the terraces below, looking up at him and Aloyse curiously. His arm began to throb in time with the drums, and he saw that the sergeant's eyes were narrowed on the spot where the arrow shaft had pierced his woolen sleeve, the bloodstain widening with his pulse.

Sergeant Aloyse was determined to keep his captain safe from the regimental sawbones. He called on a friend from another company, who'd survived Bonaparte's Egyptian campaign. The Egyptian veteran cut the arrow shaft below its speckled feathers and pushed the point through, while Guizot closed his teeth on a leather strap to keep from screaming. He gave the captain the stone point for a souvenir, then cauterized the wound with a metal ramrod heated red-hot in the fire. In the course of that operation Guizot bit clean through his leather, but he was convinced of the necessity, since Sergeant Aloyse had warned him how fast a wound might fester in this heat.

Their losses in the ambush had been light; it was more a nuisance than anything else. It slowed them down. For the next several days it was the same. Sans-Souci harassed them with snipers, surrounded their line of march with skirmishers. None of the enemy would stand to face an organized assault, so they could easily be driven off from any point, but they would as soon return. It wore upon the nerves of the French soldiers, who grew weary of the endless climbs that never seemed to achieve a peak, and irritable with their short rations. Some began to sicken from the combination of suffocating, sweat-soaked days with damply chilly nights. Others showed signs of dysentery, probably from gnawing at the hard green fruit which was all that had been left on any tree. Guizot's best comfort was that his wound showed no sign of corruption. Also, he seemed to have won his sergeant's warm respect. Aloyse was solicitous of him now, boiling water every night and fussing over his bandage.

They were meant to pacify the whole region of Grande Rivière before they moved on, but this will-of-the-wisp resistance seemed impossible to suppress. If it disappeared before their march, it sprang up again behind them. Rochambeau, of a choleric temper at the best of times, lost all patience in a week of this futile maneuvering. Concluding to leave Grande Rivière to its elusive defenders, he marched his men onto the Central Plateau, where with small difficulty they occupied the town of Saint Raphael.

Here, finally, they found stores: dried beef aplenty and more on the hoof, with barrels of flour and dried beans, yams and cassava, and all sort of fruit. There was also a good supply of *tafia*, the local rum produced by a distillery on the southern outskirts of the town. Guizot was dispatched by Rochambeau to ensure that this enterprise would continue its operations. Sergeant Aloyse could not have been better pleased with this assignment, and he had soon arranged for Guizot's company to better protect the distillery by camping within and around it, with officers taking shelter from its roof. There was a sour smell to contend with, true, but this placement gave them control of distribution to the rest of Rochambeau's troops, not to mention the easy access for themselves— though Aloyse and his brother sergeants took care that the men did not drink so much as to become disorderly.

Morale much restored, Rochambeau's troops set out the next day and by a speedily executed encirclement captured a fort at Mare à la Roche, taking nearly four hundred prisoners and half a dozen cannon. Later that day they reached Saint Michel de l'Attalaye and occupied the town with no opposition. Established at Saint Michel, Rochambeau received a dispatch that General Hardy, in the presence of Captain-General Leclerc himself, had won a hard fight at Morne à Boispins. Though Leclerc declared that this was the most formidable position he had encountered since he had first begun to make war, the French grenadiers finally carried the day, and so flushed Christophe's troops out of the town of Marmelade. Conditions thus looked most auspicious for the closing of the pincers on Gonaives.

That afternoon, Rochambeau sent Guizot with his troops to reconnoiter in the direction of the passes which opened from the Central Plateau toward the coast. They marched across great rolling grasslands, on the alert but meeting almost no one. After the mountains of Grande Rivière, the going seemed almost ridiculously easy, and the terrain was so open that the risk of ambush was nil. Now and then an oxcart crossed their way, and once Guizot saw a sizable movement on the southwest horizon, but when he inspected it with a spyglass it seemed to be a crowd of civilian refugees who'd fled the towns Rochambeau had occupied.

Comparing his map to what he could see, Guizot thought he was heading for the range of Cahos mountains, but these had hardly seemed to grow closer after an hour's march or more. Gray clouds billowed down all over the sky, though there was little wind. It was unusual for wind to begin so in this country, at such an early hour, and in this suffocating calm. Sergeant Aloyse stretched out a hand—a plump drop splattered in his palm. Guizot was ready to order their return to camp when one of his grenadiers called out and pointed down the road ahead. Raising the spyglass to his eye, Guizot discerned a short pack train, coming out of a cleft of the mountains that bounded the plateau.

"Forward," he said, feeling some degree of apprehension, though the other party appeared to be small. Sergeant Aloyse pulled his hat brim down to his eyebrows and stepped out. The pack train seemed to be coming up to them rather quickly; in fifteen minutes they had joined.

Guizot halted at twenty paces' distance and surveyed the other group, two blacks riding admirable saddle horses and leading a pair of pack mules, and one piratical-looking white man, also well mounted, with an immensely broad-brimmed hat and two colossal dragoon pistols strapped either side of his saddle.

"Where are you bound?" Guizot said. "Who are you?"

"Xavier Tocquet." The white man took off his hat and passed a palm across his forehead. Beneath the hat he wore a black-and-white patterned kerchief, knotted at the back above the leather thong securing his long hair. Something about this headgear nagged at a corner of Guizot's attention. The white man had a lean face, a long nose, and hard eyes.

"We are trading, up from the coast," he said. "Yourselves?"

"What trade?" Guizot deepened his voice. Certainly the man had the look of a smuggler. He glanced toward the mules, whose packs were well wrapped up in canvas.

Tocquet shrugged. "Cloth. Some spices and cinchona. We're trading for tobacco, if you must know." He held out his hat to catch the rain, which was still only lightly pattering. "I'm also a landowner in these parts," he said. "And as the weather is worsening, I think we'd prefer to be on our way."

With a press of his knees he urged his horse forward, as if he expected the soldiers to part before him. Guizot held up his hand.

"My commander will want to speak to you," he said.

"Your commander?"

"General Donatien Rochambeau."

"And what is the errand of your General Rochambeau?"

Guizot drew himself more tautly erect. "To subdue and capture the rebel Toussaint Louverture," he said. The phrase *rag-head Negro* appeared in his head; it was this that Tocquet's headscarf had recalled to him.

"So be it, then." Tocquet shrugged again. "I hope that you are camped nearby, as we would all do well to get out of the rain."

Xavier Tocquet had never seen himself as one to be enthralled by sentiment. Nevertheless he had lingered for twenty minutes or longer outside the makeshift gates of Habitation Thibodet. Ten years before, when Elise had finally burst out to join him, those gates had been a splendor of scrolled and gilded iron. How his heart had leapt up then . . . he had not really believed she would come, had already, somewhere in his head, left her behind.

Today she was not coming, not at all. Tocquet sat his horse; the animal shifted and crabbed under him, eager to move. Bazau had dismounted and was feeding his own horse a handful of grain. Gros-Jean had crossed the cactus fence of a yard across the road and stood flirting with a blue-kerchiefed young woman in the curtained doorway of her *case*. These two gave no sign of impatience, but there was no reason to stay.

"*N'alé,*" Tocquet said. We're going. Gros-Jean and Bazau were almost instantly astride. They filed to the east, in the warm dappling of yellow sunlight that leaked through *manguiers* planted either side of the road. Tocquet expected the weight of his mood to lift, as it always did once he'd left any place—once he was well on his way, the weight always rose from him. But today it did not, though the weather was fair and the heat diminished to a tolerable level as they climbed higher in the mountains.

That he should be so fastened to a woman! When Elise had come to him a decade previously, tousled and uncertain, with Sophie in her arms, Tocquet had known that he must be responsible for her afterward, since he had lured her wholly out of the respectability of her marriage. So he had married her himself, once Thibodet was dead. And then? Well, he might have a woman or so, elsewhere, a black woman or a mulattress. There might be a couple of outside children—but Tocquet never rubbed Elise's nose in that. Any such liaisons were kept far off from Thibodet, or from their domicile in Le Cap, for that matter. It was also possible that he'd had some love passage during his American voyage, as Elise seemed most recently to suspect, but that would be merely a passing fancy, nothing to which he meant to return.

And what of her? Had she not been as chimerical with him as he had ever been with her? If she did not care for the dull strictures of the Spanish society east of the border, she could herself be quite a stickler for propriety. The subject of their worst quarrel, and a bitter and enduring one it had been, was her brother's attachment to Nanon. And her stubbornness in digging herself in at Thibodet now, under these circumstances, was truly maddening.

But there she would remain, unmoved. Tocquet understood, as they climbed toward the pass to the plateau, that he'd never really believed today's tactic would work. Better perhaps that he should have taken Sophie with him. He did not like to leave the girl in the danger he foresaw—nor Mireille, but Mireille was too small to engage him personally. If he had taken Sophie, might Elise have followed after all? But she might be too stubborn even for that—there was no overestimating it. And furthermore, he had waited too long, so that he was no longer certain if it was safer to go or remain.

The bright sky darkened as they came up through the pass. Tocquet felt all the more hemmed in by gloom. He was used to tricky times—all times were tricky in this country—but he'd never felt such a dreary uncertainty as now. He spotted the French column before he was seen, and knew it must belong to either Hardy or Rochambeau—Tocquet was assiduous as Toussaint in gathering intelligence, and used several of the same sources. He'd meant to go to the *hatte* he kept on the plateau near Terre Cassée, but though he might have avoided the column still, he decided not to try it. On this perverse day, there was a sort of sour satisfaction in watching himself—Xavier Tocquet—run his head into a snare. Permitting himself to be made prisoner, or the next thing to it, by a callow French captain with his arm in a sling.

By the time his military escort brought him into Saint Michel, the rain was coming down in rivers. The road had become a slough of mud; the men slogged through it, ankle deep. If it kept raining through the night, Tocquet considered, the French advance would be very thoroughly bogged down. So many men would make a morass of whatever ground they moved on, in this wet. He estimated the numbers as they rode through the milling troops toward the village square—close to two thousand, by his best guess.

Rochambeau had established a headquarters in what passed for the *hôtel de ville*—a ramshackle wooden building closing off the north side of the Saint Michel town square. Guizot brought Tocquet to the foot of a long table where the French general sat, studying maps in the gray rain-washed light, surrounded by several of his staff and a black freedman Tocquet knew slightly, whose name was Noël Lory. After a moment, Rochambeau acknowledged his captain.

"What news?" he said, creaking back in his chair. "Have you explored the passes?"

"We were prevented from going so far by the rain, *mon général*," said Guizot, "but we have met this trader, whose information may be helpful—he has just come up this afternoon from Ennery."

"A trader." The small dark beads of Rochambeau's eyes fixed on Tocquet. "You are?"

"Xavier Tocquet."

"A Frenchman."

"I was born here," Tocquet said. "Likewise my father, and his father before him."

Rochambeau sniffed. Tocquet felt the little eyes scouring him for any visible sign of African or Indian blood. Without waiting for an invitation, he pulled out a chair and sat down. He took off his dripping straw hat and smoothed the brim out on the table in a shape that it might hold when it dried. Rochambeau looked at him with a certain asperity; Tocquet affected unconsciousness.

"A trader," Rochambeau said slowly. "I suppose you must trade with the rebel Negroes, as you seem to have come out of their camp."

"I have a few bolts of cloth and some spices only," Tocquet said. "No material of war." He congratulated himself that what he claimed was true—well, he'd foreseen before he set out that it would be no time to get caught moving guns—and in any case Toussaint had snapped up every gun in the country, so there were none to move.

Rochambeau stood up. He was a short man, barrel-shaped; his black shako seemed to account for a fifth of his height. With a bobbing movement, like the walk of a parrot, he went to the open arcade overlooking the square. Bazau and Gros-Jean waited by the horses and mules, just within the shelter of the roof's overhang. Rochambeau studied them for a moment, then snapped his fingers for the young captain and the pig-tailed, mustachioed sergeant who attended him. He set the sergeant to inspecting the packs. Bazau and Gros-Jean looked on impassively, making no move to assist. Rochambeau, meanwhile, exchanged a few muttered sentences with the captain which Tocquet could not overhear. He took off his black-and-white head cloth and wrung water out of it onto the floor.

"Splendid horses you have there," Rochambeau said. "Do you also trade in horse flesh?"

"No," said Tocquet.

Rochambeau strolled back toward the table. "A pity," he said. "But my captain tells me you own land in this region."

"Only a small coffee plantation, and not so very near." It was a lie; he knew that if the French came upon his *hatte* at Terre Cassée they would certainly commandeer all his livestock. "A matter of no more than forty *carreaux*, on the heights of Vallière," he said. In fact he knew of such a place, though he did not own it; it belonged to some mulatto acquaintances of his.

"Oh," said Rochambeau. "And would that have been your destination?"

"Yes," said Tocquet, lying still, for his real intention was to head southeast toward Santo Domingo City. "A little further, even, to the frontier at Ouanaminthe, where I might trade cloth for tobacco." He loosened the thong at the back of his neck and spread his hair on his shoulders to dry. Noël Lory was watching him. Tocquet had never liked him much, had never trusted him at all. It was possible that Lory knew he owned no land at Vallière, and likely he knew all about the *hatte* at Terre Cassée.

"I cannot recommend it," Rochambeau plumped back into his chair at the head of the table. "There is too much fighting in that area for a small party like yours to get through safely."

"Is it so?" Tocquet said. "I had understood that General Christophe controlled the Cordon de l'Ouest at least as far as Dondon, if not further."

Rochambeau smiled. "The rebel Christophe was defeated yesterday at Dondon, and today at Marmelade."

"Are those your victories, General?" Tocquet said silkily.

"Those battles are to the credit of General Hardy," said Rochambeau. "And the Captain-General Leclerc is himself on the march. Today Hardy has beaten Christophe back as far as Ennery, perhaps. If you are coming from that direction, I wonder that you did not meet the remnants of his force."

"I left near dawn," Tocquet said. It was happening, then, as he had thought; somehow he hadn't quite believed it, for all his insistence to Elise. "Though the distance is not so great, the way is difficult."

"How did you come?" said Rochambeau.

"Northeast of Morne Basile, through Savane Carrée." That much was true.

"Ah," Rochambeau squinted down at the map, then looked up again. "Do you know the pass at Ravine à Couleuvre?"

Tocquet reached into his short jacket for a bundle of oilcloth that held three cheroots. Under Rochambeau's disapproving stare he bit off the end of one and lit it, then leaned back to exhale a great blue feather of smoke.

"Ravine à Couleuvre?" Rochambeau's fingers rattled the map against the table.

"Yes," said Tocquet. "Ravine à Couleuvre offers another pass from the plateau to the coastal plain, though the distance is greater if you mean to go either to Ennery or Gonaives."

He leaned forward abruptly, cupping the cheroot—the map was a good one, accurately detailed, and penciled with the route he'd just described. Noël Lory must have informed him. Tocquet took in some other pencilings, which marked the advance of Desfourneaux from Plaisance and Hardy from Dondon. The three columns were almost in position to pull the drawstring tight around Ennery and Gonaives. If Rochambeau passed through Ravine à Couleuvre, he would cut off retreat to the south or the east. Then Toussaint, if he could not fight his way through, would be squeezed out onto the open coastal plain.

"Well, it is plain enough," Tocquet said, thinking that Noël Lory must have already given up this much. "If you descend Ravine à Couleuvre from Morne Barade, you will come out here"—he rapped his thumb on the map—"on the main road, in the middle of the Savane Désolée."

"And how far then to Gonaives?"

Tocquet affected to consider. "No more than ten miles."

"Very well." Rochambeau stole a glance at Lory. "I am told that the rebel Toussaint has a great depot of arms and ammunition at Ravine à Couleuvre."

Tocquet shrugged and drew on his cheroot. "That I can't say. The Governor-General does not confide to me his dispositions."

Though Rochambeau's expression turned quizzical as Tocquet pronounced Toussaint's official title, he made no comment on it. "Very well. But I cannot encourage you to continue your journey to the north. You would do better to remain with us. Perhaps you may render us some service as a guide."

"Oh," said Tocquet. "I think you will be very well guided by Monsieur Lory." He shot Noël Lory a quick, hard look to see if the man would flinch. Certainly he'd betrayed Toussaint—if he'd betrayed Tocquet's interest was a cloudier matter. All Tocquet knew for certain was that he had no interest at all in arriving at Ravine à Couleuvre as a member of this French division. He knew full well, as Lory must, that Toussaint not only had a huge arms cache there but that his men were entrenched to the eyeballs all along the gorge.

"You'll stable my horses for me, then?" Tocquet got up. "I'll just get my pistols first."

"No need for that!" Rochambeau laughed. "You are with the French army now—we shall guarantee your safety. And Captain Guizot will look to your comfort for the night."

"As you prefer." Tocquet reached through the arcade to flick ash from his cheroot into the rain—with his free hand he flashed three fingers at Bazau, then made a spiraling gesture toward the great beyond. "Take care of the horses," he said. Bazau smiled tightly, nodded as he lowered his red-kerchiefed head and turned away.

Some of the junior officers had managed to billet themselves in the houses of Saint Michel, but Guizot had missed this opportunity while out reconnoitering the ways west across the plateau. But a reasonably sound tent was erected for his use, and Sergeant Aloyse managed to requisition some planks for the floor, so they would not have to spread their bedrolls in the wet. Aloyse had also secured a couple of small kegs of rum from the Saint Raphael distillery—private stock, as he cheerfully put it. He seemed content to set himself up as Guizot's personal quarter-master, so long as he could share in what he furnished. So there was rum to offer Xavier Tocquet, who shared their shelter for the night.

After they'd consumed their evening ration of dried beef and corn-meal mush, they sat in the open doorway of the tent, drinking rum and watching the rain. For his part, Tocquet offered round his supply of che-roots. Guizot declined—he was getting a cough—but Aloyse accepted with enthusiasm. Warmed by the rum and the tobacco, he began to tell tales of the European battles he'd attended. Tocquet seemed more than interested, and Aloyse was in any case an engaging raconteur. Guizot watched them, their hawk-like faces leaning together over a sputtering stump of candle the sergeant had waxed to a board. Tocquet's long hair matched the sergeant's snaky pigtail; their heads were joined in a mutual cloud of blue smoke. Guizot felt a little set apart. He felt the beginnings of a cold—from overexertion in the heat, followed by this damp and chill. A throb in his arrow wound worried him a little, though probably it was only caused by rum—there was no sign at all of proud flesh. He watched Tocquet curiously—Tocquet had let it drop that he descended from the *flibustiers* and *boucaniers* who had made the first French settle-ments here, so he really did come from pirate blood. However, he said little more about himself, said very little at all in fact, except to encour-age the sergeant to continue if he paused.

Long after they'd pinched the candle out, Guizot lay wakeful on blan-ket and boards, listening to the sergeant's snores and the steady beat of rain on canvas. The tickle in the back of his throat held him away from sleep, and at the same time his thoughts kept crawling. General Rochambeau had instructed him to keep a close eye on Tocquet, with-out going so far as to place their visitor formally under guard. With that in mind, Guizot had laid out his blanket across the doorway of the tent. Not the most comfortable position, for it seemed to leak a little around the flap, but then it seemed to leak a little everywhere else too. If Guizot put his finger into a crack between the boards, he found half an inch of running water there. The whole of the square had been trampled to a marsh.

He occupied himself with rehearsing the sergeant's tales, and Toc-quet's occasional promptings. Most of Aloyse's listeners, Guizot included, would quiz him about Bonaparte, but Tocquet seemed more interested in the general officers now in Saint Domingue: Hardy, Humbert, Leclerc himself. After all the drone of rain on the tent was soothing. When he closed his eyes, his mind presented him the dark face of the woman who had shot him. With his fingertip he touched the stone arrow point through the rough wool of his trouser pocket. There was her face in the leaves, heavy and handsome as a stone idol, beneath the shock of untameable hair, and there again looking down upon him from the cliff top, with nothing he would call malevolence—instead a calm challenge. Did the child she carried wear that same face?

Guizot sat up sharply, and coughed into his hand. He'd been asleep, for some time probably. Now his head ached from the rum. The sergeant's snores were still resounding against the background of the rain, but the third place was empty, and water poured through a vertical slash in the back of the tent.

Quick as a thought, Guizot was through the tear in the canvas, dressed only in his trousers, wincing as his wounded arm brushed a stake. He put his left hand in his pants pocket to support the arm. The strip of cloth he'd been using for a sling was tangled somewhere in his bedding in the tent. The rain washed over his bare chest and head—he pushed his wet hair back. He could just make out a lean tall shadow slipping around the edge of the sodden encampment; by the wide hat brim it ought to be Tocquet.

The man was a spy then, as Rochambeau must have suspected all along. If he followed, Tocquet might lead him to Toussaint. Guizot might still be first to lay a hand on the raghead Negro. A flush of excitement propelled him forward, his bare toes spreading in the mud. For the moment he'd forgotten that he was nearly naked and unarmed. A sentry stood, ill-sheltered by a tree, in the southeast corner of the square, but he seemed to notice nothing when Tocquet's shadow flitted past him. Of course the rain drowned out all sound. Guizot glanced back as he passed by; the man was asleep on his feet, like a horse, gun stock propped on the toe of his boot and rainwater overflowing from the barrel.

No time for that. With the rain shutting out any light from the sky, it was almost impossible to see anything, but Guizot locked onto Tocquet's shadow: a deeper patch of darkness on the dark. Or maybe he'd deceived himself, for when he reached the crossroads at the edge of town there was nothing. He looked to the right—nothing at all. To the left a vague shape that might have been a tree, with horses beneath it? More than one horse, and a Negro voice spoke in that *patois* that Guizot had not yet learned to understand.

He stumbled in a puddle as he moved toward the sound, and at once something coiled and tightened around his throat, hauling him up backward on the balls of his heels. Tocquet's tobacco smell surrounded him. Guizot groped with his good hand but could get no purchase—his hand grasped nothing but rainwater and he was running out of air. Then the grip shifted. He gasped a breath and felt a knife point pierce the loose skin just above his windpipe.

He tried to recall a prayer, could not. The Negro voice said something incomprehensible. Then Tocquet whispered, in clear French, *I think I'm getting old.*

At the instant of release something round and hard struck Guizot beside the temple. The knife pommel? That was what he pictured as he collapsed. Though the blow was glancing, he let himself fall headlong into the mud, feigning unconsciousness, lest Tocquet think better of his moment of compunction. The rapid splashing of hooves was out of earshot within seconds, but Guizot lay still for a longer time, thoughtfully probing the lump on his head and the shallow cut on the skin of his gullet. Tocquet had spared his life, after all, and Guizot waited ten minutes, possibly fifteen, before he ran back to raise the alarm.

19

Charmed as she was by her new infant grandson, Fontelle had never meant to remain at Habitation Arnaud for long. The mistress Claudine was kindly intentioned, but her head was ever a little off balance, and she could not control the *lwa bossale* which so often climbed unbidden to seat themselves on the saddle of her head. Disorders followed, and while Fontelle admired the patience and grace of her son Moustique in guiding those wild spirits into useful or harmless channels more often than not, the commotion was wearing on her after a few days. Also, soon after Michel Arnaud had come stumbling in at the gate with his injured ankle, rumors began that a large number of French soldiers were on the march south from Le Cap.

She left an hour before first light, kissing Dieufait where he slept on his pallet. Over Moustique's snoring head she made the sign of the cross. Marie-Noelle was awake, quietly nursing the baby, whose name had not been finally chosen. Fontelle kissed them both and went silently out of the *case*. She meant to bring news of Moustique and his increased family to her daughter Paulette, at Ennery.

On the road just beyond the gate of Habitation Arnaud she fell in with a gang of cattle drovers, taking their herd up into the mountains, ahead of the French *blanc* soldiers said to be advancing, not half a day's march behind. There was much discussion among the drovers as to whether these new *blanc* soldiers had come to restore slavery or not, but all agreed it was better to hide the cows from them, since it had been proven that these new *blancs* would slaughter and roast the beef without paying. Fontelle made no comment, but sat her little donkey in silence, now and then touching it up with a short stick she carried in her right hand. In her mind she tumbled possible names for the baby. Jean-Paul. Jean-Mathieu. Possibly Jean-Pierre, in honor of his grandfather. The drovers did not pay her much attention. Her face was too long-jawed and sallow to hold their eyes, though one of the older men seemed to notice that her body was still supple and limber under the loose and colorless dress she wore to travel.

At evening the drovers stopped at Plaisance, but Fontelle stayed there no longer than to water her donkey, get a drink for herself, and refresh her face and hands with a little cool water. She did not look for a meal at Plaisance, but rode on through the deepening, greening twilight, up the switchbacks of the northern approach to Morne Pilboreau. The vast hollow of the Plaisance river valley to the east gave her a touch of vertigo, and she would look in that direction only from the corner of her eye, suspicious of spirits in the vacant air that might hope to tempt her to the brink. Earlier that day something had blown into the ear of a yearling bull, who'd then plunged over the cliff into a chasm, trailing a frayed rope's end behind him, followed by the desolate cries of his owner.

Eastward, the peaks were shrouded in rain cloud, a gray wall drifting slowly toward her as the light dimmed further. It grew colder; Fontelle took a shawl from her straw pannier and wrapped it over her shoulders. She found a boiled egg and a banana in the pannier beneath the shawl, and nibbled at these as she rode along. From beyond the clouded peaks in the direction of Marmelade she heard the thundering fire of cannon and the brighter, sharper sound of musketry.

The shooting had stopped by nightfall, when Fontelle reached the height of Pilboreau, but the crossroads was crowded by many people who had come up the trail from Marmelade to get away from the fighting there. Fontelle sat quietly at the edge of their fires and learned from listening to the talk that Christophe and the Second Demibrigade had been driven from Dondon the day before—the fighting today was at Morne à Boispins. She spread her cloth on the ground and slept for three or four hours. Near midnight, when the stars were cold, she was roused by the murmurs of the *marchandes* making ready to travel, and she untied her donkey and rode among them down the southern cliffs of Pilboreau toward Ennery and Gonaives. The moon was near full and high in the sky, but the wet wind brought the clouds from the east to block the stars off one by one until the moon was darkened too and it began to rain. Fontelle wrapped her shawl around her head, but was soaked through soon enough just the same. The *marchandes* strode either side of her in the dark, their baskets solidly balanced on their heads despite the chattering of their teeth.

Before dawn the rain abated and finally stopped, and as the road lev-

eled off from the mountain, the *marchandes* broke into a swaying trot
and sang to warm and encourage themselves as they advanced. Under
the old trees by the stream at the crossroads for Ennery, they halted and
unpacked their baskets. Fontelle, who had a little store of money, bought
a quantity of small, rosy mangoes and a stalk of *bananes Ti-Malice*. She
wished good day to her companions of the night and urged her donkey
up the trail toward Ennery. As sunlight began to leak yellow through the
small round leaves of the lemon hedges that lined the road, she began to
hear more musket fire from the ridges ahead. Though she did not much
like to be riding in that direction, she kept on. There was no other disturbance except the distant shooting, and it seemed to have approached no
nearer when she reached the gate of Habitation Thibodet.

Doctor Hébert lay spooned with Nanon, a little wakeful in the last
hours of the night. He pushed his nose into the fragrant mass of hair at
the nape of her neck, never mind the tickling. She stirred a little, did not
wake. The doctor listened to rain driving down on the roof. As the rain
began to taper off, he slept, then woke with a terrible start, his heart
throbbing at the top of his throat, it seemed. Now the rain had stopped
completely; there was a trace of sunlight beyond the jalousies. The
sound that had roused him was not thunder, then, but cannon fire, somewhere away in the mountains. Nanon caught his wrist as he jumped out
of the bed.

"Stay." Her eyes were large and liquid with concern.

"You had better get up yourself, and get the children dressed and fed."
The doctor kissed her fingers as he peeled them away. "Find my sister,
and Madame Cigny. Make ready."

"Where must we go, then?" Nanon swung up to the edge of the bed,
arching her back as she shook her hair down.

Her question was a step ahead of the doctor; he had no idea of an
answer. He yanked on his trousers, shrugged into a shirt, stuffed his feet
into his boots. At the door he paused to take his pistols from their pegs
and check their priming before he stuck them in his belt. The house was
quiet except for his own bootheels thumping down the hall. He trotted
down the gallery steps and across the yard toward the stable.

The cannon had stopped, but he could still hear small arms fire
beyond the ridges to the north. In the musty dim of the stable he bridled
a mule, then led it out and swung astride, bareback, clutching the mane.
The reversed pistol grips gouged him in the belly as he moved. Paulette
had come yawning out onto the gallery and stood there blinking at him
curiously. The doctor clucked to the mule and slapped the reins against
its neck and rode at a fast walk out of the yard, through a few spindly,
neglected ratoons of cane, and up into the coffee terraces.

The field hands were moving among the coffee trees, but slowly, hesitantly, without song. In their silence their ears were doubtless cocked to

the noise of musketry above. But in these folds of mountain, all sounds were deceiving; the ear could not reliably tell what was near or what was far. The doctor rode past Caco, standing on the fifth terrace to gape at him, his basket dangling. He wished that Riau or Guiaou was on the plantation now; Riau, especially, would be likely to know something about what that gunfire meant. Or Tocquet—it suddenly struck the doctor that Tocquet had not appeared at last night's supper table, nor had he seen him at all the previous day.

Above the coffee terraces veins of provisions twined among the cliffs, and a few long-eared black pigs were foraging. Strayed from their keeper, they'd begun to root up yams, but when the mule approached they scattered snorting into the brush. The doctor leaned low into the mule's neck to encourage it up a slope just barely short of vertical. He'd learned this technique watching Toussaint's horsemanship, though he couldn't have managed it here with a horse instead of a mule. Shale whizzed out from under the hooves, and twice the mule stumbled, slipped sideways, but finally came scrambling out onto the remains of the old Indian road that ran northeast along the ridges toward Marmelade and Dondon.

The doctor straightened, and glanced to the west. On a neighboring peak, a man was standing next to the tall flagpole of the *hûnfor*, shading his eyes to look for something in the distance. Quamba, the doctor thought. He squeezed the mule into a trot, for the going was relatively easy here. In a quarter-mile he came upon men of the Second Demibrigade, tattered and muddy and hollow around the eyes, hurriedly digging trenches or dragging deadfall timber to block the road. So occupied and exhausted they were that they did not seem to notice that the doctor had come on the scene. He halted for the mule to get its breath. By some trick of the mountain acoustics the musket fire sounded farther off now, though it must be approaching; this was clearly a retreat. There was an unobstructed view for several hundred yards to the east, and there where the road curved was some movement. The doctor patted himself for his folding spyglass, but he'd left it in the house. He flattened a hand above his brows, against the sun still low on the peaks. That figure in the general's bicorne was certainly Christophe; he recognized the silhouette. The antlike movement resolved itself into men bearing litters of the wounded toward him, with Christophe directing them, calling hoarse orders behind.

At once the doctor turned his mule off the road into the brush. If he met with Christophe now, the black general would certainly impress him to care for his injured men, and while he would not ordinarily object to that duty, he wanted to see his family safe—if that were possible. If the French pursuit were fast and vigorous, it seemed to him likely that the hasty defenses he'd seen would soon be swept away. Then the retreat would pour down on Habitation Thibodet with all its damages.

He rode the mule down the coffee terraces and pulled to a stop in front of the cane mill. There was commotion on the gallery, first Elise, then Isabelle appearing and then dashing back inside. A tall mulatto woman in a high blue turban came riding around the corner of the mill from the direction of the drive. The doctor recognized Fontelle and raised a hand to her.

"Monsieur le médecin!" Fontelle beamed at him, revealing the crooked teeth in her long jaws. Unhurriedly she dismounted and unstrapped a bulging pannier. "I have brought you mangoes, look."

Unconsciously the doctor accepted in each hand a small fragrant mango from the crossroads of Ennery. "Where have you come from?" he asked Fontelle.

"Just now from Ennery," Fontelle said. "This morning from Pilboreau. Yesterday from Plaisance, and the day before, Acul and Habitation Arnaud. There I stayed—"

"Did you pass through the fighting?" the doctor cut in.

"No," said Fontelle. "But the French soldiers were coming down from Le Cap, they say. I did not see them. Last night we could hear shooting from Pilboreau."

"The soldiers from Le Cap."

"No," said Fontelle. "They say it is other soldiers from Dondon and Marmelade. We did not see them either but we could hear their guns."

Paulette came galloping down the gallery steps and caught her mother in an embrace that rocked her where she stood. The doctor sucked in a breath, then dashed into the cane mill. In the last few months the small office behind the machinery had become Tocquet's retreat; he kept cards and a chessboard there, along with the plantation's neglected ledgers, rum, brandy if it could be found, tobacco. Sometimes he slept there, in an Indian hammock strung from corner to corner of the room, if he were on the outs with Elise, as he seemed frequently to be of late. But this morning the room was empty, air stale with the smell of old tobacco smoke. The doctor turned on his heels, watching motes of the dust he had raised turn in the shaft of sunlight through the shuttered window. The hammock was gone; Tocquet sometimes took it with him when he traveled. In an earlier time Toussaint had used this place for a headquarters, and where was Toussaint now?

The doctor heard Paul's voice shouting through the shuttered window and he ran outside to see what was the matter. Left unhitched, the mule had wandered toward a gap in the hedges, but Paul had caught the reins and was leading it back.

"Well done," the doctor called. "Just hold him there." Elise had reappeared on the gallery and he trotted up the steps to meet her there.

"Have you seen Xavier?" he panted.

"Xavier has abandoned us," Elise said dourly. "He thought there would be trouble here."

"Good God," said the doctor. "You might have mentioned it. When? Where has he gone?" Elise was staring at his hands and he realized he was still holding the mangoes.

"Fontelle brought them." He waved a mango at Fontelle, still clutched by Paulette in the yard, the donkey snuffling the dust beside them. The skin of the mango he was gesturing with had split in his grip, and now he noticed the juice of it sticky on his palm. A couple of fruit flies hovered over it. The doctor offered the undamaged mango to Elise, and when she shook her head he shrugged and laid it on the table. He wiped the other mango with his loose shirttail and took a bite. The taste of it was sharp and sweet; it was just at the point of perfect ripeness.

"What kind of trouble?" he said, when he had swallowed. "When is he coming back?"

"How should I know?" Elise said bitterly. "He wanted us all to go with him across the Spanish border, but I was certain we would be safer here, so long as Suzanne Louverture remained. And you just stand there, chewing mango!"

The doctor took a final bite and fired the pulpy seed out into the yard. "I don't know where Madame Louverture may be," he said. "But there seem to be two French columns converging on this area. That is Christophe falling back before one of them—" He pointed to the ridge. "And as much as I was able to see, he is hard pressed."

"Christophe!" Isabelle walked onto the gallery, setting down a small portmanteau to fasten the buttons of a traveling duster up her delicate throat. "*That* for your General Christophe—" She turned her head and spat with a surprising lack of inhibition across the rail into the bougainvillea vines.

"What is your plan?" the doctor said, as he took in her costume.

"To fly," said Isabelle succinctly.

But where? the doctor would have asked; hoofbeats on the drive distracted him. He whipped his head around, expecting perhaps to see an advance guard of French cavalry, though only two horses entered the yard, with Bel Argent, Toussaint's white stallion, in the lead. With a start the doctor realized that Placide, instead of Toussaint, was riding the big warhorse.

He ran down the steps to greet Placide. The second horseman, he saw with some degree of reassurance, was Guiaou. But where was Toussaint? He never allowed any other man to ride Bel Argent. If Toussaint were dead, or out of the action, would there be peace or a bloodier war?

"Doctor Hébert," Placide said a little breathlessly, checking the white stallion as it made to rear. "My father wants you. That is—the Governor-General asked me to come for you."

"Yes," said the doctor. "Very well, but where?"

"The battle." Placide pointed to the south.

The doctor felt the blood drain from his face. Here was exactly what

Tocquet had been predicting—a French encirclement that would trap Toussaint with his back to the sea. The force to the south might be Boudet, then, marching up from Port-au-Prince.

"Where is this battle?" he asked Placide.

"The battle has not yet been joined," said Placide, "but you must go and bring with you medicines and bandages."

"What of the women and children here?" the doctor said. "Where is your mother, and your brothers?" He took hold of Placide's stirrup and drew himself against Bel Argent's warm flank.

"At Sancey," Placide said.

"They can't stay there." The doctor waved his free arm toward the ridge. "Christophe is being driven back, just there—you cannot count on him to hold."

Placide cocked his head to the gunfire. "I thought Christophe was at Morne à Boispins."

"No longer."

Placide glanced between the doctor and Guiaou, hesitating. Guiaou, meanwhile, had seen Merbillay coming into the yard with her youngest child swung to her hip, and he steered his horse in her direction.

"Let your women and children go to the *grand'case* of Sancey," Placide said finally. "My mother and brothers are still there, and Morisset is with them, the commander of my father's guard. If they must leave Sancey, they will be taken to a place of safety. But you must go yourself to find my father at the headquarters in Gonaives."

"Well said, Placide." The doctor let go of the stirrup, reached for a quick clasp of Placide's hand. "I'll want Guiaou with me, to help me with the wounded." He turned as he spoke to see Guiaou bending at the waist from the saddle to kiss Merbillay's cheek and spread a hand on the head of the child she carried.

"No," Placide smiled faintly as he shook his head. "I must keep Guiaou with me." With that he beckoned Guiaou to follow and with a press of his knees moved Bel Argent into a smooth canter up the terraces toward the height of the ridge.

The women had not wasted their time since they woke, and in twenty minutes more they had set out for Sancey: Elise, Isabelle, Nanon, Zabeth, and all the children except for Paul, who insisted that, at nearly ten, he was old enough to see the fighting. The doctor finally gave in to him, unsure of his own reasons—in the turmoil, he simply didn't want to be separated from his son. He took Caco with him also, since he was Paul's best companion, and Paulette, whose nursing skill he knew. Since Fontelle had just come to see Paulette, she also joined their party. Twenty minutes sufficed for the doctor to add his American rifle to his armaments and pack enough bandages and dried herbs from the Thibodet infirmary to load a donkey. The muskets were still firing on the ridge above the plantation as they left it to set out for Gonaives.

With just a little varnishing of the plainest truth, Captain Guizot had made a determined effort to turn Tocquet's escape to his own credit. He'd given an energetic pursuit, after all, had struggled hand to hand with the fugitive, and had light injuries to show for it: the goose-egg bruise beside his temple, and the less obvious but more sinister scratch beneath his jaw. Rochambeau grumbled, but did no more than reprimand the captain, though the sentry who'd been sleeping on his feet was tied to a wagon wheel and whipped.

It rained all through that night and the next day; no movement of the troops was possible in the soup. Guizot moped under the canvas of his makeshift tent, nursing his cold, which had worsened. His head hurt also from the blow, and the tumble in the mud had done his arrow wound no good, though it seemed better after the solicitous Sergeant Aloyse had cleaned it thoroughly with scalding water. And the rum they'd salvaged from Saint Michel was a quiet comfort to both of them after dark.

In the small hours of that night the rain finally stopped, and the next day dawned clear and bright. They moved out in the middle of the morning, down the road Guizot had earlier explored, through mud still deep enough to slow them down considerably. By midday the weight of the sun was crushing, but the mud scarcely dried; it went on sucking at their boots and the wheels of the caissons. Guizot plodded onward, at the head of his men, with Sergeant Aloyse always at his back. His mind looped aimlessly, softening like butter in the heat. He thought of his companions on *La Sirène,* and Toussaint's sons—where were they now? That episode seemed to belong to some other life.

There were rumors among Rochambeau's men that Hardy had over-run Marmelade, and that Boudet was coming up the coast from Port-au-Prince to surround Toussaint at Gonaives. But where were Daspir and Cyprien and Paltre? Guizot lurched forward awkwardly, his balance unsettled by the wounded arm, clumsily riding in its sling. At moments he thought he felt Tocquet's tobacco breath on his face again, with the knife point pressed into his gullet. If he had had the fortitude to pursue, even after he'd been dropped sprawling half-stunned in the mud . . . he had the queer, unsupported conviction that Tocquet might have led him quite near to the man they sought. The words of the wager he'd made with the other three captains were hanging, always the same distance ahead of him, above the mountains that bounded the western horizon. The mountains seemed to grow no nearer, no matter how they struggled through the mud.

The rain had made the night completely lightless; to move through it was like drowning in a cave. Tocquet knew every way across the high

savanna as well as the lines in his own palm, but the night of his evasion
from Rochambeau's camp was so smothered in darkness that they did
not find their way to the passes of the Savane Carrée before dawn.
They'd abandoned the roads to cut across the grassland, where their
horses were less likely to be engulfed in the mud, but still they were
obliged to go very slowly, with direction almost impossible to determine
in the rain. Tocquet had little fear of pursuit, but all the same he chafed
at their poor progress. They'd left their pack animals, with their goods,
to Rochambeau, and this loss also irritated him as they picked their way
along.

The downpour was so heavy that daybreak brought no more than a
vague, pearly gray illumination. It was not possible to conjecture the
time, but after a period of riding through rain that felt like a waterfall,
they finally reached a cavern on the slopes of Morne Basile. An overhang
of the cliff provided partial shelter for their horses, and in the deeper
recesses a store of dry wood had been laid by for just such emergencies
as this one. Bazau built a fire and lit it; Gros-Jean dug a ration of dried
beef from the bottom of a saddlebag. All three of them stripped off their
clothing and laid it to dry on the rocks by the fire. They chewed the hardened strips of beef contemplatively; it took some time to get one down.
Now and then one of them would walk to the cave mouth to confirm that
the rain had not abated.

Tocquet was certain enough that no troops would advance through
this flood. The three of them stayed in the cave through the night, rotating a watch, though probably it was unnecessary. Tocquet woke spontaneously the moment the rain stopped, though cascades of run-off still
roared all around their shelter. Gros-Jean was watching at the mouth of
the cave. They roused Bazau and set out in the velvet dark. Presently
their way was lit by a moon the parting clouds disclosed.

At dawn there was gunfire in the hills and Tocquet had to lead them
on less familiar, more difficult paths to avoid Christophe's retreat from
Marmelade. Their going was all the more difficult for the rainwater that
still ran down every available channel. More often than not they had to
go on foot, leading the horses, coaxing or whipping them up the twisted
ascents and steep defiles.

It was past noon when they reached Thibodet, and the *grand'case* was
deserted. All work appeared to have stopped in the coffee groves. A few
people tended their provision grounds, while the rest simply rested
somewhere in the shade. Few adult men were in evidence, but the
women and children drifted over the property as if unconcerned by the
chatter of muskets just one ridge away.

Tocquet found Merbillay behind the *grand'case*, stirring an iron cauldron of *gros bouillon*. Gros-Jean and Bazau dipped up gourdfuls right
away, not waiting for any invitation. Oblivious to the glance Merbillay
fired in their direction, they sat crosslegged on the ground to eat.

"Koté madamn mwen?" Tocquet asked. Where is my wife?

Merbillay inclined her handsome head and scraped the sides of the iron cookpot with a long wooden spoon. Her youngest, Marielle, clung to her skirts and peeped, smiling shyly at Tocquet.

"Li pati pou Sancey, ak tout blan sa yo," Merbillay said, noncommittally. She has gone to Sancey, with all the other whites.

Tocquet nodded and scooped up a gourd of stew. He ate slowly, squatting on the ground by the others, and stopped before his hunger was wholly satisfied, so as to remain alert. The three of them got fresh horses, saddled up and rode on. At Sancey the situation was the same: the plantation drained of able-bodied men, the *grand'case* deserted but for servants. These latter were able to tell Tocquet that Elise and the other whites from Thibodet had indeed passed through earlier in the day. With Suzanne Louverture and some of her relatives, they'd gone further south, in the direction of Périsse.

At first Placide had been afraid that Bel Argent would be altogether too much horse of him, though to ride him was an honor he would never have declined. But with half an hour in the saddle, on the road from Sancey to Thibodet, he and the white stallion reached an understanding, and Placide knew that he would manage. He savored the impression he made on General Christophe by materializing in the midst of the mountain skirmishing, on his father's best-known mount. But despite his excitement, the elation of action, Placide could see that Christophe was in a bad way—both he and his men demoralized by their defeat at the seemingly impregnable post of Morne à Boispins. Though they were still delaying the French, though Christophe swore through his teeth he would defeat them, Placide concluded that Doctor Hébert was right: the line above Ennery could not hold for long.

The whites of the *grand'case* had already departed by the time Placide and Guiaou rode back into the main compound of Thibodet. He would have liked to continue on their trail to Sancey—to kiss his mother, take Isaac's hand one time before the battle Isaac would not share. But the family was probably already on the move, retreating from Sancey to some place of greater safety, farther south.

Guiaou had led them on the way up from Gonaives, but on their return Placide took the lead; he had taken care to note the landmarks, and now he turned through every crossroads without a fault. A dry wind swirled over the lowlands north of Gonaives, stirring white dust out of the *raket* and *baroron*, coating the two riders and their horses. Placide set a moderate pace, so as not to overtire Bel Argent. They entered Gonaives at a steady trot.

Toussaint had just returned himself, from an inspection of posts along the Ester River to the south. Placide found him on the second-story porch at headquarters, in council with Vernet, Magny, and Monpoint. He stood at attention to make his report and remained in that posture until his father put him at ease with a nod.

"So." Toussaint's hand floated over the map; he glanced up to catch Vernet's eye. "General Hardy is advancing on Ennery even as we speak. If, as it seems, Christophe cannot hold him, he may arrive to threaten us here. But another column is coming through the mountains"—his forefinger traced the main road from Pilboreau down to Gonaives—"commanded by Desfourneaux, and perhaps also by Leclerc himself." He sat back, holding Vernet's eyes. "These two forces may combine against you. It looks likely that they will."

"*Oui, mon général.*"

"You will repel them. I leave you two battalions of the Seventh Demi-brigade, a squadron of cavalry and what militia has been mustered—let that be sufficient to destroy these *blancs* who come to take our liberty. But if by any chance you cannot hold, burn Gonaives and retreat along this line into the Cahos."

"*Oui, mon général.*" Vernet saluted, turned smartly away. His boot-heels clattered down the stairs. Toussaint turned to Monpoint and Magny.

"See that your men and the horses are ready. We move within the half-hour."

Monpoint and Magny saluted and withdrew. Placide, now alone with Toussaint, cocked his head to peer at the map.

"What of General Boudet and his force?" he said. Like others around the Gonaives headquarters, Placide had heard the rumors that Boudet meant to close on Gonaives from the direction of Port-au-Prince.

"Boudet will not reach Gonaives. Boudet will not get so far as Saint Marc. Dessalines stands in his way, and Dessalines will keep him in his bottle." Toussaint's hand passed over his mouth, carrying away the smile. "Our business today is with Rochambeau." He flicked the map with a yellowed fingernail. "He means to march down out of the Central Plateau and reach the Savane Désolée, just here."

Toussaint leaned back, fixed Placide with his gaze. "If he succeeds?"

Placide gulped back a renegade heartbeat. He swallowed twice before he spoke. "He will occupy the road to Ester and cut our communications. We shall be caught between his force and the other columns advancing from Le Cap and Ennery."

Toussaint smiled openly. "So they desire. So they suppose. But Rochambeau will not reach the southern road. We will meet him here, in the Ravine à Couleuvre."

"Can we hold him there?" Placide blurted.

"We can destroy him in that place, and we will do it. We must do it. After Rochambeau has been wiped out, we will return here to support Vernet and finish all these *blancs* who are coming down from the north."

He measured Placide with his eye. "*Fé konfyans, fils-moin.* We will not fail. I have prepared for a long time to meet the invader in this ravine."

His fingernail tapped the ink checkmark that indicated the height of Morne Barade. "But to succeed, we must reach this position before night."

"And if Rochambeau should come there first?"

Toussaint did not reply at once. His eyes half closed; his hand slipped beneath the skirt of his coat to finger the beads of the rosary attached to his belt. Placide listened to the click of wooden skulls: one, two, three. He had been fascinated with that rosary as a boy, during that distant time he and his brothers had been living with their mother on the Central Plateau, seeing their father very seldom, when he came to them between his battles. It had seemed to Placide that the rosary grew longer with each of his father's absences. Toussaint's parted lips breathed out his silent prayers. *Papa,* Placide thought to say.

"*Mon général,*" he said aloud. "If Rochambeau should arrive before us?"

"*Fé konfyans BonDyé.*" Toussaint stood up. "Put your trust in God— He will not permit that to happen."

Sancey was all astir when the refugees from Thibodet arrived. Suzanne Louverture moved quietly, quickly, efficiently through that turmoil. Her glance acknowledged the white women and their children with no sign of surprise. A couple of servants were carrying small bundles out of the house, while Saint-Jean scurried back and forth through the open doorway, generally getting himself underfoot. Toussaint's sister, Madame Chancy, stood beside her two daughters; small portmanteaus waited at their feet. Beside these ladies was Isaac, no longer wearing his dress uniform, but more simply attired in canvas trousers and a loose white shirt. It was plain enough to Elise that none of them would be staying here.

Mireille squirmed on her bosom, reaching for Zabeth, who was, however, sufficiently burdened by her own infant. Sophie tugged free from Elise's other hand, and with Robert she scampered up the steps to peer in the tall windows of the Sancey *grand'case*. Elise opened her mouth to reprove her. But just then Suzanne came out of the house and turned to lock the front door with a large iron key. The children, abashed, crept down the steps to rejoin their mothers.

Silently, Elise regathered herself. She'd hoped for a respite in this place, a pause, even if they did not stay. If she'd yielded to Xavier's importunings, she might even now be . . . where? It came to her, with a palpitation, that Xavier might have waited too long for his own purposes, might well have been caught in the fighting in the hills or on the plateau.

But now Isabelle had drawn her own iron key from her bodice and was brandishing it at Suzanne Louverture. Her voice was distinctly too loud when she spoke, and her hand trembled, holding out the key.

"Scarcely a month, Madame Louverture, since I locked the door of my house at Le Cap with this. And from that house, the lock survives, but all the rest is ashes. And on whose order was—"

"Isabelle!" Elise shifted the baby to her opposite arm and moved to quell her friend. "Be silent!"

Nanon had appeared, more calmly, from the other side, and at her touch Isabelle subsided.

"Pardon," Elise said to Suzanne. "I'm sure she means to wish you no misfortune—she is unsettled by her losses."

Isabelle's breath came in quick, harsh pants. The hollow of her throat was pulsing. In all their friendship Elise had never seen her break this way. One never knew what straw would be too heavy. Nanon, a head taller than Isabelle, stood behind her, stroking the nape of her neck and her temples. She drew Isabelle's head back to rest on her bosom.

"Well," said Suzanne. "I think we have all known the changing fortunes of our wars." She touched Isabelle with a fingertip on her forehead, then raised her slack hand and folded the fingers over the key it held. "Take courage, Madame," she said. "When these troubles are ended, you may yet build another house to hold the lock your key will open."

Ten dragoons of Toussaint's honor guard were there to escort them, under command of Morisset. Horseback or riding donkeys, they all set out on the southbound trails. Morisset led them on byways Elise did not know, crooked paths that avoided the main road from Ennery down to Gonaives. Once their way was blocked for a few minutes by a long file of field hands who'd laid down their hoes for muskets and were heading at a dogtrot in the direction of the Savane Désolée.

"The legacy of Sonthonax," Isabelle said dully. Elise hushed her, with a glance at Suzanne; she knew that Toussaint had been as assiduous as the French commissioner Sonthonax in distributing muskets to the field hands, with the exhortation that these weapons were the fundamental instruments of freedom and must be kept ready for just such occasions as this.

Suzanne, if she had heard this ironizing, did not react, and Isabelle consented to be silenced. Her episode of hysteria seemed to have passed and she was calm and upright in her saddle, though she looked pale and drawn. Isaac rode beside her, offering tidbits of conversation in the clear, correct French he had learned at the Collège de la Marche. Gradually, Isabelle began to soften under his polite attentions and her own awareness that, without even trying, she'd beguiled the boy.

"Where is Saint-Jean?"

The voice was Suzanne's, from the head of their line. Isaac swiveled his head around—Elise looked too, but the youngest Louverture son was nowhere to be seen. The older children had been making a game of their progress for the last half-hour, giggling as they raced their donkeys in circles through the brush, but now the path had turned very near to the main road, and below them Elise thought she could hear the distant rattle of a military drum and the shuffle of marching feet. Sophie and Robert burst out of the bushes. Isaac repeated the question to them— "Where is Saint-Jean?"—and Robert pointed in the direction of the road.

At once Isaac was off at a canter. Four of Morisset's dragoons went after him. Suzanne had turned her donkey across the trail; her peeled stick pointed to the sky. "Isaac," she called. *"Isaac!"*

"Madame," Morisset said. "My men will bring him back to you, but we must go on, and quickly. Those are French soldiers there on the road."

Suzanne fell into her place in the line. Morisset turned them inland, leaving the trail to go cross-country, inland, with one more dragoon remaining behind at the point of their departure. They rode through dense brush, raked by the dry thorns, till they gained another, higher pathway. The sound of the drum was no longer audible from the main road. Robert and Sophie had fallen silent; they did not try to leave the group. After forty minutes Isaac and the five cavalrymen overtook the others. There was no sign of Suzanne's youngest son.

"No one will harm him," Isaac said. "He is the son of the Governor-General." But the young man's dark face looked drained of blood. Suzanne did not respond to what he'd said. Isabelle, who'd come very much to herself again, pressed her mare forward and reached out a hand to Madame Louverture, but Suzanne did not seem to see her. She faced forward, her eyes hard under the line of her blue headcloth, her face a mask.

In the afternoon they reached Habitation Cocherelle, where the balance of Morisset's squadron awaited them. Toussaint had passed that way an hour before, at the head of a battalion of grenadiers and more dragoons of his guard. He'd left word for the family to remain there till his next message might come.

Suzanne slipped down from her donkey, walked into the shade of a flamboyant tree, knelt in the dust, and folded her hands to pray. Isabelle took a few steps toward her, then stopped short. Elise and Nanon joined her. Behind them, Morisset was giving orders, deploying his men on all the approaches to the Cocherelle *grand'case*. Madame Chancy walked past the white women, but she too stopped before she reached Suzanne beneath the flamboyant. When Suzanne had finished her prayer, she rose and brushed the dirt from her skirt. She clasped Madame Chancy's hand for a moment and then, expressionless, went into the *grand'case* to begin making it ready to receive the refugees.

Elise sat on the Cocherelle gallery, with Mireille sleeping, finally, in her arms. She was exhausted beyond all reckoning, had not the will to rise and lay the baby down. Where would she lay her? Isabelle and Nanon and Zabeth were all scurrying through the house, following Suzanne Louverture's directions, beating out mattresses, making beds, or organizing pallets. Isabelle had snapped completely out of her despondency, or buried it in this new bustle. Someone had lit a cookfire behind the house; the odor of simmering *soupe joumoun* mingled with the wood smoke. In these acts of dailiness Suzanne must find some shelter. Elise could not imagine what must be in her mind and heart. She remembered Saint-Jean as she'd last seen him, grinning as his donkey darted through the *baroron*. He'd disappear, then reappear, like Sophie and Robert. When had been the last time he'd crossed her field of vision? He'd disappeared, then failed to reappear. That simple. Remarkable as it was in this country, Elise herself had never lost a child. She had not paid enormous attention to Mireille—indeed the baby preferred Zabeth, to whom she was more accustomed—but now she snuggled her closer, as she let herself slip down toward a doze.

A noise at the end of the Cocherelle drive roused her. Morisset's sentries must have challenged someone. Silence, then Elise picked out three horsemen riding toward her out of the dusky lane. The tall figure riding the lead horse wore a familiar broad-brimmed hat.

Elise ran down into the yard and clutched his stirrup. "Xavier," she said. "Dear God, you are safe."

Tocquet smiled wearily through the dust that coated his face. "And you also," he said. "And the children?"

"All safe and well," Elise said. "But for Saint-Jean—he was lost on the road. It was awful—one minute he was there and the next he was gone."

"He is found," Tocquet said, and slipped down from his horse to stand beside her. "Fortunately or unfortunately, as you prefer. General Hardy has captured him."

"What ill luck for Suzanne."

"He won't be harmed," Tocquet said. "He is too valuable as a hostage. They'll treat him kindly."

"Then Hardy's men must have overrun Ennery altogether," Elise said.

"Parts of it," Tocquet said. "It was all confusion when I passed. There was some fighting in the village, I think, and of course we were doing all we could to keep clear of it."

"How glad I am to see you," Elise said.

"*Pareil*," said Tocquet. "I feel the same. It has been a long day tracking you down. And you too, little one."

Mireille had awakened, uncharacteristically calm. She raised her head from the crook of Elise's elbow and looked at her father with wide, round eyes. Bazau and Gros-Jean had also dismounted. Gros-Jean approached, and with a cluck of his tongue he took the reins from Tocquet's hand and led the horses away behind the Cocherelle *grand'case*.

"Is that *soupe joumoun* I smell?" Tocquet said. He draped an arm over Elise's shoulder; she rested her cheek on his collarbone. Mireille turned and closed her soft hand around Tocquet's trailing forefinger. Together they began to stroll toward the house.

"Isabelle and Nanon are with you, yes?" Tocquet said. "And Antoine?"

"He was ordered to go with Toussaint, with the army—they seem to be thinking there will be a great battle."

Tocquet stopped short. "Where?"

"It hasn't been reported to me. You must ask Morisset, perhaps—he is here, with these guardsmen who are watching the house. I think they said Toussaint was bound for Ravine à Couleuvre when he left here this afternoon."

Abruptly Tocquet disengaged his arm. "That may be ill luck indeed," he said. "I was afraid of it—and Ravine à Couleuvre is uncomfortably close by."

"What do you mean?" Elise reached for his hand; absently Tocquet returned the pressure, then let it fall as he fumbled for one of his cheroots.

"Rochambeau knows that Toussaint has arms cached there," he said. "He has found someone to guide him, too. If he meets Toussaint in the ravine, it's likely he'll outnumber him. And Antoine is with them! I ought to overtake them as soon as I may."

"Whose side are you on?" Elise said, with more curiosity than bitterness, this time.

"Ours," said Tocquet. "You and me and Sophie and Mireille. Gros-Jean and Bazau and Zabeth for that matter. Why should we not include them too?" Of a sudden he smiled, in an easy way. Setting the unlit cheroot in the corner of his mouth, he reached to squeeze her shoulder. "I'm only accepting your version, after all. For the moment our fortunes are thrown in with Toussaint's, or rather our family's with his, as you argued . . . what, was it the day before yesterday?"

"It has been longer," Elise said. "Oh, I thought I would never see you again! Must you really go so soon?"

"I ought to get your brother out of it, if I can," Tocquet said. "And if Toussaint is to protect his family, it would be well if he knew for certain where they are—and that he knew the odds that face him."

He prodded Mireille's stomach lightly; the baby gurgled and reached again for his forefinger.

"But not at once," Tocquet said. "First I will take some soup if I may, and Bazau and Gros-Jean will take soup. I ought to speak to Morisset, and Madame Louverture, and see what they may have here for horses."

There was a small tavern across the road from Toussaint's head-quarters at Gonaives, and Doctor Hébert took his companions into that establishment to order a midmorning meal. He'd reported as soon as they reached the town, but Toussaint was absent and neither Magny nor Monpoint seemed to know quite what to do with him. The tavern offered stewed chicken, *banane pesé*, and greens. The doctor nagged at Paul to eat, though the boy was too excited to apply himself to the task. No one could say when they'd next sit down to a hot meal. Fontelle and Paulette worked slowly and diligently at their plates till they were empty. Neither of them spoke while they were eating. Likewise Caco ate in silence. Only Paul kept chattering, asking questions to which the doctor replied distractedly or not at all.

He ordered half a dozen baked yams, and when they were delivered he carried them out to where their donkeys were tethered at the rail to pack them into his saddlebags. That accomplished, he lingered by his mule to check the priming of his pistols and the long gun. Across the mule saddle, he saw Placide and Guiaou come trotting up to the headquarters. Guiaou took the reins of Bel Argent as Placide got down and hurried inside, and led both horses off behind the building.

Toussaint must have returned, the doctor surmised, while they were inside eating. And indeed it was not long before Toussaint himself appeared on the street. Within minutes he had formed up a battalion of grenadiers and a squadron of cavalry; with no more than a glance and a gesture, he beckoned the doctor to a place near the head of the cavalry column, just behind Placide. Magny and Monpoint repeated orders down the line. The troops strode down the block, turned through the square below the church, and soon were marching south from Gonaives along the broad, flat road through the Savane Désolée.

A couple of buzzards appeared in the sky above them as they went on—not unusual in this desert, but the doctor did his best not to look at them. They kept going through the still parching heat of the Savane Désolée until they reached the cactus fence and wooden gates of Habitation Cocherelle. From Placide, the doctor understood that Toussaint's family was expected to be here, and his own also if everything had gone according to plan, but none of them had yet arrived. He saw a chance to leave Paul in a safer place, for at midafternoon the boy seemed a little weary of the adventure they'd embarked on. Perhaps Caco might remain behind also. If only Paul's mother and brothers had been there . . . but soon it was clear that Toussaint would not wait. The troops moved out from Cocherelle, crossing the back fields of the plantations Lacroix and Périsse on a trail that diverged from the main road to climb a slow grade toward the mountains.

At dusk they'd reached the gravel shoals at the mouth of Ravine à Couleuvre. The stream bubbled merrily over the pebbles, swollen with the recent rain on the Central Plateau up above. Here Toussaint called a halt for a meal, though he forbade all fire. The men began munching such cold rations as they could discover. Doctor Hébert replenished his waterskin from the stream and passed a piece of cold yam to each member of his group. They ate sitting crosslegged on the gravel, as the darkness thickened around them. Paul finished his portion of yam, licked off his fingers, and settled in his father's lap, leaning back against his chest, quiet, though his eyes were bright and alert. The doctor felt irrationally glad of the boy's presence, the warm weight leaning back against him. He settled a hand across Paul's full belly.

At moonrise, Toussaint rose and addressed the men in a low voice, scarcely louder than a whisper, though somehow it carried to them all.

"Open your shirts," he said, with a gesture toward his own top buttons. "You will find on your bodies the brands of slavery. For ten years you have fought for freedom, and the memory of servitude has been burned off the face of this land by fire."

From the place where he'd been sitting by the stream, Guiaou stood up. The deep scars on his face and throat were silvered and softened by the moonlight. Then another man stood up, and another and another, with a wave of rustling, until all were standing. The doctor stood too. Though the boy was rather a heavy load, he hitched him up onto his hip so that he could see Toussaint's small and slightly bowlegged figure, standing under the west bank of the ravine. Toussaint had left his own clothing closed. A high collar pushed up under his chin, and his coat was closed with a wide red sash. The scabbard of his sword scuffed on the gravel, while in his hands he held, somewhat incongruously, a dandy's cane.

"The enemies who come against us have no faith, nor law, nor religion. They come again with branding irons and chains, and if their lips still promise liberty, slavery hides in their secret, constant thought. They come as strangers, to a land that will always be alien to them. Our enemies are walking toward you over fields of ash and coal. Their skins have never been marked by slavery, and their women and children are far away across the ocean, along with the graves of their fathers. You who stand against them now have seen the earth and the rocks soaked with the blood of those who have gone before you in the battle. You know how the trees and the air itself are full of the spirits of those who've left their bodies on the field. Our enemies will never prosper, for our land itself rejects them, and when they breathe our air their strength fades from them and their courage fails. Nothing in our land will ever give them comfort. Let their bones be scattered over our mountains, or tumbled in the waves beneath our waters."

Toussaint signaled with his cane, and the troops began to filter up the gorge. No more than six hundred men all told, by the doctor's best estimation, had marched from Gonaives. But as they climbed he realized that others had been waiting for them here. At every bend of the winding ravine was a new entrenchment, staked with palisades, with hundreds upon hundreds of field hands armed with muskets and dug in to the points of their teeth. Toussaint stopped for a quick word at each of these positions before pressing on. The trail zigzagged, sometimes following or crossing the stream along the floor of the ravine, sometimes scrambling to the top of the cliffs above. Along the bottom of the ravine grew ancient palms, following the twists and turns of the streambed, their roots driving through the gravel to scarce water. Many had been felled to reinforce the entrenchments, and fresh-torn wood was pale on the stumps and the hewn trunks.

At last a bend of the trail through a dark grove brought them into the open on a high bank, and in view of the rolling curve of Morne Barade, still a considerable distance farther on, at the head of the gorge. The dark hill was calm under the moon, and there was no spark of any human light, but Toussaint halted. The doctor, sitting his mule behind Placide, thought he heard a click of beads, and then the voice: "Almighty God, give me the grace to reach that place before the enemy!—just half an hour more to march."

There was moonlight enough for Placide to read the face of the watch he had brought home from France: a quarter to eleven when Toussaint halted the column under the shadow of Morne Barade. Toussaint dismounted, and with a whisper summoned Placide, Guiaou, Guerrier, and a fourth man named Panzou. On foot they moved quietly up the trail, with Toussaint leading. The trail passed into the shadow of tall trees that blocked the moon. Placide could see nothing. Almost nothing. His father's hand caught at his elbow, drew him up into the shelter of a rock.

"Stay by me," Toussaint breathed in his ear. He whispered something to the other three men, who separated and disappeared into the darkness, moving up the slope under the trees. Toussaint plucked again at Placide's sleeve, and Placide followed him, climbing up over the curve of the boulder, setting his boot toes into cracks, grasping vines that clung to the stone. A patch of moonlight revealed his father on the rock, motionless as a lizard; then he flashed forward into darkness. Placide followed, groping his way from sapling to sapling. Then he stood by Toussaint on the brink of the ravine again, looking down. There was a glitter, metal? No, it was only moonlight on the water.

Toussaint turned from the cliff's brink. They went back, picking their way to the stone where they had separated. Presently Guiaou returned, then Guerrier. Neither had encountered anyone. They waited. Placide felt his watch in his pocket. Panzou did not return.

Finally Toussaint grunted, and they all began to move back in the direction of the troops. When they came in sight of the waiting horses, Placide could not hold back the question.

"Where is Panzou?"

"I don't know," Toussaint muttered. "Maybe the enemy has taken him."

"Can they have reached Barade before us?" Placide felt a quick sharp thrust of alarm. "But we saw no one."

"No." Toussaint grasped his forearm. "And yet one feels that they are here."

"What will we do?"

"What we must do." Toussaint's gapped teeth flashed briefly in the moonlight. "Advance. Engage."

At sunset, Rochambeau's column came at last within the shadow of the hills that bordered the plateau. Slow as their progress had been through the mud, Noël Lory had led them faultlessly to the pass. On the slope of Morne Barade the going was still slippery, but easier than it had been on the flat, for water could not pool on the rising ground to make a swamp. Guizot's detachment blundered into a small settlement, too small to be called a village really—just a few mud huts with about a dozen people shouting at the sight of the soldiers, scattering with their dogs and goats, disappearing eastward into the brush, in the direction of the high savanna. Abandoned, their chickens ran cackling this way and that. With a quick burst of speed and concentration, Sergeant Aloyse ran down a hen.

Rochambeau gathered his officers on the western brow of the hill, where he stood scanning the gorge below with a spyglass. He grunted as he collapsed the instrument, then turned to Noël Lory.

"Where exactly is this powder depot?"

"It is in the ravine," Noël Lory said. "A little farther."

Guizot looked out, then down. The sun was a red blur melting on the blade of the horizon—mare's tail clouds fanned out from the burning haze. The gorge snaked away from the side of the hill where they stood. In the gloaming he could see pale strands of gravel at the bottom and dull reddish glints from the water moving in the stream. The bushy tops of palm trees pushed up from the gravel. The cliffs on either side were heavily wooded. A trace of a path running through the trees was the only sign of any human use.

"Captain Guizot." Rochambeau had turned to face him, tapping a forefinger on the tube of his spyglass. "We must hope that the spy who escaped your guard has not alerted the enemy to the direction of our approach."

Guizot cast down his eyes. "So indeed we must, *mon général.*"

Rochambeau took a backward step, then raised his voice to include all the officers in his address. "No matter if he is prepared for us," he said. "We have only slaves to fight, and they will not dare look us in the face— we who have carried our triumphs across the Tiber, the Nile, and the Rhine. We have not come these thousands of miles from our country to be defeated by a revolting slave."

He turned again to Guizot. "Captain, how goes your wound?"

Guizot stiffened his back as he raised his head. "Sir, it scarcely hinders me."

"Then you may redeem your error. Go there." Rochambeau turned to point down the slope. "Take three men of your choosing and establish a forward post."

Guizot saluted, and Rochambeau turned to his other officers to tell them where they were meant to go.

As Rochambeau allowed no cook fires that night, Sergeant Aloyse was obliged to surrender the hen he'd requisitioned to a friend in another company. He bade the fowl a tender farewell, stroking its speckled feathers where it nestled in the crook of his arm, giving its rubbery comb a last touch of his finger after he'd handed it over to the other man. The hen ducked its head at the contact, and blinked back at him.

The idea of roast chicken lingered with Guizot as he and the sergeant and two grenadiers went skating down the western hillside, into the darkness deepening under the trees. They stopped under cover of the brush, a dozen yards from the cliffs that walled the gorge, hidden in shadows around the edge of a teardrop-shaped clearing, which presently revealed the light of the rising moon.

The night grew chill. Guizot's sodden uniform congealed to his cold flesh. He swallowed mucus, suppressing the impulse to cough. Time dragged along. Always he could hear the water trickling at the bottom of the ravine. Sometimes there were other sounds more difficult to interpret. Now and again came a whistling so melodious Guizot was sure it must be human, though Sergeant Aloyse declared it to be the song of some night bird.

Then he saw the sergeant move into the moonlight of the clearing. No voice: only pant and scuffle. It looked like Aloyse was struggling with a shadow—as if his own shadow were fighting to depart from him. Aloyse crouched at the shadow's head while its bare heels drummed on the dirt. Then he sat back, his face striped in the moonlight filtered through the branches. His hands and the knife they held were blackened with wet blood. Guizot and the soldiers pressed in to look. In the center of their circle lay a black man in the rags of a colonial uniform. The trousers had been reduced to shorts and the shirt was pinned together with thorns. Above the collar, the gash in his throat gaped at the moon.

"Go to the general," Guizot hissed at the soldier to his left. His wounded arm felt numb and cold; he hitched it up a little in the sling. "Tell him we have killed an enemy scout."

The grenadier slipped into the bush. Sergeant Aloyse dragged the corpse by its heels into the shadows. Its arms still twitched in spasms of reflexive movement. Guizot was relieved to have it out of sight. No one spoke further. They resumed the places where they'd been before. With his good hand, Guizot fondled the flint of his pistol. He was aware of the bright odor of the blood spilled on the ground. His ears strained fervently toward nothing, only the ripple of the stream. Then his messenger returned, and behind him came the rustle of moving troops. Rochambeau was deploying a line down the hill.

Strangely, the shuffling of the French soldiers seemed to echo back from the ravine. Guizot sent back a request for them to halt. But from below, the sound of marching men continued. Guizot shot a glance at Sergeant Aloyse.

"Qui vive!" the sergeant bellowed, his voice deafening after such long silence. "Who goes?"

No sound, only damp expectation from the darkness beyond the leaves. Then the reply rang back at them—it seemed no more than a yard away.

"We are the Governor's honor guard!" Then, almost without a pause, "Move forward! Fire!"

20

Moonglow shimmered on the leaves as Magny marshaled his grenadiers up the trail that Placide, Toussaint, and the two other men had scouted half an hour before. This time they made less attempt at stealth, though orders were passed down in a muted tone and no one struck a light. The men, who were mostly barefoot, made little noise as they advanced, but otherwise it seemed as though Toussaint expected or even desired to be discovered.

It was Toussaint himself who replied to the first challenge. Placide, who rode a horse length behind his father, beside the climbing infantry column, heard his voice come powerfully out of the dark: *"Garde d'honneur du Gouverneur!"* and then, with scarcely a second's pause, *"Feu! En avant."*

With that, Placide's pistol was in his hand, an astonishingly heavy weight. He did not at all recall drawing it. Since there was no target, he did not fire; also his father was invisible in the shadows, lost to the moonlight, somewhere just ahead of him. The first musket volley had already gone off, and return fire seemed to come from three hundred degrees of the compass. The word *envelop* appeared in Placide's mind. He had learned the term in tactical studies at the Collège de la Marche. Had they been enveloped by French infantry? Musket balls were most certainly crisscrossing in the darkness all around him, as Magny's grenadiers fixed their bayonets and strode by.

Placide balanced the weight of his pistol toward the darkness ahead. Toussaint had reappeared in a pool of moonlight, dismounted and holding his horse off the trail with his left hand. The tip of his cane gave each grenadier a quick, encouraging flick on the shoulder as he marched by. Somewhere forward was a brutal sound of shock, then groaning—then several grenadiers came flying back. Half a dozen French infantrymen charged after them. Placide picked one of them, pulled the trigger. The dead man carried on several paces past him before he fell, inert in his downhill momentum. Placide reholstered the pistol, drew the other. But no, he ought to recharge the first pistol now, while there was time. In this flash of confusion was a glimmer of fear.

"What!" a voice shouted from below. "You would abandon your general?" Another swarm of musket balls tore through the trees. Placide looked wildly from side to side. Toussaint had disappeared during the French breakthrough. But now, below, the men were rallying, and again the grenadiers came marching forward. Toussaint, still on foot, appeared by the right shoulder of Placide's horse. The cane he'd held in his right hand was now replaced by his sword.

"Go back and find Doctor Hébert," he hissed. "Take him behind the second entrenchment."

"I won't abandon you!" Placide said hotly, as if in answer to the rallying cry that had risen from farther down the ravine. Toussaint smacked him sharply on the thigh with the flat of his sword.

"Do not think to disobey!" he snapped. "Find the *blanc* doctor and keep him safe, and keep him working on our wounded—already they begin to fall. That doctor will be worth more lives than any one man fighting here."

"*Oui, mon général,*" Placide choked. Toussaint, inexplicably, grinned up at him, then gave the horse a sword whack across the buttocks as Placide wheeled away.

Paul, who had been dozing on his donkey-load of bandages, came alert the instant the first shots sounded on the hill a hundred yards above. In seconds the deep quiet of the moonlit night was exploded into shouts and gunfire. *What! You would abandon your general?* Fontelle and Paulette wrapped their arms around each other, and Caco pressed into the flank of Paul's donkey, his big eyes bright. Just ahead of them, the column of grenadiers seemed to buckle, collapse on itself. What a fool he had been to bring Paul here, the doctor thought. They would be overrun by the French within minutes. But the column soon stiffened, then lashed forward again.

Placide broke out of the brush and rode toward them. "Come," he said shortly and beckoned as he passed, scarcely slowing his horse at all. The doctor, willing enough, swung aboard his mule and waited for the others to climb on their donkeys. He followed them and Placide, bringing up the rear. Placide led them to the bottom of the gorge, then to the first entrenchment, where after a moment of muttering some logs were dragged clear for them to pass. The field hands manning this position reached up to brush Placide's boots and trouser legs as he rode through, their smiles shining in the moonlight—it must feel like great good luck to these people to touch a son of Toussaint Louverture.

Around a tight turn of the gorge, the second entrenchment had been dug; one came upon it very suddenly. Here again the defenders opened the works gladly for Placide.

"We have arrived," Placide said, and when the doctor looked at him inquiringly, "The Governor-General has ordered that you prepare for the wounded here."

The doctor scanned the area and concluded the place was well chosen for the purpose. He began to unload the donkeys onto a humped sandbank above the rushing stream, an area partly sheltered by the overhang of the southern cliff and by the trunks of several huge palms that were still standing. He set Paul and Caco to digging a fire pit. There was a kettle in one of the packs; Paulette drew water from the stream and set it on the fire. Someone came back from the trench to complain about the light, but the doctor and Placide both argued that since the battle was already joined, the need for concealment was past.

Fontelle crumbled disinfectant herbs into the kettle, while the doctor laid out the tools of his trade: knives, pincers, the short-bladed surgical saw. Placide rode forward to the upper trench, then back again to their position. On Morne Barade, the deeper throats of cannon had joined their voices to the chorus of gunfire. The doctor walked to the lip of the second entrenchment and peered up—at just the right angle he could see around the curve to the bloom of muzzle flashes on the dark curve of the hill. Paul, who'd followed, stood at his side, trembling like a terrier. Mute, the doctor put an arm over his shoulder and led him back to the others.

By the time the water had come to a boil, the wounded had begun to dribble in. Soon they were pouring. The area of the makeshift hospital was throbbing with the sound of half-swallowed screams, as the doctor rooted balls out of torn flesh, or in the worse case sawed off a shattered limb. He used Fontelle and Paulette to hold down his patients whenever such help was necessary. As often as he might he sent Paul and Caco away, to scavenge more firewood—the fighting had not come any nearer, and Placide came back from time to time to tell them that Toussaint's line was holding, perhaps even advancing on the French position at the height of the hill.

What! You would abandon your general? Guiaou knew the voice that raised that cry—an officer of grenadiers named Labarre. Red flashes of anger pulsed behind his eyes. Magny was shouting orders from some other point, and Toussaint also was nearby, spanking men's legs with his sword's flat to urge them forward into the line. Guiaou felt his horse beginning to crab. He loosened the reins and stilled the animal with a soothing hand. Always, whenever firing began, Guiaou allowed himself a moment of stillness, for his head to sink backward, compress into a tight ball at the stem of his neck, just where the red cloth he'd put on for the fight was so tightly knotted. Then the noise of guns settled into a rhythm like drums, and behind his head Guiaou could feel the nearness of the spirit Agwé rolling him into battle like a wave. The words that tumbled from his mouth belonged to a song he'd heard in the south, sung by soldiers of Dessalines.

> *A l'assò, grenadyé!*
> *Sa ki mouri, sé pa zafè ou*
> *Nanpwen maman*
> *Nanpwen papa*
> *Sa ki mouri, sé pa zafè ou!*

Guiaou looked to his right, found Guerrier sitting his own horse. He wished that Couachy were alive and with them. But Guerrier was a good companion. Tonight they would have the chance to kill some *blancs*, certainly, and so Couachy's spirit might be nourished. The platoon of grenadiers Labarre marched past them had now taken up the song.

> *Grenadiers, to the assault!*
> *Those who die are none of your business*
> *We have no mother*
> *We have no father*
> *Those who die are none of your business!*

It was Labarre leading the song now. Guiaou looked where he was leading his men. His action flowered in his head. He motioned to Guerrier, then urged his horse out through the screen of trees, onto the open brow of the hill, where at forty yards' distance a massed square of French infantry bristled with bayonets like a cactus.

Guiaou leaned toward Guerrier and grinned. "Their bullets are dust. *N'alé!*"

He drew his *coutelas* as they charged the square. A whistling of bullets screamed by his ears, the path of each ball bending to avoid him. The horse's mane streamed back in his face. Guerrier was sitting bolt upright with his musket couched like a tilting lance. The muzzle flared, then the bayonet picked a Frenchman out of the square and flung him backward, gutted like a fish. Guiaou's *coutelas* was splitting heads—one, two—they wheeled their horses away. Labarre was behind them now, leading his men toward the outcropping Guiaou had noticed a moment earlier, above where the French had made their square, but he had not yet reached it. The grenadiers had stopped the song to put all their effort into this dash.

"N'alé!" Guiaou howled again. Let's go! He and Guerrier drove their horses again into the French. Guiaou's eyes fixed on the blade of his *coutelas*. All sound stopped. The blade flashed in the moonlight, lowered, rose blood-darkened, dull. This time when they wheeled away, Labarre's platoon had reached the ledge and were pouring fire down on the French square. Guiaou and Guerrier rode into shelter of the trees and turned their horses, breathless. Guiaou's thought surfaced long enough to wonder where Toussaint was now and if he had seen their action. Then it sank back. In the well behind his head the shadow of Couachy was smiling. And now, Magny was sending more men at a charge up the grade on the French square, which shuddered now under Labarre's constant fire.

> *A l'assò, grenadyé!*
> *Sa ki mouri, sé pa zafè ou*
> *Nanpwen maman*
> *Nanpwen papa*
> *Sa ki mouri, sé pa zafè ou!*

A volley from the charging men was quickly returned by the French. Then the two lines crunched together, struggling hand to hand. Guiaou dismounted, just for a moment, to wipe his *coutelas* on the grass.

Blood-soaked nearly to his shoulders, Doctor Hébert paused in his surgery and climbed over the sand bank to rinse his hands in the cold flow of the stream. Fontelle and Paulette were just above him, laying down a man who'd had his arm sawed off below the elbow. To the doctor's left were arrayed the bodies of four men who'd not survived their operations, their faces covered with scraps of cloth. He looked the other way, toward the fire pit where Paul huddled, firelight flashing on his still face. Caco sat by him, leaning into his shoulder. The doctor thought he saw in Paul's regard the same numb vacancy the boy had shown when they'd recovered him from the streets of Le Cap, where he'd been altogether lost for a stretch of months, till Paulette recognized him by chance and Fontelle took him in. That must be why he'd yielded to Paul's foolish pleading to come along with him this morning—he'd wanted to keep the boy near him, not risk losing him again. Perhaps Nanon had understood as much, before the doctor knew his motive. At any rate she'd bowed her head before his choice, as was usually her way.

But was this worse? Wringing water from his hands, the doctor walked down to where his mule was tethered. A good thing at least that Caco was here too—the doctor felt that the two boys lent each other strength. In one of the mule's saddlebags he found a stoppered gourd mostly full of rum. The rest of his supply was being used for anesthetic, but this much he'd conserved for his own encouragement. He drank, partly concealed by the mule's shoulder, and savored the flush in his chest. There was some commotion below, at the third entrenchment. Then, to the doctor's astonishment, Xavier Tocquet came striding up toward him, with Gros-Jean behind, leading both their horses.

"*Salut*, Antoine!" Tocquet said, sweeping off his hat. "I have been a long time coming to you."

"But how could you know where to come?"

"I found Elise at Habitation Cocherelle, where she took refuge with Madame Louverture. Nanon is with them, and the others—all safe. That smells like rum you have there."

The doctor relinquished the gourd. Tocquet tipped it high, lowered it, and passed it to Gros-Jean.

"And where is Bazau?" the doctor said. It was unknown to see the one without the other.

"I left him with the women," Tocquet said. "It seemed better. Morisset is there, with most of a squadron of cavalry, but I wanted one of ours as well. They may all have to move quickly—I don't like the odds of this battle."

"How have you calculated?"

For a moment both men tilted their heads to the noise of musketry up the ravine. Now and then a human cry forced up above the shooting.

"What strength has Toussaint here?" Tocquet asked. "Two battalions and his cavalry?"

"He left a battalion with Vernet for the defense of Gonaives," the doctor said. "Half the cavalry also."

Tocquet let go a whistling breath. "Then he must be outnumbered five to one, or worse."

"But there are a lot of field hands here, with their muskets they've brought out of hiding. There are many, too many to count. You must have passed through them on as you came up. And in the last hour, more and more of them have been going forward."

"Is it so?" Tocquet looked up toward the second entrenchment. "But still, they are untrained men for the most part. How long can they hold against crack French troops of the line?"

"What choice have they?"

Tocquet laughed drily. "Death or slavery." He passed back the gourd and the doctor drank.

"Do you believe that?"

"I believe I'd sooner Toussaint than Rochambeau," Tocquet said. "Rochambeau's approach is . . . a little brusque. If he'd held his fire at Fort Liberté, all we see now might have been avoided. But—no matter. Our families have already left Cocherelle, in fact—I hadn't thought this position would hold so long."

"It has been very well prepared, as you see."

"And with good reason." Tocquet pointed at a stone doorway set in the opposite bank; the outlines of the masonry plain enough in the moonlight.

"I wondered about that," the doctor said. "What is it?"

"A magazine," said Toussaint. "There's a cave behind—Toussaint has been caching powder there these last two years. That's where Rochambeau is going—he's got a spy who told him where it is."

"I see," said the doctor. "I suppose that means this spot will be extremely well defended."

"For as long as may be," Tocquet said. "But where is Toussaint?"

The doctor gestured wordlessly up the ravine in the direction of the firing, then spotted a horseman riding their way. "But there is Placide," he said. "No doubt he can take you to him."

Placide had spent the first hours of the battle shuttling between the hospital and Toussaint's post behind the front line, chafing at first to be held out of the action, then relaxing as he began to realize that what he was doing was of real use. On each trip down the ravine he guided the wounded to the doctor, and with each return he brought a fresh gang of field hands to be hurled into the charges. The waves of Magny's charges did not stop. Just once, they'd barely gained the summit of Morne Barade, but the French had re-formed and finally thrown them back.

Placide led the wounded men down the ravine. At moments his mind returned to the image of his gun muzzle blazing into the chest of the French soldier. That fine chased pistol the First Consul had given him. How many paces that dead soldier had dashed on before he fell.

Another hundred field workers followed Placide as he led Tocquet and Gros-Jean up, their muskets rocking in their hands as they trotted along. Magny took them in hand when they came to the old almond tree where Toussaint was posted. As the men went forward, lifting their muskets to their shoulders now, they all took up the chant that rang down from above.

A l'assò, grenadyé
Sa ki mouri, sé pa zafè ou . . .

Toussaint was hunkered on his heels by the bole of the almond tree. He squinted up suspiciously when Tocquet greeted him.

"Good evening, General," Tocquet said, and glanced at the lowering moon. "Perhaps I ought to say good morning. Or maybe it isn't good at all. I bring you news of your enemy's strength."

"Di mwen," Toussaint said. Tell me.

"I met Rochambeau some days ago at Saint Michel," Tocquet said. "I conversed for an evening with one of his captains. He landed near two thousand men at Fort Liberté. Some, I suppose, are in garrison there, but I'd reckon from what I saw that he has come to you with most of that division."

Toussaint stood up. He passed a hand across his face, then dropped his kerchiefed forehead into his palm. Tocquet drew out one of his cheroots.

"Don't light that." Toussaint raised his head sharply. "You know I do not abide tobacco. It is ill news that you bring."

"I bring news of your family also," Tocquet said. "They are safe, but on the move from Cocherelle into the mountains."

Toussaint's eyes fixed on Gros-Jean. "Sé lavérité l'ap di?"

"Yes," said Gros-Jean. "I have seen with my own eyes—everything he says is true."

"Let them go to Pont d'Ester," Toussaint said, speaking equally to Tocquet and Gros-Jean. "Say that I will come there afterward, when I have done my duty here."

As he spoke, fleeing men began to break through the post, field hands and regular troops together. Toussaint turned halfway toward Placide. Labarre came staggering up and sagged his weight against the almond trunk.

"My snipers are dead," he gasped.

"All?" said Toussaint.

Labarre nodded, wheezing for breath. Guiaou and Guerrier rode up to the tree and turned their horses tightly.

"All killed by the cannons," Labarre said. "The *blanc* soldiers are coming. They are coming fast."

Toussaint slapped his bicorne hat onto his head. "Re-form the troops on the floor of the ravine," he told Magny, then snapped at Tocquet, "Go now, and bring my message to my wife." At last to Placide: "Take these people down the gorge—and get the doctor behind the third entrenchment."

Paulette splashed a little more rum against the clenched teeth of the patient, as the doctor probed in the top of his wounded thigh. Fontelle pressed the limb to stillness with both her knees. At last he straightened, the small of his back aching and clenched. Between his pincer tips was a musket ball, blunted against a bone. He passed the instrument to Paulette and held out his empty hands—Fontelle poured hot water over them. The sound of firing seemed suddenly to have come nearer, and now there were cries and confusion on the bank above them. The doctor peered toward Morne Barade. Tocquet, Placide, and Gros-Jean were just coming through the second entrenchment.

"They've broken through," Tocquet said. "I think they've broken—" Though his visible agitation was slight, it was more than the doctor had ever seen in him. "You'd better get out of this, Antoine. The fighting has moved down to the bottom of the ravine."

"Take Caco and Paul back to Nanon," the doctor said.

"Yes, of course, and yourself with them," said Tocquet. "Come along, will you? You'll not be missed—they're going to be routed here."

The doctor hesitated, then shook his head. "I'm needed where I am."

"You're mad," Tocquet said shortly. He looked to Fontelle and Paulette, who exchanged a brief glance.

"N'ap reté isit," Fontelle said, wiping her hands on her apron. We're staying here.

Tocquet shrugged. "As you like, then. Come Paul, come Caco!" He leaned forward suddenly, grasped the doctor by both shoulders, and gave him a little shake. "Save your own life, Antoine, if you can find the time."

The doctor swung Paul up onto his donkey, squeezed his hands, and gave him a kiss on the cheek. Caco had already scrambled up behind him, not waiting for assistance. The doctor watched them all ride down and around the next bend in the ravine. The moon was dropping low over the line of their departure. When they were gone, the doctor became aware that Placide was standing by him.

"The Governor-General orders that you remove the hospital behind the third entrenchment."

"Yes," said the doctor. "No doubt that is best."

But Placide somehow was still expectant. "Doctor," he said, in a lower voice. "Have you ever killed anyone?"

"Yes," said the doctor. "More than once." He turned and touched the back of Placide's hand. "It's terrible," he said. "But better than being killed yourself."

"W'ap goumen fò, monchè." Toussaint held Labarre's head in his two hands. You have struggled powerfully, my dear.

Guiaou watched them, seated calmly on his horse. Toussaint's right hand lapped over Labarre's forehead, and his left palm cupped and pressed the base of the skull, warming and securing the spirit in its seat. Guiaou seemed to feel the same two hands cradling his own head, and indeed the name of Guiaou had just occurred in Toussaint's murmuring.

"Guiaou will bring you more men, good marksmen . . ." Toussaint's purring voice went on. But Guiaou did not wait to hear any more. With a click of his tongue to bring Guerrier, he turned his horse down the trail by which Placide had departed with the gunrunner Tocquet and his man. Soon they met the boy coming back up again, leading a hundred more field hands up from the lower trenches. Guiaou fell in with them and brought them up to Toussaint and Labarre. Already the new men had begun singing as they climbed.

A l'assò, grenadyé!
Sa ki mouri, sé pa zafè ou

Nanpwen maman
Nanpwen papa
Sa ki mouri, sé pa zafè ou!

Guiaou knew the quality of these men very well. A long time ago he had been the same sort of fighter as they. These men might charge furiously, inspired by their chant and the drumbeat in the blood. But perhaps they would not charge many times, if they met firm resistance. It was also possible that they would not hold so very long against the charge of massed *blanc* soldiers. That was the difference between these men and Toussaint's trained soldiers such as Guiaou had now become.

But these hundred men were not going into the line to meet a charge. Labarre was going to fan them out across the rim of the ravine. They would shoot down on the French soldiers filing along the bottom and cover them with fear, confusion, and death.

Guiaou turned his horse to follow Labarre. But Toussaint called him and Guerrier back, to give them a different order. The key with which the order would be enacted Toussaint took from a string around his neck; Guiaou slipped his own head through the loop. In his lowest voice, breathing into Guiaou's ear, Toussaint told him where to go, where he must leave their horses, how to find the necessary place, and how he must judge when the time was right.

Then Toussaint himself had slipped away, skidding down a path so steep and worn it was more like a ditch, now and then catching a handhold from an overhanging branch as he swung toward the bottom of the ravine, which was now heaving up a roar of gunfire. Guiaou and Guerrier followed Placide across the clifftop. Now, after all, they did overtake Labarre, who had scattered his company along the edge of the cliff to take cover behind trees and boulders there. These men did not fire in volleys, but singly, upon such targets as they could pick out in the French column advancing below. Their aim seemed to be very good, for many of the *blanc* soldiers were falling, and yet the column never stopped—if it contracted, it soon thrust forward again. Monpoint's cavalry, ranged on the wide gravel shoals beside the stream, barred the *blanc* soldiers' way to the first entrenchment. The silver helmets of his riders glowed in the light of the lowering moon. Long shadows of the surviving palms stretched over them like bars.

Then came the crump of a cannon firing, and confusion as a shell exploded among the horses below. Guiaou reined up and stared across the ravine. The French had maneuvered a couple of cannons onto the high ground there, and now the second gun discharged a round of *mitraille*. Below, the horses were bucking and whinnying, and Guiaou's own mount was uneasy beneath him. Toussaint appeared, on foot, the red and white feathers floating high above his bicorne. His movements were quite deliberate and slow, and he used his cane, instead of his sword, to direct the movements of both the horsemen and foot soldiers. So conducted, Monpoint was beginning to file his cavalry back through the palings of the first entrenchment, while another gang of field hands moved up to absorb the shock of the French advance. The French column trembled, rippled like the body of a snake. There were many, so many of these *blanc* soldiers, stretching up out of the ravine as far as Guiaou's eyes could follow them, up and over the crest of Morne Barade.

Toussaint could no longer be seen in the confusion. Except for a few fallen horses, the cavalry had all got safely away, but now the brunt of the French charge had reached the first entrenchment, and the first few *blanc* soldiers had even spilled through. On the cliff, Labarre's snipers had begun to fire faster, more wildly, though Labarre moved among them, calming them, encouraging them to take more careful aim. Some few who'd burned their ammunition had begun to hurl down stones.

"Come on!" Placide called to Guiaou, his voice nearly breaking. "Hurry!" Guiaou and Guerrier swung their horses after them, moving into a trot. Below, the *blanc* soldiers had broken altogether through the first entrenchment and were moving across the flat ground by the stream at a dead run. Guiaou looked back over his shoulder once, toward the peaks of more distant mountains beyond Morne Barade, where the black of the night sky was beginning to break up in patches of deep blue.

The doctor had scarcely time to organize his enterprise behind the third entrenchment when another stream of wounded began to come in, as rapidly as floodwater pouring down the gorge. He worked feverishly, cutting and binding, while trying to think with a part of his mind—how long since Tocquet had left with Paul and Caco, and what were their chances of getting clear of the ravine before all the defenses that dammed it gave way? But he could not manage to reckon the time. A stream of cavalry was coming back across the third entrenchment now, and word was that the first entrenchment had been overrun. He could hear the steady crump of cannon fire from the northern wall of the gorge.

Then Placide, Guiaou, and Guerrier came tumbling in upon him. The doctor was happy to see Guiaou, for both his women assistants were staggering from exhaustion. But Guiaou was not to be diverted into nursing. He gave the reins of his horse to Placide and, ignoring the doctor's importunings, trotted back toward the third entrenchment, with Guerrier following. The doctor went after them, pleading his case, but stopped when Guiaou passed the trench and slipped out through the stakes behind it. From where he stood he could see the French charge rounding the bend into the unexpected volley from the defenders dug into the second entrenchment, a hundred yards forward. A great many French soldiers fell and the rest, momentarily, dropped back. Guiaou and Guerrier, meanwhile, scurried across the bare moonlit shoal and reached the shadow of the northern cliffs. On roots and vines and out-croppings of stone they climbed toward the stone doorway Tocquet had pointed out. Guerrier crouched on the lintel, knuckles to the stone, while Guiaou hesitated in the shadow of the frame. Then the door folded inward and Guiaou disappeared inside.

The charge on the second trench had been renewed, and spent balls were pocking into the gravel just before the third. The defenders here all urged the doctor away. With a long, draining sigh, he went stumbling back toward his makeshift surgery. The stream of the wounded had been broken; perhaps none could get through the fighting around the second entrenchment. Placide muttered something to him as he rode back toward the line, something about the horses just left here. The doctor squatted by the cold kettle, looking into the faces of Fontelle and Paulette, worn and grubby beneath their headcloths. They could be seen a little more plainly now, as the moonglow dissipated into the harsher, sharper light of dawn.

At that first contact, Guizot had believed that the resistance would not be very stout—perhaps less stubborn than what they'd met at the forts of Fort Liberté, for the enemy seemed to melt away in the darkness, where they, the French, had the advantage of high ground. He'd wanted to lead his company in a quick pursuit, but Sergeant Aloyse had restrained him, warning of the likelihood of ambush.

Then as suddenly they found themselves receiving a charge from below, and actually, incredibly, were repulsed, driven backward pace by pace onto the open brow of Morne Barade—into confusion, over which Rochambeau's hoarse voice soon prevailed. The men formed a square in time to meet a charge by cavalry, or no—it was only a pair of horsemen, whom Guizot watched with his mouth agape, astonished at their mad temerity. As the riders retreated, fire opened on the French from a ridge just opposite; men fell and there was another spasm of bewilderment while Rochambeau hastily rallied his artillerymen to bring cannon to bear on that position.

The rebel slaves were coming hard, charging up the hill, shouting some song in accents that sounded like French, though Guizot could decipher no word of it. Once, twice, the wave broke on the French square and receded, then on the third or fourth time it broke through and Guizot found himself in a welter of hand-to-hand fighting, managing the best he could with his one good arm, whipping his sword to bisect the darkness rushing down on him, until at last this charge was also broken and repulsed, and the French re-formed.

A lull. The snipers' ridge had gone completely silent, shattered by the cannon. Guizot had no idea how long the struggle had lasted, though he did notice that the moon hung much lower over the gorge than before. Now, at last, the troops moved forward confidently. The rebel slaves who'd been charging them were breaking, fleeing down the hill, and with a rattle of their drums the French pressed on, wetting their boots and trouser legs as they splashed across the stream, then picking up their pace on the gravel floor of the ravine.

Rochambeau had come forward, a stout, compact figure, his black shako bobbing as he urged the men on, against the enemy cavalry which had formed to meet them here. No doubt of the general's personal courage; he moved calmly, relaxed among his troops, indifferent to steady sniper fire that had begun to come down on them again, now from the northern wall of the gorge. On the opposite cliff, French cannon had begun to speak, exploding chaos among the cavalry that faced the foot soldiers in the ravine. Guizot, in the front line, caught sight of a little man on foot among the horses, small and bowlegged as a jockey, his face ugly as a frog's. Guizot was so near he could see the tail of red kerchief that dangled from the little man's feathered bicorne. *Rag-head Negro.* He was rooted to the spot in his squelching boots, as if fixed in his place by lightning, and when he first tried to speak, no sound emerged. The little man was directing the enemy movement with fluttering movements of a light cane, as if he were conductor of some opera.

Rochambeau was passing nearby, and Guizot clutched at his elbow. Annoyed, Rochambeau shook free, glaring as if he'd strike his captain.

"Mon général," Guizot blurted at last. "Look there!—surely it is Toussaint Louverture."

Rochambeau absorbed the message. "Can it be?" he said, staring, then turning to Noël Lory, who stood, reluctantly, beside him. When Lory nodded, Rochambeau's arm swept down. "Capture him! Kill him! Either will do—forward, quickly. *En avant!"*

And Guizot rushed ahead with the others. He was near enough to see the wrinkles on the little black man's face, and it even seemed that the other, facing him, wiped away a smile. Then with a cat's agility he sprang into the saddle of a riderless horse that a cavalryman had just led up to him, and he was off, speeding up to a canter, jumping the bank of a palisaded ditch. All the cavalry had been swept away, like a curtain disclosing the array of sharpened stakes upon which Guizot was now charging, into a musket volley that rose from the trench behind.

He was knocked down in the first shock, and when he rose, he was no longer in the van. But the French charge had carried the position, though there was still some ugly fighting in the trench they had broken through. Guizot ran to overtake his company, chasing the wagging pigtail of Sergeant Aloyse. They rounded the next bend of the gorge and came up short against another trench, another wall of musketfire. The French charge broke on the new line of stakes, in a blur of stumbling, cursing, screaming. Rochambeau's voice again, loud above the others. The column pressed on them from behind.

Guizot's sling hung loose around his neck. He tried the wounded arm experimentally and felt no pain, or almost none—no more than a catch where the torn muscle moved over the bone. Someone shook him by the shoulder.

"Captain." It was Rochambeau. "Do you see there? The doorway in the cliff wall?"

Guizot squinted through the dust. He'd tumbled away from the main action. Twenty yards ahead the French infantrymen were plunging one after another into hand-to-hand fighting in the rebel carthwork. Beyond that battle line, set into the north bank of the ravine, with a stone door, with another rag-head Negro, this one nearly naked, crouched on the lintel like a gargoyle. Guizot rubbed his eyes and looked again. The darkness was dissolving quickly, and he could see more clearly in the plain gray light of the dawn.

"That is our target," Rochambeau was saying. "A powder magazine, according to this one." He nudged Noël Lory for confirmation; Lory returned a gloomy nod.

"You will secure the magazine, Captain," Rochambeau said. "As soon as the way is open, at whatever cost. Do you hear?"

"*Oui, mon général,*" Guizot replied. Sergeant Aloyse, happily, was just at his back, nodding emphatically to affirm the order.

"Excellent," Rochambeau said as he moved away. "See to your men."

Since Guizot had been so far forward when the fighting began, he'd been cut off from his company, and when he tried to rally the men now, no more than half of them reported. Surely not so many could be casualties; surely most of them had only been scattered in the confusion. Enough had been found, he thought, for the task at hand.

Guizot waited, a little anxiously, though he was happy not to be fighting in the trench. He rolled lightly from heel to toe, flexing the muscles of his thighs, thinking of the little man in the feathered hat—where had he vanished to? And probably Guizot had just been closer to him than any of his comrades of *La Sirène* had got . . .

"*Allons-y,*" Sergeant Aloyse hummed, Let's go. The trench had been definitively breached and the French troops were now pouring through. Guizot beckoned the men behind him, stumbled into the ditch, and scrambled out the other side on his all-fours, scraping the back of his hand on a splintered stake. As he emerged he broke into a run, hard on the heels of Sergeant Aloyse.

The key Toussaint had given him was loose in the lock, and Guiaou was not very much practiced in the use of keys. It took him several tries before it engaged the lock and turned. The iron-bound door sank smoothly inward, but Guiaou remained poised on the sill. The smell of the cave came wafting out toward him. He could see nothing at all inside, and yet he felt, beyond a doubt, that the lost *caciques* of long ago had served their spirits here.

"Ki sa w'ap tann?" Guerrier said from his post on the lintel. What are you waiting for? It was his good luck to stay outside and watch, though Guiaou had been honored with the more crucial task. With a grimace, he moved through the doorway and flattened himself against the wall. His heart was booming like a big *asoto* drum. In his head he sang his song for Agwé.

Mait' Agwé, koté ou yé
Ou pa we'm—

But here he faltered. *Master Agwé, where are you?—don't you see me . . .* maybe Agwé could not see him at all, here in the dark blind stomach of the earth. Here was no place for Agwé, and no place for Guiaou either.

As he clung to the wall, he began to notice that the familiar tang of gunpowder was stronger than the cave smell. This reassured him just a little. Also, daylight was coming on outside, and in a short while his eyes adjusted so that he could make out the shapes of barrels and boxes of the gunpowder stacked high against the walls and stretching back a long way into the cave.

Just as Papa Toussaint had told him to do, Guiaou pried out the top of a barrel with his cutlass and dumped a big mound of gunpowder onto the floor. The bright smell entered his nose and he sneezed. With both hands he shaped a fat, sausage-like trail of gunpowder all the way out to the stone sill. Then he turned to watch the fighting from his hidden place inside the doorway. When he faced outside, he did not feel so much frightened by the hollow darkness of the cave behind him. And Guerrier was very near—Guiaou might reach up a hand and touch his bare foot with its horny nails overlapping the lintel.

Papa Toussaint had told him that he must not light the powder unless the second trench gave way. That was where they were fighting now, with bayonets and knives and fists. It looked to Guiaou that the fight was not going very well for Papa Toussaint's people.

The boom of the French cannons seemed to come from directly above him now. On the far side of the ravine, he could see one of Labarre's snipers, firing out of a cleft of rock. He disappeared to charge his musket, then popped up and fired again. Guiaou could not make out what target the man was shooting at. But when he looked at the trench again, the French *blanc* soldiers had broken through and were swarming out over the fan of gravel just now yellowed by the rising sun. That was Guerrier's voice, roaring the alarm. Most of the *blanc* soldiers were charging straight down the gorge, toward the third entrenchment. But one heavy-set man, with a big beaky nose and a gray pigtail, was rushing right up toward Guiaou, and behind him a thinner, pale-faced man with epaulettes on his coat and a grubby white sling flapping loose around his neck, and behind that one at least a dozen more. Guerrier's musket exploded above him and he heard Guerrier shrieking because he had missed. The first man, the one with the big nose, had reached the bank and was scrabbling for handholds, beginning to climb.

Guiaou crouched and with a quick snap of both hands struck fire into the fuse he had laid. How fast the powder trail burned back! For an instant he could not take his eyes away. Then he hurled himself out through the doorway, both arms stretched for a loop of hanging vine.

That gargoyle black hunched on the lintel jumped to his feet, swung a musket across his hip and fired from that position. Guizot saw the muzzle flash, a spear-point blaze, but the hip shot did no damage. The black jumped up and down on the lintel, howling at them helplessly; he did not seem to think of recharging his weapon. Sergeant Aloyse had reached the bank and was already beginning to climb toward the stone door twenty feet above him. Higher still, at the top of the bank, a pair of cannon were firing down into the ravine—Rochambeau's cannon, Guizot realized, dropping *mitraille* and explosive shells among the retreating rebels.

He found a toehold in the rock, caught hold of a protruding root, and hauled himself up. Aloyse kicked a cupful of shale and dirt down into his face. Guizot shook his head, looked up again and saw a second black hunkered in the doorway, cradling something in his hands that bloomed into a fierce incandescent glow.

Then the black came hurtling out of the doorway, all his limbs spread wide, like a flying squirrel. Guizot did not see where he landed. In the instant that he understood what the burning powder trail foretold, he clutched at Aloyse's heel and cried a warning, but the sergeant kicked free and climbed out of his reach. Guizot dropped eight feet to the gravel, rolling across his wounded arm, and came up running as the blast threw the whole cliff up into the sky. When he looked over his shoulder, he saw a broken cannon wheel spinning down amid smaller bits of debris and Sergeant Aloyse's cartwheeling body and a great coffin-sized piece of stone that might have been a doorpost, all drifting down in a strangely retarded motion as if they weighed no more than feathers. He scrambled back, under a shower of pebbles and dirt, to the place where the sergeant had landed. The ringing of his ears shut out all other sound. He pulled up the sergeant's head by the pigtail; his face was all awash in blood. Guizot snatched the sling from around his neck and used it to mop Aloyse's face, but the sergeant swiped his hand away and sat up, coughing. His right hand pinched the bridge of his nose. Perhaps he'd been no worse than stunned. Guizot swung the sergeant's arm over his shoulder and raised him to his feet.

The momentum of the French charge had already breached the third entrenchment, and it appeared that the rebels were now in full flight. Rochambeau did a dance of rage below the tremendous gash the exploded magazine had opened in the wall of the ravine. He tore off his shako, hurled it down, kicked it away from him, then ran to jump on it. Breathless now, he stooped to pick it up, and while he knocked out the dents and brushed off the dirt, he kept urging his men forward with quick sharp jerks of his jaw.

The doctor was standing, stretching his back and watching the sun's rim push above the ridge line to the east, when he saw Guiaou and Guerrier launch themselves from that stone doorway and land rolling on the gravel floor of the ravine. Within the vacant doorway something burned almost as bright as the sun and then with a deafening, flattening boom the whole cliff blew up, scattering tree trunks, boulders, tubes of cannon, the shattered bodies of the French artillerymen. The doctor came to himself plastered belly-down on the gravel, eye to eye with Fontelle and Paulette, who'd had the same reaction as he. When he got to his feet, he saw that the French charge had already slammed into the third entrenchment.

"Retreat!" That was Placide's voice, echoing an order. The doctor looked about for Toussaint, but only found Guiaou and Guerrier, flying back to get their horses. He set Paulette and Fontelle to loading the donkeys. For the last two hours he had been sending the walking wounded down the ravine in the direction of Périsse, but those who couldn't walk would have to be left where they were, and some of their supplies would be abandoned too; there was no more time. The doctor saw Paulette and Fontelle mounted and scrambled up onto his mule.

Sixty yards lower in the ravine, Monpoint had opened a gap in his line of cavalry for the passage of Toussaint's surviving troops, and the doctor kept his exhausted eyes forward as he passed through, behind the two women. No use to look back at the legless men lying on the strand, stretching out their hands to him, or anyone else who passed. The regular troops were marching in reasonably good order, but the retreat of the field hands looked more like a rout. The doctor was too tired now to feel fear, and with the rising sun warm between his shoulder blades he even dozed off a time or two as the mule took him rocking down the gorge. But when they'd emerged into the cactus-scattered desert near Habitation Périsse, he roused himself and looked back once and saw how the sky was speckled with dark vulture's wings, spiraling and beginning to settle beneath the bushy palm crowns sprouting from Ravine à Couleuvre.

When Placide overtook Toussaint at Périsse, his father had already dismounted, beside a tall cactus hedge that lined the road which led through Marie Louise. Toussaint was whipping the air with his cane and shouting at Magny to stop the flight of the field hands, turn them, bring them back. The regular troops had already rallied here, and Labarre and several other junior officers were drawing them back up into their ranks.

"Listen." Toussaint let his cane fall into the pale dust and snatched a musket from Guerrier. "Listen to me. We have no retreat. Don't look behind you—we are in the desert, the sea at our back. What the enemy brings is death undying. They will send us as *zombi* into the fields again. Will you accept that?"

"Never!" It was Monpoint's voice ringing out. "We will defeat them here or die."

Toussaint nodded, brandishing the musket. Labarre and Magny took up the cry; Placide heard it tearing out of his own throat: *"Victoire ou la mort!"* By the third time all the men were shouting it: *Victory or death!*

"Good," said Toussaint. "They are coming."

It had been cold through the night on Morne Barade, though Guizot had not felt it much in the midst of all the fighting. Now, in the low desert they had entered, there was a dry, suffocating heat, and the sun burned out of a cloudless sky, inhuman empty blue. Guizot marched at the head of his company, just behind Rochambeau's vanguard. The general's black shako, a little scuffed from its recent mistreatment, bobbed at the head of the line. A steady tattoo of drums encouraged them. Guizot's tongue rasped over dry lips. He'd drunk from the stream before they left it, but in this heat one was sweated dry again in less than a half-hour. Sergeant Aloysc pegged along at his right, snuffling with the effort, blood crumbs blackened around his nostrils. His nose had been broken, no worse than that.

Despite his exhaustion, Guizot's heart was high. Except for a high cactus hedge on their right, this was open country, level and flat; a Negro army would never stand against them here, and what did it matter to lose the powder magazine if the enemy army could be destroyed? And the enemy was in sight, just ahead, standing with a steadfastness Guizot would not have expected.

"Ready! Aim! Fire!" Rochambeau himself gave those commands. The forward rank knelt to recharge muskets; Guizot ordered his own men to fire. There at the front of the enemy line was that same little man with the feathered bicorne, flourishing a musket now as he directed the enemy musketeers—

"En avant!"

The French were charging, bayonets lowered, and Guizot ran with them, just behind the first line, his drawn sword at the ready and his eye fixed on the feathers of that bicorne, the red plume floating high above the rest. Kill that man and the battle was won. Capture him and the bet was won. Capture him and the war was won . . . But after the first shock, Guizot lost sight of him. The enemy was holding. Then, finally, yielding a little under the pressure of the bayonets. The French advance sped to the pace of a run; it seemed as if the enemy had broken, but still Guizot could not relocate that red feather, will-of-a-wisp that his quarry was. In his excitement he'd outrun his company, except for Aloyse; the two of them were now abreast of Rochambeau's advance guard. Then came another shock, from the left this time, and Guizot realized they'd been flanked. The blacks were pushing toward them; Guizot parried a bayonet with his sword, ducked, stabbed underneath the musket barrel, spun through and away. And now again the French advance was moving.

With the enemy advance guard barely forty yards away, Toussaint had turned to whisper to Placide. "Go with Monpoint," he said. "Take Guiaou with you. The rest of the cavalry is there behind that hedge. Monpoint will hold them in reserve to break the French line when the time is right."

Placide squeezed his heels into the flanks of his horse. Guiaou was cantering on his right, while Guerrier remained in the infantry line, beside Toussaint. Monpoint had ranged his horsemen on the Marie Louise road, covered by a cactus hedge nearly twelve feet high. He did not take any action at first, but sat his horse quietly, watching the infantry clash.

At this remove, Placide's mind was clear and he could watch calmly. After the first exchange of volleys, the lines collided with bayonets—the French had a terrible skill with that weapon. There was a break in Toussaint's line, and Placide heard Labarre's voice shouting, "What! do you forget your vow! remember the Governor is among us!" Placide looked at Monpoint, nudged his horse forward, but Monpoint stayed him with a hand—it was too soon, and in fact Toussaint's line had rallied.

Placide calmed himself, forcing a deep breath; now he could see that Rochambeau had not deployed his men to take advantage of his superior numbers, and Toussaint must have seen that also: now two companies of *chasseurs* were flanking the French line on the left, moving quickly through the cover of the *raket* and *baroron*, then wheeling, doing tremendous damage with their fire before they charged. But the French were many. Too many—there looked to be two men to replace each man that fell, and Toussaint's front line was yielding again; it seemed to buckle in the middle. Placide saw Toussaint return his musket to Guerrier. He'd recovered his cane; how had he found it? The cane's tip whirled, and Toussaint's mouth worked, but Placide could hear nothing—his ears still rang with the explosion of the powder magazine in the gorge. Toussaint was staring at Monpoint.

"He means us to charge," Placide said, and felt Guiaou move up beside him. Surely this must be the intended moment, and they must seize it, or be lost.

He looked again for his father's feathered hat but could not find it.

Monpoint remained, fixed, rigid and mute, like the statue of a horseman. His eyes were glazed. Placide glanced at Guiaou, who looked hungry to ride—his nostrils flared almost as wide as those of his horse. Would the others follow if Placide and Guiaou undertook to charge? Would Toussaint then rebuke Placide for insubordination?

Then he saw Toussaint running up from the infantry lines toward the hedge. He seemed to be empty-handed now, or no, he still had the cane. He moved at a quick bowlegged trot, with Guerrier loping along a step behind him. Two men broke out of the French line, one with a long, snaky pigtail, and tried to lay their hands on him. Toussaint's hat spilled onto the ground, but he twisted away and continued. Guerrier knocked down the smaller Frenchman with his musket stock, dodged under the swinging arm of the other, and followed.

Toussaint slapped his cane across Monpoint's thigh, but Monpoint remained immobile.

"Where is your heart?" Toussaint sputtered. "There'll be no better chance than this. Let us see what the brave men of my guard can do— charge them! Charge them without delay."

Monpoint's jaws worked—in the corners of his mouth appeared a little foam of spittle. Placide followed the line of his glazed stare. Behind the line of engagement, more and more French soldiers were spilling out of the ravine, hundreds upon hundreds of them, pooling like water spilled from an overset cup.

"Victory or death, that was your sentence." Toussaint swung the slender cane across Monpoint's shoulders, so hard that it broke. "Well, if you will not ride, get down, and give your horse to me."

Guerrier appeared, proffering Toussaint's bicorne hat, which he'd just rescued from the mêlée. Toussaint took it absently and held it in one hand against his knee. Monpoint's head turned very slowly to face Toussaint. His left hand floated upward, with an equal slowness, as if some outside power lifted it.

"Death, then," his voice croaked. The left hand pointed to the French center. "I will go there to find my death."

"Find victory," Toussaint said, but Monpoint had already spurred his horse away. Toussaint slashed his broken cane across the horse's buttocks, then tossed it away. His hand rose to take the bridle of Placide's horse, then sank down, empty. *Victory or death!* had risen to a scream among the cavalry, as the horses thundered out of the lane. The wind rushed into Placide's eyes as he spurred forward among the rest, and the astonished faces of the French infantry turned toward him like pale flowers.

Captain Guizot had been clubbed in the head one time too many these last few days . . . He knew it to be so, for the idea made him giddy, had him laughing out loud even as he grabbled in the dust for a tooth that the musket stock had just knocked out. Sergeant Aloyse caught hold of him and hauled him to his feet.

"So close," Guizot gabbled, through his half-hysterical giggling. "So close, I touched him with this hand."

Sergeant Aloyse gave him a shake so hard that his jaws clicked together. The chattering stopped. "Thank you," Guizot said. He looked around for Rochambeau, wondering if his general had been witness to their near-successful exploit, but the black shako had withdrawn to the main body of French troops. The sergeant's eyes had widened, and Guizot wrenched his shoulders free, turning to see whatever it was he saw. A squadron of enemy cavalry was howling down on their right flank from an opening in a cactus-hedged lane.

"Get back!" The sergeant's voice. He and Guizot made a bolt for their closest cover in the French advance guard, but this cover was not very good—the enemy foot soldiers, emboldened by the cavalry charge, were pressing harder with their bayonets. They were cut off. The charge had divided them from the main body of the French, left them pinned between two enemy forces, and already some of the troopers near Guizot and Aloyse were throwing down their weapons and raising empty hands for quarter.

"We'd better run for it," Aloyse grunted, and when Guizot peered doubtfully at the scrum of men and horses between them and the main French body, he added succinctly, "Better to die on the field than be captured by the savages—but you do as you like."

Guizot followed the sergeant's desperate dash, dodging among the whipping hooves, leaping over fallen bodies. A black horseman with a grotesquely scarred face rode down on him, meaning to split his head with a *coutelas*. Guizot, bemused by the man's strange and horrible aspect, got his sword up to parry just in time. The horseman circled for another cut, and as he did so a gap opened and Guizot plunged into it, following the sergeant's flying pigtail. The French line parted to let them in, then closed behind them. His chest burning, Guizot fixed his sword point in the ground and bowed over the pommel, sucking for air, but before he could well get his breath the drums were beating a retreat and he had to move again. Incredibly, they were withdrawing, abandoning the field to this ragged Negro army, falling back to shelter in the mouth of the ravine.

All that had taken place in that desperate charge was a bright, bewildering swirl to Placide. He was still in possession of all his weapons, and his sword arm was tremendously sore, so he thought that he must have acquitted himself decently. What he remembered best, most fondly, was that Toussaint had moved to hold him back from the battle, then changed his mind and let him go.

A guard post had been set to observe the French where they huddled inside the mouth of the gorge. Placide rode back in the direction of Toussaint's temporary command post, in the thin shade of a *raket* tree on Habitation Lacroix. Now, in the relative quiet, he was more aware of the ringing in his ears from the explosion of the magazine that morning, but the high whine only added to his exhilaration.

As he rode in he passed some thirty disconsolate French prisoners sitting on the ground with their hands on their heads, under guard of Monpoint, who had after all survived the charge, and a couple other men of the guard. Toussaint was sitting behind his portable writing desk, opened on a section of log that served as a table. Doctor Hébert, grubby-faced and hollow-eyed, was writing something to his dictation. The shadows of pulpy, spined *raket* lay on his page.

"Ah, my boy," Toussaint said, looking up. "You come in good time to help me with my letters. The good doctor is weary, and also I must send him with our wounded to Petite Rivière. And I will soon be riding to Gonaives to see how the day has gone there."

"I will go with you," Placide said.

At Toussaint's words, the doctor stood, nodded to Placide, then stumbled slightly as he moved away, toward where Fontelle and Paulette reclined on bandage bundles by their donkeys. Placide sat down in the place he had vacated.

"No," said Toussaint. "I would have you see to the safety of the family first."

"Of course, but where are they?" Placide said, with a pang, for he had not thought of his mother and brothers since the unimaginably distant morning before.

"If it is the will of God, they have all gone to Pont d'Ester," Toussaint said. "But soon I mean to send them to Grand Cahos."

Placide looked down at the paper the doctor had been copying; the letters swam under his eyes. Some reckoning of prisoners, lists of the dead. He looked up.

"But we have beaten them, Papa—we are masters of the field. Have we not won?"

He found no smile in Toussaint's face, not even a hidden one. His father's feathered bicorne had been dropped on the ground, and dust caked in the sweat on the red cloth that bound his head. Toussaint's eyes shot over Placide's shoulder, off into the recess of pale desert, with its thorny scrub withering under the white ball of afternoon sun.

"We are masters of a graveyard," Toussaint said in a low tone. "I cannot number our losses today, no more than I can count the deaths among the enemy." He covered Placide's left hand with his right. The dry warmth was somewhat comforting, despite the words. "Nor we nor the enemy wins this day. No one wins at war."

Fort de Joux, France

November 1802

October 27, 1802

*I have received your letter of 26 Vendémiaire, concerning the State
prisoner Toussaint Louverture. The First Consul has charged me to
let you know that you answer for his person with your head. I have
no need to add anything to an order so formal and so definite. Toussaint Louverture has no right to any regard beyond that which
humanity demands. Hypocrisy is a vice as familiar to him as honor
and loyalty are to yourself . . .*

Baille felt himself flush, though not from the compliment the Minister
of Marine had strained into his warning. The paper rattled in his hand. It
was the wind, the draft that sucked around the edges of his casement,
guttered the pale flames on his hearth and the weaker one of the candle
he had lit to assist the faint light of this wintry day. He flattened the sheet
onto the table; it stuck with dampness to his palm.

*"You will have noticed yourself that he seeks to deceive you, and you
were effectively deceived, when you admitted one of his satellites, disguised
as a doctor, into his presence . . ."*

But that was not me! Baille slapped back from the table, the letter still
pinned under the meat of his hand. Still, he knew the reply to any excuse

that he might make: *You are answerable for his person with your head.* He pressed his free hand to his jowl. Dormoy had been no satellite of Toussaint, but a mere curiosity seeker—Baille, and others after him, had taken pains to assure themselves of that. And it was Colomier, not Commandant Baille, who had been imposed upon in that affair. But the answerable head did certainly belong to Baille.

You must not stop at the steps you have already taken to assure yourself that he has neither money, nor jewels. You must search everywhere to assure yourself of that; be certain that he has not hidden or buried anything in his prison. Take away his watch, if he enjoys the use of it; you may furnish him one of those wooden clocks, of the cheapest price, which will serve as well to indicate the passage of time. If he is ill, the health officer best known to you should see him and care for him—only him, only when it is altogether necessary, and only in your presence . . .

Shrinking from the pettiness of the instructions, Baille shifted on his splintery wooden chair, to loosen the band of his belt, which cut into his belly. His bowels were uneasy, though not from illness, he thought, only nerves. The business of Dormoy, foolish and inconsequential as it might have been, had conveyed this trouble both to him and to his captive. His head was heavy on his neck, and ached a little, behind the eyes. He leaned forward again, into the pressure of his belt, read on.

The only means Toussaint might have had to see his lot ameliorated would have been to cast off his dissimulation. His personal interests, the religious sentiments with which he ought to be penetrated, to expiate all the evil he has done, imposed upon him the duty of truth; but he is far estranged from fulfilling this duty, and by his continual dissimulation, he . . .

Baille revolved his head toward the window. They expected results from him, then, the Minister of Marine Decrès, and the First Consul whose mere mouthpiece the minister was—expected him to succeed where Bonaparte's best interrogator had failed. If Caffarelli, with all his famous subtlety, could not winkle an honest confession out of Toussaint—then how was Baille meant to do better than the expert, with such a program of small humiliations and annoyances? Well, he must be sterner than before, and yet he hoped he might stop short of cruelty; he had no taste for that. And though Toussaint was a puzzling figure, sometimes even alarming to Baille in his peculiar inscrutability, he could not quite see in him the author of great evil which the letter described. Still, he must not disobey. He saw above all that he would henceforth be accountable for the slight leniencies and small comforts he had so far allowed.

I presume that you have already separated him from all that might have anything to do with a uniform. "Toussaint" is his name; it is the sole appellation which should be given him . . . When he boasts of having been a general, he does nothing but recall his crimes, his hideous conduct, and his tyranny over Europeans. So he only deserves the most profound contempt for his ridiculous pride.

I salute you . . .

Baille released the letter; the edges of the sweat dampened sheet curled toward the center. He turned his face to the window again. Beyond, the last redness of the sun blazed on the ice of the opposite peak. Very soon the dark and deeper cold would follow.

"Franz!" he called. In the doorway appeared his senior corporal. "Go to the kitchen and take the prisoner Toussaint his evening ration. Take two men with you and leave them both without the door. The door must be locked while you are in the cell, and do not fail to lock every door along the corridor as you pass through it—both in entering and retiring."

"That is as usual, sir," Franz said. "You will not come?"

Insolence. "I will come later. *I* will choose my time. But tell them I will dine myself as soon as may be. Let them send me some warmed wine, if there is any potable, at once."

Having eaten rapidly and heavily, Baille sent out with his dishes the order that he should not be disturbed. He undressed only partially and took to his couch. Some hours later, he woke with a start, heart pounding, bile rising in his throat. The buttons of his trousers gouged uncomfortably into the folds of flesh below his navel. The castle bell had just struck two, though he'd only heard the echo of that clanging. Outdoors there was the boot-scuffle sound of the changing of the guard.

Baille rose, dashed water on his face from the jug, smoothed back lank strands of hair on his head. He pulled on his own boots and shrugged into his coat. His heart still fluttered disagreeably, but he thought he might soon pass on this sensation to the prisoner.

Franz was unhappy to be roused at this hour; he obeyed, but sullenly. Tonight, Baille turned out two extra members of the guard. They tramped through the lower corridors, torches held high, splashing when they crossed the wobbly planks that bridged the standing water in the penultimate vault, skimmed over now with a skein of ice. Baille left two men outside the door, entering with Franz and one other.

Toussaint sat up in his bed, looking at them alertly, out of his silence; he showed no sign of confusion, though he did seem shriveled, with the thin blanket clutched around his shoulders. He wore his clothes to bed, even his coat, Baille noted with some disappointment. No doubt it was for greater warmth.

"Build up the fire," he said to Franz. "For better light," he added. As Franz moved toward the hearth, Baille turned, drawing the key from his waistcoat pocket to double-lock the door.

"You squander my firewood, with which you are of late so stingy," Toussaint said. "What do you mean by this intrusion? It is hours yet before day."

He knows the time, Baille thought, with or without a watch or a wooden clock. Of course Toussaint could hear the bells as plainly as anyone else in the castle.

"New orders," Baille said. "You must be searched."

Toussaint passed a spidery hand across his mouth. Were the fingers slightly trembling? No.

"For what?" he said. The crooked smile, thrusting out his long lower jaw. "I have perhaps concealed here some swords and pistols, a bronze cannon—why not a squadron of cavalry?" He swept his hand around the empty cell.

"Money. Jewelry," Baille recited. "Perhaps some documents? I do not know what you may have retained, but you must understand, Ge—" he cut himself off. "You understand that orders must be followed."

"Of course."

"Get up then, please. No, leave the blanket." Baille paused. "I must also ask you to disrobe."

Toussaint stared at him strangely, his eyes glittering. He did not protest, but turned to the wall; then, as if he'd changed his mind, faced Baille, staring rigidly at the commandant as he began to unfasten his garments.

"Search the bedding," Baille said to Franz and the other guardsmen. "No, not like that. Shake out everything and turn the pallet. Yes, that's better." Meanwhile he watched Toussaint as he slipped out of the loose coat and brown peasant's trousers supplied at Decrès's suggestion. Under the soft round hat he wore even to bed, his head was bound in a yellow kerchief, which Baille had purchased for him after many requests.

"To the skin, if you please."

Toussaint stared at Baille, disbelieving, then peeled off his culotte and stood nude.

"Examine that," Baille said to Franz, who stirred the undergarment on the flagstones with the point of his bayonet. "And you, Ge—" He stopped again. *"Toussaint" is his name; it is the sole appellation which should be given him* . . . Franz would hear the strangled honorific, might report it.

"If you please, step nearer to the fire."

Toussaint complied, his eyes remaining fixed on Baille's. The commandant scanned him throat to toe. He was still fit for a man of his age, wiry, though he'd recently lost weight. Lumps of stone-gray cicatrice stood out on the velvet black of his skin—scars from the many battles which he claimed. His sex was shriveled in the cold. There was no place of concealment. But the cold affected him. Baille watched a shiver pass over the small, taut body. Well, let the victim tremble! But Toussaint breathed into the space behind his navel. Baille watched the small taut belly expand. The shiver stopped. His own breath steamed in the frosty air.

"Now turn around."

Toussaint revolved. His shoulders were just slightly stooped. The legs a little bowed, the buttocks taut. There were no scars on his back. Well, he must have always faced his enemies.

"Trouvaille!" called out the other guardsman. A find! He flourished up something from a slit in the pallet. It sparkled warmly in the torchlight.

"You see?" said Baille, though more to Franz than to the guardsman who'd made this discovery. "Bring it to me."

The guardsman stumped across the flagstones. What he presented was a single spur, chased and gilded, though the gilt had worn away from the place where the rowel turned and on the inside where it was shaped to curve around a boot heel. Baille fingered the chill metal, then glanced at Toussaint, who had turned, unbidden, to face him once more.

"With such a weapon I might overthrow my prison," Toussaint said. "Would you deprive me of a souvenir?"

"Such are my orders."

The spur clicked when Baille set it down on the table. He picked up the coat and turned out the pockets. The famous watch, but nothing more. He stroked the lining with his fingertips. Here was something—a rectangle of folded paper and the round shapes of a few coins. By what sleight of hand had he concealed these things when he was made to change his clothes? Baille felt his suspicion abruptly sharpen. He looked at Franz.

"Search the room, the cracks between the stones. Make certain there is nothing buried and no hiding place."

Franz looked at him rather coolly, but turned away before Baille could be certain of any superciliousness in the look. He drew a short knife from his belt and began to probe the masonry joints on the wall behind the pallet. The other guardsman, at a grunt from Franz, crouched down and felt the edges of the paving stones, groping his way from the bed frame toward the hearth.

Baille returned to the coat, working the paper packet toward the slit in the lining at the back. He had to bend the papers slightly to pull them through. Conscious of Toussaint's judgmental eye, Baille unstuck the several sheets from one another and spread them over the table. Three letters, crumpled and dirty at the corners, beginning to tear along the folds. The first from Captain-General Leclerc himself and the second from a General Brunet: *We have, my dear general, some arrangements to make together which cannot be dealt with by letter, but which a conference of one hour would complete . . .* Baille realized that this must be the last correspondence Toussaint had received before his deportation.

"Those documents are my property," Toussaint said. "Moreover, they are evidence to be presented at my trial—proof of the duplicity which General Leclerc practiced against me."

"Nonetheless, I am ordered to confiscate them," Baille said. Without looking at the third letter, he folded the papers together again and slipped the packet into his pocket. Then he shook the few coins from their hiding place in the lining and stacked them on the table beside the watch and the spur. Toussaint watched him, but said nothing more. The firelight behind him blackened his silhouette. Baille turned away and walked to the wall opposite the hearth—the raw bedrock of the mountain itself. Might Toussaint have quarried some cache into this? It seemed unlikely. The stone was furrowed and wormholed with the damp that constantly seeped through it. Tonight the cold had hardened the moisture into crystals that fractured the light of the fire and the torches.

"Rien de plus," Franz announced. There's nothing more.

"No," said Baille, as if he'd known this result ahead of time. He touched the rock wall with his forefinger, snapping a delicate stem of ice. Toussaint's eyes felt hard in the center of his back. Baille turned to face him.

"Your kerchief also, if you please."

Toussaint only stared at him. He seemed strangely composed, even in his nakedness. The castle bell struck three. Beyond the grille at the end of the cell, the voices of sentries exchanged their *all's well* from post to post.

"Your kerchief must also be inspected," said Baille. Toussaint looked frozen to the hearthstone. Baille took several steps toward him. So did Franz, from an opposing angle. But before they'd reached him, Toussaint ripped the yellow cloth from his head and shook it out in a circular flourish, as if to show it empty.

Yet Baille was distracted by looking at his head, which, it seemed to him, he'd never before seen bare. The forehead was extremely high where the removed cloth revealed it, rising sharply to a bald and glossy bump protruding through tight knots of grizzled hair. When Baille looked again at Toussaint's hands, they were busy with the kerchief, folding it diagonally over and over to compress it to a smaller, tighter triangle. Again he thought of some sleight of concealment. The packet of yellow finally disappeared in the pressure of Toussaint's two hands, while Toussaint raved in a language Baille could not understand— *"Madichon pou le general Leclerc! Madichon pou li! Tout sak pasé pou mal sé sou kont li! Men, l'ap mouri. L'ap mouri, mwen di, mwen wé, l'ap mouri nan pay nou. Li pa jamn soti nan Saint Domingue."*

"General," Baille stuttered. Well, now he'd pronounced the title—too late to recall it, though he felt that Franz took note.

"General! Control yourself. These demonstrations do not become you."

And Baille was struck by the extent of his own discomfort, embarrassment, even distress. After all, such a breakdown in the morale of the prisoner was surely what the new orders were intended to achieve. But Baille was positively unnerved to see it. He opened his mouth to say something more, then stopped. It was plain that Toussaint would not hear him. His jaws were clenched, the tendons stood out vibrating around his throat, and every fiber of his body exerted pressure on the wedge of cloth between his hands.

A curse upon the General Leclerc—curse him! Every evil thing that has happened is his doing. But he is dying—I say it, I see it. He is dying in our country—he will never leave Saint Domingue.

Baille gathered up the coins and the spur. He beckoned to his guards. Toussaint ignored them as they withdrew.

Nothing could be worse than the humiliation which I received from you today. You have stripped me from top to bottom to search me and see that I have no money, you have finally turned over all my linen and even searched into my pallet. Happily, you have found nothing: the ten quadruples *that I turned over to you are mine, and it is I who so declare to you.*

Toussaint paused, the quill tip poised over his paper. His ink well was nearly dry. The light was poor, though outside it was day. But day by day the sun was weaker and more distant and the hints of it that penetrated the grille that admitted air to his cell grew fainter, less convincing. He'd resumed his clothing, rebound the yellow cloth around his brow. But still the cold cut through to him, and the pain in his head was much worse. His letters squirmed across the page, awkwardly jammed against each other. He dipped the pen again and kept on scrawling.

You have taken my watch away from me along with twenty-two sols I had in my pocket; I warn you that all those objects belong to me, and you will have to account to me for them on the day they send me to the execution. You will remit the entirety to my wife and to my children. When a man is already unfortunate, one ought not to try to humiliate him or vex him without humanity or charity, without any consideration for him as a servant of the Republic, and they have taken every precaution and machination against me as if I were a great criminal. I have already told you, and I repeat to you again, I am an honest man and if I had no honor, I would not have served my country faithfully as I have done, and I would not be here either by the order of my government. I salute you—

—and Baille let the sheet drop from his hand with a grunt. Toussaint's crabbed writing went out of focus as it fluttered to the table. The prick of conscience which the commandant had once felt had also lost its sharpness. At any rate, there'd be no more such letters. With this document, Baille had also confiscated Toussaint's pen and paper. At the same time, he'd supervised another search, fruitless except to derange the prisoner a little further. Let him enjoy his silence as he might.

Toussaint shuddered under his thin blanket. The teeth that had been loosened by that spent cannonball long ago were rattling in his jaws, and the pain in his head was astonishing, a sensation so all-encompassing and pure that it transcended all division between pain and pleasure. Then, and suddenly, it stopped, and a flood of warmth welled up at him. He uncurled his rigid arms and legs and floated on the warm and buoyant surface of the fever. The frost was sparkling on the bare rock wall. Its crystals knitted themselves into a mirror. Toussaint looked toward it tranquilly, through the fog of his own breath. An element of his spirit left his body and went drifting toward the wall, but the reflection that returned to him was not his own.

Moyse, he breathed. But the one-eyed face in the mirror lost the aspect of his adopted nephew and hardened into the stiff gaze of Ghede. Baron Samedi, Baron Cimetière, Baron Lacroix . . . by all these names Toussaint had known him. He relaxed and released himself to follow the dark angel beneath the water of his own death.

Instead he found himself looking out through the tunnel of Ghede's one eye. He heard the whine of mosquito song as he passed through the vortex. Then on a gust of a warm wind he was flying up and over the cape; he caught a glimpse of Fort Picolet upside down and the waves beating on the seawall below the Batterie Circulaire as his insect body went tumbling toward the windows of the Governor's house at Le Cap. The mosquito voice hummed in his ear the story of Moyse's namesake Moses, whom the Lord did not leave to cross the Jordan in his body; never was Moses to enter the land whose promise his life's labor had realized . . . Then darkness. The room where he emerged looked curtained all in black. There were clouds of mosquitoes besides the one in which Ghede was incorporated, and Moyse was among them after all— also Macandal and Boukman and Dieudonné and Blanc Cassenave and Joseph Flaville and all the hundreds on hundreds of others who had passed through the mirror before Toussaint, remaining, invisible, just on the other side of the world we see. Pauline Leclerc batted her fine little hands at the mosquitoes, irritably, ineffectually. Her voice was small and dull in the close room.

"Leave the curtains shut. The night air is noxious, especially to an invalid."

But he could not tell whom she addressed; she seemed to be alone in the room. The bed she sat beside was illuminated by white wax tapers fixed to each of its four posts. Amid the four flames the Captain-General Leclerc writhed feverishly in the sheets which would become his cerements. The mosquito lit on his pale, waxy throat. Pauline wept wretchedly at the bedside; Toussaint felt a touch of surprise that this accomplished courtesan could feel so much at the loss of one little husband. Leclerc twitched and shuddered as the mosquito's needle-snout probed into his gullet for a final drop of blood. Pauline sobbed—could she be only acting? Then the blood was found, and all the thirst of the Invisibles joined in the frail machine of this one mosquito to share its winy taste.

Part Three

LA CRÊTE À PIERROT

February–March 1802

Vainqueurs partout, nous ne possédions rien au delà de nos fusils. L'ennemi ne tint nulle part, et pourtant il ne cessa pas d'être maître du pays.

—Lieutenant Moreau de Jonnes

Though victorious everywhere, we possessed nothing but our guns. The enemy did not hold out anywhere, and yet remained the master of the country.

21

At the center of the dawn bustle of the French camp at Ennery, Captain-General Leclerc positioned himself on a camp stool by the rolled flaps of his tent door, and extended first one foot, then the other, that his orderly might brush and polish his elegant high-topped boots. Cyprien and Daspir watched him at a little distance. Leclerc, who was perusing his dispatches, affected to ignore both the staff officers nearer to him and the orderly busy at his feet.

"That makes a week or better that he has not taken off his boots," Daspir remarked, as he sliced into one of the perfectly ripe avocados he'd managed to acquire from a passing *marchande* an hour earlier. He'd slept uneasily and awakened before daylight, his unrest channeled into hunger. During his several trips through these mountains he'd learned that the market women traveled before dawn, and today he'd put the knowledge to good use.

"You don't think he removes them when alone in his tent?" Cyprien sniffed.

"But no—our general is too much the man of honor." Daspir popped the seed from his avocado and bit into the yellow-green flesh, his top teeth scraping the inside of the peel.

"Or too much governed by his pride," said Cyprien. "Well, perhaps he does sleep in his boots—if not, his orderly would betray him."

"It must be desperately uncomfortable," Daspir said. "To wear one's boots both night and day."

"I think there are a good many soldiers in our command who would be glad to suffer so."

"Well yes," said Daspir. "I won't dispute you there." In fact, several supply ships had gone astray from the main fleet, one carrying a cargo of new boots, and for that reason a good number of the French soldiers marched in broken shoes, and a few went barefoot.

"Try an avocado?" Daspir said. "There are several, and I also managed a couple of oranges."

"No thank you," Cyprien replied. "I seldom have much appetite before a battle. Though I do hope we shall sup well tonight—in Gonaives."

"Likewise," said Daspir. He licked avocado paste from his fingers, letting the peel drop on the ground. "And may our commander pull off his boots this evening, and let his toes go free in the fresh air."

"Yes," said Cyprien. "It's been a little longer than he wagered."

What of their own wager, Daspir thought, but he said nothing of it. Cyprien was cynical on that subject, or the subject itself was cynical. And Daspir had no idea where Guizot or Paltre might be at that point. Dismissing the thought, he tore into the green peel of an orange, disclosing yellowish, juicy flesh.

Leclerc stood up, brushing his tight trouser leg reflexively. The orderly put away his brush and blacking and set himself to disassembling the tent. Daspir studied the high gloss on the Captain-General's boots. Despite his ironizing with Cyprien, he thought that Leclerc had shown himself to be something more than a mere popinjay these last few days. He had been energetic, determined, and decisive. It seemed to Daspir that the farther Leclerc traveled from his lady wife, the more these qualities strengthened in him. It might be that he deserved to win his own prize.

General Desfourneaux stooped slightly, bringing his ear to Leclerc's lips. Daspir was too far off to hear Leclerc's words or Desfourneaux's response. They'd all marched south with Desfourneaux, from Le Cap by way of Limbé, and had met with no more than harassment on this route. The worst they'd seen was sniping and skirmishing from irregulars led by Sylla in the mountains of Plaisance, and those men had not stood for long against the organized French troops. But General Hardy's division, moving westward along the mountain range from Dondon to Marmelade, had fought some hard engagements with the retreating rebel Christophe—the victory at Morne à Boispins being especially prodigious, according to Hardy's reports, which Leclerc certainly gave full credit.

Now Christophe had been pushed away to the heights of Bayonet, some distance to the southeast of their position, while Hardy had the day before joined Leclerc and Desfourneaux here at the crossroads of

Ennery. And at the same time, according to the strategy which Daspir and Cyprien had agreed was very well conceived, General Rochambeau was moving to cut off any retreat south from Gonaives. So indeed they might sup well in Gonaives tonight, with the rebellion ended and the rebel Toussaint either captured or killed.

"Captain Daspir, come to me, please." Leclerc was beckoning with his left hand as he spoke.

Daspir crossed the space between them and brought himself smartly to attention.

"If you wish, you may ride with the advance guard this morning."

"It is my honor." Daspir saluted and went at a half-trot to find his horse.

An hour later he was riding down the main road toward Gonaives, content to have stolen a march on Cyprien, who remained with the main body of the troops. The descent was gentle, and the Ennery River purled quietly to their right. Daspir was lulled by the warmth of the sun on his back; at this early hour the heat had not yet become painful. His stomach was pleasantly full of avocado and orange, and he felt confident for the day's action. When he looked at the river he recalled the image of the little Negro officer astride his warhorse, on the far side of that other stream, north of Limbé. With a little more luck he'd be as near to him today, or nearer. For surely Toussaint would be trapped today at Gonaives—no choice for him except death or surrender or to throw himself into the sea.

The downward slope fell into a trough, then began to rise, just slightly, on the other side. The river was very near on their right, while the road turned sharply around the steep flank of a jungle mountain. All was calm and quiet except for the tramp of marching feet, intermittent birdsong, and the rippling of water over stones of the riverbed. Afterward Daspir could not be certain if he'd felt that electric shock in his spine before the shooting started, but something moved him to stretch out along the neck of his horse, so that the volley passed harmless over him.

Others had not been so fortunate; when Daspir straightened he saw a dozen foot soldiers laid low on the curve of the road. There was more shooting, dead ahead of them. The advance guard had walked into an ambush. Daspir drew his sword, but he could not immediately see the enemy; the firing to his left came out of a dense cover of trees. His horse carried him around the bend, and now he saw a barricade of logs across the road—from behind this obstacle more bullets poured. Daspir's horse reared and wheeled. An enemy charge rolled down from the mountainside: a horde of screaming, whirling blacks that came out of the screen of trees with a sudden abandon that swept part of the advance guard into the river. Daspir's horse stumbled on the bank. When he glanced down, he saw a dead man floating, the body catching between a pair of stones. Daspir looked dully at the leather straps crossed on the dead man's back.

His blood rushed past him down the river, thin threads dispersing in the water.

Then they were making a headlong retreat, thrown back against the main force marching up behind them. "What is the meaning of this disorder?" Leclerc was screaming, and Daspir stammered, *"Mon général, their resistance is surprisingly stout,"* but Leclerc was not paying any attention to him, had moved on to bellow at somebody else. Daspir took off his hat and looked at it and stuck his little finger into the bullet hole—the old one from their landing at the Baie d'Acul. Today no projectile had come so near to him—so far. He felt his confidence begin to return.

Cyprien shouted something indistinct to him, an order passed down from General Hardy. The survivors of the advance guard were re-forming, bolstered by troops from Desplanques's brigade, and the drums were beating the charge. Daspir resumed his place in the van. Ahead, the men moved out at a smart trot, not wavering as they rounded the bend to confront the log barricade. With an effort, Daspir held himself straight in the saddle. The advance carried him against the logs, where he lashed with his sword against a black in tattered colonial uniform who was hacking toward his right leg with a cane knife. Infantrymen were climbing the logs. Daspir saw one fall backward, flung off as lightly as a forkful of straw by a bayonet thrust from an enormous black. But the French charge did not slacken; the men behind kept clambering over the bodies of those who'd fallen before them.

The mêlée had become general atop the barricade when Daspir felt the wind riffle his hair forward and realized he had lost his hat. The hat with its fortunate bullet hole—his talisman. He looked about wildly and saw it rolling on its edge toward the river. He was on the ground before he knew he'd dismounted, chasing the hat. A black sprang up before him, and Daspir unconsciously knocked him out of the way with his shoulder. The hat caught on a stick at the water's edge, and Daspir swooped down and recovered it. Cyprien swirled past, shouting some admonition. Daspir caught his horse's trailing reins and hauled himself back up into the saddle.

Mounted, he could see that the French charge had broken through the barricade and was pressing the retreating blacks south down the road, though not very hotly. A fair number of infantrymen had paused to drag the logs of the barricade clear of the roadway, rolling the timbers into the stream, which was now choked with bodies, both black and white. Daspir averted his eyes from that. But still he felt exhilarated when he overtook Cyprien.

"Nothing can hold back our French grenadiers," he sang out gaily.

"No . . ." Cyprien looked a little pale. "But that was a wicked ambush—they reckon that we have lost three hundred men."

After that Daspir found it harder to ignore the bodies strewn along the roadside. But soon enough they had marched past them all. The road straightened, emerging from the mountains into the dry open plain below. The enemy was a cloud of white dust half a mile ahead of them. The French army held a steady pace, but did not close the distance. Daspir checked that his hat was secure to his head and tipped his head back to look up at the vacant, cloudless blue of the sky. Then he fixed his eyes forward once again. He was hot now, from his exertion and the increase of the sun, and his throat was dry. There was no water in his reach, and the road had turned away from the river. The air he breathed felt thick and gritty in his throat.

Placide rode half a length behind Toussaint on the trail from Marie Louise to Granmorne. Though Toussaint did not look back at him, the image of his son's bewildered face persisted. How could the boy understand the victory they'd won so desperately to be a loss for all concerned? Placide was patient, however; he asked no unnecessary questions, but waited for the answers to appear to his observation. Toussaint liked that very much in him; it was a trait they had in common.

And truly it had been a victory—it still was. At the least and worst, Toussaint had broken the trap set for him. The line of retreat was now open. But to be forced to retreat was galling, especially if Gonaives must be sacrificed—though the sacrifice of Gonaives had been part of his plan from the moment he'd decided to attack Rochambeau. And the loss of so many men was bitter. But none of that was enough to explain the dreadful hollowness he felt as they climbed the spiraling trail up Granmorne. The day was bright and clear, the air fresh on the mountain, where the heat subsided the higher they climbed. A hummingbird hovered at a bloom beside the trail. But all these things were at a distance from Toussaint, as if on the other side of the mirror. As soon as the fighting had ended that morning, he'd felt his head vacated by his sustaining spirit—a dangerous emptiness, which anything else might arrive to occupy.

"Halt! Who comes?"

Toussaint squinted up the trail. The silver helmets of his honor guardsmen flickered behind the leaves. He cleared his throat, but Placide was already answering.

"We are the guard of the Governor-General."

At that, Toussaint masked a faint smile. The face of one of Morisset's dragoons appeared in a frame of green branches. "Governor! Pardon— we could not see you clearly. Come up—your family is here and safe."

"And Morisset?" Toussaint took his hand away from his mouth.

"He has gone to the help of Vernet at Gonaives, where the fighting is heavy. We have not been threatened here."

Toussaint nudged his horse forward, ducking his head below the branches. Though the distance was considerable he could hear shooting and even some shouting voices coming from the direction of Gonaives.

The town was still being defended, then. He felt the dark mood lift just slightly. Then they had come into a clearing, where Placide hurriedly slipped down to embrace his mother. Toussaint took in his Chancy nieces and their mother, and Isaac, who could not seem to meet his eyes. Most if not all of the inhabitants of the *grand'case* at Thibodet were there too, with all the white and mixed-blood children.

"Where is Saint-Jean?" he said. The harshness of his voice echoed the dread he'd carried up the mountain. Suzanne's head lowered. Oddly, it was the gunrunner Tocquet who answered the question, he who'd come in the night with the news of Rochambeau's strength, instead of anyone of Toussaint's family.

"Governor, Saint-Jean was overtaken by a column of General Hardy's division. I did not see him myself, but I have it on good authority that he is safely held by the French."

Toussaint drove his knuckles against the pommel of his saddle; the skin split between them, but he felt no pain. "An evil mischance that he was taken," he said.

"Father." Isaac was looking frankly at him now. "The Captain-General has never mistreated me or Placide, nor any of his officers—surely they would show no discourtesy to our younger brother. Be confident they will return him safe, as they did us."

"Ah, but the war is open now," Toussaint said. He looked into Isaac's darkening face, then away into the surrounding circle of trees. "Still, there is sense in what you say. We must make the best of it, and hope that your judgment is good."

Tocquet spoke again. "I can bear out your son's judgment, Governor. By what I heard, Saint-Jean has been put in the care of Madame Granville, the wife of his tutor, whom you know. So you may be comforted—he is with friends."

"You are good to tell me so," said Toussaint.

Tocquet pushed back his broad-brimmed hat and adjusted the leather thong that bound his hair at the back. "Out of your own goodness, will you tell us what has become of our friend Antoine Hébert?"

"He is safely on the road to Petite Rivière, with those of our wounded who can still walk." Toussaint saw from the corner of his eye how the pretty *quarteronne* Nanon seemed to wilt at his words; Tocquet's white woman moved to support her. "I do not hold him against his will, but you must know how urgently his skills are needed."

He turned to Suzanne. "*Madamm mwen*, you must go now to Pont d'Ester, while I—"

"Wait." Suzanne's eyes flashed up at him from under her blue head-cloth. "I will not go on so alone, and risk another mishap."

"But I must return to Gonaives, if the fighting continues there." Toussaint checked Placide with a glance, as Placide lifted his foot toward a stirrup. "No—stay here to protect your mother and the others." Toussaint drew out his watch on its chain. "If I have not returned by three, you must bring them all to Pont d'Ester, where I will join you." He glanced over the five dragoons that Morisset had left there. "Keep watch on the roads to the north. If you see French troops, you must go sooner."

Toussaint reached down for a brief clasp of Suzanne's hand. Then he turned his horse back into the trees and began riding back down the trail as quickly as was prudent. He swayed in the saddle, reins gathered in one hand, sometimes licking away the blood that ran between the knuckles of the other.

He had required to be alone, to hide from the rest of them, his dependents, the awful hollowness that had seized him. An emptiness he could now understand to have been left by the unexpected loss of Saint-Jean. But that was not all. No matter the strategic sense of it, to lose Gonaives was like giving up the ribs that covered his heart. For years he'd maneuvered to win control of this port. But that was not all either. He almost wished Placide were still with him, to hear the explanation: the loss of Gonaives would break Toussaint's communications with Port-de-Paix, where Maurepas, with the Ninth Demibrigade, had been making the most brilliant and successful resistance of any before today. Following Toussaint's orders to the hilt, Maurepas had burned Port-de-Paix at the first appearance of French ships and retreated to the gorges of Trois Rivières, where he'd handily whipped every French general so far sent against him, including both Debelle and Humbert on more than one occasion.

Toussaint held on to the thought of Maurepas as he pressed his horse to gallop on the main road north to Gonaives. He met a portion of his own troops, falling back from Périsse toward Pont d'Ester; their startled faces turned to follow him, but he did not pause. There was no fighting at the lower entrance to Gonaives, and only the lightest guard. From the few men there, Toussaint learned that there were two battles under way, one on the road that came straight from Plaisance, the other at Pont des Dattes. He walked his horse through the town to cool it, through the square before the church. Headquarters was also almost deserted, with practically every man who could walk thrown into battle. From the stable behind, he heard the racket of Bel Argent whinnying and kicking his stall door. Toussaint felt his gloom disperse a little. The white stallion might return him some portion of his inner strength, if anything would or could. He sent a runner to warn General Vernet of his coming, and saddled and bridled Bel Argent himself.

"We have fought as well as we can," Vernet said when Toussaint had reached him. "Morisset led a charge that drove them back as far as La Tannerie for a time. But there are too many for us to hold. It is Leclerc himself who presses us here, and Hardy has his whole division in the line at Pont des Dattes."

"How do you estimate their strength?"

"In all? Twelve thousand, it must be," Vernet said. "And we but fourteen hundred, and that at the start of the day."

Toussaint removed his hat and massaged the bone of his head, through the sweat-soaked red madras cloth. He looked to the west, where the afternoon sun reddened and lowered.

"So," he said softly. "We must burn the town and abandon this place. Let Morisset go back to Granmorne, where he left a small guard for my family. You will join with General Christophe as he retreats from Bayonet, and we will all reunite at Pont d'Ester."

"*Oui, mon général,*" Vernet said dismally. "It will be as you have ordered."

"*Bon courage,*" Toussaint admonished him. "Certainly we have lost some terrain, but we will still have an army."

He felt none of the encouragement he'd recommended to Vernet as he rode back toward the center of town. Rather, the black shade of doom gripped him even more tightly. It had filled the hollowness in his head with rage and a fear he could not yet name. Even the surge of the refreshed and rested Bel Argent between his knees did not raise his spirit. He had not slept these last three days, and he thought he could feel the onset of a fever, but none of that was enough to explain the despair that occupied the cavity at his center which had held his fire and strength as recently as that morning.

Despair was reflected in the faces of the Gonaives *bourgeois* who were now scurrying toward the south portals of the town, carrying whatever they could quickly bundle up or toss into a wheelbarrow, hurrying just a pace ahead of Vernet's fire-starters, who spread among the buildings with torches and *lances à feu.* Toussaint snatched up a torch from one of them and held it high. In its red blur he saw the inevitable, obvious to him at last: With the loss of Gonaives, Maurepas would not only be out of communication, but perfectly surrounded by the French. After today—after he had won today—Leclerc would have large forces free to block Maurepas's retreat by way of Gros Morne—indeed to encircle him by that route. Under such pressure Maurepas could only surrender or be destroyed, and now the black shadow that possessed Toussaint told him there was no hope or help for it.

The door of the church stood open, dark. Bel Argent, who could go up anything short of a sheer cliff, had no difficulty scrambling up the steps. Toussaint ducked his head to pass beneath the lintel. Inside his torch fumed smoke among the rafters. A sexton darted out a side door, but the priest, a white man, held his ground before the altar.

"The spirit of Jesus has abandoned me," Toussaint announced. His voice boomed along the nave. The priest raised one shaky palm, said nothing.

"How faithfully I served him, but for nothing," Toussaint hissed. "It is the servants of Jesus who make war upon me now." He spurred the horse; the priest dodged away from the iron-shod hooves. With his left hand, Toussaint ripped the carved crucifix from the wall above the altar, whirled it once around his head, then slammed it down to the stone floor.

"*Aba Jisit!* Down with Jesus! I will not serve Jesus any more!"

But the priest had fled, and the church was empty. Toussaint held his torch among the drapes until they were well ablaze, then flung it away among the wooden benches. Bel Argent was trembling, eyes rolling in the smoke. Toussaint stroked his mane and pressed his flanks more gently with his heels. The crucifix splintered under the hooves, then horse and rider moved together out the door, into the larger conflagration.

It was the shortage of cavalry, Daspir kept telling himself, that held back the French outside Gonaives through most of that day. Before his staff posting, he had trained as a hussar, so he could appreciate the *élan* of the silver-helmed black cavalry squadron that swooped down on Leclerc's troops and routed them, though but briefly, a long way up the road they'd come. The Leclerc-Desfourneaux column lacked horses enough to counter these maneuvers properly. Leclerc, beside himself at what he thought sluggishness, ran madly about, screaming exhortations as he stung men's legs with the flat of his sword blade. The French troops regained their discipline soon enough and marched back into the line. After two more hours of stubborn fighting, the opposition at the north gate of Gonaives began to crumple. But by then it was the close of the day, and when Daspir looked up he saw that the rose-colored mares' tails of the sunset sky were darkened by swiftly rising clouds of smoke and stabbed with tongues of flame.

The rebels had set fire to the town, then disappeared in the confusion. So it seemed, for there was no armed resistance as the French marched in, though every building burned. It was just as it had been at Le Cap, Daspir thought bitterly. He was weary beyond description, and ready to faint from thirst. The smoke was heavy. He masked his face with a white handkerchief; the fabric was soon blackened around his nostrils and mouth.

The rebel headquarters was evacuated; flames licked out of every window. General Hardy, who'd entered the town by way of Pont des Dattes, was calling for a bucket brigade. But the well in the town square had been plugged by the carcass of a dead bullock. Daspir dismounted, rallied a handful of troopers, and supervised its removal. It then developed that no buckets were to be found, or nearly none—any container that would burn had been added to the pyres. Besides, the men were mostly out of order, plunging through the burning houses to loot whatever they could before the fire destroyed it all. Their huzzahs of victory, loud as they were, rang strangely against this background.

Daspir sank down on the curb of the well, took off his handkerchief, and looked dully at the mask-like charcoal marks his breath had made. Seated, he was below the worst of the smoke. His horse, reins trailing, moved up to snuffle the water that had begun to pool within the well curb once the dead ox was dragged off. Daspir rinsed his handkerchief and pressed it to his temples and the back of his neck, then dared to scoop some water in the palm of his hand to drink.

With that refreshment spreading through his parched body, he felt a little encouraged. When Cyprien blundered up to him, a phantom drifting out of the smoke, Daspir hailed him with an expression of good cheer.

"We shall not sup so well as we'd hoped tonight, it seems."

"I think not," Cyprien coughed. "Hardtack for us again, if we're so lucky."

Daspir stood up beside him, covering his nose and mouth with the wet handkerchief. Darkness had completely lowered now. They were facing the church, whose walls had already been consumed, so that the framework stood out like blackened ribs against the fire that breathed inside. As they watched, most of the timbers collapsed in the back of the building, sending up a great geyser of sparks.

"Has Toussaint been taken?" Daspir asked, with small hope.

Cyprien coughed again and spat on a cobblestone so hot from the fires that his spittle hissed. "Does it look like he has been? No, the report is that he has cut his way through Rochambeau and got off somewhere to the south."

"Indeed," Daspir said. "I suppose that only means that we will meet him on another day."

There was some commotion now behind them, a beating of hooves and sudden shouting at the far end of the square, but Daspir was too weary even to turn his head that way. His stomach rumbled, and with that he remembered to tap the pockets of his coat.

"Take heart," he said to Cyprien. "I have yet two avocados and an orange."

22

At day's end at the top of Granmorne, Placide began to hear roaring and the tattoo of French marching drums, rising above the gunfire from the direction of Gonaives. He slipped out of the pocket of trees where his family was sheltered and crept onto the rim of a huge black boulder that jutted from the northwestern brow of the hill. A red fire had crowned over the hollow of the town, and beyond it the sun burned bitterly on the horizon.

It was long since his father had ridden away, well past the appointed hour of three, but Suzanne had refused to leave Granmorne until some word of him came. The whites of Thibodet had only just departed. When he looked down more steeply from his rock ledge, Placide picked out a couple of their group—Isabelle Cigny and her son—as they turned a bend of the trail leading inland, a roundabout way which Tocquet hoped might allow them to skirt the fighting and return to Ennery.

"Quelle horreur." The dull voice belonged to Isaac, who had joined Placide on the rock. What a horror. Placide said nothing. His brother had spoken in French, but the Creole word *anmè* unfolded itself in Placide's mind: bitter. There was the bitterness of his father's spirit at the destruction and death he had felt himself forced to order; now Placide felt he understood that better than before. But where was his father now?

He felt Isaac's confusion too, and turned and wrapped an arm around his shoulder.

"It is well that you stay with our mother, after all," he said.

Isaac nodded. "To the end, if it is bitter." He returned the pressure of Placide's arm. The choice of word placed them in the same spirit, closer than they had been at any time since the moment of their division. Placide recalled the internal rending he had felt that day in the headquarters of Gonaives. In his mind flashed an image of the building as it must be now, its blackened shell gnawed out by flame.

Isaac slipped out from under his arm and looked back toward the trees. "Come on," he said. "Do you hear that?"

Placide, already following, did hear the shuffle of marching feet. There were three or four different trails that led to the summit of Granmorne. He recalled how the French had overtaken Saint-Jean without anyone knowing it till too late—he'd scarcely had time to think of it till now, his youngest brother in the hands of the enemy. His mother's voice rose, though not in protest or anger; Placide could not make out the words. When he and Isaac came back into the grove, they found that General Vernet had come, leading the survivors of the Seventh Demibrigade up from the burning town below.

"Madame, the Governor-General is safe and well. He expects you now at Pont d'Ester—it's likely he expects that you would be there already."

"Yes," said Suzanne. Her voice grew milder; her head lowered under its blue cloth. "We are ready to go to him, now we know where he is—"

But Placide was distracted by the sound of hoofbeats. Morisset was coming in, bringing his battered cavalry squadron along at a dull plod. The dust-caked silver helmets glimmered in the fading light. Morisset pulled his horse up at the edge of the trees. Placide was just moving toward him when he heard the sound of cheering from the town. French voices. The voices of *blancs*, Placide thought, with an unaccustomed thrust of resentment at that word. *Blancs*, exulting over another firepit they had captured.

Morisset's helmet hung between his shoulder blades, the leather thong caught across his throat. His shallow features were turned to the wind. The sun was dropping below the horizon now, leaving trails of its red light to scar the clouds. The light from the fire in the town was stronger.

"That they should dare to cry victory after so much defeat." A muscle jumped in Morisset's jaw; his nostrils flared. Placide was near enough to hear his breathing.

"Let fifteen brave men come with me," Morisset said. "We will still show them something."

In an instant every man in the squadron had faced his horse back toward the town. Morisset, his face relaxing, detached half a dozen of them to remain as an escort for Madame Louverture. Then he raised a palm to stop Placide, who'd found his own horse and quickly mounted.

"*Monchè,* your bravery is admirable," Morisset said. "But I must answer to the Governor for your safety."

"But—" Placide stopped himself short. Obedience—first duty of the soldier. The swallowed argument lodged in his throat. Isaac was watching him from the ground, his expression difficult to read. Placide held in his horse, as the greater part of the squadron moved back onto the trail by which they'd just arrived. He looked at the backs of the men receding, the switching tails of the horses. A shimmer of their excitement washed over him; his heart still pounded.

"*Kenbe sa.*" It was the scarred one who spoke, the man who had brought the ill news from Santo Domingo City, who was so devoted to Placide's father. Guiaou. Morisset had detached him with the escort. Now he jostled his horse toward Placide's and held out a damp square of dark red cloth. Take this.

Placide only stared at him, bemused.

"*Maré têt ou!*" Guiaou said. Tie up your head!

It was his father's fashion, Placide realized, and that of many men as they went into battle. Guiaou had just pulled the cloth from his own head; the corners were still creased to the old knot. But Placide's head was larger. Automatically, he turned to the wind, letting the air carry the fabric from his forehead to the back. His fingers fumbled behind his head. Then the knot was solid, the pressure secure along his temples and at the nape of his neck. Guiaou grinned and nodded to him.

"*Alé,*" he said. Go.

Placide squeezed his heels to his horse's flanks. In a moment he had overtaken the last rider in Morisset's squadron; the man looked back once but gave no sign of disapproval. He faced forward again, and Placide closed the distance. Guiaou's *mouchwa têt* had worked for him, maybe, like an invisibility cap. Onward and downward they jogged. A couple of small bats flittered back and forth across the trail, losing themselves in the bordering trees at the end of each pass. By some trick of the land's lie, the sound of French cheering grew fainter for a time, then abruptly much louder.

It was full dark when they reached the slope of the cemetery hill on the southwest edge of town, but the moon was well risen, picking out the crypts and crosses in a cool white light, spreading shadows of the riders long across the graves. Placide prickled with something other than fear. He checked the knot at the nape of his neck. Thus the world would appear to Baron Lacroix, when that spirit arose through the cemetery. Placide's blood beat a different pattern than before.

The iron cemetery gate hung shut before them. Morisset bunched his men in cover of the wall beside it. Firelight from the burning buildings warmed their faces and the horses' manes. The cemetery was only a couple of blocks from the main square. Some effort must have been made to put the fires out, for most of the shells only smoldered now; just a few were fully ablaze. Spectral figures of *blanc* soldiers were black against the fire glow as they scurried back and forth across the streets, flittering like the bats on the trail above. Many were probably drunk by now, on looted rum.

Morisset looked over his men. His eye brushed over Placide but did not stop. As he faced the bars of the gate, his lips pulled back far enough that firelight wavered on his front teeth. At his gesture, a man got down to raise the bar from the gate and then quickly remounted. Placide checked the knot of his *mouchwa têt* once more. Something inspired him to close his left eye. His drumming pulse quickened, changed its beat; his right eye locked forward with a doubled concentration. The two wings of the gate went floating open with a squawl of rusted hinge. They charged in silence, except for the hooves.

"You there," Daspir called to a passing grenadier. "Lay down that cask!"

The soldier stopped, but only stared at the captain. Cyprien was staring at Daspir too. But Daspir, emboldened by the effect of half an orange and a whole avocado, persisted.

"Looting may be punished by death, I should warn you," he said smoothly. "In the case of drunkenness on duty, there is flogging to consider."

"*Vive la France!*" The soldier rolled the bunghole of the cask to his lips; slightly choking as clear fluid spilled from both corners of his mouth. "*Vive le Capitaine-Général!*—and three cheers for the beautiful Pauline!"

With that he loosed the cask from his hands and ran off. Daspir was on it almost before it hit the ground, tumbling it like a dog pawing a ball. Not much had spilled before he caught it up. It was only a small keg, perhaps a gallon. Daspir tilted it back with both hands and gasped at the syrupy burn of the new white rum.

"Well ordered!" Cyprien said, his eyes alight with appreciation, if it were not merely the glitter of the surrounding fires. "Well executed too."

Daspir passed him the cask with a nod. His eyes were watering with the impact of the rum, but the burn in his belly heartened him. He looked down the street behind them, thinking of further foraging possibilities— in that direction the fires had been extinguished or had not completely taken hold, so there might be possibilities. Strangely, a handful of looters came bursting out of that block now, as if they'd been shot from a cannon.

"Good God . . ." Cyprien tucked the cask under one elbow and made a quavering gesture with the other arm. "It cannot be."

Daspir wiped his eyes with the back of his wrist and saw a phalanx of silver-helmed cavalry come fuming toward him like a crew of ghosts out of the smoke. A phantasm from the long day's fight. Surely this manifestation could not be real. At first they seemed to come silently; there was a lag before he heard the hoofbeat.

"Form up the men!" Daspir looked wildly about and recognized no one of his own company. Captain-General Leclerc himself had jumped up from his camp stool by the steps of the burned church where the French had planted their battle flag, and stared at the charging horsemen with utter disbelief. Phantasmal no longer, the raiders had taken on a terrible concrete weight; they were cutting down confused and disordered soldiers all over the square.

Daspir ran toward his commander, unsure of his purpose. Leclerc was staring fixedly, not directly at him, but over his shoulder. He drew a pistol and fired it, to what effect Daspir could not see. There was a rush of air behind him as Daspir reached the church steps, and he turned to the horse bearing down on him, so near he could see the color inside the flaring nostrils. The rider was without a helmet, head bound in a red cloth, his features coppery in the firelight. *Rag-head Negro*. The flying mane of the horse cut up the face into bright lines, as one arm reached for the flagstaff.

Daspir caught hold of it with both his hands; for a moment they struggled for the flag. He didn't know if it was the horse's shoulder or the flat of a saber that sent him sprawling backward, his head recoiling from the corner of a step, hard enough that his vision broke up into whirls of golden motes. But he had not been knocked quite unconscious, and in another moment he was on his feet, shaking his head as he groped himself for damage; he seemed to have nothing worse than scrapes and bruises.

Cyprien and a couple of other captains had formed the troops into a square. The raiders, seeing their moment had passed, were wheeling their horses around to retreat. That rag-head Negro reined his horse into a curvet, so that the captured French tricolor snapped smartly on its rod. It seemed to Daspir that the rider raised his hand to him. Then he was gone with the others, into the smoldering street they'd emerged from. The French troops fired a volley after them, but no one seemed minded to give chase.

"One must grant them a certain flair, those riders." The voice belonged to General Hardy, who'd come from somewhere to join Leclerc on the steps, behind Daspir. Leclerc's only reply was muttered cursing. Those boots must cramp him now, Daspir thought, although with scant amusement. Behind the two generals, a few fire-blackened timbers of the burned church stuck up like ribs from a well-stripped carcass.

He crossed the square toward Cyprien, stepping over bodies of the recently fallen. The raiders had done a lot of damage in a short time— Leclerc had reason to curse, Daspir supposed.

"I thought you were finished," Cyprien said. "But he held his hand at the last moment, that black dragoon who rode you down."

Daspir halted and rubbed at the sore point on the back of his head. *Rag-head Negro*. But the horse was not the same, nor yet the rider; he had been taller, more lithe-seeming, longer in the leg, and his face certainly a lighter hue beneath the headcloth. One eye was hidden, squinted shut, but still that face was known to him.

"Placide," Daspir pronounced.

"What?"

"It was Placide. Toussaint's son—our charge on *La Sirène*. It was Placide who took the flag—I'd not mistake him."

"You hit your head on the church step," Cyprien said.

"I did," Daspir admitted, "but not so badly."

"Well," said Cyprien, looking doubtfully away. "I suppose it might have been . . ."

Daspir averted his own eyes, which fell as by a miracle on the little rum keg, standing upright within the well's curb, the bunghole at the top. He plucked at Cyprien's coat sleeve.

"Look there," he said. "If that is our cask of rum unspilled, then you may trust me for the rest of it."

On the road beyond the cemetery, Morisset halted to reckon up his men. There were no losses from the last encounter; the surprise had been too sudden, too complete. In the midst of a compliment on the captured flag, Morisset did recognize Placide, headcloth or no. At first his face went hard.

"Eh, boy," he said. "Did you defy my order?"

"*Gadé, papa'l ta yé kontan anpil ak sa'k li fé.*" The voice came from among the horsemen, before Placide could collect himself to reply. Look, his father will be very happy with what he has done.

Morisset's face broke toward a smile he masked with his hand before it was complete—this too his father's gesture, Placide noted.

"*N'alé,*" he said, and turned his horse. Placide, still carrying the flag, moved his own horse into the column. A couple of the other troopers reached out to brush his shoulders as they passed. The warmth of the contact ran down Placide's spine.

Once south of Granmorne, they slowed their horses from a trot to a walk. Morisset strung two men back to guard their rear, but there was not much threat; the land was still theirs at least as far south as Saint Marc. Placide dozed in the saddle, and sometimes sank completely into slumber, lulled by fatigue and the swing of his horse's smooth gait, waking with a jolt whenever his head rolled to the far limit of his neck.

They came to the camp at Pont d'Ester, bathed in the light of the midnight moon. It had rained here earlier; the river was high and the ground swampy underfoot. Placide found his father, sleeping at last for the first time in at least three days, wrapped in a cloak and lying on a piece of plank embedded in the mud. Guiaou and Guerrier watched over him with a worshipful air. Curled under the cloak, Toussaint's body looked no bigger than a cat's. Sometimes he coughed or murmured or shivered in his sleep; these motions made Placide uneasy. He took off the red head-cloth and offered it back to Guiaou.

"*Kenbe'l,*" Guiaou said. "Keep it. I will find another. It has been strong for you this day." He grinned at the flag Placide had taken.

"Thank you," Placide said. He kept looking into Guiaou's deeply scarred face as he folded the cloth to put into his pocket.

"It is Mêt Agwé who dances in my head sometimes," Guiaou said, as if replying to an unspoken question. "And you?" His eyes grew searching. For a moment it seemed that he might reach to cradle Placide's head between his hands, but he did not. "I cannot say. You should go to the *hûngan,* maybe Quamba, if we go back to Ennery."

Placide nodded, though he scarcely understood. Yet a tingle of the charge still sustained him—that feeling he was moved by another force into the actions he had taken. He was tired now and could simply accept it, whatever it was, along with his poor understanding of it.

Isaac had just appeared at his elbow. "Brother," he said. "They say you have distinguished yourself in the last raid."

"By the power of God," Placide replied.

Isaac let his eye linger on the French flag. "Come," he said. "We have found a place to sleep which is not too wet."

Placide followed him, stumbling a little in his weariness, to a spot high on the river bank where the shelter of a mango tree had been augmented by a strip of canvas stretched tight. Suzanne and her sister and the Chancy girls slept beneath it, atop the lumpy bundles of their clothes. Isaac passed Placide a blanket, only slightly damp. Placide arranged himself on the gravel.

The earth seemed to rock beneath him where he lay, repeating the motion of his horse, or even the longer sway of a ship across the waves. Placide sat up suddenly and turned his face to the lowering moon.

"Isaac," he said.

"Hanh?" Isaac mumbled and rolled up on his shoulder.

"I saw our Captain Daspir today. Him who guarded us on *La Sirène.*" Placide paused, recalling that smooth, rather soft olive face, with the eyes surprisingly cool and appraising.

"It was he who fought me for the flag at Gonaives," Placide said.

"Was it so," Isaac muttered sleepily.

"Yes," said Placide. He wrapped his arms around his knees and shrugged the blanket higher on his shoulders. Across the river, a night bird called. "I might have killed him with my sword, but something held me from it."

Isaac turned onto his back and spoke more plainly. "It is well you did not kill him."

"Yes," said Placide, "I am glad too."

. . .

Bazau and Gros-Jean lost their usual lazy manner in the descent of Granmorne—in fact both of them seemed wound as tight as watch springs. Tocquet felt the same tension hardening across his back. To be quit of the Louverture family was a relief in one way, in another way not. He still had a party of four women and eight children, if he'd counted them right, and some of them needed to be carried. Not the company he'd have chosen to slip invisibly through a war zone. Yet to the older children it was all a frolic. When Morisset's squadron descended the adjacent trail in the dusk, Tocquet had pulled his party off into the trees. What could it mean, their going back toward Gonaives? He'd had to cuff Sophie, though but lightly, to keep her quiet, and might have died of the wounded look the girl fired at him. Only her feelings were really hurt; he'd scarcely ever struck her. Of course she was familiar with Toussaint's honor guard, knew many of the men by name. They were often on the roads around Ennery and would touch their helmets to her when they passed, so she would not be thinking how some of them might love white children a little less today, especially when no one like Madame Louverture was in sight.

When Morisset's squadron was out of earshot, they walked on into the quickly thickening dark. Tocquet sent Bazau to bring up the rear, while he and Gros-Jean explored forward. Most of the time—there was nothing for it—Tocquet carried a drowsy, irritable child, his own Mireille, or one of Nanon's twins. Sophie, sullen since the slap, trudged grimly along behind Robert and Paul. The lark seemed to go out of the excursion even for the older children when they were walking in the dark. They lacked for light, though the moon was near full, because Tocquet kept them well under cover of the trees. The sound of fresh fighting reached them from Gonaives, then faded as they turned further from the town.

Elise and Isabelle had begun to bicker over something, most unusual for them. Nanon and Zabeth, meanwhile, walked in a graceful silence, as if in a dream. But after a couple of sour exchanges with Isabelle, Elise rushed forward to overtake Tocquet.

"Can we not stop?" she hissed. "The children are exhausted, my feet are burning, I am so tired I could sleep on the ground right here, and Isabelle insists she cannot take another step—"

"Isabelle could march us all into our graves, and well she knows it," Tocquet turned his face away to cover his grim smile. "It's no time to lie down on the trail," he said. "We don't know who is passing—the woods are full of fugitives from the town and probably deserters from both armies. There's those who kissed your fingers yesterday who'd think your head would look well on a stake today."

"But—" Elise clipped off her phrase. "What is that—smoke?"

At the same moment came to Tocquet's nostrils the familiar sick-sweet smell of burning cane. There was a fire glow on the horizon, just to their north, where a tall stand of bamboo bounded the trail. Tocquet pulled himself into an almond tree and climbed a few branches till he could see out. On the far side of a shallow ravine, a great house was aflame in the midst of burning fields. French soldiers in ranks on the oval drive watched the conflagration calmly.

Tocquet slipped down from the tree. Elise, Nanon, and Isabelle circled him expectantly. Tocquet passed around a few soft hulls of almonds he'd collected in the climb. "You might open these for the children," he said.

"Marvelous," said Elise, "but what did you see?"

"That is the *grand'case* of Sancey, if I am not mistaken."

"And burning?" Elise let her face fall in her hands.

"We don't know what that means to us—except that we've come farther than I knew. Wait here—" Tocquet cocked his head—he heard Gros-Jean's voice, talking to someone unfamiliar further up the trail. He turned from the women and ran catfoot through the darkness—at the next bend he found Gros-Jean with the stranger.

"*Yo té brulé Sancey?*" Gros-Jean said. Have they burned Sancey?

"Yes," came the stranger's voice.

"And Descahaux?"

"No, Descahaux is not burned yet."

"And Thibodet?"

"*Pa konnen,*" the stranger said. I don't know.

Gros-Jean turned to Tocquet in the moonlight. "You heard?" he said. "There is a *lakou* just above where we can rest."

Tocquet nodded and went back to the others. "How far?" was Elise's first response, echoed by Sophie in a still more plaintive tone, but Tocquet did not trouble to invent an answer. They went on climbing doggedly. In fact it was not very long before the stranger led them through a break in a cactus fence into a cluster of small clay-walled houses. A little dog yapped once or twice before someone picked it up and hushed it.

Silhouettes of two women emerged from one of the small, square houses, one young and one old to judge by the shape of their shadows. Their faces were featureless in the dark, their voices soft and warm as chocolate. After some murmuring back and forth, the white women and the children stepped carefully over the sill, one by one, inside. The cloth was dropped across the doorway. Through it, Tocquet could hear the rustle of their settling: a bump, a shuffle, a child's complaint, then Nanon's soothing, shushing voice.

He squatted by the corner of the cabin. The donkeys they'd managed not to lose in the days of flight were tethered outside the cactus barrier. Bazau and Gros-Jean had gone off somewhere. From somewhere higher up the ravine came the desultory tap of a single drum. Tocquet crossed his legs, half closed his eyes, was scarcely aware that he was waiting until Bazau and Gros-Jean had returned.

The sinking moon threw their long shadows toward the mud sill of the *case*. Bazau unplugged a gourd bottle and with a seemingly careless motion spilled a little on the ground before he drank. Gros-Jean did the same when the gourd was passed to him. Tocquet held his eyes aside. He knew they meant to thank their spirits, that they'd been guided safely through the dangers of this day.

What would it hurt? He spilled a little rum himself before he drank. All through the day he had been wishing for Antoine Hébert—another man, and one who could shoot. They were safe now, though; Tocquet could feel it. Tonight this *lakou* was as peaceful a place as he'd ever known. He could only wish the doctor had found as good a sanctuary. Let all the invisible ones protect him.

Tocquet lit one of his cheroots and let it go around their circle. When it was done, he slept a little, sitting with his back against the wall. At dawn he woke to the sound of cock crow moving over a steady bass tone: a woman grinding corn with a pole twice her own height, in a mortar made of a hollow stump still rooted to the packed earth of the *lakou*. She grinned at Tocquet, toothlessly though she was not old, as he got up and dusted off his trousers. He returned her smile and went down into the bushes to pee.

When he came back, Sophie had just come out of the *case*, blinking and rubbing her eyes with her wrists. She sulked a little when she first caught sight of Tocquet, then gave it up and came to wrap her arms around his waist. They stood side by side, still touching lightly, looking down the green valley.

"Where are we, Papa?" Sophie said.

"Descahaux. It is one of Toussaint's places. You see, the *grand'case* is still there." Tocquet pointed across the ravine, to a house more modest than the *grand'case* of Sancey. He did not bother to indicate the smudge of smoke where the latter building had stood, toward the bottom of the valley. On the horizon, a denser, heavier pall of smoke hung over Gonaives.

Nanon and Zabeth emerged from the house and led the women and girls for rudimentary ablutions in the stream. When they came back, the women of the *lakou* had made ready for them a deep *gamelle* of *maïs moulin* and another full of small white sweet potatoes. The white people ate silently, reverently, as the truly famished do. Today no one reproved the children for eating with their fingers. Tocquet found a coin to offer the women of the *lakou* before they started on their way.

As if electrified by their first real meal in twenty-four hours, Paul and Caco raced ahead of the others down the zigzag trail. Robert ran after them, somewhat less recklessly, while Sophie hung back with the adults today. A girl's conservatism, Tocquet thought, or maybe she remembered better than the boys how Saint-Jean had been overtaken by the French advance.

When they reached the bottom of the valley, Paul and Caco came tum-

bling back over them, Paul crying, "Soldiers! Soldiers!" and Caco adding,
"*Soldat blanc!*" Elise halted, turning to Isabelle with a worried air, but
Tocquet encouraged them to go on. "They are French soldiers, after all,"
he said, with barely detectable irony, "our countrymen."

In a hundred more paces they'd come out of the trees and stood in
view of the smoking hole that had been the Sancey *grand'case* two days
earlier. French infantry milled on the slope beyond the ruin, and
presently a young lieutenant came to inquire their business.

"We are the proprietors of Habitation Thibodet, which lies just
beyond this place," Tocquet said. "We seek to regain our home today,
supposing that it still exists."

Without comment, the lieutenant looked over all their crew.

"Does one know who burned this property?" Elise said abruptly.

"Ah, Madame." The lieutenant's eyes settled on her; he inclined his
head politely. "This place is said to belong to the outlaw Toussaint, by
whose order the towns of the coast have been razed. We thought to give
him a taste of his own tactics."

To that, no one immediately replied. Gabriel and François were
coughing from the smoke; Isabelle stared gloomily at the house key she'd
plucked from her bodice.

"And Thibodet?" Elise said finally.

"I have no knowledge of the place," the lieutenant said, as he stepped
aside and beckoned. "But by all means go and see for yourselves—we do
not mean to hinder you."

In another half-hour, Tocquet stopped below the mango trees and
wrinkled his nose.

"What is it?" Elise said.

"I don't smell smoke."

"You don't smell smoke," she repeated.

"A good sign, I think," Tocquet said. "Let us go on."

Paul and Caco had run on ahead; a few minutes later they came dashing back. Yoyo, Caco's little sister, was capering among them now.

"Saint-Jean is there!" Paul cried in high excitement.

"What do you mean?" Elise said. "Saint-Jean is where?"

"In your own house, *ma tante*—come see!" And the three of them
scampered away again.

"It is mysterious," Elise muttered, pressing a hand to her abdomen.

Tocquet took off his broad-brimmed hat and scratched at the back of
his head. "It suggests the house is still standing at least. As for Saint-
Jean—we'll see soon enough."

When they entered the back of the Thibodet compound, they found
Merbillay working around the kitchen much as usual—with Paul, Caco,
Yoyo, and now Sophie all clamoring around her for a snack of the pork
griot she was turning in her iron *chaudière*. The house was there, walls
and roof intact, and all the outbuildings. Everything was quite as usual,

except that now French soldiers were bivouacked around the area where the black army had formerly camped.

Their gallery was crowded with French officers, they saw when they circled to the front of the house. And with them, one black lad who jumped up to greet them—Saint-Jean, as Paul had claimed. He ran toward the steps, but one of the officers came forward to restrain him.

"Of course," said Tocquet. "We've been requisitioned, for officers' quarters."

"Dispossessed, you mean," Elise said darkly.

"An inconvenience less lasting, I note, than being burned to the ground," Tocquet said.

"Wait," Isabelle said, staring at the captain who stooped to whisper in Saint-Jean's ear. "I know that officer—so do you." She turned to Nanon and Elise. "Help me."

Tocquet squinted under his hat brim. Yes, that captain did seem familiar—one of the lot that had infested them here before diplomacy with Toussaint had failed. Tocquet had kept clear of them for the most part, had not bothered to remember their names. The other women, even Zabeth, had closed around Isabelle. At first Tocquet did not grasp their purpose, but when the cluster opened he understood. Isabelle had been made over, insofar as circumstances allowed: her hair tidied, dust and soot brushed from her cheeks, a red hibiscus bloom tucked behind one ear. Kicking aside her broken shoes, she tripped barefoot across the grass beside the pool, carefree as a maiden coming home from a country outing.

"Captain Daspir," she trilled. "Can it be you?"

Daspir was already trotting toward her, hat in his hand. Saint-Jean, forgotten on the steps behind him, ran down to join Paul and Caco, though one of the other officers stood up to watch him from across the gallery rail.

"*Quelle surprise!*" Daspir said. "Of course, I'd hoped to find you here. But how—"

"Oh, we have been fleeing the brigands for an age, it seems." Isabelle flashed her brilliant smile. "For that, you find us in some disarray." She lifted a fold of her stained skirt with one hand, then twirled out its stripes with a nimble pirouette. "And yourself, Captain?"

Daspir seemed mesmerized by the flirting fabric; it took him a moment to react. "Oh, I have just been sent from Gonaives this morning," he said, turning from Isabelle to locate Saint-Jean. "The surveillance of Toussaint's offspring appears to be my destiny. But—" He reached for her hand; Isabelle let him capture it. "You must be very weary from your travel—and all the hazards you have run."

"God has preserved us," Isabelle said, laying her free hand across her clavicle. "And my friends, whom you'll remember, are thankful to regain their home. Though in the present situation, as I see . . ." She trailed off, looking at the officers on the gallery.

"Oh no." Daspir pressed her hand more warmly. "No, not at all. We shall not discommode you for a moment longer. Saint-Jean is meant to go up to Le Cap tomorrow—we have the unfortunate necessity to hold him as a hostage—and as for the rest of us, never mind. Give us ten minutes and the house is yours."

23

It pleased me that the *blanc* officers gave me that letterbox where Toussaint's souvenirs had been hidden, though what use would I, Riau, have for such a thing? There was no one who sent Riau letters or trinkets of the kind that Toussaint saved. I never wanted the love of white women as some men did. I did not like the way they smelled or their thin, sharp lips and noses like the beaks of birds. Once I had some letters from white women that I found in the pockets of a *blanc* soldier who was dead. I kept those letters for a long time, and used to read them sometimes, but by the time I got the box those letters were gone. Merbillay wrote no one letters. She could not read or write her name.

Yet I took the box to an *ébéniste* and ordered the false bottom to be repaired. The woodworker was soon able to find the secret of the latch that let the bottom open or held it shut. I thought how Merbillay's eyes would shine to see it open. Yoyo and Caco would like it too.

I could not think then, though, how I was going to get back to Ennery to see them again, because Ennery was one of Toussaint's places, and now Riau was on the other side of the war from Toussaint.

So long as I was near Maillart, I did not feel so very uneasy about the place that I was in. Major Maillart had been in many battles with Riau and we respected each other as two brother officers ought to do. But Maillart had been in our country a long time. It was different with the other *blanc* officers who had just come out from France. There was Captain Paltre, who was much with Maillart in those days at Port-au-Prince. Paltre had been in the country once before, though not for long. Yet I did remember seeing him then, in the north. He had come and gone from Le Cap with the Agent Hédouville, when Toussaint chased him out. This seemed not a great thing to be proud of, but Paltre liked to boast of what he knew, and the things he had done and was going to do. His boasting was all built out of hints, maybe because there was no certain story he could tell. Maillart did not encourage this boasting, but he accepted Paltre's company anyway. I felt a mean spirit living in Paltre, and I did not think he was so important as he claimed—no more important than Riau, since the General Boudet had sent us both away when they had opened the bottom of the box.

But maybe Paltre did have something hidden behind his head. In those days at Port-au-Prince, between the battles, I went sometimes to the house of Paul Lafrance. The old man's wife would give me coffee and something to eat whenever I came, and the three daughters laughed and swung their hips at anything I said. I did not mean anything toward any one of them, but only saw the three of them together, though after a few times I could tell that Marie-Odette might like to be alone with Riau, without her sisters. But I had a respect for Paul Lafrance that held me back. Madame Lafrance was a good cook, and it was sweet to hear the voices of the girls together, but always when I left their house I would hear again in my head again the breaking voice of Paul Lafrance when he told the white officers how he would die to see his daughters slaves. How had that thought come into his head? It was against the proclamations. Still I could feel that Paltre, at least, and maybe others, would be glad enough to see those girls in chains.

Maillart would often play cards with Paltre, who did not play very well in spite of his boasting, so that Maillart usually won his money. I understood this, but I did not stay long with them when they played, and I would not drink with the two of them past the first few swallows, though with Maillart alone I would drink to the bottom of the bottle. Maybe Maillart only sat with Paltre to get his money from him at cards, because it did not seem that many thoughts were shared between them. Maillart never seemed to notice, but I felt the weight of some bad secret on a few of the white officers under the General Boudet, even the General Pamphile de Lacroix, though that *blanc* had an open heart and an open hand, was quick with his words and fond of laughter, so that everybody liked him.

It was Lacroix who told General Boudet that Riau ought to go down to the plain of Léogane to meet Lamour Dérance to see if he might bring his men to join with the French. How Lacroix came to have this thought I never knew, but it was not a bad one. I was glad to get away from Port-au-Prince for a few days too, though after the last time I was not so sure how Lamour Dérance would receive me.

Soon after, General Boudet went out of Port-au-Prince with most of the men that had come out of the French ships with him, and marched them north to fight Dessalines at Saint Marc. He left the General Pamphile de Lacroix with only six hundred men to defend Port-au-Prince, which was maybe not a wise thing to do. Dessalines had left Saint Marc by the time Boudet arrived there. As Riau had seen before, Dessalines had made Saint Marc ready for the burning a long time before, and he set fire to the tar-painted walls of every building as soon as Boudet and his army came in sight. I heard Paltre tell Maillart about it afterward and his face was pale even for a *blanc* and his voice shook in a way his boastfulness could not control. It had been the same at Saint Marc as what Riau had seen after Léogane was burned, because Dessalines had ordered the killing of all the *blancs* he could catch and left their bodies stinking and smoking on the coals of Saint Marc for Boudet's soldiers to find. I looked at Paltre's face when he told Maillart, and though he did not say so I felt certain that when he smelled the burning flesh of the *blancs* butchered at Saint Marc, he must have bent over low to vomit on his own shoes. But I did not hear him tell Maillart until many days later, and a lot of things had happened in between.

Dessalines was gone from Saint Marc by the time Boudet brought his soldiers in. He waited to start the fires until the *blanc* soldiers were in sight, and maybe he waited to cut the throats of all the *blanc colons* he had caught there too, so that the soldiers could hear the screaming from where they stood on the road, and know they could do nothing to stop what was happening, because they would not reach the town soon enough no matter how fast they ran. Saint Marc was surrounded by many strong forts and it was as good a place as any to give the *blancs* a battle in their own fashion, and better than most, but Dessalines did not mean to fight them so that day. He was following Toussaint's order when he burned Saint Marc and left it, but he must have agreed with the order too, because Dessalines, the same as Moyse, was not certain to follow an order if he did not agree.

The *blanc* soldiers were angry at what they found at Saint Marc, but they did not hurry too much to chase Dessalines. Toussaint meant for them to find ashes and dead *blanc* bodies wherever they arrived, because that would throw down their hearts and discourage them. They stayed for a day on the ashes of Saint Marc, and while they had not yet raised up their spirits enough to march after him, Dessalines was coming quickly down toward Port-au-Prince again, in a circle that moved through the mountains at Fonds-Batiste and Les Matheux, at a speed that only Dessalines could manage in such territory. But I, Riau, knew nothing of these things until afterward, because I was already gone from Port-au-Prince.

I rode out alone, with my horse well fed, and two days' dried beef in my straw *macoute*, and even a purse with some money given to me by the *blancs*. General Lacroix would have sent some *blanc* soldiers to protect me, perhaps, and to watch that Riau did not try to play any trick on the French this time, only Major Maillart persuaded him that I would be safer without any *blanc* soldiers with me, and more likely to be trusted by the people I was going to meet. Maillart looked happy enough to be staying in the town, when Lacroix would have sent him with Riau if he had sent anyone, and I was content to be away from all these *blancs* for a while, and to be out of Port-au-Prince also.

There were a few French soldiers watching Fort Piémont, and a few more in the town of Léogane. Some people who had lived in Léogane were shoveling ashes out of the holes where houses had been, or trying to raise roofs on what was left of the walls after Dessalines burned them. They did not work very quickly, and one could see that their hearts were low. South of Léogane, it was all quiet. Since Laplume had given his hand to the French, they had nothing to fear as far south as Les Cayes, except maybe from bands of maroons like the band of Lamour Dérance, but these had not taken either side yet, and they were waiting to see what they would do.

I, Riau, I was also waiting. I thought that when I left Port-au-Prince and the *blancs* behind, my spirits would return to guide me. Yet this too was only a thought I had made, and even in the plain of Léogane I could not stop my thoughts, but they went crawling everywhere all the time, like worms in cornmeal. The stillness of the plain seemed wrong, like the stillness in the hole between the winds of a hurricane.

I did not have to ride very long south of Léogane before I came upon some of Lamour Dérance's people. This time they were full of smiles, because now they recognized Riau as a friend of Jean-Pic. I let them bring me to their camp, which had moved a little since the other time. They were in the low hills now below the plain, where they might get away quickly if they wanted to, in the direction of Jacmel or of Lake Henriquillo.

So I came then to the *ajoupa* of Jean-Pic, and his *madanm* killed two ducks for us that night, and stewed them with mangoes in an iron pot. There was rice and beans too and boiled greens, so all of Jean-Pic's small children were happy, and sat in the firelight cracking bones for the marrow with the duck fat shining around their smiles. One of the boys turned over a pot and struck a drumbeat on it with one bare hand and a stick found on the ground. He was strong like a little bull in his neck and shoulders, though he had not grown very big, and I thought of Caco when I looked at him, and then the younger children. I wondered how I was going to get to Ennery again, and what might be happening there now. I know from the *blanc* officers at Port-au-Prince that the General Leclerc was planning a big attack on Toussaint at Gonaives at the same time that Boudet was going to fight Dessalines at Saint Marc, but I did not know what had happened in those battles, and I only hoped that Guiaou might be near Merbillay and the children, when Riau was far away.

I did not say much to Jean-Pic about the business that brought me to the camp, only that I had a message to Lamour Dérance from the French generals at Port-au-Prince. In the morning when we had each eaten a small piece of cassava, Jean-Pic signaled for me to walk with him. We climbed a little distance into the hills, high enough that tails of mist were lifting where we walked, till we came to a place where a stand of bamboo made a sort of arbor, a *tonnelle*. A pile of stones was on the ground beneath the bamboo, and at each of four corners around it stood a small clay *govi*.

In a moment a couple of strong men came in from another direction than us, looking all around the place, but turning their eyes from the pile of stones and the *govis* as they passed. Their fingers kept brushing the handles of the pistols in their belts, but Jean-Pic knew them and called their names, and they spoke to him in a friendly way. Then soon after came Lamour Dérance, stooping to enter the *tonnelle* and then straightening where the bamboo gave a higher space. He folded his arms tight across his chest and looked at Riau with hard eyes across the pile of stones.

I knew that Legba was inside the stones, and maybe lying underneath Legba would be Maît' Kalfou. I knew those four *govis* were there to mark the crossroads, though I did not know what *pwen* were held inside them. Also I knew that Lamour Dérance did not very much trust Riau.

"*Ginen maman nou*," I said at last. Africa is our mother. I said this because I thought I knew that Lamour Dérance had come out of Africa a *bossale*, as Riau did, instead of being born in Saint Domingue, a Creole like Toussaint. When I had said it, Lamour Dérance grunted and loosened his arms, then sat crosslegged on the ground. I sat down too and nodded at the stones. I knew the crossroads had been marked to judge Riau, but maybe it would also judge Lamour Dérance.

"Now you have come to this *kalfou* with all your people," I said. "Let your spirit show you the best way to cross for them and you."

"I am listening," said Lamour Dérance. As he spoke, a little black kitten came wandering in under the bamboo and climbed up onto his knee. With one hand Lamour Dérance rubbed the fur of the kitten, always looking at Riau. Jean-Pic and the other men stood sideways to us, by the opening of the *tonnelle* above the plain—they listened though they did not look.

"Well, it is simple," I said. "There is a French general at Port-au-Prince now. His name is Pamphile de Lacroix. If you go to him now, he will receive you gladly. You have only to help him beat Toussaint and Dessalines, and all your people will remain free as you are now—"

"How is it certain?"

I had brought a proclamation paper from Port-au-Prince with me and now I brought it out from under my shirt and unfolded it and read the words to Lamour Dérance, pointing to each word with my finger as I spoke it.

IF ANYONE TELLS YOU, "THESE FORCES HAVE COME TO TEAR AWAY OUR LIBERTY," REPLY, "THE REPUBLIC WILL NOT SUFFER THAT IT SHOULD BE TAKEN FROM US."

When I had finished reading, Lamour Dérance took the paper from my hand and held it very near his face, though not for long. He turned his head and called a name and a third man came in and took the paper away. I thought that Lamour Dérance must be sending the paper to someone who could read and be certain that Riau had read out all the words as they were truly written. Then he turned again to me. All the time his hand still stroked the kitten. This reminded me of Halalou and his white cock, so long ago.

"What if the *blancs'* paper gives us lies? *Gen dwa blan-yo bay menti.*"

"How can what they say or do be worse than what Toussaint has given you?" I said. "Now you have to hide from Toussaint all the time, if you don't want to work on the plantations. And Toussaint would make Dessalines your whipmaster."

I stopped talking so that Lamour Dérance could consider. I wanted him to have to remember how, when Lamour Dérance rose up with Moyse against Toussaint to take the town of Marigot, Dessalines had come with the Eighth Demibrigade to kill them in the mountains, there above Marigot and Jacmel. Dessalines had killed so many that for a time Lamour Dérance did not have many good fighting men in his band at all, until more ran to him from the plantations on the plain of Léogane. Dessalines had been a hard master over all of the west since Toussaint had ordered that all men who were not in his army must go back to work with the hoe. Dessalines whipped with thorny branches if the work was not done fast and well, and many said his rule was harder than any *blanc colon* had ever been.

"My son, who has nine years, works in the coffee now, at the command of *blancs* at Ennery," I said. "As Riau worked the cane at Bréda."

The little kitten raised its head and looked at me with dark blue eyes. "I thought you had forgotten Bréda," said Lamour Dérance. "When now you turn against Toussaint, who became your *parrain* in that place."

He did not say the name of Moyse, but still I heard it. I knew that he would lay the weight of my old action on me now, but it did not feel less heavy for my knowing it before. When I looked at the pile of stones it seemed to me that Legba would bring Moyse up through them, to stare at Riau with his one eye. There was nothing to do but face him.

"Moyse turned against Toussaint," I said, "who was his *parrain* also."

When I said this, Lamour Dérance folded his arms up tight again and blew a hard breath so that his nostrils flared, holding his mouth shut tight. The kitten curled in the crook of his legs, as if it would go to sleep.

"Moyse could not succeed against Toussaint then," I said. "Then, Toussaint was too strong for him." In the eye of my mind I saw Bouquart step out of the ranks and blow out his brains with his own pistol as Toussaint had ordered him to do. Bouquart had gone with Moyse against

Toussaint. I gave my head a shake to chase away that picture. "But now Toussaint cannot succeed against the *blancs*. They are too many and their power too great." And now what appeared behind my head was the picture of the ships blowing up the forts of Port-au-Prince harbor.

I began to remind Lamour Dérance how Laplume had already gone with the French and how likely it was others would do the same, so that all the south and much of the west and soon more and more of the north would be safe in the hands of the *blanc* soldiers. After that I could only repeat the words I had said before, but now they felt cold coming off my tongue. The presence of Moyse grew stronger in the pile of stones and I thought how I owed his spirit a service, as I had told Quamba at Ennery, yet all my words put me farther away from doing that service which I owed, and until I had done it nothing else I might do could prosper. Then I felt alone, and cold all over from the inside out, and the words that Riau's mouth kept making sounded more and more distant, and they had no power of persuasion. If Lamour Dérance was persuaded I did not know, because all he did was get to his feet and tell me that he must think for a time about all I had said.

He scooped the kitten up in his arms and went away through the gap in the bamboo he had come in by. The men who had come in advance of him followed. Jean-Pic and I went out in the other direction, and walked back down the trail. Now the sun was high and the mist all burned away, and hummingbirds were at the flowers growing by our pathway. Jean-Pic did not say anything about what had been told to Lamour Dérance, and soon the heat of the sun which was warming the whole plain of Léogane had warmed away the chill I had felt, under the bamboo and beside the stones.

We dug that morning in the gardens Jean-Pic had begun in this new camp, then ate a meal and slept away the hottest time of the afternoon, lying in the shade of the *ajoupa*. In the cool of the evening a man came from Lamour Dérance to say that he had finished his thinking and was ready to bring his men to serve the French at Port-au-Prince.

All the *blancs* were in a whirl when we came to Port-au-Prince next day, and this was the reason for it—while Riau was absent they had captured Chancy as he tried to pass through Petit Goave toward Jérémie. Chancy was a nephew of Toussaint by blood, not by adoption like Moyse and Riau. They caught him carrying two letters from Toussaint. One letter was to Dessalines at Saint Marc and the other was to Dommage at Jérémie, a long way out on the Grand Anse to the south. The letter to Dessalines was a copy of the same letter I had seen before in Dessalines's own hand, because it was Toussaint's way to send the same letter by more than one messenger. He would not trust a single messenger with all the words his pen set down. But the other letter never reached Dommage at Jérémie, not by anyone's hand. Dommage was a commander Toussaint trusted very much, as much as he trusted Maurepas or Charles

Belair, as much as once he had trusted Moyse. But when the French ships came to Jérémie, Dommage did not know what to do, because Toussaint's letter had not come to him, so he let the ships into the port and let the men come into the town, and he gave his obedience to the French.

Chancy could not get to Dessalines at Saint Marc because of the French *blanc* soldiers on the ways between, so he turned south to try to reach Dommage instead, and then *blancs* caught him as he reached Petit Goave. When I returned to Port-au-Prince from the plain of Léogane, Chancy was in the guardhouse there, expecting that maybe the *blanc* commander would soon order him to be shot. Major Maillart and General Lacroix and all the *blancs* there were in a big stir, because now they knew from Toussaint's letter that Dessalines was ordered to burn down Port-au-Prince no matter the cost. Now they could see too how Dessalines had tricked General Boudet away from Port-au-Prince, with most of the *blanc* soldiers. They did not know just where Dessalines was, but they knew he would be coming quickly and that he would arrive before General Boudet and his men could return. There were only six hundred regular *blanc* soldiers in the town, and these would not be enough to fight the thousands Dessalines was bringing.

For that, General Lacroix was very glad to see Riau's return, with the big band of Lamour Dérance and his maroons, and the band of Lafortune who was with them too. After Riau's talk with Lamour Dérance had ended under the *tonnelle*, Lamour Dérance had carried his words to Lafortune, and the two of them decided to go over to the *blancs* together. Lafortune's people made double the number of Lamour Dérance's men, and we were so many coming back to Port-au-Prince that at first the *blancs* feared it was Dessalines surprising them from the south. But when Lacroix once understood what had been done, he looked as if he might kiss Riau, though in the end he only clasped my hand very tight in both of his. Major Maillart gave me a big clap on the back which was his fashion when he was pleased, though when he took his hand away I saw the fingers trembled a little. They had all been fearful of what Dessalines might bring to them, in spite of all their soldiers in the country and all the cannons on their ships.

Now, the *blancs* at Port-au-Prince had already heard the men of the Eighth Demibrigade were coming against them from the direction of Grande Rivière, while Dessalines had reached Arcahaye, which was not very far off at all. Lacroix told Lamour Dérance and Lafortune that if their men could beat the men of the Eighth, they might take anything the men of the Eighth had, if it was clothes or boots or guns or money. Lamour Dérance and Lafortune accepted this idea easily, and so General Lacroix sent out some of his *blanc* soldiers to meet the Eighth from the front direction, while Lamour Dérance and Lafortune circled through the hills above the town to catch them from behind.

I, Riau, went with Lamour Dérance and with me came Major Maillart and a couple of other *blanc* officers who wanted to see how the thing would be done. Those maroons could run fast on the hill trails no matter how steep, even carrying muskets and the cartridge boxes the *blancs* had just filled from their armories. I took off my boots and strung them over my shoulder because I could move better without them on those trails. The *blanc* officers were soon red-faced and breathless, though Maillart got along better than the rest, since he was better used to the country.

It was the Eighth Demibrigade that had cut up Lamour Dérance's people near Marigot before, so they carried that anger into the battle, though the Eighth had been commanded by Dessalines in that battle, and today it was Pierre Louis Diane who was at the head of the Eighth. Pierre Louis Diane expected to meet the French *blanc* soldiers and expected that their numbers would be small, but when the maroons rushed on them from behind, they were not ready and soon they were full of confusion and fear. A lot were killed in the first few minutes and more than a thousand captured. Then the men of Lamour Dérance and Lafortune took everything from the dead and the prisoners too, except Pierre Louis Diane and his officers. They were sent by General Lacroix to be held prisoner on the ships that waited in the harbor.

Chancy was still shut in the Port-au-Prince guardhouse, but Pierre Louis Diane and his officers were put onto the ships. I saw that Lacroix knew the danger was not finished for him and his men yet, because Dessalines had not yet come. The story of Dessalines and of all the *blancs* whose throats were slit on his order or by his own hand had traveled a long way before him by then. By nighttime, the men of Lamour Dérance and Lafortune were not much use to the *blancs* any more because they were having a big *bamboche* at the edge of the town in their happiness at plundering the Eighth Demibrigade, with rum and fires and drums and dancing. Only I went with Jean-Pic and a few of the others who were not drunk or ridden by their spirits, with Maillart on the order of Lacroix to lay ambushes on the roads from Arcahaye. At the same time Lacroix had got the captain of all the ships to send many of his sailors from the ships into the town to help defend it.

The moon was high and bright enough that we saw easily to shoot at Dessalines's scouts when they appeared on the road from Arcahaye. A few fell in the first shooting, and the rest scattered quickly away along the road they had come. At the same time we could hear shooting at Croix des Bouquets too, but it did not go on for long at any of these places. Some fires could be seen on the Cul de Sac plain, where Dessalines's men were burning whatever *cases* they might have missed burning the last time they passed that way. At the sight of the fires, all the *blancs* in the town began to cry *Dessalines! Dessalines is coming!* and the hand of Major Maillart got very tight and hard on his sword grip and the ends of his mustache were quivering, but Dessalines did not come. He had heard what had happened with the Eighth that day, and he knew now that the *blancs* were more ready for him than he had hoped. So he went away across the plain of Cul de Sac, killing and burning whatever he passed and driving some white prisoners ahead of him toward Petite Rivière. At Petite Rivière he would meet Toussaint, who had fought a big battle at Ravine à Couleuvre three days before, but I did not know any of that until later.

Now all the *blancs* at Port-au-Prince were happy because they were safe and the town was saved from Dessalines's torches, and Boudet brought his soldiers back from Saint Marc again not long after. They were all filled up with victory because they thought Toussaint had been beaten hard at Gonaives and Dessalines was running away too, though they had all been much afraid of Dessalines the day before. The truth was that the *blancs* were not winning yet so much as they said, because though they had taken Gonaives and Saint Marc there was nothing left for them in either of those places but dead bodies charred on the hot coals. Also the *blanc* commanders were all telling each other lies about how many soldiers they lost in their fights, especially at Ravine à Couleuvre, where Toussaint had killed hundreds more than General Rochambeau confessed. Also they had not succeeded to trap Toussaint at Gonaives and make him prisoner, which had been their plan. Instead Toussaint had gone away into the back country with all his army, to meet Dessalines with all of his. .

I saw the face of Captain Paltre grow a sick gray color when he spoke across the card table of what they found when they entered Saint Marc, what Dessalines left there for them to find. Then to encourage himself Paltre took a big drink of new white *clairin*, carelessly so that he coughed. *Let him choke on it*, I thought, where I sat in the corner cleaning my pistol, in shadows apart from where the *blancs* played cards. To encourage himself, Paltre then told a story he claimed he had heard when he was here before with Hédouville, though the story came from an early time, when an English army held Saint Marc and Port-au-Prince and other towns between them on the coast. Then the Count of Bréda had joined the English, hoping they would give him back his lands and slaves again, which they had promised though they could not ever do it. One day the *mulâtre* Lapointe, who commanded for the English in Arcahaye, offered to buy from the Count his *old nigger*. When the Count asked what he was talking about, Lapointe said, "Why, your old nigger Toussaint, who calls himself Louverture—I will buy him, general as he is." As Paltre told the story, Lapointe paid the Count eight hundred *gourdes* to own Toussaint. Yet though Lapointe and Toussaint both still lived, Lapointe had not yet been able to get control of what he had bought, though Lapointe had now gone over to the French. But this part, Paltre did not say.

All the *blanc* officers at the card table laughed loud when Paltre had finished telling this story. All had come with the new ships except Maillart, who did not laugh. He was still for a moment, completely still, then he laid down his cards so their faces showed, and picked up some money the cards had won. Of all those *blanc* officers only Maillart seemed to know that Riau sat in the shadows cleaning his pistol while they played and talked, though his back was turned to me the whole time, and only Maillart seemed to know when I got up from my stool and walked out of the room. I was not wearing my boots when I went out, and my bare feet made no noise.

Two times in those days I had heard the name of Bréda. I was still a very young man when I ran from there to be with the maroons. I was not so much older than my son Caco now. I had scarcely fifteen years. But I did not know my age for certain because the day of my birth was lost in Guinée with my mother and my father there. When I thought of Pierre Louis Diane and the others held prisoner on the ships in the harbor, I felt the cold choking weight of the iron collar on my neck when I was taken from the hold of the ship that brought me out of Guinée to the barra-coons outside Le Cap, where I was sold to Bréda. In slavery time at Bréda the *blancs* all talked before us so, before Riau or any slave, with no care at all for what they said, as if we had no more understanding of their words than a horse or a dog would have.

Only Maillart respected Toussaint, though he had gone over to the other *blancs* as soon as they and he had met in Port-au-Prince. He seemed to do it without thinking. I did not know what was behind his head. He and I had not spoken of the choice he had made. Maybe he had not even seen that crossroads when he passed it. But when I left the card players I began to doubt the way that I, Riau, had taken from that *kalfou*.

Chancy was kept then in an old *cachot* for soldiers who had dis-obeyed. There was a hole in the stone floor of a fort, round with a stone rim like the rim of a well, and beneath it a square room all made of stone. There was not any other way in or out and no light except what came in through the hole. Chancy was down there in the dark. Once a day they lowered a bucket with bread and water on a rope and once a day if he was lucky they pulled up a bucket where he made his *kaka*.

Then I with Maillart and Paul Lafrance and some mulatto officers who had taken the side of the French *blanc* soldiers made a story about Chancy for the ears of Lacroix, because it was easy to speak to him, and then with his help the story came to General Boudet. Chancy was a *mulâtre* himself, the child of Toussaint's sister with a *blanc* in Les Cayes as it was said, and the story we made told that he had fought with the mulattoes when Rigaud made war on Toussaint, and that afterward, not long ago, Toussaint had put him into prison—so he was not so loyal to Toussaint as the *blancs* would think from catching him with those let-ters. Now, there was enough truth in this story for it to be believed, yet Toussaint had adopted Chancy as if to be his son when the war with the mulattoes was finished, and there was no one who loved Toussaint better than Chancy, and though Chancy had been in prison for a time it was only because Toussaint was angry at him for making love to a married woman. But these things the *blanc* generals did not know. On the strength of the story Chancy was let out of his *cachot* and given the freedom of Port-au-Prince, on his parole that he would not run away to go back to Toussaint. All among us liked Chancy, and no one wanted to see him shot for carrying Toussaint's messages. I made certain too that Chancy understood that Riau had helped him to get out, in case he might bring that word to Toussaint later on.

Chancy got a bath and a clean uniform and went with me to visit the daughters of Paul Lafrance. Madame Lafrance was there to give us lemonade with plenty of sugar and she gave us pieces of *griot* with a good sauce *Ti Malice,* and Paul Lafrance was with us too. One of the old ones was in the room with us all the time, because they knew Chancy too well to leave their girls alone with him. Chancy was a fine-looking young man, with clear skin and the hair of a *blanc,* and he had some education so that he spoke gracefully in proper French, and with wit enough to keep the girls laughing. I saw Marie-Odette begin to give him many of her smiles. But though everyone was laughing and glad, whenever I looked at the smiles of the girls I remembered what Paul Lafrance had said to General Lacroix, and the face of Lacroix as it had looked across his shoulder when he embraced Paul Lafrance, and I heard an echo of what Lamour Dérance had said, *Gen dwa blan-yo bay menti.* Lamour Dérance had sold himself to the *blancs* anyway, but still his words hung in my ears: Maybe the whites are lying.

24

Though he'd been offered a bed in the town of Petite Rivière, Doctor Hébert preferred to camp on the knoll above, where most of Toussaint's wounded from Ravine à Couleuvre reposed within the walls of the old English fort. Fontelle and Paulette had found themselves a lodging below, but each morning they appeared to aid him in his nursing, walking slowly up the gentle grade which rose imperceptibly from the town. When they reached the fort, Fontelle immediately set to boiling water, but before they began the work of cleansing wounds and curing dressings, she cooked the doctor a fresh egg or a green plantain, or sometimes (if foraging had gone well) both together.

The fort was rectangular, enclosing no more than a few hundred feet, with the main gate oriented toward the negligible slope to the town. Only when within the walls did one recognize the real height of the place. Below the long wall to the southwest, a cliff dropped off abruptly. Below, a dizzying distance below, the great river of the Artibonite made a slow muddy coil around the base of the hill.

This peak, which the people of the region called La Crête à Pierrot, marked the beginning of the Cahos mountain range, which stretched eastward into the interior, toward Mirebalais and the Spanish border. Just to the west was a small *bitasyon*, with little *cases* and corn plantings quarried into the more steeply rising mountainsides in that direction.

On the day of his arrival, the doctor had arranged for the people there to help raise some *ajoupas* for himself and the wounded men. The fort had been left unfinished when the English withdrew from the colony, and it was not in much state of defense. There was no garrison but for the wounded, and except for the powder magazine there was no shelter either.

Yet the doctor found himself better here than in the town. The air was fresh and it was cool, chilly at night, in fact. The chill and the breezes sweeping the hill discouraged the mosquitoes. Sometimes he went down to the town to sup—there was a community of whites at Petite Rivière, and a couple of surgeons who lodged in the house of one Massicot, but he always returned to the hilltop to sleep. It was convenient to be near his patients, and in the worse case, if trouble erupted below, he might slip away east on the mountain paths.

As for what had happened at Gonaives or Ennery, no news came for several days. The doctor tried not to fret about his family. He knew that Fontelle must be suppressing similar thoughts, and her people were more widely scattered. For the moment it was calm enough in the surrounds of Petite Rivière, and it looked riskier to leave than to remain. He thought it most likely that the inhabitants of Thibodet were still with Madame Louverture and her relations, but he could not know where they might have found their refuge. If he stayed where he was, surely Toussaint would come with some intelligence. Yet when the commotion of an arrival did begin, the people in the town and outlying *bitasyons* all began to cry, *Dessalines! Dessalines k'ap vini!* Dessalines is coming!

The doctor straightened from his work and went to an embrasure where a rusting six-pound cannon tilted on a broken carriage. Below, the sluggish river reddened in the setting sun. Voices echoed up from the town, which was mostly hidden from him by a screen of trees, and he heard the weary tap of a drum and the whistling of a single fife. A bend of the road below the town brought the approaching column into his view. When he put his spyglass to his eye, he saw that a couple of hundred white civilians were limping along, pressed by Dessalines's troops, their heads drooping like the heads of slaves in a coffle.

He did not hurry the evening round, but when it was done he washed his face, put on the cleanest shirt at his disposal, and went down with Paulette and Fontelle to Petite Rivière. With them came one of Toussaint's soldiers, Bienvenu. The doctor had been treating him, successfully so far, for wounds of *mitraille* in his right arm and shoulder. Bienvenu carried his right arm in a sling, but as he was glad to demonstrate, he could still aim a pistol and wield a *coutelas* or a *bâton* in his left. He'd assigned himself to the doctor's protection, out of gratitude and old acquaintance; Bienvenu had joined Toussaint's forces by the intercession of Riau, and from Riau the doctor knew that Bienvenu was a fugitive from Habitation Arnaud, whence he'd fled before the risings of ninety-one, though he didn't know if Bienvenu knew he knew it. Glad as he was of the extra eyes and arm, he carried his own pistols too, hidden in his waistband under the loose tail of his shirt.

As they walked down, the velvet darkness settled over them, while above, the stars began to brighten. With all the bustle of the arriving troops, the feeling in the town was still and grim. No sign of the *blancs* Dessalines had marched in, and the doctor noticed that the only white face on the street was his own. He bade a quick good evening to Fontelle and Paulette (the mother seemed eager to get the daughter out of view of the new-arrived soldiers) and went on alone with Bienvenu.

At Massicot's house the door was barred and the shutters closed. The doctor forebore to knock loudly or long. When there was no reply to his first soft taps, he slipped around to the fenced yard in back and let himself in at the wooden gate, leaving Bienvenu outside. Fanfan, Massicot's fattening hog, snorted and rolled a long-lashed eye at him, but did not move from her wallow in the fence corner. Presently the back door opened a crack and Massicot peered out.

"Oh," he hissed, beckoning the doctor in. "I did not know you—I thought it was Dessalines's men come to steal my pig."

The doctor slipped sideways through the half-open door, which Massicot at once pressed shut and bolted. In the front room the surgeons sat in darkness, as no one would venture to strike a light.

"What news?" the doctor said, yielding to the general impulse to whisper.

"Gonaives is burned, and Saint Marc too," Massicot croaked hoarsely. "Dessalines's people have just been driven back from Port-au-Prince. Oh you'll see, they are desperate men! They will certainly take my pig."

"And your life along with it, you old—" Someone shushed the surgeon who had blurted this reproach. If Massicot had heard, he did not seem to take offense.

"Dessalines came with prisoners, I thought I saw," the doctor said.

"Many," said Massicot. "Some from as far off as Gros Morne, but he has been sweeping them in all across the plain. Lucky they have not been massacred. There were hundreds killed at Verrettes, we have heard. They are all shut up in the old cotton warehouse, if it is not the brickworks."

"I had better go and see what can be done for them," the doctor said. Massicot caught at his sleeve as he made for the back door, but did not follow him into the yard.

Bienvenu hung over the fence, admiring Fanfan in the starlight, his good hand cupped over his navel. The doctor grunted to get his attention, and they went on together. It was only two blocks from Massicot's to the square; Petite Rivière was a very small town, with no more than forty houses, though many of them were solidly built of brick or stone. Under the eyes of Dessalines's soldiers, they crossed below the doors of the church. The doctor pulled his hat down over his face and put his hands into his pockets; he felt eyes on his back as they went by. His pistol barrels scraped against his pelvis as he walked. A block ahead, he made out the figure of Père Vidaut, the village priest, flanked by his two acolytes, and he picked up his pace to overtake them. Père Vidaut was vested as if for the mass, and his two black acolytes carried cross and candle.

"Whom are you attending, Father?" the doctor said when he'd caught up.

"Those unfortunates that Dessalines has herded into the old cotton warehouse," the priest replied. "It is too close for so many in that place—they will suffer much, even by night, and if they are kept through the heat of the day . . ."

"What chance have they to be released?"

"I don't know." The priest dropped his shoulders. "Madame Dessalines has come as well, and she has a gentle heart. Maybe she'll have some influence with her husband. But *monsieur le général* appears in an especially thunderous mood."

As the priest's voice trailed away, they came along the wall of the cotton warehouse, out of use since cotton planting had stopped with the wars and the desertion of the plantations. A familiar face popped up in a small, square window in the brickwork as the doctor passed.

"*A l'aide!* Help us!"

The doctor stopped, letting the priest go on. Framed in the window was the face of Bruno Pinchon, whom the doctor knew slightly from the region of Port-au-Prince.

"You are far from your plantation," the doctor said, somewhat reluctantly. He had never much liked Pinchon; the man feared ill fortune and seemed to attract it. "How do you come here?"

"By mischance. I was visiting—"

There was some turmoil inside the building, and Pinchon's visage was replaced by that of the naturalist Descourtilz.

"He was visiting me," Descourtilz said, with a queasy smile the doctor could just make out in the starlight. "We were taken on the road from Habitation Rossignol-Desdunes to—well, it is no matter. In all the Artibonite there is no hiding place any more. Our color betrays us everywhere."

The doctor nodded, slightly chilled. Descourtilz was also a medical man, and they'd once dined together at Gonaives, pleasantly enough, discussing the anatomy of the local crocodile, of which Descourtilz had been making a study. Like Pinchon, Descourtilz had come out from France during a lull in the fighting, seeking to recover family property under Toussaint's regime—most likely it was that common circumstance that threw them together. The doctor preferred Descourtilz to Pinchon, though both excited his sympathy now.

"We have got to get out," Descourtilz said flatly. "We are packed in so, no one can sit down, and if he did he'd suffocate."

"I understand you," said the doctor. The porthole through which Descourtilz peered was one of only four in the long brick wall. "The priest has already gone around to the front. I'll see what he thinks may be accomplished."

In front of the warehouse, Père Vidaut had met a dozen-odd *femmes de couleur* who had come bearing food and water for the prisoners. The guards had opened the door to admit them, but when the doctor made to follow, the priest motioned him away.

"You may not get out again so easily," he said. "Better to return by day."

"And yourself, Father?"

The priest smiled thinly, one hand on his stole. "I will trust to my cloth," he said. "And to God's grace."

The doctor bowed and made his retreat. A stranger's face hung in the window where Descourtilz's had been. He went on without pausing, Bienvenu a pace behind. No one molested them on their climb to the fort, but the doctor was happier than ever to have Bienvenu's company.

Next morning the doctor jerked up from his mat at the sound of voices disputing and a loud clatter of metal on stone. He crawled out shirtless from beneath the palm fringe of his shelter. Bienvenu and a couple more of the walking wounded were arguing, beside the wall, with a platoon of Dessalines's men who'd arrived with mattocks, shovels, and hoes. Behind them daylight bloomed quickly over the plain, and in the wooded mountains to the east all of the cocks were crowing, but it was still cool enough that the doctor's bare chest and arms broke out in gooseflesh.

One of Dessalines's men shook a hoe at Bienvenu, who skipped out of reach, twisting to shield his wounded arm, then advanced again with *coutelas* drawn in his left hand.

"*Dousman,*" the doctor said hastily, taking a step forward. The quarrel paused as both men turned toward him. "What is your trouble?"

By the inner wall, Paulette was on her hands and knees, blowing up the flames of the fire Fontelle had just kindled beneath the iron kettle. A couple of Dessalines's men stood near, watching the girl's derrière and the egg and two plantains Fontelle had brought with roughly equal interest. The doctor glanced at that situation; then Bienvenu's voice recalled him to the argument.

"They want to knock down the walls of the fort!" Bienvenu said hotly. "They say, by order of General Dessalines they will do it, but here are all the wounded of Papa Toussaint."

Paulette straightened from the fire and moved toward the wall, swinging her skirt away from the men who watched her. One of them reached slyly for a plantain, but Fontelle knocked him away with an elbow, then backed him farther off with the hot iron spoon she held.

The doctor looked for a captain of the crew. "What are your orders?" he said.

"Tear down the fort, and retreat to Grand Cahos."

"A moment," said the doctor. He walked to the open gate and looked out. Dessalines was coming up the slope from the town, in his general's dress regalia, riding a big bay stallion. The doctor hurried back to his *ajoupa* and stooped in to find his shirt. At the same time he flipped over the mat he slept on to cover his long gun and two pistols. By the time he straightened, tucking his shirt, Dessalines had dismounted and stood beside his horse, squinting into his silver snuffbox.

"General." The doctor bowed. Dessalines stirred his tobacco thoughtfully with a fingertip, then closed the box without taking any.

"Your orders are?" the doctor asked.

"Destroy the fort so that the *blancs* cannot use it," Dessalines pronounced.

"But these wounded are here by order of the Governor-General."

Dessalines's eye bore down on the doctor. "Toussaint ordered you to bring them to the fort?"

The doctor swallowed. "To Petite Rivière."

"Well, *ti blan*, little white man, I give you time to move these wounded while my men tear down the walls."

"And your orders for the town?"

"*N'ap boulé tout kay yo,*" Dessalines said carelessly, glancing toward the screen of trees below the gate. He clicked a fingernail on the snuffbox lid. We will burn all the houses.

The doctor spread his empty hands in the air. His mouth opened, but no words came. The image of Descourtilz's face, caught in the small bricked window of the cotton warehouse, flicked across his memory. Fontelle approached, with the boiled egg and two steaming plantains arranged on a banana leaf, but the doctor's appetite had fled. He dropped his hands and nodded in the direction of Dessalines.

"No, better that you offer it to the general."

But Dessalines shrugged off the food. At his gesture, his captain stepped up and took the boiled egg from the leaf, then broke off half a plantain. The rest was divided bite by bite among the men who held the mattocks. The last man sailed the empty leaf over the parapet. Bienvenu, who stood quietly with his *coutelas* hanging behind his left thigh, watched the leaf go fluttering down over the river.

Someone raised a pick and brought it down. The point drew sparks from the stone, but dislodged only a few shreds of mortar. The man who'd struck looked disconsolately down at his jolted arms. Dessalines shifted his stance and cocked his head. The doctor's ears strained for whatever sound he heard: horses. Dessalines dropped the snuffbox into his coat pocket. A moment later, the first horseman was pulling his mount up sharply within the gate. "Look out, the Governor is coming!"

The doctor recognized Guiaou, holding one of Toussaint's pennants on a whipping bamboo staff. Then Toussaint rode in himself, flanked by Placide and Morisset, and followed by two dozen riders of his guard.

At once the doctor was washed in relief. But when Toussaint slipped down from Bel Argent, he crumpled against the saddle skirt—only his grip on the stirrup leather held him up. Dessalines watched, his posture emptied of all intention, his face entirely blank. Finally Toussaint pulled himself upright and took a shaky step away from the white stallion. He was pouring sweat, but his face was bloodless.

"Sir, I see you are taken with fever—" the doctor began, but Toussaint passed him stiffly, unheeding. The doctor glanced up at Placide, whose grave face hung above his horse's head.

"What is this work?" Toussaint demanded.

Dessalines repeated what he had told the doctor.

"No," said Toussaint, "no." He fisted a hand, then opened it, then wet a forefinger with his tongue and raised it to the wind. He turned on his heels, holding the raised finger to the points of the compass. When he'd completed the revolution, he was again facing Dessalines. The movement seemed to strengthen him a little, or at any rate when he next spoke, his voice no longer quavered.

"Let them deepen the ditches around the fort," he said, gesturing at the men with their mattocks. "Shore up these walls, within. I have brought a few more cannon. We will stand here, and let the *blancs* shatter themselves against this mountain." His voice was low and tight on those last words, but then he smiled, unexpectedly, moving his hand quickly to wipe away the smile. He moved a step toward Dessalines and put a hand under his elbow.

"Come," he said, drawing the taller man toward the powder magazine. "Let me tell you how it will be done."

Most of that day the doctor spent shifting his wounded to new shelters hastily raised on the slopes of the *bitasyon* behind the fort, for Toussaint confirmed the order that all of them should be moved. That was more easily accomplished than to get them all down to the town, and despite Toussaint's arrival the doctor could still picture Petite Rivière burning, given what Dessalines had said. For the moment, he left his own bivouac within the walls where it had been. Bienvenu, without saying anything, unrolled his own sleeping mat beside the doctor's.

Dessalines came away from his conference with Toussaint looking well pleased. He swung onto his horse and rode to the town, while Toussaint remained in the fort throughout the day, with Placide and Guiaou following him, overseeing the digging of ditches and the placement of cannon that were being dragged in. Though the doctor, Fontelle, and even Placide besought him to rest, to seek the shade, to take a *tisane* brewed against his fever, Toussaint ignored them all; he would only crumple, for a few minutes, when the fever turned to wracking chill, and jumped back to his feet as soon as the chill had passed.

Once the wounded were resettled, a little after noon, the doctor gave up the struggle with Toussaint and walked down to the town himself. Outside the priest's house behind the church, he encountered Madame Dessalines, and made her his deepest bow. The lady returned him a nod and a warm smile. It had not been quite a year since Dessalines had married Marie Félicité Claire Heureuse Bonheur. The couple had begun to celebrate their marriage, the second for them both, here at Petite Rivière. Though the doctor had not been present, he was familiar with the tale. Everyone had been feasting and singing and dancing the *carabinier* when messengers arrived with the news of the Moyse rebellion. At once Dessalines had abandoned his bride to enter the field of those new battles. According to rumor, their courtship had begun on a battlefield too, when Marie Félicité had presented herself to Dessalines with a plea that he allow some water and medicines to be sent into the town of Jacmel, which he was then besieging.

Père Vidaut stood in his doorway, watching her go. When she'd turned the corner, the priest motioned the doctor inside. They passed through two simply furnished rooms and emergèd into a tiny enclosed garden at the rear, where they sat in the shade of the one almond tree. An acolyte served coffee, cassava bread, and some fruit. The doctor ate with a sudden hunger, and told the priest of the work under way at the fort. In the course of the morning more troops had arrived, one phalanx commanded by Magny and another by Lamartinière, and both Morisset and Monpoint were present, each with a squadron of cavalry, so there was a great concentration.

"So," said the priest. "On our side, with the help of Madame Dessalines the captives have been paroled to the town, though they may not leave its limits. As to what will follow . . ." He shrugged. "It's rumored that Leclerc's columns are not very far off."

"Toussaint doesn't seem to mean to retreat," said the doctor. He recalled Dessalines's project to burn Petite Rivière, but maybe that plan too had been altered by Toussaint's arrival; he did not mention it to the priest. From a few words dropped by Placide and Guiaou, he'd gathered that Toussaint had just come from a lightning tour of his posts inland along the Artibonite and through the mountains from Mirebalais—all these still held, but it appeared that Petite Rivière was to be the first point of strong resistance. The doctor began to wish he were elsewhere. But what were his chances now of slipping away? What Descourtilz had said weakened his confidence in the project of escaping into the mountains alone.

He left the priest and went to call on Massicot. The house was calmer than the day before, with shutters open to the breeze. Massicot stood in

the backyard, lowering blackened strips of banana peel to the grateful
jaws of Fanfan. Descourtilz and Pinchon had found berths among the
surgeons here. They'd had an unpleasant journey to Petite Rivière, the
doctor learned, chivvied along by Dessalines's troops on the retreat from
the embers of Saint Marc. Many had seen their properties burned as
they crossed the Artibonite valley, and a few had been killed, either for
an example or only on the whim of Dessalines.

"A terrible man," Pinchon said tremblingly. "A savage! If he opens his
snuffbox, one's life depends on whether he finds his tobacco damp or
dry . . ."

"*Condui li pissé,*" Descourtilz muttered.

"What?" said the doctor.

"Take him off to piss," Descourtilz repeated, smearing his thin, sweat-
sticky hair back over his round head. "That is his phrase if one is to be
killed—it's your own blood you'll be pissing."

"Or, *fé pyé-li sauté tè!*" Pinchon said with a shudder. "Make his feet
jump off the earth—have you heard that one?"

"Gentlemen," said the doctor. "These strike me as unhealthy
reflections."

"What would you?" Pinchon lapsed into a sulk. Descourtilz only
shrugged and looked toward the rear window.

"One might get away, perhaps?" the doctor said. "What do you know
how it is in the direction of Ester, or further to the north?"

"Oh," said Descourtilz. "The arrival of French troops is rumored
hourly, yet always they seem to come too late. The inhabitants of Saint
Marc were butchered while General Boudet looked on, so we hear—
from a distance just too great for him to intervene. Our guards drank
themselves unconscious one night before we came here, but though we
might have got away there was no place to run to—nowhere in all the
country to hide from these marauders."

"And that old fool cares only for the safety of his pig," Pinchon said,
with a bitter jerk of his jaw toward the backyard.

"It occupies his mind, I suppose," the doctor said. "Well, Toussaint
has come, at least—he is not likely to mistreat us."

Descourtilz snorted. "Toussaint prefers not to bloody his own hands,"
he said. "He leaves that work to some other to do, and turns his face
away."

"You oughtn't to speak ill of him," the doctor said. "He's your best
hope."

He took his leave and found Bienvenu waiting for him outside the
back fence, ready with remonstrances for his leaving the fort without an
escort, even by broad day. At this moment Bienvenu's solicitude made
the doctor feel all the more confined. His own chance of escape from this
situation was probably no better than Descourtilz's. Toussaint was also
his own best hope, and Toussaint looked dangerously ill. With Bienvenu,

the doctor climbed slowly to the fort, his limbs leaden in the afternoon heat. The ditch outside the walls was now so deep that Guiaou had to lay aside his shovel and span it with a plank for the two of them to cross.

Men were dragging new cannon to the reinforced embrasures, but no one paid the doctor any mind. In the shade of his *ajoupa,* he furtively scratched a shallow trench by the wall and there interred his long rifle, wrapped in a cloth, then spread his sleeping mat over the loose dirt. His pistols he hid in his straw *macoute,* under the packets and bundles of herbs. If Dessalines should catch him armed—no, Descourtilz was right, at least for the moment. There was no flight, and resistance would certainly be fatal.

The fort had emptied when he came out of the *ajoupa;* everyone was working on the ditches outside. The doctor set his hands on his hips and arched into the ache at the small of his back, turning in the direction of the sun that lowered over the powder magazine. A silhouette emerged from beside the building; the doctor squinted and shaded his eyes. The afterburn of the sun's glare spread a black cross over his vision, and out of the cross Toussaint emerged, staggering blindly toward the doctor.

"Dessalines!" Toussaint moaned, unaware that anyone looked or listened. "*Sé Baron pou moin li yé.* Dessalines will betray me to my death."

But this must be delirium. The doctor turned to track Toussaint as he passed, still incoherently murmuring. The illusion of the black cross still burned across his eyes; it must be only a sunspot. Toussaint passed through the gate and tottered over the plank that bridged the ditch. The doctor watched him wander into the twisting trails of the *bitasyon* beyond.

That night he slept very poorly. A whistle of a night bird or the rustle of wind-stirred palm leaves was enough to bring him bolt upright, gasping, one hand scrabbling in the *macoute* for the blunt comfort of a pistol grip. For that, he checked his wounded often, though he did not go armed when he left the fort to find them in their new shelters on the edge of the *bitasyon.* Where Toussaint had got to, no one seemed to know. The doctor half suspected that he'd crawled off somewhere to die.

But maybe it was more likely he'd gone in search of one of those old women around the region whom he trusted to cook and care for him. When he rematerialized in the fort next morning, his fever seemed to have broken and his eyes were clear. He poured himself into the organization of the defenses with all his old accustomed energy. Though he would accept no treatment, day by day the doctor saw him strengthen.

In the space of four days all was ready to his satisfaction, and on the morning of the fifth Toussaint called his commanders into the fort. By then they included Dessalines, Lamartinière, Magny, Monpoint, and Morisset, and as many men as the walls would contain pressed into the fort behind him. Toussaint addressed them formally, as he had at Ravine à Couleuvre. No one seemed to mind the doctor, who sat crosslegged under the leafy fringe of his *ajoupa*—or maybe Toussaint wanted a *blanc* witness.

"I am returning to the north today," he declared. "I must get news of Maurepas, and I will bring Christophe with me as I pass to Leclerc's rear. If God wills it, I will return with Maurepas and the Ninth Demibrigade to relieve you here. Till then I confide the defense of this place to your valor!" He swept his arm toward the eastern mountains, which the rising sun had just cleared. "This place and all the lines it covers. There is a good supply of powder here, and Dessalines will get more from the reserve at Plassac. General Vernet is coming to you soon with dried beef and beans and urns for water. *Bon courage!*"

Dessalines made no reply, but looked off over the parapet, rather moodily, the doctor thought. Perhaps he was thinking of his wife, who would likely have to leave Petite Rivière, if this sort of siege was to be expected. It was Monpoint who stepped forward.

"General," he said, "you may leave without worry—we who remain will be worthy of your confidence, dead or alive."

There was a cheer, then Morisset added—"All I regret is that I, your old companion at arms, will not go with you through the dangers you are going to meet!" But he was smiling as he spoke, and among all the men the mood was elevated.

Toussaint stepped forward to clasp Morisset's hand, then turned and kissed Placide quickly on both cheeks. The senior officers returned his salute, and Toussaint walked briskly through the gate and crossed the ditches. Astride Bel Argent, he touched his hat brim.

"*Kenbe là*," he called. Hold on. With that he turned the white stallion on the trail to the interior. One company of dragoons spurred their horses after him, and seven infantry companies marched behind. The balance of the force Toussaint had brought—one infantry batallion and the two cavalry squadrons of his honor guard—remained at Petite Rivière.

So too did Dessalines remain. He stood looking dourly over the parapet at the slow muddy wind of the river below, half-consciously fidgeting with his snuffbox. If Toussaint's oration had roused the same feeling in him as in the other officers, he concealed it well. The doctor watched the snuffbox move from one pale palm to the other. Dessalines looked up and caught his eye. Feigning unconcern, the doctor broke the glance. He gathered his instruments and herbs and, with Bienvenu, left the fort to walk to the new camp of the wounded at the edge of the *bitasyon* behind. If he felt eyes drilling into his back as he passed through the gate, at least no one moved to hinder him.

Fontelle had established her cauldron in the spot to which the wounded had been moved. There proved to be as good foraging here as in the town, and it was more out of the way of the new influx of troops. Already she'd cooked a quantity of small yellow sweet potatoes for their breakfast. They ate and set to the work of changing dressings. The doctor kept away from the fort all that day, though it was near enough through the sheltering trees that he could hear picks slamming into the soil and men grunting as they dragged cannon into place. Toussaint had brought heavier guns, eight- and twelve-pounders mostly.

At evening, with Fontelle and Paulette and Bienvenu, he walked down to Petite Rivière. Clouds were hurrying over the sky, blotting the stars as soon as they appeared. A stray guinea hen, covering her chicks, darted across the trail ahead of them. As the hen took shelter in the brush, a military drumbeat began in the town below.

"They are beating the general." Bienvenu cocked his head to the drum. His gait picked up the rhythm. The doctor felt a cold bolt run down from the top of his skull to the place in the ground where his heel struck. All day he had managed not to think of what Toussaint's departure might portend. Now whatever it was had begun. He reached for Fontelle's and Paulette's hands and squeezed them briefly, then let go. Fontelle walked with her turbanned head held high, eyes fixed on the way before them, her long face angled toward the sound of forty drums. Though less obviously than Bienvenu's, her pace seemed influenced by the beating.

By unspoken accord they went to the church, circling to the rear, since the drums were loudest in the square in front. The door was shut but they found Père Vidaut in the house behind, stuffing a few garments into a cracked and moldy leather portmanteau.

"What has happened?" the doctor said. "What is happening?"

"I can't be sure but I fear the worst," the priest said shortly. Neither of his young black acolytes was anywhere in sight. "This morning they rounded up all the prisoners from the plain into the warehouse again, and now they are hailing them into the square—I interceded for the release of a few. But I can do no more here now. I am going to seek the protection of Madame Dessalines."

He pulled the portmanteau shut by the handles and turned to face the doctor. "You'd have done better to stay on the height," he said. "Among your patients—where your value as a doctor would not be forgotten."

"What of the surgeons at Massicot's?"

"Gone to ground, if they are wise." The priest paused. "I got Descourtilz out of the warehouse. He may have gone to Massicot's—I don't know. But follow me—there's not much time."

They crossed the dooryard to the rear of the church—the priest darted in through a small portal behind the altar. In the stale darkness within he groped for chalice and salver and stuffed them into the portmanteau atop the wads of his clothing. The doctor could barely distinguish his movements in the dark. Fontelle and Paulette were pressed against his back. Through a chink in the closed front door came a bar of torchlight from the square.

"Wait," said the priest. "What's that?" Voices had been raised beyond the church door—the doctor recognized Dessalines and Lamartinière. The priest moved lightly to the crack and the doctor followed. Their heads knocked together as they both stooped to peer.

The doctor lowered himself to one knee and found a wider gap before his eye. He could hear the priest's hoarse breathing above him. Through the crack he saw the hundreds of white prisoners who'd been herded into the square, half naked most of them, arms bound with rags of their own shirts. Their faces were drawn and haggard in the torchlight. Just below the church steps were two men who looked utterly possessed by panic, both wearing soiled and sweat-stained French uniforms, one army and one naval.

"No," said Dessalines. "From tonight, we hold no prisoners. These two will follow all the rest."

Lamartinière had turned to face him. "You will be answerable to the Governor-General if they are harmed," he said. "As I will be." He laid a hand on his sword grip. "As I am."

"Ah," the priest breathed. "Sabès and Gimont."

"Who are they?" the doctor whispered.

The priest's lips rustled at his ear. "Prisoners—hostages. Lamartinière brought them here when he came. They have been kept under guard apart from the rest. Gimont is a naval officer, Sabès an emissary—they brought messages to Port-au-Prince before Boudet landed his troops there, but Lamartinière took them captive and has held them till now . . ."

"And you know all this?"

"Dessalines sent them to confession this morning," the priest muttered. "Now I know why."

The doctor pressed his eye socket to the crack. Dessalines's face was knotty and dark. His fingers fluttered on the lid of his snuffbox. But then he let out a short harsh laugh.

"Your respect for Old Toussaint has grown," he said to Lamartinière, who faced him, vibrating with resolve. "Well, save your blade to kill the *blancs*. You may send this pair to Toussaint's camp at Grand Cahos if he wants them so much—only get them out of my sight, and quickly."

As Lamartinière loosened his grip from his sword pommel, Gimont, the naval officer, fell onto his knees, gasping. Sabès bore the shock of relief with less demonstration. A couple of Lamartinière's men came up quickly to lead them away. But Dessalines had already turned to his men in the square. Though the doctor could not make out his words, they were received with loud shouting and wild brandishing of torches. Then the soldiers closed in and began to press the bound prisoners out of the square, toward the edge of town. More fifes shrilled, echoed by trumpeting conch shells, and many of the men began to thrust their torches into the eaves of the buildings that they passed. The drums had gone on beating the whole time.

"We can't wait longer." The priest pulled away from the door and moved toward the altar. "They will burn the church too before they are done. Let me take these women to Madame Dessalines—they won't be molested if they aren't caught with you."

"What a comfort," the doctor said drily. "Well, but you're right." He squeezed Paulette's hand. Fontelle gave him a quick hard hug.

"If you can get to Nanon or Madame Tocquet—" He forced a smile. "Tell them I am waiting out this trouble at La Crête à Pierrot."

"God defend you, then." The priest made the sign of the cross. The alley behind the church was still calm when they came out. The priest led the two women quickly away; Bienvenu drew the doctor in the opposite direction, toward the fort.

"Wait," the doctor said. "First I want to see if there is anyone at Massicot's."

Bienvenu tugged his elbow mutely; the doctor shook free. Bienvenu folded his arms, shook his head heavily three times, then followed him. They met no one on the way but white people scattering from their houses—apparently the local whites, as well as the captives from the plain, had been elected to the massacre. The back door of Massicot's house burst open as they reached the fence.

"Thieves! *Murderers!* Stop!"

Fanfan the pig was squealing even more desperately than her master, for two men with *coutelas* had hemmed her into a fence corner. Massicot rushed up and threw himself on the back of one. Half a dozen others appeared and swarmed around them. The struggling men toppled, rolled on the ground. The doctor slipped a hand into his straw *macoute* and covered his pistol grip, but there was no clear shot, and in the shadow of the fence, no one had yet noticed him; he could watch everything that was happening as one observes a dream. Massicot's greasy gray hair came loose from its queue—a big square hand had pulled it loose. "Fanf—" he started, and trailed off in a gurgle. The black hand raised his severed head and jammed it down on a pointed fence paling.

The roof of the house burst into flames and several of the surgeons came rushing out the back, closely pursued by a dozen more of Dessalines's soldiers. Most scattered in the alley, but one jumped up into the limbs of Massicot's mango tree. The doctor crouched in the shadow of the fence, hiding his face from the burst of firelight. Bienvenu hovered over him. Two black soldiers circled the *manguier*, jabbing at the surgeon's calves with their *coutelas* points.

"Shoot him," said one, and the other replied, "Don't waste the powder." A third soldier made a leap and caught the surgeon around the shins and dragged him down, screaming like a girl. One of the others opened his belly with a *coutelas;* the surgeon went on screaming and tossing his head as the black men stirred his guts out onto the ground.

Fanfan's squeals were silenced now. A crew of men huffed as they lifted her to hang from her back trotters from a branch of the same mango tree. Blood drooled from a wide fatty gash in her throat. Someone took a *coutelas* and disemboweled her, rather more fastidiously than they had the surgeon. Impaled on the fence pole, Massicot's head gaped upon the scene, its slack jaws revealing many blackened, rotting teeth.

Bienvenu snatched at the doctor's arm; they ran across the alley and dove into a low hut, rolling in dust and dirty straw and feathers. The doctor's hand came up sticky with a broken egg. He shook it loose and wiped it on the straw and found that he was grasping someone's forearm—Descourtilz, half hidden under straw.

"Has Massicot lost his pig at last?" said Descourtilz, but a black man on the other side hushed him at once, as Bienvenu covered the doctor's mouth with his hand and camouflaged his head with a handful of dung-smelling straw. For some time they lay silent there, the doctor inhaling Descourtilz's sour breath, for they were nose to nose. The flames of the burning house came flickering through the lattice of the chicken coop. The doctor could not lose the image of Massicot's head, the dead stare on the carcass of his Fanfan, expression dulling as the eyeballs dried in the heat of the blaze. The dream-distance had been torn away, so that the doctor had to struggle not to vomit in the straw. Two silhouettes blocked the firelight on the lattice, then with a chuckle someone threw in a torch. Straw and the roof were alight at once. The doctor lunged and broke the lattice with his shoulder and came up running, scattering smoldering straw. Descourtilz must have made off in the other direction; he seemed to have drawn off pursuit.

Flanked by Bienvenu, the doctor ran till he was winded, then slumped panting against the hot stone wall of a burning house, pressing a hand against the stitch in his side. Dessalines's men had broken into the rum stores and were drunk and had lost all discipline—the prohibition against wasting powder forgotten, they fired their overcharged guns in the air or into cows and chickens or anything that stirred. A gang rounded the corner and bore down on the doctor and Bienvenu.

"*Aba blan!*" the lead man shouted. Down with the whites! He swung his blade at the doctor's neck. The doctor twisted away as he ducked—not far enough, but the blade was stopped by the bone at the top of his skull. The blow set off a chain of colored lights across his brain, and both ears rang amazingly. He was down on his knees and elbows, blood pouring into his right eye.

"*Ann koupé têt tout blan yo!*" Let's cut off the head of all the whites!

The *coutelas* swung down, and stopped with a clang. Bienvenu's blade had parried it.

"*Li pa blan,*" said Bienvenu, in a deep and terrifying tone the doctor had never before heard. He's not white.

"*Pa blan?*" the leader hesitated.

"Li gegne peau clair anpil anpil," said another of the group. He has very, very light skin . . .

"Gegne peau clair men li pa blan pou sa!" Bienvenu insisted. He spun his *coutelas* to clear the leader's blade. The leader took a step back from the doctor. Everyone was looking curiously at Bienvenu, and one of them reached out to touch his sling.

"Where were you wounded?"

"Ravine à Couleuvre." Bienvenu drew himself up tall. "I fought the *blancs* there with Papa Toussaint, and this one was there with us." He gestured at the doctor. "This is the one who cares for my hurt, and for many others who were hurt there."

"Oh, oh." A murmur went round. Someone handed Bienvenu a bottle of rum. He covered the broken neck with a rag of his shirttail as he drank.

The doctor stood up wincingly and probed the side of his head. The *coutelas* must have been quite dull. Though the cut bled freely, it was shallow, stopped by the bone. No fracture, in his estimation. Bienvenu passed him the bottle and he took a long pull, not minding that the sharp edge cut his lip.

"Santé, tout moun," he said. Your health, everybody. He took another gulp of rum and his own blood.

"Li pa blan?" some doubter asked again.

"Fé li chanté!" said another man. Make him sing! He capered in a loose ellipse, hopping on one leg and clapping as he chanted.

Nanon prale chaché dlo . . .
crich li casé . . .

Nanon's going to look for water
but her jar is broken . . .

With a last clap and a giggle he broke off.

"Li pa blan," Bienvenu said authoritatively. "He doesn't sing either. Now, let us pass."

"Ou mêt alé." The leader stepped aside and nodded. *You may go.*

Halfway up the slope to the fort, they were overtaken by several horsemen. The doctor had no more strength to run; he turned around to face his doom. But the patrol was led by Placide Louverture.

"Doctor Hébert!" Placide blurted. "You should not have left the fort. It is not safe for you tonight."

"No." The doctor's exhale was almost a sob. He looked down at the blazing roofs of the town. It was not so spectacular as the fire at Le Cap, because Petite Rivière was so much smaller. However, a few of the screening trees had caught fire from the roofs. From the darkness of a shallow gulch to the north of town came frequent intermittent screaming.

"No," said the doctor. "It's not safe." He felt sure that if he began to laugh or cry he would never be able to stop, so he did neither. With one shaky hand clutching Placide's stirrup, he made the rest of the climb to the fort.

Next morning he woke to an aching head and a pall of ill-smelling smoke rising from the charred foundations of Petite Rivière. On the hilltop, all was quiet. The sentinels in the fort went about their business in good cheer, quite as if there'd been no massacre the day before, and they let Bienvenu and the doctor through the gate without any questions.

Bienvenu assumed Fontelle's place at the kettle; he insisted that the doctor clean and compress his own wound before he attended the others in the camp. When he'd completed the morning round, the doctor returned to the fort in time to see Descourtilz walking up the hill, a lancet held high in his right hand and a roll of bandages spooling from the crook of his left arm. These medical emblems gained him an unchallenged admission at the gate. He found the doctor by the wall above the river.

"Ugh," he said as he came to a stop and looked over the walk in the direction of the fuming ruins. "So you too made it through, I see—we are the lucky pair. What a bloody business—have you got anything to eat?"

"Of course," said the doctor and produced a couple of small potatoes from the morning meal. Descourtilz laid down his bandages, stuck the lancet into his belt, and bit into the first potato savagely. "Forgive me," he said, glancing sidelong at the doctor, as wind from the river riffled his black hair around his head. "I—"

The doctor waved away the apology. He'd awakened himself to the wolf-like hunger that a brush with death inspired. Unconsciously he fingered the stain on his bandaged head.

"What happened?" Descourtilz mumbled through potato.

"Someone wanted to chop off my head," said the doctor. "The program of the evening, as you know."

"Too well," said Descourtilz. His unshaven neck pulsed as he swallowed.

"But you have certainly had your own adventures," the doctor suggested.

Descourtilz wiped his mouth with the back of his hand and looked off over the river and the plain. The doctor noticed that his face and hands and forearms were dotted with drops of dried blood from a webwork of fine scratches.

"Oh," he said. "I survive by miracles—I would scarcely credit them myself, if I heard them from another."

"What of Pinchon?" the doctor said reluctantly.

"Dead," said Descourtilz.

"Well," said the doctor. "He always thought himself unlucky. I suppose that in the end he was."

"You might say so," Descourtilz said. "We were caught up together when all of us paroled to the town were locked up in the depots again. Père Vidaut came and winkled me out of that place, just before the killing began, and Pinchon too, for he stuck to me like a barnacle. We were made to appear before Dessalines, and he ordered that we must die with the rest. By that time they had already begun bayoneting all those who were left in the warehouse, I think. Then Madame Dessalines, who is a saint, spoke up for me, and said I might be useful as a doctor, and so she stayed his hand for a moment. And when Dessalines was distracted, she took us to her own chamber and let us hide under the bed. But then Dessalines came there too, with some of his officers—if one may call them that, the savages—to plot the massacre. He showed his whip scars, and reminded them all of the abuses of slavery, to stir their blood thirst. The whole time my leg hung out in the light, because Pinchon had got in under the bed first, and would not make me enough room, so finally someone saw it, and I was hauled out, and Pinchon too. They cut Pinchon to pieces there in the bedroom while I watched, but somehow, I can't say why, Dessalines sent me away to his wife again."

Descourtilz cleared his throat. "I had run enough risks in that house, I thought, so I ran to seek shelter at Massicot's, but the old fool would keep opening the door to see that no one bothered his pig. Well, they set the house on fire in the end, all the same. By the grace of God that old Negro you found with me in the shed appeared—Pompey, I shall never forget his name, though I didn't know him when he first approached me—in fact I thought he meant to kill me, but it seems I had cured him of something once, or so he believes. After that chicken house was burned, he got me away from the murderers and hid me in a hedge full of thorns—you see I have been scratched to ribbons—and so I passed the night."

"And the priest?" the doctor said. He was thinking of Fontelle and Paulette and what might have become of them in Père Vidaut's care.

"If he still lives, I don't know," Descourtilz said. "But he is a brave man, and determined—he kept coming to the prisons, though the guards would beat him, and he got many people out, with bribes or by pretending to have orders, as he did with me. I don't know what became of him after that. I would be dead if not for him, I know. What barbarity it has all been." He looked again at the cushion of smoke above the town, with its rank smell of charring flesh. "But I think the worst was when I was lying half under that bed, waiting for them to discover me, and the whole time Dessalines and his men were talking of nothing but death . . ."

The doctor looked where Descourtilz was looking. He fingered the folding spyglass that lay in his pocket, but after all there was nothing down by the town that he wanted to see more closely.

That afternoon Dessalines marched out of the town with a good number of the men Toussaint had left him. Descourtilz was sent away at the same time, to go with ambulances to the neighboring peak of Morne Calvaire, but no one gave any instruction to Doctor Hébert. Maybe Bienvenu had been telling the truth the night before and he had somehow lost his whiteness. With no mirror, there was nothing to remind him of his color, now that Descourtilz had gone. The soldiers in the fort were friendly toward him; indeed he seemed to move among smiles. No one seemed to remember last night's bloodbath, though most of them had probably been a part of it.

The garrison left in the fort was light: a total of seven hundred men, about, under command of Lamartinière and Magny. The two cavalry squadrons were still somewhere outside the fort, though there was no sign of them, and Placide Louverture must still be with Morisset, the doctor thought. But none of that cavalry appeared for the next two days. Maybe Dessalines had abandoned Toussaint's plan and there would be no great battle here after all. There was, so far, no sign of any French approach.

Three days after the burning of Petite Rivière, the doctor was roused by Bienvenu from his afternoon siesta and hustled to the wall. Bienvenu needed his sling no longer—he could gesture expansively with his right arm. The doctor rubbed his eyes and wiped his glasses and looked where he was urged. The camp was evacuating itself from the hillside opposite. Most of the wounded from Petite Rivière had either recovered or succumbed by now, though some still went limping on sticks and rough crutches. And in fact the whole *bitasyon* was emptying out: children and the old and infirm carrying bundles on their backs, women balancing baskets of hastily harvested yams and corn on their heads.

The doctor couldn't guess the reason for this exodus, till Bienvenu took the spyglass from him and crossed hurriedly to the embrasures overlooking the Artibonite. Well past the river and below the town, he could now make out a worm of dust, sidling along the road across the plain. When he recovered the spyglass from Bienvenu, he could make out French battle flags and a few horsemen riding back and forth along the infantry column.

They were still an hour off, or more, but the atmosphere in the fort had electrified. The artillery men were all priming their cannon, laying out charges of *mitraille*. The doctor retreated to his *ajoupa*, where he turned back a corner of his sleeping mat and dug his fingers in the loose dirt to touch the cloth-wrapped barrel of his rifle. If he ran down to meet the French column, would he get a bullet in the back as he left the fort? He touched the scab on the side of his head. Maybe it would be better to follow the people of the *bitasyon* to the trail they were taking deeper into the mountains. Or simply sit it out where he was.

Before he could come to any conclusion, the gate of the fort had been shut. He watched the advancing column until daylight faded. The French had camped somewhere below the town. Lamartinière and Magny were rushing back and forth between the fort and the surrounding ditches and new watch posts just established further out from the walls. Attack would most likely come at dawn.

The doctor lay awake for a long time on his mat, wondering how Fontelle and Paulette had progressed on the road north, trying to picture them bringing the news to Nanon or Elise or Paul or Xavier Tocquet that Doctor Hébert was *waiting out the trouble at La Crête à Pierrot*. The doctor had studied the column well enough before darkness to reckon its strength at two thousand or better—two thousand crack French troops of the line against a few hundred of this black army and no more than a dozen cannon at the embrasures of this little fort. The place would be overrun in an hour. Yet he thought he had a chance to survive, if the French grenadiers identified him as white, if the defenders did not decide, in some rage of defeat, to blow up the powder magazine.

The new sentry posts were quietly alert below the walls. In the woods to the northeast, firelight was trembling—probably against orders the doctor supposed, when he got up around midnight to relieve himself. The stars of the Great Bear hung from the top of the sky, illuminating the body of a sergeant who'd been caught asleep at his post and tossed on the ground before the trenches to encourage others not to doze. Bienvenu did not have guard duty—he slept innocently, profoundly, on his mat beside the doctor's. When he resumed his own place the doctor was expecting several more hours of insomnia, and so he was very much surprised to wake at first light and find Bienvenu gone. A rattle of musketry drowned out the usual morning cock crow.

The doctor ran to a parapet and raised the spyglass to his eye. He picked out the back of Bienvenu's head in the middle of a skirmish line deployed across the slope between the fort's ditches and the burned shells of the town. Since Bienvenu had brought him safe out of the massacre, the doctor had felt the liveliest interest in his well-being, but this skirmish line was going to be destroyed in the next few minutes—there were only a hundred men or so, lightly supported by snipers in the trees on either side, against two thousand French grenadiers already charging with bayonets lowered, and doubtless enraged by the carnage they'd found in whatever was left of Petite Rivière. The slight grade of the ascent did not slow them at all. The skirmishers shot off their muskets, fell back, turned, and ran for the fort—it was the rout the doctor had expected, though all around him the cannoneers had begun to light their matches. Lamartinière and Magny ordered them not to shoot—they'd only mow down their own retreating men if they fired now. The doctor fixed his glass on Bienvenu, who had not been shot, had not been bayoneted, who incongruously seemed to be laughing as he rushed to the edge of a ditch and tumbled in.

"Feu! Feu!" Lamartinière and Magny cried with one voice. The whole skirmish line had vanished in the ditches, so there was nothing now between the cannon mouths and the French charging into point-blank range. The doctor had picked out two generals on the field, and both went down in the first volley of *mitraille*. One got up and staggered away, supported by subalterns, as the cannons went on crashing, recharging, firing again . . . but the other lay on his back where he had fallen, pumping blood from a huge wound in the chest. There were hundreds more musketeers who'd all along been hidden in the trenches and they now kept up a steady fire, while cannons recoiled, recharged, belched more *mitraille*. Some black troops, surprisingly, were covering the French retreat. The doctor twisted the lens of his spyglass and made out the insignia of the Ninth Demibrigade—Maurepas's men from Port-de-Paix. Could Maurepas have surrendered?

Then Lamartinière screamed for the firing to stop, and as the cannonade and musket volleys faded away, a trumpet or a conch shell sounded. Out of the woods northeast of the slope, the cavalry of Monpoint and Morisset appeared to sweep the field. Through his spyglass the doctor discovered Placide, riding down a fleeing French grenadier, cleaving his head with a saber as casually as if splitting a length of firewood, then riding on to slay the next. He lowered the instrument and let the scene blur. When he looked again, the field was empty except for the dead—at least four hundred of them.

The whole business had taken less than one hour. All the men in the trenches were laughing and cheering, and the cannoneers were hugging each other. The doctor felt neither joy nor sorrow. He stood, the spyglass hanging numb in his left hand, until Bienvenu appeared and called to him, then gave him a nudge and spoke again, "Come, Doctor, please, you must come now, they are just bringing in the wounded."

25

In Toussaint's eyes the low stone outline of the powder magazine took on the aspect of a tomb, and from its farther end there bloomed the black cross of Baron, as it were wrapped in chains. Reasonably there was no cross, but reason had no application. His reason had been unseated by the fountain of dread that gushed up in him, responding to the black-toothed powers that rushed on him from without. Blood was the conduit of the dread expanding with every beat of his pulse. His heart clenched tight; his head ached terribly. The black cross burned against the sky.

He could not think it only a trick of sun or fever or the two combined. Baron was manifest in the cross. Toussaint's spirit had been sucked out of him. He was nothing, an empty bottle, wind whistling in the uncorked neck. All at once the warmth of fever drained from him too and in the shuddering chill that followed, he sank against the rough set stones of the magazine wall. The darts of pain his chattering teeth fired in his damaged lower jaw struck him from a long way off, though he wanted to reach toward the pain, restore himself in his body. His eyes were closed, the sun red on the lids. The black cross went on blazing behind his eyes. The deep drumbeat of his heart kept pumping out the fear. Within the cross's junction point appeared Baron Cimetière, wearing the face of Jean-Jacques Dessalines. His lips were parted but his teeth still set together, and from behind the teeth came the shrill and stuttering gravedigger's cry—*ke-ke-ke-ke-ke*—or was it the cry of a hawk overhead? *Dessalines has sold me!* Toussaint thought, or said. Somehow he had risen, moved away from the wall of the powder magazine; he was no longer cold but hot, his whole head swimming. *Dessalines is my Baron . . .* Had he spoken aloud? . . . the little white doctor looked at him strangely as he passed, and seemed to speak, but Toussaint did not hear. *Dessalines has sold me to the French.*

He staggered out the gate, and almost tumbled into a trench in progress that he'd ordered to be dug, but at the last moment he regained his balance and wobbled onto the narrow trail that led into the *bitasyon* east of the fort. High on a cane pole ahead of him was the small red square of a *hûnfor* flag. As he walked toward it, it disappeared, hidden by the branches of the trees. He was passing among the wounded from the battle at Ravine à Couleuvre, and it seemed that some of them stretched out their hands to him and that he heard them call the name they gave him, *Papa Toussaint*. He did not stop. He must take his weakness out of sight, hide it from all view.

But someone was following him. He turned, with an effort that pained his head, and saw Guiaou. At that he felt a flicker of gratitude, far off on the horizon. Guiaou would never sell Toussaint. The trail ascended as he followed it. The fork he'd chosen led neither to the *hûnfor* nor to any dwelling of the *bitasyon* but came instead to a little spring. Low to the ground, the water bubbled out of an ogive slit in the rock. By the spring someone had placed a triple *govi*. Toussaint touched a fingertip to the water—cold shot up his arm to the shoulder. With that shock came a moment of clarity, and he saw that in the moist ground around the spring, behind the *govi*, and among stones on the slope above, grew *armoise*, *bourrache*, and *romanier*.

Dessalines had not sold him yet. Nor had Baron yet taken him, down to the gate of death. Those two things were yet to come. And he had yet some way to travel before he reached that crossroads. At that understanding Toussaint began to feel a little calmer. The dark beating of his fear and helplessness shrank, folded in on itself, and rolled a little distance from him. He stooped and plucked a bud top of *romanier* and rolled it in his fingers and smiled at the fragrance.

Guiaou appeared on the path behind him, advancing slowly, but with no hesitation. More terrible than the deep knife scars that plowed the side of his face was the alarmed concern that poured out of his eyes. Toussaint had seen that look many times since Ravine à Couleuvre, flowing out of any eyes that saw him weakened by the fever: Suzanne, Saint-Jean, Placide, and any of the many others who had invested all their future hope in what Toussaint might achieve in the quick passage through these violent days. Most of all Isaac, who doubted his own decision, who envied his brother Placide now—Toussaint had seen it—less for the gallant figure he cut in the honor guard, for his chance at adven-

ture and glory of arms, but more for his having been moved by his spirit
to express, fully and unreservedly, the love for his father which Isaac certainly also felt. And so many others had recently regarded him so, down
to the least soldier of his armies. Even the *blanc,* Doctor Hébert, had that
look in his eyes just now.

These ideas wavered before him as Guiaou came up. Both his eyes
were clear, though one hid deep in the furrows of scar.

"Mon général," Toussaint heard him say. "Why do you wander? You
are unwell and ought to rest."

"Fey yo . . ." Toussaint could not succeed to finish his sentence. *The
herbs.* His sore tongue stuck in his head. He opened his hand to disclose
the crushed floret of *armoise.*

Guiaou leaned near, for the daylight was fading, then nodded. *"W'ap
chita isit la—m'ap vini."* He gestured; the old wounds on his warding arm
aligned with the knife scars on his face, the scars all rimed with white,
like salt. Sit down there and I will come. Toussaint reeled in the direction
indicated. A short way across the slope from the spring, a stand of bamboo arched over a gentle hollow in the ground, filled with dry leaves of
the bamboo. A sort of natural *tonnelle,* an arbor. Toussaint stepped
within it, achingly lowered into the twisted, rustling leaves. Guiaou had
understood and was gathering herbs around the spring—not only the
romanier, Toussaint saw, but the *bourrache* and *armoise* too. But of
course he had sometimes assisted the *blanc* doctor, and so must have
learned some of the uses of herbs that Toussaint had taught the doctor
himself long before. So the virtue of his own teaching returned to Toussaint now. This thought encouraged him. He sank backward, resting
against the close-grown, springy canes of bamboo. There was still a little
red sunlight filtering through the fluttering leaves. He felt his fever
shooting up. The crisis. He saw Guiaou as he had presented himself for
the first time years ago, with his scars more freshly healed, cured by the
salt of ocean waters. Guiaou had walked halfway across the country to
join Toussaint's army. Before that he had fought for the *colons,* though,
in the regiment known jokingly as the Swiss. As a reward the white men
had taken the Swiss to sea in a ship and cut them to pieces and thrown
them to the sharks. Few but Guiaou had survived, perhaps none. Guiaou
had brought the story to Toussaint, though maybe he had not understood it perfectly—had not seen how the *colons* could not dare return
slaves to the field who had learned war. Guiaou, maybe, saw just the pure
monstrosity and not the cause behind it, but that was enough to hold
him ever faithful to Toussaint.

When he first came, Guiaou had been afraid of horses, and of water,
but now he rode with the best of the cavalry, and he would cross water
too, if Toussaint asked it of him. And surely there were dozens and hundreds and thousands of others in and out of the army whose spirits were
as strong for Toussaint as was Guiaou's. Against the others, those with

different hearts, who would not return to the field any more, who would not work beyond their daily need of food, who believed freedom to be a license to laziness, who preferred *marronage,* and libertinage, to any duty of citizenship. And at their head had been Moyse. How Toussaint had loved him . . . He had delayed his arrest for weeks after the rebellion had been crushed, hoping at least that Moyse would recognize his danger and leave the island, but Moyse had waited, stubborn as ever (and certainly he had known very well what was sure to come), to be made prisoner and brought before the firing squad. Toussaint's thoughts were rushing, spiraling, as the fever rose toward crisis; he knew this but still could not control the thoughts. Guiaou had gone to Santo Domingo for Toussaint, and returned with the terrible news that Paul Louverture had given way to the French, and only because Toussaint's letter had not come to him. But Guiaou had not been obliged to cross water. Only mountains. *Deyè mòn gegne mòn.* Behind mountains always are more mountains. And Guerrier. Guerrier had gone to Santo Domingo with Guiaou, was it not so? There was some resemblance between these two, though Guerrier bore no scars. The readiness of Guerrier to lay down whatever tool he'd used before and take up the musket Toussaint offered him. Take up his musket for Toussaint.

"Koté Guerrier?" he said as Guiaou reached him, carrying herbs bundled in one hand and in the other the three-Marassa pot from beside the spring. Where is Guerrier? He felt anxious as for a small child, some helpless thing.

"Li byen," Guiaou said. He is well. Guiaou sat down crosslegged and took Toussaint's head into his lap. "Guerrier is near us, *mon général*—he is at the fort." Guiaou held the herbs close to Toussaint's face so that he caught their scent.

"B—Boulé . . ." He wanted to tell Guiaou to boil water and prepare a *tisane* with the herbs he had gathered. But the words would not come out. Guiaou dipped his fingers in the Marassa pot and stroked cool water against Toussaint's temples. Why had he moved the Marassa pot from its place beside the spring? The cold was painful, but after the shock he felt relief. Parts of his being which the fever made it impossible to focus clearly together began to drift apart and float away from each other as separate spheres. As the strain of binding them together was relaxed, a warmth of calm grew within him. Guiaou would never sell Toussaint. Guiaou would be faithful to him always. Guiaou sat listening to the lizards ticking through the dry leaves of bamboo as it grew dark. He had understood that Toussaint meant for water to be boiled and a *tisane* to be made. He had helped in such preparations with the white doctor. But for the moment there was no fire, and he had needed the Marassa pot because there was nothing else to carry water. Also, for now at the height of the fever, maybe cold water was best. Later, when the *tisane* was more urgently needed, something would appear to serve the need. Guiaou

went on laving Toussaint's temples with the water from the spring. Presently he pulled his hands up to his chest and wet the insides of his wrists as well, there where the pulse beat fast and hot, so close under the skin. The general was now sleeping. Almost peacefully, it seemed. It might be that the fever had peaked, though he was still very hot. Guiaou glanced toward the sound of a lizard in the leaves and saw instead a little boy's face peeping through the canes at the far end of the *tonnelle*. Then another face, a girl's, bright with curiosity. They remained for a moment, then flicked away lightly as two birds.

Guiaou had said nothing to the children. He had only smiled. But after they had been gone for a time, after it was fully dark, the boy and girl came back again, each carrying a bundle of firewood (the little girl balanced her firewood on her head), and behind them an old woman lugging her tripod and kettle. Between the mouth of the *tonnelle* and the spring, the old woman built a fire and boiled water to make the *tisane*. Also she filled bottles with hot water and placed them into Toussaint's armpits and under the arches of his feet.

In the morning when he woke Toussaint was hungry. The fever seemed completely to have passed. But before he returned to the fort and his men, he walked in a circle around the *tonnelle* with a stalk of *armoise* in his hand, then steeped the herb and washed his own feet in the liquid carefully, before he pulled back on his boots. With a smile he quickly hid behind his hand, he told Guiaou and the little boy and girl and the old woman grinning with her gums that if one used *armoise* so before a long, exhausting journey, one would feel neither fatigue nor any temptation to give up the course.

Dessalines! The dread Toussaint had felt at the worst of his fever was now gone. Once something that occupied one so completely, devouringly, had departed, one could not properly remember it any more. Still Toussaint knew, as his modest force circled through the mountains north from Petite Rivière, that he had touched upon a deep root of power there at La Crête à Pierrot—a force that Dessalines would draw on. Dessalines and all the others who would mount resistance there. They would bring this force up from the earth and water into open air where it would flower into flame. Toussaint's own death was hidden in it somewhere, and maybe the death of Dessalines too. But a great many of the *blanc* invaders were going to die first, there at La Crête à Pierrot . . . maybe all of them would die.

Most of the invading *blancs* were still drawing tight the empty noose they had devised—empty since Toussaint had slipped out of it, after Ravine à Couleuvre. Now the slip knot would close on La Crête à Pierrot, and then let them see if their rope was strong enough to hold what it had snared. Meanwhile, the *blancs* had left the terrain they'd occupied on their passage south too lightly garrisoned.

Though most of the honor guard cavalry had been detached at Petite Rivière, some horsemen still were following Toussaint, under command of Pourcely. Toussaint had picked Guiaou and Guerrier to bear his standards, riding on his either side. Behind the cavalry, the infantry companies under Gabart were stepping out smartly, and as they passed through the mountains they gathered more men—field hands and even some maroons Toussaint was able to rally to fight the *blancs,* armed with muskets distributed during the time of Sonthonax, or cached more recently in these hills by Toussaint himself, from his trade with the North American Republic.

They crossed the central plateau with tremendous speed, for now Toussaint's rear guard reported that General Hardy's division had been sent to pursue them, while Leclerc took his main force further south. At that news, Toussaint only laughed and with a pressure of his knees moved Bel Argent into a canter; diversion of French troops from the south was just what he wanted, and they would not catch him now, till he was ready to be caught. The tiny garrison Rochambeau had left at Saint Michel bolted at first sight of black horsemen sweeping the tall grass of the high savanna toward the town, abandoning almost all their stores as they ran for Ennery.

The stores unfortunately were scant, though there was a little powder and shot. Toussaint spent most of the night in Saint Michel, rising two hours before dawn to lead his men onward, excepting a small detachment he left to mislead Hardy toward Saint Raphael. By daybreak they had entered the canton of Ennery, where Toussaint's mood turned very dark, as they rode through the wasted fields of Habitation Sancey and halted before the burnt and collapsed timbers of the *grand'case* there. Soon Guiaou came riding down from the heights with the word that Descahaux was still intact, but this news did not alter the grim set of Toussaint's jaw.

Toussaint hardly needed spies as such, for anyone in the roadside *cases* was eager to tell him that the *blanc* soldiers from Saint Michel had come stampeding through the night before, to infect the similarly small garrison at the village of Ennery with their panic. Quickly he ordered Gabart to march the infantry southwest of the *bourg,* while he himself rode straight in with the cavalry. Resistance was token when the horsemen charged—the French garrison was so quickly routed from Ennery that most of them escaped Gabart's encircling movement, though some were killed by long-range shots as they ran pell-mell down the road toward Gonaives.

In twenty minutes this fight was over, and the only vestige of French authority left in Ennery was Leclerc's most recent proclamation nailed to trees in the sleepy square. Toussaint leaned out from Bel Argent's back to rip a copy from its nail. A couple of women and small children peered out curiously from the corners of the houses as he scanned the document, then recoiled as he crushed it in one hand.

"Outlaw—he declares me outlaw! The brigand who has burned my house—it is Leclerc who is the outlaw, and if I wish it I will take back Gonaives from him this very day."

Toussaint threw the paper over his shoulder and dug his spurs into his horse. The wind blew the wad toward Guiaou's face; by reflex he caught it in one hand. He unrolled the crumpled paper and smoothed on his saddlebow, squinting painfully at the letters.

Art. 1er—Le général Toussaint et le général Christophe sont mis hors la loi; et il est ordonné à tous les citoyens de leur courir sus, et de les traiter comme rebelles à la République française . . .

"What does it say?" Guerrier had ridden up beside him, with curious eyes—he remembered that Guiaou had been able to puzzle out certain proclamations during their journey on the Spanish side of the island.

Art. 1—General Toussaint and General Christophe are outlawed, and all citizens are ordered to pursue them, and to treat them as rebels against the French Republic . . .

To tease the letters into their words made Guiaou's head go spinning, and he saw nothing in those sentences of any importance to himself or to Guerrier.

"More lies of the *blancs*," he said with a smile; then, tossing the paper back into the wind, he urged his horse onward to follow Toussaint.

Tocquet had meant to go alone to Gonaives for salt. Despite the recent devastation, he guessed that the markets would be functioning at some level by this time, even on the ashes of the town. Or if not, he could go on to the salt pans themselves, farther south. It was that possible extension of the journey that made Tocquet assume that the women would all stay behind at Thibodet. An outing to Gonaives would no longer be the party of pleasure it might have been just a couple of weeks earlier, and on the roads farther south, who could know?—Rochambeau had claimed a wholesale victory over Toussaint at Ravine à Couleuvre, but the stories coming in from people that lived in that region were quite different. By all *those* accounts, Toussaint had got away with most of his army undamaged, and where that army was now, no one could say for sure.

But since their reunion on the day of that battle, Elise had not wanted to let him out of her sight, or as Tocquet sometimes thought, didn't want to let herself out of his sight. Ordinarily such attachment would have soon made him restless, but now for some intangible reason he found that he rather appreciated it. Maybe it was an effect of war. In any case, the mission for salt was Elise's idea from the start. It was Elise who had schemed for the pigs of Thibodet to be herded off into the jungle and hidden, by Caco and a cohort of children, from the French soldiers who'd settled all over the plantation like, as she put it, a plague of locusts. "They might have plundered Sancey for provisions," she said, "and if they were so profligate as to burn it instead, I don't see why we are obliged to feed them here."

Now that the French had marched off to the south, Elise had declared the hogs should be slaughtered—preserved meat would be easier to store and conceal than all that meat on the hoof. Tocquet would have dried all the pork on the *boucan,* but Elise held out for at least a few hams salted in the European way, and she wanted to sample the salt for herself. And Isabelle, who was bored and irritable since her Captain Daspir had marched off with the rest, insisted on coming along as well. So only Nanon remained behind to keep the children.

What pleasures Gonaives had once offered were now, as Tocquet had predicted, no more. The restaurant where he and Elise sometimes dined had burned down to its foundation, though eventually they did find the management serving meals from iron tripods on the waterfront, where the sea wind blew the clouds of ash away from the kettles and the clientele. In the center of Gonaives, a few gangs of soldiers and sailors worked slowly, feebly, at the reconstruction of the headquarters and a couple of other key buildings, amid swirls of ash that mingled with the dust. Isabelle and Elise had wound their heads and faces with long scarves, so that they resembled a pair of Bedouin bandits. Tocquet and Bazau and Gros-Jean each wore an extra *mouchwa* tied over his face, and by the time they'd succeeded in buying their salt, the cloth was black with ash around the nostrils.

The ash blew inland from the waterfront, and they could uncover their faces to eat. From the kettles they took bowls of *riz ak pwa,* plantain, and a little boiled fish with peppers, and ate sitting on low, rough-carpentered chairs made from green wood in the countryside. All of them fell to with frank appetite, even the women, Isabelle sorting bones from fish with her tongue as efficiently as any old black *grann* from the mountain. They had almost finished, and Tocquet was beginning to consider a cheroot and a short glass of rum, when the work gangs came pounding from the square toward the landing, dropping their implements as they ran.

Toussaint! The army of Toussaint is at the gate!

Bazau, his face empty, got up to calm a pack mule loaded with salt—the animal had begun to jerk its head against the tether, distressed by the sudden commotion. The women were staring at each other, more in surprise than in alarm. Now the armed contingent of soldiers began to come running up from the post, in the same disarray that the work gangs had been, though no one looked to be pursuing them.

Tocquet got up and dusted off his trouser seat and caught the arm of a corporal who was frantically hauling the line of a little shallop moored to the *embarcadère*. "What is it, friend?" he asked. "Is Toussaint here—did you see it with your own eyes?"

"Yes!" the corporal declared. "He has been on our heels from Saint Michel to here and all of his black devils with him."

"And all of them ravening to drink human blood?" Tocquet kept his tone neutral, but Bazau slumped into the side of the mule, to bury his laughter in the sacks of salt.

"Yes, and thousands of them," the corporal panted. "They have massacred Leclerc at Petite Rivière, down to the last man."

"Who told you so?" Tocquet said more sharply.

"It's on the wind." The corporal shot a quick look around their faces, then jumped down into the boat. All along the *embarcadère* his fellow soldiers were doing the same, in such a hasty confusion that several of the boats risked capsizing. On one of the warships moored farther out, a cannon coughed out a plume of smoke—a signal, maybe, as there was certainly no enemy in view.

The corporal looked up from the rocking shallop. "We are all lost if we don't get off this cursed island. Are those white women? They had better come too."

"Well, yes." Tocquet looked to Elise. "I think I mentioned that there might be trouble. You might best wait it out on one of the ships, while we see what it amounts to."

"Nonsense," Elise said. "I won't leave you so."

"Even if it is my bidding?"

"If I were so biddable, sir, I would never have come away with you in the beginning." Elise's color was up in her cheeks and her eyes were bright; she looked well, with the wind ruffling her hair. Tocquet turned from her and spat into the water, to signify an annoyance he didn't entirely feel. Then he looked at Isabelle.

"I won't," she said, before he could speak. "Nanon is alone at Thibodet and I won't leave her and I won't leave the children."

"You had rather die?"

"Yes." Isabelle stuck up her chin. "I had rather die if it comes to that."

"Well damn you both for a pair of donkeys!" Tocquet snapped. "I never saw such stubborn women." He looked toward the shallop but it had already pushed off, the men leaning into their oars as they pulled for the ships. A black-backed gull swooped down and knocked one of their abandoned bowls into the water and rose with a scrap of plantain in its beak.

"Come on then," Tocquet said. "Get yourselves mounted, if you won't hear reason, and we'll see what it is we have to face."

They saw no sign of Toussaint until they'd reached the Pont des Dattes, where they found his corps ranged on the other side. It was nothing like the horde that corporal had been gibbering about—Tocquet took in that much at first glance. Toussaint had only a light force of regular troops and cavalry, though still probably enough to overwhelm the little French garrison left at Gonaives. Behind the regulars waited some hundreds of wild-looking men from the mountains, many of them armed with muskets which looked very much like the ones Tocquet had recently brought in from Philadelphia.

"*Salut*, Governor, good day to you." Tocquet raised his hat two inches from his head and then replaced it. "You may advance with no fear if you like—the French have already taken to their boats."

"Have they done so?" Toussaint, sitting his white stallion, touched his hat brim lightly.

"Yes," said Tocquet. "The town is yours for the taking, though I can't say there's very much left to take."

"None of this ruin is my doing!" Toussaint said hotly. "I did not tell the Captain-General Leclerc to force his way on shore with cannon and sword. No more did I order General Rochambeau to slaughter all my garrison at Fort Liberté—"

"It is not our doing either." Isabelle unwound her scarf to reveal her face—her voice emerged sharp and clear. "We have lost much in this struggle ourselves, and seen our homes destroyed."

"Yes," said Toussaint with some impatience. "I know you, Madame Cigny—I am familiar with your losses."

Isabelle stopped, one hand on her throat, where she wore the key to her gutted house in Le Cap, along with her other amulet.

"Leclerc's men have burned my house as well," said Toussaint shortly. "There is next to nothing left of Habitation Sancey." His eyes shifted. "And you," he said. "Xavier Tocquet. How will you judge between me and the Captain-General?"

"I won't," said Tocquet, his voice quiet. "I do not judge such questions. We have known each other for a long time, Governor, and you know me as well as that."

"For the love of God!" Isabelle said. "We know you to have a compassionate heart, Governor—surely you mean no harm to this man, who is now our only protector."

"For a weak and helpless woman like yourself?" Toussaint covered his mouth with his hand.

"And what of my brother?" Elise, too, unwrapped her head, and shook her blond hair down on her shoulders. The spark of amusement left Toussaint's eyes, and it seemed to Tocquet that the black general sank more remotely into himself, as he turned his head rather stiffly toward her.

"He who has saved the lives and limbs of so many of your soldiers, Governor, and served you tirelessly for so many years. Where is he now, my brother?"

"Doctor Hébert was safe and well when I saw him last at Petite Rivière," Toussaint said. "It is my heartfelt wish he may continue so."

"Petite Rivière!" Isabelle hissed. "We have just heard that Leclerc and all his men were destroyed by your armies at Petite Rivière."

"Did you indeed?" Toussaint smiled on her openly. "Well, that may be. But if it has already happened, I have not been told of it."

He wiped away the smile, then glanced over his shoulder with a snap of his fingers. "Guiaou—Guerrier."

The two rode up quickly.

"Escort these people to Habitation Thibodet."

"Oui, mon général." Guiaou saluted.

"You will be seen safe home," Toussaint said, turning toward Tocquet.

"Accept our thanks," Tocquet said. He was sweating a little, in spite of the breeze. "And can we safely remain there?"

"That has become a difficult question," Toussaint said. "Though through no fault of mine. Recall: before the Captain-General landed, you might remain peacefully at home or travel wherever you would in the colony, without fear. But now . . . You might do better to go north."

"To Le Cap?" Isabelle put in.

"Yes, to Le Cap," Toussaint said, tightening his reins as Bel Argent began to sidestep. "But you must do it quickly."

Descahaux had been set to rights by the time Toussaint returned there in the late afternoon. The French soldiers had not much disrupted the place; possibly they had not realized it was one of his personal properties. Suzanne and the family always preferred the more comfortable situation of Sancey. There was nothing so very grand about the *grand'case* of Descahaux, though the house was well placed to catch the breezes and offered splendidly wide views of the mountains ranging behind each other on all sides. *Deyè mòn gegne mòn . . .* Toussaint came here for solitude, or sometimes, admittedly, for trysts.

He'd instructed Guiaou and Guerrier to scout further on the ways from Ennery to Marmelade, once they'd deposited the *blancs* at Thibodet, and at sunset they'd come back with the news that the road was open. The French general Desfourneaux occupied Plaisance. But Toussaint would only have to knock in a few French pickets to reach Marmelade from Ennery, and that would be his movement for the following day. Though he was happy to have frightened the French into their boats, it was against his strategy to reoccupy Gonaives so soon—bitter as it had been to lose the port. When all the French had been destroyed or driven from the island, he would rebuild Gonaives, but for now he'd draw his strength from the mountains.

I lift up my eyes unto the hills, whence cometh my hope. There was the Bible's answer to *Deyè mòn gegne mòn.* He rose from his caned chair and took a few steps to the gallery rail. Dusk settled into the long, deep valley; the mountains ranged away toward the horizon in blue-green shades of smoke. He turned and faced Gabart and Pourcely, who sat quietly in chairs on the opposite side of the gallery from the table where Toussaint's writing implements still lay. In the confusion he'd been separated from the most skilled of his secretaries: Riau, Pascal, Doctor Hébert, but there was a young *griffe* in Pourcely's command who wrote a fair script, and Toussaint had already dictated his order to Christophe, before the light began to fail. Christophe would rally the Second and Fifth Demibrigades and move north, raising men in the hills of Grand Boucan and Vallière and Sainte Suzanne and Port Français; in a few days' time he should be able to start insurrection on the Northern Plain, and possibly even threaten Le Cap.

But Toussaint was distracted by the thought of Tocquet and the two white women—why couldn't he leave them to look to themselves? Something about them continued to pick at him, though he bent his mind back to his tactics. Sylla was harassing Desfourneaux in the mountains of Plaisance, though Sylla's force was negligible, and Romain was fighting a similar campaign in the heights of Limbé—there were two old maroon leaders who'd kept their faith with Toussaint's army, unlike the *magouyè* traitors: Laplume, Lafortune, Lamour Dérance. If not for the treachery of those three, Dessalines would almost certainly have destroyed Port-au-Prince. Toussaint forced himself past his rage at their betrayals. To the matter at hand. From Marmelade he might drive Desfourneaux from Plaisance, or better yet, with Sylla's support, annihilate him altogether. Then he would press on through Gros Morne and finally, finally rejoin Maurepas and the Ninth, who'd been resisting so brilliantly on the northwest peninsula, according to the last Toussaint had heard. But that had been many days ago, and since then there were rumors that Maurepas had surrendered. Toussaint had feared that outcome since his communications with the northwest were broken by the loss of Gonaives, but he would not accept it. He needed Maurepas and the Ninth, for that was the force he'd bring back to surround Leclerc, once the Captain-General had been baited into concentrating his whole army on La Crête à Pierrot.

A warm scent of *callaloo* floated from the rear of the house across the gallery. Toussaint watched Pourcely and Gabart react, each man shifting his weight, recomposing himself, folding his hands across his stomach. At Descahaux lived one of those ancient incorruptible *granns* whom Toussaint trusted to prepare this dish for him—toothless, wizened as a wadded parchment, her bones as light and fragile as the hollow bones of a bird. Tonight he'd leave his usual regime of bread and water and with his officers enjoy the comfort of *callaloo*.

The two white women nagged at him, though—the suddenness with which they'd disclosed their faces from the dust-guard scarves, and Elise shaking out her yellow hair. What token had she given him?—the little painted pendant, whose portrait, now that he thought of it, much more resembled Isabelle Cigny than the blond Elise. There was a trace of the *racine* of Africa in that Madame Cigny, though so faint she might not know it herself. Tocquet had it too, along with a touch of the Indian, blood of the old *caciques*, and Tocquet almost certainly did know it. Toussaint felt no great indebtedness to Tocquet for the guns he had brought, knowing that he'd sell wherever there was profit. Tocquet was a pirate, descendant of pirates; he had no loyalty but to his own interests, but this was a quality which could be respected, once it had been understood. Though Toussaint rather liked Tocquet, he felt no special interest in his survival. There was something else. Quite suddenly he recollected the rumor that Isabelle Cigny had had a liaison with Joseph Flaville; it was even whispered that she had hidden herself in the mountains to bear his child, before Flaville was executed for his part in the Moyse rebellion.

Moyse again! He came at Toussaint from all sides. A drum was beating, in the direction of Thibodet, low in the valley. Moyse arose from the very same places where Toussaint liked to cache his own reserves. He flattened his hands on the gallery rail and looked out, believing he felt Moyse's spirit rising in that drumbeat, in the evening mist and the last calls of the doves under the eaves, and brightening with the stars above the mountains. Possibly the wandering of Moyse's disembodied soul could be more dangerous than Dessalines's spirit still acting in its body.

Toussaint was moved to cross himself. At once the idea returned to him, as if from an outside agent—*one must order the spiritual thing before the material thing can be ordered*. With that, the matter came clear to him, though it wasn't the flash of Elise's eye, or the proud toss of her head as her hair came down from the folds of the scarf. Toussaint's *amours* with white women had never really touched him in that way; he was moved toward them by curiosity rather than passion (much like his *blanche* partners, as he knew well enough). In the end, they were political encounters. No, but it was what Elise had said about her brother. And Toussaint had gíven her a somewhat false answer, for in fact the doctor was in quite a dangerous situation. Toussaint had left him in it because he would certainly be needed where he was—he could make himself quite useful, and at bottom he was willing to serve. The doctor was loyal to Toussaint as few *blancs* had ever been, but Toussaint could not guarantee his safety now—through no fault of his own, that much was true; without the violence of the Captain-General none of these other *blancs* would have had anything to fear.

He could not save the doctor now, but there was something he could do. Returning to the table, he lit the lamp, dipped his pen, wrote out a few quick lines, and signed below. He blew on the page and passed it over the flame of the lamp to make certain that the ink was well dry. Guiaou appeared on the gallery just as Toussaint was thinking of sending for him. He folded the paper and beckoned Guiaou within a whisper's range.

"Do you know that *blanche* at Thibodet, the woman of Tocquet?"

"*Oui, mon général.* I have just left her."

"Can you give her this letter when none of the other *blancs* will see?"

"But of course, *mon général.*" Guiaou slipped the paper inside of his shirt.

"Go now, if it is not too late." Toussaint masked a smile with his hand. "You need not return before morning." He knew Guiaou had a woman at Thibodet.

"It will be as you say, *mon général.*"

And Guiaou was gone. Toussaint, content, pushed back his chair. His mind was clear of the nagging thought, and tomorrow's actions seemed more evident to him now. Also he knew that the old *grann* was waiting to serve the *callaloo.*

"*Ann manjé,*" he said as he turned to Pourcely and Gabart. Let's eat.

Nanon and Paul were dressed to travel, as Elise was too; the ladies would not linger in *déshabillé* this morning. The weariness of it!—Elise's head felt leaden. It was too exhausting to leave Thibodet now, where the house was still intact, the fields still in some sort of order, though there'd been a considerable exodus of able-bodied men from the *atelier* since the most recent wave of disturbances had begun. Now that they'd been relieved of the French troops quartered on them, they might have enjoyed some days of peace here—but of course that was all a fantasy; Toussaint had said as much himself. There was nothing for it but to go back to Le Cap, and scrape what shelter they might out of those ashes.

She thought of Toussaint, astride the white charger at Pont des Dattes. It was only a picture in her mind, with no feeling attached to it, though it had a certain weight. Her thoughts divided, moved past the image, and rejoined. Tocquet was down at the stables, organizing horses and donkeys for their caravan, and Isabelle was packing her valises in the house. The children had breakfasted and then scattered. Only Nanon had retained Paul at the table, to compose his weekly letter to his father.

"But, Maman," the boy said, his ivory face disconsolate. "Is it not useless to write now? How shall we send it?"

A fair question, Elise thought. She would have been lost for an answer herself. She watched Paul fidget with his cup; half-finished *café au lait* gone scummy. Nanon should make him drink up that milk; it would be hard to come by at Le Cap, no doubt. Along with other privations and discomforts they could certainly expect. It made her queasier to look at that cup. But Paul was not resisting the letter out of sheer sloth, she imagined; it must certainly distress him to think of his absent father.

"Maybe we will give it to a bird," Nanon said, with a faint curve of her full lips. Her hands were folded demurely on the table's edge, and her head slightly bowed, so that she seemed to be looking at the point of Paul's chin. It was her habit, Elise knew, to avoid, almost imperceptibly, the eyes of white people.

"The *malfini* will find your father when he looks down from the top of the sky," Nanon said. "Or maybe we will give this letter to one of these little brown doves, who are so careful."

"But really, Maman," Paul said sulkily. "There is no bird who will carry a letter."

"*Kouté,*" Nanon said, listen. Her voice was still gentle, but she raised it enough to look her son full in the face. "To write to your father will put you in the same spirit with him, and even if we cannot send the paper, it may be that your thought will reach him still."

Paul glanced at Elise, though not so petulantly.

"Your mother is right," Elise said. She placed her fingers over her mouth for the moment it took her to swallow the sour bubble forming in her gullet. "Do as she says."

Paul nodded and picked up his pen. There was merit in Nanon's way of thinking of the thing, Elise considered. Between herself and Sans-Souci there'd been no letters, no exchange of tokens. There, the name had slipped out of its oubliette in the depths of her brain. Was he still alive at Grande Rivière? And if he were, what difference? No news, no word, no bird to carry messages. Quite likely she did not even wish that there were. She pushed the name back down where it had come from. Paul's quill scratched upon the paper. Someone was watching her, she felt, from beyond the pool below the gallery—from the lemon hedge that bounded the yard. But before she could make out who it was, Merbillay came striding onto the gallery, carrying the coffee tray, her head held high and her height exaggerated by the long striped kerchiefs that swept her hair up into a cone.

Queen of the kitchen that she was, Merbillay almost never served at table; her manner was a little too imperious for that. Merbillay had spent too much of her youth as a maroon ever to acquire the submissiveness one wanted in a house servant. Where was Zabeth? She must be readying the infants for this day of travel. In fact, Elise had set her to that task. Elise had not ordered any more coffee, and wanted none. Her first cup had seemed to disagree with her. But Merbillay tilted the hot black stream from the silver spout, bracing her free hand on the table. The edge of her palm pressed warmly, insistently, against Elise's hand.

Then somehow Merbillay's hand had completely covered Elise's with its warmth, but between their palms, there was some object: a folded paper. Elise looked up, meeting Merbillay's eyes, calm and inscrutable beneath the embroidered hem of her kerchief, and as their contact sundered she slipped the paper to her knee, beneath the table's edge. The letter was twice folded, but unsealed. At a rapid glance she could just make out the backward loop enclosing three dots which finished Toussaint's signature.

As Merbillay withdrew from the gallery, Elise smoothed the paper against her knee. The watcher now stepped clear of the hedge: Guiaou.

She had not recognized him at first, because he had put aside the honor guard uniform in which she had grown used to seeing him, and now stood shirtless in a pair of canvas trousers. Of course his ghastly scars made him unmistakable once he had stepped into the rapidly warming sunlight. And the morning was getting on, Elise thought abstractedly, and they should be setting out very soon, given the length of the road ahead. She nodded to Guiaou, who seemed to have been waiting for that, for at once he turned aside and slipped away through the nearest gap in the hedge.

But Riau had been here too, Elise realized. She had not consciously recognized him either, for he too had been out of uniform, but she certainly had seen him with Merbillay, last night or the night before. There was something for Isabelle to study, and maybe for Elise herself: the apparently effortless grace with which Merbillay could manage those two men.

She feigned a cough, raised her hand to her collarbone, and pushed the letter down into the space between her breasts. Paul was busy writing, and Nanon gave no sign. If she had seen, Elise felt sure, Nanon would say nothing.

26

At Port-au-Prince it was quiet enough for some days after Dessalines had been frightened away by all the men of Lamour Dérance and Lafortune and the *blanc* sailors who came out of the ships on the harbor, and after General Boudet came back from the ashes of Saint Marc with all the French *blanc* soldiers he had taken with him there. Quiet, yet I, Riau, could not rest easily, though there was no danger that I saw in those days. We did not see any fighting for a while though there was talk of it in other places. No one came to attack the town again, and Dessalines was supposed to have gone off through the mountains toward Mirebalais, killing any *blancs* he could find on the plantations because he was so angry at being shut out of Port-au-Prince a second time.

Yet when I lay down to sleep at night, my *ti bon ange* stayed trapped inside my head. It could not get out to wander in the world of dreams, but stayed between the bones of my skull beating its wings like a bird in a jar, while Riau's open eyes bored all night into the shadows under the roof of the *caserne*. In the daytime, after such a night, I walked as if a *loup-garou* had bitten a hole through my chest to suck all my insides out so the *loup-garou* could travel in my skin. Or maybe some enemy had hired a *bokor* to send his dead against me. If I had really believed so, I might have looked for a *hûngan* that I might pay to turn the curse away, but I did not know any *hûngan* near Port-au-Prince well enough to trust, and I did not really believe I had been attacked by a *bokor* anyway. I thought my trouble came from my own spirit, or from some spirit that I owed a service which I had not done, and the truth was that I knew well enough what kind of service it was.

At the same time it seemed to me that maybe I had been the good servant of these French *blanc* soldiers for too long. If I had not brought Lafortune and Lamour Dérance in from the plain, Dessalines could have burned Port-au-Prince when he came, and so weakened the power of the *blancs*. The *blancs* recognized the worth of what I had done for them. Maillart especially, for he understood that Dessalines would have put his head on a spear if he had been able to overrun the town that time, even though at other times he and Dessalines behaved as brother officers, especially when Toussaint was near. But the power the French *blanc* soldiers held began to worry me more and more. However much they declared that all our people would be free forever under their law, I did not like to see how they loaded Pierre Louis Diane and all his officers with chains and held them prisoner in the stinking bottoms of the hulks out in the harbor. Also I could not stop seeing the eyes of the general Pamphile de Lacroix when Paul Lafrance asked him so plainly if he and all the French *blanc* soldiers had not really come to bring back slavery? His eyes showed there was something hidden behind his answer even if he, Lacroix, did not like it. Maillart saw nothing of that, I thought. Maillart had an honest heart for a *blanc*, but he could blind himself without any effort to anything he did not want to see. Probably he had learned this skill from being the lover of such a *blanche* as Isabelle Cigny. Maillart hid no deception of Riau, but Captain Paltre and other officers who were friends of Paltre would smile behind their hands when they looked at me, and as my bad nights made me weaker, it seemed to me more and more that these *blancs* were the *loup-garou* that wanted to suck out all my blood and swallow my flesh and finally walk the world inside my skin.

All the *blanc* soldiers were planning a big battle where they would catch Toussaint at Petite Rivière, and make him their prisoner or kill him. That was where they all believed Toussaint had gone, after they chased him out of Gonaives. Leclerc, the little *blanc* general who stood above all the rest, had come down from Le Cap with a lot more men and was meaning to fight this battle himself. But I, Riau, I did not want to go to this battle at all. It was one thing to try to get out from under Toussaint's rules and laws, and another to fight against him face to face.

Then Jean-Pic had a quarrel with his woman, and he came into Port-au-Prince from the camp of Lamour Dérance on the plain to look for Riau. He did not tell me so very much about this quarrel, but it made him want to go north again for a while, which was our old country, where Jean-Pic and Riau had been maroons together long ago before the risings. I thought I had been too long among these *blancs* anyway and maybe it was a good thing to go north, at least as far as Thibodet.

So I found for Jean-Pic a uniform coat with only a few patches and those in the back, and a pair of trousers not too worn. He had brought his own horse with him from the plain. I could not get him any boots, because the *blancs* had not brought enough boots for themselves. Jean-Pic liked the look of boots, but he would not have liked to wear them for long. The hide of his feet was harder than boot leather from all the years he had been walking all over the country.

To leave Port-au-Prince all I needed to do was offer to take a message to the commander at Croix des Bouquets. But before we rode in that direction, I found Chancy. I told him I was going to Toussaint and would take a message to him, if Chancy wanted it so. Chancy was still a prisoner of these French *blanc* soldiers, though they had made the whole town his prison now instead of that dark *cachot* beneath the fort, and he was bound by his promise not to run away, but he could still write a letter, secretly, to tell Toussaint what had happened to him, I said. Chancy was happy with this thought, and he did write the letter and sealed it with wax, and then I hid it in the lining of my coat. I did not mean to go to Petite Rivière at all, where all the *blanc* soldiers were getting ready to bring their battle, but I thought that where the *blancs* expected they would find Toussaint would probably be the last place he would go.

At sundown Jean-Pic and I reached the post at Croix des Bouquets and left our message there. Then instead of returning to Port-au-Prince we rode on across the plain of Cul de Sac. It was dark by the time we began to climb Morne Cabrit, and the moon was new, and it rose late. Still the sky was clear and the stars so bright we could ride without fear of falling off the rocky trail. I looked at the stars and remembered the *blanc* doctor Hébert and how he had told me that the stars were named after the old spirits of his own country. He had told me some of those names, sometimes, though I did not remember them now. I wondered that night if he was looking up to see the same stars that I was, from some other place in the country. That night I did not feel the *loup-garou* eating away at my insides any more, and at dawn when we stopped to sleep under cover of the trees, I slept easily, and through most of the day.

I thought it was better to travel through the mountains, since the French *blanc* soldiers had taken all the coast from Port-au-Prince to Gonaives at least. Even in the mountains it seemed better to travel by night. After we crossed the Artibonite River we heard that Dessalines and *blanc* soldiers under Rochambeau were chasing each other all through the mountains of Grand Cahos, but we kept away from both of them and so came on a bright morning to Ennery and Thibodet.

Guiaou was not at Thibodet when I and Jean-Pic came there. Guiaou was away somewhere else, following Toussaint, so I went at once to stay in the *case* of Merbillay, as Guiaou would have done if he came when

Riau was not there. It seemed long since Riau had been with Merbillay. Between that morning and the noon meal we lay in the quiet cool of the *case*, because all the children had gone out, and I had sent Jean-Pic for Zabeth to find him a place to sleep somewhere, so Merbillay and I were alone. We spoke little in that time, and when I woke she had gone down to the *grand'case* to begin her cooking for the *blancs*. There was no sound but the buzzing of a wasp from a mud-daubed nest on the wall of the *case*, and outside the voices of children.

Caco was waiting for me outside the *case*, and so were Yoyo and Marielle. I kissed the little girls on their lips. They sat looking at me with big eyes in the shade of an *ajoupa* roof Caco had built out from the back door of Merbillay's *case*, and listened to Caco talk. Caco had a lot to tell, because he had been to that big battle at Ravine à Couleuvre, traveling with the doctor and his son Paul. He had not done any fighting himself but he had seen a lot of it, though Tocquet took him and Paul out of that place before it was all finished.

It was from Caco that I learned all of the news. There were not many men of fighting age left at Thibodet now, because they had all uncovered the muskets Toussaint had given them to hide and gone off to one battle or another, and there was not much work happening on the plantation, even though the *blancs* had come back to the *grand'case* when the fighting had finished at Ravine à Couleuvre and all around Gonaives. There was no one there to work but women and old men and children and these only worked their own provision grounds. There had been a lot of French *blanc* soldiers here too, Caco told me, with all of their officers staying in the *grand'case*, but they had all marched away south a couple of days before Riau and Jean-Pic came there.

In the weeks that I had been away, Caco had grown. I saw that he was big enough to be in the fighting himself, if it came to that. His eyes missed little, and he spoke with a good understanding of what his eyes saw. But I did not want him to go into the fighting. When I looked at Caco and his sisters, I only wished that the fighting would stop.

Zabeth found a place for Jean-Pic in the *ajoupa* where Michau stayed, not far from the *grand'case*. This Michau was a house servant who came down from Le Cap with all the *blancs* when the *blancs* had to run away from there. In the evening we all gathered by this *ajoupa* and Merbillay gave us food she had saved from what she had cooked for the *blancs* that night. There was a lot of *griot*, and other good things too. They had just killed pigs on Thibodet, which was where the *griot* came from, and Caco had a story to tell about how he had helped hide those pigs from the *blanc* soldiers when they were there. It was a good feast that we had that night, and afterward I went to the *case* with Merbillay and the children. I slept well through the night because I was tired from the fast traveling, even though I had slept part of that day.

In the morning I learned that Jean-Pic had plenty of sleeping room in that *ajoupa* because Michau, he thought, had slipped into the *grand'case* to stay with Zabeth. At that I remembered from the night before that Zabeth's eyes had seemed brighter, and her smile deeper, than at any time since Toussaint told Bouquart to shoot himself. I was glad for Zabeth then. I would have liked to stay another night in the *case* of Merbillay, but my service would not wait, and in the morning I went up the hill to find Quamba.

Though Quamba was a nearer friend to Guiaou than to Riau, sometimes he came when Riau was there with Merbillay. He would eat whatever there was and sit playing his bone flute in the darkness, and some of the children might sing and dance. But this time Quamba waited for Riau to come to him.

The *hûnfor* was on the point of a hill above Thibodet, and one could see a long way from it, even as far as Sancey, which was still smoking because the *blanc* soldiers had burned it for revenge against Toussaint. I stood beside the *kay mystè*, shading my eyes to look. I knew from Caco that the *blancs* had not burned Descahaux, which was another one of Toussaint's places further up the gorge, but I could not quite see Descahaux from where I stood.

It was cool still, because the sun had not long risen from the mountains, and the breeze still came across the hilltop, hard enough to snap the red flag on the long cane pole above the *kay mystè*. When I turned from looking at the smoke above Sancey, Quamba was waiting by the cross of Baron, with both his arms folded across his chest.

"I have come to make the service that we spoke of," I said to him.

Quamba did not move. "You don't give yourself much time," he said.

"No," I said. "But now the spirit will not let me rest."

Then Quamba opened his arms and smiled. *"Ba'm main'ou,"* he said. Give me your hand.

I took the hand that he held out and held it lightly as he held mine.

"Well," Quamba said, as he let it go. "We can begin."

Before Riau was stolen out of Guinée, I served the spirits of my family there, but I was only a small boy then, and afterward I remembered almost nothing of that service. At Bréda we were all made to follow the cross of Jesus, and even Toussaint—Toussaint most of all—pretended to serve Jesus only. After I ran away from Bréda, in those first days of my *marronage*, it was Achille, the *hûngan* among our band, who taught Riau to serve the *lwa*. In the years between that time and this one, I had gained some *konesans*, a knowledge of the sacred things. Since Merbillay had lived here at Thibodet, I had learned many things from Quamba, and the spirits gave me much through Quamba's hands. Quamba tore the leaves of Ayizan to hide my face and made the bath to clean my body and made the bed of *mombin* leaves for me to lie on. Quamba saw my *gros bon ange* go into the *govi*, and saw that *govi* touched by fire. From all this Riau rose up *hûnsi-canzo*, with Ogûn Ferraille the master of his head. But to take the *asson* there was more.

Again I lay on a bed of leaves, in the shadow of the *kay mystè*, till I no longer knew the rising or the setting of the sun. How many days it was I did not know for certain, but maybe it was less than all the nine, because with the *blancs* bringing war all over the country there were not so many days to spend. What happened through those days I will not tell. When it was finished, Quamba put the *asson* in my hand. I closed my fingers on its neck, and heard the bead strings clashing on the body of the gourd, but it was not my hand or Quamba's that moved so. It was the *lwa* that moved through me.

Then I would have gone back to Merbillay's *case,* to rest a little while beside her living flesh. But by the time Quamba raised me up, Guiaou had come, and Toussaint himself was not far off. Toussaint had returned to Ennery, and chased away the few *blanc* soldiers who had stayed there, and now he waited on the hill of Descahaux.

Now there was really not much time. We did not make a great assembly. Quamba and Riau prepared alone. There were no drummers and no dancing, but at dusk, after he had stretched a cloth from the door of the *kay mystè* toward the cross of Baron, Quamba sounded the drum himself, lightly, steadily, till Papa Loco came to him. With the *lwa* there came also some people in their bodies, Merbillay, Caco, Jean-Pic, Zabeth, Michau, and Guiaou himself. All these sat quietly on the one side of the cloth with Riau, their backs toward the hill of Descahaux. As we waited for it to begin, it seemed to me that Toussaint's eye was on us too, or that his spirit had let him know what we were doing. But that thought did not frighten me.

Quamba held the *asson,* with Loco on the other side of the cloth where we could not see him. He did so because, he told me, since it was Riau who had the questions, it was better for Quamba to bring the dead from beneath the waters this time.

Then we heard water gurgling from one jar to another, and a sound like the voice of a drowning man. But it was not Moyse who spoke. Bouquart was the first to come, and Zabeth was the first to speak to him.

"Who killed you, Bouquart?" Zabeth's voice was choked and shaking. "Who was it brought your death to you?"

Now, I knew the answer to that question, and Zabeth too—there was no mystery. After Moyse's rising was put down, Toussaint told Bouquart to step from the line and shoot himself, and he did so, and this Zabeth had seen with her own eyes, and Riau had seen it too, but maybe her grief was no sharper than mine. Bouquart was father of Zabeth's Bibiane. But it was I, Riau, who cut the iron from Bouquart's legs when we came out of Bahoruco together here to Thibodet, and his freedom was the work of my own hands.

Sé blan yo ki té touyé moin, Bouquart's voice croaked. It was the whites who killed me.

Zabeth wept. Michau held her head against his chest, till all his shirt was wet with her tears. Merbillay and Guiaou stroked the fingers down her back, and Caco held her hand. Bouquart's answer seemed strange to me. Yet I saw how this answer freed Zabeth from her hatred of Toussaint. Now she could give her hatred to the *blancs*, who had no faces. And the sense was this—it was the *blanc* slavemasters who stood behind Toussaint and moved his hands to make those actions. That was the reason Moyse made the rising at that time.

Then Bouquart went into the *govi*, and his voice stopped. Now it was dark, and the stars were coming, and I, Riau, felt the whirl in my head I knew through the days I had spent lying on the leaves with my face turned up to the emptying sky. But I held on to my own head now, till everything came steady. Moyse was the next to come. I could not mistake his voice, though his throat was full of water.

"Ki moun ki té touyé w, Moyse?" I said, and heard the choking in the sounds I made. Moyse, who killed you? Riau, Riau, might be his answer. Because although it was Toussaint who gave the order that Moyse be shot, Riau's hands had worked in that affair. Riau's voice loosed Guiaou to betray Moyse's rising to Toussaint. If Moyse accused me, he would be just, though I never let myself know it before now.

Moin-même, said Moyse. *I killed myself. Toussaint gave me time to run away, but I would not go. And when I came before the firing squad, it was I myself who told the men to fire.*

I thought of it. These things were true. I had been there myself at Port-de-Paix, and heard Moyse's voice give the order to the men who shot him. But I did not think that was the whole truth of his death, and Moyse had cursed Toussaint, also, before he died.

A different spirit is with Toussaint now, Moyse said, although I had not asked the question. I did not quite know how to ask it. But Moyse was ready with his answer just the same. *You have seen how hard Toussaint has turned against the blancs,* he said. *And these soldiers in the ships have surely come to bring back slavery, no matter what they say. If you would keep your freedom, follow Toussaint.*

Moyse went into his *govi* then, and I knew that my own face was all wet with tears, though I had never felt them begin. I was shivering too, like the leaves of the high palms that shivered in the wind above the *hûnfor,* but after a little time it stopped.

There were more dead who stood behind Moyse, a great many more. Quamba had not called them but still they came. Most of them were men who'd died in Moyse's last rising. They kept on coming for a long time, and in the end Quamba did not have jars enough to hold them.

My horse was well rested after all that time I spent lying in the *hûnfor.* Caco had kept him fed and watered, and brushed his coat to a red gleam. Caco had ridden him a little too, though he did not think I knew it, and he had not ridden him too far or too hard.

The morning after that night when Moyse spoke, I rode to Descahaux. There was some chance that Toussaint might order me shot, I was thinking, while my horse climbed up the path. Twice before I had run away from Toussaint's army, and shooting was the punishment for that. It was Moyse who received me back the second time when I returned, and as I went riding to Descahaux, I heard an echo of his voice in my head. Toussaint would not shoot a good officer now, said that drowned voice of Moyse, when there was war with so many *blancs,* and so many of his men were getting killed in battle.

Also I had the letter of Chancy to give Toussaint. As I had hoped, this letter told how Riau had helped Chancy to get out of his *cachot* where he was waiting to be shot in Port-au-Prince. And beyond that I thought it was not likely Toussaint could know that Riau had been the one to bring Lamour Dérance and Lafortune to the side of the French *blanc* soldiers, to attack that column of the Eighth and frighten Dessalines away. Toussaint might only believe that I had been held by the *blancs* there in Port-au-Prince, the same way that Chancy was held.

Toussaint asked me many questions after I had read this letter, and I answered him—that I had not been able to take his message to Laplume in time, before Laplume had sold himself to the *blancs* after all. I told him how I came to Dessalines before Saint Marc was burned. I told him a little of the fighting I had seen at Port-au-Prince, and how the cannons of the ships blew up the forts. I told him how Major Maillart seemed to fall in with the *blancs* who had just come, since after all he was himself a French *blanc* soldier. Then Toussaint asked me more questions about the French *blancs* I had seen, the quality of their officers and the number of their men. Each one of these questions I answered truly, and any lies I gave to him were hidden underneath the things I did not say.

All this talk did not last so very long, because Toussaint was hurrying to go to Marmelade. When the talk was done, he gave me his long jagged smile and hid it quickly with his hand. Then he told me he would name me to his honor guard. Guiaou was standing by him all this time, and at Toussaint's word Guiaou stepped forward to give Riau a guard's uniform, with the silver helmet. These things not long ago belonged to a man who had been killed at Ravine à Couleuvre, but what his name was I never knew. There was a hole in the front of the coat and a bigger hole at the back. The cloth had been washed and scrubbed so only a few brown spots remained, but the holes had not yet been mended.

I bowed to Toussaint to show the honor that I felt. In Toussaint's guard, Riau would keep his rank of Captain.

Then I took the coat back down to Thibodet. Merbillay smiled as she sewed up the holes, because now both her men belonged to Toussaint's guard, and that to her was a great thing. It did not take her long to finish and it was not yet noon when I was ready to go and join Toussaint. All the children looked at me round-eyed when I set the silver helmet on my head. I picked up each one of them to kiss, even Caco, though Caco had grown heavy to lift. Maybe if I saw him again, I could not lift him.

Jean-Pic met me at the gate of Thibodet, and he smiled very wide in his beard when he saw my honor guard uniform and helmet. We rode together to join Toussaint. His men were already on the road, but there were not so many. From Guiaou and Guerrier I learned that he had left most of his guard, especially the horsemen under Monpoint and Morisset, to protect the fort at La Crête à Pierrot. He had still some companies of the guard footsoldiers, and some companies of the Fourth commanded by Gabart, but it did not seem a lot of men to fight these French *blanc* soldiers. I remembered how they had gone over the wall of the fort of Léogane like ants and how they were not stopped any more than ants by how many of them were crushed. But we did not meet so many on the road to Marmelade, and those we did meet ran away soon. They looked surprised and frightened to see us come, as if they had not expected us at all.

So Toussaint took Marmelade without much fighting, and made his headquarters there as he had been used to do for a long time. That night to Marmelade there came a letter from Dessalines that told how he had fought a battle with Rochambeau in the mountains of Grand Cahos and that there was a lot of fighting around the fort of La Crête à Pierrot. So maybe the French *blanc* soldiers had all gone south, or most of them. But that same night we learned that there were more *blanc* soldiers at Plaisance and that probably we would have a fight with them next day.

Before the sun came up next morning, Toussaint sent men out to take the next fort on the road to Plaisance, which stood on a hill of Habitation Bidourete. There were two companies under Gabart and another two under Lafontaine, and I, Riau, went with them, though most of the guard stayed back, under command of Pourcely, because Toussaint wanted to keep them fresh for fighting later in the day. There were not many *blanc* soldiers in that fort, though they were stubborn, and by sunrise we had killed many and driven off the rest. More soldiers came to try to help them, but still there were not too many, and we killed some and drove away the others. But by the time Toussaint had come up with Pourcely and the rest of our men, news had come that the *blanc* general Desfourneaux was on his way from Plaisance, leading fifteen hundred men.

Then Toussaint divided the men he had in two. Half went with Toussaint and Gabart in a column to the right, from Habitation Bidourete toward Habitation Laforestie. These were all men of the Fourth that they led. The others, the men of the honor guard, were sent to the left, led by Pourcely. But Toussaint sent Riau ahead of them all, up onto the mountain above Plaisance, to look for Sylla, who was supposed to be fighting the *blancs* somewhere in those hills, and try to bring his men to our battle.

I got Toussaint's leave to take Jean-Pic with me, and we rode very fast together across the fields of Habitation Bidourete and Habitation Laforestie, cutting through gaps in the hedges or jumping the hedges when there were no gaps. Toussaint had sent Pourcely by the back roads to come upon Desfourneaux from behind. But Jean-Pic and Riau were coming in front of the French *blanc* soldiers. When we crossed Habitation Laforestie, we began to hear their drums as they came on, though they were not yet in sight of us.

So we came safely as far as the path that climbed the eastern wall of the mountain. It was steep, and we needed to let our horses go slowly at first, because they were already hot from the gallop across the fields. If we stopped we could look down and see the *blanc* soldiers moving quickly across the low ground to the rattling of their drums. Beyond them was the Plaisance river valley like a wide deep bowl, with the green of trees and blue of the mountain mist wrapped around each other like veins in stone. Some of those *blanc* soldiers saw us too. There were puffs of musket smoke from their column, and a moment later the sound of their shots. But we were too high on the mountain for their muskets to reach us.

Soon we met watchmen of Sylla on the mountain, and they were in a big hurry to get us off the trail. More *blancs* were coming that way, they said, though we could not yet see them. Our horses did not want to leave the trail, and Jean-Pic had to get down and drag his along by the reins, with one of Sylla's men following and pushing it from behind. But I stayed mounted, leaning forward, my weight all the way forward and low and my face pushed tight into the horse's mane. I had learned this way of riding from Toussaint, and though my horse's hooves slipped in the shale, the horse kept climbing, till finally we came into a flatter place in a notch of the mountain, where there was a stand of old *acajou*.

Sylla was waiting, between those old trees, but he did not have many of his men with him there. He had sent for them when he saw what was going to happen in the valley, but they were far off, on the other side of the mountain, where they could ambush supply trains on the road between Limbé and Gonaives. Until more men came there was nothing we could do but watch what happened from where we were. Sylla had a long-seeing glass, which he passed around among us, but I could see well enough without the glass, and voices carried a long way in those hills.

The shooting had already started by the time we got our horses hidden in the *acajou*. The *blanc* general Desfourneaux had a lot more regular soldiers than Toussaint did, though it was hard to know just how many men of the hoe had joined Toussaint with their hidden muskets, on the way from Ennery and Marmelade. Toussaint was much outnumbered, that was plain, and even so he had divided his men in half.

Yet when the fighting started on the right, Toussaint and Gabart broke the French advance and drove them back. Those French *blanc* soldiers had to retreat, but they kept tight in their lines and squares. Even when Toussaint sent a charge of horsemen on them, he could not break them up. These were tough soldiers. But if Pourcely's men came upon them from behind as they were falling back, I saw they would be in a bad place—Toussaint might wipe them all out then, and that was the way he had planned it.

I was watching, with my heart swollen high in my throat, to see the men Pourcely was leading come out of the woods on the left. But Pourcely was a man of Jean Rabel, on the northwest coast, and he did not know his way very well through the Plaisance valley or these mountains. He got all his men lost in the bush somehow, and that is why they never came where they were meant to be. Instead, Desfourneaux's *blanc* soldiers began to work their way around to Toussaint's left, because Pourcely was not there to stop them, and soon those *blanc* soldiers began to get up on the trail that Jean-Pic and I had just ridden across a little while before.

Then Toussaint must have understood what was happening, because he took his horsemen and a lot of Gabart's foot soldiers across to the left. We could see well enough it was Toussaint, because of the one red feather set high above the white feathers in his hat, though he was riding a different horse today, not Bel Argent. The French *blanc* soldiers were getting ready to meet him on the trail, not far below where we were watching from the grove of *acajou*. There were black soldiers in the front of their line, and they were near enough for me to see that they wore uniforms of the Ninth Demibrigade, the soldiers from Port-de-Paix.

That meant that Maurepas must have surrendered, or been killed or captured by the *blancs*. That would be very bad news for Toussaint, because he had set a lot of his hopes on joining with Maurepas. But I did not have much time to think about this much before Toussaint himself came riding around a bend of the trail below.

Now I did take the glass from Sylla's hand, to see if Maurepas was among the men of the Ninth who were with the *blancs* now, but if he was I did not see him. It looked like the man leading the Ninth was Lubin Golart, who had been commander of the Fourth Battalion of the Ninth for a long time. Golart had always been against Toussaint, since the war against Rigaud or even before. He was leading his old battalion now at the head of the French *blanc* soldiers, but there were a lot more men of the Ninth with him now than just that one battalion.

Toussaint came around the bend of the road with a lot of his horsemen around him, but when he saw the uniforms of the black soldiers, he rode on to meet them all alone. Golart gave the order to fire, but the men of the Ninth did not obey, not even the men of the Fourth Battalion. Though Toussaint rode within twenty-five paces of the line, those soldiers did not fire. Golart screamed at them till foam from his mouth ran down his chin. Golart was crazy as a mad dog then. He had tried to kill

Toussaint in a hundred different ways before, and now Toussaint was so close his men could almost touch him with their musket barrels and still they did not fire. I wondered why Golart did not shoot his own gun at Toussaint, but at that moment Toussaint's spirit was too strong for him.

"Soldiers of the Ninth!" Toussaint's voice was so loud and large we could all hear it plainly where we were hidden in that *acajou*. *"Will you dare to fire upon your general and your brothers? Only the* blancs *are our enemy!"*

And maybe Golart was an enemy too, I thought. It was a new thing for Toussaint to speak so boldly against the *blancs*. He had not been saying that before these French ships and soldiers came. But the men of the Ninth all lowered their muskets and began to shout, *Vive le Gouverneur! Vive le Gouverneur!* It even seemed that some of them were weeping. I thought that the Ninth was all going to come over to Toussaint's side again then, and Desfourneaux's soldiers would be wiped out after all. *Long live the Governor!* all of them were crying. But all at once the French *blanc* soldiers began to shoot down the men of the Ninth from where they stood behind them. Those soldiers of the Ninth were all confused when the bullets came from behind that way, and a lot of them were killed in the first firing, and the rest were scattered, down the hill and among the trees.

Then there was nothing to stop the French *blanc* soldiers from shooting straight at Toussaint and his men. The ground was all against Toussaint. The *blancs* were on the high ground here, and could shoot from cover of the rocks and all the tight bends of the trail, the way Toussaint had taught all of us to do, but it seemed these *blanc* soldiers understood how to do it too. These were the toughest *blanc* soldiers I had seen.

Jean-Pic had taken out his pistol, but Sylla stopped him with a hand on top of his arm. Sylla's men had not yet come from the other side of the mountain, and there was nothing our few shots could do, except to tell those *blancs* where we were hidden. We watched then, and did nothing more. I, Riau, had seen a lot of battles, but this one was very bloody. I did not see how Toussaint was going to live, among all those bullets falling on his people like a rainstorm. I saw a bullet strike a captain of dragoons who rode beside Toussaint, and Toussaint caught him out of the saddle, and carried him away on his own horse. The horseman passed through the line of foot soldiers Toussaint had brought, and that line held a little while before the French *blanc* soldiers pushed it back.

What I could not see from where I stood, I found out later from Guiaou and Guerrier. That night, with the darkness to hide us, Jean-Pic and I found our way back to Toussaint again. By then he had given up the fort at Bidourete to the *blancs*, and was getting ready to go south, with Pourcely's men, who had missed most of the fighting, and what was left of the men under Gabart. Toussaint was going to lead them south next day, back along the way we had come. I did not speak to him that night, though I watched him from a little distance, sitting by the fire. Toussaint was always made sad by any deaths among his soldiers, but tonight he seemed more angry, at Golart and the men of the Ninth who had turned against him, and at Pourcely for leading his men to get lost, though he tried to swallow his anger at Pourcely. With all that, Toussaint did not seem so much discouraged yet.

Another messenger had come from Dessalines that day, and Guiaou had seen him shot off his horse just as he rode up to Toussaint. That had been when Desfourneaux's soldiers were still attacking hard. Toussaint carried that messenger off too, though he was wounded to his death, and he bled all down the front of Toussaint's coat. But the message was in writing and it told we were not beaten yet. All our men were fighting still, around La Crête à Pierrot.

27

Michel Arnaud came abreast of his cane mill and paused for a moment to stare at the idle building. A little brown wren had nested under the eaves; she put her head out and turned the black bead of her eye toward him, then withdrew, into the cobwebbed shadows. Arnaud shrugged and walked on, depending a little more on the stick he carried in his left hand as the trail grew narrower and the ground more uncertain. He'd only sprained his ankle in the disastrous fall that had destroyed his horse— not broken it, which was a bit of good luck. In these last days the swelling had almost completely receded, thanks to the hot soaks that Cléo and Claudine forced him to endure morning, noon, and night, but the joint was still weak and he must go carefully. He did not heal as fast as he had done when he was younger.

In his right hand he held an unsheathed *coutelas*, and as he progressed toward his distillery he swiped at the brush overgrowing the trail. Most branches only bent from the dull blade, springing back into place after he had passed. What did it matter? The effort made him sweat, though it was still early morning. He stopped for a moment to rest and listen, but heard only birdsong, and the drone of children reciting some lesson for Claudine in the school beside the chapel. No drums, no shots, no war cries. He went on.

The area around the vats was suffused with the sour smell of fermenting cane. Half his crop was fermenting in the field at this point, but here at least there was some profit in it. The chief refiner touched his forehead in greeting as Arnaud limped toward the coils. He'd shifted his talents to distilling rum because they no longer had labor enough to make sugar. The fields were as empty as the mill. From an *atelier* of many hundreds, barely two dozen adult men remained, and many of those were halt, lacking a hand or a leg or an arm . . . In the old days, Arnaud had practiced amputation, as a punishment for runaways, or thieves sometimes. Many of those men stayed by him now; he fed them, and they worked as they could.

As for the rest—they'd abandoned the mills and the fields, if not the plantation altogether. Arnaud was confident that a good many of his erstwhile mill and field hands were still living on the place, getting their sustenance from its provision grounds, or at any rate were frequent visitors. Many had uncached their muskets and gone off to join Toussaint, or some other leader, in fighting Leclerc's army. In the *mornes* above Limbé, whose green rising Arnaud could see from where he stood beside the coils, Romain led a quasi-maroon insurgency against the French.

And be damned to the French! Arnaud snapped mentally—as resentfully as if he were not French himself. But he was Creole, and more and more these new arrivals struck him as invaders, and it was a bungled invasion at that. He might have shared this complaint with Bertrand Cigny, except that Cigny was dead. They'd got the news a few days earlier, from an exhausted squadron of Leclerc's cavalry, the men drooping in the saddle from fatigue and slow fever. They'd come with a wagon to purchase rum for the troops, and had with them Isidor, Arnaud's old houseman who'd disappeared a decade before, in the midst of the risings of ninety-one. They brought the news of Cigny's death but not his body, though they'd seen it by the scorched wreck of Cigny's house at Haut de Trou, impaled, disemboweled, the genitals cut off and stuffed into the bearded mouth . . .

Arnaud thrust the point of his *coutelas* in the ground, took up a clay cup from a flat stone beside the blade, and held it under the coil, interrupting the drip into the barrel. He rinsed his mouth with the oily white rum and swallowed. The refiner watched him carefully. Arnaud nodded as the thread of warmth worked through him. The rum was good. And *Grâce, la miséricorde*, for poor Bertrand Cigny. Arnaud shook the last drops onto the ground and replaced the clay cup on the stone. Lord, have mercy . . . Though Arnaud had never been remotely devout, he sometimes caught himself muttering prayers unconsciously, as if Claudine's religious mania had infected him. What happened to Cigny might have happened to anyone. Might still. There were not enough of the French troops to occupy the ground they had ostensibly reconquered, and so for planters on their land there was no security at all, except, in Arnaud's case, for whatever safety might derive from the peculiar prestige of his

wife among the people that surrounded them. Since they'd fled the
smoking ruin of Le Cap, there'd been much pilferage on the borders of
Habitation Arnaud; their fruit was stolen, their pigs and goats were
driven off, but no one had attacked the house, and there had been no
burning.

For no reason at all, his heart began to pound, and his palms and temple broke out in a cold, itching sweat. He had these attacks quite often
now, though usually at night, when he must turn to his wife's mute comfort, for Claudine woke by some instinct whenever one of Arnaud's ter-
rors began. By day it was worse—one could not wait for daylight; there
was no term to the terror and nothing to expect. He would have liked to
drink more rum, but he knew it would not help. The refiner was still
watching him, besides. Over the rush of his blood and the drum of his
heartbeat, he heard the creak of wagon wheels, a single wagon coming
to a halt in the ruts beyond the crusher and the vats of mash. His cane-
cutting crew—such as it was. One of the men unhitched the mule from
the wagon and led it to the crusher's turning pole. Another, whose right
arm ended in a stump, began to load cane stalks into the chute, using his
left arm to gather the cane from the wagon into the crook of his right
elbow.

Arnaud lent his own arms to the task. The wagon driver clucked to the
mule, and the reddish iron cylinders of the crusher began slowly to turn.
Arnaud kept pulling cane from the wagon, careless of the blade-like
leaves that slit his arms, and pushing it into the chute, leaving it to the
amputee to guide the stalks into the crusher's teeth. He could not now
recall if the man had lost his hand to a punishment or some cane mill
accident—he seemed to bear Arnaud no resentment, either way. In the
old days Arnaud would never have put a hand to such work, not if he
were the last man standing on his plantation. But now the physical effort
pulled his mind out of its screaming spirals. His heartbeat leveled, and
his sweat turned honestly warm. Now he could better understand what
had moved Claudine to carry water to the field hands, under the noonday sun. Though recently she'd given up this practice, since there was no
one in the fields.

At noon, Arnaud helped the refiner seal a head on a filled cask, then
dismissed the men for a siesta. He took up his stick and the *coutelas*,
ringing the flat of the blade against the iron rim of the rum keg. There
was some reasonable profit there, though nothing like what white sugar
would have brought. But soldiering was thirsty work, and the military
wagons did come steadily.

Beside the chapel, the school lean-to was empty, the children scattered to some other shade. In the shadows of the open chapel, Moustique
stood muttering half audibly, before the altar shelf, which was draped in
black. About Moustique's skinny, stooping shoulders was draped the
stole which Claudine had clumsily embroidered for him. He chanted for

the soul of Bertrand Cigny. Claudine had set him to this work, thrice daily, for some period of days—a funeral rite without a corpse. It was strange how little the boy resembled his father, the Père Bonne-chance, who had been burly, low to the ground, strong-built as a badger or a little black bear. Père Bonne-chance had once saved Arnaud's life, inveigling him out of the hands of rebel slaves who certainly would have killed him. Later on, the priest had been executed for collaboration, and nothing Arnaud tried could stop it. *Grâce, grâce, la miséricorde* . . . If there was any truth to religion, Père Bonne-chance was with the martyrs. Arnaud got no comfort from praying for himself.

Moustique was looking at him now, since Arnaud had drifted to a halt before the chapel. There had always been someone looking at him—no corner of this country was without at least one pair of watchful human eyes—but until recently he had never noticed it. He nodded, blinking sweat out of his eyes, and as he was facing the shrouded altar, he fumbled the sign of the cross before he turned away. A trio of speckled hens scattered from his feet in the dust as he walked on toward the *grand'case*.

Isidor and Cléo sat on the gallery, much at their ease, as if they were the masters there. Claudine was nowhere in view. Arnaud looked up, above the roof tree, and saw her step up to the cleft in the rock where he'd cached his weapons of last resort, that watch post. It was where she often went at noontime now—against all persuasion she must make that climb in the fiercest blaze of the day's heat. Rail-thin she stood, arms hanging slack, her garment fluttering from her bones in the breeze that combed the height. She was looking toward the mountains of Limbé.

Arnaud lowered his head and walked on. In some way he would have liked to join her. But even the lesser climb to the *grand'case* seemed to wind him. He limped up the steps, his stick's tip booming on the boards, and dropped into a low wooden chair such as market women used to squat above their wares. He closed his eyes, and presently felt a cool pressure against his temples—Cléo's fingertips, dampened in the glass of water she had brought to him unbidden. He was too hot, she murmured. The cool fingertips pressed dispassionately on the insides of his wrists and then released, and he heard her long skirt swishing away across the floor. He sipped at the water, set down the glass. He had slept poorly. For so long he had been indifferent to any danger. Hazard might move him to anger but not fear. Now that indifference had all worn away, leaving him exposed and raw. If the wind stirred the palm leaves, he was startled. But the breeze had died, and for the moment it was utterly calm. He settled his weight in the chair and dozed.

Tocquet had rushed them out of Thibodet before dawn; at daybreak they were passing through the drowsy *bourg* of Ennery. By the time the sun had fully risen, they were mounting the south slopes of Pilboreau. Tocquet would not let them dismount at the market on the height, though both Sophie and Isabelle complained with some sharpness. He only bought them all warm cassavas they could munch in the saddle as they rode on.

Never had Nanon seen Tocquet show such an obvious tension. She was accustomed to his lazy, cat-like confidence. Now he more resembled a cat that knows itself pursued by some more dangerous hunter. He rode in silence at the head of their line, watching, watching, ceaselessly scanning the trees and rocks either side of the trail, down the long descent and the deeper distances of the Plaisance river valley. Gros-Jean and Bazau, bringing up the rear, had none of their usual joviality, but were as grim and silent and watchful.

In this atmosphere, the conversation Isabelle and Elise attempted soon expired. The children were also uncharacteristically subdued. Paul especially, Nanon thought. He had been moody for nearly two weeks, ever since the battle which parted him from his father. Was she wrong, Nanon wondered, to urge him to write letters which could not be sent? Her conviction was that this exercise would not only keep the doctor alive in Paul's mind, but also somehow protect his life in reality. This much she believed, though she could not have said why. But whether it helped Paul, in the short run, was more doubtful.

She watched the boy, riding his donkey—he was pale and drawn, his ivory skin bloodless, his mouth a thin line. Robert too was silent and watchful. Of course he had witnessed the destruction of Le Cap, to which they were now supposed to return. Gabriel and François were too small to understand what was happening, and Isabelle's Héloïse probably was too, but of the three older children only Sophie retained her usual belligerent energy. There was no foolishness of straying from the road this time, as there had been on their flight south from Thibodet— not that Tocquet would have allowed it now. Of course, that was how Saint-Jean had been lost, and Paul would not have forgotten that, though certainly he'd be missing Caco more. Caco was his closest friend, but he had stayed behind at Thibodet.

Nanon watched Tocquet as she rode, following the movements of his head, letting her eyes linger where it seemed to her that his did. In this way she was able to pick out a band of armed men, all black and ragged as maroons, slipping through the trees a half a mile below the road. From the direction that they moved in came a muted sound of gunfire, so faint in the distance it could barely be distinguished. Tocquet made no remark on what he'd seen, though Bazau muttered something to Gros-Jean. Nanon kept silent. If Elise or Isabelle or the children noticed anything they did not say so.

Gabriel and François rode in straw panniers slung to either side of Nanon's donkey, which she sat sidesaddle in the country manner. François traveled quietly, looking all around with large eyes, while Gabriel kept trying to climb out, for the first hour or more of the journey.

Yet after all François was the first to grow pettish, whimpering loudly enough to draw Tocquet's reproving glance. Nanon gave him lumps of raw sugar to quiet him, and rather envied Zabeth—the infants in her charge were small enough to nurse to sleep, awkward as it might be to nurse them while balancing on a donkey.

In the early afternoon they reached the *bourg* of Plaisance, which seemed almost deserted, though a handful of French grenadiers watched the crossroads. From the soldiers they heard that General Desfourneaux had marched most of the troops out of town that morning, to confront a black army led in person, it was said, by Toussaint Louverture. Tocquet would not let them stop longer than the time it took to water their horses—and for Zabeth to change the babies by the well side; the glance Zabeth gave him set him a pace back. Elise approached him then, and argued in a low tone that they might very well stay here for a time, to let the children stretch their legs from the saddle, and when Tocquet pointed irritably at the sun, Elise suggested they might even stay the night, since the French soldiers would certainly have returned to Plaisance by then.

"They are not guaranteed to return victorious," Tocquet said shortly, and Elise fell silent. They rode on.

At a fork in the road above Limbé they found four black women with bunches of bananas on offer, and a little way from them two colored women sat on the ground, eating bananas in the shade of a *flamboyante*. The younger woman quickly got to her feet as they approached, and Paul brightened when she called his name. It was Paulette, with her mother, Fontelle.

Nanon found herself looking all around for the doctor, for surely he must be here with them somewhere—she knew Tocquet had left them together when he brought Paul home from Ravine à Couleuvre. But the doctor was nowhere to be found. He'd been safe at Petite Rivière when they last saw him, Fontelle said, and had charged her to give Nanon that word. She and Paulette had meant to bring their news to Thibodet, but Toussaint was threatening Gonaives when they came there, so when he withdrew they had decided to press on their way north—they hoped to reach Habitation Arnaud before night.

"But Antoine," Nanon blurted. "Why did you leave him?"

"He preferred to stay," Fontelle said, though not quite meeting Nanon's eyes. "He would not abandon all those wounded soldiers. But Bienvenu was always with him—and Toussaint would never let him come to harm."

Nanon's heart constricted. Fontelle knew something that she did not want to say. And Toussaint was not protecting anyone at Petite Rivière today, if he was engaged in battle with Desfourneaux on the way to Marmelade . . . But Nanon swallowed the rest of her questions. Paulette was walking the rim of the ravine beside the road, one arm draped over

Paul's shoulder, and whispering in his ear. Whatever she might know, Nanon could tell from his expression that she was not saying anything to upset him, and it would be better to leave it so.

Fontelle and Paulette rode on with the rest of them, but after the first excitement of their meeting, the pall seemed to deepen over them all. There was no talk. Tocquet wanted none, and his mood prevailed. Behind them a cloud bank had shut off the sun, dark rain clouds lowering on the heights of Limbé. Some part of the tension certainly came from the sullen charge of the air before rain. But instead of a downpour it was men who flowed around them with no warning—wild-looking men, though some wore shreds of uniform—they seemed to come from all directions, and pressed upon the riders from all sides. One of them snatched the bridle of Tocquet's horse, but Tocquet knocked his arm away with the barrel of a long dragoon pistol that had suddenly appeared in his hand. He must have been waiting for his death all day, Nanon understood in a rush of recognition, scanning all points of the horizon to see from what quarter it would appear. Bazau and Gros-Jean had drawn their weapons too; Michau, the porter, had only a knife. They were four men against more than fifty.

"Romain! Romain!" Elise was shouting as she rode down toward Tocquet. She had the quirk of riding in trousers, astride like a man, and with something of a man's authority; she guided her mare with her left hand, while with her right she tore a paper out of her blouse and flagged it high above her head.

"*Mwen rélé Romain!*" she said. "Where is Romain?"

"*M'la,*" pronounced a guttural voice. I am here.

The man who spoke was heavy-set, with a long torso and short legs, and heavily bearded. The matted hair of his head and beard was all teased into little russet points. He wore the rags of a colonel's coat, and looked up at Elise with yellowish eyes.

"You are Romain?" she panted. "Read this."

Romain took the paper from her hand, as if reluctantly, not shifting his eyes from her at first. Tocquet's horse shied sideways, hooves skidding on the road as the hindquarters bunched. He pointed his pistol toward the sky as he reined the horse up. Romain now began to read, quite slowly, following the lines with a blunt fingertip.

The woman who bears this letter is Madame Tocquet of Habitation Thibodet at Ennery. Respect my order to let her pass, with her husband Xavier Tocquet and anyone else who may accompany her.

Signé

TOUSSAINT LOUVERTURE
Governor-General Saint Domingue

"Well." Romain looked from Elise to Tocquet, then back at Elise, whose blond hair had slipped down from under her hat. "You may pass, then." He handed her back the folded paper; Elise tucked it back in the throat of her blouse.

"Where are you going?" Romain said.

"Le Cap," Tocquet said, but Elise interrupted.

"Tonight we stop at Habitation Arnaud," she said.

"Yes," said Romain. "It is safe there. For one night. But maybe you should not stay longer. Le Cap, yes, maybe Le Cap will be better for you."

"Will you explain?" Tocquet said.

Romain looked to the right and left. "Christophe is in the mountains," he said. "At Pont Français and Sainte Suzanne and Haut Limbé and Grand Boucan and Vallière." He raised one hand and slowly let it fall. "Christophe is in the mountains now, but tomorrow he may be in the plain."

"I see," Tocquet said. "We're grateful for your courtesy."

"Yes," said Romain, and turned toward his men. *Bay tout moun-yo pasé,*" he said in a louder voice. Let all these people pass.

It was a full fifteen minutes before Tocquet said anything more at all, time enough for him to smoke all of one of his black cheroots and let the ash and last charred shreds of tobacco fall on the road behind. Then he turned in the saddle toward Elise.

"You impress me very much, Madame," he said brightly. "And still one wonders how you came by such a safe-conduct."

It seemed to Nanon that Elise colored considerably; there was even a flush on the back of her neck. "Suffice it to say that it is a good thing for us all that I do have it."

Tocquet cocked one eyebrow at her, but at the same time he seemed to be swallowing a laugh. Certainly his humor was now lighter than before. "Yes, I think it is sufficient," he said, then squeezed his horse's flanks and rode a little way forward.

In the event, it did not rain. The clouds broke up and through a rift in them a shaft of the declining sun stretched down to touch the green of the northern plain like a gilding finger. The cool breath of the evening *serein* carried them through the gateposts of Habitation Arnaud. There was a sudden stir in the *grand'case*, when they were spotted, and Cléo rushed off to look for Arnaud. The children slid down from their mounts and tottered around on rubbery legs, the smaller ones mingling with the small children of this place. Amid the flurry of arrival, Isabelle stood staring rather sourly at the chapel, where Moustique was garbling a service, before the sole audience of the rigidly upright Claudine.

"What is this mummery?" Isabelle said. She must be blistered from the ride, Nanon thought, for her tone was very sharp.

"He's saying the mass for your late husband, Madame," Arnaud said, with an equal sharpness at first, then breaking off in confusion. "I'm sorry," he said. "I—I didn't mean to tell you so . . ."

"Oh," said Isabelle, putting two fingers to her lower lip. "Oh." Everyone seemed to have stopped to stare at her.

"I never treated him well," she said. "He was quite a dull man, I know, but never was unkind to me."

Elise reached out a hand to her, but Isabelle, for whatever reason, collapsed instead on Nanon's bosom. She wept. Nanon, surprised at first, began to stroke her hair and murmur. Elise's hand still hovered in the air, until, with a quick self-conscious movement, she drew it back. She was hurt, as her eyes showed, before she turned aside. Nanon would have liked to comfort her too, perhaps more than Isabelle, whose burst of emotion had surprised her—the snuffle of wet sobs on the bodice of her dress. She softened herself to draw it all in. She had sheltered in the Cigny house on several occasions, sometimes for quite long periods, so she'd had good opportunity to observe their married life. If not for Nanon's intervention, Isabelle would have had to present Monsieur Cigny with Joseph Flaville's bastard: black Gabriel. That affair had been kept the most deadly secret; as for her frequent liaisons with white men, Isabelle had barely observed the form of trying to conceal them.

And yet one could not know another's heart. Nanon and Doctor Hébert were not demonstrative, except when they were alone. At first she'd seen the doctor as a funny little fellow, harmless and easy enough to lead. By the time she'd discovered herself mistaken in that early judgment, she'd also realized that the doctor had strengths and advantages as a protector that no one could have guessed from a first impression. But the larger feeling had wanted a much longer time to take root and grow.

Claudine had appeared, with dry whispers and a few frail caresses. She led Isabelle into the house and settled her on her own bed. Nanon stayed with her for most of an hour, until she fell asleep. It was nearly dark when she quietly returned to the gallery, where the others had gathered around, though there was just enough light for her to see bats flickering across the sky above the yard. Arnaud was debating some point with Tocquet, who stabbed the tabletop with his finger as though it were a map.

"But the rumor is impossible," Arnaud said. "Christophe cannot be at Vallière and Pont Français at the same time—there's the whole Northern Plain between."

"I'll give you that," said Tocquet. "He cannot be in six places at once, no matter what devil may possess him. But he may have raised irregulars in all those places, by riding the circuit or sending messengers—how many men did you say have disappeared from your place alone in the last days? And Christophe is only the emissary of Toussaint in the whole affair—"

"Toussaint was soundly beaten at Ravine à Couleuvre," Arnaud said.

"He was not," said Tocquet. "Leclerc may claim it, but I saw enough of it myself, and I know the outcome by certain report. Rochambeau was driven back to the ravine at the last, and he lost as many men as Toussaint did, if not more, and you know Toussaint has larger numbers to begin with. But the real point is that Toussaint will never be soundly beaten until his army is destroyed, and he got his army away whole from Ravine à Couleuvre."

"But there are defections from him everywhere," Arnaud said. "Maurepas has submitted, with all the Ninth Demibrigade."

"Excellent," said Tocquet. "Then we should be safe at Port-de-Paix, if we could get there." He paused. "Well, Toussaint will be set back by that, no doubt, but he won't be incapacitated. He was fighting today on the road from Marmelade. He has drawn Leclerc off, and most of his troops and his generals, to some concentration at Petite Rivière—which I'll wager will prove to be a diversion. Meanwhile Toussaint has got around them all!—and is on his way north with who knows how many men."

As he spoke, Tocquet sketched lines of movement over the blank table-top; Arnaud stared as if he saw the places inscribed there.

"Between him and Christophe they may well sweep the plain, as I have no doubt is their intention," Tocquet said. "There are not enough French troops between here and Limbé to make up a police force—you tell me yourself that Romain alone gives them more trouble than they can contain. Who commands at Le Cap, now that all Leclerc's senior officers have marched to Petite Rivière?"

"The mulatto," Arnaud said with some faint air of derision. "Boyer."

"Ah." Tocquet sat back, and touched a finger to his lower lip. "So . . . Boyer is not to be discounted. But I wonder if Leclerc may come to regret having introduced all these Rigaudins back into the field. Pétion, Villatte, Léveillé—not to mention Rigaud himself. There will be complications. And how many men can Boyer have left to his command? With so many marched off to the south? They may think they've drawn Toussaint tight in their bag, but you know that he is a clever old cat, and I think he has already slipped out of it."

"If you think Boyer is so feeble, why do you insist on going to Le Cap?" Arnaud said.

"A fair question." Tocquet laughed, rather hoarsely. Two dead stubs of his cheroots lay in a saucer by his hand. "I admit that during the recent misfortunes, Le Cap has lost much of its attraction. But it was Toussaint who suggested we go there, and I believe that he does not personally wish us harm. I think Toussaint is going to Le Cap himself, if he can, and I think he means to burn and murder his whole way there." Again the dry laugh. "If you had a ship waiting on the Baie d'Acul, I'd suggest that we all sail for Jamaica. As it stands, Le Cap is our best resort. If Boyer holds it, well and good. If he does not, there are ships in the port. Or we may treat with Toussaint if there's no way out."

Nanon looked at Tocquet in some surprise, then lowered her eyes. It was strange to think that he'd allow himself to be driven from the country. Arnaud had turned his face toward his wife, who sat in the shadows, her eyes glittering from the light of the candles on the table.

"It is indifferent to me," she said.

Arnaud's gaze wandered over the other faces. He looked uncertain, to Nanon, and somehow diminished. He had aged in the short time since she'd last seen him, a mere matter of weeks. Or not so much that, but a shade of the old man he might live to become was hidden somewhere behind the face he presented now.

"We'll sleep on it," Arnaud said and lifted his glass of raw rum.

Nanon slept soundly; she was never a restless sleeper, even when troubled, and even when there was such small comfort in their lodging. The house Arnaud had raised after the burning of his plantation in ninety-one had only one bedroom, and Isabelle recovered herself enough to refuse Claudine's offer of her bed. All the people from Thibodet slept in a couple of *cases* by the chapel, near the little *case* inhabited by Moustique and Marie-Noelle and their children. There had been such evacuation from Habitation Arnaud that it was no trouble to find room for them. Elise grumbled a little, but under her breath. Isabelle was silent, the children subdued, Robert and Héloïse mute before the death of a father whom, Nanon reflected, they had scarcely known. All were drained from the long day's ride. Nanon stretched out on a woven mat. She was briefly aware of Paul lying wakeful beside her. Then, the great dark.

Behind the eye of her dream, she was aware that it might have been the tale of Cigny's murder that raised these images: details that Arnaud had kept from Isabelle, but which Nanon had heard him mutter to Tocquet. It did not matter. The dream eye glided over the ground as if on the soundless wings of an owl, over the ruin of Petite Rivière, which smoldered and fumed in its ashes. It was night, overcast or moonless, but the mild slope above the town was spotted with greenish-yellow lights the size of candle flames, each picking out the mangled carcass of a *blanc*, and there were hundreds of them strewn across the hill. The owl wings lumbered over the wet air. At first sight Nanon recognized the body of Antoine Hébert, though all its members had been scattered, and the head was gone. Only his glasses lay across a little stone, the witch fires gleaming on cracks of one shattered lens. Beyond the ditches, in the shadow of the fort's wall, a pack of wild dogs waited: *casques*. They were huge and brindled, their heads dropped low beneath heavy shoulders, eyes red-glowing. The dogs were coming toward the bodies. Then the dream eye sheered away.

Nanon sat up with an ugly jerk, wrenched upward in the swirl of a terrible scream. After a moment she could know the voice had not been her own, for the inside of the *case* was quiet. Paul breathed softly in sleep beside her, and no one else had stirred. Perhaps she'd dreamed it. She sat with one hand covering the pounding of her heart. It was very dark inside the close little room, but after a while she began to discern the outline of the curtained doorway. There was a different beat behind her heart, in time with it: a drum somewhere outside the *case*, sustaining a single steady stroke. When her heart had stilled, the drum continued.

She got up then, picked her way over the other sleepers, and pushed out through the curtain. Above her was a pantheon of brilliant stars. The night air cooled the sick sweat of her dream. Bazau sat crosslegged by the doorway, a musket cradled across his knees. He nodded silently to Nanon as she passed.

The drum had stopped, but not before she'd marked its direction. In starlight she walked behind the chapel, toward candles flickering deep in the bamboo, and entered the mouth of the *tonnelle*. Under the arched and woven stalks it was very dark, and the stars were hidden, but at the entrance of the *hûnfor*, four candles were placed on the cardinal points around Legba's stones. Nanon stopped there, a hand to her throat.

"Ou mêt antré." It was Moustique's voice. You may come in.

Nanon stepped past the stones and candles. Here the space opened to the dome of stars. Before certain niches, other lamps were lit, but Nanon did not look at these too closely. Isidor sat near the drum, and Cléo and Fontelle were also attending. But Nanon's attention went to Ghede, crouched like a cricket at the far edge of the peristyle, greedily scooping up rice and beans from a plate between his legs, with the help of a big wedge of cassava. The *loa* was incarnate in the body of Claudine Arnaud, but Claudine had never known such an appetite. She wore man's clothes, black shirt and trousers, and her head was tied up in a deep purple cloth, skewed to cover her left eye.

Nanon stopped before Ghede, a few paces distant.

"I dreamed my husband's death," she said.

Ghede looked up. His open eye fixed her in her place.

"Your sleep is a mirror," Ghede said. "Sometimes, all you see there is your own fear."

"Let me keep him, Ghede," she said, her voice trembling slightly. Then, after a pause, she said more steadily. "I would give all I own."

Ghede dropped his cassava on the plate and licked his fingers. With one long stride he closed the distance between them. Though the body he used was thin and angular, Ghede's hips rolled in a fluid, boneless, lascivious motion, pelvis thrusting, out and in. Nanon remained motionless till this movement stopped.

"Ou pa vlé viré ak moin?" Ghede asked her. You don't want to dance with me?

"Non, merci." Nanon curtsied. No, thank you. Her knees felt watery as

she rose, but Fontelle and Cléo had come to support her on either side. Ghede did not seem dissatisfied. He nodded to her and crouched again over his plate.

Fontelle and Cléo guided Nanon toward the opening of the *tonnelle*, their hands warm on her elbows, arms close round her waist.

"If it's not his time," Moustique said as she passed, "Ghede won't take him."

Though the stars had barely begun to dim when Nanon emerged from the *tonnelle*, Arnaud's *grand'case* was alight. Tocquet had come out of the *case* and with the help of Bazau and Gros-Jean was hustling packs onto mules. Arnaud was busy hitching a wagon. One by one the older children stumbled out of the *case* and sleep-walked to new resting places in the straw spread on the wagon bed, between the few barrels of rum Arnaud's remaining hands had loaded. Zabeth and Marie-Noelle settled in the straw with their infants; Nanon lifted Gabriel and François in to ride with them.

By the time the sun was hot overhead, the Northern Plain had begun to burn, all across the cane fields from the coast. The smoke grew heavy, and the sea breeze carried it across the road, thick with flakes of ash and hot cinders. The travelers masked their faces with dampened cloths. People began to come streaming out of the cane, in flight from the smoke and fire. Tocquet and Arnaud quizzed a few of these as they crossed the way and learned that Christophe was advancing along the coast road from Terrier Rouge, driving Boyer back toward the gate of Le Cap. They were fighting plantation to plantation across the whole plain too.

After a muttered consultation, Arnaud and Tocquet picked up the pace. The road they traveled converged at Le Cap with the road by which Boyer was retreating, and if Boyer was really routed, they would do well to get there before him—before Christophe had sealed the entrance to the town.

Claudine drove the wagon, eyes fixed on the edge of the sky, holding the team at a steady trot. The road was rough, and the smaller children began to whine at the jolting. Nanon and Isabelle and Elise rode close by the wagon. Tocquet and Bazau trotted in the rear, keeping an eye on the road behind, while Arnaud and Gros-Jean cantered ahead to reconnoiter. Until they reached Haut du Cap, no one interfered with them. They were in sight of Le Cap's first defensive earthwork when a large armed band swarmed across the road.

At the sight of them, Arnaud felt his resolve harden. Now the danger assumed a material form, his terror was gone. He was thrilled, even, at the rushing return of his confidence—his self, as he'd been accustomed to know it. Though they'd been riding hard for an hour, there was still a reserve left in his horse. He could empty his pistol, then ride on wielding his *coutelas* till he had broken through or been killed. But the wagon and the women would not make it through.

Arnaud reined up, and Gros-Jean beside him. The man who seemed to lead the band was missing his right ear. A faded brand of the *fleur de lys* on his left cheek marked him as a thief, most likely, or a runaway.

"You are Michel Arnaud," he said. "We know you."

"*Wi Wi, nou rekonnen'l,*" came other voices. Arnaud heard his name move through the band. Arnaud felt a little surprised, for his face was covered to the eyeballs in a dampened kerchief to filter the smoke. He was intensely grateful not to be afraid. Nor did he feel the blind, consuming anger which had often carried him through such moments, only a near-indifferent calm. He studied the first man who had spoken, but could not recognize him. That did not mean that he might not have lopped off that ear with his own knife, or planted the brand on that face with his own iron, long ago in the time of slavery.

A few French sentries showed themselves within the earthwork. They meant to do nothing, Arnaud could tell; there'd be no sortie, no rescue. Probably they were too few. From across the Haut du Cap river, which was partly concealed by a stand of cane to their right, came a noise of shouting and gunfire. The branded man's head revolved in that direction.

"Christophe," he said. "There is Christophe—he is chasing Boyer."

The noise swelled as it approached. Arnaud sensed the sentries in the earthwork were attending to it also. He touched his pistol grip for a moment, then pulled the masking cloth from his nose and mouth and dropped it, then dismounted, letting the reins trail. He took a step away from his horse.

"I am Michel Arnaud," he said. "If you have some account with me, we may settle it now." He opened his empty hands, a few inches away from the pistol and *coutelas* strapped to opposite sides of his belt. "But let these others pass on to the town."

The branded man was hesitating. He still seemed to be distracted by the noise of the fighting beyond the slow brown drift of the river, though nothing had yet come into view. The cane, and smoke rolling over it, obscured everything. Arnaud coughed. Behind him there was a crash, and though he didn't like to take his eyes off the branded man and the others he faced, he risked a quick glance over his shoulder. At Elise's urging, Sophie and Zabeth had rolled one of the rum barrels over the rails of the wagon; it spurted a little bright liquid through a cracked stave as it landed, and a good number of the band swarmed eagerly over it. Claudine, meanwhile, stood up from the box, her skin pulled tight to the bone of her face, staring a thousand miles through the horizon, her left hand with its missing ring finger raised palm out as if to test the wind.

Arnaud faced forward. Now he heard Claudine's name, whispered around the band. Some of the men who blocked their way were looking up at her with a kind of awe.

"Give us all the barrels," the branded man said.

Arnaud shook his head. "One."

"Don't be a fool, man!" Tocquet had ridden up to the head. "Give them the rum and get on your horse." He turned to the branded man. "Take all the barrels and welcome to them, but as we go." As he spoke he leaned down to catch the harness of the lead mule in the team. At his urging the wagon creaked slowly forward. Arnaud vaulted into his saddle with the verve of a youth of twenty. The branded man made a fishtail motion with his arm, and the men in front of them began to shift out of the road.

Two of the band had jumped into the wagon and were rolling barrels off to their fellows who walked behind. They paid no attention to the women and children crouching in the straw of the wagon bed. Ahead, Arnaud saw with enormous relief that the sentries were dragging the heavy wood gate of the earthwork open. Half a dozen muskets were leveled in their direction, though, and one little four-pound cannon.

"Get those brigands off your wagon!" one of the sentries shouted. One of the men jumped down at once, though three barrels remained to be unloaded. The second man ignored the call. Grunting, he hefted a barrel to the rail and rolled it over. Gros-Jean rode up and tapped him on the shoulder.

"*Fok ou desann,*" he said, and pointed to the soldier who held a lit fuse above the touch hole of the little cannon. You must get down. The second man glanced in that direction, flashed Gros-Jean a quick grin and jumped off the wagon, leaving the last two barrels behind.

Arnaud counted his party as they came through the earthwork—all were present and accounted for. The guard was very light here, as he'd suspected, no more than a platoon and short-handed at that. A little determination would suffice to overrun this post. But through the closing gate he could see that the men of the band were doing nothing more than rolling the rum barrels further out of musket range. Then the gate was closed, and the sentries had waved them on their way. Around the next bend of the road appeared the stone gate posts of the town itself.

"Ah, Michel . . ." Tocquet rode up alongside Arnaud, and reached to touch him lightly on the shoulder. Thrown together as they'd often been, the two men didn't naturally like each other much, and it was rare for Tocquet to use Arnaud's first name. But Arnaud understood that the quick touch was meant both to compliment his courage and to reproach him, lightly, for his recklessness. He faced Tocquet, who still looked at him curiously.

"I never owned my strength," Arnaud said, surprised to hear himself utter it.

"No man does."

Though Arnaud expected Tocquet to have spoken, the voice belonged to Bazau, who flanked him on the right. He glanced at the black man, but

Bazau was looking through the gate posts, his profile calmly smoothed of all expression. They cleared the gate to the sound of hooves and harness and the more distant noise of fighting toward the coast. None of the three of them said anything more as they continued their way across the fire-blackened Rue Espagnole.

28

The little painted pendant went on troubling Maillart, for he couldn't determine what to do with it. As it would certainly be compromising to Antoine Hébert's sister, he ought probably to have got rid of it—tossed it into the canal with the rest of the trinkets out of Toussaint's trophy box. The order to treat any white woman who'd consorted with a black as a prostitute had rather shaken the major. There'd be more than one colonial dame brought low if that directive were broadly applied. More than one of Maillart's own acquaintance. He wondered, too, what lay behind it, what other disagreeable orders there might be.

And still the pendant's image reminded him so of Isabelle that he could not quite bring himself to dispose of it. It was not her portrait, yet it recalled the brightness of her eyes, the coyness in that finger laid over lips stung red by kissing. At moments he thought private, he'd cup the pendant in his hand and study the image on the small ceramic disk, wondering where Isabelle was now, if she had reached some place of safety. He was confident she had, for Isabelle was a cat who fell on her feet, though by this time she might have consumed a few of her spare lives. He'd caught young Captain Paltre a time or two, peering over his shoulder, trying to see into his palm, but then Maillart would fold his fingers over the teasing face and drop the pendant back in his coat pocket. He could not quite control the habit of worrying it between his thumb and forefinger there, but the surface of the disk was thickly glazed, so that this handling did not wear away the image.

They'd been on the march out of Port-au-Prince for several days, since news had come that General Debelle had been pushed back, with surprising losses, from a little fort above Petite Rivière. Maillart knew the fort, and thought little of it. The place was well chosen, to control a key point of entry to the interior via the Grand Cahos, but the fortification itself did not amount to much, and though it stood on a high cliff above the Artibonite River, it was too easily attacked across the inconsequential slope rising from the town.

And yet it seemed to be their target. Captain-General Leclerc appeared to believe that here Toussaint had gone to ground. Maillart did not much think so. Toussaint did not willingly put his back to any set of walls. But maybe he'd been forced to it; it might be true, and so the major kept his opinion to himself. For the past two days they'd been maneuvering inland, and General Boudet had detached the advance guard to press as far east as Mirebalais, under command of the Adjutant-General d'Henin, who'd taken some losses capturing a small redoubt, then found the town in ashes. D'Henin returned to Boudet gray-faced, with a tale of three hundred white corpses weltering in their blood where they'd been hacked to death on Habitation Chirry, and all the countryside in flames.

Now, toward the close of day, Boudet's reunited division moved along the south bank of the Artibonite toward the town of Verrettes. Maillart contrived to feel mildly optimistic on this ride, despite the nervous whispering of d'Henin's men. He rode along to Paltre's left, fingering the pendant in his pocket. Verrettes was scarcely more than a village, but pleasantly situated not far from the river, and there a major might commandeer a roof for the night, perhaps even a bed. Perhaps there would also be supplies to requisition. They'd been traveling since Port-au-Prince on moldy biscuit from the ships. Though Maillart had some skill in supplementing such rations, the pace of their march had been brisk enough that he'd been able to supply himself with no more than a few pieces of fruit.

His stomach responded to the thought of a regular meal with a couple of interested growls. Maillart tightened his diaphragm and stood up in his stirrups, peering ahead. On the outskirts of Verrettes a skirmish line had appeared, and a few shots were fired, though at such long range that the balls were spent when they reached the French column. Pamphile de Lacroix ordered the drummer to beat the charge. The skirmishers, mostly un-uniformed field hands, scattered easily enough, though some still sniped at the French flanks from the trees.

"We are not so terrifying as we were," Lacroix muttered, as he made his way back down the line to Maillart.

"That band of irregulars presents us no real threat," the major replied.

"No," said Lacroix, with a distant smile. "But I don't like their confidence."

The departure of the skirmishers revealed a pall of smoke. Maillart's heart sank. Verrettes was burned too—yes, the houses were destroyed from one end to the other, he saw as they rode to the central square. The Place d'Armes was carpeted with the bodies of white men, women, children. Some preserved an attitude of supplication in their deaths, kneeling slumped against the walls, their empty hands stretched out for mercy. The blood was not yet dry on the ground. Maillart saw a woman who seemed to have been slain by a bayonet or a lance that had first passed through the trunk of the infant she held to her bosom. He looked away quickly but there was nowhere safe to look except for the darkening sky.

Captain Paltre leaned sideways out of his saddle and puked on the ground, then straightened and rode on, his eyes glazed, a trail of vomit at the corner of his mouth. Maillart wished he would collect himself enough to wipe it away. Paltre had reported a similar scene when he'd entered Saint Marc with Boudet's division, just shortly after Dessalines had put the town to bayonet and torch. Apparently he was not yet hardened to such spectacles.

Buzzards walked comfortably among the dead, shrugging their black wings, like old men stooping in black tailcoats. From their attentions, many of the corpses stared from empty eye sockets. Against a tree in the center of the square, something flopped and groaned. Lacroix hurried in that direction, then called for a farrier to come with tools to draw the heavy nails that transfixed the white man's palms to the living wood. His swollen tongue hung out of his mouth. Maillart gave him a drink of water.

"Who did it?" Lacroix said.

"Dessalines," the man said thickly. "This morning, Dessalines was here." When the second nail was drawn, he slumped to the ground in a faint.

"He won't live," Lacroix said grimly.

"Most likely not," Maillart agreed. He was trying not to look at Paltre, who sat dumbstruck astride his halted horse. Somehow the smear of vomit by Paltre's mouth distressed him more than all this scene of carnage.

"My Christ." Lacroix swept his arm around the panorama. "The reports don't give one a proper idea . . ."

Maillart said nothing.

"They are not human," Lacroix said. "Whoever did such thing cannot be human."

"Don't say that," Maillart heard himself blurt. "Never say it."

Lacroix looked at him curiously, perhaps somewhat suspiciously, but Maillart said no more. And anyway the order was coming down the line to evacuate the ruined town.

He had no appetite that night, not even for his ration of hardtack. They camped on the south bank of the Artibonite, squared off in battalions, to protect their equipment and horses at the center of each square. At first the men had been moved to anger by the massacre, but after nightfall their humor turned uneasy. At midnight Maillart was roused by Paltre's nervous movements. Apparently there was a little gunfire around the edges of their camp, and the sentries were shooting back into the dark.

"It's nothing," Maillart snapped at Paltre. "They won't attack us in this strength. They only mean to steal your sleep."

With that he rolled over, and flattened his cheek against the leather of his saddlebag. But after all it was not so desirable to reenter his nightmares just now. He lay feigning sleep for Paltre's benefit, remembering what he had said to Lacroix that evening. To declare the enemy less than human opened the door to every horror. Dessalines must have told himself the same today, before he put his victims to the bayonet: *These are not human.* Maillart had not been able to hold himself back from touching that woman, stabbed to the heart through the child she held. He had touched her on the cheek. The skin had been warm, perhaps only from the sun, but it seemed to hold some fading warmth of life.

. . . that they should have always before them the hell that they deserve— a phrase from Toussaint's letter, which Chancy had been caught carrying. If the message had been intercepted, Dessalines was certainly acting in its spirit all the same. And certainly there was a human intention behind it. It was terrible, but not insane. In fact it was quite a lucid intention, plain and bright. Though he liked Pamphile de Lacroix a great deal, Maillart could never say so much to him. It might after all be taken for treason. Besides, his own ideas confused him. He wished Antoine Hébert were near. Antoine would have known better how to put it. Really this style of thinking was more in the line of the doctor than Maillart. Maillart did not like it when his thoughts boiled so. The activity of the thoughts stopped him from sleeping.

Or even Riau, if Riau were here now. He would say nothing on the subject, or very little, but Maillart thought Riau would understand what he himself could not formulate. Riau had a facility for acting and being without any sign of reflection, and this the major had always appreciated. But Riau had taken a message to Croix des Bouquets and had never come back from that errand.

Maillart sat up suddenly. Of course, Riau had gone back to Toussaint. He had known it from the second day Riau failed to return to Port-au-Prince, but had not recognized the knowledge. Well, there was nothing to be done about it. The next time he and Riau met, they probably would be obliged to try to kill each other. Such was the soldier's lot. But tonight, Maillart felt resentful of it. It seemed more difficult to shrug it off than it had been when he was younger. This obligation was the most atrocious aspect of it all, he thought. But it could not bear much more thinking.

Eclair snuffled across the earth toward him, raised his head and whickered. Maillart clucked his tongue, stretched out again, balanced his head on the saddlebag. Above him, stars revolved in spirals. Eventually he slept.

In the morning a handful of deserters from Toussaint's honor guard crossed the river, meaning to come over to the French. They'd lured their captain along on some pretext, though apparently he was not privy to their scheme to change sides. Among this party, Maillart recognized Saint James, one of the very few white men who rode in Toussaint's guard. By Saint James's account, discreetly murmured to Boudet and his staff, Dessalines had recently conducted at Petite Rivière a slaughter similar to the one they'd just come upon at Verrettes.

Boudet had been in a cold fury since the evening before, and at this news he rounded on the captain, who had been arrested but not yet restrained. *"How many men have you murdered at Petite Rivière!"* With these words Boudet snatched the captain's arm. They struggled, chest to chest—then Boudet sprang back with a cry. He had been bitten in the thumb, bad enough to bleed. The captain meanwhile rolled under the belly of the horse from which he'd lately dismounted, scrambled through the legs of other horses, and ran full tilt for the river. He was a good swimmer, Maillart took note, and a swift one. Though musket balls plowed up the water all around him, none of them seemed to find a mark. The captain emerged on the far bank and went on still at a run. Some were still shooting at him, though the range was doubtful. Maillart had his own pistol drawn but did not discharge it. Then the black captain's running stride developed a hitch. A lucky shot must have struck his leg. Awkwardly slowing, like a loose-wound clock, he managed a few paces more and then collapsed.

"We'll get him when we cross the river," Boudet said.

Saint James and the other men who'd come with him led Boudet's division up the river to the ford they'd used themselves that morning. Snipers harried them from the woods as they marched, and a few horsemen rode feints along their flanks. Maillart learned from the scouts that these were men of Charles Belair, the same who had broken his sleep with their raid the night before. Boudet's troops were hot to pursue these harassers. After what they'd seen the day before they wanted blood. But Boudet and Lacroix kept them close in their ranks and marching forward.

On the north bank of the ford the enemy appeared in sufficient force to trouble them with musket fire across the river. Boudet formed his advance guard under command of Pétion, and ordered him to lead the crossing. A number of Pétion's grenadiers were grumbling that it was always they who had to march in the van and risk the fire of ambushes. Pétion turned on them and snapped, "It is your glory to have this place of honor—now be silent and follow me."

Indeed, Pétion was the first man into the river and the first man across. Maillart watched him with an interested respect. Pétion was a mulatto and an old Rigaudin; he'd just come out from France on the same boat that carried Rigaud and his other partisans. He looked to be quite a capable and courageous officer, though Maillart was content, for his own part, to be marching well behind the vanguard.

He joined the detachment that returned to the area of the bank where that black captain had fallen. Though the leaves where he'd lain were all soaked with his blood, the man himself was nowhere to be seen. Maillart supposed someone must have carried him off, for by the amount of blood soaking the ground, he'd have been too weak to shift on his own. Angry at his escape, a few of the soldiers kicked up the bloody leaves.

The ambushes had been swept away by the time they rejoined the main advance. Boudet and Lacroix and most of the men were eager to press on to Petite Rivière, where they hoped they might engage Dessalines. But Saint James and the others who'd deserted with him told the French generals of a large powder depot in the vicinity, and Boudet decided it would be best to capture it if possible.

With Belair's raid, many of the men had got little sleep the night before, and marching under the full sun told on them quickly now. Soon their heavy wool uniforms were sweated through, so that all of them smelled like soggy sheep. In the mountains the trails became too steep and narrow for them to continue dragging their few cannon. Boudet called a halt to bury the artillery, that the enemy might not discover it. Despite these delays, they reached Plassac a little before noon.

A howling came from across the gorge from them—some number of black irregulars appearing on an open bend of the trail that climbed the opposite hill. Lacroix shaded his eyes to look.

"Can it be Dessalines?" he said.

Maillart accepted the spyglass Lacroix offered him and squinted into it for a moment. "I recognize no uniforms," he said as he lowered the instrument. "These might be anyone, but—"

"If we could only come at him now . . ." Lacroix was flexing both his fists.

"Blow up the magazine," Pétion said. "That will hurt them as much as anything, whoever they may be."

Boudet nodded, then gave his orders. A couple of Pétion's grenadiers laid the fuse, as the rest of the troops marched down the defile. Maillart turned his head as he passed and saw the flame hissing backward. At the bottom of the descent they halted and looked back to see the magazine erupt from the mountainside with a tremendous flash and roar. A little stone dust rained down on them. A few of the men cheered, while others cursed Dessalines. The echo of the explosion persisted in Maillart's ears as they went on. He could just see the last of the black irregulars rounding the bend of the trail out of range above them, like the tail of a banded snake slipping into the jungle. They saw no more of the enemy for the rest of that day, though sometimes they were fired upon from cover. By sundown they had come within a cannon shot of La Crête à Pierrot.

Doctor Hébert sprang awake at first light, with the unpleasantly startled feeling familiar to him since the killings at Petite Rivière. He lay face down, palms flat on the mat, until his heartbeat slowed. Under his hands was the softness of the earth he'd broken to bury his weapons. At last he sat up and sniffed the damp air. The chatter of crows came from beyond the parapets. He wished for coffee, uselessly. Rations were already short. General Vernet had not been able to supply them with the quantity of water expected. And the night before, Dessalines had returned to the fort in a towering rage. A French advance had crossed the river near Verrettes and cut him off before he could reach Plassac; he'd been unable to resupply from the powder magazine there, and feared the French might have discovered it.

Amidst the crow talk began the thin scrape of a violin tuning. The doctor wished the man would desist. His head ached slightly, for want of coffee. He got up, though, and walked toward the sound. The naturalist Descourtilz squatted by the wall, talking to the violinist. Dessalines had brought in an odd assortment of Toussaint's musicians the night before: two trumpeters, a drummer, and the violinist—white men all. It seemed that Toussaint had abandoned his whole orchestra on some plantation nearby, in the hurry of his march north. The others had tried to get away to the coast, but these four had stayed behind, to be scooped up by Dessalines.

The doctor knew the violinist, from Toussaint's fêtes at Le Cap. What was his name? Gaston, possibly. He nodded, rendered a thin smile. Bienvenu also looked on, fascinated, as Gaston scraped his bow across the strings. The other musicians lay sprawled and snoring beside their instruments on the ground.

"Look there." Descourtilz tilted his chin toward one of the embrasures. The doctor peered along the cannon barrel. Tucked in the river's bend, below the fort, was a long column of French soldiers marching toward the trees that screened the town of Petite Rivière. The doctor felt a certain chill. He took his face away from the embrasure, lips formed in a silent whistle.

"Yes," said Descourtilz. "That looks to be an entire division."

"I think you're right," said the doctor. "Most likely they are maneuvering to attack from the direction of the town."

"A pity Dessalines has come." The naturalist looked pale and shaky. "He'll murder us before he'll see us rescued."

The doctor shook his head as he glanced at Gaston. Better to leave such thoughts unvoiced. If the violinist was alarmed at Descourtilz's remark he did not show it, but went on scraping out some melancholy air, under Bienvenu's rapt gaze.

"Come," the doctor said to Bienvenu. "Let us build up the fire." There were some wounded men to be tended, from the engagement with Debelle a few days before. His own head wound needed its dressing changed also, though now it was nearly closed. Descourtilz might lend some assistance and take his mind off his fretting. But Descourtilz was staring at the powder magazine.

"Christ," said the naturalist. "*Now* what does he mean to do?"

Dessalines was striding up toward the magazine, a blazing torch in his right hand. Lamartinière and Magny walked on either side of him. The few hundred soldiers of the garrison followed, like iron dust drawn by a magnet.

Dessalines pushed open the door to the magazine and peered inside. A sulfur smell came wafting out, wrinkling the doctor's nose. The torch in Dessalines's hand sputtered and sparked. Descourtilz flinched against the wall and reflexively covered his ears with his hands.

"Open the gate," Dessalines said in a ringing voice. At the lower end of the fort, two puzzled sentries swung the two halves of the gate slowly outward.

Dessalines sat down on a pyramid of cannonballs beside the magazine's open door. He held the torch with both hands between his knees and narrowed his eyes on the flame. Now he spoke in a much lower tone, so that everyone must press closer and lean in to hear him.

"I will have no one with me but the brave," he said. "We will be attacked this morning. Let all who want to be slaves of the French again leave the fort now."

He thrust the torch with both hands toward the open gate. A few heads turned, but no man moved in that direction.

"I don't suppose we are included in that invitation," Descourtilz muttered. Gaston, who'd lowered his violin, merely gaped.

"Let those with the courage to die free men stay here with me," said Dessalines.

A cheer went up: *We will all die for Liberty!* The doctor noticed that Marie-Jeanne, Lamartinière's wife, cried the affirmation as loud as any man. She was a tall and striking colored woman; he was rather astonished to see she was still here.

"Quiet." Dessalines chopped a hand in the air to cut off the cheer, then swung the torch toward the magazine's open door. "If the French get over the wall, I will blow them all to hell, and us to Guinée," he said. "Now, all of you, get down against the walls, and no man let himself be seen."

In the cool damp of the early morning, Maillart got up and washed his face in the river and moved out in the midst of Boudet's column, his bones a little creaky from sleeping on the ground. On the cliff above them, the unremarkable fort was quiet, half hidden in lifting swirls of morning mist. Boudet's men filed into the strip of woods outside Petite Rivière. A stench of smoke and scorched flesh lowered over them; this town had been burned, like the others.

Boudet called a halt outside the town. With Pétion, Maillart, and Saint James, he rode out of the ranks up the low grade until they were just out of musket range of the first earthwork, outside the fort. Cannon mouths showed at the embrasure, but no guard was visible anywhere. There was no flag flying anywhere, though Maillart thought he could pick out a thin thread of smoke rising somewhere within the walls.

Boudet scrutinized the position with a spyglass. "It looks deserted," he declared. "These murderers will not stand to fight. I think they've spiked their guns and run away."

"Beware an ambush," Pétion said softly.

"What ambush? Their defenses are all apparent here."

The sun broke fully over the peak of the hill and the walls of the fort. Raising one hand, Boudet shaded his eyes against the blaze.

"Leclerc is supposed to come out from Saint Marc to join us," he said, twisting in the saddle to look toward the west. "No sign of him as yet . . . I think we may as well take this place. We'll carry it, if it's manned or not."

They'd ridden halfway back to their ranks when firing began in the trees to the west. Pamphile de Lacroix, scouting through the woods above the town, had come upon an enemy camp and, as it seemed at first, routed it. The blacks were in full flight as they broke from the trees and rushed across the open slope toward the fort, with the French troops pursuing them full tilt, already hooking and thrusting with their bayonets.

Boudet gave a quick order to send his own men into the charge. Maillart could feel the force of their rage as the first line swept around his horse. This charge would wipe out the shame and horror of the Verrettes massacre, wash all that away in blood. But then the fleeing blacks all jumped down into the ditches and the cannons of the fort belched out *mitraille* across the suddenly cleared field.

A hundred men must have gone down in that first volley. Maillart's heart flipped over in his chest. But the line closed up its gaps at once and kept advancing, the pace of the charge barely slackened, all the way to the edge of the first ditch.

"There, there! is that Toussaint?" It was Captain Paltre who spoke, jockeying his horse up to Maillart's.

The walls of the fort now swarmed with the enemy. Dessalines appeared on the rampart, brandishing a sword in one hand and a torch in the other. He'd stripped off coat and shirt to show his scars, but still wore a tall hat with fantastic plumes.

"It is Dessalines," said Maillart, "but he will do." He drew his pistol. A dozen shots were fired at the black general at the same time as his, all of them without effect. By the legs of Maillart's dancing Eclair a couple of grenadiers, felled by *mitraille*, were trying to drag themselves backward, but the infantry line trampled them down as it moved ahead. Paltre galloped his horse to the rim of the first ditch, jumped down, and with a wide sweep of his arm skimmed his hat beyond all the earthworks, over the wall and into the fort.

"Follow me," he called out hoarsely, and plunged into the ditch. Amazed, Maillart saw him emerge on the other side. He crossed the other ditches miraculously unharmed and pulled himself to the top of the wall. About thirty other grenadiers had followed him, making a wedge across the ditches. Maillart rode to the edge of the earthworks, undecided whether to join the assault on foot. On the rampart, Dessalines split a man's head with his sword and at the same time jabbed his torch into the face of another soldier assailing him. Maillart loosed his reins to reload his pistol. Another grenadier reached the top of the wall and was pierced by ten bayonets at once. A black smashed Paltre in the face with a musket stock and Paltre crumpled over backward into the ditch. Another round of *mitraille* roared from the cannon. Maillart's horse bucked and threw him.

He floundered on the edge of the ditch, fumbling to recover his pistol among the milling feet of the infantry. The charge had broken under the last round of *mitraille*. Paltre came swimming up from the ditch, his face pouring blood from a broken nose. Maillart caught the back of his collar and hauled him out. He stood, supporting Paltre with one hand, the unloaded pistol dangling from the other. All around him the ranks had been shattered into complete disorder.

From the walls a trumpet sounded, a drum rolled, and the gate swung open. Laying planks across the ditches, the blacks now charged the French with their bayonets. In the mêlée, Maillart's horse brushed by him and he managed to catch the trailing reins. He mounted and dragged the half-stunned Paltre across the withers. Halfway down the slope the French had re-formed and returned to the charge, repelling the blacks, pursuing them again. Again they disappeared into the ditch, and this time the volley of *mitraille* did such terrible damage that the French could not rally.

Maillart saw General Boudet sitting on the ground, hands wrapped around the toe of his boot and blood streaming through the fingers. He rode toward the wounded general, but before he could reach him another horseman had caught him up and was carrying him out of the fray. Behind the retreat of their general, the French line completely shattered. Again the trumpet sounded from the walls, and this time it was answered from the forest to the west. Out of the trees came galloping several hundred horsemen of Toussaint's honor guard, sabers shining in the full morning light.

Maillart recognized Morisset at the head of the cavalry, and he thought he saw Placide Louverture riding behind. He drew his own saber. But he was encumbered by his wounded passenger, and the French infantry had been stampeded completely by this fresh cavalry charge. Nothing for it but to ride to the rear, if there was any rear to ride to. Morisset's horsemen pursued the French to the town and into the plain beyond it. For a few dreadful minutes Maillart believed that Boudet's whole division was about to be completely destroyed. But then they found themselves supported by Leclerc himself, just marching in from Saint Marc with Debelle's division, now commanded by General Dugua.

Maillart deposited Paltre behind the newly solidified infantry line. At the sight of the French reinforcement, Morisset had withdrawn his cavalry up the Grand Cahos road. The French advanced again, to the town and beyond, and halted just out of range of the fort's cannon. Now the French tricolor flew from the walls. From within the fort came wild shouts of triumph from the blacks. The wide slope below the ditches was strewn with six hundred French corpses.

In the moment before the battle was joined, Dessalines had stirred up the sleeping musicians from the ground with the point of his sword. It would be a rough awakening, the doctor thought, to open your eyes to Dessalines bestriding you, probing your ribs with his blade, a torch smoking in his other hand, his old whip scars writhing on his back like fat white snakes. When Dessalines bared his torso for a battle, it was a bloody sign.

But at first Dessalines seemed in great good humor, as if he anticipated some fine entertainment, a favorite dance like the *carabinier*. He tickled the musicians into a row, though he did not yet command them to play. The doctor watched from the shade of his *ajoupa*, Descourtilz crouching beside him there. The cannoneers squatted low beside their gun carriages. At Dessalines's signal, the fuses had been lit.

Outside the fort came a roar like the wind. The French troopers were shouting their indignation as they charged. Descourtilz got up to peer over the wall, and the doctor cautiously followed suit. He was in time to see the retreating black skirmishers dive into the ditches just under the walls.

"Feu!" Dessalines's voice boomed, almost simultaneously with the cannon. The guns recoiled and the air filled with burnt-powder smoke. Grapeshot tore great gaps in the ranks of the French. A week previously, Debelle's troops had broken at this moment, but these new soldiers did not falter. They closed their ranks, and when the second volley laid waste to them again, they closed ranks once more and kept advancing.

At the first volley Dessalines had prompted the musicians to strike up a martial air by smacking them on the calves with the flat of his sword.

The drum and trumpets made themselves faintly heard, but the violin was completely inaudible over the noise of artillery, however desperately Gaston sawed it. Dessalines moved behind the players, grinning. The French advance had come to the edge of the ditches. The doctor saw an officer with a dimly familiar face sail his hat over the walls of the fort, then charge after it, with some shouted exhortation. There was a humming around his head, like bees; he didn't realize it was bullets till Descourtilz pulled him down from his perch.

Together they crawled toward the wall of the powder magazine for better cover. But Dessalines, who'd lost his smile, had resumed his post by the open door. "Turn them back!" he shouted, "Or—" He shook his torch toward the open doorway. Half a dozen French grenadiers had reached the top of the wall and were fighting hand to hand with the defenders there. Dessalines appeared to change his strategy; with a shout he rushed into that fight. The doctor saw him dance atop the wall. A bullet sheered off one of the tall feathers in his hat, but except for that he seemed untouchable.

Then Dessalines came panting back and ordered the musicians to sound the charge. Unbelievably, the gates were pushing open for a sortie. The doctor risked another peep over the wall. Now it was Dessalines's men chasing the French down the slope, jabbing bayonets in their kidneys. The French made a rally, turning the tide, but *mitraille* blew away this charge like the others, as the blacks again took cover in the ditches. And now, as the trumpets continued to blare, Morisset led the cavalry out of the woods to sweep the field.

The doctor dropped down to the earth of the fort. Though the cannons had quieted, his ears still rang. Descourtilz hunkered by the *ajoupa*, scraping together a heap of the musket balls that lay on the ground like hailstones. Finally the trumpeters stopped blowing, one of them laying his palm over his deflated chest as he lowered his instrument. Dessalines was leading a cheer, stabbing his torch high into the air. Black soldiers in the highest state of excitement were dancing their victory on the edges of the parapets. Bienvenu returned to the doctor, breathless, sweating, streaked with blood that seemed not to be his own.

See to the fire, the doctor reminded himself, and the herbs and poultices and bandage rolls. Behind Bienvenu came the fresh wounded; there would be much work to do.

Captain Daspir was riding with Leclerc's staff when they met Boudet's division in near-complete rout by the black cavalry, a hundred yards below Petite Rivière. There passed a moment of sick confusion; then Daspir and Cyprien set themselves to rallying the fresh troops into squares, as the fleeing men took cover behind them. In fact the cavalry charge did not press them very hard once their lines were well formed, but retreated up the road west of the town.

"What is the meaning of this?" Leclerc was sputtering. "You yield before these unorganized savages?"

He was berating General Boudet, who came hopping toward him on one leg, supported by a lieutenant on his left, his hurt leg swinging, his face drawn and pale with pain.

"See for yourself," Boudet said through his gritted teeth, and sank to a sitting position on a cartridge case. A surgeon knelt before him and began cutting away the blood-stained leather of his boot.

"Forward," Leclerc ordered, trembling. Daspir and Cyprien joined the march, which proceeded south of Petite Rivière. In the ravines between the town and the river they discovered the putrefying corpses of several hundred slaughtered white civilians. Some of the men began to curse, others to vomit, but Daspir had no reaction left in him, after similar scenes at Saint Marc and elsewhere, although here the odor was most unpleasant and the corpses hopped with vultures and crawled with flies. He exchanged one stupefied glance with Cyprien and rode on. Presently they reached a new scene of carnage: hundreds of fresh-slain French soldiers carpeting the slope below La Crête à Pierrot.

Stunned silence obtained as the men moved into line. Above, the noonday sun was broiling. Within the fort, the French flag snapped on a long staff. Cries of mockery came from the walls. Daspir's heart thumped uncomfortably against his ribs. His mouth was brassy; he took a sip of tepid water from his canteen. The black cavalrymen had also flown the tricolor, he remembered. A youth with a red headcloth had carried it into the charge.

Leclerc shook his head slightly as he surveyed the field, his small, delicate features stiff with anger. "We will avenge these men within the hour," he said, then turned to Daspir and Cyprien. "Go back and bring up the ammunition wagons. Who commands in Boudet's stead, Lacroix? Let him bring what men he finds able to the field."

They left Leclerc conferring with General Dugua, who had assumed the wounded Debelle's command. Their detour to avoid the ravine of the massacre brought them nearer to the dully smoldering ruins of the town. Cyprien covered his face with a scented handkerchief; Daspir simply tolerated his cough as they passed. He rode toward the supply wagons, but paused a moment to watch the surgeon working over Boudet's foot. The general had had his toes shot away, it appeared, and he also had a nasty suppurating wound on one hand. Behind him, a weathered-looking officer with long mustaches and a major's epaulettes was remolding a captain's broken nose between his thumb and forefinger. Daspir took a second glance at the wounded captain and recognized the disfigured Paltre.

"My God, what has happened to you?" Daspir jumped down from his horse at once. Paltre made an effort to answer but could only spit out blood.

"Be still," Maillart said and turned to Daspir. "It's all from his nose, he won't die of it. A friend of yours? He's a lucky man, and a brave one too—if not a bit of a fool. You might go get his hat for him, if you're returning to the attack."

"His hat?"

Maillart straightened and offered his hand; Daspir clasped it briefly.

"He threw his hat into the fort and tried to go after it," Maillart said. "It's a miracle he's hurt no worse than this. I think every man who followed him died."

Daspir gaped. Paltre struggled up and spat out more blood.

"I'm going," he said. "If Daspir goes, I go back too."

"Calm yourself," Maillart said. "You've proved your courage! You can't go on till the bleeding stops. There's no sense in it."

Daspir opened his mouth to explain their bet and the competition. Was it likely Toussaint was in that fort? Leclerc had certainly thought to find him when they marched this way from Saint Marc. He would have asked Paltre to confirm it, but at that moment Cyprien rode up to remind him that he should be hurrying the wagons up to the line.

The fort was silent, motionless, though the cannon mouths breathed a little smoke, and Maillart's ears still hummed with the din of the recent battle. The carpet of dead men on the slope appeared to wriggle. Maybe it was only the shimmer of the broiling noon heat. But no, a couple of wounded men were trying to crawl down the slope to the new French line. Three men broke from Leclerc's ranks to help them, but one was immediately picked off by a marksman hidden in the fort—dead before he hit the ground, though his heels still drummed in the dust. The other two soldiers shook their fists as they skipped back. Another long shot dispatched one of the wounded men who'd kept on crawling.

There's a man with a rifle, Maillart thought. He considered his friend Antoine Hébert, such a surprisingly good marksman with his long American gun. The notion momentarily froze him, but of course the doctor would not be anywhere near this place and would not be firing on the French if he were; he was always reluctant to use his unexpected talent against human life. But surely the sniper in the fort must be armed with a similar weapon.

Leclerc had brought a good number of black troops with him out of Saint Marc, men of the Ninth Demibrigade, incorporated into Debelle's force after the surrender of Maurepas. Some hailed from the Thirteenth Demibrigade as well. Leclerc had put them in the front line, but they seemed a little reluctant to advance across this killing ground. Maillart knew these were no cowards. He had trained some of them himself, in earlier days, when Toussaint first began to organize a real army. Under Maurepas they'd repulsed both Debelle and Humbert, defeated them really, and inflicted considerable losses too. In fact, Maurepas might never have surrendered if Lubin Golart had not turned his coat and joined the French generals. Golart had been a subcommander of the Ninth and was able to bring his regiment over to the French; he'd hated any partisan of Toussaint's ever since the War of Knives; and moreover he knew the terrain around Port-de-Paix as well or better than Maurepas. These men of the Ninth were brave and well trained, Maillart knew, well seasoned in battle also, and if they hesitated now it was because they knew what was going to happen.

As Leclerc should have known also, or at least Dugua. Maillart's mind began to race. He was still quivering from the shock of Boudet's rout and his own forced flight before that cavalry charge. The same thing that had happened to Boudet this morning must have happened to Debelle the week before. Dugua ought certainly to have learned that much when he assumed Debelle's command. Now Leclerc was re-forming his line, replacing the black troops with French, who were all more than eager enough for a charge. Leclerc was going to march blithely into the same trap for a third time.

A mostly naked black man appeared on the wall of the fort, wearing Paltre's hat, and a rag of a breech clout. He capered like a goat on the parapets, dancing the *chica*, wriggling his spine and flapping his arms, thrusting out his chest and hooking his pelvis upward. From inside the walls came clapping and chanting and laughter. The man's muscles gleamed as if they had been oiled. A few men fired from Leclerc's lines, unbidden, but he ignored the shots. Finally he turned his back and gave his buttocks an infuriating wriggle before he jumped down into shelter behind the wall. The hat was raised once more, twitched teasingly, before it disappeared.

"Take that fort!" Leclerc, livid with rage, was screaming. He stepped ahead of his line, whipping his sword forward and down. At once the line swept past him. Drums beat the charge. Maillart watched Captain Daspir riding into the stream. He held his own horse back. Someone bumped against him—Paltre, who'd managed to remount. His nose was held in place with a blood-soaked bandage which gave him the look of a demented *agouti*.

"I'll get my own hat back," Paltre muttered and rode forward.

Maillart grasped at him, angry—he was moved to pursue, but held himself in. Better not to let his anger sweep him along, as it was sweeping everyone else on the field. He had never liked Paltre much anyway, not since the days of Hédouville, but today he'd been impressed with the young captain's lunatic bravery. And since he'd invested something in saving Paltre's life, he didn't like to see it wasted now.

Yet he stayed where he was and watched, a little surprised at his own detachment. Leclerc's small, incongruously dapper figure was setting an example for his men. He was well to the fore, his life on the line, urging, encouraging. It was what Napoleon would have done, in the days when his men worshiped him as the Little Corporal. Maillart had heard those tales from a distance. The men who'd landed at Port-au-Prince with Boudet were full of them. But it was an ill moment for Leclerc to be enacting such a dream, however bravely. This charge was driven by rage, contempt, and incomprehension of the enemy. Most of the troops had been piloted over the country by overseers or landowners of Arnaud's old stripe, who still somehow managed to believe they had only to show their slaves the whip to return them to abject submission. In the end it was misleading guidance.

The former slaves stood calmly, neck deep in the ditches before the fort, elbows bracing their muskets on the ground. They held their fire till the very last moment, and when they did fire the effect was withering; yet the French charge did not abate. Now it was all hand-to-hand fighting in those trenches, and the momentum of the charge had carried a couple of dozen grenadiers to the base of the wall. But now, of course, came the *mitraille*, mauling the French advance beyond the ditches. The storming party was cut off and would be slaughtered.

"Look there." It was General Lacroix, leaning into Maillart's shoulder and pointing as he shouted in his ear, toward a small round hilltop north of the fort, covered by a sparse grove of slender trees. "Do you see that eminence?"

Maillart nodded.

"Take the seventh platoon of musketeers there," Lacroix said. "I'll wager you can do some damage from that place."

Maillart saluted; Lacroix thumped his shoulder and moved on. The maneuver was accomplished quickly enough, and proved to have been very well conceived. From the little hilltop Maillart could see plainly down into the fort, boiling like an anthill disturbed by a boot. After a moment he discerned that no cannon were aimed to cover the hill, and that Dessalines sat on the step of the powder magazine, conducting the fight with a lit torch he held in his right hand.

"Kill that general," Maillart said and fired his own pistol among the muskets, but too quickly. The range was a little long for these small arms; cannon would have been more useful. Dessalines lifted a hot musket ball from the ground at his feet, then smiled up at the hilltop. At once he got to his feet and ordered two cannon to be rolled to the embrasures facing the hill.

Maillart reloaded, fired again, again to no effect. Either the range was simply too long or Dessalines was protected today by some enchantment. He could hear the black general's voice very plainly, bullying his cannoneers—*what do you mean by this sluggishness!* Yet they seemed to be bringing the guns around quickly enough. One of Maillart's musketeers jostled him and pointed. Beyond the fort, below the bluff, some hundreds of black irregulars were climbing from the river bank onto the main battlefield to attack Leclerc's left flank. It was not a very well-organized movement, but there were a lot of men involved in it, and Leclerc's men were already falling into disarray under the constant battering of *mitraille*.

Dessalines grinned, and over his shoulder Maillart noticed a miserable quartet of white musicians sweating out one of his favorite martial airs, and unbelievably he thought he got a glimpse of Doctor Hébert flashing from the cover of one *ajoupa* to another, a roll of bandage trailing from his arm. He most definitely saw Dessalines, himself, lower a flame to a touch hole. *Mitraille* snapped the slender trunks of half the little trees on their hilltop. One of the musketeers dropped to the ground, clutching his knee.

"Retreat!" Maillart saw to it someone helped the wounded man away. There was no hope for this position once cannon had been brought to bear on it, though it might be worth trying to return with their own artillery.

Mitraille still raked the main battlefield below the fort. Returning, Maillart saw Daspir's horse shot out from under him. He rode in. Daspir was pinned, one leg caught under his saddle and the horse's withers, trying to pry himself loose with his sword. As Maillart reached him, the horse rolled away. Daspir's leg must not have been too badly hurt, for he was able to scramble up behind with a little assist from Maillart's arm.

Excellent, Maillart thought, now I own two of these reckless puppies. He looked around but did not see Paltre. To the left of the field, the new black irregulars were enthusiastically bayoneting those of Leclerc's troops too bewildered by the *mitraille* to resist in an organized way. In fact, the whole situation was fast becoming desperate. General Dugua, bleeding in two places, was being carried off the field on a stretcher. Pamphile de Lacroix had joined Leclerc, and Maillart spurred his horse in that direction. Behind, Daspir lurched off-center, then quickly regained his balance, pressing his chest into Maillart's back.

Morisset had made it a point of honor for Placide to carry the flag he'd captured in that last raid on Gonaives into all subsequent engagements. Sawed short for the purpose, the flagstaff could be seated securely in a long scabbard strapped to the saddle, leaving Placide's hands free to shoot or strike. In the first charge of that morning, he'd fired no shot and struck no blow, though he'd ridden down several of the bolting French troopers, and maybe they'd been killed by the hooves of his horse, or finished off by others riding behind him.

When the column of fresh troops appeared from the west, Morisset had pulled his cavalry out of the battle; they rode to the shelter of the woods beyond the town to rest their horses. Placide got down and walked his mount to cool for half an hour before he let it drink. This reflexive action calmed him as much as it did his horse. He unfastened the red headcloth Guiaou had given him, mopped off his face with it, and folded it in a triangle to put in his pocket. The electric thrill of the fight still ran all through the guardsmen; the grove was heavy with the odor of their anger and sweat, mingling with the hot smell of the horses.

Only one squadron of cavalry had entered the first charge; the second, commanded by Monpoint, waited in reserve. The two commanders watched the second French advance on the fort from the cover of the trees.

"Which one is Leclerc?" Monpoint asked Morisset, but neither man had ever seen the French general.

"There," said Placide, pointing to where Leclerc had just stepped out of the ranks, to initiate the charge. Morisset grunted an acknowledgment. He shaded his eyes to squint at Leclerc where he stood with Dugua, directing the battle.

Somehow the sight of Leclerc drained Placide of all feeling, even that uncategorizable quaver that the recent action had left in his limbs. He felt as empty as a bottle, washed and let dry. Through this emptiness, action might flow without thought. When the French charge faltered at the ditches, and Gottereau had brought his throng of armed field hands to take their share in the slaughter, Monpoint began mounting the men of his squadron for another charge.

"Let me ride with them," Placide said suddenly.

Morisset looked at him, uncertain at first. Placide turned into the wind, opened his headcloth into the air that fanned back over his head, and tightened the knot on the base of his neck.

"Go, then," Morisset said. "Do you need a fresh horse?"

Placide shook his head. "No, mine has rested." Though the bay he rode was not Bel Argent, it did come from Toussaint's personal stable, and Placide thought it stouter than most of the honor guard's horses, though the guard was generally well mounted. Morisset stretched out a hand and brushed the knot of the headcloth, letting his hand slip down from Placide's shoulder as Placide trotted away.

They entered the field at a gallop from the Grand Cahos Road. Placide, a length behind Monpoint, managed the staff of the flag with his left hand and the reins with his right. At the first shock he seated the staff in the scabbard, switched hands on the reins, and drew the sword Napoleon had given him. His eye had tightened on Leclerc from the moment they rode into view. Later he would reason through his motives: how Toussaint always took care to blame Leclerc personally for this war, rather than the French nation or its leader. How strangely suitable it would be all the same for Leclerc to be struck down with the weapon Napoleon's treacherous hand had placed in Placide's. But at this moment there was no such notion in his head; there was nothing at all, only the wind flowing in and out of the bottle.

Maillart was a dozen yards away when the little group surrounding Leclerc disappeared in a cloud of dust. At first he thought the Captain-General had been directly hit by a cannonball or an exploding shell.

Later on it turned out that the ball had struck somewhat short and thrown up a fist-sized stone into Leclerc's groin; not a lethal injury but more than enough to flatten him. Daspir picked him out first where he lay, and scrambled down from Maillart's horse, landing at a run. He'd managed to hang on to his sword amid all the confusion when his own horse had been shot down. Now the trumpets blared from the fort behind them and were answered again from the tree line across the way, and already the silver-helmed horsemen of Toussaint's guard were thundering down on them. Daspir had learned to flinch at this sight. He forced himself to keep going. Leclerc lay foetally curled, breathless, clutching his groin, his pale face smudged with dust. Maillart fought to control his dancing horse. He could not see General Lacroix anywhere. He turned Monpoint's blade with his own as the black commander barreled past him, thinking, *Damn it! Remember all the rum we've shared?* The next rider carried Maillart's own flag, and he thought, *Riau, Riau;* it was what he had dreaded, and Riau often wore such a red rag into battle, but the face under the tight band of the headcloth belonged to Placide Louverture.

Maillart was frozen. He would not strike the boy. But Placide was riding for Leclerc, whom Daspir had assisted first to his knees, then, unsteadily, to his feet, as Placide rode down on him with his head floating empty under the red cloth and his whole being poured into his right arm, the force and direction of the blow. Daspir just managed to get his own sword up, awkwardly angling his blade above his own head, like raising an umbrella in a rainstorm. Placide's falling blade snagged on Daspir's hilt, and Daspir, with his arm crooked over his head, unbalanced by Leclerc's weight on the other side, felt the muscle tear behind his right shoulder in the instant before Placide's horse struck him in the back and knocked him winded into the dirt.

Look at him ride, Maillart was thinking, imagining that Toussaint would feel the same surprised pleasure if he could see his son now. Placide had managed to turn his horse in an unbelievably short space, the animal's hindquarters scrubbing the ground, then thrusting up again into the charge. Unconsciously, Maillart spurred up Eclair. He'd have to meet Placide this time, now that Daspir had been knocked out of the action and Leclerc stood bewildered, dust-blinded, no weapon in his empty hands, with Placide bearing down on him, admirably single-minded on his target. As Maillart recognized that he himself would be inevitably too slow, too late, the cavalry commander Dalton appeared from the dust cloud and snatched Leclerc across his saddlebow like a sack of meal (due to the nature of his hurt, the Captain-General would be unable to bestride a horse for many days). Placide's sword flashed through the space where Leclerc had been a split-second before, with such force and penetration that the point hacked a divot from the ground.

Maillart rode by. He could not wheel his horse in twice the time it took Placide—the boy was going to catch him from behind. But instead Placide rode past, ignoring Maillart, bent on Dalton as he carried Leclerc away. All of the French were routed again. Daspir popped up under Maillart's horse, spitting a mouthful of grit. When Maillart caught his right arm to help him up, Daspir's face went a stark, cold white. He managed to scramble up behind Maillart, then fainted dead away from the pain as soon as he was seated.

To his surprise, Maillart saw that he was overtaking Placide now. He did not raise his weapon. It was too difficult, when he had to hold the unconscious Daspir on by clamping the arm wrapped around his waist. He passed Placide. They were running, all the French were in full flight; they would not stop before they reached the ferry landing at the river below the town. Placide was losing ground on them, Maillart could see over his shoulder. Now only a splotch of the red rag was visible, now only the flag high on its staff. Then he was gone. At last Placide's concentration admitted the voice of Monpoint, shouting for him to slow down, turn back. He had too much outdistanced the rest of his squadron, and now the bay was flagging. He drew on the reins and walked the horse, still staring after the stampeded French army. The only thought his mind would hold was that, after all, he had been wrong not to have changed horses.

The two trumpeters and the drummer were wind-broken and exhausted from blowing and beating through the whole day's fighting. Gaston, however, sat up crosslegged like a grasshopper, still bowing his fiddle through slow, melancholy, country airs that scarcely varied one to the next. The noise was nerve-wracking, but it did mask the screams of the men of the Ninth, who had been turned over to Lamartinière after their capture.

Bienvenu had passed a hard day in the fighting, and the doctor excused him from nursing duties, that he might go to watch the tortures which were this evening's entertainment for the troops. During the day the doctor had got some nursing help from Marie-Jeanne Lamartinière, when she was not occupied by sniping on the wounded French below the walls, using a long rifle much like the doctor's, with a skill all the men applauded. Yet when she nursed, there was a forcefulness in her calm that seemed to make a man stop bleeding at her touch.

This evening, however, Marie-Jeanne had gone to join her husband. Encouraged by Dessalines, himself somewhat irritated by a chest wound he'd acquired from falling against a stake, Lamartinière was visiting the worst punishments anyone could imagine on the men of the Ninth who'd turned their coats to fight for the French. From all this, the doctor had averted his eye, but Descourtilz spied on the proceedings for a little while, then crept back to the doctor's post to whisper the details: "The first was skinned alive, then they tore out his heart and drank his blood; the second was castrated and had his guts pulled out of his belly into the fire while he still lived; they broke all the bones of the third and then—"

"Shut up, for Christ's sake," the doctor said. "Be quiet and help me with these bandages."

Descourtilz left off his narrative and joined in the work. They had organized a hospital shelter along the north wall of the powder magazine. The area was easiest to protect from the sun, and if Dessalines did blow up the fort, the end for the wounded would at least be quick.

At the opposite end of the fort, most of the garrison clustered around the men who were being tortured. Lamartinière had taken a high tone, at the beginning: "I want to have the satisfaction of destroying, myself, these miserable traitors who've served in the ranks of the French, against the liberty of their brothers." But as he moved into the work, a blood rage transformed him; he ceased to resemble his civilized self. The throng of men blocked the doctor's view, though if he glanced in the direction of the moaning, he could see the red flickering glow of the fire at the center of the ring. The crowd expanded or contracted, shuddered or rippled, shouting or sighing its appreciation of each fresh extravagance of cruelty. Above it all, the violin whined.

"How do you turn your back on such monstrosity?" Descourtilz finally said.

"It won't be altered by my looking at it," the doctor said. The work was finished; he sat on the ground with his back against the rough stone wall of the magazine. A few stars gleamed above the shattered saplings on the hill beyond the wall. He scratched at the edge of his head wound, under the bandage.

"In ninety-one I was prisoner in the camps of Grande Rivière," he said. "What I saw there is most likely beyond the imagining of anyone here. And I missed being done away with here as narrowly as you, down there in the town . . ." He hesitated. "In the end I think there's no good facing it. I know it's there. But I don't want my mind filled with the images."

The violin struck a sour note, then limped back into tune. The throng around the torturers sucked up a very deep breath.

"They are all savages," Descourtilz said bitterly.

"They are a people of extremes," the doctor said. At that moment he believed that he might rip someone's heart out himself if the action would win him a drink of rum. He felt that Descourtilz's assertion was wrong, but it was difficult to articulate his reasons.

"When this festivity is over," he said, "they'll be as mild as little children, most of them."

"Not Dessalines," said Descourtilz, and paused. "I know what you mean—but isn't that the most horrible thing of all?"

"No," said the doctor. "No, I don't think so."

Descourtilz merely grunted, then stretched out on his side. A few minutes later, Gaston left off his fiddling. It was finished; the men were drifting away from the embers of the fire. Bienvenu came slinking along the wall toward the doctor's *ajoupa*, a little abashed, like a dog that's done mischief.

"*Gegne clairin*," he said, offering a gourd. There's rum.

The doctor took the gourd with an inexpressible gratitude. After his first gulp he discovered his fingers had got all sticky with blood from brushing Bienvenu's hand. Quickly he scrubbed them off in the dirt. Bienvenu had gone to sleep instantly, peacefully; he lay on his back and snored. The doctor took another, more contemplative swallow of rum and weighed the gourd in the palm of his hand, guessing it to be half full at least. Carefully he stoppered it and put it out of sight, in the straw bag where he kept his healing herbs.

Though he was exhausted, he could not sleep. Maybe it was the blood smell steaming from Bienvenu that disturbed him. For half an hour he twisted one way or another on his mat. At last he sat up and took one more short sip of rum, then began walking along the wall in the direction of the gate. The stars were now brighter overhead, and he could pick out a few constellations: the Corona Borealis, Hydra, the Crab. By the last coals of the bonfire, Dessalines and Lamartinière sat muttering. The doctor turned his face from them as he passed. The rum put a distance between him and the idea that had come to him on the mat: he was not very likely to leave this situation alive.

At an embrasure beside the gate he stopped and looked out along the cannon barrel. Under the rounded roof of stars he could discern some indistinct movement among the hundreds of corpses scattered over the field. His glasses were smudged, but when he took them off to clean them they slipped through his numb fingers, rang off the cannon barrel, and went spinning away. When he leaned out to snatch for them, he overbalanced and was falling too, whirling, nauseated . . . he saw the glasses shatter against a stone. Then he was on his feet again, suffused in the warm smell of Nanon, and Nanon was handing him his glasses.

The doctor blinked and caught his breath. He steadied himself against the wall. Where he'd thought he'd seen Nanon stood the commander Magny, looking at him with mild interest or concern. His glasses were in his hand, unbroken. He polished them on the hem of his shirt and put them on.

"Dogs."

Was it himself or Magny who had spoken, or maybe the sentry who had just joined them from the gate? In any case the dogs were there, great bristling, brindled *casques* out of the mountains, packs of them, moving among the cadavers to feed.

"It is not acceptable," Magny said. He looked at the doctor, as if for confirmation, but the doctor could not draw his eyes from the view. In the bluish light of the icy stars, the wild dogs hunched their shoulders and lowered their heads and jerked their jaws to loosen and gulp cold chunks of human flesh.

"We'll put an end to this." Magny turned and muttered something to the sentry. Ten minutes later they were leading a sortie from the fort, to drive away the dogs and pile the bodies between stacks of wood for burning.

29

In the days since the battle at Ravine à Couleuvre, Sergeant Aloyse had adopted a more tender attitude toward Captain Guizot. Before, he'd treated the captain with the sort of kindness a grown man might show to a boy at risk of hurting himself. But since Guizot had dragged Aloyse clear of the wreckage of the exploding powder magazine, the sergeant mixed a measure of respect with his concern. Indeed, Guizot found that his various prodigies of activity that day, however slim their actual result, had won him admiration from more than a few. His orders were obeyed with more alacrity by all his men, and General Rochambeau, when he addressed his remarks to Guizot, no longer alluded to the escape of Xavier Tocquet.

Their instructions were to proceed inland, across the Grand Cahos mountain range to the town of Mirebalais: a key, so it was told, to controlling the interior. Toussaint might retreat to this pocket of the mountains, some had speculated. It took them two days, however, to begin the march. There were enough French dead to be buried that Rochambeau was moved to lie about their number in his report, and time was needed to get the worst wounded in condition to be evacuated to Gonaives, and the more lightly wounded fit enough to march with the division.

All symptoms of the cold Guizot had carried down from the rainy plateau disappeared the day after the battle, but his arrow wound from

Grande Rivière swelled and began to fester. All through the day, the puncture leaked a putrid matter into its bandage. By nightfall the captain was usually somewhat feverish. Sergeant Aloyse cared for him and helped him conceal the worsening injury. The chief medical officer of Rochambeau's division had succumbed to fever on the march from Saint Raphael, and his instruments were now manipulated by a man more skilled as barber than surgeon, if one judged by the ugly stumps of his amputations.

They limped into the Cahos mountains, hindered by inaccurate maps and unreliable, perhaps treacherous, guides. Maybe no map could ever convey the interminable twisting and spiraling of the jungle pathways that always only revealed another more demanding ascent beyond the peak just mastered. As for the guides, all they ever would say was "It is a little way farther." Still, it was a relief to leave the stinking battlefield in the ravine, where vultures still worked to pick the corpses from their shallow graves in the loose gravel of the shoals. And though it was cold where they camped on the heights, the incidence of fever lessened as they climbed. If not for his fear of losing his arm, Guizot might have felt optimistic.

Was Toussaint ahead of them, flying to Mirebalais? Guizot had actually brushed his sleeve, on the desert plain of Périsse. But their intelligence was none too reliable—they hardly knew the whereabouts of the other French divisions. The switchbacks of the trails twisting through the Cahos mountains left their compass needles spinning beyond reason. The endless self-resembling turnings of their movement were punctuated by ambushes every so often—quick skirmishes offered by mobs of half-naked, barefoot blacks, sometimes led by men in more regular uniform and sometimes not. These were Dessalines's men, was the rumored report, though the notorious black general did not reveal himself in person. Other rumors told that Dessalines had engaged with General Hardy on the slopes of the mountain called Nolo, and been beaten back eastward toward Mirebalais, but Rochambeau's scouts could not certainly confirm those rumors.

The ambushes and skirmishes did small damage so far as casualties were counted, and yet they wore away at the morale of Rochambeau's men—to be picked, constantly harassed, by an enemy that would not stand to fight. Guizot was increasingly aware of how rapidly this army of shadows always parting before them closed to reoccupy the territory over which Rochambeau had just passed. He knew Sergeant Aloyse was aware of that also, though the two of them did not discuss it.

Toussaint was not waiting for them at Mirebalais; not even a cat had been left alive in that place. A pall of smoke hung over the cleft in the mountains, above the pocket of river valley where the town lay in its ruins. Miles before they'd reached the place, they knew they'd find no shelter there. The plantations too had been put to the torch for a half-mile radius around the town. They entered at sundown, eyes burning, coughing from the lingering smoke. Guizot had tied a dirty kerchief over his face; it soon grew black around the nostrils, but it did little to block the foul smell of his own festering wound. Oddly, there were no human corpses in the town, though the wells had been stopped with the carcasses of draft animals.

They camped a quarter-mile upriver, on the right bank of the Artibonite. Aloyse hauled water and worked on Guizot's arm with hot compresses, until the captain had slipped into a feverish sleep. In his dream he saw the hurt arm blackened to the shoulder, rot spreading across his chest to corrupt his heart. But when he woke the wound looked little worse than it had the day before and the fever had slackened; his mind was clear. A messenger from the Captain-General had reached Rochambeau at dawn: they were to move northwest again, along the right bank of the Artibonite toward the coast. They'd find the enemy brought to bay at last when they joined Leclerc at Petite Rivière.

With that envoy came the news of the massacre at Habitation Chirry; it was there that Dessalines had marched the whites of Mirebalais to be butchered. Later that morning their line of march traversed a ridge that gave them a long view of pale mutilated bodies scattered over the burnt stubble of what had perhaps been a cornfield, three hundred dead of every age and sex with the vultures among them still more numerous. Rochambeau would not stop for a burial detail, and the men did not protest his urgency, but tramped on doggedly, burning eyes fixed ahead. They marched for an hour after dark, but when the sky clouded over they were obliged to camp, near enough to Verrettes that the rot-stink of that other field of massacre reached them from across the river, borne on the south wind, mingling in Guizot's nostrils with the rot of his own arm.

Plagued by mosquitoes and the throbbing of his wound, he was tottery, giddy, when he rose next day. Rochambeau would not wait for a cook fire. They chewed their moldy hardtack on the move. An hour's march had settled Guizot into the rhythm. Midmorning, they struck friendly pickets who let them know Pamphile de Lacroix was established on a line to their left, while dead ahead the enemy had been trapped and mostly surrounded in a little fort. Rochambeau was too excited by this news to pause for an account of the earlier days' engagements. Guizot had no objection to the haste of their advance; the images he'd so briefly glanced over at Chirry still burned behind his eyes.

After another forty minutes' march, he and Aloyse were sent forward to reconnoiter and saw through the trees that covered them a small redoubt on a little knoll, defended by fresh-dug earth supporting roughly pointed logs, occupied by something under two hundred men, by Guizot's quick estimation. Beyond the redoubt and a little below it was the masonry wall of a more substantial fort, and beyond that a passage into the empty air; Guizot supposed that a bend in the river must lie below.

In another moment, Rochambeau had come up from the rear to join them. From under cover of the trees, he studied the redoubt with a spyglass. Behind the earthworks, a black corporal looked up curiously. Perhaps a flash of sunlight had glinted from the lens, but he seemed uncertain of what he had seen, and Rochambeau quickly lowered his instrument.

"Captain," said Rochambeau, "I think it would be small trouble to you to sweep away that little emplacement."

"None at all," Guizot replied. The blood beneath his infected wound pulsed like a drumbeat, and though he still felt somewhat dizzy, he could feel his anger hardening.

"Good," Rochambeau said. "Then let us set about it."

In the morning after that long day's battle, Doctor Hébert woke to find that Magny's effort to burn the bodies on the slope outside the fort had been less than completely successful. Yet the smoke from the fitfully smoldering fires had been enough to discourage the dogs, unless they'd been moved to retreat by the rising sun. The doctor turned from his embrasure and set about heating water for a change of bandages. Descourtilz and the musicians were still snoring on their mats. By the steps of the powder magazine, Dessalines was conferring with Magny and Lamartinière. He gestured toward the knoll above the fort, where the French had briefly appeared the day before, and Lamartinière nodded several times, snapping his heels together.

Dessalines was leaving the fort on a mission to bring more powder from Plassac, the doctor overheard—if by chance that depot had survived. Below, they were opening the gate for the sortie, but Dessalines stopped on the threshold, and called out another order. Half a dozen men broke out of his small contingent and scooped the remains of the prisoners of the Ninth who'd been tortured to death the night before onto a square of canvas, dragged it through the gate, and tumbled its contents onto the slope beyond the ditches. The doctor could not quite restrain himself from watching the procedure. Some of the bodies were dismembered, as Descourtilz had reported; his eyes clung to a severed forearm fetched up against a stone, stiff fingers stretching upward from a bloody palm.

During this operation, Dessalines seemed to think of something. He called Lamartinière to come to him, leaned down from his horse, and proffered his right hand, as if to be kissed. But instead he pointed to one of several heavy rings on his fingers. Lamartinière took note of it and nodded.

A few scattered shots came from the French lines as Dessalines rode out. But the honor guard cavalry showed itself in force at the tree line opposite, and that was enough to discourage any serious pursuit. In a moment Dessalines's little force had vanished in the trees.

In two days' time, Lamartinière had raised a tidy little redoubt on that knoll above the fort, buttressed with earthworks and *bwa kampech*. For want of proper tools, most of the digging and chopping was done with *coutelas*, but still it went quickly. Lamartinière manned the fort and installed four of the cannon from the fort, then settled in to wait, day after day. There was no attack upon them anywhere. The French could be seen maneuvering in the distance, well out of range of either battery. Apparently they were in for a rulebook siege.

The departure of Dessalines left Descourtilz more cheerful, though Doctor Hébert was not so much encouraged by it. Sicge tedium weighed upon him drearily. Both food and water were running short. At first, some of the more daring black soldiers managed to slip to and from the river at night, but in a few days French maneuvers had closed that breach and the next water-foraging party did not return. With water rationing, the wounded did poorly; many had begun to die.

Lamartinière had put his men to cutting brush around the redoubt. Their long knives hacked through the heat of the day, clearing broader fields of fire. Outside this new perimeter, the doctor was sometimes allowed to ramble, in search of healing herbs to replenish his stores. Sometimes Descourtilz went with him, and always Bienvenu and one other man from the black army, though this other man changed from one excursion to the next. Meanwhile, Lamartinière's men had finished their clearing and turned to deepening the ditch around the redoubt. The doctor knew that Descourtilz's mind was on escape, but there was no such possibility. Even Bienvenu would sound the alarm, and the second man was there in case Bienvenu should waver.

The slope below the fort heaved with vultures' wings from dawn to dusk, and a greasy black smoke bled into the air from the ravines below Petite Rivière. At dusk, sometimes the dogs returned, their heavy brindled shoulders hunching. Marie-Jeanne Lamartinière picked off a few of them with her long gun, until her husband told her to stop wasting ammunition. Thereafter she only stared at the dogs balefully, her two hands twitching on her hips.

One afternoon the doctor was shocked out of his siesta by the crump of a single artillery piece from the direction of the town. With Descourtilz he hurried to the wall beside the gate, to see a heavy iron sphere loft into the air, fall short, and roll back down the slope, its fuse whipping and spitting sparks. When the shell went off, the nearby corpses jumped; a dozen vultures lumbered into the air and circled.

The doctor snatched out the joints of his folding spyglass and brought it to his eye. In the lens's round he could make out the figure of Pétion, lately returned from his exile in France, directing the adjustment of the *obusier*. When the match was lit, the doctor had a great impulse to flinch, though he knew there was no point. Descourtilz nudged his elbow, and the doctor passed him the glass. The second shell was flying over their heads; it landed squarely within the fort and spun with its fuse sizzling.

Marie-Jeanne Lamartinière moved toward it as quickly as any of the men, but Magny caught her arm and held her back. A couple of horses whinnied nervously, edging against their tethers by the upper wall. The doctor watched, half frozen; it seemed to have been instantly understood by all that no water could be wasted on extinguishing this thing. Three men hauled it off the ground and began to carry it toward the nearest embrasure. There was a moment of awkwardness because a cannon was in the way. One man was blown to indecipherable bits when the shell went off, showering the bystanders with blood and ribbons of shredded flesh. A second, who'd lost his grip in falling over the gun carriage, was not hurt at all, while the third had his two hands hopelessly mangled. The doctor found his breath and ran to stanch the bleeding, almost colliding with Marie-Jeanne, who'd rushed in with the same purpose.

Lamartinière's redoubt was now returning fire, effectively enough to silence the *obusier*, at least temporarily. Pétion would doubtless be trying to move this gun to some more advantageous position. As for the shattered hands, there was no saving either one of them. He found his straw sack and retrieved his saw. It needed three men besides Bienvenu to hold the wounded man, and Magny ordered the musicians to strike up the liveliest air they knew, in hope of muffling his screams. Finished at last, the doctor left Bienvenu to bandage the stumps and crawled to stretch out on his mat. His stomach boiled, but he swallowed it back and finally lost consciousness.

When he woke, it was already dark; he lay motionless but for the blinking of his eyes. Bienvenu's voice droned in the darkness, giving the news of the evening's scout to the man who'd lost his hands that day. Apparently General Hardy had brought in a French column to join the siege line north of the fort. At his arrival, Morisset and Monpoint had withdrawn their cavalry and ridden off in search of Toussaint. "Papa Toussaint will come," Bienvenu's whisper kept assuring. "He will come to kill all these *blancs* and make us free."

Cautiously the doctor rolled back a corner of his mat and pushed his fingers into the dirt until they stopped on cloth-wrapped steel. The touch of his octagon rifle barrel scarcely reassured him. He withdrew his hand and let the mat fall into place, wondering whom he'd fire on when the end came, if he fired at all.

To the right of General Lacroix's line, two hundred cadavers of white civilians slain by Dessalines for many days had been stiffening, then deliquescing, in their clotted blood. The stench grew more unbearable every day, and every day there were more flies. Lacroix put Major Maillart in charge of burning the corpses. It proved to have been a bad idea, for the bodies burned sluggishly, incompletely, and blanketed the area with a stinking black smoke that choked the men all across their lines. The cloth Maillart tied across his nose and mouth did little good. At least he had the advantage of light cotton clothing. Most of the men, Lacroix included, had come out wearing woolen uniforms, and the foul miasma sank deep in the wool, and seemed like it would linger forever.

Lacroix was the senior surviving officer, after Leclerc, whose dangerously bruised groin kept him mostly confined to his tent. For an hour a day the Captain-General would tour the developing siege positions, moving on foot as he could not possibly bestride a horse, biting his lips to hide his pain. Then he'd disappear into his convalescence. The task of encirclement thus fell to Lacroix.

To Maillart, Lacroix made the observation that in war as in agriculture, it was foolish to try to tear out a huge boulder all in one piece; better to use patience to chip away at it and carry it off by shards. Toward that end, Lacroix detached General Bourke to cross the river and block the ford southwest of the fort. By this passage the rebels had got reinforcement on that one day of pitched battle which had been so disastrous for the French. With Bourke in place, they could no longer even fetch water from the river, much less cross into the open country beyond. Bourke held the position without much difficulty, though lightly harassed, mostly at night, by the troops of Charles Belair, who still maintained an elusive presence south of the Artibonite. When General Hardy's division arrived to flush the honor guard cavalry out of the woods above the town, it seemed that the net must soon draw tight.

Maillart spent his days riding from post to post—his familiarity with the terrain made him valuable. Lacroix had put the captains Paltre, Cyprien, and Daspir mostly in his charge, to be instructed in the lie of the land. Maillart observed the junior officers with a degree of ironic distance. There seemed to be some rivalry among them, though he could not quite devine its source. Paltre and Cyprien he remembered from the season the mission of Hédouville in 1798. He had distinctly disliked both of them then, for an unseasoned pair of wastrels, arrogant without cause and overly given to the vices of women, rum, and gambling (and for Maillart to register such a reproach was in itself extraordinary). These weeks of real and terrible warfare seemed to have embittered Paltre, to judge from his dour muttering through his broken nose, while Cyprien seemed simply to have hardened. Daspir looked a little less touched by it all. There was a softness in his cheeks and mouth, a concupiscent expression that reminded Maillart of Michel Arnaud as a younger man, ten years ago, before the slaves revolted. Yet in Daspir's eyes there was a cool steeliness of regard that ill matched the rest of his expression. Puzzling, but Maillart liked him best of the three. Despite his sprained shoulder he rode the lines willingly, managing his horse with his left hand—and he was an excellent horseman.

They kept their movements comfortably out of range of the fort, though still within view of it. It was a glad thing to ride away from the pestilent smoke of the corpses smoldering in the ravine below Petite Rivière. From within the fort a couple of horns and a drum regaled them with the popular airs of the French Revolution; if he listened closely Maillart thought he could make out the thin whine of a violin as well. Cyprien and Paltre seemed positively offended by this choice of music, while Daspir was merely perplexed. The three of them, guided by Maillart, spent much of their time scouting for a better position for Pétion's guns. Lacroix was resolved that a steady bombardment would be the best solution to the siege, but the most opportune spots from which to launch shells were all covered by the small new earthwork the defenders had hastily erected. Though the blacks in the larger fort were conserving ammunition, fire from the little redoubt was extremely vigorous whenever a French uniform came within range. With a borrowed spyglass, Maillart studied the work and reported to Lacroix that it had been well surrounded by trenches, in the same style as the main fort.

Then, around noon on March 22, another still, hot day of siege, a cannon barrage erupted from the woods east of the redoubt. Lacroix jumped out from under the square of canvas where he'd been sheltering from the midday sun, and shaded his eyes to stare toward the fort.

"We have no troops in that direction," he said and turned to Maillart and Daspir, who were standing by. "What did you see up there this morning?"

"Nothing," said Maillart, who had indeed seen nothing unusual when he'd reconnoitered the area a little after dawn. But in less than five minutes a rider came pounding in to announce the arrival of General Rochambeau.

At this news, Lacroix grinned at first. "Why, if he can silence the cannon they've got there—" Then his face changed. "No, but he will try to rush the trenches. I know him." He turned to Maillart. "Go and stop him."

In seconds Maillart and Daspir were in the saddle, bearing orders for Rochambeau to sustain his cannonade but not to risk an infantry assault. Maillart had got the idea right away. Twice already the French had fallen into just this trap, and tales of Rochambeau's recklessness had percolated all through the army; some grumbled that if he'd been more temperate at Fort Liberté, the burning of Le Cap would have been avoided.

But now as they rode too hastily across Hardy's front lines, the main fort did open fire on them, so they were forced to take a longish detour under cover of the woods. The horses were slowed almost to a walk to weave a way between the trees, and yet the cover seemed too thin, with grapeshot snapping branches all around them. From further off the artillery battle continued to resound, then suddenly fell silent. Maillart and Daspir broke cover and cantered the last quarter-mile in a dread whistling silence. With all that they arrived too late; Rochambeau had already launched his charge.

Guizot was crouching in the undergrowth, shoulder to shoulder with Sergeant Aloyse, trembling like a terrier from excitement, anger, and nerves. After a closer look at the enemy's armament, Rochambeau had countermanded his first order and decided to commence with his own artillery. It took some time to bring the seven cannon they'd dragged across the Cahos mountain range to bear, and Guizot had trouble restraining his men, all hot to avenge the civilian massacres they'd seen on the march from Mirebalais.

As for Guizot, he felt much the same. Who might command the fort he faced no longer interested him. The slight, small figure of Toussaint Louverture had become abstract, the cloth that bound his murderous head shrunken smaller than a red pinpoint, deep in Guizot's mind. Before him was only the enemy and the only thing to do was kill. As the cannon bellowed all around him and the gunners shouted encouragement to one another, he held his eyes fixed on Rochambeau's black shako. Then at last the barrage ceased; the guns of the redoubt had stopped returning fire. Rochambeau swept his gloved hand forward, and Guizot nudged Aloyse as he lunged to his feet and into the open.

He charged at the head of his grenadiers, stumbling over stubs of recently cut brush. Thirty yards away, the redoubt did not look impressive: an earthwork hastily shoveled up and studded with crudely pointed logs bristling outward. An outer ring of loosely molded dirt was scarcely knee high, and the whole thing looked practically undefended. Guizot's excitement rose; from a distance he heard his own voice howling. Then, when they'd closed half the distance, the ground sprouted rows of musketeers like dragon's teeth. Completely covered by the trench, their barrels braced on that insignificant ring of dirt, they fired with a fine precision.

The first shock passed over Guizot like a wave, washing him in a nausea like that of his first days at sea. Yards short of the trench, the charge had broken and he himself seemed the only man still upright in what had become a field of bleeding casualties. Except Aloyse, who clawed at him, eyes ringed with white, shouting hoarsely, "Turn back, turn back!" Guizot's ears were ringing; bullets were still whistling by. The men behind the higher earthwork had loosed a volley while those in the trench reloaded. Guizot turned and scrambled after the sergeant's bouncing pigtail. He was stumbling over corpses now, and it seemed to take him years to reach the trees.

Ten paces into the cover he encountered Rochambeau, stamping his high boots and spitting with rage. "Captain, what do you mean by this dishonorable flight? Return your men to the assault!"

Guizot, numb and breathless, had no thought but to obey. He turned in a half-circle, drawing wind to call an order, but before a word could leave his lips he saw he had no men to rally. Except for himself and Sergeant Aloyse, every last soldier of his command lay dead or crippled on the field.

Rochambeau was arguing now with a cavalry major who'd just ridden up: a tall, raw-boned fellow with a graying mustache, his face and hands weatherbeaten to the color of old brick. Behind this man was Captain Daspir, right arm in a sling, who on sight of Guizot slipped down from his horse and came to him.

The notorious Rochambeau cut no impressive figure in Maillart's eyes. He was so short that his shako and boots seemed to account for a quarter of his height. His uniform fit sloppily on a pudgy body and the same doughiness was in his face, which wore the expression of a petulant child. At first, he did not want to hear the order Maillart brought, arguing that Pamphile de Lacroix was not his superior, while Maillart did his best to explain with due deference that for the moment Lacroix spoke for Captain-General Leclerc—and that in any case the folly of charging the entrenched redoubt was now more than evident on the field before them. But now General Lacroix had arrived himself. A short distance behind him came Pétion's artillerymen, sweating and grunting as they hauled their guns and carriages up the hill—a maneuver which Rochambeau's attack had finally made possible.

"General, General," Lacroix was saying. "What is this impetuosity? Did you not receive my order?"

"What would you?" Rochambeau jerked his gloved hand toward the redoubt. "How many niggers can there be in that ant hill? A hundred? Two hundred? Would you imagine they could hold against my grenadiers?"

Pamphile de Lacroix pressed his fingertips to his temples, with an odd delicacy, as if holding together a fractured skull. "Indeed," he said in a low voice, "there cannot be more than twelve hundred men all told in that redoubt and the fort together. And we surround them with twelve thousand. They give us odds of ten to one and yet . . ." Lacroix turned to survey the field. "Include those men you've just sent to the slaughter, and they have cost us fifteen hundred men in pure losses."

Rochambeau looked ready for another hot reply, but Maillart interrupted, speaking to Lacroix. "*Mon général,* the message did not reach him," he said. "Unfortunately, we arrived too late."

At that both Lacroix and Rochambeau subsided. It was quiet, except for the cry of a hawk wheeling high in the air above the blood-soaked field.

The man who'd lost his hands to the shell had taken gangrene. Corruption climbed his forearms to the elbow and beyond. Without sufficient water there was little the doctor could do; he could not properly clean the wound or change bandages and dressings as often as required. He did not have the heart to take the arms off at the shoulder . . . which likely would only delay the outcome, in any case. And there was nothing at all for the pain. Yet the man was stoic, in his way; he did not cry out and seldom even whimpered, only stretched out his necrotic stumps to show to anyone who passed, as if he begged handlessly for charity. It really might have been best to shoot him, but the doctor could not uncover his weapons for that, and if he did Magny would not have allowed him to waste a shot.

At last, on the morning before Rochambeau attacked the redoubt, the man died. In a dull silence, Bienvenu found men to help him roll the body through an embrasure and let it drop over the cliff above the river. As the body unfolded its limbs to fall free, the first cannon sounded above the redoubt.

Descourtilz and the musicians crept to the wall to watch the action, but the doctor only squatted by the powder magazine, which offered him some protection against stray projectiles. If an odd shot chanced to blow up the powder, at least the end would be very quick. He brooded, his tongue rasping over dry lips, on the handless man who had just died. The action that had cost him his life deserved a more respectful burial, but they could not keep corpses in these walls.

The guns went silent in the redoubt, followed by shouts and the tearing sound of volleying muskets. Crouched with arms wrapped around his knees, the doctor listened for Marie-Jeanne's rifle, a clearer, truer note than any musket issued. That morning, the Amazon had gone to join her husband in the redoubt with her long gun, cartridge box, and a sword as long as one of her legs strapped to her waist on a belt of steel. Every time her rifle sounded, a French grenadier was certainly dead.

Presently the shooting stopped and Descourtilz joined the doctor, his face drawn and gray.

"The idiots tried to charge the trenches," he reported. "You can't imagine the destruction."

I don't want to imagine it, the doctor thought, but said instead, "How many?"

Descourtilz shrugged. "See for yourself."

But the doctor remained sitting where he was, perhaps for as long as half an hour. In that time there was no shooting. One could even hear birdsong from the wooded areas, with now and then a human voice calling some instruction. At last the doctor went to join Descourtilz and Bienvenu, who stood peering from opposite corners of one of the embrasures. The redoubt was still; no man showed himself above the earthworks. Over the dead and dying men a cloud of yellow butterflies was settling, drifting down like flower petals, like the snow the doctor hadn't seen these last ten years. Among the powdery yellow wings were a few white ones, picked out with small crimson dots.

"How strange," Descourtilz exhaled.

"It's the blood." The doctor's voice was harsh in his dry throat. "I don't know why, but it's the blood that brings them."

There came an explosive crump and a whistling rush of air, then a shell dropped out of the sky square into the redoubt, throwing up dirt and splinters when it blew. Descourtilz and the doctor ducked reflexively behind the wall, but the next shell fell in the main fort, blasting iron in all directions, shattering the forequarters of a horse.

"Pétion!" came a shout from down by the gate. "There is Pétion!"

Bienvenu was on the screaming horse in a flash, letting the blood from its throat with his *coutelas*. Several other men ran up to help him skin and dress the meat. Descourtilz and the doctor still huddled by the wall. Now and then another shell landed in the fort, but the main bombardment was directed at the redoubt. The doctor dared not lift his head to see, but the damage must certainly have been dreadful. And the butterflies, driven from the field, were streaming west like a plume of yellow smoke.

All afternoon the shelling continued; it ended only after dark. Two hours after nightfall, Lamartinière crept in with the remnant of the two hundred men who'd manned the redoubt, now too shattered to be held any longer. Lamartinière looked sick with exhaustion; Marie-Jeanne seemed a little brighter, though her dress was torn and bloody and her face was streaked with dirt. They dined that night on horseflesh half roasted, half dried over small hot fires, and after this repast, Magny ordered the musicians to strike up the "Marseillaise."

At dawn they saw that the French had used the cover of darkness to occupy the redoubt Lamartinière had left. The earthworks had even been a little reconstructed, to form a semicircular battery bearing down on the main fort. The doctor felt his stomach drop before the first shell fired.

"Pétion! Gare Pétion!" The cries from the defenders were half rage, half respect and grudging admiration for a dangerous adversary. Lamartinière and Pétion were both mulattoes, though Lamartinière had remained loyal to Toussaint when Pétion threw in his lot with Rigaud. With Magny, Lamartinière now supervised return fire from the cannons of the fort, but Pétion's guns were too well emplaced to be dislodged.

All day the bombardment went on and on. It was too dubious to try to throw the shells out of the fort before they blew. A new system developed, as if spontaneously. When each shell landed, one man rushed at it crying, *"M'alé nan Ginen!"* and covered it with his body. I am going to Africa! The doctor couldn't say where these men went for certain, but when the shells exploded very little of them remained in the fort.

One shell, one man. There were now some nine hundred defenders surviving. No man who covered a shell in this fashion lived, except in rare cases where the shell did not explode, but the injuries to others tended to be less than fatal. Still, the doctor felt too demoralized to treat these lighter injuries at first. There seemed to be no point; the scope of the problem surrounding him was too large for his mind to contain a solution to it. It was Marie-Jeanne, who'd laid down her rifle for a bandage roll, who by example and her urging got him to return to his work. Bienvenu and Descourtilz also worked tirelessly through the day, bandaging and when necessary sawing. Without water, without sufficient nourishment, these men would almost surely die, but there was nothing to do but move against that probability, keep on swimming against the tide. Deafened by the roar of shelling, the doctor did his duties automatically. He'd fallen into a kind of trance, almost as comforting as drunkenness, though his small reserve of rum had been exhausted long ago.

At night when the shelling had finally stopped, they ate the balance of the horsemeat and sang French patriotic songs till they were hoarse. The doctor stretched out, thinking he would never sleep, and woke from a tomb of black unconsciousness with Descourtilz's sour breath in his ear.

"Come on. We're going over the wall."

The doctor sat up cautiously. Behind Descourtilz he could just make out the figure of one of the trumpet players. Bienvenu was asleep, or pretending to be, on his mat nearby. The doctor scrabbled in the dirt for his rifle, then thought better of it.

"No," he said. "I'm staying."

"You're mad, then," Descourtilz hissed. "No one will survive another day of this—it's not so far to the French lines."

"But I'm engaged here," the doctor said. For some reason he pictured Tocquet riding off down the river, the dwindling back of his son Paul.

"With what?" Descourtilz's barely audible whisper still managed to convey exasperation.

"With this." The doctor stroked his hands over the velvety darkness surrounding them. "With all of it." He didn't know himself what he meant. "Go on, then." He took Descourtilz's hand for a moment. "*N'a wé,*" he said, not sure if the naturalist would understand the Creole. "*Si Dyé vlé.*" If God wants it, we'll meet again.

Descourtilz slipped off without saying anything more. There was some rustling, a choked breath, one thump, then another, outside the wall. No one had sounded any alarm. The doctor lowered his head to the mat.

In dream he met the man who'd lost his hands but now there was no gangrene; the stumps had healed and the man displayed them only to demand the doctor's witness. He saw that these were no battle wounds but a punishment dating from slavery time. In dream the shock of this spectacle set him to weeping, but when he woke to the slate-gray light of dawn, his mind was clear and he felt calmer than he had for many days. He sat crosslegged in the shadow of his *ajoupa,* wishing distantly for a cup of coffee, a tot of rum, or best of all a glass of cool, clear water. Yet none of these wishes seemed so important now, and though he wondered whether Descourtilz and his companion had been killed either by black sentries or the French, that did not seem to matter so much either. He listened to the liquid calling of the crows in the trees beyond the redoubt, and as the morning mist began to lift and fade into the bluing sky, he watched the men Lamartinière had sent to raise red flags on every corner of the fort.

Now that Guizot had completed the quartet of captains, Maillart learned for the first time what had been their relation on the voyage out. After nightfall had stopped the shelling, they all sat around the embers of the fire that had warmed their evening rations, sharing a bottle of *clairin* and telling their war stories. Maillart clucked to himself in quiet astonishment as the story of their bet emerged. That these four pups should have thought themselves capable of capturing Toussaint Louverture— well, but he supposed he must have been as young as that himself one time, if it were a long time ago. The rum warmed him to a certain sympathy with the four captains, though he felt distinctly more in common with Sergeant Aloyse, who was nearer to his own age and experience. But the sergeant was not at all convivial; he sat glum and silent beside his pack, nursing his drink, his beaked profile harsh in the starlight. Maillart had been given to understand that he'd lost the last of his old companions in that foolhardy assault on the redoubt.

Daspir twirled a finger through the bullet hole in his hat. "At least I can claim to have seen him first," he said. "Though I did not get my grip on him."

"But we were the closest to bringing him in, you and I," Cyprien said. "At Gonaives—as you said yourself. We might have had him."

"But you didn't," Paltre snuffled sourly. By the luck of his billeting to Port-au-Prince he'd got no glimpse of the quarry at all, and seemed to resent it.

"And I?" Guizot put in, with a drunken giddiness. "I touched him, with these hands." Only his right hand lifted when he made to raise them both; the left slipped from his lap and dangled. The other three looked at him doubtfully. That one had better stop drinking, Maillart thought.

"What nonsense," Paltre said. "We have none of us succeeded."

"There is still time," Cyprien pointed out, reaching for the bottle. "So long as the old rag-head remains at large."

Maillart glanced about the group. The lack of enthusiasm was striking. And no wonder, since they were surrounded by nearly two thousand corpses of their people, slain in evidence of the old rag-head's determination. In former times, he might have said as much aloud, and begun a quarrel. Now he only wished he were somewhere else, though he couldn't precisely imagine where he wanted to be.

"What an ass I was to propose it!" Guizot burst out. His eyes glittered oddly. "I had no idea—none of us did. It is all folly." He winced with another effort to lift his left arm. "I'm sorry," he said, faltering. "At this hour, I . . . forgive me. I am no company." He moved to where he'd spread a blanket and lay down.

Maillart and Aloyse exchanged a glance, then both of them moved toward Guizot together. Not drunkenness, Maillart thought as he touched his forehead; it is fever. Sergeant Aloyse was loosening the captain's sleeve.

"Well," said Maillart, after a moment. "This gentleman is in need of a sawbones." He coughed. "In my opinion."

Daspir turned his face away. Paltre and Cyprien both looked a little nauseated, but they kept staring at the suppurating wound.

"A fine young man, and brave," said Sergeant Aloyse. "I would not like to see him lose this arm."

"To save his life?" Maillart said. But the sergeant was doggedly changing the soiled dressing—with a certain skill, Maillart took in. As the wound was handled, Guizot moaned a little in his feverish sleep.

"Sea bathing," Maillart said. "That cleans a wound." Of course the sea was too far off. Where the devil was Antoine Hébert? He'd liked to have had the doctor handy for more than one reason. Yet if he were dead, somehow Maillart thought he would know it.

"I had a packet of herbs against proud flesh," he said. "But I used it all on General Lacroix."

The sergeant glanced up at him.

"I don't know their names to look for more," Maillart muttered.

The sergeant shrugged. He'd finished the bandage.

"Come on," Maillart said. "Let's take a turn."

The killing ground on the slope below the fort was pale with rags and bones under the starlight. The bodies there had mostly been picked clean, though the odor of corruption lingered. Maillart saluted the pickets and passed outside the line, walking a little way up the grade. Daspir and Aloyse trailed him. When Maillart stopped, the sergeant passed him.

"Better not go farther," Maillart said. "There's a marksman up there who can see in the dark, I swear."

Aloyse stopped. "But what do I hear?"

Maillart turned his ear to the fort. On the night there came to him a frail melody of a violin and a chorus of ghostly voices singing.

Allons enfants de la patrie
Le jour de gloire est arrivé
Contre nous de la tyrannie
L'étendard sanglant est levé . . .

"My God," said Aloyse. "They are singing the 'Marseillaise.' "

He turned abruptly to Maillart. "I sang that song across Italy and Austria and in the streets of Paris—with my brothers in arms, who today are all dead. Wherever we sang it we came to set the people free." His voice cracked as he turned toward the music. "No enemy of ours could sing that song." Again he faced Maillart. "Can you tell me, Major, what have we come here for?"

Maillart looked at Daspir, who lowered his eyes. Aloyse was gazing toward the fort and singing himself now in a half-whisper.

Aux armes, citoyens . . .
Formez vos bataillons . . .
Marchons! Marchons!
Qu'un sang impur
Abreuve nos sillons . . .

He broke off.

"We're following orders," Maillart finally said, but it didn't really seem an adequate reply.

Guizot and Aloyse both slept through dawn reveille, though Paltre wanted to roust the sergeant.

"He wakes to grief," Maillart said. "Let him alone."

With Daspir he rode to scout the environs of the fort. Already men were dragging caissons of powder and shot and shell up the hill to Pétion's guns. Maillart and Daspir dismounted to enter the reconfigured earthwork on foot. Mist silently lifted from the walls of the fort. Maillart wanted to cling to the quiet, before it was torn by the day's bombardment. The sun, as it cleared the mountains, picked out a blood-red flag on every corner of the walls.

"What's that?" said Daspir, a little nervously. "What does it mean?"

"No quarter," Maillart said. "No surrender." He cleared his throat and spat on the ground. "It means they'll fight until the last man dies."

30

The red *mouchwa têt* Guiaou had given to Placide was plastered to his head with sweat and caked with dust. On the shortened staff wedged in the scabbard by his left knee, the French tricolor he'd wrested from Daspir hung slack. At day's end it was still very hot, and the air heavy. He rode four places back in Morisset's cavalry column, down the switchbacks leading to the pocket in the hills which held the town of Marmelade. Above the horses, swirls of reddish dust rose into the setting sun like smoke.

Toussaint waited, as if expecting them. He'd set a camp table under an ancient almond tree at the edge of the town square. Placide dismounted, finding his legs gone soft beneath him. Guiaou, who'd stepped out from Toussaint's side to catch the reins of his horse, sustained Placide with a hand beneath his shoulder. He smiled to see that Placide wore the headcloth, and Placide, from the depths of his fatigue, did his best to return the smile.

He would have gone to Toussaint then, but Morisset was ahead of him, saluting before the camp table, then sitting down at Toussaint's gesture, to commence making his report. Placide turned aside and led his horse to water. Guiaou caught up the reins before the horse could drink too deeply, and began to lead it slowly around the perimeter of the square. Placide sank down and crossed his legs, beneath a yellow palm.

Presently he unknotted the red cloth from his head and rinsed it in the stone basin of the well and squeezed a little cool water from it: a drop on his wrists and temples and the hollow at the base of his skull. In the twilight a little breeze began and cooled him further, but the air was still so harshly arid that the red cloth dried quickly. He folded it into a small neat triangle and held it under his hand on his right knee.

He only knew that he had dozed when he heard the church bell ringing. Startled, he scrambled to his feet, slipping the red cloth into his trouser pocket. Now Toussaint came to him, wordlessly kissed both his cheeks, and led him to the church. Placide sat on the front bench between his father and his officers: Morisset and Monpoint, Gabart and Pourcely. His head was still heavy; the readings and chants of the vespers service braided into dream images that rushed upon him whenever his eyes slid shut: the upward rush of foot soldiers' faces as his horse crashed down on them, the endless serpentine coils of the mountain trails, and suspended at each turn a wooden skull like those on the rosary Toussaint manipulated with one hand while the priest intoned the scripture . . . then suddenly, a vista of the sea, and the wounded sphinx-like face of Lasirène turning her half-human countenance toward him, then away, disappearing beneath the waters with a pump of the jeweled flukes of her tail.

Morisset roused him with a nudge, to take communion. The dream image still glittered behind his eyes as he knelt before the chalice and the plate, and it seemed that it organized all his confusion into sense. But at the taste of sour wine he lost the sense of it. He got up and followed his father and the others out of the church. They were all going in to supper, but Toussaint held him back a little, beneath the almond tree.

"What can you tell me of what you have seen?" he asked.

"But you must have already heard it all from Morisset," Placide replied, dismayed at a tinge of querulousness he heard in his own tone.

Toussaint covered his mouth with his hand. It was full dark now, and the wind shivered the branches of the almond tree.

"From Morisset I heard that you disobeyed my order and rode to Gonaives from Grand Morne on the night after we drove the enemy back from Périsse."

"Forgive me." Placide lowered his head. A couple of almonds had fallen in that rising wind; he pushed the fleshy pod of one through the dust with his boot toe. "I could not stop myself."

Toussaint took his hand away from his jaw. "Morisset has also told me that you acquitted yourself very well at Gonaives that night—and since, around La Crête à Pierrot."

"I am happy to have his good opinion," Placide said.

"Yes," said Toussaint and turned into the wind. Invisible in the tree limbs overhead, the settling crows squawked and whistled. "I was impetuous myself, when Gonaives was burned. In my anger and my disappointment, that day I abused God. But now again I pray both day and night, that BonDyé favor our cause."

"May God hear your prayer," Placide said. "It goes hard for our people at La Crête à Pierrot. Morisset must have told you, but the garrison there has been cut off from water now for days, and Dessalines was driven back from Nolo, so he cannot relieve them. They are surrounded by an ocean of the enemy."

"And just so, God has delivered the enemy into our hands." Toussaint smiled openly into Placide's astonished face. "Look well, they have nearly abandoned their defenses in all the rest of the country to wear themselves out upon that rock, and now it is we who surround them— I, and Dessalines in the Cahos, and Charles Belair below the Artibonite. By tomorrow night, or the next at the latest, I'll close my grip on the Captain-General, though he does not suspect it."

"I might have killed him," Placide said. "I nearly did, but my horse was spent, and could not overtake him."

"Yes!" Toussaint clapped him on the shoulder. "But God shows his hand in your failure too, for it will be better that I take him as a prisoner, and return him to France, that he may account to the First Consul for the violence he has brought to our country—this war he has waged on us for no just cause."

Placide's weariness split away from him like a husk of an almond lying on the ground. The passionate comprehension of his dream washed over him again. It seemed to him that all his father said was possible.

From behind the house across the square, where Toussaint had made his headquarters, there streamed an odor of rice and beans, simmering with pork fat and onion and hot peppers. Placide's nostrils could pick out each ingredient, he thought, and he felt a pang at the hinge of his jaws.

"*Ann manjé,*" Toussaint said. Let's eat. He touched Placide's arm to guide him toward the house where the table would be laid for them, where the other officers had already gone. "And afterward . . . we'll move tonight, upon the Captain-General at La Crête à Pierrot."

"You planned it all," Placide said. "From the beginning."

"Not quite." Toussaint wiped away another smile. "But since Ravine à Couleuvre, I planned it so."

With that he stopped and faced his son. He needed to look up a little, for Placide was distinctly the taller.

"But you," he said. "You would do better to go to the Cahos to join your mother and Isaac. You are too much exhausted from these battles."

"No," said Placide. He held Toussaint's deep eyes with his. "I'll ride with you."

On the morning of March 24, Captain Daspir rode with Maillart and General de Lacroix to visit the posts surrounding the fort. He could handle his horse well enough with his left hand, though his right was scarcely serviceable. In raising his arm to shield Leclerc, he'd sprained his right shoulder severely enough that still he could not draw a sword or lift a pistol. It was beginning to rankle him a little that the Captain-General had so far failed to take any notice of his sacrifice.

It was quiet at first along the lines, but then, when the dawn light was strong enough for Pétion's artillerymen on the knoll beyond the fort, the bombardment recommenced. Birds fled, shrieking, across the river, over the surrounding lines. Maillart shaded his eyes with his sun-baked hand, looking up at the shells crashing down within the walls. Each sent a shower of earth and gravel splashing over the parapets. On the corners of the fort, the red flags of "no quarter" stirred slightly in the morning breeze that was rolling the mist back from the mountains.

Then there was a pause in the shelling, and they rode on through the sudden silence. Beyond the ringing of his ears, Daspir began to hear a regular whacking sound, accompanied by the grunts of a laboring man, from the post they were approaching. The sound was like that of a woodsman laying an ax into a tree, but what trees there had been at this turn of the riverbank had long since been cut and trimmed to fortify the siege lines. When they came around the bend of the river, they discovered an infantry sergeant, stripped to the waist, panting and sweating as he beat an ancient Negro from his shoulder to his buttocks with a cane.

"Why, he'll kill him," Daspir said, in his surprise. A number of men stood watching the flogging, among them the brigadier who commanded the post. Also an old black crone looked on from several yards distance. Rags of a striped skirt hung from her withered hips. She leaned heavily on a crooked stick and held a small black pipe, unlit, between her gums. If the spectacle of the beating distressed or impressed her, she gave no appearance of it.

"Here, you, whoever you are," Lacroix snapped. "Stop that at once." He turned to the brigadier. "What do you mean by it?"

The sergeant stopped beating and leaned on his cane. The old man turned on his side and drew his knobby knees up to his chest.

"This pair was trying to get up to the fort," the brigadier began, with a gesture that included the black crone, and all at once several of the bystanders began to dispute that version, saying that the old couple had been seen coming out of the fort instead. General Lacroix hushed the dispute with a gesture.

"At all events, we take them for a couple of spies," the commander said.

Lacroix shrugged away the accusation, and stooped to help the old man up. At first, the old man did not seem to take the meaning of the hand extended to him. Then he did grasp it and struggled to his feet. Lacroix let go his hand and took a pace back from the rank smell of him—the scent of corruption even reached Daspir where he sat his horse several yards away. The old man had a full head of stone-white hair turned gray with dirt and matted with debris. There was no iris to his eyes; they were all black pupil floating in the yellowed whites. The dark eyes gave him an unearthly aspect.

"They've been searched," Lacroix said. "Interrogated?"

"There's no sense in anything they say," said the post commander. "We meant for the stick to encourage their tongues."

Lacroix glanced at Maillart, who took a step forward, wrinkling his nose.

"*Di mwen, granpè, sa w'ap fè isit?*" he said. Tell me, grandfather, what are you doing here?

The old man turned his strange eyes on Maillart and bleated like a sheep. Maillart looked at the crone and rephrased the question for her. She made no reply at all, only mumbled her pipe in her gums from one side of her mouth to the other, always staring into the middle distance across her hands folded over her stick, with a gaze of rapt senility. Of a sudden the shirtless sergeant shifted the stick to his left hand and smacked the pipe out of her jaws with his right. The old woman seemed almost unaware that she'd been struck, though she missed the pipe, and searched for it with her rheumy eyes, and finally found it on the ground some yards away. In agonized slow motion she leaned over to retrieve it, working her way hand over hand down the cane she leaned on. Finally Maillart crossed the distance, retrieved the pipe, and offered it to her. He said something more to her which she seemed not to comprehend at all. He laid the pipe in her wrinkled palm and folded her fingers over it.

Perhaps she's deaf, Daspir thought, as he watched this comedy. He wrapped his left arm around himself, reaching to rub the torn muscle below his right shoulder blade.

"A pair of idiots," Lacroix pronounced. "What harm can there be in them?"

"They had this," the sergeant said. He opened his hand to reveal a silver ring strung to a loop of greasy cord, depicting a big dog's head or maybe a bear's. Mouth open in a fanged snarl, it appeared to slaver. It had two chips of a dull red stone for its eyes. The officers passed it hand to hand; it made a solid weight in the palm. Maillart looked as if he would speak when the ring came to him, but he kept his silence and handed the ring to Lacroix.

"It does us no credit to molest such crippled simpletons, or rob them of their treasures," Lacroix said. "Let him have his ring, and let them go."

A little sullen at this rebuke, the post commander opened the loop of string between his hands. The old man turtled his head through it, whimpering a little as if this movement pained him. The ring dropped into the hollow of his collarbone. Then the sergeant handed him his cane.

"So," Lacroix snorted. "You were beating him with his own stick?" But the sergeant did not seem to hear him; he had turned away to button up the tunic he'd resumed.

Daspir watched the old couple creep toward the bank of the river, leaning heavily on their canes, both of them bent almost double. The bombardment had not yet recommenced, and the ringing in his ears had almost stopped. It was here that the rebels of the fort had come for water, until the establishment of this post put a stop to it. Now the light was flat on the river's snake-like turning and a wind riffle on the water had a scaly glitter. The old man and old woman had waded chest-deep. Feeble as they were, they must surely drown, Daspir was thinking. But the movement of the water seemed somehow to ease their limbs.

"They swim quite well for a pair of cripples," Maillart remarked.

Lacroix was staring, his lips parted, though he did not yet speak. Daspir noticed that the old couple had relinquished their canes and let them drift downstream away from them. When they came out on the opposite bank, it was as if they'd been bathed in the fountain of youth. They jumped to their feet and began dancing the *chica*, bumping hips and bellies and buttocks, shouting a stream of insults at the French across the river.

"Shoot them!" Lacroix slapped his palm against his trouser leg. A volley began, but to little effect. The old couple were running with startling agility up the difficult slope from the riverbank to the fort, the old man displaying the exuberant capers and bounds of a young goat. Bullets thumped into the ground all around them, but none of them found the target. The fort's gate opened, and someone ran a plank across the ditch to let them cross.

While Lacroix and the post commander were expostulating with each other, Daspir turned quietly to Maillart. "I thought you recognized that ring," he said.

"I may have done," Maillart said thoughtfully. "I may have seen it on the hand of General Dessalines."

At the notorious name, Daspir felt a cold shock in his vitals. "Why didn't you say anything?"

"I don't know," Maillart said, and turned his face up to the fort. "You'd do as well to ask me why they sing the same songs in there as we do."

To that, Daspir had no reply. No one else in their small group had anything more to say, as they rode disconsolately along the riverbank toward the next post. Soon the bombardment began again, covering their silence. Daspir had tended to attach himself to Maillart since they'd first met in these killing fields. The man had likely saved his life, after all, and even without that, though Cyprien and Paltre despised him no little for his long moldering in colonial service, Daspir saw the value in Maillart's experience, and besides he instinctively liked his ways. It would be very unpleasant not to be able to trust him.

. . .

Doctor Hébert had not slept in three days. His eyes were wedged open by a combination of hunger and torturing thirst and by the mad unpredictability of the bombardment. They shelled two or three times a night, with little accuracy but frequently enough to break the rest of everyone in the garrison. By day the shells did much more damage, and at whatever hour they started to land, the fort's defenders all began to swirl within the walls, looking for shelter, though there was little to be found; they could only swim in circles like fish in a barrel.

A fresh bombardment began a little after dawn. In the moments following the discharge of the *obusier*, the doctor's heart clenched tight and his airways constricted. He was hunkered, his back to the wall, just beside the tatters of his *ajoupa*, which had several times been raked by exploding iron. The first shell landed not three feet from him, but the doctor did not move, only looked at it indifferently. Bienvenu jumped up from his side and threw his body to cover it. Then indeed the doctor's heart began to pound—he couldn't bear to lose Bienvenu, who'd shielded him from so many dangers. But already the man's skeleton was thrown into harsh black relief by the red glare of the explosion, and he'd flopped over onto his back, jerking like a fish out of water. A fountain of blood splashed from his chest. The doctor knelt over him, pressing the blood back, trying to gather it into the shattered pump of the heart. The trumpets started, with the drum and the almost inaudible violin; whenever the bombardment began, Lamartinière exhorted the musicians to *play! play!* . . . ever brighter and gayer airs. The only necessity was to stop the bleeding; the doctor would stop it with his whole weight. Blood was bubbling up around his wrists. Bienvenu shook him by the shoulders. The doctor looked up at him, bewildered.

"Let him go," Bienvenu hissed. "You have to let him go—he's dead."

Bloody to his shoulders, the doctor crept back to his place against the wall. Bienvenu remained at his side, whole, as yet unhurt . . . so it had not been Bienvenu blown to bits just now, but some other, someone the doctor did not know. Unless Bienvenu's presence now were the hallucination, the other the reality. It had become increasingly difficult to distinguish, these last days. However, the shelling seemed to have stopped. The sound of birds was audible, beyond the walls. And the music stopped, which was also a relief. The grasshopper whine of the violin had grown unbearable, though it was always faint. Sometimes the doctor thought he heard it when it was not really playing at all. There were times when he wished a shell would demolish the violinist, or his instrument at least.

Bienvenu squatted, facing him, his dark face furrowed in concern. The grayish yellow foam around his mouth came from the musket ball he was sucking. Many of the men had taken up this practice as the shortage of water became more severe.

"Don't do that," the doctor said. "It will make you ill."

Bienvenu only looked at him sadly. Lead poisoning had added an

extra dimension to the experience of the men who sucked the balls—
who were already sufficiently deranged by starvation, dehydration, and
exhaustion. The doctor groped in his pocket and to his surprise discovered in the lining a pair of English pennies. One of these he proffered to
Bienvenu.

"Take this," he said. "Use this instead." He held the brown circle
between thumb and forefinger, in what suddenly struck him as a parody
of priesthood. That notion inspired a desire to laugh, but he bottled it
up—one must not open the door to hysteria.

Bienvenu spat the sloppy musket ball into his hand and accepted the
penny in its place. The doctor laid the second coin on his own tongue.
After a moment, a little saliva started. He felt his dry lips cracking under
the heat of the ascending sun. From the red aura of his closed eyelids
emerged a white-haired Negro who held out to him a paper inscribed
with letters of blue fire. The doctor recognized the hand of his son Paul,
but here was no ordinary recital of the week's events. *Grâce, la miséricorde, Papa!* The letters flamed into his face. *Grâs-o, Grâs-o, n'ap mandé
grâs-o . . .* The doctor recoiled. I am not God! his mind burst out. May
God forbid that I should be invested with the powers of a god.

Like as not there was no God.

With that thought his eyes rolled open. Beside him, the violinist Gaston was masticating a strip of leather cut from the leathers of his boot.
He offered another to the doctor. If he let his eyes go out of focus, the
scrap of leather more or less resembled a strip of meat dried on the *boucan*. But the doctor had no appetite for it. For the moment, the copper
on his tongue sufficed him. It occurred to him to wonder whether copper
was more or less toxic than lead.

Gaston passed the strip of leather to one of the trumpeters, who
accepted it with all appearance of gratitude.

"I won't be needing these boots anyway," Gaston said, gesturing at the
shredded uppers. "Nowhere to walk!" But then the violinist noticed that
Marie-Jeanne Lamartinière was coming with the water ration, and he
fell silent in anticipation.

The doctor took the penny from his mouth and held it in his hand.
Marie-Jeanne gave water with a silver serving spoon that hung from her
sash on a fine chain. From the gourd she carried she filled the spoon just
short of the brim and slipped it between the jaws of Bienvenu. The doctor watched his Adam's apple working. Then his own turn came; he
stretched up his open mouth as meekly as a baby bird, his eyes fixed on
the short knife which rode in her sash between the spoon chain and her
sword. Two days before she'd slit the throat of a man so maddened by
thirst he'd tried to snatch the water gourd from her—done it as neatly as
any peasant woman letting blood from a hog or snapping the head off a
chicken. It had been a mercy killing, for the others of the garrison would
surely have torn the offender limb from limb.

Marie-Jeanne's shadow passed over him. The doctor held his water ration in his mouth as long as he could before he swallowed. Gaston gulped his straightaway, washing down his meager meal of shoe leather.

Now Marie-Jeanne had refilled her gourd and was coming to help the doctor tend his wounded. For each, a spoon of water inserted through the burning lips. The doctor steadied each head as Marie-Jeanne gave the water, and Bienvenu restrained the limbs of those most likely to convulse. There was nothing else to be done for them. No fresh bandages, no more herbs, no water to brew them if they had existed. Most of the wounded were well off their heads from fever or unremitting pain. Sometimes the doctor tried to quiet the loudest of them with massage or comforting whispers. Sometimes he thought he'd do as well to strangle them.

As they worked, the doctor stole glances at Marie-Jeanne, admiring her as one might admire an icon. Starvation had burned her beauty brighter. The white bone of her skull shone through her ivory skin like spirit. As they worked, her spidery fingers might by accident brush his, and when this happened she would often smile at him. For all she was exhausted as the rest of them, there remained an energy in her touch which could for a moment restore his will and sense of purpose.

Then there was musketry from the direction of the river, followed by a commotion at the gate. Marie-Jeanne straightened, letting the spoon drop against her skirt, the gourd neck dangling from her right hand. The doctor stood up too, to see the arrival. He recognized the white-headed man who came dashing in as one of Dessalines's elder officers . . . and also as the messenger of his hallucination earlier that day. But in this reality the envoy brought no letter from Paul. Instead he went straight to Lamartinière, saluted, then drew out of his tattered collar a cord which held a heavy silver ring.

Toussaint rode out of Marmelade near midnight, his white stallion Bel Argent flanked by the cavalry of his honor guard. Placide found his place among their ranks, near Guiaou, Riau, and Guerrier. He'd slept for nearly two hours after the meal, and felt himself somewhat restored. Sometimes indeed he did doze in the saddle, but when he popped awake from these short respites he felt in full possession of his faculties. At one of these awakenings he remembered his red *mouchwa tèt* and in the darkness bound it to his head.

Their progress was not as rapid as Toussaint would have wished, for most of their infantry was composed of armed field hands, who far outnumbered the regular troops. These men, though eager to fight the *blancs*, lacked the training needed to carry them on a fast forced march through the mountains.

For that reason they did not reach the north edge of the Savane Désolée before first light on March 24, and Toussaint, unwilling to expose his force in that open country by day, began circling southeast under cover of the hills. All during the day he continued to rally more men from the *bitasyons*, uncaching more muskets from their scattered hiding places. As their numbers grew, the march grew more disordered, and Placide, with Morisset and two dozen of the cavalry, rode to the rear to urge these foot soldiers onward, for all the world as if they were herding cattle.

At midafternoon Toussaint called a halt, to wait out the harshest heat of the day. While the men foraged bananas from a plantation on the slopes, Toussaint sent more messengers to search out Dessalines and Charles Belair. Though he'd sent other dispatches both last night and that morning, no word had yet come, and the silence seemed to worry him. Placide volunteered to go to Dessalines, but Toussaint refused him, on the pretext that he did not know the country well enough, and sent Riau in his place.

By sunset no news had come from any quarter and Toussaint put his men back on the march. They moved for four hours as the brief twilight deepened into darkness and halted again in a flat, dry country called Savane Brulée, not far at all now from Petite Rivière. Toussaint sent for Morisset and Guiaou and Guerrier and ordered them to go forward to scout the French rear. This time when Placide asked to accompany them, Toussaint allowed him to go.

As they drew near the lines surrounding the fort, Placide began to smell the charnel stench from the ravines below the town, blended with smoke from the half-successful burning. The odor was fainter now, though a pall hung heavily over the place. A waxing half-moon had begun to rise, throwing enough light to pick out their silhouettes a little too clearly. At the pole of the sky, the Great Bear hovered. They darted across the Cahos road and into the shadows of the trees beyond. Here in these woods the honor guard cavalry had sheltered in the first days of the siege, but now Hardy's division had occupied the ground and pushed the siege line beyond the woods in the direction of the fort.

"Come back," Morisset hissed in Placide's ear. Cautiously they moved west of the road and began to circle down below the town, working their way behind the lines of General Pamphile de Lacroix. As they came near the heaviest smell of the ravines, Morisset reined up his horse and after a moment's hesitation dismounted.

"What?" Placide asked him.

"We may do better on foot," Morisset told him. "There are enough black turncoats among these *blancs* now. We might deceive them if we are seen—but leave your helmet here."

Guerrier remained near the ravines, where the reek might discourage investigation, holding four horses and three helmets. Morisset, Placide, and Guiaou crept ahead on foot. They'd climbed perhaps two hundred yards when an artillery piece boomed and a fishhook of sparks curled down into the walls of the fort from the knoll above it. A moment's darkness, then the explosion flowered. Placide did not know if he imagined the moan that followed, or if it came from inside himself.

"Keep quiet," Morisset hissed urgently. "This way." They were all a little blinded by the flash. A voice spoke out harshly, ahead and to the right.

"*Qui vive?*"

Without hesitation, Morisset stepped out into the glow of a torch just illuminated. Placide moved with him.

"We belong to the Ninth," Morisset said and saluted.

The sentry was black, but a French corporal sat on a stone behind him. The black sentry ran his eyes up and down Placide and Morisset.

"Those are not uniforms of the Ninth," he said. His expression shifted, then was replaced by Guiaou's face. The headless corpse of the sentry took a step forward and went down on one knee to reveal Guiaou behind him, wiping his *coutelas* clean with his fingers and thrusting it back into his belt.

"Hurry," Morisset breathed. Placide stepped over the body of the Frenchman, who lay dead against the stone where he'd been sitting. Guiaou ground out the fallen torch with his bare heel.

The half-moon glared down on them like a beacon now. The ruined town of Petite Rivière was off a little distance to their left. To their right appeared a large square tent that glowed from lamps inside it. When the tent flap lifted, Placide could recognize plainly enough the diminutive silhouette of General Leclerc, waving both hands like a conductor as he spoke to a taller officer who faced him. The tent flap fell, leaving Leclerc inside—the taller man strode directly toward them.

Placide drew himself up and saluted; Captain Daspir made as if to return the salute, but a hitch in his right arm prevented him from completing the movement. He nodded distantly and passed on without breaking his stride. His footsteps beat toward Lacroix's lines, then suddenly stopped. Placide caught Morisset's sleeve but could not speak.

"*Aux armes!*" came Daspir's voice. "A spy! A spy!"

Then the three of them were running hard in the direction they had come from. The commotion in the camp was not very far behind them, but then, within a minute, firing broke out on the line to the right, beyond the tent they had discovered, in the direction of the river. From the volume, there seemed to be quite a number of men engaged, but they did not stop to study the situation. By the time they rejoined Guerrier they had shaken any pursuers.

"That was his tent," Placide panted. "Leclerc. We've found him."

"Yes," said Morisset. "But what was that shooting on the line?"

"A gang of the field hands passed this way," Guerrier told them. His voice was muffled by a rag he'd tied across his face to block the stench. "A little while ago, I couldn't stop them. It may be that they followed us from Savane Brulée."

"*Toute grâce à Dieu!*" Morisset said, and Placide saw his smile gleam in the moonlight. "If not for them we'd likely have been captured."

"And what of them now?" Placide turned his face toward the shooting, which seemed to be slackening a little.

"Let them look to themselves—they weren't ordered here," said Morisset. "And we must go back quickly to make our report."

In the course of the long blistering afternoon in the fort, a chorus started up among the wounded. *Bay nou dlo oubyen lamò!* A man with a head wound had begun it—there was nothing wrong with his lungs. No effort of the doctor's could quiet him, and soon the others had taken it up. Give us water or give us death!

"Well, maybe we should kill them," Bienvenu murmured.

The doctor looked about the area. Of the nine hundred men Dessalines had left to man the fort, half or more were now dead or incapacitated. They'd been starving for days, but no one dared name the notion of surrender. It seemed indeed that no one desired to. Yet the arrival of Dessalines's ring was certainly an event of some significance. Lamartinière was in close council with Marie-Jeanne and the surviving officers now.

"Not yet," the doctor mumbled. Then, shifting his penny from his sore tongue, "Let us wait till night, at least—I think that something is going to happen."

An hour after nightfall, Marie-Jeanne came to let the doctor and the musicians know that the fort would be evacuated. The doctor had drawn that conclusion some time before, since the men had spent the afternoon making cartridges and packing their ammunition boxes to the brim, and Marie-Jeanne had been offering water every three hours instead of every six, and by the cup instead of the spoonful. The wounded had at last got enough water to quiet them temporarily. They had not deduced, as the doctor had, that they would certainly be left behind when the able-bodied men marched out of the fort.

Still, Lamartinière held the garrison waiting throughout three quarters of the night. The doctor lay on his mat, unable to sleep. He watched the half-moon rise above the walls, saw the Great Bear lumbering up the dome of the sky. Gaston offered another meal of shoe leather, which the doctor declined, reasoning that he'd either be dead or in range of better provisions soon enough. There were a couple of bombardments, around eleven and one o'clock, but neither lasted long or had much effect.

Two hours before dawn, Marie-Jeanne returned to him, with Bienvenu following her this time. She gave the doctor her water gourd and indicated the two remaining vases, tucked against the wall of the magazine. No need for any explanation; this reserve would easily last the time remaining.

"You might come with us," Marie-Jeanne told him. "Lamartinière would accept your coming. But I think you will be safer here."

The doctor considered for a moment. "I'll stay with our wounded," he said.

Marie-Jeanne inclined her head.

"If you should make it safely to Le Cap," the doctor said, "please, if you would, find my wife Nanon and my son Paul, and tell them . . ." He couldn't think what she ought to tell them. "Say I was well when you left me here and that I will come back to them as quickly as I can."

"I'll do it," said Marie-Jeanne. *"Si Dyé vlé."* She opened her arms and the doctor stood to receive her embrace. Drily she kissed him on both cheeks. The bones of her fingers were hard against his spine. It was an odd thing he had noticed lately, how flesh shrank from the fingers first— though Marie-Jeanne's whole person was now thin as a wraith. The doctor wondered if he'd ever hold Nanon again. Marie-Jeanne released him and walked away down the slope.

The doctor settled his back against the wall. Bienvenu squatted next to him, as was his wont.

"Go on," the doctor said.

Bienvenu seemed to hear nothing.

"Go," said the doctor. "The *blancs* will kill you if they find you here." He gave Bienvenu a little nudge. Bienvenu got up and collected his weapons.

"Kenbe là," he said. Hold on. He walked after Marie-Jeanne without looking back.

Around the gateway the men sang softly, no French verses now, but Creole songs to honor their old gods of Africa. The doctor was sure of this, though he could not make out the sense of the words. If God wills, Marie-Jeanne had told him, she would deliver his message. Of course his own chances of survival were probably better than hers at this point. He watched, under the moonlight, as her bones carried the veil of her flesh out through the gate, shoulder to shoulder with her husband, leading that whole throng of walking skeletons.

The musicians seemed palpably unburdened by the departure of the troops. Gaston began to jig in the lacy, gnawed remnants of his boots. He tucked his fiddle under his chin and sawed out country dances.

"Be quiet, can't you?" the doctor finally snapped. Then, more softly, "You'll wake the wounded."

Gaston shot him an injured look, but laid the fiddle down. He went to the vases and, somewhat ostentatiously, dipped himself a gourd of water.

The doctor was digging up his rifle; it seemed that the hour for that had at last arrived. He brushed the dirt from the cloth that had shrouded it and sat with the octagon barrel cool against his hands. All at once firing broke out from the direction of the town, and the doctor jumped up and joined the musicians at the embrasures. Strangely, the muzzle flashes seemed to be located *behind* the French lines—surely if Lamartinière had made it so far, he would hurry his retreat without seeking an engagement.

As the doctor formed that thought, there was another eruption of musketry, on the near side of the encircling line, a little to the west and closer to the fort. He exchanged a puzzled glance with the violinist.

"What do you make of it?" Gaston said.

"I don't know," said the doctor. If there was an effort to relieve the fort, then wouldn't Lamartinière have stayed inside it? But after all he didn't really know what meaning had been attached to Dessalines's ring.

When the firing stopped, he went to his mat and loaded both his pistols and the rifle. After a twenty-minute silence, shooting began on the hill above them, much nearer this time, so close the doctor could hear the curses of men taken by surprise. Eventually the racket ceased. The four musicians stretched out on the ground and soon began to snore.

The doctor sat crosslegged with his weapons arrayed on the mat before him, remembering his parting words to Bienvenu. If he called the Frenchmen *blancs*, then what had he become himself? Dawn might bring the answer to that question. Exhausted as he was in every fiber, he hadn't the least desire to sleep. Though he'd finally drunk something close to his fill, he still held the penny on his tongue, the copper taste bitter and bright. At the worst it might be enough to pay his way across the Styx. He watched the stars begin to fade, and streaks of blue bleeding upward into the black of the night sky.

"*Aux armes!*"

Maillart ran toward Daspir's voice, not twenty paces from him in the dark.

"A spy! A spy!"

Maillart collided with Cyprien and Paltre. Then Leclerc himself emerged from his tent to hear Daspir's stammered account—three intruders from Toussaint's force—he waved his left arm in the direction they had gone. At Leclerc's order, Cyprien and Paltre dashed off to organize pursuit, while Leclerc limped back into his tent, still ginger with his sore groin. Maillart remained by Daspir.

"How are you certain they came from Toussaint?" he said. "There're blacks aplenty in our own ranks. Are you sure you did not mistake them?"

"So help me God, one of those men was Placide Louverture," Daspir declared. "I crossed the Atlantic with him—I know his features well enough."

"Well then—" Maillart began, but before he could complete the sentence his head snapped around to the sound of firing, behind Lacroix's lines, to the left. Behind the lines and at a point none too well defended. Maillart experienced a flash of pure terror. If Toussaint had really arrived, in sufficient force, the French would find themselves doubly encircled, and their whole force might go swirling down the vortex centered on La Crête à Pierrot.

"Come on," he said, batting at Daspir to start him moving. They ran toward the shooting and found Lacroix directing the defense himself, with a good success. Whoever was attacking was discouraged after a few volleys. Likely it was no more than a feint. But just as their effort dwindled, new muskets began nearer to the town—an attack on the earthworks there from the direction of the fort.

"They've come out of their hole at last," Lacroix cried, flushed with excitement, and with Maillart and Daspir in tow he hastened toward the new point of attack. The men of the Ninth had spent much effort on fortifying this line, reinforcing the earthworks with timber—they'd understood better than anyone else just what they were likely to confront. Maillart was grateful for the pains they'd taken now, as the skeletal warriors began boiling up from the surging darkness—there was some hand-to-hand fighting atop the works, but only a few could press so far, and these were slain or tumbled back. After fifteen minutes of hard struggle the attack evaporated as suddenly as it had begun.

"Do we pursue?" Daspir blurted.

"No," said Lacroix. "We'll not be caught in that same trap again." He paused a moment to get his breath. "We'll keep to our lines," he panted. "There's nowhere they'll get through them. And sunrise will find them naked as worms up on that hill."

Unless they go back to the fort again, Maillart thought, but he didn't say it. The three of them waited a quarter-hour more, straining their eyes and ears into the dark. Then firing commenced on the hill above.

"Ah," said Lacroix. "I think they've gone to visit Rochambeau." With a thin smile he added, "I'll warrant he'll be ready to receive them."

Captain Guizot, once the night's second bombardment had been terminated, went to lie quietly on his blanket. His wounded arm would not let him really sleep, but he drifted in the half-consciousness of fever. On his closed eyelids replayed images of shells bursting in the fort. No sight was more glorious, especially by night. Guizot had conceived a bitter hatred of the black defenders, who'd annihilated his whole company with a few minutes' worth of grapeshot, all but himself and Sergeant Aloyse. Every night he went to Pétion's battery to watch the shells pour down, and afterward those fireworks bled through his delirium in still more luridly explosive colors. Beyond it all, apart from it all, the throb of his arm ticked like the pendulum of a cabinet clock. No longer pain, but just the regular, maddening beat. For the last day he had not allowed even Aloyse to examine the wound. He kept it hidden inside his coat. In fact, the arm had swollen till his coat sleeve bulged like a sausage casing and he would have had to cut it off to remove it.

For that reason he was more completely dressed than most when the sortie from the fort struck Rochambeau's lines a little before dawn. He bolted straight up from his blanket and ran for the general's tent, cradling his bad arm with the good one, across his belly. Since the destruction of his company he'd been billeted to staff. He found Rochambeau stuffing his chubby legs and the tail of his nightshirt into his trousers. Purple with agitation, the general had no more to say than "Fight them! Hold them!"

With Aloyse at his side, Guizot scrambled toward the noise of fighting, to find that their earthworks, much less substantial than those of Lacroix opposite, had already been breached. What came through was a swarm of figures from a nightmare, stiff-legged and jerky-limbed as marionettes, skull bones cutting through the skin—they looked all nails and teeth as they swept forward screaming. Once their muskets had been fired, they let them drop on their slings and fought on with their long knives. The French fell back and the blacks poured through. On the crest of the wave of them rode a tall gaunt Amazon with piercing gray eyes, gesturing, striking through the breach with a long sword. To all the actions of the men there was a weird, unified rigidity, as if they had no awareness of their own but responded as one to the woman's will. Shoot her, Guizot thought, and maybe the rest will lose their animation. He let his hurt arm fall limp to his side, but somehow failed to draw his pistol with the other. What if she were not real at all? He would be firing at a phantom.

Then they were gone, all those survivors, streaming through the French camp into the heavy bush behind it and finally vanishing into a steep, vine-tangled ravine that writhed its way into the Cahos mountains. After what had happened to him in the mountains of Grande Rivière, Guizot was not eager to pursue, and no one else seemed moved to follow either.

Rochambeau appeared on the scene for the first time since the attack had been launched. Not troubling to greet his own soldiers, or even to look at them, he walked toward a wounded black who'd been felled by a musket ball through the knee, and gave him a rattling kick in the ribs. The black curled up, hugging his body with a moan, then uncoiled with the speed of a striking snake. The blade of his *coutelas* scored a white line on the general's boot top as Rochambeau skipped back out of range. The black was up on an elbow, *coutelas* at the ready. Anyone might have shot him but no one did. Not Guizot nor Aloyse nor anyone moved to interfere. Rochambeau advanced with his own surprising speed. He trapped the black's knife hand under his boot, set his sword point in the hollow of his throat, and leaned on the hilt with all his weight.

Guizot was inspired to look anywhere else. After a moment, Rochambeau sighed and stepped back, sheathing his blade and kicking the blood-clotted dust from his boots. Hand on his sword hilt, he addressed the various subalterns who'd gathered around this scene.

"Shame, gentlemen, shame on you all."

At that, most of the junior officers looked at their shoes or away into the air, except for Guizot, who now fixed his eyes on Rochambeau's twisting features.

"Let the sentries, if any survive, be shot at sunrise," Rochambeau said. No one replied.

"Does no one hear me!"

"*Oui, mon général*," an aide-de-camp squeaked. "It will be done."

"The enemy has cut his way through us." Rochambeau paced, stamping the dirt with his blood-stained boots. "You have allowed him to get away with his whole ragtag band of a few hundred wild niggers—when he is surrounded by twelve thousand crack troops! He leaves us nothing but his dead and his wounded—and two thousand of our best men dead upon this ground."

He cocked a forefinger and aimed it between Guizot's eyes.

"Captain Guizot," he said.

Guizot tensed. Until this moment he'd not been certain that Rochambeau actually knew his name.

"As well as anyone, you know the shame of our losses here."

"It is so, *mon général*," Guizot croaked.

Rochambeau glanced at his watch and then at the sky. "I give you command of a fresh company for this morning," he said. "I think you'll find small resistance now in the fort. If you succeed, that company shall remain your command for the duration." He looked down at the body of the black man he'd just killed, then raised his eyes to the captain again. "I believe you will know how to do your duty."

With the thrill of the news his scouts had brought him, Toussaint's whole person trembled like the body of a terrier on a hot scent. He caught Placide by his upper arms. "You're certain it was him. Leclerc!— and you can bring us to that place."

"Yes, I am sure of it. Morisset too." Placide was stammering in his own excitement. "We were seen by one of the captains who escorted us on the voyage, and yet they could not overtake us when he had raised the alarm."

"But they may be forewarned by him." Toussaint covered his mouth with one hand.

"There was an action on the line as well," Morisset mentioned.

"From the fort?" Toussaint wheeled toward him.

"No." Morisset glanced at Guerrier. "It was some of the field hands who overshot our position. Probably some of those we'd armed today."

"No matter, no matter." Again Toussaint's face began to shine. "What confusion they may cause is all to our advantage now. But we must strike with no delay."

He turned to Guiaou, who went flying off to fetch Bel Argent almost before Toussaint could complete the order. Morisset went with Monpoint to get the whole cavalry into the saddle. Toussaint was looking critically at the sky, where the stars were still bright on a black velvet ground. But before Bel Argent could be led up, a rider came galloping into the torchlight, pulled up his horse in a swirl of dust, and jumped down before his mount had stopped moving, lurching to catch himself against the trunk of a palm. Guerrier hurried to take the helmet he was fumbling from his head. Freed of the helmet, Riau wiped sweat from his face with his palm.

"What news of Dessalines?" Toussaint rapped out.

"I couldn't reach him." Riau straightened from the tree trunk and spread a hand over his sternum; the hand heaved outward with the force of his breath. Toussaint allowed him a moment of respiration.

"Lamartinière has left the fort," Riau said finally. "I crossed his rear guard going up the Cahos. They couldn't hold out for lack of water—they say Dessalines sent word for them to leave. Lamartinière cut his way out through the army of Rochambeau. There are nearly five hundred left of the garrison." Riau sucked in a fresh breath. "Lamartinière is going up the Cahos to join Dessalines," he said. "But I thought I ought to come to you first."

"Too late!" Toussaint said. His voice burned. When Riau's face went vacant, Toussaint raised his eyes to him and said, "Not you, Riau, you have done right." He stopped and lowered his head. "So the fort has fallen."

Guiaou, who was just leading Bel Argent into the ring of torchlight, stopped cold, bewildered by the collapse of the atmosphere. Riau found the reins of his exhausted horse and discreetly led the animal away. The others had all vanished too. Only Guiaou and Guerrier remained with Placide and Toussaint, who sank down, somewhat unsteadily, onto a chunk of timber, and dropped his face in his two hands.

Placide felt a sickening, giddy spin. If his father lost his certainty, nothing stood between himself and the void. He had not recognized that until now. And why, why could they not still act? But he found he could think his own way through it. With all the field hands they had raised, Toussaint alone was still handily outnumbered by the seasoned French troops gathered at Petite Rivière, and now that the fort was empty they could spend their whole strength on repelling Toussaint's attack. Moreover, by now they were likely to have the same intelligence that Riau had just brought. The project had been daring from the start; now it was truly, absolutely too risky.

Toussaint removed his hands from his face. He adjusted the knot of his blood-red headcloth, replaced his hat, and stared beyond the circle of light, eyes unmoving and unblinking, for what felt like a very long time. Placide stole a glance at Guiaou. Both Guiaou and Guerrier were waiting as easily as the big white horse—so easily one could not say they were waiting at all. Placide found himself a little encouraged by that. He tightened his headcloth at the base of his skull, and laid a hand on Bel Argent's warm, breathing flank. His mind came to a steadier balance.

Then Toussaint snapped onto his feet, lithe and limber as a cat.

"Find General Gabart and rally the men."

"All of them?" Placide blurted.

"Yes! Yes, all." And Toussaint whipped away into the surrounding dark as Placide hurried to execute the order.

By daybreak the men were all assembled, and Toussaint addressed them in triumphant tones.

"The French army has been destroyed at La Crête à Pierrot!" he declaimed. "We'll have no more trouble from them here. They are finished, and the *blancs* and their soldiers in the north have no one to defend them now. Go north!—my brothers, my friends, my children—go north to drive the last of the *blancs* out of our country. Drive them into the sea they came from. Wipe them out of creation!"

At that the men all roared and clashed their knife blades in the air; some fired off their muskets (though the officers tried to prevent that) while others blew shrill blasts on conch shells. By sunrise the mass of armed field hands was hurrying north toward the passes of Ennery and Marmelade, with a few squads of cavalry and a handful of regular troops to guide them. But Toussaint, with Placide and his senior officers, with his honor guard and most of the regular troops that remained to him, headed instead into the Cahos mountains by the route Lamartinière was supposed to have taken.

At daybreak the doctor gave a water ration to the surviving wounded. Three men had died in the course of the night. Among the rest, about a dozen would surely die no matter what this day brought—they were too far gone to come back now. The others, just under thirty of them, had lighter wounds and might recover, given medicine and proper nourishment and rest. That thought inspired the doctor to a twinge of hope.

Gaston helped him carry water to the wounded. The doctor was a little surprised at that. Till now, all the musicians had given the hospital area a very wide berth.

The three dead men he dragged a little apart from the living. He straightened their limbs, folded their hands across their chests, and finally weighted down their eyelids with scraps of iron scattered from the shelling. He had no strength to do more for them, and Gaston offered no aid in this endeavor.

When the gray dawn light began to yellow with the sun, they heard a harsh voice ordering a charge outside the fort, and then the pounding boots across the empty ditches. In a few seconds, a pair of French grenadiers had rolled over the ramparts and were opening the gates to admit their fellows. The doctor wondered why it had not occurred to him or the musicians to throw the gates open earlier. Maybe they were simply too dulled by the habits of siege.

The company that came hurrying in, muskets at the ready and aimed in all directions, was led by a peculiarly dead-eyed young captain, who wore his left arm in a sling. The four musicians struck up a rusty version of "La Marseillaise" to welcome them. The captain did not seem much gratified. He drew his pistol and fired a shot over their heads. The music came to a sudden stop.

"So it's you who taunted us with that tune," the captain said.

"Come now, we are loyal Frenchmen like yourselves," Gaston protested. "We have been prisoners here all this time—we only played what they forced us to play."

The captain didn't look to be impressed by this argument; on the contrary he was taking a better aim at the violinist. But a pigtailed sergeant caught his shoulder and murmured something in his ear, and the captain lowered his weapon and turned away from the musicians. In place of the pistol, he drew out his sword and began to advance on the area where the wounded lay. One of the three dead bodies tripped him up, and the captain kicked at it as he stepped over. The iron scraps fell from the corpse's lids, and the eyes rolled open, round and pale.

The wounded man on whom the captain had fixed his advance got up, to the doctor's astonishment, for he didn't believe that man could stand. He backed to the wall and held out his empty hands.

"Pitié pou mwen," he said. Have mercy on me.

The dead-eyed captain thrust his sword so hard that it chipped mortar from the wall when it came through the wounded man's back. With an effort he pulled free the blade and used it to signal the troopers coming up behind him, their bayonets at the ready.

"Carry on," the captain said, and almost simultaneously the doctor shouted, "Stop it!"

He was on his feet, holding both his pistols at hip height. He'd shifted the penny from his tongue to speak more clearly, and held it now between his cheek and gum. "How can you kill these men—they are wounded and offer no resistance."

"It wasn't I who raised those banners." The captain jerked his jaw toward the red flags of "no quarter" hanging dully from the corners of the walls. Now the doctor could see that the captain's eyes were not only lightless but floating in fever.

"The men who raised those flags have left the fort," he said. "You have already killed them, maybe, as would be your right if they attacked you. But these—"

"Carry on," the captain repeated, and the men behind him marched stolidly on the wounded, bayonets lowered. A surprising number of men the doctor had thought wholly incapacitated managed somehow to reach their feet. Some held out their hands for mercy, others scrambled and uselessly groped for anything that might be used for a weapon of defense.

"Stop it," the doctor said again. He could not make his voice carry. "Stop this slaughter . . ." It did not stop. A short, stubby man in a general's uniform topped with a black shako had just come at the gate below, and at his appearance the grenadiers seemed urged to wield their bayonets more fiercely. The general, however, paid no apparent attention to the massacre taking place, but toured the embrasures, pursing his lips at the cannon Lamartinière had been compelled to abandon.

"And you," the captain said to the doctor, who noticed he had sheathed his sword and again produced his pistol. "You who are so attached to these murderous rebels—are you not one of them?"

"He's been their prisoner, like ourselves," Gaston called from where he crouched beside the water vases, against the wall of the powder magazine. "He's nothing but a doctor."

"Oh?" said the captain. "Then how does he come by those arms he carries?" He raised his pistol and bit his lip as he steadied the wrist of the hurt arm in its grubby sling. The doctor took in that his left arm was hideously swollen; suppuration stained the sleeve. But this thought was idle. He knew he could shoot the captain between the eyes before he could fire, and have a ball left in his other pistol for the pigtailed sergeant, or maybe the general in his shako (though the general would be a longer shot), and he knew he would do none of these things. The feverish captain, however, looked very likely to shoot him.

There was nothing more to say. The doctor flipped the penny to the center of his tongue. Now there were no survivors. The tangle of new-bayoneted corpses by the wall now stood for the sum of his labor here, and yet these dead were still his own. Their bodies swam before his eyes and merged into a single skeletal figure, white-eyed, grinning, dressed in formal black, approaching the doctor now with an oddly delicate courtesy. Baron de la Croix, or Baron Cimetière—he whom the blacks worshipped as Lord of the Dead and of the graveyard. It was time for the doctor to offer his coin. But strangely, Ghede was shaking his head and turning down his palm in a gesture of refusal. With a clatter of hooves, Major Maillart cantered up through the gate, nearly bowling over General Rochambeau in his haste. He slapped away Guizot's pistol with the flat of his saber. The pistol discharged when it struck the ground, and one of the grenadiers shouted in alarm as the ball snapped by his ankle.

"Antoine!" he cried. "My Christ, how did you come here?"

Maillart jumped down and threw an arm over the doctor's shoulders. Holding him so, he turned to Guizot.

"What do you mean by it?" he said. "This man is one of *us*—and my oldest friend in this country."

But the captain did not seem to register this question. He made no effort to recover his pistol either. His face was rigid, and he did not seem to be aware of the tears that rolled over his cheekbones and splashed on the ground beside his boots.

"Let him be," the doctor said. "You can see he's not himself."

He slipped out of Maillart's embrace and took a step toward Captain Guizot, reaching for his empty hand.

"I'm only a doctor, you see," he said. "You'd better let me have a look at that arm."

Fort de Joux, France

March 1803

The snow continued to sift down, blunting the edges and points of the parapets and towers into indistinct, soft rounds. Amiot walked the battlements, gazing in the direction of the chasm and the sheer cliff wall beyond it, though both were completely hidden now, obliterated by the shifting curtains of snow. In fact he could not see a yard beyond his nose. It had been snowing for three days straight, and yet to Amiot it felt more as if the snow had never stopped since the first of January, when he'd relieved Baille of his command of the Fort de Joux. The snow obscured the light of the dawn, though Amiot knew, from the recent tolling of the castle bell, that dawn was soon to come.

Like every sound, the bell's tones were swaddled and muffled in wrappings of snow. There was no wind; the whole world seemed afloat. The snow had risen halfway to the tops of Amiot's boots, so that it was real labor to trudge through it. When the light grew strong enough, he would order the soldiers to clear it away.

He passed a sentry, his hat made shapeless by the snow collected on it. Amiot was perhaps invisible to him, for the sentry did not salute as he passed by, but only coughed into his hand. Amiot decided not to notice this small dereliction. He had after all been pacing this area for upward of a half an hour. When he reached the corner of the wall he stopped and turned. What was the end of his exercise? Since his last search of Toussaint's cell, he'd not been able to return to sleep.

Amiot inhaled profoundly, snow stinging his nostrils, drawing cold threads of the thin mountain air to the bottom of his lungs. In a moment he felt the invigoration of the deep breath coursing in his blood, but his mind remained remote from that refreshment, heavy and drooping. Truly, there was something debilitating in this duty. Amiot had felt only contempt for Baille when he'd departed, a man grown old beyond his years in a few months of untaxing service—who'd never had heart for the regime he was required to impose. Without a trace of sympathy or inter-est, Amiot had watched Baille's figure shrink and stoop away, but now he began to feel that the miasma of the former commandant's weak will still infected the rooms which he himself now occupied.

Indeed, he'd ordered two searches that night: the first at midnight, the second at four. In the course of both, the prisoner had been stripped to the skin, his few belongings shaken and tumbled, his clothing picked over with a needle, the crevices of his cell probed with the point of a knife . . . as usual. It was all too usual, perhaps, to be effective. Of course there was no object to find; the prisoner could not have kept a fly's wing hidden against such an onslaught of investigation. It was in his mis-shapen head that something might still be concealed . . . some final shred of information, an idea or a thought.

The searches were meant to dislodge that last secret, be it the hiding place of Toussaint's rumored treasure, or some further detail of his deal-ings with the English . . . who knew what. But Amiot suddenly thought, where he stood in the snow, that perhaps the searches were too regularly spaced; he bore them himself by timing them closely to the changes of the guard, but Toussaint was also an old soldier, and would be as used to that routine. It was Amiot's rest that had been disturbed; after midnight he'd slept but lightly, and after four not at all.

There was the difficulty. Amiot could alter the rhythm of the searches. Make them only an hour, or less, apart. But he must attend each search in person. No man had leave to enter or open Toussaint's cell except in Amiot's presence. Then what if he should lose his controlling grip on his own mind before Toussaint lost his? But surely that was hardly possible. He, Amiot, was the stronger. Certainly he was the younger. He had sur-vived many bloodier battles, and would win this one in the end.

"Sir, it is time."

Amiot started. The falling snow was still thick all around him but now it swirled with a milky light. Day had not broken, but rather infiltrated, while he was . . . what? Had he been asleep on his feet like a horse?

"Time?" Amiot twitched at the dimwitted sound of his reply. It was the guardsman Franz who'd addressed him, his lump of a nose shining red in the snow.

"The prisoner's morning meal is ready."

"Of course," said Amiot. He must attend this service too, without exception. He spread his lips in a freezing smile. "And let us organize a search."

"Another?"

Amiot searched the other's face for superciliousness, found none. And yet he did not like this guardsman. Franz was Baille's man; moreover, Amiot suspected him of secret sympathy for the prisoner. Franz had a wife and at least one child in a neighboring canton of Switzerland, and on his days of leave he managed to make his way to rejoin them—even in such weather as this. It did not do to post such a man so near to home and family. Franz was insufficiently uprooted; he retained the mute resistance of a peasant standing on his miserable plot. But much as Amiot studied him, he found no clear evidence of insubordination.

"Yes," he said, in his most clipped tone. "Another."

While the search detail was organized, Amiot waited by the fire of his bedchamber, rubbing his hands over the uncertain flames, relieved as the feeling burned back into his fingertips. Reckless to stand so long in the cold, unconsciously, but this time there would be no harm. His feet were number still, at first, but by the time Franz let him know that all was ready, he could feel the dampness of melting snow along the seam of his boots, and his feet ached reassuringly along the descent toward Toussaint's cell.

A skein of ice had formed across the planks that traversed the standing water, frozen now to slush, on the floor of the second vault. Amiot slipped and had to catch himself with a palm against the chilly wall. Franz glanced back at him, expressionless, then looked away. Setting his teeth, Amiot marched ahead. He carried the ring of keys himself, and relocked every door behind them once they all had passed it.

Then he was turning the heavy iron key in the lock of the last cell door. At a light push it swung silently inward. At his arrival this door had grated loudly whenever it was shifted, but Amiot had ordered the hinges oiled.

In the wide hearth, Toussaint's fire was ash. A vague snowy light, filtered through the grating at the opposite end of the cell, was enough to reveal the prisoner asleep, or at least unmoving under a tangle of bedclothes.

"Toussaint!" Amiot called, loud with false heartiness. "Your breakfast is served—it is time to rise."

In a tunnel of blanket an eye appeared, just one. No other movement.

"*Réveille-toi!*" Amiot cried gaily. Wake up! At his gesture, one of the guardsmen crossed the room and twitched away the blanket. Another set down the covered trencher of thin oatmeal just to the side of the doorsill. He'd brought five guardsmen, in addition to Franz, and they spread along the walls of the cell, holding their torches high.

Toussaint had now swung to a sitting position on the edge of the cot, his left arm folded over his chest. He'd been fully dressed beneath the blanket: the brown woolen trousers and smock, the baggy coat, a round hat over the tails of the yellow kerchief he always insisted on wearing, apparently two or three pairs of socks. As if he'd been lying there ready for escape . . . but of course, it was only the cold that plagued him. With all that clothing he still seemed to shiver.

"Well, get up then," Amiot told him. "You may put your clothes on the back of the chair."

Toussaint uttered a terrible cough. It took a long time, and shook him from his heels to the top of his head. At such times it seemed there was no more Toussaint at all, but only the cough animating the body. Then the paroxysm dwindled, or Toussaint succeeded in calming it.

"You have searched me twice tonight," Toussaint said. His voice was thick with phlegm but otherwise neutral. "Once at twelve and again at four."

"And so?" Amiot raised his eyebrows high with his smile, but Toussaint did not rise to the lure of mockery.

"It is morning now," said Amiot. "Another day."

Toussaint stood up and began to disrobe, draping his garments over the chair as Amiot had told him. Amiot watched to see if he still trembled in the cold but found no sign of it. At last the old man stood naked, all except for his yellow kerchief on his head and a sling he'd recently affected, which supported his left arm.

"Forward march," said Amiot. "You know the way."

Toussaint stepped out ahead of him, erect, his pace secure. Once he stopped, at the spasm of another cough, but this time he suppressed it, held it back unuttered. He was still master of himself, Amiot thought grudgingly, if nothing else. When the spasm had passed, he nudged Toussaint between the shoulder blades with a short, silver-tipped ebony stick, to press him toward the doorway. At the threshold he turned back toward his men.

"Search everywhere," he reminded them. "His clothes, his bedding— don't forget his food."

"His food?" Franz glanced from the trencher chilling by the door to Amiot's face. Might that be counted as insolence?

"You heard my order," Amiot said. "Search his food."

Toussaint waited, standing in the center of the adjoining cell, which had been briefly occupied, once before, by his so-called valet, Mars Plaisir. Or he was not waiting at all but simply standing there with the calm indifference of an animal, even to his own nakedness. All furnishings had been removed, and of course there was no fire. Amiot circled Toussaint, tapping the silver-shod stick into his palm, searching for any sign of a tremor in the cold. There was none. He used the silver tip of his stick to lift Toussaint's testicles and probe between his stringy buttocks. Nothing; he had expected nothing. He'd got the idea of these indignities from horrified descriptions of colonial slave markets published by Les Amis des Noirs. Finally he commanded Toussaint to open his mouth wide and hold it open. For fear of his breath, Amiot did not look very closely inside, but used the stick's tip to roll Toussaint's upper and lower lip away from his few remaining teeth.

Throughout, Toussaint remained as unresponsively still as a mahogany carving, his web of scars like errors of the carver's blade. Amiot felt his own battle scars beneath his clothing. Though Toussaint was so much the older, he had come late to military life, so perhaps his years of service were no more than Amiot's. Amiot's scars twisted like red worms on his pale skin, and if he chanced to look at them he remembered pain. Toussaint's scars looked like curls of foam on a still black sea, and Amiot could not imagine that he felt them.

"Franz!" he called. "Come here, I want you."

In a moment Franz had appeared.

"Support his 'injured' arm," Amiot ordered him. As Franz complied, Amiot slipped the sling from Toussaint's left wrist and pulled it a little roughly over his head. The sling was contrived of a rag of old shirt, greasy at the points of contact with wrist and neck. Amiot rolled the cloth this way and that. There was nothing to be found in it.

Franz was supporting Toussaint's elbow, and clasping his left hand with what Amiot took to be excessive gentleness. Let Franz be sent away to some other post!—and why not Saint Domingue? It seemed the war was going poorly there. Captain-General Leclerc had been dead since November and Rochambeau, his successor, was hemmed up in a few coastal towns by renewed rebellions. The demand for reinforcements was unceasing, and rumor told that men had died there by the thousands. Why should not Franz become one more of those, if Amiot found a pretext for his transfer? Up to this moment, though, Franz had followed his orders faithfully, to the letter if not in the spirit.

Annoyed, Amiot reached to snatch the yellow kerchief from Toussaint's head, and was struck by a pulse of fear. How was this? He lifted his hand again and again felt the stab of anxiety.

All except fools knew fear on the brink of battle. Amiot knew it well enough, and had learned to plunge through it, like a dive into cold water. But here there was nowhere to plunge.

It was only his poor night's sleep that weakened him. A passing thing. And there was no importance to the kerchief. Such a grubby cloth could hide nothing but head lice. Let it be. Amiot tendered the sling to Franz, allowed him to help Toussaint rearrange it. Together they walked the old man back to his cell, where, to be sure, the other searchers had found nothing to report.

Toussaint's fire had been rekindled and built up, and the trencher of gruel laid on the hearthstone to recover something of its warmth. Amiot had ordered neither of these things. That had been Franz, exceeding his duty. Amiot shot a cutting glance at the guardsman, then ordered them all to leave the cell.

"Good day, Toussaint," he said with another large smile and locked the door behind him.

The snow had stopped when they emerged, and the wind picked up. Amiot refreshed himself with a gaze over the brilliantly gleaming Juras, into the ice-blue sky. But the wind bit him with its bitter edge. Furling his cloak around him, he went indoors. He ate three-quarters of a taste-less omelette and drank three cups of heavily sugared coffee, then turned to the clerical work of the day, a review of the reports he had been mak-ing these last weeks:

28 January: Toussaint suffers pains in different parts of the body, which accompany little surges of fever. He has a very dry cough.

9 February: Louverture, whose health had got better the last several days, complains of his stomach and does not eat as usual.

19 February: The prisoner has vomited several times, which relieved him. However, he has a swollen face.

4 March: The detainee is always in the same state of indisposition. He has a swollen face, complains endlessly of stomach pain, and has a very strong cough.

Amiot rolled the papers through which he'd been leafing and thrust them into a pigeonhole. He sat back, with his ankles crossed, and looked at the cobwebbed ceiling until a belch from his breakfast escaped him. Then he bent over the desktop again, found a clean sheet of paper, and dipped his pen.

19 March: The situation of Toussaint is always the same, he com-plains constantly of stomach pains and has a constant cough. For some days he has carried his left arm in a sling by reason of his pains. For three days I have noticed that his voice has very much changed. He has never asked me for a doctor.

Amiot laid his pen aside. Under Baille's command, Toussaint had had half a dozen rotten teeth drawn by a dentist, at his own request, and had been examined by a doctor more than once—in Baille's presence, of course, and apparently on account of Baille's excessive solicitude. Amiot watched his ink dry on the page. If Toussaint did not request a doctor, Amiot would furnish none. And if he did—

A tap on the door broke his chain of thought—the morning mail. Amiot emptied the bag out on the table and turned over the contents. Little of interest but a packet from a friend in Paris, containing a pam-phlet which recently had been printed not by the Amis des Noirs this time, but by some reincarnation of the old colonial Club Massiac— where Saint Domingue's exiled planters, furious at the failures of Ro-chambeau and Leclerc and ever more hopeless of regaining their lands, could spill their vitriol against Toussaint.

His Parisian friend had marked out a few lines for his special atten-tion, perhaps in jest, or perhaps in all seriousness. Amiot narrowed his eyes at the passage: "... *he* ought to *be chained alive to a stake, exposed by*

the wayside so that the crows and the vultures, charged with the vengeance
of the colonists, can come each day to devour not his heart—for he has
never had one—but the reborn liver of this new Prometheus."

Having resumed his trousers and shirt, Toussaint stood with his bare
feet on the hearthstone. The anger he'd held tight in the bottom of his
belly drained out toward his extremities. It warmed his fingertips more
than the fire. And thanks to Franz, the hearthstone had warmed at least
to his body temperature or a little above.

He was tired now. His sleep twice broken. And it had been an effort to
use that tight-folded packet of rage to repel Amiot's searching hand from
the yellow *mouchwa têt*. Though the headcloth had its own protective
properties. *Pa touché!* Let the commandant so much as lay a finger on
the knot in that yellow cloth, and Maît' Kalfou would hound him to the
very bottom of his dreams.

Disagreeable as the searches were, there was relief, a kind of novelty,
in leaving the cell. Even to be naked in another room, and alone—for
Amiot's attentions conveyed no human presence—meant no more than
the nuisance of a circling dog.

The emptiness of that other cell still held traces of the spirit of Mars
Plaisir. Before he had been taken off to some other prison, the valet had
been permitted to attend his master here. They passed their hours in
praise of Suzanne and Placide and Isaac and Saint-Jean. Through the
vestiges of Mars Plaisir, Toussaint still could feel a hint of his wife and
his three sons, whenever he was led naked to that space.

Where were they now? He knew they lived, but his inner eye would
not reveal them. He knew he would not see them again in the body.

A chunk of wood collapsing in the fire broke him out of his half-
dozing state. A handful of coals, glittering red as jewels, had scattered on
the hearth. Painfully, Toussaint stooped for the fire shovel and scraped
the coals back into their bed. He tensed his diaphragm to hold back the
cough and waited for the wave of it to roll past him.

Pain was general now, all through him. There was the pain of all his
joints, from the ague of his fever, or only from the cold. But that was
nothing. No real threat. The dangerous pain began behind his left eye
and flowed under his cheekbone, and back along his lower jaw. It occupied his temple and the tube of his ear, crawled down through his left
lung and, from the bottom of it, gripped at his entrails. Bending and
stooping set off this whole recoil, so he avoided those movements as
much as he could.

From where he crouched now he could reach the trencher, so he took
it up, meaning only to dump the contents into his slop jar. The gluey oatmeal was almost inedible even when fresh and warm (Amiot was meaner
with sugar than Baille had been), and after the guardsmen had stirred
through it, in search of some ludicrous fantasy of contraband, Toussaint

had no taste for it at all. But when he lifted the lid he discovered, atop the mush he had expected, a piece of sausage and a chunk of pale yellow cheese.

That was Franz, the old guardsman. His doing. Toussaint flushed with a sudden feeling. It had struck him earlier, in the other cell, that Franz had somewhat absorbed the spirit of Mars Plaisir. He'd taken his hand in the way of Toussaint's own people, with warmth but no pressure. There was no *blanc* on earth who clasped a hand that way.

He sat down on the chair by the hearth, bit off a small piece of the sausage and rolled it in his mouth, looking for a pair of teeth sound enough to manage it. A bright burst of saliva started up at the first taste. The flavor of garlic was very strong. He chewed, painfully, thoroughly, before he swallowed. The cheese interested him also. But he laid the trencher on the table and waited to see what would happen.

Franz was a seasoned soldier, that much was evident from his bearing, from his age and the long pigtail he still wore. Toussaint supposed he had likely fought with the first *sans-culottes*, and maybe he had been with Bonaparte in the days before Napoleon had exalted himself to the status of First Consul. The more Toussaint's body weakened, the more Franz grew solicitous of him, though in extremely discreet ways none other could detect. In Franz's eyes he thought he saw the gleam of devotion of men like Guiaou and Guerrier. The need and the trust he had found in such faces had driven him a long way over his road—it had become a part of his own power.

His entrails clenched to expel the sausage. Toussaint lunged across the room to vomit in the slop jar. Empty, he replaced the lid and leaned his weight on it. At last he recovered enough to stand, to rinse his mouth with water and settle himself again into the chair.

Somewhere during his bout of nausea, he'd counted seven strokes of the castle bell. If there were no surprise searches in the meantime, which depended on the will of God, he'd have five hours before the trencher was removed. In that time he would pass the food through his system in one way or another, so that Franz's action would not be discovered. Probably the cheese would be easier to keep down.

He drifted as his fever rose. The fever was a sort of padding against the pain. The pain belonged to someone else, was trapped in Toussaint's body, at the bottom of a well. Now the faces of Guiaou and Guerrier hovered before him: Guiaou with his terrible scars which left his eyes the more expressive, and Guerrier's broad features animated wholly by the same mute trust in Papa Toussaint. The truth was that men like these were rare. Riau was the more common type. Riau who would never give himself entirely, who held something always hidden behind his head, who always remained a *marron* in his heart. Moyse had always been the same. These latter days, when Moyse's one-eyed visage floated up, Toussaint could say to him, *la paix*. No more than I, you did not live to cross the Jordan. But without you, without five hundred thousand like you, we could not have won. God's peace be with you.

And the absurdity of Amiot's program of searches . . . The giddiness of rising fever made Toussaint want to laugh. There was no contraband information left to discover, any more than there was an object to find. The *blancs* already owned every piece of information. They knew everything and understood none of what they knew.

Toussaint tightened the knot of his *mouchwa têt*. Firm pressure worked to dam the flow of pain through his head. With a fingertip he checked the tiny fold of paper beneath the cloth just above the knot. Here he had cached his final testament—let Amiot find it after his death. A footnote to the long, dissembling memorandum he'd composed for the First Consul—no more than a line or two, but sufficient to make sense of all the rest.

You thought I was deceived by Brunet's letter. Fool, I knew what was to come. I knew when you faced me, you faced one leader. When you removed me, you would face five hundred thousand.

Outside, the wind had risen. Now it moaned across the grate. With the wind, a puff of fine snow spiraled through the grate into the cell. A dusting of snow on Toussaint's face refreshed him momentarily from his fever, like the touch of a cool cloth. A scatter of snowflakes settled on his open hand, prickling at the skin like furry legs of bees. Then the flakes melted and joined in a droplet which magnified the crossing of lines on his palm. Toussaint let his arm go slack, spilling the water onto the ground, as fever washed him into sleep.

Part Four

THE ROOTS
OF THE TREE

March–June 1802

*Que La France envoie des forces ici, que feront-elles? Rien.
Je voudrais qu'elle envoyât trois, quatre, ou cinq cent mille
hommes; ce serait autant de fusils et de munitions pour nos
frères qui ne sont pas armés. Quand nous avons commencé
à battre pour notre liberté, nous n'avions qu'un fusil, et puis
deux, trois et avons fini par avoir tous ceux des Français qui
sont venus ici. Ainsi si l'on en envoie des autres, ce seront
des armes pour remplacer les vieilles.*

—Moyse, *Mémoires de Général Kerverseau*

*Let France send her forces here, what will they do? Nothing.
I wish they would send three, four, or five hundred
thousand men: it would be that many more guns and that
much more ammunition for our brothers who are not
armed. When we began to fight for our freedom, we had
but one gun, and then two, and then three, and we finished
by having all of the guns of the French who came here. So
if they send more, that will only be arms to replace the
old ones.*

31

The ash in the shell of Elise's house had been settled by the rains, and much of it already shoveled away. In what had been the back garden, Michau and another man worked a saw twice as long as either of them was tall, patiently rocking it through the length of a huge log. One by one, they were trimming new timbers to span the fire-blackened masonry wall, and cutting planks to rebuild floors. Paul had been helping them until twenty minutes before, when his mother had told him to get out of the afternoon heat and also, by the way, to write his weekly letter.

We are building back Tante Elise's house, Papa, he wrote. *Madame Isabelle is building her house also. Even though Monsieur Bertrand is dead, Madame Isabelle is making her house faster than we are making Tante Elise's house, and she says that it will be even grander than it was before the fire.*

He paused, went back and scored out the clause *Monsieur Bertrand is dead,* so heavily that the blot made the paper soggy. Then he stopped writing altogether and listened to the noise of the saw. The garden had been razed by the fire, but a row of *bananes loup-garou,* which Elise had planted on a whim, had come back already, spreading broad leaves along the rear wall to make a little shade. Paul sat there, in a low wooden chair with a woven seat—they'd bought a dozen such, along with mats for sleeping, at the market which had regenerated on the ashes of the Place Clugny.

Paul tried to collect his concentration. The sentence still made sense without the clause he had gouged out, yet his mother would require him to recopy the whole because of this error, before she stored it in her flat straw sack, there being nowhere to send it. He wrote, *Grâce, la miséricorde, Papa! We pray each day, I and Maman and my brothers, that you are safe and will soon return.*

At this his thoughts scattered. François and Gabriel did not properly pray. They were too small for that devotion. And Nanon would object to the expostulation, *Grâce, la miséricorde,* for reasons too cloudy for Paul to follow, though he knew it would happen. His fingers twitched on the edge of his sheet. Before his eyes, the yellow *cocotier,* which had been burned, had managed to push up a pale green frond, and over this a blue dragonfly was hovering, delicate to the point of transparency. This vitality encouraged and at the same time somewhat frightened him; he was troubled because there was no reason for the fear.

A commotion began at the front of the house: Madame Isabelle had come, with news of an arrival at the harbor—they were all going down to see, Elise and Nanon and the children. Zabeth called into the back garden and Michau answered briefly before he went back to the sawing. Paul remained where he was, though he knew he would have been forgiven his task, for a time, if he ran to join this excursion. But . . . he had not seen his father since the battle at Ravine à Couleuvre. There he had expected to witness something like a tournament, but instead it had been more like a hog butchering—only with guns to add to the squealing, confusion, and noise. Paul had been safe away at Thibodet when Le Cap had burned this time, so it was not possible that he should remember flames shooting up through the roof of Tante Elise's house, where he gazed abstractedly now. His father had passed through that fire, though not Paul . . . but Paul had been here when the town was burned in ninety-three. His father and mother had carried him through it, riding on a donkey. Paul had heard this story many times, though he was too small to remember it, smaller even than François and Gabriel were now. But maybe that passage explained the flames that were dancing now behind his eyes.

He signed his love to the letter and folded it hastily, smudging the ink of the last lines. With the letter in his hand he went out into the street. No one had noticed his departure, and if they had they would have thought he was going to the fort. Instead he went up the hill, through the Place Montarcher, where the fountain had again been set flowing. A few black women glanced his way incuriously as they lifted their water jars to their heads. He passed them, stepping out quickly despite the heat, and hurried past the heat-wracked iron gates of the Government compound, hoping to outdistance the fear that shamed him. He was nearly nine years old.

As a smaller child, he'd lost both parents for a time. Nanon had taken him when she went away to live with another man, a pale colored man with lots of freckles, in the days when Doctor Hébert was no more to Paul than a pleasant human smell and a warm touch. This freckled man had treated him with a careful consideration that masked his dislike, and one day he had taken him to Le Cap without his mother. He'd told Nanon that Paul was to be put into a school, but he said nothing at all to Paul on the whole journey down from the mountains, and they did not go to any school, but instead to a bad house, where the bodies of women were sold to men, though Paul had not understood that part until later. He had understood much sooner that he would not survive there, and so he had run away after a while, and lived as a beggar in the streets of Le Cap. Not in the fashionable precincts where he was walking now, for here he found nowhere to hide himself, but further down, in the *banlieues* between Marché Clugny and the graveyards of La Fossette.

He turned downhill from the Rue Espagnole and found the crooked trail that climbed the brow of Morne Calvaire. Somehow the little *cases* that lined this shaly path had escaped the torches of Christophe's soldiers. These days, the inhabitants were furnishing their labor to the reconstruction of other parts of the town, though most of them were sleeping now, through the hottest part of the afternoon. Paul was not suffering, despite the effort of the climb, though he felt a little lightheaded by the time he reached the top. He stopped by the three wooden crosses that stood before the shell of the church, and turned into the wind to cool himself. He looked back down the path, as for a shadow.

Caco had told him stories of the *djab*, bad spirits astray that might pursue and torment a person, most often by night but sometimes even by day. Paul missed Caco, who had stayed behind at Ennery. Neither had found anything to say to the other about what they had seen at Ravine à Couleuvre. If Caco missed his own father, and Riau was mysteriously absent from his *lakou* more often than not, he never said anything about that either. Now, as Paul looked down the empty trail he'd climbed, it came to him that his *djab* today was no more than a thought that he could not properly identify, though he knew it was bound up with the letter and the impossibility of sending it. Nanon kept all his letters in her special flat *macoute*, against the day his father would return.

A sighing sound rose from the waterfront, and Paul raised his eyes to see. A crowd had gathered along the *embarcadère*, and all the people sighed in gratification, as Madame Leclerc was borne ashore in a litter, from the shallop that had carried her from her ship moored in the harbor. She had returned this day from Port-au-Prince. The dumpling of a little boy who followed her must be her son, Dermide—Paul had not met him but had overheard Sophie and Robert discussing his petulance and cruelty.

The figures on the waterfront were diminished to the size of puppets; yet Paul could make them out quite clearly from where he stood. There was the mayor Télémaque, and Madame Isabelle and Tante Elise, both women holding huge bouquets of flowers. Apart from them, among strangers, stood his mother, holding the hands of Gabriel and François, while Sophie and Robert and Héloïse stood by. At this distance Paul could not see Nanon's face but he knew her eyes would be slightly downcast, for she never looked directly toward a center of attention, and showed pleasure only by the slightest curve of her wide lips.

Another moan of joy from the crowd, as Madame Leclerc's slippered foot touched the ground and she came up standing from the litter. A green speck rode on one of her fingers; she cupped it with her other hand. Paul realized that it must be the bird Madame Isabelle had given her. That would be a triumph for Madame Isabelle. And indeed, Madame Leclerc went to her first of all the group and kissed her cheeks, then turned to bury her face in Tante Elise's flowers.

Paul looked farther out over the long oval of the harbor. Besides L'Océan, which had delivered Madame Leclerc, there was another new ship on the moorings: La Cornélie. He had no idea what its presence signified, but he took note. In the time of his orphanage, he'd learned to remark the arrival of every new boat, which might mean propitious times for begging.

He'd meant to give his letter to the breeze that always blew here, but now . . . Behind him, a few charred timbers were all that remained of the roof of the church. The walls had mostly survived, though smoke-stained and cracked by the heat. No fire burned here today, except the sun.

Behind the church another path tracked down the hill among little cases and ajoupas that also had not been burned. Paul went that way, the letter crumpled in his hand. A hen and her chicks scrambled up from a dust bath and scattered out of his way as he passed. Where the trail went through the hûnfor, a few of the shield-shaped panels of woven palm that enclosed the area had been set aside. Paul walked into the sense of safety he'd been seeking; the feeling washed over him like warm water. There were no drums today, no dancing. The place was given to ordinary use. Paulette and Fontelle were laying out wet clothes on the rocks to dry, and among them Paul recognized a few of his own garments and some of his mother's. Somewhat more to his surprise, he saw that Madame Claudine lay sleeping on a mat on the western edge of the peristyle where the palm panels threw a little shade; he knew she frequented this place, but this was the first time he had ever seen her with her strange eyes closed.

What drew him now were the small fires flaring from the mouths of several cup-sized iron pots, arranged around the poteau mitan: in each a blue flame set within an orange one, like the pattern of a feather. He moved toward the pots, confident now, stooped, and held his letter to the nearest flame. The paper blazed up all at once. Just when it would have scorched his fingers, he rose, twisting away from the pots, and released the wafer of ash into the wind.

"Sa w'ap fé?" The vast figure of Maman Maig' filled the portal of the *kay mystè*. Behind her, the small red and blue squares of cloth danced on their strings. What are you doing?

"Mwen voyé youn let pou pè mwen," Paul said, unabashed. I am sending a letter to my father.

Maman Maig' seemed to find nothing strange in this reply. *"Vin' pal'ou,"* she said. Come here so I can talk to you.

Paul approached, and Maman Maig' took his head into her enormous, cushiony hands. Often she would do so when they met, and no matter how much he had grown since their last encounter, her hands always contained his head completely. He had the feeling that she could remold all the bones of his skull as she pleased, as if it were clay or bread dough.

"Sa w gegne?" she said. What's the matter?

"Mwen pè pou pè mwen," Paul said. I am afraid for my father. In stating the fear, he ceased to feel it. He understood now that any *djab* pursuing him would have been forced to stop outside the peristyle.

"Wi, mwen sonje'l." Maman Maig' still held his head. Yes, I remember him.

"Ou rinmin li. Li rinmin'w tou," she told him. You love him. He loves you too.

Paul nodded, his jaw pushing against her fingers. Maman Maig' released his head.

"L'ap tounen, wi," she said. *"Si Dyé vlé."*

She touched his shoulders lightly and let him go. When Paul turned from her, he saw that Madame Claudine was sitting up cross-legged and looking at him. She did not speak, but her eyes seemed to confirm what Maman Maig' had said. He will return if God so wills.

As he crossed the peristyle, Paulette smiled at him and offered her hand. Paul took it and for a moment pressed it to his cheek—never mind that he was nearly nine years old. It was Paulette who had recognized him in the streets in the time of his begging, and brought him here for shelter, until Tante Elise had finally come for him.

I will carry water for Maman Maig', he thought happily. He knew the *djab* no longer followed him. He had gone out the lower gate of the *hûnfor*, which the *djab* had been unable to cross. He would bring Maman Maig' water from the fountain of Place Montarcher. He knew this gesture would please her, though the children of the *lakou* got her plenty of water from a nearer source.

The Batterie Circulaire was manned by colored gunners sent there by the General Boyer. Paul knew a couple of these men, and sometimes they would smile and wave to him when he passed below the wall, but none of them were smiling today. They were staring across the water at *La Cornélie* and muttering gloomily among themselves. A shallop, different from the one that had conveyed Madame Leclerc to shore, was just putting out in the direction of that ship. The shallop was heaped high with cargo and manned by *blanc* sailors from the fleet, who seemed to be having difficulty in their transit, though the water in the harbor was reasonably calm.

The crowd which had received Madame Leclerc had now dispersed. Paul walked along the empty *embarcadère*. The tide was in, and where two waves collided in a corner of the sea wall, a column of water erupted with a noise like a cannon. Paul went on with the pleasant taste of salt on his lips and the sting of it on his cheek.

A wagon had stopped on the *embarcadère* before the Customs House. The wagon was drawn by a single mule, and the driver sat stone still on the box with the reins loose in his hands. A tall woman was standing beside him, shading her eyes to look out at the harbor. At once, Paul felt an interest in her. In her posture was something of the haughtiness of Madame Claudine, but this woman had broader shoulders and stronger bones, and there was a greater air of calm the way she stood, looking fixedly at *La Cornélie*, though Paul could also feel that she was angry. He moved nearer, his footsteps silenced by the waves beating on the sea wall, until he was standing just below the wagon rail.

The *blanc* sailors in the shallop were managing their sail in an unusually lubber-like manner, and suddenly the shallop rolled so far that it took in water over the starboard gunwale and seemed like to founder. Some of the cargo looked to have gone overboard in this mishap. A number of other small boats converged, and in this confusion the shallop slowly righted itself.

"Trickery," the tall woman said. "They are stealing the goods of Madame Rigaud."

She must have been speaking to the man on the box, but he made no reply. He sat motionless, sighting on *La Cornélie* through the long ears of the mule. He had a rich brown skin, darker than the woman's, and a beard trimmed short and square. Paul felt somehow that he knew these people from long ago. It was the same feeling he'd had when he met Maman Maig' for what he'd assumed was the first time.

As this notion crossed his mind, the woman looked down and took him in. Her gray hair was swept back from her face in rays like the petals of a sunflower.

"Paul," she said, after studying him briefly. "It is Paul, I think. The son of Nanon."

"Yes," said Paul. "Nanon is my mother."

"And your father is that *blanc* doctor," the woman said. "A strange man. I remember him."

Paul nodded. For a moment he wondered if the mention of his father would allow the *djab* to recover his trail. But his mind remained tranquil as he looked up at this tall colored woman.

"I am Madame Fortier," she said. "And here is my husband, Fortier, who has no conversation. You were at our house in Dondon with your mother, long ago. You were much smaller then, but still I know you." She stretched down her hand. "Come up here where I can talk to you."

Paul took her hand and pulled himself up onto the wagon. Madame Fortier sat down on the box, tucking in her skirt to make room for him.

"Do you know what is happening out there on the water?" she said.

"No," said Paul. He looked at the shallop, which was again under way for *La Cornélie*.

"General Rigaud is on that ship," Madame Fortier said. "The *blanc* Leclerc has had him arrested on some pretext and now he will be deported to France. That little boat has all the goods which Madame Rigaud brought out to start her life here again with her family. Those *blanc* sailors have pretended to capsize the boat so they can say that the goods were lost under the sea, but in reality they have already stolen them."

Madame Fortier took a deep breath while Paul considered this information. "Rigaud and his family will go to France as paupers now. That is how the *blancs* are, always. They pile trickery onto their treachery, and then more betrayals on top of that. And do not think that they are finished. No, they have only just begun."

"You talk too much to a little boy," Fortier said, without turning to look at them. His gaze was still centered between the ears of the mule.

"He is small, but he has intelligence," Madame Fortier said. "His father has very much intelligence, however peculiar he may be, and his mother . . . no fool. You would see it in his face if you looked at him."

"So much the worse," Fortier said, without turning his head. Instead of hostility, Paul heard a dry hint of amusement in his voice. And he liked how Madame Fortier spoke of his father in the present tense. It made him feel that Maman Maig' 's prediction would work out favorably.

"We took no part in the quarrel between Rigaud and Toussaint," Madame Fortier said. "But it is difficult not to become entangled in such complications."

In his mind, Paul was fretting over a few unclear memories aroused by her mention of a house at Dondon. He could remember coffee trees, on a steep terrace. The freckled man had brought them there, he thought.

"There is no peace in our mountains now," Madame Fortier said. "Not at Dondon and not at Vallière. Neither the *blancs* nor Toussaint's people seem to be able to hold either one of those places for more than a week. First it is Sans-Souci, and then the *blancs* climb up from Fort Liberté, and then perhaps it is Christophe and then more *blancs* coming out from Le Cap . . . well, it is very troublesome." She waved her hand. "Most of our workers have gone off with Sans-Souci, and the rest have been frightened away by the *blancs*, or conscripted by them, one or the other . . ."

"Sans-Souci will never give in to them," Fortier said unexpectedly.

"No," said Madame Fortier. "He won't. But Sans-Souci does not know

how many *blancs* there are in France. If enough of them are willing to
come here, they may kill him."

"Toussaint did not know how many *blancs* there were in France
either," Fortier said.

"No, he didn't," Madame Fortier said. "But now who is putting too
many words in the ears of this little boy? I don't think I have ever heard
you talk so much, before company."

She turned to Paul again. "I have not been to France myself, but one
of my sons was there. Jean-Michel, though more likely you knew him as
Choufleur—I can't think that you remember him very fondly, if you
remember him at all. He told me there were more *blancs* in France than
there are trees on this island, and France is only one of their countries.
You see that many of these *blanc* soldiers were sold to the French from
other lands of the *blancs*. There is one called Germany and another
called Poland."

But Paul's thoughts were now skating away from her talk. Choufleur.
That had certainly been the name of the freckled man: Choufleur. He had
forgotten that name a long time ago and did not want to remember it
now.

"Choufleur could not keep out of the quarrel between Rigaud and
Toussaint," Madame Fortier said. "He did not choose the winner's part,
and so . . . he will not trouble you or your mother any more. You don't
have to think about him."

Paul looked at her. She had tracked his thoughts more closely than
any *djab* Caco had ever described.

"Well, you can close your mouth now," Madame Fortier said. "It hap-
pens that my son owned a house in the Rue Vaudreuil, and since it is difficult to stay in the mountains, we are going to see how much of it may
still be standing, after the fire. My husband does not care for town life"—
she laid her hand on Fortier's back—"but maybe we will only stay a little
while. Where are you living?"

Paul gave her the address of Tante Elise's house.

"So," Madame Fortier said. "We may as well take you there—it is
not so very far out of our way." She looked at Fortier, who expressed no
opinion.

"But just now I am only going over there," Paul said, and pointed to
the Governor's house, which was only a couple of blocks from the Customs, up from the waterfront.

Madame Fortier arched her eyebrows at him.

"*Mami* is there now, I think," Paul said. "With Tante Elise, and
Madame Isabelle Cigny."

"Well, indeed," said Madame Fortier. "That is an interesting connection. You had better go and exploit it. Go see if your ears can hold any
more."

Paul nodded and scrambled down from the wagon. Madame Fortier
reached down to squeeze his hand.

"You are welcome to come and see me," she said. "Your mother too." Her face grew momentarily grave. "Or maybe it would be better that I call on you."

Paul nodded again as she let go his hand. The back of his head felt like the Fortiers were looking at it as he walked up from the Customs, toward the new gate of the Governor's house, which had just recently come from the blacksmiths. But when he looked over his shoulder, the mule and wagon had gone. There was something . . . his mother would not want to go to that house, though not because of Madame Fortier. But by good luck he knew the guard at the gate of the Governor's house, and he was able to leave this bothersome thought outside it.

He could hear the voices of the other children in the inner courtyard, and he went toward the sound. There he found the smaller ones, François and Gabriel and Héloïse, playing with Dermide around the rectangular stone tank that held the turtles. Paul had heard a story that these turtles had lived through the fire. Though the force of the heat had parched the water out of the tank, the turtles had found enough mud to hide in at the bottom. But other people said that those turtles had been baked in their shells and that these were new ones, brought from somewhere else.

Paul watched Dermide—the little prince, as he'd overheard Sophie and Robert mockingly call him. As a prince might have done, he wore a red sash over a blue velvet suit that must be very uncomfortable in the tropical heat. His face was patchy red and sweating. And yet he watched François, who was walking the rim of the turtle tank as if on a tightrope, with a certain craftiness. When François came to the corner and began to turn, Dermide lunged and pushed him in.

Paul hurried to see that his little brother was all right: François had landed on his knees, but the tank was shallow and though the splash had wet and dirtied him to the neck, he was much more offended than hurt. His eyes were angry, but François's anger was never very effectual. Paul shifted his attention to Gabriel, who was a little smaller than his twin, and did not resemble François at all, or anyone else in Paul's family. Though he was only two years old, his movements were more smoothly organized even than those of the older children. He strolled toward Dermide, who was twice his size, and shoved him so pointedly in his blue velvet belly that Dermide toppled over onto his back, landing hard enough to knock the wind out of him. By the time he found the breath to shriek, Gabriel had distanced himself from the scene. He'd taken Héloïse by her pale hand and led her over to investigate the turtles, though they'd all tucked up inside their shells at the commotion.

Paul looked quickly toward the adults, who sat around several little iron tables on a tiled terrace shaded by an arbor. His mother, who was sitting a little apart from the white women, raised her head enough to see that François was not seriously damaged and that Paul was near him. The pretty woman with the green parakeet on her shoulder must be

Madame Leclerc, but she was too involved in her conversation with
Madame Isabelle to give Dermide's predicament more than a passing
glance. It was Sophie who, miming a grown-up sigh, got up from the
table where she sat with Robert and came to help Dermide to his feet
and stop his crying.

Arm over Dermide's plump shoulders, Sophie led him through the
passage into the outer garden. Paul helped François out of the tank and
dried and cleaned him the best he could, then took him in the same
direction. There was a faint sooty smell in the passage but since much of
the Governor's house was built of stone it had survived the burning better than most buildings, and Madame Leclerc had devoted much energy
to restoring it, so that the only differences Paul really noticed were in the
decoration. The smaller trees of the outer garden had been destroyed,
but Madame Leclerc had sent soldiers to dig up a lot of young palms in
the countryside and planted them here as replacements. The great
trunks of the older trees were scorched, but they lived still and had
begun to put out new leaves. François and Dermide and Gabriel and
Héloïse scattered and hid from each other among the new palms, whose
long fronds were whispering now, in the cooling evening breeze.

"I'll watch them," Sophie said, officiously enough to irritate Paul.
Then he noticed that Robert had also come into the garden, so he left
them alone and went back inside, slipping quietly along the covered
arcade at the perimeter of the inner courtyard. The adults were all busy
in different conversations and did not notice him.

Monsieur Xavier Tocquet, whom Paul did not address as Tonton no
matter how married he was to Tante Elise, sat with General Boyer at one
of the iron tables; he had just offered the general one of his black cheroots, and Boyer had accepted it, but held it unlit, staring at it moodily
as he rolled it in his fingers.

"It was well worth the trouble to bring him here," Boyer said, "to send
him away again with such an insult."

"And the cause?" Tocquet lit his own cheroot and blew out a flower of
fragrant smoke. Paul recognized, from what Madame Fortier had told
him, that they must be talking of General Rigaud, aboard *La Cornélie*. He
turned toward the wall behind him, where there was an interesting old
map of the town to look at, but kept an ear bent on the conversation.

"Why," said Boyer, "it is Laplume at the bottom of it all. It was he who
claimed that Rigaud would raise rebellion on the Grande Anse, beginning in the region of Les Cayes."

"But Rigaud never got farther south than Saint Marc since he
returned this time," Tocquet said.

"No," said Boyer. "Leclerc—the Captain-General did not trust him
enough to send him back to his own country. But Rigaud was not going to
raise any rebellion against the French. He has proved his faith to France
plainly long ago—and he would join any effort against Toussaint."

"That much is certain," Tocquet said.

"Yes," said Boyer. "Well, you know that Laplume had taken over Rigaud's house at Les Cayes, with all its furnishings."

"I didn't know it, but go on."

"It is true. And Rigaud was so assiduous in petitioning for the return of his property that Laplume wanted to get him sent out of the country. For that he raised this rumor against Rigaud."

"And Leclerc accepted this tale with no inquiry?"

"Judge by the result," said Boyer. He hesitated. "The style of this action is as distressing as the substance. The Captain-General told Rigaud that they were going together to the Grande Anse by sea. Rigaud boarded *La Cornélie* in all confidence, in the harbor of Saint Marc, and only then was notified that he was a prisoner. Leclerc had gone aboard another ship—he has never faced the man he accuses."

"Ah," said Tocquet. "These developments must be encouraging for Pétion, and yourself, and the others who sailed on *La Vertu*."

"The proverb says that virtue is its own reward." Boyer colored slightly. His brocade coat collar seemed to make his neck more stiff. "I have carried out the order punctiliously—a soldier has no private thoughts. Madame Rigaud and her children are being sent aboard *La Cornélie* even as we speak."

"Of course," Tocquet said. "No one would think of questioning your loyalty." He leaned forward to light Boyer's cheroot. "I have no part in this military, and I want none."

Boyer puffed. "You remind me of another matter," he said. "There is rebellion on La Tortue—a rising in favor of Toussaint. The garrison at Port-de-Paix is . . . for the moment it is not well placed to subdue this trouble, since there is also unrest at Trois Rivières."

"And so?"

"They say you are very familiar with La Tortue," Boyer said. "If you would, perhaps, accept a commission . . ."

"Is the French corps thinned so badly as that?" Tocquet made a sound between a laugh and a cough. "We've heard it was disastrous at La Crête à Pierrot but—in any case, I have just told you I want no part of the military. My thoughts are my own. I am no soldier."

Boyer smiled. His sidewhiskers rustled against his collar. "There are those who say you are a bandit, Monsieur."

Paul grew tense in his shoulders and his scalp. One did not safely trifle with Xavier Tocquet; everyone knew this. But from the corner of his eye he could see that Tocquet only returned the smile.

"I think you mean a pirate, General. I may fairly be called a pirate, for I descend from the *flibustiers* of La Tortue, without whom all Saint Domingue would still attach to the crown of Spain."

"I meant no offense."

"You certainly meant to prickle me, General. But I am not offended."

Tocquet produced a flask from an inner pocket and, at Boyer's nod, dropped a little rum into the general's coffee and then into his own.

"Martial Besse will command the expedition to La Tortue," Boyer said. "Perhaps you know him. He also sailed on *La Vertu.*"

"Not well, but . . ." Tocquet's eyes grew distant. "I may help you in this affair—as a guide, but no commission. It is a long time since I have been on La Tortue."

"Oh, do, do help us." Madame Leclerc switched in her seat at the adjacent table and draped a languid arm in Tocquet's direction. "I have heard that La Tortue is the most charming island, and I do very much desire to see it." She put a long trill in the *r* of *desire*, and fixed on Tocquet her most vivid smile. Paul was impressed, in a way unfamiliar to him, by the smile and the rolling *r* and the softly rounded alabaster arm. But Tocquet's eyes remained detached.

"Madame, I will render what service I am able," he said, still without looking directly at Madame Leclerc. His regard seemed to pass between her and Tante Elise, away above the turtle tank and the high wall beyond it. Paul felt that his aunt was pleased with Tocquet's unresponsiveness, but Madame Leclerc was not at all pleased.

"You were speaking of General Rigaud, I think?" she said. "I heard that he was so very piqued at the surprise of his arrest that he flung his sword overboard from the ship, rather than surrender it. Can it be true?"

She tossed her head and intensified her smile. Boyer twitched. A spot of color appeared below his cheekbone. "I am not informed of any such detail," he said. Tocquet made no comment, but masked himself in a cloud of tobacco smoke.

Madame Leclerc seemed to be preparing another sally, but before she was ready, the green parakeet hopped down from her shoulder to her wrist and spoke to her: *"Comme tu es belle."*

"Ah," said Madame Leclerc. "My pet is always complimentary. Unlike some." She shot another glance at the two men, then turned her pretty shoulder to them, drawing herself in on the bird. Paul was staring frankly now. He had heard of birds that talked but never met one.

"Come here, boy." Madame Leclerc had not appeared to be looking at him, but she had certainly been aware of his eyes. Paul glanced quickly at his mother, who almost imperceptibly nodded. Madame Leclerc was beckoning to him with a graceful curve of that languid arm; a triad of silver bracelets tinkled on the wrist unoccupied by the parakeet.

"Just put your finger behind his feet . . ." And the lady's soft fingers were on his forearm. Paul was perplexed by her touch and the sweet scent of her and the close focus of her attention. It was easier to concentrate on the bird.

"Yes, like that," she said. "You see?"

When Paul touched the back of the parakeet's scaly legs, it took a neat backward step onto his forefinger. He smiled. The little claws were tickling him.

"Don't show him your hand from the front," Madame Leclerc warned. "He will peck it. And his beak is quite sharp."

The parakeet screwed its head around and blinked one eye at Paul.

"Comme tu es belle," it declared.

Madame Leclerc began to giggle. Isabelle and Elise tittered along with her; Nanon looked up briefly from her basket of sewing.

"It may be that he is a little indiscriminate," Madame Leclerc said. "But he is unfailingly determined to please."

She turned to Isabelle. "As for his singing, well—" With a jingle of bracelets, she clapped her hands sharply. "Moustapha!"

The man who presented himself was not named Moustapha at all. Paul had known him as a porter on the waterfront and he knew very well that his name was Baptiste. Today he was not so easily recognizable, though, for he had been costumed in a Chinese silk robe that strained at his shoulders and stopped short at his knees, and crowned with an ill-balanced turban fastened in the center of his forehead with a large red glass brooch.

But Paul was more struck by the thing he was carrying: a box of a silvery metal set with brass inlays representing songbirds on ornamental sprigs. A crank stuck out of the side, as if it were some kind of a grinding machine, but on the top there was a bird cage.

"Go on," Madame Leclerc told him. "Put him in."

Paul hesitated. He didn't want to see the talking bird ground into sausage.

"Well, it won't hurt him!" Again, the chiming of her laughter. "It hasn't seemed to help him much, but it won't harm him."

Baptiste was smiling encouragingly from beneath the ridiculous turban, so Paul put the bird into the cage and latched the door. The parakeet hopped up onto the small swinging perch and sat there, shrugging its shiny green shoulders. Baptiste balanced the engine upright on its post and turned the crank. Out came a fragile, metallic melody, one which Paul had heard Madame Isabelle singing to Héloïse from time to time: "Ah, what shall I say, Maman?"

Rapt, he reached to touch the yellow inlays on the box. Baptiste smiled more broadly and shifted the machine, presenting the crank handle to Paul's hand. Paul turned it, shyly at first, then with more vigor. The music played fast or slow according to the speed of the cranking. But the bird was unmoved by the tune at any tempo. It swung on the perch, closing first one eye and then the other.

"Perhaps he is not musical," Pauline said, still laughing, throwing back her head. "Or perhaps he needs a better music master—one who knows the birds of this land." A new thought seemed to come to her, and she leaned forward to tap a finger on Isabelle's arm.

"Do you know?" she said. "Another curiosity—a band of musicians were found alive in the fort at La Crête à Pierrot. Frenchmen all, and the only survivors. Four or five of them, and one other white man, I was told . . . I believe he was supposed to be a doctor—"

Paul's hand slipped away from the crank. Tante Elise had interrupted Madame Leclerc with questions: Where had this doctor gone to now? Did anyone happen to know his name? But Paul attended only to his mother, who'd forgotten both her sewing and her usual sidewise decorum; she was looking at Madame Leclerc head on, with her lips slightly parted and her eyes warm and bright.

32

No one knew which spirit was walking with Toussaint, or at least I, Riau, I did not know it. No one had ever known for certain what spirit was master of his head, and maybe Toussaint wanted to be always his own master, like a *blanc*. He would not give his head completely up to any *lwa*. Always in the days of Bréda, and afterward when he was strong, Toussaint talked of Jesus as if Jesus was his only one. But Jesus was the spirit of the *blancs*. I, Riau, had not been there at Gonaives, but those who were had told the story—how Toussaint tore Jesus down from the cross, and cursed him and rode over him with the hooves of his big horse Bel Argent, before he set fire to the church. And still before I heard this story, I knew that Toussaint had his other *lwa*, but he was always secret in that thing.

After La Crête à Pierrot had fallen, and the French *blanc* soldiers were swarming all over the place where our people had been, Toussaint's eyes were rimmed with red, and he was twisted up with rage and sorrow. There, as at Ravine à Couleuvre, the battle had not gone as he planned or wanted. The French *blanc* soldiers had left many dead around La Crête à Pierrot, much more than we, even after they had killed all our wounded they found lying in the fort when Lamartinière had gone. They had lost so many that the General Lacroix had to march back to Port-au-Prince with wide empty spaces hidden in the inside of his column, so the weakness did not show. But I, Riau, heard that from Maillart a long time afterward, so maybe Toussaint did not know it either. Whatever he knew, it seemed that all those dead *blanc* soldiers were not enough to feed the spirit that was with him then.

One saw that day that he was old, and tired from his long riding and hard fighting, though the spirit that was in him forced him on. I thought that Ezili Jé Rouj was with him that day, after Lamartinière received Dessalines's ring and fought his way out of the fort with the men he had still able—she who would claw at her own face and maybe even tear her own eyes out when things had not passed as she wished them to. No man should be too long with Ezili Jé Rouj, for she is one to ride her horse to death when she is angry, and she is almost always angry, but Toussaint rode under her as far as the mountain east of La Crête à Pierrot, Morne Calvaire, where Dessalines had finally come.

Then Toussaint's eyes were red and furious and his mouth was bitter when he spoke. If Dessalines had waited only one more day to send his ring to Lamartinière, then Toussaint might have struck the French from behind their lines, and Dessalines too from the other side, so that they would have killed every *blanc* in the French army, or at least have captured the Captain-General Leclerc. Dessalines listened without saying anything back, but his knuckles were gray on the snuffbox he clutched in his left hand, and I saw what it cost him to keep his tongue still. He had fought as hard in those last weeks as Toussaint or anyone, except perhaps for Lamartinière and the others who had been trapped in the fort, and I saw too that he was getting sick from fever.

But the spirit of anger left Toussaint, and he smiled on Dessalines, and spoke to him more calmly. Dessalines was too strong a leader for Toussaint to treat him poorly now. Toussaint sent Dessalines down to Marchand where he could cover the road that ran from Saint Marc to Le Cap through the Savane Désolée. But we rode on into the Petit Cahos, where Toussaint's family was. During that ride, we stopped in the day's worst heat at Toussaint's *habitation* at La Coupe à l'Inde, where he kept many horses, and Toussaint left Bel Argent there, since the big horse had been ridden too hard for too long and needed to be rested. Others of us who needed to changed our horses there as well, and then we rode on toward the Grand Fonds.

Then and in the days that followed, no one could see what spirit was with Toussaint. He was smooth like the surface of the ocean when the big fish has gone under and the circle that his tail makes has already disappeared.

When Dessalines came to Marchand at last he was very sick with the fever, so that for some days he could not stand, and when he did get up again he found that no more than sixty soldiers were with him still, or so the story was told later. Dessalines shot two of the captains who brought him this news, and after he had done that, the other captains who still lived found him enough soldiers to make him more content. But at that time Toussaint had gone to Grand Fonds, where he had sent his family when the French *blanc* soldiers first came down through Ennery, so he did not know exactly what Dessalines was doing. Suzanne and Isaac were staying there, at Habitation Vincindière, but Saint-Jean who was the youngest son had been made a prisoner of the *blancs*, while they were running from Ennery. Placide was with the other officers, Gabart and Pourcely and Monpoint and Morisset, at Habitation Chassérieux, where Toussaint made his headquarters now, a little way from Vincindière.

In the early morning we were riding into the clouds over the Petit Cahos mountains, where the wet gray fog lay thick among the trunks of old palm trees and tall pines. We had to go carefully along the trails because there were ravines so well hidden in the fog we could only know their places by their echoes or the sound of rushing water deep inside them. But when the sun had risen, the fog turned pale and floated away, like fingers of a hand letting go of the mountains, so that by the time we came to the plateau of Chassérieux it was very hot. Here a lot of people who had run away from the French *blanc* soldiers in the Artibonite had come, and they had put up *ajoupas* all over the flat ground there, and other soldiers had come there too, away from different fights with the *blancs* all around the country.

Toussaint did not go at once to find Suzanne and Isaac at Vincindière. He raised a tent in the center of the flat land among the people, to make shade against the midday sun, and he called for men who knew how to write. I, Riau, was one, and another was his son Placide.

First Toussaint gave us words for Bonaparte, who was the chief of all the French *blanc* soldiers in France. He had a letter from Bonaparte that he must answer, and in this answer he said that Bonaparte should take away the Captain-General Leclerc, and send someone else to talk to Toussaint, because it was Leclerc who had caused all the trouble and fighting, when Toussaint had never intended to make any trouble with the *blancs* at all. This letter took a long time to write because of the way the words had to be twisted, and after that we had to write another one, to the General Boudet who had gone down to Port-au-Prince again, after the fighting around La Crête à Pierrot.

The sun had left its height by the time these letters had been copied out and all the words put in their places so that they satisfied Toussaint. Placide and Toussaint got back on their horses then, and they rode on to Vincindière. I found Guiaou, who had been riding with Toussaint that day the same as I, and together we raised a little *ajoupa* to share. I had been camping with Jean-Pic before, but Jean-Pic had run away after Toussaint's big bloody fight at Plaisance. He wanted to go north to a place where there was no fighting. Guiaou had been much with a new man called Guerrier, who had traveled with him across the Spanish bor-

der, when Couachy was killed by some trickery of the *blancs*, but this
night somehow we decided to camp together.

We had to go some way off from the flat ground of the plateau before
we found sticks and leaves enough, because so many people had already
come there. Guiaou made a place flat with his *coutelas*, on the edge of a
ravine, and there we planted the forked sticks and put the cross-sticks in
the forks, and laid the long palm leaves across them. There we had shelter from the rain, if there was not too much wind, and it did rain a little
before the end of that day, but by darkness it was clear again, with many
stars bright above the mountain.

No one was singing or drumming in the camp that night, and there
was not much talk around the cooking fires, or the talk was low, and
there was not very much to cook, because all the people had run so fast
from the French *blanc* soldiers. It seemed that their spirits were low to
see Toussaint running from the *blancs* himself, because that was what it
looked like he was doing. And the stories that were being told about La
Crête à Pierrot would not make anyone want to drum or dance.

Guiaou had no food with him at all, but I had saved a piece of cassava
bread, and I shared this with him. We did not talk at all while we were
eating, or afterward when we lay down to sleep. I was thinking of Toussaint, and in my mind I saw a picture of him meeting Suzanne and Isaac
at Vincindière, but I thought how he must still wonder about Saint-Jean,
if the *blancs* who held him were treating him with kindness. With that I
began to think about Merbillay's children at Ennery, if they were safe
and well themselves, and I knew Guiaou must be thinking the same
thoughts, but we did not say anything about it.

Guiaou was asleep sooner than I was, or so I thought from the sound
of his dreaming. For a long time, I could not send my thoughts away,
though I tried to let them go into the sound of running water I could hear
at the bottom of the ravine where our *ajoupa* was made. Guiaou called
Toussaint *Papa*, as many people had begun to do, but I, Riau, had known
him longer, though sometimes I addressed him as *parrain*. For a long
time the words of the letters we had written that day ran in my head, and
I wondered how many of us Toussaint might sell to save his children.

When I first came to Port-au-Prince with Maillart, I had seen the messenger Sabès, who had come out of the ships with another *blanc* named
Gimont, with messages from the General Boudet who waited on the
ships in the harbor. Lamartinière had made them prisoner then, though
they came only as messengers. Later on they had come close to being
killed many times. Lamartinière treated them well at first, but Dessalines
would certainly have killed them at Petite Rivière, and there were people
who wanted to kill them at Chassérieux too, because the anger against
all the *blancs* was very high; only Isaac had come over from Vincindière
to protect them. It may be that he had known those two *blancs* on the
ships that he and Placide had ridden over the ocean, or maybe he knew

that Toussaint would not like Sabès and Gimont to be killed, even though Isaac had not taken Toussaint's part against the French *blanc* soldiers.

It was hard to see what Toussaint's part was now, and maybe he was trying to hide it in the fog he turned between his hands. When he came back to Chassérieux the next morning, the first thing he did was order that Sabès and Gimont be brought before him. He did not really need to send for them at all, because they had been at Vincindière the whole time, where Toussaint had spent the night. Isaac had brought them there, where they would be safer, after he had got them away from the people who wanted to kill them at Chassérieux. But I thought Toussaint must want all the people at Chassérieux to hear what he would say to these *blancs*, because he spoke to them outside the tent, loud and before all the people.

Toussaint did not look old or tired any more that morning. He was dressed in his finest uniform, one that he would never wear to ride, and he wore the big sword longer than his leg, on a velvet belt with many bright and colored stones. All our men were gathered around his tent when Fontaine brought Sabès and Gimont in, because the other officers had told them to come there. The men were sitting on rocks, or cross-legged on the ground, with knives and guns laid on the ground in front of them to show there would be no more killing just then, and farther off some of the women and children who had come up from the Artibonite were listening too. I sat on a stone beside Guiaou and listened.

Toussaint told Sabès and Gimont that they had never had any bad treatment from him, and that they had seen how well he treated all his *blanc* prisoners. It was hard for me not to look at Guiaou when Toussaint spoke so, though I held my eyes straight forward, and I saw from the tight jaws of the two *blanc* officers that they were having trouble too. Sabès and Gimont had seen a lot of unarmed *blancs* and women and children get butchered, at Savane Valembrun and Petite Rivière and probably a few other places too, even if Toussaint did not like such things to happen when he was there himself to see them. But Toussaint was still talking, saying again how he had done all he could do to stop this war from happening, and how all the war and trouble was really the fault of the Captain-General Leclerc.

Then Sabès could not keep his tongue still any longer, and he said to Toussaint all in a rush that none of the trouble would ever have happened if Toussaint had not disregarded the authority of Leclerc, and that he and Gimont had suffered a lot, and seen a lot of very bad things happen to other *blancs* along their way, which was as much as saying Toussaint lied. We heard a little whisper go around the men at that, like a small breath of wind on a still hot day, but Toussaint raised his eyes and the whisper stopped. I thought that Sabès must be a brave man, or maybe a little crazy, to speak as he had spoken then, though it was truth. But Toussaint tried to hide his anger. He talked still more, telling how he had been named Governor-General of Saint Domingue by Bonaparte, chief of the soldiers in France, and that Leclerc had appeared to attack him the way a pirate appears on the ocean. Gimont was a captain of a French boat, and Toussaint finished by saying to him, "If you command a ship of state and if, without giving you any notice, another officer comes to replace you by jumping on the foredeck with a crew twice the size of your own, can you be blamed for trying to defend yourself on the afterdeck?"

Sabès and Gimont did not say anything more after that. Toussaint had already told them that they were going to be sent down to General Boudet at Port-au-Prince, to carry the letters Toussaint had written, and they would not have wanted to make him change this idea. Toussaint had horses given to them, and they rode out of Chassérieux toward the coast, with a small guard, while Toussaint went inside his tent, and the ring of people who had been listening broke apart.

After all that had happened since the French ships came, most of our people were thinking that any *blanc* was an enemy, so I did not know what they thought about all Toussaint had said that morning. But I, Riau, because I had copied them, I knew the words of the letter Sabès and Gimont were carrying to Boudet, and they were smooth as glass—*The rights of man, which shelter them from all arrest, give me no right to consider them prisoners. I desire that you should act in the same way with regard to my nephew and aide-de-camp Chancy, who is at Port-au-Prince.*

However well Toussaint liked his sister's son Chancy, the person he would most want to trade for was his own son, Saint-Jean, but while Boudet held Chancy in Port-au-Prince, Leclerc himself kept Saint-Jean hostage at Le Cap, and it was Leclerc that Toussaint had spent the morning blaming, in place of all the French *blanc* soldiers. I did not know what he might have to trade to Leclerc for Saint-Jean, so his intention was very hard to see. These were troublesome thoughts, and maybe others in the camp were having them too. The men had rested a little now, enough to wonder what they were going to have to do next, and no one spoke about it, but all could feel a spirit of confusion in the air.

But on the afternoon of that same day, four riders came in a cloud of dust that we could all see from a long way off. They brought the news that the General Hardy, who was moving from La Crête à Pierrot toward the north coast, had passed through La Coupe à l'Inde and raided Toussaint's *habitation* there, and among a lot of other things he had taken Toussaint's white horse Bel Argent.

Toussaint did not hide his anger then, and all at once everything seemed clear. Before an hour had passed all of our men were hurrying north on the way Hardy had taken, except for a very few he left to guard Vincindière. Even without Bel Argent, Toussaint rode faster and harder than any of the men he was leading, but he and Bel Argent were like one animal when they were together, and we saw he would do anything to get

him back. Another thing was that Hardy had been the man who captured Saint-Jean on the road out of Ennery, so maybe Toussaint had two
points to take to him that day.

It was better to be moving than to wait and think. General Hardy was
moving fast, for a general with a lot of prisoners and baggage, but Toussaint was following even faster. At Saint Michel, on the Central Plateau,
the people told us the French *blanc* soldiers had passed through that day
and they were marching for Dondon. It was already night when we
reached Saint Michel, and so we rested a few hours there.

When they saw us come into the town, a few dozen men of Saint
Michel came in from the woods where they had been hiding since Hardy
came. They had muskets, but they had been afraid to fight, and the man
who led them was shaking his head, saying that these men were not like
any other *blanc* soldiers he had ever seen. They could run through the
bush and climb the mountains as fast as any man among us, and the
leader of Saint Michel even said he had seen some of them pull down
wild horses by their ears and ride them without a bridle.

Guiaou and Guerrier looked sideways at each other when they heard
that part, but Toussaint only laughed and said, "I have already told you,
Bonaparte has sent his very best men to fight us. They have done wonderful things in Europe and they may work wonders here for a short
time, but the fire of our sun will weaken them quickly and you will out-
last them all at the end."

We slept a few hours with these words of Toussaint, but before the
light of the next morning we were going after Hardy's soldiers again.
When we had passed the quarter of Bassaut, Toussaint found a *morne* to
climb, and from the top he could see where Hardy had stopped his men
on the outside of Dondon.

Then it was noon, and Hardy would let his soldiers rest through the
heat, we thought, but we were not resting. Toussaint sent Riau and
Guiaou to look for General Christophe, who had been fighting in these
mountains with what was left of the Second Demibrigade, and also a few
hundred men of the hoe who had taken up the guns Toussaint had hidden in the mountains. By good luck we found Christophe before too
long, on the slopes of Morne La Ferrière, which was not so very far above
the town of Dondon. Christophe knew already that Hardy was there, but
he did not have men enough to fight him by himself.

Toussaint's order was that Christophe should attack Hardy from one
side while Toussaint himself attacked from the other. Christophe was
ready enough to try this plan, now he knew Toussaint had come, and he
began to move his soldiers down the mountain toward Dondon, but
Hardy had put his men on the march again before we knew about it, and
they struck us before we were ready for them, on the road coming out of
Dondon.

Christophe had not many regular soldiers left in the Second Demibrigade, and the men of the hoe who carried guns for him would not stand when the French *blanc* soldiers made a wall of bullets by firing on them all at once and then ran at them with their bayonets shining like steel teeth. Christophe could not make them stand. They scattered into a grove of palms, and Christophe had to run away himself, with the French *blanc* soldiers running after him hard, so that for a little while it seemed like he would be captured. And I, Riau, though I had a good horse, I felt their bayonets close behind me, as I rode away with the palm leaves whipping across my back, and my face rubbing against the mane of the horse because I had ducked down to hide the bullets singing over me. I had not been in any close fighting with these French *blanc* soldiers before then, though I had seen some big fights from a distance. It seemed as terrible to face them as the chief at Saint Michel had said, when they were so quick and so fierce, and a hundred of them could move almost as one.

But once in the woods it was all different. The trunks of the trees broke up the charge of the French *blanc* soldiers. They began to stumble and separate from each other and they did not know how to shoot very well among the trees. I saw then that they did tire quickly, as Toussaint had said, after their first big try. The fear that was with me went away, and I caught up with Guiaou and Guerrier at the edge of the trees, where a narrow road went off among coffee terraces. Guiaou was tightening the knot of his *mouchwa tèt*, getting ready to turn against the French *blanc* soldiers again. He and Guerrier did ride down on the *blancs* and cut a few of them with their *coutelas*, before Hardy could get his own horse soldiers to come up. Hardy's men were in trouble now, with our men shooting them one by one from behind the trees, and Christophe, who had got away, was forming up his regular troops to go back into the fight.

But I, Riau, I rode as fast as I could around all this fighting, back toward Dondon, to let Toussaint know that it had begun. Maybe he knew already from the noise, or he was watching somewhere from the top of a *morne*. I met Placide with Morisset, leading the riders of the honor guard into the battle. In place of his silver helmet, Placide today wore a red *mouchwa*, and from the wideness of his eyes and the far distance they were looking, I thought some spirit was in his head, one strong enough that I could feel it too. Everything seemed calmer to me then, and the noise of the fighting was farther off, as if I heard it from under water. Placide was carrying a French three-colored flag into the fighting. I sent my message on to Toussaint by another man and turned to ride with Placide and Morisset, moving up to the head of the line to show them where to find the enemy.

The French *blanc* soldiers ran from us when Morisset's riders smashed into them, and Toussaint's foot soldiers were coming up very fast behind. We chased them through the pass which drops through the

Black Mountains from Dondon, down the snake-back road onto the low ground of the Northern Plain. In that open country, Hardy formed his men into squares again, so that we could not attack them so easily, but they were still retreating, and as fast as they could, and they had left many dead under the trees and by the roadside. Hardy had dropped a lot of what he had taken at La Coupe à l'Inde, and a lot of the animals he had stolen were scattered, so that we could catch them later on, but Bel Argent was still with him as he hurried to Le Cap. That horse was not easy to keep up with. For some reason Toussaint decided not to keep chasing Hardy after darkness came, even though he had not got back Bel Argent. Our men were all tired from long hours of running and fighting, but we had beaten these *blanc* soldiers who looked so strong, and we had driven them all out of the mountains, even if we had not been able to catch and kill them all as Toussaint would have wished.

After that day the French *blanc* soldiers could not hold on anywhere in the mountains of the north. In the days that followed, Toussaint took over all his old posts from Grande Rivière to Marmelade. From what I had seen in earlier times, I thought he would be thinking that if he could fight through from Marmelade to take Gonaives again, he could cut the country in half the way he had done when he was fighting other *blancs* before, the English or the Spanish. These mountains were the root of Toussaint's power, and I think the spirits that sometimes walked with him were sleeping there, maybe in the old caves of the *caciques* beneath the mountain of Dondon. A man who knew the caves could walk from Dondon to Marmelade underneath the ground, if those old spirits were willing to let him pass. And wherever Toussaint went in the mountains now, he shouted to all the people there that the *blancs* had come to make us slaves again, though he had not said anything about that to Sabès and Gimont.

Toussaint made a headquarters at Marmelade, and no *blanc* soldier came any nearer to him there than Gonaives. There were no *blancs* at all in the mountains by then, because those on the *habitations* who had not been killed in all the fighting had run away to the towns on the coast. Sometimes there was talk of French *blanc* soldiers at Plaisance again, but if they came there they did not stay long, because Sylla was behind them there, with the men he had fighting in the hills above Limbé, and Toussaint kept his own men going back and forth between Marmelade through Limbé to Acul, because, unless he could take Gonaives back from the *blancs*, the Baie d'Acul was the only place where he could touch the sea. So the only part of the country the *blancs* could really hold was the low ground of the plain around Le Cap, and even there Toussaint kept trying to start risings in the *ateliers*, with his story that the *blancs* were sure to bring back slavery.

I did not know how the *blancs* were doing in the rest of the country, and maybe they had been more successful there. Toussaint wanted

Dessalines to take back the ground around La Crête à Pierrot from them, but he had not yet been able to do it.

Only a few days after our big fight with Hardy's soldiers in the pass below Dondon, Sans-Souci came into Marmelade with a lot of French *blanc* soldiers he had taken prisoner in a fight around Grande Rivière. Boyer, who was a colored general who had been with the party of Rigaud before, brought fifteen hundred French *blanc* soldiers to fight Sans-Souci at Sainte Suzanne and other places, but Sans-Souci had beaten them all and driven them back into Le Cap, even though these were new soldiers who had just come over on new ships from France.

This news interested Toussaint very much, and it seemed bad to me at first. I did not forget how strong those ships had looked when they were blowing up the forts of the harbor at Port-au-Prince, and how those French *blanc* soldiers would run all over everything, like ants, when they were fresh. How could we ever kill them all, if they kept pouring out of France?

A lot of our people wanted to kill Sans-Souci's prisoners right away, and I don't think Sans-Souci would have been unhappy to see them die. There was not anyone who hated the *blancs* more than he did, except for Dessalines. But Toussaint treated these prisoners very well. He killed cows for them to eat, and he found shoes for the ones who did not have any shoes. A lot of them had come from France without shoes, we heard, or else their shoes broke very fast on the rocks of our country. They said they had come without enough guns either on their ship, which interested Toussaint very much also. There were four hundred of these captured soldiers. He asked their leaders a lot of questions, and when he had taken their knives and guns away, he gave them the freedom of the quarter of Marmelade, as it would have been *liberté de savane* in slavery time. These *blanc* soldiers did not have a clear idea where they were, and there were too many of our people around them for them to try to get away.

These French *blanc* soldiers spent their days running races and climbing trees and jumping from one rock to another or across the streams in the ravines, or practicing fighting against each other with their hands. I did not see any of them pull down a wild horse by the ears, but they were very active and strong. Our women and children came out to watch them from behind the trees, laughing and covering their mouths with their hands. Some of our men began to worry again about how many such soldiers might still be coming from France. But Toussaint only looked at the sky and hid his smile inside his long fingers and told anyone who asked him that the rains would be coming very soon, and then we would see all these strong *blancs* made weak and dying from the fever.

Not long after Sans-Souci had gone off to Grande Rivière again, to fight any more *blanc* soldiers he might find there, Chancy came to Marmelade with letters to Toussaint from the General Boudet. Toussaint did not tell anyone what was in these letters, but read them secretly inside the house where he was living in Marmelade. Chancy did not know exactly what was in the letters either, but he knew Boudet had waited for word from Leclerc before he sent the letter to Toussaint. Chancy was not certain, but he thought that maybe Boudet's letter might whisper to Toussaint that he could change his coat and come over to the side of the *blancs* at Port-au-Prince.

The *blancs* had been trying those tricks all over the country since their ships first came, the same as I, Riau, had done with Lamour Dérance and Lafortune, and as others had done with Laplume. Even Christophe, after our fight with Hardy at Dondon, came with a letter to show Toussaint— this letter was signed by Leclerc himself and it promised Christophe whatever he wanted if only he would catch Toussaint and sell him to Leclerc. That was strange, because Christophe had burned Le Cap, and only he and Toussaint were made outlaw by the paper Leclerc sent out after that. That paper did not say anything about the other generals. But Christophe had also a copy of his answer to show Toussaint, and it was full of angry words.

You propose to me, Citizen General, to furnish you the means to secure Toussaint Louverture: that would be an act of perfidy on my part, a betrayal, and this proposition, degrading as it is to me, is in my eyes a mark of the insuperable repugnance you must feel if you believe me insusceptible of the least sentiments of delicacy and honor. He is both my chief and my friend. Is friendship, Citizen General, compatible with such a monstrous cowardice?

Toussaint only nodded and stroked his jaw when he had seen these words of Christophe to Leclerc, and his eyes were looking a long way off. Maybe he was not as pleased with Christophe's words as Christophe had expected. I wondered how he would be reading Boudet's words now.

I asked Chancy if the French at Port-au-Prince had become so weak that maybe they did not want to fight Toussaint any more, but Chancy did not really think so. It was true that General Boudet was hurt at La Crête à Pierrot and had not yet recovered. Pamphile de Lacroix had come back from that fight with big holes hidden inside his lines where men who were dead now should have been marching. And Lamour Dérance, when he heard that Rigaud was arrested and sent back to France, had abandoned the *blancs* at Port-au-Prince and taken all his people into the mountains again. Even so, Chancy did not think that the *blancs* felt in much danger at Port-au-Prince, and Toussaint had lost a lot of our men in those fights too.

It was beginning to hurt my head to have to be wondering what Toussaint was going to do. Maybe he had not wanted anything more than to get Chancy free in return for Sabès and Gimont. Maybe he only kept these captured *blanc* soldiers so well because he hoped to get Saint-Jean back in return for them. Yet it seemed that even four hundred of them would not be worth so much. When they began to talk to our people, and especially to some of our foolish young girls who began to go to them at night, it seemed that they had been brought here almost as slaves were brought out of Guinée. They were not chained inside their ships, but they did not have good shoes or clothes or enough food and they had been told lies about where they were going and they were forced to fight.

No one but Toussaint knew for certain what he meant to do, and maybe even Toussaint was not sure. I, Riau, had changed my coat more than one time, the way my spirit moved me.

But in those days my spirit felt very far away, even though Quamba had helped me take the *asson* not so long before. I was fenced in all alone by all my thoughts, and lonely, so I wanted to get out of that fence and go down to Ennery again, and not only to see Merbillay and the children.

I was not going to run away this time, in case Toussaint would have me shot when I came back. I would have to come back, I thought, because it looked like there was nowhere free in the whole country between Toussaint's people in the mountains and the *blancs* on the coast. But I knew Toussaint would want to know what was happening on the road between Ennery and Gonaives and so I offered to go and see for him, and Toussaint accepted this offer.

Before I left, Guiaou gave me a big tortoise shell he had found in the woods to take to Yoyo at Thibodet, and a smaller one for Marielle. The small shell had the bottom piece along with the top and Guiaou had stopped the holes with clay, with pieces of the tortoise's backbone still inside to make a rattle. When he had given me these things, Guiaou seemed happy enough to stay in the camp at Marmelade with Toussaint.

It was easy riding from Marmelade to Ennery, and I met no *blancs* at all on my way to Habitation Thibodet. I did not find anyone in Merbillay's *case* when I got there at the end of the day, though I called and knocked on the edge of the doorway. When I stooped and went inside, the air of the room seemed as if no one had been breathing it for a long time, and almost all the things were gone except for the *paillasses* on the floor. My *banza* hung still from the roof pole. I took it down and touched a string and bent the sound with a finger of my left hand. The *banza* was dusty on the wooden neck and the gourd shell of its body. I carried it outside and sat down to play on the ground near where my horse was snuffling in the dust, until some children came. When I asked them where Merbillay had gone, they pointed down the hill to the *grand'case*.

By the time I had walked to the steps of the *grand'case* it was almost dark, and the stars were beginning to show above the hill where I had tied my horse. There was still enough light for me to see something moving in the pool the doctor had made there long ago. When I moved to look nearer, I was quick to jump back, because the thing which was there was a big *cayman*, resting among the flowers of *bwa dlo*. Only his eyes showed above the water, and two points of his nose, and I thought I could see the shadow of his body just underneath. I thought he was more than six feet long. But then it was too dark to see, and someone was lighting the lamps on the gallery.

When I turned toward the light, there was Merbillay, holding the burning splint in her hand for the lamps. She was wearing her finest headcloth, the one with the gold fringes, to swirl her hair on the top of her head, and she had on one of the *blanche* Elise's dresses.

"Bienvenu, mon capitaine," she said. When I came up the steps she gave me a courtesy, like a *blanche*. Sometimes Elise gave Merbillay her old dresses, but what she wore tonight was a new one. When she gave me her hand, it was dry and cool and pulled a little way from mine. Everything she had been doing unfolded all at once inside my head.

Merbillay was staying in the bedroom of Tocquet and Elise, which was the best room in the house. She had put Caco in the other room at the front, where sometimes the doctor would stay, and the smaller children in the back where Zabeth used to keep the babies. Zabeth had gone off with the *blancs* to Le Cap, and something had made Merbillay believe that this time they were not ever coming back to Thibodet.

She had made a fine meal to serve at the table of the *blancs* on the gallery. As Captain Riau of Toussaint's army, I had sat down at that table sometimes before. This night I sat to eat with Merbillay and the children. The food was even better than what she cooked for the *blancs*, *lambi* with green cashews and rice cooked with cinnamon and milk. Some other people who were living at the *grand'case* sat down to cat with us, while others served the table as Zabeth used to do. The *grand'case* was all full of people who had come from the *cases* above the coffee terraces, and they had made a lot of disorder inside.

When we had finished all the food, I gave Guiaou's shell to Yoyo and Marielle. Yoyo ran away under the starlight toward the spring high on the hill, because she wanted to try her shell for a water dipper. Marielle went inside the *grand'case*, shaking her shell against her ear and smiling. Then everyone else went away from the table, and Merbillay asked me to come with her into the bedroom of the *blancs*, but I would not go.

"If you are afraid of the *blancs*," she said, "they will not be coming back any more."

I did not give her an answer to that. All the plates were still on the table between us, sticky with milk and oil from the food. There would be flies in the morning, if no one took them away. Maybe what Merbillay thought was true and the *blancs* were finished in this country, but if that was coming it had not happened yet. Maybe her picture of the future was true, but that picture had not yet come clear. Nothing was clear. If Toussaint had raised too much trouble for ordinary *blancs* to travel to Ennery, still Xavier Tocquet would go anywhere he wanted to go, with Bazau and Gros-Jean, or alone if he wanted. But that was not the reason I would not sleep in the *grand'case*. I had thought about lying down with Merbillay for many days before I left Marmelade, but I did not want to lie in the bed of the *blancs* and be covered with the *fatras* of their old dreams.

"You make good food, like you always do." I rubbed my stomach with one hand and smiled as I stood up. "I will be in our old *case* whenever you want to find me." Then I kissed her hand, like a *blanc* myself, before I went away.

There was a pull in the bottom of my belly that made my legs want to turn around and go back to her as I climbed up the hill, but I thought maybe it was better to keep away from any woman for a few more days, so that maybe my spirit would come back to me. I could not think what moved Merbillay to start living in the *grand'case* as she had done. Maybe there was a third man in it somewhere, but I had not seen any sign of that, and Merbillay was not the kind of woman who would hide it.

I took the *banza* out into the starlight and sat down near the door to play it. Some of the same children who were there in the afternoon came to listen, and in a little while Caco came too, and sat down so near me that his shoulder was touching my shoulder. Then we heard Quamba's bone flute whistling in the dark and coming nearer, and Quamba crossed his legs to sit down and play until we had finished the tune. Quamba let the flute drop on the string that held it around his neck, and I leaned the *banza* against the wall of the *case*.

"I have been dreaming, or there is a big *cayman* in the pool by the *grand'case*," I said.

Caco laughed and rolled his head against the wall.

"You can laugh," I said. "But that is dangerous for the little children, like your sisters. Why does no one kill this *cayman*?"

"All the guns have gone away to shoot *blancs*," Quamba said. "If you want to kill a *cayman* that big with a knife, Riau, you are welcome."

"He is not hungry." Caco could not stop laughing. "Maman gives him a chicken every day. Or sometimes the leg of a goat."

"Well," I said. "I am glad there are chickens enough at Thibodet to feed a *cayman*." Of course I had my pistols with me, so I could shoot the *cayman* myself if he was there by daylight, but I thought maybe I would leave him alone.

Then Jean-Pic came out of the darkness toward our *case*. He was almost at the door before he noticed that Riau was there.

"I thought you had gone north, to our old country," I said to him. Jean-Pic and I had been maroons together long before, in the hills around the edges of the big plain outside Le Cap.

"I was in the north," Jean-Pic said. "But there was too much trouble, so I came back here. I didn't see you there, Riau."

"It looks like you saw where my bed was," I said, but I was smiling in the dark.

"Oh," said Jean-Pic, "I was sleeping in the *ajoupa* of Michau, because he went north with Zabeth and the *blancs*, but yours is a better house, and it was—" He stopped himself because he did not want to say the house was empty, and looked over his shoulder toward the *grand'case*.

"You can sleep here," I said. "There is still room enough for you."

Then Quamba got up and went away and the children scattered, all but Caco, who came into the *case* with me and Jean-Pic. I let the cloth fall across the doorway and stretched out on a *paillasse*. The cloth held a pale milky light across the door. I could hear Jean-Pic and Caco breathing not far off, although it was too dark to see them.

"Too much fighting in the north," Jean-Pic said. "I went to Grande Rivière to get away from the *blancs*, but Sans-Souci found me and made me fight them still."

I heard Jean-Pic's head shaking against the straw of his *paillasse*. "Woy!" he said. "Sans-Souci likes to fight too hard. With him, you have to beat the *blancs* or die. And they are tough, those new *blanc* soldiers."

"Lamour Dérance has left the *blancs*," I told him. "I heard it from Chancy. He took all his people back from Port-au-Prince to the mountains. He was angry because the *blancs* arrested Rigaud and took his sword and sent him away to France."

"I heard they did that, in the north," Jean-Pic said. "I don't care anything about Rigaud. Rigaud is the same as a *blanc* to me."

"Yes," I said. "But he is not the same as a *blanc* to the *blancs*."

"I would like to see Matilde again," Jean-Pic said. Matilde was the woman he had in Lamour Dérance's band. "Maybe I will go and look for Lamour Dérance, if he has gone back to the mountains."

Jean-Pic was chewing his beard in the dark. "What I would really like is to go back to Bahoruco," he said. "If the *blancs* have not run all over it already, or people fighting the *blancs*."

He didn't say anything more after that, and so we slept. My sleep gave me a foolish dream about a *cayman* sitting at the table on the gallery of the Thibodet *grand'case*, eating a chicken with a fork. In my dream it troubled me that the chicken still had all its feathers, and was bleeding on the tablecloth. All the chairs were standing on their heads, like the chests and the bed in the bedroom. I woke thinking these were the thoughts the *blanche* Elise might have, if she saw how Merbillay had turned her house all upside down, but how had these thoughts come into Riau's head? In the old days Riau would have killed every *blanc* in a house like that and burned it down and danced on the ashes and never dreamed about it.

But it was pleasant to hear Caco breathing near me in the dark. When I slept again, I slept without dreaming.

Next morning Jean-Pic had decided to go south. He could not get a horse at Ennery, or even a donkey. They had all been taken off by the French *blanc* soldiers or ours. I rode him double on my horse as far as the crossroads where the road from Ennery strikes the big road up the coast. The mango sellers at that *kalfou* told us that a lot of French *blanc* soldiers were coming up the road, so we hid my horse in the ravine of the river of Ennery and crept up to the roadside to watch from behind the trees. A lot of soldiers did come marching up the road from Le Cap, and Captain-General Leclerc himself was leading them.

Jean-Pic went south when they had passed, on foot, among a gang of *marchandes* who were taking fruit to Gonaives. They were singing as they went, but I did not want to go any nearer to Gonaives that day. I bought mangoes and took them to Merbillay's *case*. I found Caco to watch my horse, and then I took off my boots and walked with my bare feet to the top of the hill where the *hûnfor* was.

Quamba's woman was sweeping the ground when I came in. She smiled at me, and laid down her broom and went away. I sat down on the hard dirt of the peristyle, under the square red flag that snapped on its long pole in the dry wind. The door to the *kay mystè* was open. Inside in the shadows I could see the new *cannari* we had made, though which was for Bouquart and which for Moyse I could not tell. I did not feel the *konesans* I thought I used to have.

After a while, Quamba came up.

"The house is yours, Riau, if you want to make a service," he said.

"I know it," I said. "I am only waiting."

Quamba went inside the *kay mystè* and did something there, I don't know what, and then he went away. I stayed where I was until after dark, until the stars had moved halfway across the sky. What I expected I did not know. I wanted to feel my spirit guiding me again, and no longer be the prisoner of my thoughts.

Before the night was finished I went back to Merbillay's *case*. I had not been near the *grand'case* or seen Merbillay all day. But when I pulled the cloth back from the door, I saw that Yoyo was sleeping on the *paillasse* near Caco. That made me smile. The shell Guiaou had sent to her was by her on the floor.

In the morning I ate mangoes with Caco and Yoyo and then I rode again to the Ennery crossroads where the mango sellers were. There I learned from the *marchandes* going up and down the big road that there were plenty of French *blanc* soldiers at Gonaives, and ships on the harbor with their cannons. In the afternoon I rode back to Thibodet and let Caco take my horse while I walked up to the *hûnfor* again. All afternoon I sat where I had sat before. At nightfall Quamba passed and put out the *maman tambou* and the *asson* and a pair of ringing irons where I could reach them if I wanted, but for the first time in my life I was afraid to touch these things.

Yoyo brought Marielle to Merbillay's *case* that night, so all three of the children were sleeping there with me. Marielle woke and cried for her mother, but Yoyo shook the turtle shell and sang to her and made her sleep again. I lay awake, thinking of Guiaou. We both knew Guiaou was Yoyo's father, as Riau was Caco's. Which one of us was father of Marielle we did not know for certain, but we had agreed that both of us would be, though we had tried to kill each other first. Once Riau was much more like Guiaou. When the spirit came it filled his head completely and left no place for doubts or thoughts to quarrel with each other. Guiaou was like that still, but now Riau was different.

I slept through a long part of the next day, and climbed to the *hûnfor* after the heat was less. This day the wind blew from the sea, and it was not so dry. The red flag on the tall cane pole was stretching for the mountains. At the end of the day a little *malfini* came on the wind from the west, and turned into the wind above the *hûnfor*. The wind was so strong that the hawk hung in the air above my head without moving, and my vision rose into the eye of the hawk. In one direction I could see as far as Gonaives harbor where the ships of the *blancs* were waiting with their guns, but invisible beneath the water Lasirène was swimming, and her tail was big and strong enough to overturn those boats. It came to me that Lasirène was the spirit with Placide Louverture, the day we fought the soldiers under Hardy. I saw the green *mornes* and the dark hollows between them rolling back to the east until the clouds had swallowed up the trees. There was the black scar on the ground where Habitation Sancey had been burned, and around some bends of the ravine the *grand'case* of Descahaux was still standing. I could even see as far as Marmelade, where Toussaint was, if I could not see what Toussaint was planning.

When the sky grew darker there was the smell of rain, although it did not rain this night. I touched the drum so that it spoke one time, and lifted the *asson* just enough to stir the seeds inside the gourd, and touched the irons together once, then sat with a piece of iron in each of my open hands. One was a curved piece from a collar, and the other a nail that had closed that collar around some man's throat. By tossing the curved piece in my hand and striking it with the straight one, I might make a ringing sound to lead the drums. But I held the irons silent, feeling them warm the points at the center of my palms. It was dark, and now the hawk was gone.

After the darkness had settled, Quamba came and sat across from me, waiting for me to speak.

"If I made the service before I was ready," I said, "it was because the spirit of Moyse was pressing me."

"The spirit will pardon you that, if it is so," said Quamba.

All at once I felt a weight come off my back, and the irons in my hands grew very warm. I felt again what it had been like when Riau struck the irons from Bouquart's feet, but this feeling was mixed with a picture of Bouquart shooting a bullet through his own head at Toussaint's order, and Toussaint seemed to be watching too as the hammer struck the iron from Riau's throat when Riau was brought a slave to Bréda. That part was so long ago I could not be sure. I had not then known Toussaint's name.

"Toussaint may be for freedom, and yet still deal with the *blancs*,"

Quamba said, like he could see everything in my head clear as if it were written on the ground between us. "That was always Toussaint's way."

"I am tired of those twisted ways," I said. "Moyse's way was simpler."

Quamba followed my eyes through the door of the *kay mystè* where the *cannari* of Moyse and Bouquart stood silent and invisible among the others.

"Moyse has gone beneath the waters," he said. "Toussaint is still here."

The iron grew warmer in my hands and spread its warmth to the bottoms of my feet. Quamba wrapped his hands around my head and set his fingertips in the place where my head hinged to my neck. *"Ki jan ou yé?"* he said. How are you?

"Nou la," I said. We're here. I meant not only Riau and Quamba but the spirits of Moyse and Bouquart too, if they were silent, and above them Ogûn, the master of my head, Ogûn Feraille. Ogûn was there with a quiet strength, different from his strength for cutting. He had not turned Riau completely out of his head but was there, sharing the head with me so that I did not feel uncertain.

I knew Riau would go back to Toussaint, but that would be another day. Merbillay was there when I came back to the *case* from the *hûnfor.* No one would know she had been away, except that she was still taking a few of her things out of a bundle. There were some crabs boiling in a pot with hot peppers on a small hot fire behind the *case,* enough for us and the three children. When I slept that night touching Merbillay, I did not dream of any *cayman,* though probably that *cayman* was still waiting at the bottom of the pool. It was a good thing that Merbillay had left the *grand'case,* because the next day the *blancs* did come back to Thibodet after all, not Elise or Tocquet, but Doctor Hébert and Maillart, with some other soldiers.

33

"Elise!" the doctor called. "Elise?" He continued further into the hall of the Thibodet *grand'case*, glancing into the rooms on either side. "Zabeth?"

The bare boards echoed back at him. He felt the abandonment of the house. And there was something else, not disarray exactly, but rearrangement. The bedrooms he peered into all looked to have been pulled apart and then quite recently reassembled. The difference was subtle, hard to identify. He stepped out onto the gallery in back.

"Merbillay?"

But there was no one in the kitchen compound behind the *grand'case*. The blackened fire circle was cold outside the vacant shed. He turned back into the house. Framed in the front doorway at the far end of the hall was the figure of Major Maillart, fists to his hips, waiting for some service or acknowledgment. Then the major paced away from the door, leaving a vacant square of morning light.

The doctor would not call Nanon's name aloud. It struck him as unlucky to do it. He didn't want that name to echo back with no response. She was not here. No one was here. Spiders shimmered in their webs in the high corners of every room. Most of Nanon's clothes remained in her armoire, but she had always been inclined to travel light.

"Antoine!" Maillart's voice, urgent, from outside. Beyond came a wordless, astonished shout from Bienvenu.

"Antoine!" Maillart called, "come quickly!" The doctor rushed onto the gallery. A dragon was heaving itself out of the pool, crushing the long stalks of *bwa dlo* to either side, or no, it was a great *cayman*—the largest he had ever seen. It moved deliberately toward Captain Guizot, with the manner of a dog expecting to be fed a scrap. Guizot took a step back, then drew his sword. The doctor walked down the gallery steps, stumbling on one of the risers, his eyes fixed on the *cayman*. Such an awkward-appearing thing, and yet it moved with a beautiful, fluid quickness.

Captain Guizot gained confidence enough to poke the *cayman*'s snout with his sword point. The *cayman* snapped. The width of its jaws and the rows of its teeth sent a gasp around the group of onlookers, all their party who'd ridden up that day from Gonaives. The *cayman* gathered itself and lunged with a startling alacrity at Guizot, who staggered backward, tripped over his own boot heel, and fell. The doctor felt the weight of his pistol in his hand, and yet he hesitated. He wanted to observe the *cayman* alive for longer. For weeks or months if it were possible. Never before had he seen such a specimen. But he also felt a certain interest in Captain Guizot, whose left arm he had saved from gangrene—it would be a waste to see him eaten by the *cayman*.

Guizot kicked at the probing snout, then scrambled backward in the dirt; he didn't seem to have room to get his feet under him. The *cayman* whipped forward, jaws slicing toward the knee above the boot leather. The doctor braced his pistol and shot it through the left eye. The *cayman* convulsed, and Maillart raised his own gun for a second shot, but the doctor stopped him, hand on his wrist.

"The skin," he said, and Maillart lowered his pistol. For a minute or more the *cayman* went on thrashing, clawing the dirt. The heavy ridged tail thumped spasmodically. At last it lay still. A black dribble from the penetrated eye caked the dust beside its head.

"What shooting!" Guizot had scrambled to his feet, was dusting himself off with slightly quavering hands. He stooped and recovered the sword he'd dropped, his eyes always fixed on the doctor, who felt a little self-conscious under this regard. Since he had succeeded in treating Guizot's infected arrow wound, the young captain always looked at him rather too worshipfully. Probably he was also embarrassed by how near he'd come to dispatching the doctor along with all the wounded men Rochambeau had ordered slain in the debris of La Crête à Pierrot.

"Indeed," said Maillart. "It is very well placed."

The doctor nodded absently. "We'll have the whole hide off him." A sadness settled over him as the rush of action faded. The hot yellow diamond of the *cayman*'s unhurt eye was beginning to cool and glaze. Descourtilz would have loved to see such an animal in action, the doctor thought, he who had made such a study of the *cayman*. He wondered if Descourtilz were still alive.

A small crowd had materialized out of nowhere, as always when anything of interest took place—women and children smiling, giggling, nudging each other as they looked at the long, scaly carcass of the *cayman*. Now the doctor found Merbillay in the group and near her Caco, Yoyo . . . what was the name of her youngest child? The little girl came slowly forward. Then with sudden daring she touched her fingertip to the *cayman*'s hide, shrieked, and ran back to her mother's skirts.

And where was Paul? The doctor was about to put that question to Caco, who would be likely to know something, but before he could speak he saw Riau come striding down from the coffee terraces. When Riau noticed Maillart, he looked for a moment as if he would veer off in another direction, but instead he came on and embraced the doctor.

"You have lost flesh," Riau said as they held each other at arm's length. Maillart was inspecting him with a certain curiosity from where he stood.

"Oh, it is only from a few days of shoe leather at La Crête à Pierrot," the doctor said. Though he was no longer so skeletal as he and the other survivors had been when they left the fort, he knew his eyes were hollow still, and his clothes hung slackly on him. "I'll soon recover."

"*Fok'w pran sang.*" Riau shook his head. "You need to take some blood—Merbillay!"

And Merbillay quickly went off to wring the necks of a dozen pigeons and set her daughters to kindling the charcoal. Quamba, encouraged by a few of the old men bystanding, was sharpening a *coutelas* on a stone, preparatory to gutting and skinning the *cayman*. The doctor stooped to help him with the difficult, delicate work around the head—he wanted the skin off in one piece. Merbillay returned for the butchered joints, and marshalled some children to carry them off to be tenderized in great vats of papaya. The skin of the *cayman*, once finally stretched on the outside wall of the cane mill, was three feet longer than the door was tall.

In the midst of this work the doctor had learned as much as he could of his family—all the whites had left Thibodet for Le Cap some weeks before, and that was as much as anyone knew of them; no word had come back since, not that any was expected.

But the scent of roasted pigeon distracted them all from this subject as they settled around the table. Merbillay brought out a platter of nicely browned birds, with a plate of greens and stewed sweet potatoes. Then she vanished toward the rear of the *grand'case*. Riau, however, joined them for the meal. He had gone to his dwelling while the pigeons cooked, and put on the tunic of his uniform for the occasion. Indeed it was the coat of Toussaint's honor guard, the doctor took note, an elegant costume, only a little worn, with a couple of holes in it meticulously darned. Tearing into the breast of his pigeon, Riau urged the doctor to follow his example. Pigeon meat was believed to fortify the blood. But the doctor, whose stomach was still shrunken from the siege of the fort, approached his bird more cautiously, nibbling on the end of a drumstick.

"You've wandered a little way out of your road," Maillart remarked to Riau, once his first hunger had been blunted by pigeon and potato.

Riau only looked back at him blandly.

"I mean the road from Croix des Bouquets to Port-au-Prince," Maillart pursued. "It does not ordinarily pass through Ennery, no?" Maillart pulled shreds of meat from the ribcage of his bird with the point of his knife. "We were a long time waiting for you to come back from the delivery of that dispatch."

Belatedly, the doctor kicked him under the table.

"Maybe Toussaint is still waiting for you to come back from your mission to Port-au-Prince from Point Samana," Riau said smoothly.

Maillart froze for a moment, then shrugged. "It may be so," he said, and forced a laugh. "I accept your point. But possibly you are the one who can tell us, Riau, more exactly what Toussaint may be expecting." He scraped his chair away as the doctor kicked at his ankle once more. Guizot had laid aside his fork and was looking from Maillart to Riau, bemused.

"No one knows for certain what Toussaint thinks about." Riau smiled tightly. "But maybe he is expecting a bad answer to the question Paul Lafrance asked of your General Lacroix."

Maillart seemed to flush a little, though the normal baked-clay shade of his complexion made it hard to tell. "And how would he know of that question if not from you?" he muttered. But he seemed to have lost confidence in his needling, and when Riau did not answer, he let it drop.

"And the way north?" the doctor asked Riau. "Is it secure?"

"There has been some fighting around Dondon," Riau said. "But that was a few days ago."

"I don't think we mean to go so far east," said the doctor. "I was thinking more of the road to Le Cap through Plaisance and Limbé."

"The Captain-General Leclerc marched up that road not long ago," Riau said. "He may have met some trouble . . . perhaps at Limbé, or in the mountains before. But he had a lot of soldiers with him."

"And how do you estimate the chances of a group the size of our own?" the doctor asked.

For a moment Riau appeared to be looking at the inside of his head. "I think you would get through," he finally said. "If I go with you."

The doctor nodded and returned to his plate. Chewing slowly, carefully, thoroughly, he was able to dispatch about two-thirds of his pigeon.

"You ought not to pick at Riau like that," the doctor told the major later, when they'd both retired for a siesta following the midday meal.

"Riau has gone back to Toussaint—I can smell it," Maillart grumbled from where he'd piled up on the bed. "Riau is an incorrigible *marron*—he has more desertions than I have fingers on both hands. In France he would have been shot long ago."

"You don't want to see him shot any more than I do," the doctor said. "Besides, we need him to get safely to Le Cap, it seems."

"It ought to be quiet enough, when Leclerc has just taken a division that way."

In this country, the doctor thought, such an army may pass, but when it has passed it is as though it had never been there. He kept this observation to himself. Maillart had put in for a leave in order to accompany him, and probably he did not like to think that Riau must also be depended on. The doctor rocked slowly in the hammock he'd chosen in preference to a bed—he thought it cooler, and the weather was heavy. He watched a pair of geckos walking on the ceiling.

"What was that question of Paul Lafrance?" He peered at Maillart, between his bare feet. The major seemed to stiffen on the bed.

"A suspicion that Leclerc has come here to restore slavery."

"Ah," said the doctor. "At La Crête à Pierrot, it was treated as a fact, not a suspicion. That was the thing they all cried from the walls."

"But it's not true," Maillart blurted. "You've seen the proclamations."

"Not everyone who's seen those proclamations believes they tell the truth." The doctor hesitated. "Leclerc has other orders, maybe, that he has not revealed."

"I am not so much in his confidence," Maillart said, his voice barely audible; he seemed to be speaking to his bolster. "But—"

He cut himself off. The doctor peered at him through the notch of his big toe. Maillart seemed to be fidgeting with something at his throat. The doctor eased his head down into the hammock. Maybe it would be better not to pursue the topic, though he felt there must be something to pursue. But he didn't want to make his friend miserable, and possibly he'd be better off not pondering the matter himself. The light had dimmed in a green, watery way, and the atmosphere was still heavier than before.

"It will rain, I think," the doctor said.

"I hope it rains soon." Maillart rolled onto his side. "One can barely breathe."

A wisp of something barely visible detached from the spot of ceiling between the two geckos and came drifting down toward the hammock with a faint, increasing whine. As it came near it resolved into a mosquito. The doctor pinched it, glanced at the blood dot between his thumb and forefinger, then sifted crumbs of the insect body onto the floor and closed his eyes. A dream rushed up suddenly, full of black vomiting. In Port-au-Prince, before they'd started up the coast, a few cases of *mal de Siam* had been seen among the new French soldiers, and the doctor had felt a quick touch of his own recurring fever. Now in his sleep he was sweating heavily and abrading his face against the hammock's mesh. But when he woke it was dark and considerably cooler; the rain he'd expected had already begun.

In two days' time they were riding north, with four pack mules following their horses. The doctor had loaded up some extra clothes for Nanon and Elise and all of the children. From what had been left, none of them seemed to have packed for a long absence. One of the mules bore the skin of the *cayman*, scraped and salted though far from fully cured; it had been some trouble to find a mule that would accept it.

The river of Ennery was running high, and the south slopes of Morne Pilboreau were refreshed and a little greened by the rain. As they mounted higher the terrain grew more dry; a hot wind breathed over the height from the Savane Désolée to the south. Ascending the tightening turns of the trail was like climbing the internal windings of a conch shell, the doctor thought, down to the bleached-shell white of the stones above and below. Beyond the peak, it was damper, greener. The crossroads market there seemed to be functioning as usual.

They halted, to rest their horses and the pack train and to stretch their legs. The doctor bought a basket of avocados to carry with them, and enough fat, juicy oranges to share around the group. As he bit into a halved orange, Maillart joggled him in the ribs.

"Look there—"

To the east the road coiled across a ravine and curled around a mountainside in the direction of Marmelade. The doctor spat out an orange seed, found his spyglass, and focused it on the switchback opposite. In the orb of the lens an indistinct scaly gleaming resolved into the silvered helmets of a dozen riders there.

"*Garde d'honneur,*" the doctor said, passing the glass to Maillart. The honor guard.

"Toussaint's?" Guizot's voice was startled. He looked back and forth between Riau and the distant horsemen; Riau today was crowned with the same silver helm. And the doctor was certain that they must be getting a similar scrutiny from the guardsmen across the ravine. But when Riau raised an arm and swirled his open hand in a fishtail spiral, the guardsmen wheeled their horses and rode out of sight around the bend.

Maillart exhaled. "And there you have it," he said. "I'd wager a month's pay, if there were any pay, that Toussaint has reoccupied Marmelade." He glanced at Riau, then at the doctor. "Very well—you are justified," he said. "Riau has already proved his value to us, and before the day's half done."

"Quite so," said the doctor. "I think we'd better go on."

Maillart was already headed for his horse, but Guizot remained planted, staring bemused out over the dizzying drop into the Plaisance river valley. The doctor rather enjoyed his uncertainty. When he'd first seen the young captain, bearing down with his bayonet, he'd seemed altogether too sure of his intention.

"Toussaint is there?" Guizot said, still staring toward the bend in the road where the guardsmen had disappeared from view. "Just there?"

"One never knows for certain where Toussaint may be," the doctor told him, "if he is not before one's eyes." He stopped, recalling the strange scene he'd witnessed in Place Clugny, a few nights before Le Cap was most recently burned. "Even if he is before one's eyes . . ."

Riau was strolling idly toward them. Guizot still gazed, as if mesmerized, over the giddy plummet into the valley and beyond it to the turquoise recession of mountains into cloud. A wind sprang up and swept the height and rocked the three of them like trees.

"Beware of vertigo," the doctor murmured. "It may call you, pull you down." He felt Riau's attention and went on, in spite or because of it. "The people here believe this air is full of spirits," he said. "If you hear them, do not listen. Look away."

They rode through Plaisance without incident, and on toward the hills of Haut Limbé. As the light yellowed toward a sunset orange, deep shadows of the trees advanced across the road. In the opposite direction, market women returned toward their villages in the hills, lightfooted, singing and swinging their steps as they passed by, with lightened baskets balanced on their heads.

On an ascent, the shadows thickened, grew legs, and swarmed across the road. It was too steep, too late in a long day, for them to get any sudden speed out of their horses up the grade, and before they could recognize it, they had been surrounded by a hundred men. One held the headstall of the doctor's horse; the bare shoulders of many others pressed closely all around. His avocado basket had emptied quickly, green ovals passing from hand to hand. Maillart twisted in his saddle, looking back at him with a discontented stare. But the doctor made no movement to object to anything that was happening. His pistols were close at hand, but it would have been folly to reach for them. In fact he felt nothing but an eerie calm.

A man with a large, shaggily bearded head emerged from the bush and moved idly toward them. The others all seemed to defer to him. *Romain, Romain,* some whispered as he passed. He stopped by the doctor's horse and stroked a finger down the octagon barrel of the rifle which hung in its sling by his right knee. Romain peered up at the doctor, grunted, and moved on. Some of his lieutenants were fishing into the loads of the pack animals. One, discovering the rolled *cayman* skin, started back with a cry.

Romain walked toward him. A pair of men loosened the strings that secured the skin and unrolled it, backing away from each other to keep it from dragging on the ground. The slack skin of the *cayman*'s legs went dangling; the onlookers murmured as they circled it. At the release of the raw odor, the mule pulled to the length of its lead and stood tossing its head, fighting the man who held it.

Romain touched the *cayman*'s eye hole, on the groove where the bullet had entered.

"*Ki moun ki té touyé'l?*" he said. Who killed it?

"Him," Riau pointed out the doctor. Romain raised his head to survey him again, and took another long look at the heavy rifle. His eyes were as murky yellow as the *cayman*'s had been.

"This *blanc* is a doctor," Riau announced. "Also a *doktè-fey*. He is a doctor for Toussaint. He was with Toussaint at Ravine à Couleuvre, and with Dessalines at La Crête à Pierrot."

Romain walked the length of the *cayman*'s skin, heel to toe, his hand gliding over the surface of the green leather. The ends of his hair locks were finished with small white cowrie shells that ticked together as he moved.

"With Dessalines too? *Kon sa, sé pa blan li yé.*" At this remark several men laughed, Riau included. Like that, he is not a blanc. The doctor let himself relax a little, though he also wondered what credit this statement would be worth to him if and when they returned to precincts controlled by Leclerc's army.

Maillart had untwisted in his saddle and loosened his reins. At Romain's signal, the two men furled the *cayman*'s skin, fastened it, and began to load it onto the struggling mule where it had been before. The mule settled down once the bundle had been securely tied.

"*Kité tout moun yo pasé,*" said Romain. Let them all pass.

They rode on, escorted now by a couple of dozen of Romain's men, a few of them mounted on donkeys or small ponies, most trotting along on foot. In an hour's time they could see, from the heights of Limbé, the red sun lowering over the calm expanse of the Baie d'Acul below them. By the time they had reached the low ground, darkness had covered. Heavy clouds had rolled over from the mountains and blotted out all light. Riau and Romain's men seemed to make their way onward by sense of smell; the doctor simply let his horse be carried along in their current.

When they reached the gateway of Habitation Arnaud, they heard drumming beyond it. The wind stirred in spirals in advance of the coming rain, and the air in the doctor's lungs felt thick as water. Romain's men scattered across the compound when they emerged from the *allée;* cries of excitement now mingled with the drums. The doctor and his group hurried for the shelter of the barn, with raindrops already smacking the dirt around them. Once inside, they turned to face the deluge that came down. Now there was nothing to see but roaring water. The doctor took a calabash bowl from his medical bag and held it at arm's length into the rain, then drank and passed it among the others.

When at last the rain had stopped, they left their horses tethered and walked out under a canopy of stars. The drums had not resumed, but there was some hubbub in the direction of the cane mill. The doctor glimpsed a flicker of lamp or candle light on the rise where Arnaud had rebuilt his house. He walked in the direction, and the others followed him.

Cléo and Isidor sat on the narrow puncheon porch, each smoking a small round pipe. A bowl of well-picked fishbones sat between them on the floor, with a little cat watching it from beyond the eaves of the roof. Cléo looked at them indifferently as they came toward the small circle of light; she did not rise.

"Monsieur and Madame Arnaud?" the doctor inquired.

"*Tout blan-yo pati,*" Cléo said. All the whites have left. She squinted at the shadow where he stood, then nodded, with a half-smile. "Is it Doctor Hébert? You are welcome. You may stay."

The doctor stepped onto the wooden floor. Riau followed him, stamping his wet boots.

"*Sa ou gegne pou nou manjé?*" Riau said. What have you got for us to eat?

"*Pa gegne anyen anko.*" Cléo shrugged. There's nothing left. The doctor's stomach grumbled at this remark. His avocados, he recalled, had dispersed themselves among Romain's men. He searched for expression in Cléo's handsome ivory face, but found no hostility, only disinterest. He put his head into the house. The air smelled damp and rather uninviting.

"Take any room except the first," Cléo said from where she sat.

"Thank you," said the doctor. His throat itched for rum. Riau appeared at his right hand.

"We can go down to look for Moustique," he said. "If they start that *bamboche* again, we may find something."

The four of them retraced their steps down the trail by which they'd come. As they neared the cane mill, the doctor noticed other shadows milling ahead of him, beyond the building, and caught the sharp smell of fermenting cane. Arnaud's distillery was in service. His mood began to brighten.

"Have you got money?" Maillart whispered in his ear.

"Of course," said the doctor. Maillart pressed his shoulder. Brushed by damp branches, they reached the distillery's coils. A line had formed for gourds of fresh *clairin*. The doctor found a coin to pay for his.

"*Santé,*" he said, swallowing as he passed the container to Maillart, who drank and passed it to Riau. Guizot hesitated when the gourd reached him from Riau's hand, then took it and drank his measure and coughed.

"*Dousman alé loin,*" Maillart said unexpectedly. He clapped Guizot on the back, then moved past him, returning toward the open ground beyond the cane mill on the trail they'd come by. Guizot looked to the doctor for some explanation.

"It means . . . don't drink your rum too fast," the doctor said. He collected the gourd, took another small swallow, and stopped it with the plug of rolled leaves. Guizot was still looking at him, his starved face pale in the starlight.

"Or, 'the softer you go the sooner you'll get there,'" the doctor said. "That would be another way to put it. It is one of Toussaint's favorite proverbs. Along with *patiens bat lafòs.*"

"Patience beats force?" Guizot's laugh was harsh, incredulous. He shook his head, then fell in behind the doctor, who was following Riau and Maillart.

Unerringly Riau led them toward the smell of roasting goat. A *boucan* had been set up among the little *cases* by the church, and women were serving out peppered goat with plantains baked whole in their skins. Romain's men got their portions first, and Riau with them; the three *blancs* lagged a little behind and were served among the women and the children.

Then they drifted toward the sound of the drums, each balancing a shiny green plantain leaf which did duty as a plate. Guizot bit into a piece of his goat and choked on the peppery gravy.

"*Dousman alé loin,*" Maillart chided him again. There was the slightest edge of hysteria in the laugh Guizot returned. The doctor looked at him with a distant concern. In this country, a mind too singular was easy to break.

A few people seemed to look askance at Guizot's uniform—there was enough firelight here and there to make it more visible than might have been preferred—but any hostile muttering was soon hushed. Maillart and the doctor were already reasonably well known in these parts, and Romain's safe-conduct seemed to hold for all three *blancs* here. Besides, the mood was sufficiently amiable. It was a *bamboche,* as Riau had said, a party of pleasure rather than any more serious ceremony. A wooden fife carried a melody above the drums, and the airs it played were old French country dances, though grafted onto rhythms out of Africa. Riau, who'd dispatched his meal very quickly, had stepped out to dance with one of the girls. The doctor felt Guizot begin to soften beside him, under the influence of hot food and drink. The young captain had been tense as a terrier all day, and such an effort was exhausting.

The doctor cleaned his fingers as best he could on the plantain leaf and let it drift away from him. He stooped for the gourd he'd held between his feet while he was eating. As he drank, Moustique appeared at his left hand. The doctor swallowed and offered the gourd. Moustique held it for a moment without drinking.

"*Ba'm nouvel'w,*" the doctor said. Give me your news.

"All is well," Moustique said. The doctor studied his profile. Moustique was still rail-thin as ever, but had outgrown his gawkiness, and seemed much more comfortably settled in himself.

"Your family?" the doctor inquired.

"Marie-Noelle has taken the children to Le Cap," Moustique said. "That is why you do not see them here. They went with Monsieur and Madame Arnaud and Nanon and Madame your sister with her husband, and all the children too. Also Madame Cigny went with them. They are all well."

He paused. The doctor felt the rum flushing through him along with the gladness of relief. He'd come to Habitation Arnaud thinking that the others would have stopped here, but had not dared put that question to Cléo and Isidor. And if Moustique had sent his own wife on with them, the doctor's instinct was that they must all in fact be safe.

"They are all well except for Monsieur Bertrand Cigny," Moustique said. "He was killed when Sylla's men struck his plantation, and his own *atelier* rose against him." Moustique inclined the gourd and let a drop fall on the ground, then made the sign of the cross before he drank. He offered the rum to Maillart, who did not at first seem to notice it. His eyes had widened at the last news, and he covered the lower part of his face with a fist.

Guizot was paying no attention; he stood rapt, watching skirts whirl by in the dance. The girl Riau had chosen was exceptionally pretty; the doctor's eye was on her too. Her slender back curved over the crook of Riau's arm like the stem of a wild flower. She dipped, came straight, and spun away from him, her dotted calico spinning out from her slim hips, her eyes bright in a dark chocolate face. Riau caught her close again, stooped to whisper something in her ear. The girl protested, laughing, beating her palms lightly on his chest. Riau leaned closer, urging still, and the girl's face quieted and resolved. She broke from Riau and moved boldly toward Captain Guizot, eyes shining on him. With a phrase of Creole he could not understand, she caught his hand and pulled. Guizot remained as obdurate as a post.

"Dance with her, you idiot," Maillart said. He'd recovered himself enough to take his tot of rum. "If you'd turn away a *belle* like that, there is no place for you in the French army."

Guizot yielded and let himself be drawn among the dancers. He had a reasonably quick step, the doctor noticed, and though the girl was infinitely more graceful, she adapted herself so flawlessly to him that soon Guizot was lit by an unconscious smile.

Then the music halted and dancers drew back. Into the orb of the space they opened stepped Cléo and Isidor. As the fife took a minuet, she returned a courtesy to his bow, and they began a *pas de deux*. Cléo was not so fluid as the young girls, but more accomplished, achieving grace with a smaller, more neatly contained effort. The younger people all stood by, swaying and smiling and clapping to the drum beat. It was quite as if the master and mistress had come down from the *château*, the doctor thought, to lend a little honor to a peasant festival.

And surely, the rusty frockcoat draped upon Isidor was the property of Michel Arnaud, while Cléo's gown was some long-closeted finery of Claudine's.

As if this couple had slipped into the skins of the absent others. The doctor was startled by that thought. He felt a scaliness creeping over him, and was struck by the oddly vivid fantasy that he was being absorbed into the skin of the *cayman* he had shot. Surely he had not drunk so much as that—yet his fingers were numb, accepting the gourd from Maillart. It was the drums. The drums were doing something to the back of his head where it joined his spine. He could no longer hear the fife, though he could see the man who was playing it.

Moustique had turned away from the dance and was walking off into dim starlight. The doctor followed him, trailing the rum gourd from his knuckles, into the mouth of a green brushy tunnel. As the drums grew more distant, the vertigo against which he'd warned Guizot also receded.

The doctor emerged with Moustique into a circle open to the sky. In the shrubbery walls of the enclosure were numerous little niches lit by candles. Moustique went to one of these and began to spoon water over several squat clay jars. In his movement was a preternatural calm.

"What do they hold?" the doctor asked.

"Spirits of the ancestors."

"Have you got the Père Bonne-chance in there?" The doctor's voice missed the jocular note he'd tried for. Indeed it seemed he could scarcely croak. "Your father?"

"No," Moustique said. "His spirit wants to be with the saints of Jesus in the sky. These are Fontelle's people, out of Dahomey."

As he spoke, the doctor felt himself grow sick with fear. He knew that Moustique's chapel was built on the site of some old horror and that something connected that emplacement to this one. He was also quite sure that Nanon had been here, very near to where he now stood, and not very long ago, though he did not know the source of any of these certainties. But the fear drained out of him, lanced like a boil. He could still feel a hollow where the fear had been, there in the soft spot on the bottom of his brain.

He stood before another leafy niche, where a candle illuminated an image of the Mater Dolorosa, long bright sword piercing into her heart. Below it hung a loop of pearlescent, pale blue beads, and framed by the beads was a fragment of mirror. When the doctor looked into it, he saw nothing. Where his reflected visage should have been was empty air.

The thrum in the back of his head intensified. The doctor turned toward it, but of course it was always behind him. Riau had entered the peristyle and stood, relaxed but motionless, in the same pose he'd had with the girl.

Something changed in the tone of the distant singing. The drums had opened a deeper throat.

Jé mwen . . .
mwen pè gade
Jé mwen . . .
Mwen pè gade sa-a . . .

The doctor became aware that Riau was centered on a filament that ran through the top of his head through his coccyx, through the bottom of his heel. It coursed from the bottom of the ocean to the starlit crown of the sky with Riau's whole being suspended on it weightless as a thread.

My eyes . . .
I fear to see
My eyes
I'm afraid to look at that . . .

The doctor's own body began to turn on the same axis as Riau's. The drum beat in the back of his head was lost in its own overtones, the hum of bees, urgent stroking of thousands of butterfly wings, and the song dropped into a heart-wrenching minor key.

Mwen vini lwen . . .
Kouman yo yé
Kouman yo yé
Mwen pralé lwen
Kouman yo yé
Kouman yo yé a . . .

He was aware that his body was falling, the gourd released from his numb arm to offer an oblation of spilled rum in a neat circle on the ground. He was no more with his body, but surging upward on that invisible filament with a flowering rush of speed his body, the whole circle of Moustique's peristyle shrinking away in the bright disappearing lens of a spyglass reversed. In the center of the vanishing orb Cléo and Isidor appeared to dance like marionettes, like insects—a whistling emptiness replaced them. The stars churned into a whirlpool of silver and from the vortex stepped Nanon, unfastening her bodice, her face calm, compassionate, certain. She opened her heart, reached in with both hands, and presented to the doctor, of all strange things, his glasses.

"You fainted," Maillart said.

"What?" The doctor was somewhere beside the source of his own voice.

"You fainted," Maillart said patiently. "Christ, what a night."

"I was watching the dancing," the doctor said. There had been something more but he couldn't remember it.

"You are not yet restored enough from the siege," Maillart suggested. "Or maybe it's a relapse of your fever."

The starry vortex whirled again before the doctor's eye. He blinked and saw the ordinary ceiling. There was a rocking feeling in his head as if he had been too long on a boat. What were those words the drum had carried?

> I come from afar,
> How are they?
> How are they doing?
> I'm going a long way
> How are they?

Now he was lying in a bed, not a hammock, with four posts solidly planted on the floor of one of the back rooms of the Arnaud *grand'case*. With a start, he snatched for his glasses, and as he grasped them the whole string of events from when he'd left the *bamboche* to when he'd collapsed in Moustique's peristyle came into alignment.

His watch had been laid on the table beside his glasses. The doctor covered his pulse with his thumb and watched the second hand tick off a minute.

"I don't have fever," he pronounced.

"Well and good," said Maillart. "You're fit to travel?"

The doctor sat up and swung his feet to the floor. He felt unusually calm and clear, as if his odd fit of the night before had somehow rinsed his brain.

"Yes, I think so," he replied.

Early light came leaking through the jalousies covering the windows, striping over his bare toes. He could hear Cléo's voice somewhere else in the house, murmuring to Isidor. The sound reminded him strangely of last night's vacant mirror. Surely, one day all trace of his doing and his being would be effaced, but somehow this thought did not disturb him now.

"Riau has gone," Maillart said. "With his horse and his gear."

"Yes," said the doctor.

"What—he can't have told you he meant to leave us."

"No," said the doctor. "But he has brought us far enough. We won't have any trouble on the plain today." He polished his glasses and settled them on his nose. "Probably Riau has gone back to Toussaint at Marmelade, as you suspected."

Maillart snorted as he stood up, stamping his feet down hard into the heels of his boots. He took his exasperation out of doors, and on the gallery poured himself the dregs of Cléo and Isidor's coffee pot.

Romain's men had filtered away during the night or the early morning. Maybe Riau had moved among them. At any rate there was no one now to be seen in the compound but women, children, a few halt old men. And here came Moustique with Guizot from the direction of the *cases* by the little chapel—Moustique shouldering an unwieldy bundle more or less the size of himself. A little boy trotted under the end of it, raising it above his head.

"You're coming with us today, then?" Maillart said.

"Yes." Moustique huffed as he swung down his load. The child swung himself astride the bundle, grinning. Maillart turned to Guizot.

"I trust you passed a restful night?"

Guizot only blinked at him, slowly and dreamily. Maillart rather envied him his girl. He himself had been wholly taken up by the doctor's crisis. But the young captain's air of beatitude was so innocent that Maillart found it difficult to sustain his annoyance.

They were on the road before the sun had cleared the treetops, and might have made very good time to Le Cap, had not the doctor insisted on detouring to the shore of the Baie d'Acul so that Guizot could bathe his healing wound in seawater. In the end, all of them went in swimming— the doctor and Guizot and Moustique and the gaggle of boys that trailed along to help them with their pack train, a couple from Thibodet and the rest more recently acquired at Habitation Arnaud. Maillart did not know their names. Only Maillart remained on shore, one hand on his weapon, keeping watch.

Sweat prickled him under his uniform. There was no sign of any life except for a couple of spotted pigs that came grunting down the trail they'd used themselves to wallow in the shallows. The strand was lined with sea grape and small almond trees. Around the further curve of the bay the jungle was a dense and featureless green wall. And if any enemy were to catch them here, their whole wet, naked party would be killed or captured soon after Maillart got off his one shot and perhaps half a dozen cuts of his sword.

He loosened his belt and let the heavy scabbards it supported settle to the ground, then shrugged out of his coat and his shirt, cupping the pendant at his throat to hide it from Moustique, who'd chosen this moment to come glistening out of the water. The situation reminded Maillart uncomfortably of the doctor's probe about secret orders. He slipped the pendant into his pocket and rolled his trousers around it. Then he dashed into the water, plunged under, swam a length or two, and surfaced to look back. Moustique was dressed and keeping watch after all, with Maillart's long dragoon pistol balanced on his bony knees.

All the broad expanse of the Baie d'Acul was a still, glassy mirror surface, returning the brilliant blaze of the sun. Near the mouth of the bay a pod of porpoises broke the horizon line into dark running curves, reminding Maillart of thoughts he'd like to drown. So long as he was active in the water—splashing the black boys and even Guizot—he was sufficiently distracted. The day was calm and sweet, and the doctor's peculiar sense of safety seemed justified.

Later, though, when he'd resumed his clothing and remounted, Maillart could not lose consciousness of the pendant strung round his neck on its frail gold chain. He'd taken to wearing it so for fear of losing it, though like as not it would be better lost. The light touch of the disk on his collarbone recalled the coy painted face with the cautionary finger laid across the lips. When he thought of Isabelle unhusbanded, his heart flopped and rolled in his chest like a puppy, yet this sensation merely confused him; he didn't know what to make of it or the circumstance. And the secret of the pendant was not Isabelle's. Maillart did not enjoy the possession of secrets. If he considered, he thought it probable that there was some darker secret, deeper than the order Boudet had revealed and which Maillart had tied up in the pendant—a secret he had no desire to discover.

34

"I have made one of the most painful campaigns it would be possible to make," Leclerc had reported to his brother-in-law from his temporary headquarters at La Crête à Pierrot, "and I owe the position in which I find myself only to the rapidity of my movement."

Billeted now to Leclerc's staff, Captain Daspir had the opportunity to overhear this snatch of dictation. Since then, the Captain-General had somewhat recuperated from the strains of his difficult campaign. His bruised groin had healed enough that he could ride a horse again. At Port-au-Prince he had spent a few apparently festive evenings with the beautiful Pauline, before she returned by boat to Le Cap. One would thus surmise, as Cyprien whispered to Daspir and Paltre, that Leclerc had taken his boots off more than once—though Toussaint Louverture remained very much at large.

Their movement was rapid enough, Daspir reflected as they flung themselves once more over the mountains in the direction of Le Cap. But their speed never seemed quite equal to what the enemy could sustain. Leclerc's sense of urgency was probably stimulated by the knowledge that Pauline's ship would have reached Le Cap before him, and reports from the north had been troubling, especially in the last few days. In committing so much of his force to the pursuit of Toussaint from Gonaives to (as he'd supposed) the Artibonite, Leclerc had left Le Cap defended only by Boyer's sprinkling of colonial troops and the sailors in the fleet, and there was no word of the reinforcements from France that had long been expected there. Meanwhile, both Toussaint and Christophe were said to be ravaging the Northern Plain, along with a dozen other rebel chiefs of lesser notoriety.

Yet when they crossed the mountains, there was no enemy to confront. Snipers and skirmishers harassed their column as it wound through Plaisance and Limbé, but these hill bandits would not risk an all-out engagement with a division marching in such strength. Where the road leveled out, north of Limbé, all was peaceful, the warm morning sun dappling fields of cane and corn which were still standing, ripening. Market women gathered at the crossroads to offer their wares to the passing troops. Daspir bought a stalk of the tiny sweet yellow bananas he had never seen anywhere else but this island, and a stalk of cane to peel and chew—a practice he'd learned from watching the black soldiers of the Ninth who now marched in their company. He traded sections of his cane to Cyprien and Paltre for a future share in the two large gourds of *clairin* on which they'd pooled their resources. With these provisions they went on reasonably content.

Beyond the Baie d'Acul the aspect changed: fire-blackened fields rolled away from the road they traveled, clear to the horizon of the north coast. The wood of Daspir's cane stalk, drained of sugar, splintered in his mouth. He spat the pulp into the road. At the time of his first landing, this country had not been so devastated as now, though there had been some burning when he rode this way before. The orange he'd plucked from a slightly scorched hedge was the first fruit he had tasted in this land. Today there were no oranges whatsoever, and all that remained of the citrus hedges was a persistent stubble. The stone gateposts of the plantations that they passed were all soot-streaked, their iron deformed by the heat of burning. Except for the contour of the mountain to their left, Daspir could pick no familiar feature of their progress.

A little way short of Haut du Cap they came upon a large band of black irregulars in open insurrection, who fired one ragged volley at their column and then bolted. As the terrain seemed to offer them no shelter, Leclerc ordered a pursuit. Yet the burned fields, flat and featureless as they seemed, proved to be laced and wormholed with ditches and creeks into which their attackers swiftly disappeared. The three captains had to pull up their galloping horses at the steep bank of a stream, and then quickly dismount under fire from an unburnt patch of brush forty paces distant.

Paltre, furious that his horse had been shot in the hindquarter, turned his brace of pistols on the brush pocket. Daspir and Cyprien crawled toward it belly-down, under cover of Paltre's intermittent fire. The brush was vacant when they reached it; only a scatter of torn cartridge paper proved that the snipers had been there. A few muddy footprints showed the path of their escape down the streambed.

"As well try to track snakes in a swamp." Cyprien spat ash from a pinkish hole in his soot-blackened face.

"*Makaya! Gadé Makaya!*" An equally soot-powdered black was rushing toward them in a high state of excitement, waving his arms and shouting, "Watch out for Makaya!" Daspir, whose nerves were already jangled, would have shot him if Cyprien had not caught his arm.

"That's one of the Ninth—he's one of ours," Cyprien hissed in Daspir's ear, though he was simultaneously pulling him down into the cover of the streambed.

"*Sé moun Makaya yo yé,*" the black soldier babbled as he rushed by, high on the bank. They are Makaya's people. He seemed to have lost or thrown away his weapon.

"And who is Makaya?" Daspir whispered.

"One of the brigand chiefs hereabouts," Cyprien said. "I know no more."

As soon as they started back toward Paltre, they were raked again by musket balls—now from a ditch between them and the road. The same volley knocked down Paltre's wounded horse and he let the other two slip; they cantered off through the ash with their reins trailing. For the next half-hour, Cyprien and Daspir were pinned down in the brush patch and completely cut off from the infantry. They didn't know if Paltre were dead or alive; all they could see was the pulsing flank of the downed horse. The other horses had drifted to the edge of the stream. Daspir crept around under cover of the bank and managed to catch both of them.

The voices of Makaya's men and the men of the Ninth continued to halloo up and down the ditches, amid sporadic gunfire and the occasional howl of a wounded man. Any movement on the open plain stirred up such whirlings of ash that the content of the action was invisible in the cloud. Cyprien and Daspir crouched back to back with the horses between them and each of their pistols trained toward the nearest bend of the streambed. Daspir had passed his left arm through the loop of his horse's reins, and used it to support his right hand on the pistol grip. The torn shoulder still pained him, though he no longer had to carry the arm in a sling. No one appeared, and the noise of skirmishing receded to the north. After ten or twelve minutes of calm, they cautiously emerged from their cover and found Paltre unhurt, curled against the belly of the wounded horse, which was quietly bleeding to death beside him. Cyprien put it away with a shot between the eyes, then took Paltre up behind his saddle.

"Look there," Daspir alerted the others, when they'd ridden perhaps two hundred yards toward the road. A gang of Makaya's men had swarmed out of the ditches and were busy flaying the dead horse and dressing out joints of meat with their *coutelas*. One scurried away with the saddle, which Paltre had forgotten to salvage. With a curse, Paltre pulled out his pistol and fired, scarcely aiming. The men scattered briefly, then returned to their work.

The rest of Leclerc's column, similarly disconsolate, was re-forming on the road. A good number of Makaya's men had reappeared in the open, just out of musket range to the south, blocking the roadway to Morne Rouge. They capered rudely, sounded their conch shells, swirled long whips fashioned from the tails of bulls. Leclerc's teeth clenched, and his hand crawled on the pommel of his sword. But the men were drained from their bootless pursuit and half-choked on all the ash they'd inhaled. Moreover it was now very late in the day, and heavy clouds were blowing in from the mountains to the east. Leclerc ordered their march to continue toward Le Cap.

They reached the gate with the rain coming behind them in a neat line across the plain, like the blade of a knife scraping crumbs from a table. The troops moved out smartly along the Rue Espagnole. Civilians turned out to cheer them, with some real enthusiasm, lining the streets under the balconies of houses beginning to be rebuilt. A few young women even had flowers to toss. Word was that Hardy had been whipped from Dondon to the gates of Le Cap a few days earlier, so Leclerc's arrival in force was more than welcome.

Most of the division turned uphill in the direction of the barracks there, but Paltre, Daspir, and Cyprien continued with Leclerc and a few other staff officers in the direction of the Governor's house. The rain blew after them; the streets were clearing in its wake. Daspir tossed his reins to a groom and hurried under the portico. Here, thanks to Pauline's pressure, prodigies of restoration had been achieved: the roof retimbered, walls freshly plastered, and any trace of soot whitewashed away. Pauline turned a cool cheek to Leclerc's embrace. With her was Isabelle Cigny; Daspir went toward her and began to bow over her hand, but Leclerc's voice arrested him.

"You'll frighten the ladies, Captain." Leclerc laughed harshly. "Why, you look like one of our blackamoors."

Daspir touched a finger to his cheek and looked at the soot on the ball of it. But he was no worse than the others, especially Paltre, who was covered in horse blood along with the ash. He drew himself rigidly upright, snapped a salute at his commander, and stalked out blindly into the hammering rain.

There was no ash left on him by the time he'd crossed the block to the barracks of the Carénage; it was as if the rain had peeled him, though in his angry discontent he scarcely noticed it. He went into the barracks and sat down on the edge of a wooden bench, trembling from exhaustion as much as the wet and chill. Upset as he was, he scarcely noticed his trembling either. Why had Leclerc retained him on staff if he couldn't stand the sight of him? He had probably saved the Captain-General's life at the moment when Placide—Placide!—would have cut him down. And yet—well, there was the heart of it, Daspir saw in a quick cold flash: his presence could only remind Leclerc of that moment of his helplessness, and of course the embarrassing wound to his groin as well. For that, Leclerc could not help but make the preferment Daspir had merited a misery to him. An absurd position, Daspir thought, but he saw no way out of it. He rolled his head against the wall and dozed.

A few minutes after the rain had stopped, Cyprien came in whistling and announced that they were bidden to an evening *chez* Isabelle Cigny.

"I won't go," Daspir said gloomily.

"What? Don't sulk," Cyprien said. "You don't want to rust all night in barracks."

Daspir shrugged and stared at the floor. He felt a scratch in the back of his throat; no doubt he'd take cold from the wetting he'd got. Cyprien sat down beside him and shook him by the shoulder.

"She asked for you particularly," he said.

"She did?" Daspir looked up.

"She did indeed," said Paltre, who had come in with Cyprien and was now doing his best to clean the front of his coat with a wet handkerchief. "And we're told it's not a favor to ignore."

Pauline flinched as the parakeet stepped from a fold of the tunic she sported onto the bare curve of her shoulder; she made a moue of exaggerated pain. The tall, cool mulattress Nanon went to her and stroked a finger down the bird's legs; it took a backward step to this new perch.

"*Comme tu es belle,*" the parakeet said, turning the bead of its eye on Nanon.

"Faithless—betrayer!" Pauline chided the bird, then shifted her attention back to Xavier Tocquet. "Do tell us more about La Tortue."

Daspir inspected Tocquet with a certain interest. He reclined in his chair with the air of a crocodile basking in shallow water, completely at ease but not especially responsive. A shadow of suspicion had passed over him, for he was thought to have been one of Toussaint's arms suppliers, and yet more recently he had been of great service to the expedition in putting down the late rebellion at La Tortue.

"It is as pleasant an isle as you imagine, Madame," Tocquet informed her.

"Oh!" said Pauline. "I do so want to see it."

Tocquet smiled on her lazily, distantly. "No doubt a visit can be arranged," he said. Daspir saw how Pauline was piqued at his indifference to her.

"I have heard the island might be a good situation for a hospital," Leclerc said.

Tocquet put his fingertips together and rolled his head indolently toward the Captain-General. "It well might be," he said. "For convalescents, certainly."

"But it is a most agreeable place for people in the best of health!" Isabelle began telling a tale of her excursions to La Tortue—edenic idylls she had passed there as a child. The blonde, Elise Tocquet, put in a word or two as well, for Isabelle had taken her there at a later time. In season, one might find quantities of turtle eggs in the sands of the beach—the island took its name from the numbers of big sea turtles in the waters surrounding it, and the meat of the turtle was also delectable if properly prepared. There was wild fruit aplenty on La Tortue, and wild pigs and goats loosed on the island by filibusters generations gone, which could be succulently roasted on the *boucan* . . . and meanwhile one's slaves prepared a bower where one might pass a night under the stars. Of course, that had been a more innocent time, before the present troubles had begun . . .

Daspir watched Isabelle, less engaged by her vivid descriptions of delicacies than by her movements, the snap of her dark eyes, the shape of her lips which were so full (though her mouth was small), the wing-like gestures of her hands. Had she really asked for him especially? Cyprien might have deceived him on that point, only to cheer him, and to assure his company at this evening's entertainment. Both Cyprien and Paltre were now rather drunk, having dipped heavily into their rum gourds before presenting themselves here. Daspir had partaken more cautiously, on the chance that Cyprien's hint might be true.

But Isabelle did not make him a particular target of her conversation— indeed she was more flirtatious with almost any other man in the room— Tocquet excepted, but Leclerc especially. And if her eyes did sometimes seem to linger on Daspir's face, he might have merely imagined that . . . There was something, just below the line of her quite daring *décolletage,* that shifted with the rising of her breath and pressed against the cloth. Now when she turned her head toward Pauline, a gold chain lifted against her throat, so fine it was almost invisible.

He must not stare. Daspir looked around the room at random. The Cignys had not rebuilt with such exactitude as Pauline Leclerc had been able to command, but certainly they must have some resources. There were a new roof and new floors smelling of fresh wood, though Isabelle apologized for the boards being covered with painted canvas rather than the rugs lost in the burning. The walls were all bright with fresh paint and each of the round-topped doorways of the salon framed a new wooden door, now folded open onto the balcony with its new railings of filigreed iron. The afternoon downpour had freshened the air, but still mosquitoes kept floating in through the open doors. Daspir winced, crushing one against his neck, and lowered his hand with its bright dot of blood.

Claudine Arnaud, who sat beside her husband in a straight wooden chair against the wall, seemed to look with disapproval on this action. Furtively, Daspir crumbled the mosquito beneath his chair. Madame Arnaud sat painfully upright, stiff in a black silk dress that rustled if she moved a hair, though for the most part she held herself perfectly still, silent, her three-fingered hand curled in her lap inside the whole one. Of course her every look seemed disapproving, no matter what came before her long sharp nose and glittering eye. She was reputed to be quite mad, though tonight she did not give much sign of it, unless her silence was a sign. She said nothing, and let the other women's prattle shower over her.

For the past ten minutes, Paltre, sitting with his legs sprawled a little too widely for politeness, had been half-surreptitiously kissing his fingers to Nanon, and now abruptly he crossed the room to join her on the small striped sofa where she sat, though she did not seem to much welcome his company. A closer look at the talking bird was his pretext, but his real mission seemed to be to get a hand on her haunch. Of a sudden, the bird flew into his face and scratched it. It rather looked to Daspir as if Nanon had launched it there.

"Putain!" Paltre flailed the bird from his face and started back, then clutched the crotch of his tight white trousers to make it plain that his "Whore!" was no random expletive, but quite personally intended. Daspir found himself on his feet, his two hands tightening, but Leclerc had also drawn himself up to his meager height.

"Captain Paltre!" he rapped out, and Paltre deflated, turning away from Nanon, who sat with her knees together and her head lowered. The posture reminded Daspir of how he'd borne his own humiliations recently.

Leclerc bowed to Isabelle. "I must ask that you excuse us," he said. "We have a tour of duty to perform."

Isabelle arched her neck and simpered something which Daspir did not catch. Leclerc had already stooped to touch Pauline's fingertips. He beckoned crisply to Paltre, who followed him out of the room. As their boots went thumping down the stairs, Nanon also rose and silently departed.

"La pauvre!" Pauline coaxed the parakeet onto her wrist and fondled the feathers between its wings. Poor thing! The bird hunched its green shoulders uncomfortably.

Daspir sat down, a little confused by his own reaction. But Isabelle was certainly looking at him now. It was not her flirtatious glance, but something steadier, more decided. Though he did feel an inward flutter, he had no difficulty holding her gaze; in fact it communicated to him something of her certainty. She caught her lower lip and let it go, reddened and plumped by the white points of her teeth. Daspir's response to this tiny gesture was so vivid and ardent that he had to sit up straighter and cross his legs to cover it. But by then Isabelle had rejoined the ladies' talk.

"Captain-General," Paltre began, as soon as they had reached the street. "I beg you to understand—I know that colored wench of old—"

"It is the hospitality of Madame Cigny you have abused," Leclerc gritted, without looking at him. "Never mind the mulattress."

"But—"

"Be silent!" Leclerc said, and Paltre obeyed. Biting his lips, he walked a pace behind the Captain-General. They were afoot, as they'd left Pauline's conveyance stationed at the Cigny house. It was no distance, in any case, either to the Governor's house or the barracks of the Carénage. But Leclerc did not seem to be going there. With Paltre still trailing him, he strode up the grade, crossing the Rue Espagnole and marching on toward the Champ de Mars.

At the hospital gate, Paltre dared to pluck his sleeve. *"Mon général,"* he whispered urgently. "It is unwise to visit here. You must have a better care for your health, for here there is contagion—and you just lately recovered from a fever."

An aged black had already begun to unwrap the chain from the bars of the gate. Leclerc looked at Paltre coldly.

"If you are afraid," he said, "I will dismiss you."

It seemed to him that Paltre blanched in the light of the stars that turned above them. Then the captain saluted and so took his leave.

Leclerc watched him descending the street, surprised that he'd chosen to swallow that last remark, with no attempt at redeeming its implications. Could the risk of infection be so great? Paltre had more experience of the colony than did Leclerc, having been here previously with the mission of Hédouville . . . but that was a useless thought. Leclerc's pride stiffened him—he pulled his collar straight and marched through the gate the old black had dragged open for him.

No physician was to be found within the hospital walls. Whatever rogue was in charge of the place must have slunk away to his own dwelling. Leclerc was so short of medical officers that he'd been forced to fall back on the local barber-surgeons, who were by and large a sorry lot. He'd not brought out sufficient doctors with him, and the mortality of those who had come had been shockingly high. In every letter to the First Consul or the Minister of Marine he petitioned for more medical men, but then he asked for many other things he also did not get.

Stooping over a cane, the old man shuffled after him into the hospital yard. Among the sick and wounded men there drifted half a dozen black or colored women, dressed and coiffed in white. Their movements flowed on the night breeze, in a manner both peaceful and a little eerie. Whenever Leclerc came near to one, she turned a brief and brilliant smile on him, then ducked her head away into her modesty. His response to these smiles was a slight catch in his chest.

The masonry walls enclosing the compound were still blackened and cracked from the fires, and the destroyed roofs were not yet reconstructed. Rags of sailcloth, or more often merely palm leaves, haphazardly covered the charred beams. Of course it was a scandal. But even without the fire and destruction the ailing men would not have had roofs enough. In their hundreds, they lay in the open courtyard, under the chilly stars and the shivering leaves of the tall palms, exposed to the dangerous night miasma.

He walked among them, following the floating courses of the white skirts and white headcloths of the nurses. The old man limped behind him with his cane. There was hardly enough room between the pallets for Leclerc to set his feet. He had five thousand men in all his various hospitals, by the latest count. Here and elsewhere they were laid low by dysentery or, still more fatally, the fevers. Some survivors of amputation were recuperating here, but in this murderous climate no one wounded in the body cavity was likely to live long enough to reach a hospital. He had almost five thousand dead on top of those out of action in the hospitals, and more of these were battlefield casualties than he would ever disclose to the First Consul—it was simply not credible that so many veteran soldiers could be killed outright in the mere suppression of a slave revolt.

Wherever a man was lucid enough to recognize him, Leclerc stooped to offer his hand, with a few words of encouragement, or perhaps some joke. He did not like to touch these infirm people, though he thought he hid his repugnance well enough. Paltre's warning had perhaps polluted his mind. And, with the dysentery and the rotting wounds, the odor was very disagreeable, and worsened by the stench of the ravine beyond the northern wall.

Here Leclerc paused before a row of bodies stacked like cordwood. The smell was rank. He swallowed phlegm.

"How did these men die?" he inquired of the nurse who stood by him.

"*Lafièv.*" Her cushioned lips softened away the *r* that should have finished the word *fever*. The deep rich timbre of her voice both thrilled and a little disturbed him.

"Let them be buried more quickly," he announced. "Their proximity is dangerous to those who still live."

"Yes," said the nurse. "In the morning the cart comes."

"Every morning," added the old man, who was always following. He smiled agreeably at Leclerc, over gnarled hands coiled around his cane. His head was fully covered with close-cropped white hair, and Leclerc could just make out a pattern of finely etched scars that scrolled around the natural wrinkles of his face.

"Every morning the cart takes the dead away to La Fossette," the old man said.

A cloud of tiny mosquitoes floated over the wall from the ravine and settled like a veil on Leclerc's face. Frantic for a moment, he batted them away. A sickly heat suffused him. He was faint. The whine of the mosquitoes seemed to separate into words, but when he had recovered a little he recognized a woman's voice singing, one of the nurses who stood over a small fire near the gate. Though the words had the sound of French, he could not make the least sense of them. That was the worst of their damned *patois,* it made one think one had lost one's mind. The song was resonant, keening, and how he wished she would not sing it—the melancholy of this tune would depress and agitate the dying men. Yet he was walking toward her, into the music that poured from her throat, or no, he meant to be returning to the gate. Now he had passed the gateway, and the old man was still smiling doggedly through the bars as he refastened the chain.

The song faded as Leclerc walked down the hill. Now his head cleared, and he felt cooler, though still clammy. He fingered the welts of fresh mosquito bites along his jawline and his throat. True enough, as Paltre had reminded him, he had suffered from fever not long ago; true also that it tended to recur. Still, for the moment he felt sound enough. The sky above him had steadied from its recent tilting; he could pick out the Great Bear and the Corona Borealis. The pain in his injured groin was no more than a hitch, these latter days. Let this mission be soon completed and he'd be whole and well as ever.

A sentry saluted him from a post on the corner of the Rue Espagnole, looking a little surprised to see the Captain-General walking alone at this hour of the night. Leclerc smiled at him enigmatically and went on, his mind reaching forward to the correspondence he ought to complete before he slept tonight. The rhythm of his steps beat out the phrases of a letter he'd sent the Minister of Marine a few days before, when he was still at Port-au-Prince: *Toussaint is not an ordinary man. He has force of character, and a large head. And if he had been, like ourselves, a witness to the events which happened in Europe during the last ten years, if he had not been spoiled by the successes he obtained over the English, and if he had begun with a better idea of the power of France, this country would be lost to us beyond return.*

And this by-no-means-ordinary man had just driven Hardy out of Dondon, and cost him four hundred and fifty men in the bargain—while in practically the same breath he told Boudet in Port-au-Prince that he, Toussaint, remained unswervingly loyal to France, while the carnage and destruction of the colony was all to be blamed on Captain-General Leclerc. Outrageous, yet Leclerc had ordered Boudet to make a temporizing reply, leaving the door ajar for negotiation. If he did not receive serious reinforcement soon, it might be better to come to terms with Toussaint, who remained capable of causing a great deal of trouble, despite the costly victories Leclerc claimed in the Artibonite campaign just concluded. Though certainly he'd prefer to see Toussaint's impressively large head lolling out of a hangman's noose . . .

At the gate of the Governor's house the guard admitted him silently; Leclerc forebore to ask if Pauline had returned. When he reached their private chambers, he found that she had not. In the adjacent cabinet he lit two candles and took up the letter to the Minister of Marine he had begun before going out that evening, and reviewed his complaints about the reinforcements he'd recently had by way of *La Zélée* and *La Tourville*. A scant eight hundred men—their number a mockery of the thousands he'd requested and desperately needed—ill clothed and unshod and without a single musket to arm them. Moreover, fully a third of them had gone direct from the ships to the hospital.

Another blanket of mosquitoes unfurled over his hands and forearms. He killed a dozen, slapping the palm of each hand on the back of the other. The insects did not start up fast enough to save themselves, if they were battening on a vein. But these black rebels were the same as the mosquitoes. No matter how many one destroyed, there were always more and they arrived from all directions.

Stop that thought. In search of something more constructive, Leclerc fastened on the evening's discussion of La Tortue. The idea of a hospital there bore further investigation. It sounded quite a salubrious place. Perhaps he'd visit personally, maybe even with Pauline. Let him once acclimate his men and he would win this war definitively. Leclerc shook off the chill that had come over him. He lifted a pen and dipped it in the well. *I will restore a bit of order here,* he wrote, *for thus far we have walked in chaos and ruin.*

When they departed from the Cigny house, Daspir and Cyprien lingered a little on the far side of the street, for the spectacle of Pauline embarking in the sedan chair contraption she favored was worth the observation. She'd decked out five more blacks in the same feathered turbans and robes as her "Moustapha"—all fine, strong men who bore these costumes with a dignity that made them somewhat less ridiculous.

"It is her fantasy of the Mameluke style, I suppose," Cyprien said in a low tone.

Daspir glanced at him, half curious. Cyprien claimed to have been with Bonaparte for a time in Egypt, though he looked a little young for it. Daspir himself was far too young to have joined that campaign. But at the moment he was so distracted by his image of Isabelle that even the sight of Pauline's artlessly engineered disarray barely held his attention.

Four of the turbaned blacks had raised the litter by its poles, and stood there stolid as a team of plow horses, while the other two lifted her aboard, settled her, packed striped cushions and shawls around her. At the crook of her finger, Moustapha handed her the parakeet, which settled on her wrist to preen. On the balcony of the Cigny house, two female figures appeared to raise their small hands in the last *au revoir.* Instantly Daspir picked out Isabelle, the smaller one, though he could not make out her face within the silhouette, and he could not tell if she saw him at all.

Maybe her looks and gestures had meant nothing after all. Pauline's litter bearers were trudging away—Moustapha processing ahead of them with a torch, and the sixth man bringing up the rear. The women left the balcony, and the slim doors closed in the arch behind them, though light still glimmered at the cracks.

"The night wears on," said Cyprien. "There was a little night life here, before . . ."

He yawned, with a slightly morose air, and Daspir followed him along the outer wall of the Cigny house, whose rows of lower archways were shuttered dark and tight. A faint scorched smell still clung to everything, despite the renovation. When they reached the corner, a sound behind him made him halt. It was like a hiss, in the form of a whistle. When Daspir turned, a door had opened, though there was no light behind it. Isabelle's serving woman Zabeth stood with her hip cocked out of the door, just pulling her fingers from the corners of her mouth.

"Ah," said Cyprien. "If not the mistress, why not the maid?"

He gave Daspir a shove that wrenched the sore spot behind his shoulder blade, though he knew it was meant for encouragement. Indeed it was to him, Daspir, that Zabeth beckoned. As he approached, she melted into the doorway. With scarcely a tick of hesitation he stepped into the narrow passage. But Cyprien must have misconstrued the situation, for there was a man with her, another of the house servants. He closed the door behind Daspir, and beat the heavy iron hook into its eye with the heel of his hand. Now there was no light at all, and Daspir felt a quick thrust of alarm. He could smell the other man's sweat alongside his own odor (of which he was suddenly, uneasily conscious), and the woman's sweeter, muskier scent, all mingled with the persistent smell of burning. Zabeth brushed his fingers and he moved in the direction of her touch, no longer afraid, though the other man was still somewhere behind him in the dark. He balanced himself with one hand on the roughly plastered wall.

Then they were climbing the tight turning of a stair. The man's voice said something indistinct from the lower level where he had remained, and there were other voices vaguely audible from elsewhere in the house, and a peal of Isabelle's laughter. Above the stair there must have been some ghost of light, because he could see the fabric of Zabeth's dress, stretching rhythmically over her haunches and her undulating back. The dress was pale yellow, he remembered from when she'd served the coffee tray in the salon, but in this darkness he could not have told the color.

She opened an inner door, and Daspir stepped through it, feeling a curtain brush over his arm and shoulder. Zabeth's fingers were outlined in a red glow. She had lit a candle in the cup of her hand, and now set it down beside a bed that almost completely filled this tiny chamber. Daspir's shins were nudged into the bedding, while his back was against the wall. From beside the door Zabeth surveyed him, swaying a little from her hips. Her smile was bright, amused, like her eyes. The yellow dress brought out the dark luster of her skin. The dress was demurely buttoned up to her collarbone, but Daspir's eyes caught on the rounds of her breasts swelling into the fabric, and his breath caught in his throat.

Zabeth clicked her tongue and Daspir, startled, met her eyes. Was it up to him to reach for her? She let out a husky laugh, then slipped out under the curtain, leaving him there. He heard the tap of the door closing. More distantly, Isabelle's voice rose for a moment, the light, bright tone of her parlor chatter.

Daspir looked about himself. This was no maid's room, certainly. The furnishings were far too rich. The wall hangings were real silk, his fingertips verified. And then? His heart punched hard into his ribs and he drew a long breath to quiet it.

With an odd feeling of stealth he undressed, a little hindered by his arousal, and stowed the roll of his clothing in the narrow space between the bed and the wall. The sheet was of an extraordinary cool smoothness when he slipped under it. What means it must have taken to create this luxury here—and how had it been done, so soon after the fire? Even under the sheet, Daspir felt an uneasy sense of exposure. Perhaps it would be better to put out the light.

In the darkness, the whole extent of his day from dawn to darkness and on to this moment came rushing up at him. Despite his excitement, he was soon asleep.

Dream covered him with the body of Paltre's dying horse; the animal galloped over him with all its weight. Hot blood poured burning over his loins. He struggled and bucked upward, unable to free himself. The animal had the torso of an Amazon, with breasts larger and heavier than he had expected. They bore down on him with stone-hard points. Between the breasts was a man's organ too, with the testicles, but small like a child's. The discovery puzzled him; he hadn't known it was like that. He burst awake into the crisis of their *jouissance*. She'd covered his mouth with her hand to muffle the noise he must have been making, but now she released it, and his panting breaths mingled with the rush of hers. She relaxed and let her weight settle meltingly over him.

It was still pitch dark in the little room. Tentatively Daspir stroked a hand down the bumps of her spine and over the curved rise of her buttock. This was a woman, not a centaur. Isabelle gave a pleased little moan at his touch. Then she pushed up and rolled free of him. Daspir reached for her, a little too quickly, and gasped at the catch in his torn shoulder.

"You are hurt," Isabelle said.

"It is nothing," Daspir said, a little shy, though he knew his injury was worth a boast.

"But you were valiant. I have heard the story. Here, let me." The balls of her fingers found the sore spot at once: the size of a coin, expanding and dissipating as her touch circled outward. Daspir sighed. He was surprised at the strength of her hands. All the while her voice kept murmuring.

"You were valiant in his defense, and yet the Captain-General is unkind to you—yes, I saw how he used you today, and I had the story from *chère* Pauline too. It is only his hurt vanity—it piques him worse than your shoulder pains you."

"Was it for that you—" Daspir began, but Isabelle shushed him.

"Don't ask for reasons," she said.

"From the first time I saw you, I—"

"Don't," she said, and kissed him deeply. But there *was* something hard between her breasts; he could certainly feel it as she pressed against him. He worked up a hand and felt a flat shape of flesh-warmed metal.

"What's that?"

"The key to this house—in its former state," she said. Quick as a fish, her hand glimmered between his legs. "And now, I beg you—do stop talking."

When they had finished, Daspir fell into a deep, velvety, dreamless sleep, and when he woke, the charcoal sellers had begun to cry their wares in the streets beyond the walls. There was light now in the room, from a small window set high in the wall, filtered through a red cotton cloth. Isabelle was watching him with a neutral, cat-like concentration. As the tinted daylight grew it picked out elements of her aging: marks of childbirth around her belly, the breasts ever so slightly drooping, thread-fine lines circling her neck and framing the corners of her mouth and eyes. A pattern printed in the cloth across the window repeated itself in shadows on her skin. All these details inspired in him an awful tenderness. Also, since most of his prior experience had been with busy harlots, he had seldom had such leisure to study a woman completely unclothed.

"What do you see?" he asked, as she kept looking at him with an equal interest.

"Your eyes," Isabelle said reflectively. "Your eyes don't fit your face."

"I don't understand you," Daspir said, faintly annoyed.

"Look here," she said and touched his cheek, then the groove of his upper lip, as if her fingertip might serve him as a mirror.

"Your mouth, and all your features really, are merely sensual. Good-humored enough, ready for pleasure, a little greedy, I should think." She smiled. Masked in the projected shadows of the cloth, her face was for a moment a little frightening. "Except the eyes. The eyes are deeper, stronger. Maybe harsher too. It may be that I see some resolution there."

"Well, I don't know—"

"You mustn't mind my fancy," Isabelle said. "In the end, your face will grow into those eyes. Only give it time."

It seemed she saw some future in him. Pleased with that thought,

Daspir let the topic drop. When she leaned in to kiss him lightly on the forehead, something swung out from between her breasts: the key he'd grasped earlier, yes, but something else too, dangling above the key. He caught it as she withdrew from him.

"Careful," Isabelle said sharply. "You'll break the chain."

Daspir squinted, ignoring what she'd said. He liked the sensation of holding her near him by the force of her own reluctance to break away. His thumb and forefinger enclosed a small, hard gray stone penis, carved in such convincing detail that he let it go as if it had burned him.

"Where the devil did you come by that?"

"A souvenir," Isabelle said distantly. Mercifully, she'd covered the pendant with her palm. "It does not concern you."

She dragged a chemise from the tangle of bedclothes and pulled it over her head and shoulders. Daspir admired the lift of her arms and the sharpness of her nipples against the fine silk. The pendants also made a bulge against the fabric, which reminded him of his first hallucinated awakening. He reached for her hip, but she pushed his hand away.

"It's too late," she said. "You had better go."

"Of course," Daspir said. "Your husband." Though as he spoke it occurred to him that the man had not appeared in the salon the night before.

Isabelle lifted a glass of water from beside the candle stub and looked at the disturbance of its surface. "That isn't the question," she told him. "My husband is dead."

35

Astride his horse, the doctor could look over the wall that enclosed the courtyard of his sister's house. From the carpet of ash that had been the garden, some greenery had begun to push itself up: broad leaves of *bananes loup-garou*, and a feather frond of the yellow *cocotier*, around which a couple of pale butterflies were floating in the humid air. A scorched limb of a tree that overhung the rear corner of the wall was also budding a few fragilely folded leaves. The house itself did not quite look habitable, though the roof had been retimbered, and stacks of pale rose clay tiles stood ready to be tiled over the new wood. Inside the shell of the building, a saw groaned slowly, then stopped with the sound of a falling plank. Michau stepped out into the courtyard, bare-chested and gleaming with sweat, and smiled up at the doctor, squinting in the afternoon sun.

"Where are the ladies?" the doctor asked him.

"They have been staying with Madame Cigny." Michau knocked sawdust from his hands. "Here it is not yet ready—but soon."

"I'll look for them there, then," the doctor told him. He touched the brim of his hat and clucked to his horse.

"But now they have gone to La Tortue," Michau added.

"Oh?" said the doctor. "And for how long?"

Michau shrugged and looked away. "I don't know." He wiped at his temples with a scrap of blue cloth. "They have been already gone some days. It was Madame Captain-General who invited them."

The doctor touched his hat again and turned his horse back into the street. Guizot fell in behind him. Maillart had ridden ahead; already he had turned the corner, doubtless bound for the Cigny house and the same disappointment.

The doctor's head swirled with fatigue, now that the expectancy that had carried him this far was deflated. He'd felt a little unhinged all day from his queer fainting spell the night before, though the swim at the Baie d'Acul had refreshed him for an hour. All through the day's ride he'd felt that Moustique was studying him for some reason, but Moustique had detached himself from their group as soon as they entered the gate of Le Cap, and hurried toward Morne Calvaire to look for the women of his family.

He met Maillart coming back along the street, on foot and leading his horse. Behind him the shadow of Zabeth withdrew into a doorway of the Cigny house.

"They're away," the major said glumly. "Gone to La Tortue."

"So I've been told," said the doctor. "Do you know their mission?"

"To gather mushrooms and turtle eggs . . ." Maillart fanned himself with his hat. "I don't know, really—it is some fancy of *la belle Pauline*, apparently. But even Xavier is gone—I find that strange."

"We'll find ourselves beds here, at least," said the doctor, clambering stiffly down from the saddle. "If all the rest of them have vacated."

"I don't know," said Maillart, centering his hat back on his head. "I may just go along and look in at the barracks. And you—" he glanced up at Guizot. "You'd better come along with me, to report."

Alone, the doctor watched them down the street. It was the first time Guizot had been separated from him since he'd begun treating the arrow wound, and even now the captain allowed himself a backward glance over his shoulder. The doctor knew he ought to get out of the sun. His horse had shoved itself up against the house wall, into the edge of shade the overhanging balcony provided. Certainly he ought to water and stable his horse, but something, perhaps only his lassitude, seemed to hold him where he was.

A strange shimmer rose from the corner where the yellow sunlight spangled the white dust lying in the street. The doctor took off his glasses and began to clean them on his sweaty shirttail. Into the shimmer glided the figure of a tall woman with a water jar balanced on her head. Quickly he stuck his glasses back onto his nose. It was Nanon, much as she'd seemed when he'd first truly looked at her—her graceful gliding progress, the cage of a pet monkey steady on her head, when they'd chanced on each other in the Marché Clugny almost all of ten years ago. What had happened to that monkey? Destroyed in the first burning of Le Cap, most likely, or maybe it had managed to escape. It had always been a troublesome creature. But now, Nanon's movement toward him was so abrupt that the water jar went flying from her, releasing a wave of bright water and painting a dark round stain on the dust.

There was the sweet shock of their contact, flesh on flesh, wrapped silkily on bone. Again the doctor's mind went reeling through his visions. "You were with me," he mumbled into the cloth of her bodice. "All through the worst of it you were with me still."

Inside the house, the doctor and Nanon looked in for a moment on Gabriel and François where they slept. It was the hour of the afternoon siesta. Nanon invited him to rest, to bathe—Zabeth had retrieved the jar unbroken and gone to fetch more water. But the doctor wanted to see Paul, who had gone to Morne Calvaire. Together they walked in that direction, lightly swinging their linked hands.

The church on the hilltop where the doctor and Nanon had been married had lost its roof to Christophe's conflagration. A stick-and-thatch shelter had since been built against one of the smoke-stained walls, and in its shade sat Claudine Arnaud, still as a snake in her rusty black dress. Moustique's little boy Dieufait pressed into her hip and lightly stroked her hands.

"She did not go with the others to La Tortue?" said the doctor.

Nanon shook her head, smiling as she looked away. "Such parties of pleasure are not to her taste."

It was always windy on the hilltop; the doctor reached to brush Nanon's hair out of her face. He stumbled a little on the path, because he could not stop looking at her. Then he was almost knocked off his feet by Paul, who came charging out of the palm palisade of the Morne Calvaire *lakou*.

"Moustique has come, and told me you were here," Paul blurted. "He says you were at all the battle at La Crête à Pierrot."

The doctor held him at arm's length by his shoulders. "So," he said, teasing a little. "You didn't want to visit La Tortue with Sophie and Robert?"

"Oh yes, but we waited for you, Maman and I. Maman said she knew you were going to come."

The doctor tried to catch Nanon's eye, but Paul was pulling him by the wrist into the enclosure of the *lakou*. Fontelle and Paulette and Marie-Noelle abandoned the laundry they had been peeling from the rocks to fold and came clustering around him. Even Maman Maig' rolled her great bulk upright and smiled at him broadly, before she settled herself back down on her low stool.

Moustique was unpacking a number of squat, cloth-covered clay jars and arranging them around the rainbow-striped central post. The doctor slipped out of the cluster of women and walked in that direction. Among the jars lay a shard of mirror which for a long time he had carried in his own pocket—he was interested to see that it was still there. Moustique was watching him again, with the same half-smile, his face half averted. There was still that faint electrical charge between them from the night before. As the doctor leaned in to look at the mirror, a shadow darkened it, and he felt an odd touch of foreboding.

"A ship! A ship!" Little Dieufait came galloping down from the church, beckoned at large, and ran back up the hill. A gaggle of the smaller children of the *lakou* went after him full tilt. Paul followed at a somewhat more dignified trot. Nanon and the doctor walked after them.

Claudine now stood at the brow of the hill, gauntly erect beside the three crude wooden crosses that had been restored to that spot after the fire. Her hair blew out behind her in the stiffening evening breeze. The cloud that had covered the sun blew clear of it, and light fell harshly on the whitecaps of the harbor. Among them *L'Océan* had dropped its anchor and the men were lowering the sails. Two longboats were rowing from ship to shore. The doctor reached for his spyglass and took a closer look: the dark woman's head was Isabelle Cigny, and the fair one was his sister.

"They're back." Absently he handed the glass to Paul. "Let us go down to greet them," he said, half-reluctantly, for a touch of that queer premonition clung to him still.

Daspir sat in the bow of the first longboat, facing the other passengers, enjoying the light salt spray on the back of his sunburned neck and covering Isabelle with a dazed smile of sexual satiety. This excursion had certainly been his happiest interlude since he first disembarked in Saint Domingue. Pauline, in collaboration with Isabelle no doubt, had been shielding him from Leclerc's ill-treatment. The Captain-General, for whatever reason, had redirected his most unwelcome attentions to Paltre. It was Paltre, and sometimes Cyprien, who'd accompanied Leclerc and Xavier Tocquet in the search for sites for the hospital Leclerc meant to install there. Meanwhile, Daspir had been free to accompany the ladies, mushrooming, flower-gathering, and the like . . . and Isabelle had introduced him to more than one mossy and secluded bower.

The boat knocked against a piling of the dock, and Daspir, startled from his revery, climbed out and secured the bowline. The second boat was still no more than halfway from ship to shore, since it had taken a long time for all of Pauline's paraphernalia, with the lady herself, to be stowed in it. Daspir stooped and stretched down to help Elise up the ladder from the boat, then gave his arm to Isabelle. She swayed against him for a moment as she came up onto the dock, depending on his elbow, then let go and assumed her independent balance. Her release was just sudden enough to perplex Daspir a little.

Their arrival had attracted the usual assembly of small black children and waterfront idlers. Daspir picked out Doctor Hébert on the far side of the street, standing with the gorgeous mulattress Nanon. There too was

Guizot, who raised his hand with a watery smile, and beside him Major Maillart, fingering the end of his mustache as he studied Isabelle with an interest that made Daspir slightly uneasy. The wind was twisting, raising dust and small specks of debris in spirals from the ground. As the red sun lowered toward the ridge of Morne du Cap, the wind hurried darkening clouds across it. Daspir had learned to feel the tension of this moment, when it would either rain or not. He felt his spirits lift and twist, without knowing which way they would blow.

Paltre might have had something of the same perturbed sensation. "Ah, the good doctor," he said, raising his hat with a queerly fixed grin. "I see you're reunited with your whore."

The doctor seemed to wobble slightly as he rolled across the street toward them, like an egg wobbling when it rolls. He was a small and oddly shaped and unimposing figure, and yet he moved with a startling efficiency. A length of stove wood was in his rising hand, and Daspir had just time enough to register its splintered edge before it smashed full into Paltre's face. Paltre reeled backward, arms whirling, and might have pitched into the harbor if Cyprien, just climbing up from the boat, had not broken his fall. Unstrung, Paltre collapsed against Cyprien's legs. A woman had screamed—Elise—though more from irritation than fear, Daspir thought.

"You are speaking of my wife," the doctor said. The length of stove wood quivered in his hand. Xavier Tocquet pulled himself from the boat onto the dock and surveyed the scene, running his thumb along the edge of his lower lip. Daspir made a protective gesture toward Isabelle, but she had moved a step farther away from him and would not let him catch her eye. He looked at Nanon, standing alone on the opposite side of the street, head lowered as in meditation or prayer. Beside her was a stack of split wood and Daspir thought distractedly that it must be destined for shipboard stoves, since all cooking in the colony seemed to be done with charcoal.

Paltre took a bloodstained hand away from his nose and plucked a splinter from his cheek, where the wood had raked it.

"You all saw him strike me," he said as he scrambled onto his feet. "You saw him strike me in the face."

Paltre dropped his hand to his pistol grip, but Cyprien caught him by the wrist.

"I will have satisfaction," Paltre spluttered, as he struggled to free his hand.

"That you will," the doctor said. He brandished the stove wood, and Paltre, still unable to loose his weapon, quailed away from it.

"Pistols. I choose pistols," the doctor said. "Tomorrow at dawn at La Fossette."

He let the wood fall clattering from his hand and walked away. Daspir watched him take Nanon's arm and lead her past the half-restored façade of the Customs House toward the interior of the town.

"Wait," Cyprien called. He was still restraining Paltre, and Daspir moved to help him. "Who stands with him? Major, is it you?"

"Yes," said Maillart, at parade-ground volume. "I stand second to Doctor Hébert." With a shock, Daspir perceived that Isabelle had crossed the street to stand beside him.

"But you must agree that all this, this—an absurdity," Cyprien blurted.

"On the contrary," Maillart boomed. "I find everything in good order. Your comrade will have the satisfaction he requires tomorrow."

"But allow us twenty-four hours more," Cyprien said. "Let tempers cool."

"My friend is already cool as the dew," said Maillart, then stopped to consider. "But I will speak to him. Later tonight, I'll look for you."

"We are in the barracks of the Carénage," Cyprien said.

Maillart nodded. He slipped a hand under Isabelle's elbow and guided her away. There was an old familiarity in the way she fit her step to his. And Daspir had begun to think of Maillart as his friend . . . he did not know what area of his confusion to attend to. Isabelle looked back once, but he could not read her glance, and then Tocquet and Elise had blocked his view, as they too moved off from the dockside. Maybe he had never read a glance of Isabelle's aright.

Guizot was crossing the street toward them, his features contorted with concern.

"What lunacy," Cyprien began, turning on Paltre. He cut himself off. No one had noticed Leclerc's boat docking, but now the Captain-General himself had emerged on the quai. As often after private colloquies with his bride, he looked both irritated and sapped of all strength. He brushed down his coattail and frowned at the four captains.

"What is this disorder?"

"Captain Paltre." Cyprien bowed, with a sick smile. "He has . . . a recurrence of his injury." He waved a hand at Paltre, who had covered his nose with a white handkerchief into which he was vigorously bleeding.

Leclerc stared at them balefully. "Get him settled, then, and come along to Government House. Don't tarry." He marched off, flanked by two of his other adjutants, passing the file of porters who were coming down to retrieve all Pauline's baggage. From below the dock they could hear her tittering voice as Moustapha and the others pulled and heaved her up the ladder.

"Come on," said Cyprien. "Let's get out of this."

They found a tavern a block from the waterfront. For form's sake Daspir ordered brandy but was quick to accept four cups of *clairin* in its stead. He had not tasted a real brandy since . . . when? The last of his bottles had been drained in some bivouac on a march he no longer remembered.

Paltre had stopped bleeding by the time Daspir set the cups down on the table; he sat with his head tilted back against the top rail of his chair, delicately massaging the crushed cartilage of his nose.

"What the devil did you want to challenge him for?" Cyprien said and gulped at his *clairin*.

"He struck me! You saw it, you all did." Paltre righted his head to speak, and a little blood trickled over the black crust that ringed his left nostril. "He has broken my nose again, I think—God rot him."

"Anyone would have struck you, after that remark," Daspir told him.

"What I said was only the truth." Paltre looked at Cyprien. "You remember the wench as well as I do, from Choufleur's house in ninety-eight. He used to lead her around on a chain, and offer her favors to any who wanted them. She would drink from a bowl on the floor like a dog."

"I remember," Cyprien said. "You've made sure her husband remembers it too."

"How should I know he had married the bitch?" Paltre snapped. "It's not an idea that would come to most men." He snorted, then quickly clapped the handkerchief over a fresh flow of blood from his nose.

"It must be that I remember Choufleur's house more clearly than you," said Cyprien. "I recall most plainly when this doctor came for his woman there. Choufleur challenged him the same as you have done. The doctor threw up a playing card and shot the pips out of it with his pistol. I mean to say, it was the *same hand* as threw the card that fired the pistol."

Guizot exhaled a hollow whistle. Paltre looked palely at Cyprien.

"I don't remember that," he said.

"Then you must have been blind drunk," said Cyprien. "I was drunk too, but I'll never forget it. I never saw such shooting in my life."

Paltre folded the bloodstained handkerchief and ran the crease of it through his fingertips. "He is a traitor anyway, your doctor. He was fighting with the rebels at La Crête à Pierrot."

"Oh, for Christ's sake," said Guizot. "He was their prisoner."

"So he claimed afterward," Paltre said. "When your bayonet was at his throat. But I remember him from earlier days, and he was always as thick as molasses with Toussaint—as much as Pascal, certainly, or any of the other collaborators who've been deported for it."

"You'd stand to be deported yourself," Cyprien said, "if Leclerc should get wind of this *affair of honor*."

"*I?*" said Paltre. "Come, what can you mean? Any of that crew around the Cigny house might be sent off well ahead of me. Xavier Tocquet for one—he smuggled guns for Toussaint these last four years and everybody knows it." He smiled unpleasantly at Daspir. "Just one word in the right ear and your beauty Isabelle would be shipped to France as the harlot she was—consorting with black officers. Oh yes, she entertained them without reserve—and everyone knows that too."

Daspir heard the crash like a distant gunshot. It was his own fist that had come down on the clay vessel that had held his rum, and smashed it to a sticky powder. Paltre seemed to be transfixed by Daspir's gaze, and

Daspir felt a hardness in his own eyes he'd never been aware of, something like what Isabelle claimed she had seen, the first night they'd slept together.

"Look at us," Guizot said, his voice slightly trembling. "We meant to be good comrades when we came. We were going out just the four of us to bring in Toussaint Louverture—do you not remember? And look at us now, at each other's throats, and everyone's." He pushed up his sleeve to the shoulder, revealing a red-and-white spiraling scar. "I'd have lost my arm, if not for that doctor—and you want to kill him, or make him kill you. Where's the sense in it?" Guizot shook all over, as if from an ague. "Where's the good sense of any of this war?"

"Be careful what you say." Cyprien leaned forward on his elbows, lowering his tone, as he looked uneasily about himself. Conversation had halted among the other soldiers and sailors in the tavern when Daspir smashed the cup.

"Guizot is right," said Paltre. "We oughtn't to quarrel among ourselves." He forced a smile toward Daspir. "You've spilt your drink," he said. "Let me buy you another."

"All right," said Daspir. He lifted his fist, unrolled it, and began picking small ceramic shards out of the edge of his palm.

"Another round," Paltre called. The tavernkeeper, a *griffe* who sported three gold rings in his left ear, brought over the jug and a replacement cup. Paltre paid for the rum and also for the cup Daspir had broken.

"But I won't be deported in any case," Paltre said, when all had drunk. His voice resumed something of its sullenness. "Not with so many good officers dead."

"No," said Cyprien. "You'll only be buried. Tomorrow at sunrise in La Fossette. Or the day after, if they are willing to wait so long."

Paltre looked at him, rolling his cup in his hands.

"*You* challenged *him*," said Cyprien. "He has the first shot. And I tell you, I saw him put a bullet through the hole of the nine on a nine of clubs."

"What's your solution, then?" said Paltre.

Cyprien leaned a little forward, setting his fingertips on the tabletop. "Apologize."

Paltre let out a hoarse laugh and pushed his chair back. "*Apologize?* You must be joking."

"Of course," said Cyprien. "You'd rather die."

The doctor had not known that he would act until he came to himself standing over Paltre with the echo of the insult and his reply still ringing in his ears. He didn't even know how the chunk of stove wood had come to be in his hand, but all of it seemed to be inevitably the outcome of that sense of fatality he'd brought down to the waterfront from Morne Calvaire. He walked homeward, Nanon's hand clenched in his

own, suffused in his feeling of *déjà vu*. Now she would not look at him.
And after all, it would not rain. The wind was dying as the clouds went
drifting back over Morne du Cap. He knew the night would be calm and
clear.

At the Cigny house, Nanon retired, complaining of a headache. The
doctor poured three fingers of rum in a glass and carried it into the inner
courtyard. Here the ash had been plowed under, and there were fresh
plantings of hibiscus and the red brushes of Indian ginger—also some
shoots of aloe, which Isabelle liked to use on her skin. In twenty minutes'
time he heard the noise of others coming into the house from the street,
and presently Maillart's voice broke the stillness of the evening air.

"Such a rogue you are for dueling, Antoine." Maillart carried a bottle
of rum, with glasses for himself and Tocquet, who sat down on the stone
sill where the doctor was sitting. Maillart poured them each a measure.

"You have the first shot," he said. "I do suggest that you spend it well—
don't fire in the air as you did the other time."

The doctor fixed him with his eyes. "I don't intend to."

"That's the spirit." Maillart frowned into his glass. "In fact they have
asked a day's delay . . . what do you think?"

"It's all the same to me," the doctor said. He set his rum down on the
stone, took off his glasses, and polished them on his shirttail. "Well, I
don't know," he said as he replaced the glasses on his nose. "Really I suppose I'd as soon have it over."

"I'd feel the same," Maillart said. "I am to meet them somewhere
tonight. I'll let them know your preference."

Tocquet reached into his shirt and fanned out three crooked black
cheroots like a hand of cards. The doctor accepted one of them, though
he did not ordinarily smoke. Tocquet struck a light and the three of them
put their heads together above the flame.

"Cyprien and Paltre . . ." Maillart blew a smoke ring toward the darkening sky. "I remember those two cubs from the time of Hédouville. They
used to come sniffing around this house, the pair of them. Cyprien looks
to have seasoned a bit, but Paltre . . ." He sniffed. "I will not miss him."

"Nor I," said the doctor, and swallowed a cough. The tobacco was
making him slightly dizzy. Inside the house a hand bell jingled and
Isabelle lightly raised her voice. Maillart lifted his head toward the
sound.

"I believe I'll look in on the ladies," he said. He replenished his glass
and went indoors.

The hush of the courtyard where they sat was dotted with calls of the
brown doves from the eaves of the houses up and down the street. The
sky had darkened to its deepest blue, and the doctor squinted up at
the brightening stars as if from the bottom of a well. Tocquet's large,
warm hand settled over the back of his neck.

"How goes it?"

"*N'ap kenbé.*" The doctor used the Creole form that went for either *we* or *you*. We're hanging on.

"I saw that fellow Descourtilz in town, a week or so ago," Tocquet said. "He made it sound as if things were a touch difficult at the end, there at La Crête à Pierrot."

"Descourtilz was not there at the end," the doctor said. The sourness of his own tone surprised him. It was as if Descourtilz's escape had amounted to desertion, though there could be no reason in that judgment.

"I'm not especially fond of him either," Tocquet said. "He has done you a service, though, in convincing everyone hereabout that you were both held in that fort by extreme duress. There was some suspicion you were giving aid and comfort to the enemy."

The doctor laughed and sipped his rum. Tocquet's cheroot had made him very giddy.

"And you?"

"I take your point," said Tocquet, releasing his long smile into the dark. "But lately I have been of some use to the Captain-General, in guiding a mission to subdue the rebellion at La Tortue. Besides, Leclerc's situation is delicate. Between disease and the battlefield, the force he brought with him has been halved, no matter how he may try to conceal it. He must take his friends as he finds them, now." Tocquet sharpened the coal of his cheroot by rolling it against the edge of the stone sill, and left the ash to powder on the ground. "Leclerc has learned of your value too—you may expect to hear from him, I think."

"Yes," said the doctor. "That saved me at La Crête à Pierrot, and Descourtilz too. Even Dessalines in his worst passion would not kill a doctor there." He drained his glass. "At the end, I think my worst risk was to finish skewered on a French bayonet."

In his mind's eye appeared unbidden the grubby drawn face of Captain Guizot as he'd first seen it, bearing down on him above the blood-dark, guttered blade. Behind, a whirl of other pictures waited, the vortex into which he fell with every sleep. Tocquet's hand was still warm between his shoulders, and Tocquet's eyes were curiously upon him, though the doctor knew he would not speak the question.

"What can I tell you?" he said. "You know that sort of thing as well as I. You've lived it, but you still can't imagine it."

"Well put." Tocquet's hand massaged the muscles of the doctor's neck, then lifted. By now the stars were brighter, and the doctor, looking upward, could piece together the geometry of Perseus and Andromeda.

"You mean to kill that Captain Paltre, don't you?"

"Assuredly," said the doctor.

"I know you will defend yourself," Tocquet said. "And yet I'd thought you would not kill by calculation. Choufleur, for example, was a much more dangerous enemy than Paltre."

From the doctor's mental kaleidoscope emerged the image of Placide Louverture, framed in an embrasure of La Crête à Pierrot, tails of his red *mouchwa têt* streaming out behind his head as he stooped from the saddle to hack down one or another French infantryman. Evidently his attitude toward taking human life had evolved since the doctor last spoke to him at Ravine à Couleuvre.

"Perhaps I've changed," he said.

Tocquet nodded. "You have that right."

"Do you disapprove?" The doctor's cheroot had expired from inattention. He set it down on the sill beside his empty glass.

"Hardly," said Tocquet. "I'd have left Paltre dead on the waterfront, had I been in your place." His cheroot glowed red, close to his face, then faded. "But your ways have never been my ways," he said. "There are times I feel the slave of my own practices. Perhaps, of the two of us, you are more free."

"I didn't know you thought so," said the doctor.

"It just now came to me." Tocquet dropped the stub of his cheroot and crushed the spark out with the toe of his boot, then raised his nose to the scent of roast pork that wafted out of the house behind them. The brass jingle of the bell sounded once again.

"Come on," Tocquet said, getting to his feet. "You'd better feed up— you've gone thin as a rail since we last met."

Zabeth opened the front door of the Cigny house and held her candle high to illuminate the faces of Daspir and Guizot, who squinted in the sudden flare. With a quick sly smile at Daspir, she stepped aside and beckoned them in.

"A beauty, that one," Guizot said, with a somewhat exaggerated connoisseur's air. Daspir did no more than nod. There was, perhaps, an extra swing in Zabeth's step as she led them up the stairway toward the second-floor salon, but he thought that Guizot had spoken a little too loudly, and he was aware that Michau had appeared to stand silently in a doorway on the passage below.

Major Maillart was on his feet the moment Zabeth had opened the door for the two captains, moving quickly to halt them on the threshold. Over his shoulder, Daspir caught a glimpse of Elise and Isabelle sitting together on a striped divan. It might have been a trick of the quavering light, but both of them looked a little guilty, as if they had been caught in some conspiracy. Isabelle's mouth pulled tight around her teeth and though she had certainly recognized Daspir, there was no particular warmth in her regard.

"Come, gentlemen," Maillart was saying. "You need not bring your business here. I would have come to find you, in another hour." He backed them over the threshold, pulling the door shut behind them. Zabeth had vanished from the scene, but still there was not space enough for the three of them on the narrow landing. Daspir stumbled down to a lower step, and had to catch himself on the rail. He did not at all like the way Maillart's long shadow loomed over him.

"Let us go down to the street, shall we?" Maillart said. "The matter is better discussed in the open air."

Daspir turned and started downstairs, grateful for the darkness of the stairwell, which covered his angry blush. Michau still stood in the doorway on the ground-floor passage, watching impassively as they went by. On the street Maillart stood facing them, casual, almost uninterested, as if his only real concern had been to herd them out of the house. Was it possible, Daspir thought, that Isabelle no longer wanted to receive him? If so, he had Paltre to thank for it—it was Paltre who forced Isabelle to side with her friends, her house guests, in the quarrel he'd provoked. Or Daspir could blame himself, to a degree, for under the present circumstances he and Guizot would have done better to send up their names and wait below, instead of bursting in as they had done. But he had been too eager—too anxious, he might even say—for maybe it was Major Maillart who presumed too much, who might have particular reasons of his own to put himself between Daspir and Isabelle.

"As you are here," Maillart said, "I may as well let you know that Doctor Hébert prefers to settle this affair tomorrow, and hopes that Captain Paltre will accommodate him."

Guizot shifted his feet and cleared his throat. "We are charged to tell you that Captain Paltre regrets his impetuous remark and will offer an apology, if it were acceptable."

"Really?" said Maillart. "It is very unusual." There was a touch of sarcasm in his tone, but he also seemed to have been genuinely startled.

"Look," said Guizot, dropping his formal manners. "We all stood shoulder together at La Crête à Pierrot. In the larger struggle we must stand together still. Surely there is some way to resolve the quarrel without bloodshed. The waste of it all is appalling to me." His voice cracked. "If not for your friend I'd have lost my arm, and maybe my life along with it."

"Yes, all right," Maillart said. "I've nothing against the two of you." He put a hand on Guizot's shoulder and glanced at Daspir a trifle more coolly. "I know it can't have been easy for you to bring such a message here. But Captain Paltre's remark was odious, rather than impulsive. And . . ." Maillart stepped back and looked up at the sky for a moment, then again at the two captains. "You should know that my friend is a peaceable man, and ordinarily he is very slow to notice an insult. But when you have once roused such a man to anger, it is difficult to alter his disposition. I have never seen him so determined as he is now."

"You mean?" said Guizot.

"I'll present your offer," Maillart said slowly, and raised his eyes to the glowing doorways of the balcony above. "But not, I think, tonight. Tomorrow it might have better hope of success. If not, Captain Paltre must plan to keep his appointment in twenty-four hours' time."

With a nod, Maillart stepped back into the house. Michau shut the door behind him. There was the sound of the hook scraping into its iron eye. Daspir and Guizot walked back the way they had come, in the direction of the Carénage. From a block distant came the muted sound of the waves beating on the *embarcadère*. Neither spoke until they were crossing the arched stone bridge that crossed the ravine.

"Do you think Paltre will go through with the apology?" Daspir said then.

To that, Guizot merely shrugged. And Daspir knew there was no definite answer to his question. The only sure thing was that Paltre was plainly unwilling to face *certain* death for his point of honor. Otherwise he was in such a volatile state that no one could predict what he might do. For that, Cyprien had stayed with him tonight, to supervise his drinking himself unconscious.

"Did you ever suppose he deserved to be shot?" Daspir said.

"Paltre?" Guizot said. "I don't know. Lately I wonder if anyone deserves to be shot."

In spite of himself, Daspir let out a dry laugh as they turned into the barracks gate. "Now that's a very odd thought for a soldier."

As soon as Maillart had shouldered Guizot and Daspir down the stairs, Nanon gathered up her sewing, rose from her chair, and retired from the room with a ghostly calm. Conversation had faltered, but Isabelle, with much tossing of her head and fluttering of her hands, forced it back to a semblance of life. The doctor sat in the stupor of his exhaustion. In five more minutes, when Maillart had still not returned, he pleaded fatigue and excused himself.

Nanon's small room beneath the eaves was dark. The doctor groped his blind way into it, trailing a hand along the angled ceiling. Just as he had shrugged out of his shirt, she caught at his waistband and pulled him down. Her mouth fastened hot and tight as a lamprey's into the hollow below his breastbone. They coupled with a wild ferocity, with no words. When they had finished, the doctor dropped into darkness like a lead weight, but twenty minutes later he shot awake with his heart pounding and a sick tightening in his gullet.

Since La Crête à Pierrot he had known many such awakenings. He'd learned a special concentration which could slow his heart and ease his breathing. *Tonight let us be merry,* he repeated like a silent prayer, *for tomorrow we die.* It was strange how this sentence always did soothe him. At his side, Nanon slept peacefully, drawn up into herself, turned away from him. She had a talent for deep sleep, no matter her trials. It was only one of her several accomplishments. The doctor replayed the details of their embraces, detached as though he were some voyeur watching. It had been a virtuoso performance, much aided by her experience and expertise. They knew each other's likings very well, and could anticipate each other's movements, like a pair of long-familiar dancers, but for all of that each of them might have been anyone to the other that night.

After all he had hoped for, and even had begun to taste when they first found each other that afternoon, it was a bitter disappointment. But the doctor divorced this feeling from his heartbeat, watching the round of faint starlight cast by the unglazed round window on the angle of the ceiling and the opposite wall. Tomorrow he would want a clear eye and a steady hand. It was Paltre who had turned their love to lust, and the doctor looked forward to killing him for it. The thought relaxed him, and he slept.

A little before dawn the doctor rose, slipped on his drawers, and crept downstairs bare-chested, carrying his pistols wrapped in his shirt. On the ground floor he lit a candle and sat at the dining table, to clean and sight the pistols. Somewhere on an upper floor one of the smaller children began to whimper and was shushed. A few minutes later, Zabeth appeared, up before her accustomed hour. She must have been up and active for quite some time, for she served the doctor a bowl of steaming *soupe giraumon*, with a fried egg and a boiled plantain. He smiled his thanks, and ate with good appetite. The pistols lay barrel to butt by his right hand, but Zabeth appeared to take no notice of them, though doubtless she was perfectly well aware of his program for the day.

Maillart arrived with the first light at the windows, a little later than the doctor had expected him.

"They will be waiting for us at La Fossette," he said.

"No hurry," Maillart said. He looked from the doctor's bowl to Zabeth, who brought him his own portion.

"What do you mean?" the doctor said. For the first time that morning he felt a little restive. He very much wanted to be on his way before Nanon or his sister appeared.

Maillart interrupted his spoonfuls of soup. "We are not expected at La Fossette today," he said. "Captain Paltre has offered an apology."

"An apology?" The doctor sat back.

"If you reject it," Maillart said, "the encounter will take place tomorrow."

"Let him cut out his own malicious tongue," the doctor said. "I will accept that as a token of repentance. Otherwise, he will have the satisfaction he has asked for."

"I surmise that you mean to reject the apology," Maillart said. "Yes? For form's sake, I might just remind you that the Captain-General takes a dim view of dueling at present—officers of whatever quality being in short supply."

"That is no concern of mine," said the doctor.

"So be it, then." Maillart pushed away his bowl. "Captain Guizot is waiting for you in the street. On a different errand—it isn't his fault. The Captain-General requests your presence at the hospital."

"I'll be going then," the doctor said, happy enough to have something to occupy his time. He got up from the table, holstered his pistols, collected his straw sack of herbs, and went out to the street.

Leclerc had sent a coach for him. Sergeant Aloyse sat on the box. Guizot stepped down and held the door for the doctor, then climbed in after him. Sergeant Aloyse snapped the reins across the horses' backs and the coach creaked around the corner and up the slope toward the Rue Espagnole.

"The position is awkward—" Guizot commenced.

"We needn't speak of it," the doctor said. He faced strictly forward, his eyes tight on Aloyse's salt-and-pepper pigtail.

"But I—"

"We needn't speak of it," the doctor said. His throat relaxed as he turned toward Guizot, with an involuntary smile which reminded him that, after all, it was more pleasant to save a life than to take one.

Leclerc awaited them already, just within the hospital gate, which the old guardian began to drag open as soon as the coach appeared. Though the doctor had seen him several times from a distance in the aftermath of La Crête à Pierrot, this was the first time the Captain-General had appeared to take any direct notice of him.

"Doctor Hébert," he said, "I am most pleased to make your acquaintance. I am told that you are expert not only in the treatment of wounds but also in dysentery, and these devastating fevers which we suffer."

"I fear my skills may have been exaggerated," the doctor said, barely attending to this formula as he uttered it.

"I have heard also that you have come through many trials at La Crête à Pierrot."

Leclerc's look was sufficiently pointed to remind the doctor of what Tocquet had said the night before. "Like all who survived that experience," he said, "I must thank God and my guardian angel."

"To be sure," said Leclerc, with a beckoning gesture. "Do walk this way, and give me your opinions. I must tell you that our expedition suffers a terrible shortage of qualified medical men, and here especially I am not at all satisfied with the arrangements—"

"I would resume charge of this hospital if you wish," said the doctor. "It had been my responsibility, before your landing."

"That was my very hope," said Leclerc, rubbing his hands together. As he spoke, the rising sun cleared the hospital wall, spreading a band of warmth. They were walking along the rows of patients on their straw mats on the ground. A few of the nurses came up to greet the doctor with quick hand clasps and shy smiles. Behind them, Guizot and Aloyse were maneuvering the coach out of the gateway, so that the cart from La Fossette could come in.

"Mortality from these fevers is very troubling to us," Leclerc said. "I am told that you have an unusual skill in treating them."

"There are some local herbs effective against certain fevers," the doctor said. "In the case of malaria, cinchona is best." He stopped and looked at Leclerc more closely, noting his skin tone, a slight discoloration of the whites of his eyes, the ghost of a tremor at his fingertips.

"I might recommend such a course to you, Captain-General," he said. "Unfortunately, cinchona must be imported. I had laid in a good supply just before your arrival, but I am sure it has all been incinerated. And now I don't know what merchant ships, if any, may be calling at our ports."

"I will look into it," Leclerc said. They resumed their promenade. The old guardian, having closed the gate, now stumped along behind them with his stick.

"And there," said Leclerc, as they reached the wall above the ravine, with a gesture at this last row of moribund patients. "For that fever, what is your specific?"

One of the nurses had stooped to help the nearest man, catching a spew of his black vomit in a gourd. Delicately she wiped his lips and laid his head back on the mat, then pressed his arms to still them, for they writhed in a fading convulsion.

"None," said the doctor. "That is *mal de Siam*, the yellow fever. There is no treatment. Few survive."

"And what accounts for the survival of those few?"

"I do not know," the doctor said. "I am myself a survivor, but I don't understand the reason any more than you do." He paused, looking down the row along the wall. At the lower end of it the grave tenders had begun to lift corpses onto their cart.

"The yellow fever spreads very rapidly among those newly arrived to the colony," the doctor said. "You may expect it to grow worse with the spring rains. The best solution is to send your new men quickly into the mountains. The bad air of the marshes on the coast promotes the fever."

Leclerc turned his face toward the wall, fingering his long silky side-whiskers. The doctor observed his handsome profile. Leclerc was no taller than himself, he noticed, perhaps not even quite as tall. He knew that most of the French troops were already unfit to march into the mountains by the time they arrived, and he expected that the mountain posts were too insecure for his advice to be very safely followed.

"At the least these men should be quarantined once they have taken the yellow fever," he said. "That the contagion may not spread to others here, who might have better hope to recover."

Leclerc faced him. "And you suggest?"

"There are the old slave barracoons at La Fossette," said the doctor. "I don't know how well they survived the fire, but they were distant from any other buildings."

"I would not send my troops to the barracoons," Leclerc said crisply.

"And such proximity to the cemetery would be disheartening, is it not so?"

But they'll mostly die anyway, the doctor thought, and it would be more convenient for the burials. Instead of saying it aloud, he raised his eyes to the hills above the wall.

"These victims might be carried to the height of La Vigie," he said. "The transport is more difficult, but the air is more salubrious once they arrive. There is no shelter up there since the fire, but if you can furnish me men and material . . ."

"I will see to it." Leclerc drew out his watch and snapped it open. "Doctor Hébert, you give us hope. I will call on you soon again, but for the moment, please excuse me."

The doctor bowed, and Leclerc withdrew. He climbed into the coach with Guizot and drove out through the gate behind the graveyard cart.

For the remainder of the morning the doctor surveyed arrangements at the hospital. It seemed to him that the nurses were doing almost everything that could be done—though there were too few of them; too many women had been frightened away by the yellow fever. He would need to recruit more, and he would need to organize an herb gathering, and the supply of fresh water and ordinary grains for those with dysentery also appeared to be insufficient.

The women had even saved his hammock for him; it had been rolled up and stored. At midday he strung it in the accustomed place, and dozed through the hottest hour of the afternoon. When he awoke, he left the hospital and strolled down toward the waterfront, zigzagging block by block, for he was in no special hurry to return to the Cigny house. At the lower gate of the Morne Calvaire *lakou,* he happened upon Paul, who shouted with pleasure and ran to greet him. The boy bumped his shoulder against the doctor's hip, and stuck close to him as they moved a little awkwardly along the street toward the Batterie Circulaire.

"Papa," Paul said. "I wrote you the letters. All the time you were away I wrote the letters."

"Do you have them still?" said the doctor.

"No," said Paul. "We could not send them, so I sent them up in smoke." He pulled away from the doctor's side and looked up at the hill of Morne Calvaire.

"Well," said the doctor. "Maybe we were near in spirit then."

Paul turned toward him, smiling, knocked again into his hip. The doctor draped a hand over his shoulder.

"Papa!" Paul said. "Do you remember Madame Fortier? She is a *grande dame de couleur*—she is very tall?"

"I remember her," said the doctor, with a vague sense of foreboding. "I am surprised that you do."

"But she is here now, at Le Cap—I saw her only a few days ago," Paul said.

It was unusual for him to be so talkative, the doctor thought. Ever since that time he had spent abandoned in these streets so long ago, he had been, though apparently calm and contented enough, quiet and a little withdrawn.

"She said she would come to visit Mami," Paul continued. "But she has not come, or I did not see her—Papa, can we go to her house? It is in the Rue Vaudreuil."

"Now?" said the doctor. "What do you want to go there for?" He knew very well where the house must be and had no desire at all to visit it. "And it is far—too far to walk."

Paul only brightened. *"M'ap chaché bourik pou nou!"* He ran back toward the lower gate of Morne Calvaire. I will look for donkeys for us.

The doctor looked after him, feeling somewhat dour—his sister would have reproved the boy for blurting out Creole instead of good French, and Paul *was* running a little wild. Probably he ought to be in school, but then the schools had all been burned, their masters scattered. Now he came bursting back out of that gate, leading two donkeys with their woven straw saddles. A little girl in a red dress glared after him, fists to her hips.

"Wait," said the doctor. "Did you just take those donkeys from her?" But the girl had disappeared into the gateway, and Maman Maig' stood where she had been, smiling and waving them on their way.

The Rue Vaudreuil was some considerable distance, but it was pleasant to ride along the harborfront. At the end of the long quai, they swung up into the town and circled out around the hum of the market at the Place Clugny. The house they were looking for ought to have been in the next block, but the doctor could scarcely recognize the work in progress that stood in its place—the original had been all built of wood, and so the fire must have razed it. Before it had been rather garishly painted—a bawdy place, run by Choufleur as a bordello and gambling house, much frequented by the most dissolute French officers in Le Cap. But now . . . the doctor would not have even been sure of the location, if Madame Fortier had not appeared, to open a new iron gate set into a wall rebuilt waist-high.

"Ah," she said, looking up at the doctor. "I had been wondering if you would come."

"I didn't know we were expected." The doctor hopped off his donkey and followed Paul in through the gate. "I hope we do not trouble you. It was a fancy of my son's."

"An inspiration," said Madame Fortier. "You are quite welcome. Though we are in disorder here. At this hour I have only water to offer you."

"We wish for no more," said the doctor, whose throat was in fact rather dry from the dust the crowds had raised around the market.

"Agnès!" Madame Fortier raised her voice. *"Poté nou dlo tannpri!"*

In a moment a slender girl of perhaps thirteen appeared with a blue-tinted bottle and a couple of glasses, which Madame Fortier took from her hands.

"My niece, Agnès," she said. "I present Paul Hébert, the son of Nanon and of this gentleman."

Agnès stood poised, light as a deer, her lips slightly parted. Her hair hung in loose waves around her honey-colored face. She was meltingly pretty, the doctor took note.

"What are you looking at?" Madame Fortier said. "Go on—take him into the garden."

Agnès plucked at Paul's wrist, withdrew her hand quickly with a laugh, then covered her mouth with her fingers, looking abashed. With a glance at his father, Paul trotted after her, around the corner of the house, where a gang of carpenters was raising the frame of the roof above the second story. The lowering sun silhouetted them sharply—one turned the point of his beard toward the doctor and raised a hand. Uncertain, the doctor returned the wave.

"You will excuse Fortier, I am sure." Madame Fortier squinted at the carpenters. "One hopes to achieve the roof, before the rains begin. But come," she motioned. "There is shade."

The doctor followed her to three low chairs grouped under an almond tree in the corner of the wall. The trunk was scorched but the leaves were full—it had not been so much damaged in the fire. As if unconsciously, Madame Fortier spilled a little water from the bottle onto the struggling grass before she poured their glasses full and gave one to the doctor. She set the bottle on the empty chair between them.

The doctor sipped his water, clean and sweet and just a little lemony. From behind the house the voices of the children rose and fell. They were out of sight beyond the garden shrubbery. The doctor felt nothing at all of what he had expected here.

"It will not be so opulent as when you knew it before," Madame Fortier said. "We lack for time, and hands, and material—well, all that you know." She swung her hand in an airy circle toward the clatter of reconstruction of other houses beyond the wall. Within this enclosure, the plan of the house which the Fortiers were restoring was much the same as it had been before, though only a quarter of the ground floor had its solid walls; the rest was a skeletal framework. But—he had expected to be smothered in these images, and instead he had to force himself to re-create them—there he had entered, and there was the gambling table, where Choufleur presided over the cards, and there the spot nearby where Nanon stood, the chain locked around her neck drooling links to the floor, looking through the doctor with her dead eyes, without a ghost of recognition.

"The place held evil memories for me too," Madame Fortier said. "In my youth, I was much mistreated here by my son's father."

"The Sieur de Maltrot," the doctor said. "I wonder that you should return here."

"With all the fighting, one cannot peacefully remain either at Vallière or at Dondon," she said. "Besides, I own it, since my son is dead. I own it with everything it holds. *Sa nou wé ak sa nou pa wé yo.*" All we see and all we don't.

The doctor turned to look into her face. "You've done something here. It's not what I expected."

"I asked for the *mambo* from Morne Calvaire to send away the most troubled spirits." Madame Fortier took out her short black pipe and packed it from a small drawstring bag of tobacco. "Those who remain are more beneficent. We offer them water, no rum or blood."

The doctor nodded, watching her light the pipe. "It does feel peaceful," he admitted.

"Yes," said Madame Fortier. "One hears that you mean to kill that Captain Paltre."

"News of my business seems to travel widely."

Hammers clattered on the roof tree, then stopped. The doctor looked toward a cloud of blue butterflies hovering above the shrubs that closed the garden.

"It surprises me a little, I suppose," she said, twin plumes of smoke streaming from her nostrils. "You would not kill my son, though you had the chance, and though he surely would have killed you. And he had done you many injuries—he did his best to destroy Paul, and almost did destroy Nanon." She smiled absently, then drew again on her pipe. "I liked it that you would not kill my son, though were I in your place I probably would have killed him. And he was going to die anyway, that was sure."

"Yes," said the doctor. "He was killed by Dessalines." He'd been himself a reluctant witness to that action.

"I know it," said Madame Fortier. "But why then will you kill this Captain Paltre?"

"There are certain injuries which can only be washed out in blood."

"Why, you might have had that precept from me." Madame Fortier laughed cheerfully, and blew out another wreath of bluish smoke. "But consider fire—fire too can purify. You see, the walls here have no memory. There are not even any more walls."

The doctor said nothing. In part he thought that she was right, but there was a knot in him that refused her meaning.

Paul's head popped into view around the corner of the house. Then came Agnès, chasing him, laughing. They both disappeared between a huge hibiscus in the garden.

"He is prospering, your boy," Madame Fortier said. "Have you thought of his future?"

"What do you mean?"

"He will not marry anyone on the order of Héloïse Cigny, you know. Sophie perhaps, but there the kinship is too close for comfort."

"He's eight years old," the doctor said, concealing his amazement.

He'd never have thought Madame Fortier observed such details of his household—or that she had the opportunity to do so. "I can't say I've felt pressed about such questions."

"The years go quickly. And the difference between him and Agnès will shrink as they grow older."

"Why, you do us a great honor there," the doctor said, feeling a blush spread from his face to his throat. "And certainly, the girl is charming, at this glimpse."

"She will also have a little property."

"Well. There is time enough for all that."

"Except that tomorrow you may be dead." She tapped the doctor on the forearm. "The whole world knows what a marksman you are, but if BonDyé should withdraw his favor, your shot may fail and his succeed."

"Of course," said the doctor. "We are none of us promised tomorrow. But I wonder that you should be so concerned for Captain Paltre."

Madame Fortier laughed much louder than before. "I have no concern for that *blanc* at all. The person who concerns me is Nanon. You must not think that you are doing this for her. Neither you nor I have any notion what men came to this house when Choufleur held her here. You do not know their numbers or their names, and you could not possibly kill them all."

"No," said the doctor, feeling the knot of his anger tighten and bulge. "But when I have killed this one, the others will be disposed to silence."

"That is one way of looking at it," Madame Fortier said. "Perhaps not the best." She knocked out her pipe on the leg of her chair and stood up. When the doctor rose, she offered him her hand.

"My son burned Nanon right down to the ground," she said. "And still she came back greener than before. I know you had a hand in her survival. Don't leave her lonely now."

Riding with Paul to return the donkeys to Morne Calvaire, the doctor went adrift in an inner fog. Again he saw the swirling mists of La Fossette at dawn, the only other day he'd fought a duel. At the moment he'd first confronted Choufleur he'd believed Nanon was lost to him forever. When, after all, she'd returned to him, he'd been so drunk with happiness he could not think of harming anyone. He'd fired his shots into the air, while Choufleur, by luck or the grace of God, had missed him. But now he did not feel at all the same.

The donkeys delivered, he and Paul returned on foot toward the Cigny house. At this late hour of the afternoon, clouds had gathered again over Morne du Cap and were thickening over the south end of the harbor. The wind was swirling and stirring the dust, and people were emptying off of the streets, though in the end it probably would not rain. As they turned into the last block, the quartet of young captains was approaching from the opposite direction. At that, the doctor's hackles rose.

Michau had opened the door for them. The doctor gave Paul a little nudge.

"Get inside."

"But where are you going?" Paul turned on the threshold, raising his ivory face.

"Nowhere," said the doctor. "Go in now. Your mother is waiting." That last was an invention, but Paul did go in. The doctor thumbed the string of his medical *macoute* off of his shoulder and passed it to Michau as he shut the door. Then he stepped into the middle of the street, running his hand around his belt to assure the readiness of his pistols.

"Wait!" called Guizot. "We only want to talk to you."

"I'm no assassin," the doctor said. "Speak your mind. I did not expect you before tomorrow morning, that is all."

Guizot's heart shrank at that declaration. He had doubted the hope of his peacemaking project all day. The doctor had given him no encouragement during the coach ride to the hospital, and Guizot had not learned anything at all from Maillart. Though once he'd seen him, from a distance, walking across the Place d'Armes, it seemed the major did not hear his call, or had even intentionally ignored it. At last he and Cyprien and Daspir had prevailed upon Paltre to make this visit, though without assurance of how he would be received. Unfavorably, as it looked now. But it was a little late to withdraw. Guizot exchanged a quick glance with Cyprien and together they urged Paltre a pace or two ahead.

"Doctor Hébert," Paltre began stiffly. If there were more words, they had caught in his throat. The doctor studied him in silence. Severe hangover would have been his first diagnosis. The scab where the stove wood had scraped his cheekbone was very dark against his greenish pale skin, his eyes were hollow, and he was sweating a nauseous aroma of stale rum.

"Doctor Hébert," Paltre repeated. "Allow me to present my most—"

"My most humble," Cyprien prompted from a pace behind.

"—my most *humble* apologies for my heedless speech of yesterday afternoon. Allow me, I—I—"

"I beg you," muttered Cyprien, looking uneasily up at the Cigny house.

"—I beg you, allow me to recall those words, to swallow them as if they had never been spoken."

The doctor sustained his passionless stare. He could not find the tight coil of his anger. In its place was only a draining fatigue, a deep weariness of the whole situation.

"As my excuse, I must plead *mal de mer,* the seasickness from which I often suffer, and which did plague me on the sail from La Tortue, along with the exhaustion of a long campaign—all that must have confused my senses, so that I mistook your lady wife for someone altogether different, who wholly lacks her modesty, her chastity, her grace. Far it would have been from me to injure your wife's reputation, whether in word or thought or action—"

"I accept your apology."

The voice came from above. Both the doctor and Paltre looked up sharply. Nanon stood on the balcony, with Isabelle and Elise on either side, each woman framed by a narrow arched doorway behind her. The spiral of the evening breeze loosened strands of their hair and fluttered the hems and sleeves of their garments.

"Madame Hébert," Paltre said. His eyes darted anxiously among the three women. A blend of hatred and fear fumed out of his pores, with the stale rum. "It is most gracious of you," he choked out.

He bowed to the women, then turned to the doctor, holding out his hand. The doctor stared at it till it wilted.

"Your apology has been accepted," he said to Paltre. "You may go."

When Paltre's hand dropped, it settled on his sword hilt. His Adam's apple pumped in his throat. For a moment the doctor willed him to draw. But Cyprien and Daspir closed in on either side of Paltre and brushed his hand free of his weapon.

"Come on," said Cyprien. "It's over."

Paltre turned and walked away between his two companions. Guizot lingered for a moment, looking at the doctor, who finally acknowledged him with a nod and a half-smile. He understood that Guizot must have put some effort into this reconciliation, and maybe it was better to end it so.

Nanon now stood alone on the balcony, her hair stringing loose from her chignon and blowing across her face in the dampening wind. Perhaps Paul had sensed something and gone to fetch her, the doctor thought. He went indoors and climbed to join her. The knot of his anger had been sundered, but he was not sure what it left him to say. She faced him, her brown eyes warm and wild. The wind blew her loose gown tight against her: a simple, tea-colored dress with the round collar ornamented with an embroidered trumpet vine of her own sewing. A spatter of raindrops blew into her face, and the doctor felt the cold dots on his bald spot.

"After all that has been between us," she told him, "no thought and no word and no opinion matters but yours and mine."

"Yes," said the doctor. "I suppose that was what Madame Fortier meant to tell me, in her way."

"Madame Fortier? I had heard she had come to town."

"I called on her this afternoon—Paul took me there. She sends her greetings to you." The doctor paused, thinking what he had said was true enough to the spirit of their encounter, though Madame Fortier had not been so explicit. Nanon moved a little nearer to him, trailing one hand along the iron railing of the balcony. He looked down. "It seems that she and every one I've spoken to since yesterday has wanted to dissuade me—and I suppose it's better so."

"Of course it is better," Nanon said. She looked down at the point on the street where the four captains had made their appearance. "You ought to have taken his hand," she said. "He will resent it that you did not."

With that she raised her eyes to his. She was so near that he could feel her warmth.

"I don't know, perhaps I should have," the doctor said. "But before God and before all the world, I will take yours."

36

We did not know what spirit it was that bore the doctor to the ground that night at Habitation Arnaud. The spirit strung its power from beneath the waters to the top of the sky, so that he hung like a fish on a line, but after that it did no other action, spoke no word. Moustique was there, who was both *hûngan* and *prêt savann*, and Moustique might have coaxed the *lwa* to speak its name through the doctor's mouth, but he did not. I, Riau, I saw the spirit split the doctor's head as a sprout divides the two halves of a seed, and from his shoulders bloomed a black sunflower, but nothing more followed. As he was *blanc*, maybe the doctor did not have the strength to carry one of the great *loa* on his head. So his legs collapsed beneath him, and the other *blancs* carried him away into Arnaud's *grand'case*, and his *ti bon ange* returned to him in sleep, to the place in his head where the spirit had driven it out.

When the doctor awoke he was himself again, but I, Riau, was gone. I did not need to be with those *blancs* any more, and so I was going back to Toussaint, though not by the straightest road. I did not know just where I was going, and yet the way before me was clear.

I rode through the forest of Bois Caïman, where Boukman had called down all the *lwa* a dozen years before to help us drive the *blancs* out of our country. There were not many people there this time of year, but every space between the old trees hummed with spirits. A *blanc* might move through air all full of spirits and never know that they were there, as a *blanc* will not notice a cloud of mosquitoes before the mosquitoes begin to bite, unless it was a rare *blanc* like the doctor, who had grown some *konesans* between his ears. Then too there was Claudine Arnaud. Moustique had built that *hûnfor* to feed the *loa* who came to her, and they were always hungry, her Ghedes and Erzulies.

In ten years the *mapou* had grown larger, there where the *mambo* cut the throat of the black pig, where Boukman, ridden by his spirit, cried into the burning sky, *Kouté la libèté k'ap palé nan kè nou tou!* Toussaint was there, though hidden in the shadows. He did not try to show his face or hand that night, though I, Riau, had seen him. I saw the mosquito settle on his cheek. Since then Toussaint should have carried Boukman's words with him, as Riau carried them always—listen to liberty that speaks in the hearts of us all.

Wind shook the high limbs of that *mapou*, and I turned my horse to ride away. As I left the clearing the thought came to me that the *loa* who brushed the doctor might be the same that walked with me, an Ogûn, not Feraille but Balendjo, the one who walks with a traveler. Riau was glad that Ogûn Balendjo was near, to carry him across the plain when he came out from under the old trees of Bois Caïman. There it was open country, and too close to all the French *blanc* soldiers at Le Cap, but it was the shortest way to Grande Rivière and that was why I took it. A patrol of *blanc* horse soldiers saw me from a long way off, but they did not have one horse as good as mine, and when they chased me their horses bogged in the low ground, because only I, Riau, knew where the dry trails ran between the boggy places.

There were mosquitoes in the wet land of the plain, or maybe this one mosquito had followed me out of Bois Caïman, I thought. He whined around my head but did not bite, and I did not try to crush him because his voice brought me the memory of Macandal, who flew off on the wings of a mosquito when the *blancs* burned his body at Le Cap. They thought that was the end of Macandal's plan to kill all the *blancs*, but all of our people who saw that mosquito cried out *Macandal sové!* We had been forced into the square to see him burn, but what we cried was Macandal is free! Those words were singing in my body, and everywhere I rode was Macandal's country, the place of his *marronage*, and Riau's too, in the time before our rising. From a long way off the thought reached me that if Macandal were not just one mosquito but a thousand times a thousand, he would drink the blood of all the *blancs* until they withered and dried up and blew away across the sea, like the burnt *bagasse* that blew from the burning cane fields. Many of those fields lay burned around me where I rode.

As I came into the valley of Grande Rivière, a dozen of Sans-Souci's men rose out of the ground like smoke, and they were all around me and my horse before I knew. The spirit of Macandal had so filled Riau's head that I did not have clear eyes to see them coming. Now when I shook my head and looked for that mosquito it was gone.

The men took me through the *bourg* of Grande Rivière and on into the hills to the *grand'case* of a coffee *habitation* that the *blancs* had run away from long before, where Sans-Souci sat on the gallery, eating chicken. When I came there he called my name and shared his food with me. He stood up to take my hand when I climbed the steps to his table, and I saw how small he was, with short arms and legs like the legs of a turtle, and yet the force in him was so great he always seemed twice bigger than he was.

Riau had last seen Sans-Souci when he brought his *blanc* prisoners to Toussaint at Marmelade, and that was not so long ago, but still Sans-Souci wanted to know where Riau had been and what he had done since. I told him that I had seen the *blanc* general Leclerc going up the road with all his soldiers to Le Cap, and Sans-Souci grunted and said he knew Leclerc was there. I did not tell him about the doctor and Maillart and those people on the road. They would have got to Le Cap anyway, by the time Riau had come to Grande Rivière.

"Pa wé Christophe?" Sans-Souci asked me. You didn't see Christophe?

I told him I had not seen anything of Christophe or his men that day, because I had come across the plain where I would not expect to find them. Christophe commanded the posts of the mountains from Marmelade to Grande Rivière, which Toussaint now named the Cordon du Nord, and Sans-Souci knew that as well as Riau did. In Toussaint's order of the army, Sans-Souci was in Christophe's command since before Leclerc came with all his ships and soldiers. But I thought that Sans-Souci would never be commanded altogether by anyone but himself and his own *mêt'têt*.

"You came across the plain alone?" Sans-Souci said. "If the *blancs* are so weak, Christophe ought to come out of the mountains and drive them straight to the walls of Le Cap."

Sans-Souci looked like he wanted to spit when he said this, and he did break a chicken bone and throw it over the gallery rail. A little dog came out from under the steps and began to crunch it, and then another dog came from behind the house to fight the first one for the bone. It was getting so dark I could not see the dogfight very well. Maybe it was true that the French *blanc* soldiers were weak enough in the plain that Christophe could beat them, but it was always dangerous to fight the *blancs* in the open country where they themselves best liked to fight, and no one knew exactly when more soldiers came into Le Cap on new ships, and Toussaint had ordered Christophe to stay in the mountains. Sans-Souci was staying in the mountains himself. But I did not say any of those things to him then.

"I got across the plain because the *blancs* are slow and I have a good horse," I said.

Sans-Souci showed his teeth in a way that was not much like a smile. "If he needs to run away from the *blancs*," he said, "I think Christophe could outrun your horse on his two legs, Riau."

At that I laughed, and Sans-Souci laughed with me. His laugh was easier than that smile had been. It was true that in the beginning of the big fight with Hardy, Christophe came so close to getting made prisoner by the French *blanc* soldiers that he had to run away barefoot through the bush, because he had thrown away his boots and his coat and his general's hat so those *blancs* would not know just who it was that they were chasing. But afterward Christophe had turned his men to face the *blancs* again, and helped to beat them.

"Maybe Christophe spent too long holding the dish for the *blancs* to help themselves," Sans-Souci said when he had finished laughing. "Maybe that is a habit he can't break."

I did not make any answer to this at all, but only moved my head in a way that might mean either yes or no. The dogs had stopped fighting by then, and it was quiet, because the bone was gone. I looked across the gallery rail to the hill where coffee trees stood. There was just enough light to still see the trees and see how they were all covered with vine. Nobody had been tending those trees, and if Toussaint saw them so he would be angry, and Dessalines would have whipped the *commandeurs* with thorns. Now it was so dark I could see only the shape of Sans-Souci's head, but not his face. Maybe Sans-Souci really did not trust Christophe, or maybe he only meant to test Riau.

Sans-Souci came out of Guinée, in chains like those that were hammered onto me. He was Congo, like Dessalines, and I think he must have been older than Riau when he was taken, old enough to know something about the Congo way of fighting before he came. Christophe was Creole, born a slave, as Toussaint was born, though Christophe came from one of the English islands. Before our rising, Christophe worked as a waiter in the Hôtel de la Couronne at Le Cap, and that was what Sans-Souci meant to spit on him for now. But in those same days Christophe had also gone across the water to Savannah to fight for the *blancs* there, and he had learned something of the *blanc* way of fighting, and fought well enough that he got his freedom for it. That was the story which was told. Soon after Boukman called the *lwa* to help us fight the *blancs*, Sans-Souci led men into the mountains, and I had crossed his road in those first days, when he held a camp at Habitation Cardinaux and was very hard on the *blanc* prisoners that he took. Christophe stayed on the *blanc* side at that time. He fought under the French *blanc* general Laveaux and never joined with our side until Toussaint and Laveaux had joined. He had been put over Sans-Souci then, and there alone was reason enough for Sans-Souci to hate him.

Since La Crête à Pierrot there was too much of this kind of quarreling. I, Riau, had seen it with Toussaint in Marmelade not long before, when

Dessalines tried to undo Charles Belair in the eyes of Toussaint. Dessalines told this story to Toussaint, that Charles Belair meant to go over to the French *blanc* soldiers to the south. With Dessalines, Charles Belair was holding a line in the Grand Cahos mountains, the same as Christophe held the Cordon du Nord, and if that line was broken then the French *blanc* soldiers could come from Port-au-Prince to reach Toussaint at Marmelade, and maybe even at further places, like Saint Raphael on the plateau. It was true that Charles Belair received a letter from the General Pamphile de Lacroix at Port-au-Prince, and for that, Dessalines said that Toussaint must order Charles Belair to be shot. But Charles Belair brought to Toussaint both the letter from Pamphile de Lacroix and a copy of the letter he had sent back. Pamphile de Lacroix asked Charles Belair to come over to the side of the *blancs*, just as Dessalines had said, but in his answer Charles Belair refused. It was the same as when Christophe had got a letter from Leclerc asking him to help trap Toussaint, but Christophe had answered that he would not do it.

Toussaint took Charles Belair out of the Grand Cahos then, and sent the Colonel Montauban to take his place beside Dessalines. People whispered that Toussaint was showing more favor to Charles Belair than to Dessalines, by keeping Charles Belair near him at Marmelade, and maybe it was so, or maybe Toussaint better trusted Dessalines to hold that cordon of the Grand Cahos, and wanted Charles Belair close under his eye because in truth he trusted him less. Still there were people beginning to whisper that Toussaint meant Charles Belair to be Governor-General after him.

That was if we drove out the *blancs*, or made some peace with them. Toussaint had his letters too, that came to him from the General Boudet, and everything that was in those letters was hidden behind Toussaint's head.

"I think Christophe does not have much more heart to keep fighting the *blancs*," Sans-Souci said. I could not see his eyes any more, but I felt them searching for me in the dark. "Christophe is tired of sleeping on the ground in these mountains." Sans-Souci made another sound like a laugh. "He would like a soft bed in the Hôtel de la Couronne."

I noticed Sans-Souci was not sleeping on the ground at all, and probably Christophe was not either. The Hôtel de la Couronne had been burned down a long time ago anyway, not by Christophe when Leclerc came, but in the fire of our first rising many years before. Maybe Sans-Souci wanted Riau to carry his idea of Christophe to Toussaint, to wound Christophe in Toussaint's spirit.

"Maybe you are right," I said. "Christophe is more used to the town than the mountains."

Then a girl came out from the *grand'case* to take away the chicken plate and give us some cassava with guava paste. Sans-Souci stopped talking about Christophe then. When we had eaten the bread and guava, I drank a glass of *clairin* with Sans-Souci, and then I went down to be certain that my horse was well. There was a small pond where the horses were watered, and in the last light I saw bats fly low and skim across the water, moving faster than my eye could follow.

I went to the room in the *grand'case* where Sans-Souci had told me I could sleep. Some other men were there already, talking quietly in the dark. I did not start any talk with them, but lay down on an empty mat. My thoughts came fluttering across my head like the bats had moved across the pond, with the arms of the trees above them reflected in the water.

I was very tired from this long day of riding, so my sleep was very deep, and it filled up like a well with a *grand songe*. In this dream I was Riau no longer, but I was in the spirit of Toussaint, lying in a small stone room as close and narrow as a grave. Toussaint lay like a dead man lies beneath the earth, waiting for the *bokor* to come to raise his body up to slavery, waiting without light or breath. Through the stone walls I heard the whistling of the *siffleur montagne* and the part of me that was still Riau knew this sound came from outside the dream, and wanted to move toward it, but the cross of Baron pressed down more heavily on the stone so that the walls closed in more tightly and I could not bend my legs or move my arms or even raise my chest to breathe, but the voice of Toussaint screamed through my lips, *Dessalines! Sé Baron pou moin li yé!* Dessalines is my Baron! Then out of the shadow of Baron's cross came the shadow of a long, cloaked figure riding, and hidden in this cloak of darkness was the face of Dessalines, only it was one-eyed now, like Moyse's face had been—

I sat up shaking and sweating, as if I had taken a fever, though I had not. I thought I might have screamed for the other men in the room to hear, but they were all still breathing quietly with their sleep. In the first blue light of morning, I could see their faces. I saw a mosquito settle on a blood vein on the back of my hand, and moved to crush it, but then I did not. I sent the mosquito away on my breath, thinking it could go to drink the blood of *blancs*. The only sound was the sound of horses in the yard.

I went out to the gallery then, without waiting to put on my boots. My head was still full of the dream of Dessalines, so at first it seemed to me that Dessalines was there, but instead it was Christophe getting out of the saddle. Then I saw that Sans-Souci had come to stand on the gallery next to me. He had put on his boots and all his uniform to receive Christophe and he was pushing the power that was inside him outward, to make himself seem bigger than his body was.

Christophe drank coffee with Sans-Souci, and gave him orders for the time he would be gone. He was going to see Toussaint at Marmelade, but for what reason he did not say. Sans-Souci said little when he took his orders. The power around him was large and dark. My head was still muddy from the dream, but by the time Christophe finished his coffee I had saddled my horse and joined the other men who were riding with him to Marmelade.

I did not know why my dream should show such a fear that Toussaint had for Dessalines. There was no stronger or fiercer general than Dessalines in all the army, especially since Maurepas had given his head to the *blancs*. Maybe it was only a false picture that came from the mirror of the dream to my eyes.

We rode into Marmelade with the rain, and as all the men hurried to get into shelter, I came with Christophe and some of the others into the hall of the house where he had made his headquarters on the north side of the square. Christophe took off his hat and his coat to shake the rain from them. He sat down at the table facing Toussaint, who had called for candles to be brought in, because the rain had made it dark. The light inside was watery with the rain, and the rain made a big noise on the roof which covered the words of Christophe and Toussaint, but still I could hear most of what they said.

Christophe took a paper from his shirt, another letter he had got from the Captain-General Leclerc, he said. Toussaint unfolded the paper and held it under the candle's light, looking down his nose at it. Then he began to read, in a loud voice that rose above the sound of rain: *The code is not yet in existence; I am working on it at this moment. The First Consul was unable to draw up a code for a country which he did not know and about which he had received contradictory reports. But I declare to you before the colony, and before the Supreme Being whose witness one does not invoke in vain, that the foundations of this code are liberty and equality, that all Blacks shall be free.*

Kouté la libèté k'ap palé nan kè nou tou. Those words of Boukman sounded in my ears again while Toussaint read, but I did not know if I trusted the words of this *blanc* Leclerc so well. In some other place in my head I heard the words which Paul Lafrance had said to General Lacroix at Port-au-Prince, before I came back to Toussaint again. That seemed like a long time ago, but still those words were clear.

It looked like Toussaint was not well satisfied with the words Leclerc had sent. He stopped reading and dropped the letter on the table and spoke to Christophe in the same loud voice that reached all the other ears in the room.

"He may claim he is writing a law to safeguard our freedom," Toussaint said. "But until that law is written and declared to France, whatever he claims means nothing."

"Yes," said Christophe, *"Oui, mon général,* of course you are right—but I believe the Captain-General is true to his word, for when I met with him at Haut du Cap, he let me go back to my men without hindrance, just as he promised there—"

Christophe was pointing to the letter on the table, but Toussaint had caught it up and crushed it in his hand. Toussaint was on his feet, and Christophe too, but Christophe was flung back away from the table as if the force of Toussaint's words had pushed him.

"You *met* Leclerc? You dare to meet Leclerc without my order?"

I had not seen such a *djab* climb on top of Toussaint's head since the day when he ordered Bouquart to step out of the line and shoot himself. But if he ordered the same to Christophe now, I thought that maybe Christophe would not obey. It looked like Toussaint was going to burn the letter in the candle flame, but then he stopped himself and let the ball of paper roll on the table. Then for the first time he seemed to know that others were there listening.

"Guards!" he shouted. "Clear out this room."

I saw this order was for me, since Riau belonged to the honor guard now, so I turned and helped to herd the others out into the square. Some went away, but I stayed under the shelter of the balcony in front of the headquarters house, watching the rain pour down over the empty stones of the square. With so much noise of the rain I could hear nothing from inside, but Christophe stayed there for a long time with Toussaint.

When the rain had stopped I went looking for Guiaou, and found out he had gone down to Ennery, one or two days before. Instead of Guiaou I met Bienvenu, who had come up from the Cahos with a message that Dessalines had fever again and was resting at his house in Marchand, leaving the longer part of the Cahos line to the Colonel Montauban. It was a long time since I saw Bienvenu, before La Crête à Pierrot, and I was glad to see him now. He had a woman who was cooking *callaloo*, and gave me some of it in a gourd. We sat to eat in a place where an overhanging ledge of rock had kept the ground dry from the rain, at the edge of the road from Marmelade to Dondon, where many of our soldiers camped.

Bienvenu told me a lot of things I did not know about what happened at the fort of La Crête à Pierrot. He was glad to know from me that Doctor Hébert was still alive and had got safely into Le Cap. Bienvenu knew that Rochambeau had killed all our wounded men with the bayonet when the French *blanc* soldiers came into the fort at the end, so he thought maybe the doctor had been killed too. I had not known before that Bienvenu had put so much work into protecting the doctor's life.

"I have more happiness for you," I said. "Michel Arnaud is still alive too and safe in Le Cap with the doctor."

"Is it so?" Bienvenu rubbed a place on the back of his head as if this word had made it ache or itch. "And the crazy one, his woman?"

"She may be crazy, but her spirit is too strong to let her die," I said. "Maybe neither one of them will ever die."

I was wrong in that idea, but I would not see it until later. Bienvenu kept rubbing that same spot on his neck, where I, Riau, had struck with my *coutelas* to break the metal cage Arnaud had locked around his head to stop him eating in the cane fields. Bienvenu ran away from Habitation Arnaud, so long ago before our rising and in my time of *marronage*, but the cage had spikes that caught in the bush, and it was I, Riau, who set him free. If not, the dogs of the *maréchaussée* would have caught him. I could already hear them when I found Bienvenu in the bush. It was a trick to measure the blow of the *coutelas* so it broke the cage but not his neck. Another time Riau had set Bouquart free of the iron *nabots* forged to his legs, but then Toussaint had killed Bouquart.

Bienvenu had reason to wish Arnaud dead, because in that time Arnaud was known as the cruelest of slave masters. Maybe I was wrong to tease Bienvenu about it. The woman took our gourds away and began to wash them from a jar of rainwater, singing softly to herself as she washed. I would have liked to stay near the softness of that song, but I went away to sleep in another place so Bienvenu could be alone with the woman.

The next day Christophe rode out of Marmelade, with most of the men who had come with him. They rode out the same way they had come the day before, along the road to Dondon. Toussaint had ordered Christophe back to the Cordon du Nord, and ordered him not to do any more talking with Leclerc.

By noon that day Guiaou had come back from Ennery again. Merbillay sent with him a basket of the small, sweet rose-colored mangoes of Ennery, and these Guiaou shared with Riau. In the hottest part of the day we slept in the shade of the ledge where Bienvenu was camped. Then late in the afternoon Placide came to wake us. Riau and Guiaou were ordered to go with Placide and Toussaint out on the road toward Dondon.

I never knew what was Toussaint's purpose in going on that road that day, though later I thought that maybe he already knew what was coming to meet him there. Sometimes he rode out with Placide to teach him things about the country and his way of moving through it and of using it to fight the *blancs*, and sometimes he would bring Riau into that talk. But today Toussaint sent Riau and Guiaou ten horse lengths ahead of him, while two other guardsmen in their silver helmets rode at the same distance behind. With Toussaint and Placide were Chancy and Charles Belair, but we were too far apart from them to hear any of their words.

The time of the heavy rains was not yet come, but it was going to rain again that day in Marmelade. Gray clouds sank over the tops of the *mornes* to the northeast, and Guiaou and I looked at each other because we could both smell the rain on the wind. Then Guiaou held up one finger.

"Listen," he said.

I turned my ears up the road, but I heard nothing. We had stopped before a bend where the road turned to follow the curve of the *morne* we were climbing. Behind us, Toussaint and the others had stopped. They were passing a spyglass among them and pointing to something down in the ravine we could not see.

"*Kouté,*" Guiaou said again. Listen.

I thought I heard the wheezing of the horse before I heard the hoof-beats, but before I had well understood either sound the rider rushed around the bend, so fast that our two horses were frightened, and Guiaou's horse almost went over the edge into the ravine. Guiaou sawed on the reins to bring his horse back, and his lips and the edges of the scars on his face turned gray. The rider pulled his horse to a stop just before it knocked into our horses. Its split hooves knocked small stones into the ravine. When the horse hung down its head, strings of white slobber hung out of its mouth, and mixed with it were threads of blood. I saw he had killed this horse with hard riding. It made my stomach tight to see it.

"Where do you come from?" Guiaou said. He still could not stop his horse from dancing. He was holding the reins too tight.

"Sans-Souci," the rider said, breathless. "I have a message—where is Toussaint?"

But by then Toussaint had already come up. Behind him, Placide's face showed a moment of fear, but then he gripped in his right hand the red *mouchwa têt* Guiaou had given him, and his face closed.

"What is it?" Toussaint said, in his most gentle voice.

"I come from Sans-Souci," the rider said. "Christophe—" He stopped for breath. This rider was almost as windbroken as his horse. Whenever I looked at that horse my stomach shrank tighter. I wanted to shoot it and push it into the ravine where I would not see it any more. There was nothing to do but shoot it, but I knew we must take it back to camp, because there were men there who had not tasted meat for many weeks.

"Christophe has given up to the *blancs,*" the rider said. "He has given up all his posts, from Dondon to Pont Français. Grande Coupe, Mornet, Grande Rivière . . ."

"Grande Rivière?" Toussaint said. "Where is Sans-Souci?"

"He got away to Cardinaux. Christophe would have killed him, but he got away," the rider said. "He has still a few men with him. Perhaps two hundred."

Toussaint made the sign of the cross with a small movement, as if he hoped no one would see. He held his two hands over his heart.

"What a misfortune," he said slowly.

Toussaint was looking out across the ravine to all the clouds thickening in the sky. His hands lowered, and one of them reached under his coat to touch the string of small wooden skulls he always kept hanging from his belt. We heard the skulls clicking one against the other.

Then Toussaint turned to Placide, as if he would explain to him, but Placide had learned enough by then to know the meaning of what had happened. With all those posts in the hands of the *blancs,* there was nothing to protect Marmelade any more, or the passes to the Central Plateau. It was for nothing now that we had beaten the General Hardy at Dondon. Toussaint had made a lot of plans. When the rains flooded the

Artibonite River, he meant for Dessalines to take back La Crête à Pierrot. Vernet was supposed to take back Gonaives and Toussaint himself would ride from Plaisance to Limbé. Then the *blancs* in the north would be cut off from the *blancs* in the south and Toussaint could beat them one by one. But now none of these things could happen. Sans-Souci might hang on in the mountains, but he would have to run after every fight. I remembered how well Sans-Souci had received Riau two days before, and I almost wished I had not left him.

Toussaint stood quietly, very calm, except for the clicking of the skull beads. Maybe his lips moved in some prayer to Jesus. I could not see what was behind his head, and if he was truly surprised by what had happened I never knew. Another day, when Toussaint rode down to Marchand to bring the news to Dessalines, Dessalines rose up in anger from his fever bed. Dessalines was one of very few who dared show his anger before Toussaint.

"I know him," Dessalines said, when Toussaint told him what Christophe had done, "and he would never do this thing without your order."

The day Sans-Souci's rider came, we led the ruined horse down to the place where Bienvenu was camped. Bienvenu and Guiaou bled it, skinned it, boiled the brains, and roasted the meat of it on the *boucan*. I, Riau, I ate my share, though without pleasure. I needed strength for when Toussaint would call me to copy letters late into that night. And afterward I could not sleep, lying in the dark beside Guiaou, who in his trust of Toussaint always slept deeply. Words of the letters flew like bats among my thoughts. Maybe Christophe had betrayed Toussaint, as it appeared, as Toussaint wanted it to appear. Or maybe he gave Christophe a secret order, in the headquarters room behind the rain, to give in to the *blancs* while Sans-Souci kept on fighting them. That was much like a thing Toussaint would do, to work with both hands, to use one hand against the other. But I could not see his reason for it now. And it did seem that Toussaint really felt betrayed. I, Riau, I wrote for him until the candle wax ran down and hardened on the table, copying angry, bitter words to send Leclerc. The letter ended this way—*Whatever might be the resources of the French army, he would always be strong and powerful enough to burn, ravage, and sell very dearly a life which had also sometimes been useful to the mother country.*

37

When Maillart's eyes opened, he found Isabelle quietly watching him from where she reclined on the fringed cushions of her secret chamber, naked except for the sheet that swirled around her hips. She had lit a scented candle which left one side of her face in shadow, while catching a glow in both her dark eyes. Maillart thought he glimpsed some wistfulness there, an echo of the sadness he felt himself as he roused from his brief postcoital slumber. The small, close room was still hot with his smell and hers, the musk only partly covered by the sweet overlay of the candle.

When he reached for her, she pulled away. "It's late." Her voice was cool, but without real sharpness—only detached. God only knew what was in her heart; this thought was a habit to Maillart now, having passed through his head so many times. As she twisted free of the embrace he'd attempted, the house key strung around her neck dropped between her breast and ticked against the carved stone penis there. This latter memento no longer disturbed Maillart as it once had done, though at first it had quite unmanned him.

"As you like," he said. He groped for his trousers, then stood to pull them on, awkwardly balancing in the narrow space between the bedding and the wall. Isabelle put out a hand as if to steady him, light fingers probing his thigh muscle through the fabric.

"Now then, the day's getting on, as you say." Maillart squinted up at the single veiled window, which really gave next to no clue to the time. Likely it was only a little after dawn, for he could still hear the cries of charcoal sellers in the street outside the house, and the first scent of coffee was just rising from below.

Isabelle let go of him and reached for her crumpled chemise. As she raised her arms to the sleeves, her breasts lifted around the pair of pendants, cool metal and cold stone, and Maillart felt a pulse of fresh desire, but he suppressed it. He buttoned his shirt and crammed the tails into his trousers. Isabelle tossed back her crown of dark curls and gathered it with a ribbon at the back of her neck. The movement brought the cloth of the chemise tight against her dark nipples; between them the stone pendant bulged.

"I have another token for you," Maillart said as he put on his coat. Isabelle turned toward him, curious, raising her chin as she lowered her arms. Maillart felt in his coat pocket and spun the china pendant toward her on its filament of fine chain. Now the moment had come, he felt a little loath to give it up. He'd worn it around his own neck for most of his way across the country, but taken it off for this tryst with Isabelle, not wanting any interruption. She pulled the pendant toward the candle's flame, drawing him after her, for his wrist was still engaged in the chain. The same flash of sadness touched him again when he saw the crow's-foot marks around the corners of her eyes.

"But this is the one I gave to Elise," she said. "Do you mean to tell me—"

Maillart felt a flush warming his throat. "I did not have it from her so directly," he said.

Somehow they'd both released the chain; the pendant fell on the bed between them, too light to make a sound.

"I'd better tell you." Maillart sat, gingerly, on the edge of the bed.

"Indeed you had," said Isabelle.

"We found it in a box of souvenirs at Port-au-Prince. I and General Boudet and a few others—it was in Toussaint's cabinet there."

"Toussaint? You mean—" Isabelle's face, with its roundly parted lips, quite resembled the image painted on the pendant, except that her look was frank astonishment, rather than the coyness of the painting. "I had no notion," she said. "None."

"So much the better." Maillart looked at the tapestried wall. "There is an order, I heard there—any white woman known to have consorted with the blacks is to be defamed as a whore and shipped to France."

Isabelle detached her fingertip from her lower lip and tapped the china pendant with her nail.

"Well," said Maillart. "None but I could have known its provenance. And no one missed it when I took it from the rest, there were so many . . ."

"Really so many?" Isabelle stared at him.

"Yes, with locks of hair and all of that, and some women had even been foolish enough to write letters."

"The foolishness of *some women* knows no bounds." She paused. "You're telling me Elise was not so foolish."

"No. She was not." Maillart swallowed. "And General Boudet is a gentleman. He burned everything that would take a flame and threw the rest into the canal—yet I thought I ought to preserve this for you."

"It is kind of you," Isabelle said abstractedly. She gathered the pendant and chain in her palm. "I suppose Elise might still be denounced." She caught Maillart's reluctant eye. "As I might be."

"Oh, surely not." But Maillart could not hold her gaze. He was memorizing a pattern of the tapestry: some European bird with its throat open, vomiting an inaudible song. "That wretched Paltre," he blurted out. "He goes around muttering, and who knows who listens. He saw too much in this house, I fear, when he was here with Hédouville in ninety-eight."

"If only Doctor Hébert had done away with him." Isabelle's hand clenched on the pendant.

"He can't be killed if he won't fight," Maillart said. "We are not murderers."

"Of course not," Isabelle said, but it seemed she had scarcely heard him. From the rear of the house, the voice of a cock was repeating its dawn cry. Isabelle's fingers curled and uncurled over the pendant like the legs of a starfish.

"Let Paltre say one word openly against you and I'll stop his mouth forever," Maillart said. Then, in another burst of irritation: "I don't see why you let that Captain Daspir hang about, mooning like a lovesick calf."

Isabelle's laugh was bright, but harsh. "You've no call to be jealous of *him*," she said. "He is only a very young calf, as you say."

"Yes." In spite of himself, Maillart grinned into a fist. "But someone seems to have given him the notion he's a bull."

This time Isabelle laughed wholeheartedly, and a little too loudly for discretion. "Oh . . ." She caught his hands in both of hers. "How good it is to laugh." Her voice lowered. "But now you really *had* better go."

The hidden stair curled down to release Maillart into the garden. Nanon and Zabeth were giving the smaller children their breakfast at a small table under the portico, but no one appeared to notice the major, as he glided quietly toward the side gate. Only Gabriel, walking among fresh planted sprigs of aloe, looking for snails, glanced up and caught his eye. A handsome boy, black as he was, and stout for his small size. Maillart smiled and winked at him, and on further thought gave him an English penny from his pocket before he let himself out onto the street.

There were the hollow eyes of Captain Daspir, bearing down on Maillart from across the way. Maybe he had been standing there sleepless all night, shifting from one leg to the other, like a stork. Maillart sent him an easy smile, stretched luxuriously in the gathering sunshine, and touched his hat to the young captain before turning his back and walking away in the direction of the Place d'Armes. As a younger man he too had skulked on the borders of Isabelle's other assignations, and known all the torments Daspir's haggard face now expressed.

But Isabelle had told the truth; he had no reason to be jealous of Daspir. The one man who had earned his jealousy had been dead since last November. Joseph Flaville. Maillart had really quite liked Flaville, respected and even admired him a little, though it had shocked him to the bone when he learned that it was he who'd presented Isabelle with the ever-so-unusual stone pendant she still wore. But where had he seen that face so recently that it now came before his eyes? Flaville was dead since last year's fall—executed for his part in the Moyse rebellion. But— Maillart stopped dead in the center of the Place d'Armes, half aware of the crows that had started up squawking into the trees at his approach. Gabriel, who'd looked at him so closely in the garden—there was the child who now wore the face of Joseph Flaville.

When Maillart had departed, Isabelle sat for several minutes, cross-legged on the rumpled bedclothes, stirring the chain around the pendant in the palm of her hand with a fingertip. At last she rose, slipped on a robe, and went down to the boudoir she had occasionally shared with her late husband. There she rang for a maid to assist her in dressing and arranging her hair. Héloïse came in with the maid, to ask permission to go with Sophie and Robert and Paul to the beaches on the road to Pico-let. Isabelle refused, a little curtly.

"And tell the others they are not to go either—not alone." She cocked a critical eye at herself in the mirror before which she sat, at the same time catching a glimpse of Héloïse behind her, as the girl's face crumpled in a sulk. Isabelle clicked her tongue, then forced herself to relax the expression that had furrowed the space between her eyebrows.

"Ou prêt, madamn," the maid informed her, her face floating above Isabelle's in the mirror's shadow, impassive. You are ready. Isabelle dabbed a little scent on a handkerchief, and in her vexation crushed it in her hand. She could hear Héloïse crying in the garden.

Paul and Robert interrupted her as she was collecting her parasol in the foyer, but she began lecturing them before either could speak.

"I *will* not have you go so far alone," she said. "It isn't safe along that strand—not for young children."

"I'm twelve years old," Robert said hotly.

"And by the grace of God you may live to manhood," said Isabelle, with an air of finality. It was not the risk of drowning that concerned her in that place. Because there was little danger of an attack on Le Cap by sea, Fort Picolet was undermanned by the quite drastically weakened

French army, and there were rumors of black rebel marauders crossing the headland from the numerous unsecured areas in the direction of Pont Français and Acul.

Robert stamped his foot and opened his mouth to snap a retort, but Paul nudged him and spoke in his place, with that silky politeness of which he was capable. Four years younger than her own son, Paul had much more self-control, and Isabelle mistrusted him a little for that; Robert had his hot temperament straight from her.

"Madame, we never meant to go alone," Paul said. "We would meet Moustique and Paulette at Morne Calvaire—maybe Fontelle too—they will be with us on the beach."

Isabelle hesitated. Her mind was not much attached to this problem; she wished she could have slipped out of the house unnoticed. Nanon's silhouette appeared at the opposite end of the hall, framed in the doorway to the garden. Héloïse leaned into her, stifling her sobs against her skirt. "I can go with them," Nanon said. "I think I ought. They are too confined here, really, and a sea bath would be a good thing for the little ones."

"Well, if you would undertake it . . ." Isabelle let her resistance slip. She forced a bright jingle into her voice. "Only take care that no one is abducted! And don't be too long in the full sun."

As she spoke she crossed the hallway to give Héloïse a pat on the head. In the same impulse she kissed Nanon's cheek. "Elise has gone out?" she whispered.

"Yes," said Nanon. "Since half an hour. She has gone to see to the work in her own house."

As the distance was short, Isabelle went on foot, carrying the parasol with its handle wrapped in the scented handkerchief, though in truth she was so accustomed to the smell of ordures and decay and stale smoke that she seldom troubled to raise the scented mask to her face. In Elise's garden, some freshly planted flowers struggled to bloom. Hammers clattered on the second-story wall, where Michau supervised a gang of four carpenters. When Isabelle appeared in the gateway, Michau pointed her to a rebuilt room on the ground floor at the back, where the doctor was now storing some of his salvaged books and journals and herbs and specimens. Elise sat there at a round three-legged table, perusing a large gray-bound ledger by the light slanting from the aperture of an unglazed window beside her.

"Well!" said Isabelle, as she took a seat. "There's an unaccustomed study. You are preparing to join your brother as a nurse?"

"He will soon need more of those than he's got," Elise said absently. "But no." She raised her hollow eyes to Isabelle.

"You don't look well," Isabelle said. In fact Elise looked distinctly nauseated, as she had every morning for the last ten days or two weeks.

"I am not well," Elise said. "I am—" Her face shattered, and she began to wail, tears pumping out of her reddening face. Isabelle moved her stool around the table and put an arm over Elise's shoulders. "There now, stop. You'd better stop—they'll hear you."

"Who could hear anything with those infernal hammers!" Elise shrieked. "I feel like they're hammering right on my head."

But she did begin to swallow her sobs, and let Isabelle dab tears from her face with the scented handkerchief.

"Now then, now then," Isabelle kept saying, in the same rhythms she'd have used with an hysterical Héloïse. "What can it be, then? What is it?"

"Oh, nothing," Elise said. "Nothing, only the end of my life."

Isabelle caught herself. Somehow she felt uneasy to pursue. For distraction, she scanned the open ledger, though without taking in the sense of the words.

"That does not resemble your brother's hand," she said.

"It isn't," Elise sniffled. "It is the work of Abbé Delahaye—he gave some of his notes to Antoine for safekeeping since there has been so much turmoil at Dondon." She picked up a trefoil of dry grayish-green leaves that had been pressed between the pages, and when it crumbled her sobs broke out again.

"Useless," she said. "None of it's any use."

Isabelle looked past her trembling hand to the page. Under the dust of crumbled leaves the plant was more vividly rendered in a drawing that must also have been the work of the priest. Below was inscribed in his frail cursive: *thyme à manger—avorticant, used according to Toussaint Bréda by Women who wish to be cured of Pregnancy* . . .

"*O,*" sighed Isabelle. The syllable seemed to pull a hole clean through her. "You don't mean—"

"I do." Elise clenched the leaves in her hand to powder. "That is the very thing I mean."

"It is a long time since anyone called him Bréda," Isabelle said. "I suppose those leaves really have lost their virtue."

Elise did not respond. She pushed the leaf crumbs around on the page. Isabelle leaned back, though the stool had nothing to support her, and raised her arms to loosen the third chain clasped around her neck. The movement brought the china pendant out of her bodice, into the hollow of her throat. Elise's face drained with the recognition.

"You never shared this conquest with me," Isabelle remarked.

"No," said Elise. "I thought it indiscreet."

"*Entendu,*" said Isabelle. She laid the chain and pendant on the page of the open ledger and smoothed a hand down over her bosom. "By the grace of Providence and Major Maillart, I can return you your indiscretion more or less intact."

"Maillart knows, then?" Elise covered the pendant with her hand.

"He will say nothing. He means to protect you. Apparently he has learned that Leclerc bears some secret order for the deportation of all white women known to have consorted with the blacks."

"Oh *Bon Dieu*—"

"But—" Isabelle said. "Maillart has kept you safe. There is no evidence . . . and if even I did not know?"

"No evidence? Consider this." Elise wrapped her hands around the bottom of her belly and leaned forward as though she would vomit.

Isabelle bit into her lower lip. "The father is certainly Toussaint?"

"No," Elise. "That was just the one time, and—it was safe enough. No, the father is almost certainly Sans-Souci, and very certainly not Xavier, who was absent for a full six weeks on that errand after guns in Philadelphia—"

"I see," said Isabelle. She spread her fingers over her throat. "But yet— to kill your unborn child?"

The hammers stopped just as she spoke, so that her words rang louder than she'd meant. Elise stared at her angrily from her red eyes.

"You may well talk," she said. "You had all your joy of Joseph Flaville, and went away to bear his child in secret, and afterward fobbed the bastard off on my brother."

"Who told you that?" Isabelle said in her first shock. The hammers had resumed their pounding. Elise pressed her palms to her temples and grimaced.

"None but my own eyes," she said, and looked away.

Isabelle drew her slim torso very straight and folded her hands into her lap.

"You will recall that I also had the pleasure of seeing Joseph Flaville blown to ribbons by a cannon load of *mitraille*," she said. "On the order of your own recent lover, it appears. As for Gabriel, I nearly died bearing him, and if not for the charity of Nanon and Madame Fortier, I would not have survived. And with all that I had to give him up."

"You have him in your household even now."

"But never to be mine." Isabelle's voice broke.

"I'm sorry," Elise said. "Your reproach stung me, I suppose."

"I meant no reproach." Isabelle raised a hand but her palm seemed to stop on an invisible membrane between her and the other. "It's only that I fear for you, Elise. That action you consider would wound you in your body and your heart." She swallowed. "You must know that I would never judge you. I think you have never judged me."

At that Elise did open her arms and the two women leaned together, rocking each other on their half-balanced stools, cheek to wet cheek.

"But what can I do?" Elise murmured damply into Isabelle's ear. She pushed back, breaking the embrace. "I can't get away to the mountains to bear the child secretly—we are all trapped here together in this town."

"I do see that." Isabelle touched a finger to the corner of her mouth, then reached to shift the pendant from the open book. She folded the worn gray cover shut. "But whatever it is, you cannot treat yourself so," she said. "It's plain you don't have knowledge enough, and in that matter I have none."

"What, then," Elise said dully.

"I'm not certain," Isabelle said. "But first, let us go to your brother."

It was very hot when they stepped into the street, and Isabelle began to wish they had arranged for some conveyance. They might have done so at her own house, but Elise seemed stubbornly determined to walk. As if overexertion in the heat might put a natural end to her predicament, and indeed it might.

Isabelle drew closer to Elise, to share the shade of her parasol. When they entered the Place d'Armes they crossed ways with Cyprien and Paltre, walking in the direction of the Governor's house. As the women went by, Paltre looked at them sneeringly, then passed some remark to Cyprien behind his hand.

"The bloodsucker!" Elise whispered as they walked on. "How I wish Antoine had shot him, as he meant to do."

"No more than I," said Isabelle. She flexed her grip on Elise's upper arm. "Keep up your courage. Hold your head high." Though she thrust her own chin up with that remark, she felt herself bared and wretchedly exposed by this encounter. It seemed to her that Paltre's eyes still probed her from behind, but she would not look over her shoulder now to see if it were true.

In the rising heat, Doctor Hébert moved slowly, deliberately, among the rows of sick and wounded men. There had been a recent hatch of fat black flies to add to the irritation of the mosquitoes that boiled ceaselessly up from the ravine. The flies increased the risk that wounds would be infected, and the doctor had just finished curetting one such when one of his nurses called to him from the gate. Stiffly he got up from his knees and passed his instruments to another of the women aiding him, who plunged them into a bowl of scalding water. Isabelle was calling out to him cheerily from the gateway, and the doctor moved toward her, swabbing his sweaty face with a large blue handkerchief.

"My dears," he said. "I'm delighted to see you, but you shouldn't have come." He looked uneasily over his shoulder toward the wall where his barely breathing fever victims lay.

"We ought to be sufficiently proof against the fever," Isabelle said. "But do let us find a little shade."

The doctor led them beneath the tree where his hammock was strung. Nearby a kettle of fragrant herbs was simmering on its tripod. Elise sank into one of the low chairs. Another of the women, murmuring at her flush, brought her a gourd of cool water.

"Sister, you do not look well," the doctor said. In fact Elise's face seemed to reflect the nausea he'd felt himself when scraping maggots from that wound. "You shouldn't stir out in such heat."

Elise said nothing. Her flush had faded, leaving her face pale beneath its sheen of sweat. Maybe she was not so acclimated against fever as

Isabelle supposed, the doctor thought. The water seemed to choke her when she sipped it.

"It's for that she came," Isabelle said, a little shortly. "Well, I'll leave you." She moved away, in the direction of the gate.

"What is it then?" the doctor said softly, feeling the first twinges of real alarm. "It could not wait till evening?"

"It has already waited far too long," Elise said. She glanced at the woman who'd given her the water. The doctor motioned her away.

"I am with child," Elise announced, once the nurse was out of earshot.

"A blessing," the doctor said, though he felt his tongue thicken in his mouth.

"A curse," Elise said. "The child will be the color of your Gabriel."

Abruptly the doctor sat down on a stone beside her chair. He looked absently toward Isabelle, who stood with one hand on the rust-red iron of the gate. She'd laid her parasol aside and the sunlight pouring through the bars seemed to have bleached the features from her face.

"Why should I look for help from you?" Elise said bitterly. "I set myself against Nanon, and drove her out, and drove out Paul—"

"Don't reproach yourself," the doctor said. "That was long ago and has been forgotten." He twisted his sweaty handkerchief into a rope between his hands. "The trouble is, I haven't the skill for . . . what you require."

"You have your potions."

"But you say you have waited too long. When was—when was your last—"

Elise told him.

"It's as I thought," the doctor said. "It's not my practice, but I think that after such a time, the herbs will not be effective."

"Then I am ruined," Elise said. "If Xavier does not kill me."

"Hush," the doctor said. "I've got to think." But he could not summon any useful concentration. It seemed an age ago he'd seen her dancing at the Governor's house, wilted over the bend of Sans-Souci's arm. He had said something to her then, but there was no use recalling it now.

"It's not my practice," he repeated. "It's not a skill I've cultivated. If it must be done, I think you had best go to Maman Maig'."

"Why not admit you are afraid to do it!" Elise jumped up. The doctor too was on his feet.

"I am afraid to see you die of it," he shouted. But Elise had whirled away from him and was stumbling toward the gate.

Huddling under the parasol, the two women had almost reached the waterfront before Isabelle could coax from Elise the burden of the doctor's message.

"He may be right," she said when she had heard it.

"To put me in the hands of that black witch?" Elise snapped. "I'd just as well throw myself into the sea."

Through a gap between the buildings they could see spume flying up from the waves smashing into the rocks below the Batterie Circulaire. Isabelle caught Elise's wrists and pulled her to a stop. The parasol tilted from her grasp and though the hooked handle caught on her elbow, the bright fabric scuffed into the ground.

"Maman Maig' is an expert midwife—and I know you have seen it for yourself, whatever else you may think of her—*Stop* it!"

Elise was wagging her head like a mule; a hank of her pale hair came loose and flapped from side to side across her cheek. Isabelle caught her chin and held it still.

"If not for such a one as her, I would have died, with Gabriel," she said. "Now listen to me. You must follow your best hope. I will go with you to Maman Maig'."

Elise pulled her chin free and tucked it. "I'm afraid," she stuttered. "I'm so afraid."

"Of course you're afraid," Isabelle told her. "Only a fool would not be." She repeated the words softly, as if they were soothing, and pulled the parasol upright. Elise let herself be guided by her hands.

At the foot of the nearest trail that climbed to Morne Calvaire, Maman Maig' sat in the shadow of an overhanging boulder, behind a sagging, waist-high wooden gate. Half blinded by the glare of the sun, Isabelle could not make out the huge black woman's expression in the shade, even when Maman Maig' got up to her feet to address them.

"*Sa ou vlé?*" she said. Her tone was neutral, her face almost invisible in shadow. What do you want?

Elise said nothing, but gathered her hands at the waistband of her skirt.

"*Sé sa. Renvoyé youn pitit,*" Maman Maig' said, in the same flat tone. You want to send away a child.

Elise simply dropped her head and let it hang.

"*Ou mêt monté,*" said Maman Maig'. You may come up.

She tugged the gate open and beckoned Elise through. A set of hand-hewn steps made a tight curve around the boulder toward the *lakou* above, and when Maman Maig' moved, Isabelle saw Paulette rising from an upper step; the girl held out her hand to help Elise. For the first time it struck Isabelle as slightly sinister that they had fallen into this path to Morne Calvaire, rather than the higher way that passed the crosses and the church. But she pushed the thought down as she moved to follow. Maman Maig' blocked her with a heavy arm.

"*W'ap reté,*" she said. You stay.

She pulled the gate shut behind her and turned away, her vast black body closing Isabelle's view of the ascent.

For several minutes after Isabelle and Elise had disappeared from his view, the doctor remained in the portal of the hospital, gazing vacantly in the direction they had taken. His mind cranked in quick constricted circles. He ought to have stopped Elise, but how? The risk of abortion was not acceptable. The risk of bearing the child no more so. Tocquet's reaction could in no way be predicted. At least Tocquet was for the moment away from the town. If Elise could also be got away—to Thibodet or somewhere more remote—but that was hardly possible now, and Tocquet was not the creature of habit Bertrand Cigny had been; there was nowhere on the island he could be guaranteed not to appear.

When he became aware of one of the women patiently waiting at his elbow, he made some half-audible apology to her and walked out through the gate. Two blocks down the hill he realized he had forgotten his hat, but it didn't seem worth the effort to climb back for it. He shook out the blue handkerchief and tied it over his bald scalp to stop it blistering in the sun. Maillart fell into step with him as he crossed the Rue Espagnole.

"You look peculiar with that head rag," he said, and then, when the doctor did not respond to this jocularity, "What's the matter?"

The doctor didn't seem to have heard that question either. They walked on. Maillart was sufficiently used to his friend's impenetrable reveries, though this one seemed colored with unusual foreboding. They said no more till they met Isabelle coming the opposite way along the Rue du Gouvernement.

"Where is my sister?" the doctor blurted, seeing that she was alone.

"She has followed your suggestion," Isabelle said. Her hands worked on the handle of her parasol. She looked over her shoulder toward the rise of Morne Calvaire.

"By herself?" the doctor said.

"Maman Maig' turned me away. But she is not alone there. Paulette is with her." Isabelle's expression flickered. "Oh, the *children*—I think they have gone to the beach alone, on the road to Picolet—if they have defied what I told them. Paulette was meant to go along, but she did not." She turned to retrace her steps, but the doctor caught her elbow.

"Wait," he said. "You would do better to go home. You have already been too active in this heat, and the sun is at its height. We'll see to the children and let you know afterward."

"Oh," said Isabelle, wilting a little. "I just now thought—Nanon is with them. I forgot she volunteered to go."

"Nanon?" said the doctor. "So much the better. But we are walking that way, all the same."

"Or I might walk with you," Maillart offered.

"No, no." Isabelle renewed her smile. "I have only a little way to go. But you must bring me your news later."

She spun the parasol gaily as she turned away. The two men watched her to the corner. If she'd seemed to falter when she first encountered them, now her steps were quick and sure. On her left shoulder, concealing her whole head, the parasol continued to revolve.

· · ·

Beneath the shaded portico of the Governor's house, Daspir waited, a little impatiently, for Cyprien and Paltre to return. Dermide raced up and down the stone-floored gallery, awkwardly rolling a hoop with a stick, his hot face patchy red and white. The space was too confined for this exercise, and crowded with basketwork furniture Pauline Leclerc had recently acquired, and Dermide seemed to take special pains to collide, again and again, with the legs of Saint-Jean Louverture, who leaned against a piling of stone, looking with a certain stoical indifference across the flagged courtyard toward the gate.

The company of Dermide was the worst cruelty of Saint-Jean's situation, Daspir thought. Otherwise the young hostage had been quite kindly treated ever since Hardy captured him on the road from Gonaives—if adoption into the Captain-General's family were to be considered a kindness. Dermide was now smacking his stick against the older boy's calves, but Saint-Jean, his eyes distant, paid him no mind.

Guizot appeared in an inner archway; Daspir acknowledged him with a nod.

"Where are the others?" Guizot said. "We ought to have started an hour ago." He stepped past Saint-Jean, out into the open, and squinted fretfully up at the sun.

"There," Daspir gestured. Cyprien and Paltre were just being admitted by the sentry at the gate.

Before they could be on their way, Pauline rushed down, to tighten the string of Dermide's straw hat, and drape him with a strip of cloth against the sun. Cooing, she pressed two gigantic hampers of food on the captains, then caught Daspir by the arm.

"Do be careful of the sun," she said.

"Of course, Madame," said Daspir, unbending. Before Isabelle, this contact would have thrilled him. Now he had to subdue his impulse to pull away.

"Ought you not to take a carriage?" Pauline's face was a mask of concern. "Perhaps my litter? Or no, I shall want it myself, I think . . ."

"Not at all, Madame—it is no distance, and the boys are so restless, the walk will do them good." Carefully Daspir disengaged his arm, for he now saw that Leclerc had ridden in at the gate.

The four captains saluted the Captain-General as they passed, and Dermide imitated them, eliciting a smile from his father. Saint-Jean went by obliviously, eyes already fixed on the sea. Pauline called from the shade of the portico: "Be careful of sharks! and the urchins, especially." On the street, the captains made a formation around the two boys, which was constantly broken by Dermide rolling his hoop out of it. Paltre had the task of chasing the hoop, muttering as he dodged between the heavy hand-drawn barrows and mule carts hauling up goods from the port.

Once they had passed the Quai d'Argout, traffic on the street dimin-

ished. The road became a wide expanse of dirt, rippling over the indenta-
tions of the coast. Dermide lost interest in his hoop, and persuaded
Saint-Jean to carry it for him. Daspir shifted his heavy fruit basket from
one hand to the other.

"We've got wares enough to open a market stall," he grunted.

"And we'll be carrying half of it back again," Guizot said.

There were others on the beach before them—a gang of children of all
ages, splashing in the shallow water. A gangly mulatto youth stood watch
on the shore, holding an ancient musket whose barrel was bound to the
cracked stock with wire. The woman standing with him looked very
much like Nanon. Daspir sucked in his stomach, hoping Paltre would
not notice her. He set down his basket in the shadow of a sea grape, well
short of the other group, and shaded his eyes to look at the swimmers.
Certainly these were the children of the Cigny house: Robert, Sophie,
Paul . . . Daspir had not learned the names of the smaller ones. The maid
Zabeth sat cradling an infant in the shallows, but Daspir saw no sign of
Isabelle.

"Nursemaids again," Paltre grumbled, plumping down into the coarse
sand. He shot a challenging look at Guizot. "Here's what's come of your
fine notion to capture Toussaint Louverture—now we've got the *least* of
his brats to look after . . ."

Daspir checked to see if the boy had heard, but Saint-Jean was standing some distance off, upwind, and the wind was fresh. Ignoring Dermide's anxious teasing, he stripped off his clothes and walked down to
the water. There he was relieved of the pestering, for Dermide was hesitant to go in. He dithered on the water's edge, retreating from the dying
ripples, as Saint-Jean swam away from him toward the other children.

"I don't know about that," Cyprien was saying. "A shrewder general
than the one we've got might use the boy in a trap to snare Toussaint."

"What, here?" Paltre turned his head to spit.

"By no means impossible," said Cyprien. "There was a raid two nights
ago that carried as far as Morne des Capucins."

Daspir looked about himself. "If you're serious," he said, "I think our
ambush is a little undermanned."

"He's not serious," Paltre snorted. "They never raid by day." But he too
seemed to be inspecting their surroundings somewhat more thoroughly.
"Who's that scarecrow?"

He pointed toward the youth with the musket, whose figure for the
moment blocked Nanon's. Guizot shaded his eyes to look. "It's only
Moustique," he said. "He traveled here with us from a plantation of
Acul." On the point of mentioning the doctor, Guizot cut himself off. "No
harm in him," he said. "I'll just go say hello."

As Guizot made his way across the sand, Daspir pulled off his boots,
shoved up the hems of his tight trousers, and waded shin deep into the
water. He'd hoped for a flash of refreshing cold, but under the sun these

shallows were tepid. There was no risk of sharks whatsoever—this bathers' cove was closed from the ocean by a reef augmented with a wall of mounded stones, but he did look carefully for urchins before he took each step. One day he'd seen a black child skewer a foot on the long, dark shiny spines—and if any such thing ever happened to *dear Dermide* they'd never hear the end of it.

Saint-Jean and Paul were dunking each other, and suddenly Sophie erupted from the water behind them, laughing, shaking back her salt-weighted hair. There was something in that movement that reminded Daspir of Isabelle, and certainly the white shift she wore for a swimming garment clung to her most revealingly in the wet. Sophie caught his eye and sobered and concealed herself again beneath the water. Embarrassed, Daspir looked away. Dermide was hopping down on the hot rocks of the sand. Finally he found the courage to wet his feet, though he came in no deeper than his ankles. Beyond him, two men were coming from the direction of the town, one with a major's epaulettes and the other wearing a blue headcloth and a pair of spectacles that glinted in the sun.

Daspir walked briskly out of the water. Guizot was standing with Moustique; Cyprien sat by Paltre, drawing circles in the sand with a fingertip.

"Who's that coming?" Cyprien said, glancing up.

"I believe it is Major Maillart," Daspir said. "It looks like Doctor Hébert is with him."

"Come after his yellow wench, no doubt," Paltre said. He tossed up a handful of sand, which blew in the direction of Nanon and her group.

"Ignore them, can you not?" said Cyprien. "Or still better, why not walk down to see who's standing the watch at Picolet?"

"I've no reason to skulk away from such people," Paltre said hotly. "I've as much right to be here as they."

"You haven't self-control enough to avoid another quarrel," Cyprien said shortly.

"But why should I have to give way before them?" Paltre snapped. "They're collaborators—the lot of them."

"Not Maillart," Daspir said in his most reasonable tone, though his throat was swollen with resentment of Maillart.

"You think not? He commanded for Toussaint, and took his orders from black officers—Cyprien, you saw it too. And your precious doctor did that devil's correspondence for him." Paltre jumped up and pointed to the water. "Look at that litter of half-breeds they call their children. Evidence enough to ship those bitches back to France—the fair one and the dark one too."

"Enough." Daspir's hand clenched on his pistol grip. Guizot, seeing the trouble, ran up behind him to catch his wrist.

"And more than enough," Cyprien hissed. "Come on, Paltre—go look over the post at Fort Picolet. And you, Daspir, you may as well go back to the town."

Daspir let go of his pistol and in the same motion shook free of Guizot's grip. "We ought not both to leave you here," he said, with a wave of his arm toward Dermide and Saint-Jean.

"No, it's all right." Guizot pointed toward the road, where a handful of noncommissioned officers had just appeared. "That is Sergeant Aloyse there, with some of his people. You may consider that they have relieved you. And there is no trouble likely here by day."

Cyprien was nodding his agreement. Daspir watched Paltre, trudging grimly across the beach in the direction of the fort, his boot heels slipping in the sand. He picked up his own boots and started in the opposite direction. When he passed Maillart he snapped him a quick salute, and briefly took the hand the doctor offered him. Half-consciously he acknowledged the salutes of Aloyse and his companions. Where the road climbed from the beach, he sat down and hastily brushed sand from his feet before slipping his boots on, and took a last hard look at Maillart before he headed back toward town. In fact, he had thought of a way to spend this unexpected morsel of free time in a way that might be advantageous to himself.

The ocean air swept away the pall of sickness which the doctor had been breathing all that morning. He stood facing the shimmering lagoon, inhaling deeply with his arms crossed over his chest, recalling that someone, perhaps Riau, had advised him one ought to breathe ten times each day before the sea.

Nanon had waded shin deep toward the children, holding her skirt bundled about her hips. Sophie made a sudden lunge and pulled her under. Nanon's yellow dress bloomed on the water like petals of a sunflower. Her laughter carried back to him on the sea breeze. The doctor began counting the heads of the children. Zabeth had carried the two infants into the shade next to Moustique. In the further distance the doctor made out a uniformed figure scrambling up the rocky path to Fort Picolet.

"You probably ought to have killed that wretch," Maillart said.

"What?"

Maillart pointed. "There. That's Paltre."

"Sharp eyes," the doctor said. "It was your idea I shouldn't."

"Theirs, actually." Maillart nodded toward the sea grape where Cyprien and Guizot had settled.

"So we have the whole quartet," the doctor said. "Let's stop where we are, then." He backed up and sat down on a chunk of stone in the shade of an overhanging almond tree.

"Guizot's a decent fellow," Maillart said.

"Of course. But I don't want to talk to any of them, not now."

"What's on your mind?" Maillart looked away as quickly as he'd spoken. It was not his habit to press a point so. But their meeting with Isabelle troubled him, together with the doctor's mood. The doctor made him no reply. Maillart stared at the point of rock where Paltre had disappeared, then lowered himself to the stone beside the doctor.

"You shamed him," he said. "He'll never forget it. He sees it in the eyes of everyone he meets, whether they throw it up to him or not. And I mislike the way he slinks about. He'd do us any harm he could."

"He shamed himself," the doctor said. "And what harm do you suppose he can do us? He won't stay here forever, in any case."

Maillart saw he'd come upon his subject from another angle. Perhaps this subject would lie in every road he might choose to take. He cleared his throat, but was distracted by the sight of Nanon rising from the water. The wind plastered the yellow cloth of her dress against her legs and torso. She caught up the wet rope of her hair and twisted it over her shoulder as she arched her back. My God, what a beauty she still is, Maillart thought. It was a rare thing to see her so completely at ease. The children were coming out of the water too, scattering across the sand. Paul and Saint-Jean spun each other down, wrestled for a moment, and got up again, kicking up showers of sand as they raced on. Gabriel, meanwhile, was galloping toward the doctor and Maillart, naked and unconscious. He smashed into the doctor's side, backed up and made another charge into Maillart. Then he shook his head, wriggled all over with his satisfaction, and trotted back toward the water's edge, where the milder François waited for him.

Maillart rubbed the point of impact on his upper arm. "That's no ordinary child," he said. "I swear his bones are made of stone." And there was the subject again, lying in his path like a boulder.

"Antoine," he said. "Have you never seen the boy isn't yours?"

"He's mine because I claim him." The doctor gave Maillart a quick, sharp look, then lowered his head and picked up a fallen almond. With the ball of his thumb he dug into the soft husk for the nut shell. Nanon and Sophie were parading past, arm in arm, letting their garments dry in the sun and wind.

"He isn't Nanon's either, in that sense." The doctor took off his glasses and shot another glance at Maillart. "He's Isabelle's."

Maillart swallowed. "Yes. I know."

The doctor flashed him a startled smile. "I didn't know you knew that."

"I didn't know you knew it either." Maillart shook his head. "She'd let me know she was with child by Flaville before she went off to Vallière with Nanon. In fact I helped to arrange that expedition."

"Why, you astonish me." The doctor pulled the kerchief from his head and began to polish his glasses with it.

"Surely I'm no more astonishing than you," Maillart said. "Bertrand

Cigny—God rest him!—overlooked a great deal, but he wouldn't have missed her giving him a child the color of Gabriel. And Isabelle—well, I can't say I was pleased by her news, but I found I would have done anything to help her."

The doctor replaced his glasses and went on studying Maillart's face through the lenses.

"I thought the child had died at birth, or had miscarried," Maillart said. "Well, I was ready enough to believe it—but now . . ."

The doctor nodded and looked away. "He's growing into Flaville's face."

"It's so," Maillart said somberly.

"Flaville was a strong man," the doctor said.

"I thought well of him," Maillart said. "In spite of everything." He gazed down the beach to the point where all the children had begun to gather around a couple of hampers Cyprien and Guizot were unpacking. Dermide was doing his best to start a quarrel with Saint-Jean over a ripe mango, but Saint-Jean backed away and let him have it. Nanon had settled some distance from the rest of the group, but when Moustique carried her a napkin full of food she accepted it. Zabeth came to join those two beneath the shade tree they had chosen.

"It's strange," the doctor said. "One doesn't look for such peculiar histories to repeat themselves."

Although the sun was bright as ever, Maillart felt chilled as if it had vanished from the sky. "Your sister," he said.

"Indeed, my sister." The doctor shook his head. "She came to me this morning—I don't know what prompted her."

But I do, Maillart thought. "You see?" he said. "That's how that miserable Paltre might scheme to get his own back."

The doctor looked at him. "What do you mean?"

"Leclerc has a secret order—on proof of any such liaison a white woman is to be disgraced and deported to France."

The doctor clicked his tongue. "What other secret orders has he got?"

Maillart didn't answer. He looked at the water, where Sergeant Aloyse paddled among his comrades, his gray pigtail floating on the water behind him. Guizot crossed the strand toward them, signaling them to come share in the meal. Maillart watched as the sergeant stood up and shook bright drops of water from himself like a dog. He remembered Aloyse's misgivings beneath the walls of the fort at La Crête à Pierrot, and the extent to which he'd shared them, but none of that bore thinking of now.

"Paltre has a suspicion of Isabelle, I know," he said, to stifle one ugly thought with another.

The doctor laughed harshly. "Elise wouldn't need to be betrayed by Paltre. As you can see, she's got no place to hide."

"How do you suppose Xavier will take it?" Maillart said.

"No idea," said the doctor. "It's as well he's gone to La Tortue."

"I don't suppose he'll stay there six months."

"No," said the doctor, rubbing the few sprigs of hair that remained on his freckled head. "She came to me in hope I would . . . arrange the problem. But it lies outside my competence."

Maillart passed a dry tongue over his lips. "That's why she's gone to the midwife, then."

"Yes, exactly."

"Is it safe?"

"No," said the doctor. "You wanted to know what was on my mind? Well, there you have it."

He stood up, brushing sand from his trousers. Guizot caught sight of him and beckoned. The doctor shook his head.

"No reason to refuse that offer," Maillart said. "That lad Guizot's as loyal to you as a spaniel, ever since you saved his arm, and Paltre has gone off—to the devil, we may hope."

"I never asked for a spaniel." The doctor cocked an eye at him. "And do you suppose I have an appetite?"

"No more than I do," Maillart said and spread his hands. "But one must eat to live."

"I suppose you're right," the doctor said. In fact the suddenness of his rising had left him a little light-headed—he had not eaten much that day, and Guizot did mean well. Still he felt hesitant to join the others. Again he folded his arms and faced the sea, watching the surf foam on the line of rocks that closed the cove, and counting his breaths carefully, though he was too distracted to know when he'd reached ten.

Daspir found the Cigny house all shuttered tight against the peak of the afternoon heat. He hammered on the door three times before he heard the reluctant scrape of the iron hook. The maid who peeped out through the crack was a stranger to him, and nowhere near as attractive as Zabeth. Madame Cigny was not receiving anyone at this hour, she told him, though he might come back in the evening if he wished. She closed the door on Daspir's boot toe, which he had thought to insinuate across the sill. As he struggled to pour himself into the narrowing gap, he heard the brassy jingle of a bell from within, and Isabelle's voice calling rather irritably for the maid to admit whoever had come.

The door yielded in, and Daspir lurched in, stumbling in the shadows of the hall. As his eyes adjusted to the dim, he saw her looking down on him from the top of the stairs. When she recognized him, she clucked her tongue and looked away.

"Well, come up, then," she said, but without much enthusiasm. She moved away from the upper stair rail. Daspir climbed, twisting his hat in his hands. Isabelle motioned him to her striped love seat, but sat herself in a straight chair across the room.

"I see I have disturbed you," Daspir said, unable to suppress the petulance in his tone.

"Oh," said Isabelle, her voice heavy with lassitude. "It is only that I did not expect you at this hour."

"It's plain enough that I am not the person you expected." Though his voice was tight and low, his jealousy was surging. It was Maillart who had turned her affection from him, Maillart who always seemed to interpose himself between Daspir and Isabelle these latter days. How had it happened so rapidly? Daspir had been moved to hurry here when he saw that Maillart would tarry on the beach—had been struck by what a rare opportunity that circumstance presented.

"It's true," she said.

Daspir's heart slammed. The doors over the balcony were also shut tight, and he could not read her expression in the shadows where she'd placed her chair. It was true, then; she had chosen Maillart over him.

"I thought Madame Tocquet might have come," Isabelle said. "But it is no matter. I meant to rest, but I could not. The heat." She turned over one hand. "It seems so airless."

She stood up rather suddenly and moved to open one of the doors which gave onto the balcony. A bright sword of light flashed into the room; Daspir flinched and blinked his eyes. Isabelle was holding the top of her negligée closed around her throat. The harsh midday light picked out the fine lines in her face. She must be ten years older than he, Daspir thought. He had reflected on this probability before, but now it occurred to him for the first time that she must be nearer to Maillart's age than his own. Yet after all it was not Maillart she had expected. And she was beautiful, and she had guided him to pleasures he had never before imagined, much less known, and also she was rich, or would again be rich once this rebellion had been definitively put down. This latter point was not without significance—to others as well as himself, Daspir had lately begun to realize.

The negligée was familiar to him. It fastened with two dozen tiny buttons down the front, concealed beneath a fold of cloth, and he had spent delectable periods teasing them open one by one, parting the garment slowly from her skin, as she whispered and shivered beneath him . . . but when he looked at her now, he could sense little of the treasure beneath the cloth. Her movement was leaden, and she did not come anywhere near him as she returned to her solitary seat. It did not seem at all likely that she would soon take his hand and lead him to her inner chamber.

"Well, I *have* disturbed you," he said. This time his tone was not so sour.

"It is no matter," Isabelle repeated. She was gazing past him, into the fierce light beyond the balcony; the intensity of the light made her dark eyes seem pale. "I am restless, as I told you. Weary, but restless." She tossed her head, but without vivacity. "It is the very definition of *ennui*."

"I came to warn you," Daspir said.

"Oh, did you?" Isabelle took her chin in one hand, curled a little into her chair, and looked at him with the expression of a faintly interested cat. The neck of the negligée opened when she released her hand, and an instant of real yearning left Daspir momentarily speechless. He fingered the bullet hole in his hat. At other times, in other moods, Isabelle had affected to admire this souvenir, but now it struck Daspir as almost shameful—to have escaped death so narrowly by mere dumb luck.

"It's Paltre," he finally said. "He means to defame you. He means . . . he suspects . . ." He felt the heat spreading over his cheeks. He ought to have chosen his words more precisely, but on his way here from Picolet his mind had gone blurry with the heat and the excitement of the idea that propelled him. Isabelle studied him with that same cat-like detachment. She had lowered her hand from her chin to the space between her breasts, where it must cover that distressing carving she'd strung there. Why would her first thought be to reach for that? As a sickly sweat broke out on his temples, Daspir considered for the first time that Paltre's ugly hints might have some truth to them. If Isabelle had stretched her ice-pale skin against a black man, and let his darkness cover her . . .

"You needn't say it." Isabelle's manner softened slightly. "Though it is good of you. I have been warned."

Maillart, Daspir thought again. But for some reason he felt no stab of jealousy this time. He pushed the other image from his mind. It was all Paltre, his meanness and his spite.

"I thought to offer you my protection," he said.

"Oh no," said Isabelle. "There's no solution in this dueling." Again she seemed to harden slightly. "It isn't that I would regret the loss of your Captain Paltre, but even if you did away with him, others of his kind would come."

"It wasn't that I meant to offer," Daspir said. He got up, dropping his hat to the floor, and crossed toward her on the creaking boards, feeling at once stiff and a little dizzy—it was all so much more awkward than he had pictured it, when she was so unbending to him now. His joints popped as he sank to his knees and scrabbled in her lap for her limp hands.

"Marriage," he croaked. All at once he lost track of the phrases he had composed during his rush across the town, but then as suddenly they began to return. "I would offer you the protection of my name, and of my sword. And of course, as well, my undying love and affection—"

When he twisted his head to look up at her face, he saw that she was truly startled and, still worse, a little amused. If she laughs, he suddenly thought, I will strike her. All in a whirl he realized that he might not be able to stop himself, that he might go on to beat her senseless, and that this capacity was one of the qualities unknown to himself which she'd perceived with her first long look into his eyes.

Isabelle did not laugh. The twinkle of amusement left her face and she held his gaze quite seriously.

"It is better to marry than to burn," she finally said. "That is the dictum of Saint Paul." She smiled, but faintly; this smile was not particularly for him. "Yet marriage never hindered my burning—this you know." She disengaged her hands from his and used them to cradle the back of his head.

"You are a good man," she told him soberly. "One day you will marry a faithful wife. Not me."

Daspir relaxed. He seemed to have no argument against what she had said. He felt that she was wiser than he, and though he couldn't quite grasp it at the moment, he was sure that she'd seen something in the future it would be better to avoid.

Resistance drained out of him. He was very tired, so much so that he closed his eyes and dropped his head onto her thigh. Isabelle's hands lightened on the back of his neck. She sighed. Under his cheek, the muscle of her leg warmed and loosened. A thread of song came in from the street.

> Palé O, Palé O
> La fanmi Asefi a palé O
> Asefi ki jeté youn pitit sèt mwa . . .

Isabelle jumped up and darted onto the balcony. Whatever she saw from that vantage moved her to dash as quickly down the stairs, leaving Daspir sitting on his heels, touching the edge of his jaw where her knee had popped when she sprang up. There was a clatter and bustle in the foyer below. Daspir collected his hat from the floor and went down.

Elise Tocquet had just come in. On her right was Claudine Arnaud, moving in that rickety, marionette-like way that Daspir always found alarming. She lent Elise some symbolic support, but Elise seemed mostly to be depending on Zabeth on her right side. The song leaked in through the door behind them.

> Asefi ki jeté youn pitit sèt mwa
> Asefi ki jeté youn pitit sèt mwa
> Pitit se byen O, palé O . . .

Isabelle's face contorted terribly. "Stop that singing," she shrieked, and lunged through the door, raising a small tight fist at the urchin in a ragged skirt who ducked away but went on grinning, mocking, chanting.

"Stop her!" Isabelle cried—more shrill than Daspir had ever heard her voice. The carter who must have delivered the women raised his whip, and the other maid, the ugly one, came hurrying through a side door, brandishing a broom.

Palé O, Palé O
La fanmi Asefi a palé O
Asefi ki jeté youn pitit sèt mwa . . .

The maid charged with the broom raised high, and the girl dodged and danced around the corner, her flashing bare heels white with dust.

Though Daspir had picked up a little Creole since he'd come, he could understand nothing in this song. But the women all seemed perfectly deranged by it. They'd left Elise to her own devices, standing with one fluttering hand on the lower stair post, trying feebly to raise her foot to the first step, so that only Daspir was watching when her eyes rolled white into her head and she collapsed backward onto the floor. He moved quickly down the stairs to assist her, but when he stooped, the battlefield smell repulsed him. A dark fluid pooled and spread around her hips. Blood. The blood smell pushed him back; then Isabelle had come between them, blocking his view, lifting Elise's ankles, while Claudine stood against the wall like a scarecrow. The ugly maid crouched to catch Elise around the waist, and as they began to raise her, Isabelle turned and snapped at Zabeth—"Go back! Go back at once and fetch Maman Maig'!"

Daspir followed Zabeth into the street. Someone, probably Claudine, knocked the door shut behind them as soon as they were through it. The cart had already groaned away, and he and Zabeth stood staring at each other round-eyed on the vacated street, but still imprinted on his vision was the picture of Elise on the floor with the blood spreading so rapidly around her on the floor. The blood had seemed to come from nowhere. When blood ran out of wounded men like that, they died.

"What was it?" Daspir said. "What was it she was singing?"

Zabeth, her eyes still fastened on his face, half-whispered an echo of the tune.

Talk about it, talk about it
Plenty-girls family will talk about it
Plenty-girls threw off a seven-month baby
Plenty-girls threw off a seven-month baby
Children are wealth, O, talk about it. . . .

Zabeth clapped her hands over her mouth and stared at him for one second more. Then she dropped her hands, picked up her skirts, and ran as fast as she could in the direction of Morne Calvaire.

38

Since dawn Guiaou had been mounted, with most of the others of the honor guard, and waiting for the order to ride. The night before, word had passed that Toussaint meant to strike Grande Rivière, to recapture the arms depot that Christophe had just surrendered to the French. Guiaou had stayed up late into the night, making cartridges and polishing all the metal parts of his musket, then slept for five hours, and risen with the morning mist. All the guardsmen were sitting their horses, which were restive, ready to move, but Toussaint was nowhere to be seen and no one else appeared to lead them anywhere. At sunrise, a couple of dispatch riders came clattering in on the road from Dondon. The guardsmen parted to let them through, and they rode on toward the center of town.

After some more time had passed without anything happening, Guiaou dismounted. Many of the other guardsmen had already done the same. Magny and Monpoint and Riau had gone down into the town with the dispatch riders, and no commanders were with them now, and no one knew what was going to happen. Guerrier paced up and down between the horses. Guiaou wished he would stop walking. At last, when the sun had grown warmer, Guerrier stretched out in the shade of the cliff above the road and spread his *mouchwa* over his eyes.

Guiaou had eaten little the night before, and nothing at all that morning. His stomach was drawn tight for fighting, but now it all began to loosen. He had lost the point of his concentration, and began to feel tired and uncertain. He sat down cross-legged and began to sharpen his *coutelas* with a small, hard stone he carried in his cartridge bag, even though the blade was already sharp enough to shave the little hairs from his leg.

The sun had just begun to spread into Guerrier's patch of shade when Riau came with a new order. About half the guards were dismissed for the day. The rest would ride with Toussaint, but to Marchand instead of Grande Rivière. What their reason for going there was, Riau did not tell, but it looked like they would not be fighting the *blancs* that day. Guiaou relaxed on the back of his horse, let his heels hang, and after a little while on the road he let himself doze. During his few hours of sleep last night his head had been charged with pictures of the fighting he was waiting for today. Now he was tired, and his head drained.

They went by the back ways through the mountains, hiding themselves from the open ground of the *rizières* above Ester. By the time they rode into Marchand, the shadows had grown long. Madame Dessalines stood in the doorway of her house and smiled at Toussaint and bent her legs inside her skirts as he got down from his horse. Toussaint ordered most of the guard to go and water and rest their horses by the well in the square, but he kept Riau and Guiaou and Guerrier with him, along with Monpoint and Placide Louverture. Madame Dessalines led them all into the house together.

Toussaint and Monpoint and Placide sat around a long mahogany table, while Riau and Guiaou and Guerrier stood in the shadows of the inside wall, looking through the tall, narrow doorways at the sunlight reddening on the dust of the road outside. Placide Louverture unfastened the red *mouchwa têt* Guiaou had given him and folded it into a careful triangle and pressed it between his hands before he put it into his pocket. Guiaou felt happy when he saw Placide do this.

A girl brought in cool water from the well. Madame Dessalines poured water into glasses for the three men at the table and the girl gave the clay jar to the standing men to share, smiling at them shyly as she went out. Then there was the sound of hooves outside, and Bienvenu, who had left Marmelade two days before, opened the door for General Dessalines.

When Dessalines had taken his chair at the far end of the table from Toussaint, Toussaint took a paper out of his coat. He held it out toward Dessalines, but the table was too long for him to reach. Monpoint and Placide passed the paper down. But instead of looking at the paper, Dessalines was looking at Guiaou and Guerrier and Riau. Guiaou did not like to have the eyes of Dessalines upon him so.

"Let them stay," Toussaint said. "There is no secret here today that any of my men cannot know."

Dessalines turned his eyes to Bienvenu, who began to close the first of three sets of doors that let onto the street. Guiaou moved to help him with the others. Now at last, Dessalines took up the paper.

"I don't see well in this light," he said.

"It's you who have shut out the light," Toussaint said. "Riau—"

Riau came forward and Dessalines gave him the paper, and when Madame Dessalines brought in a lamp Riau held it near to the light and began to read.

I see with pleasure, citizen general, the part you have taken to submit yourself to the arms of the Republic—

Riau stopped, for a moment, as if his tongue had frozen in his head. The lamplight flickered. Guiaou, who'd felt his stomach shrivel at these words, watched Dessalines breathe out a long wind of ill humor and sink more deeply into his seat. Riau was watching him too, his brown eyes calm in the yellow lamplight.

"Read it, then," Dessalines said. He drew his snuffbox from his coat pocket and laid it on the glossy surface of the table.

Those who have sought to deceive you about the true intentions of the government are much to be blamed. Today, we must not preoccupy ourselves in reviewing past evils. I must only concern myself with the means of returning the colony, as quickly as possible, to its former splendor. You, the generals under your orders, as well as all the inhabitants of the colony, need not fear that I will seek out anyone for his past conduct. I cast the veil of oblivion over everything which took place in Saint Domingue before my arrival—

" 'The veil of oblivion . . .' " Dessalines batted the snuffbox from one hand to another on the tabletop. Toussaint nodded for Riau to go on with his reading.

Everyone here has a new career to pursue now, and in the future I will not recognize anyone but good or bad citizens. Your generals and your troops will be employed and treated the same as the rest of my army. As for yourself, you wish for rest; you have earned your rest; when one has borne the government of Saint Domingue for several years, I imagine anyone would need it. I leave you free to retire to whichever of your plantations suits you best—

"You are running to your doom," Dessalines said. Guiaou looked at him. His features were heavy, mask-like, rigid—eyes wide so that the white showed around them—it was almost as if a spirit had taken him where he sat. He held the snuffbox under his left hand now, with a grip that might have crushed it. Guiaou could not keep on looking at him any more than he could have held, for more than a couple of seconds, the stony gaze of Baron Samedi. He shifted his eyes to Riau, who seemed to remain calm under the awful mystery he had unlocked from the letters on the paper.

"You are wrong," Dessalines said. "Sooner or later our whole people will rise up against the French all as one."

"I know it," Toussaint said. Guiaou's eyes turned to him. The yellow madras cloth made a tight line above his eyes. He stroked his jawbone as he spoke, as if the words pained him when they came out. "But Christophe has undone us. Now the Cordon of the North is lost, we must come to terms, if only for a time."

"Christophe," said Dessalines. "Christophe would never have dared to burn Le Cap without your order. And he would never have taken his head to give to the *blancs* at Le Cap without your order either. This I know."

"Believe as you choose." Toussaint's voice was hard. With his next words, it softened slightly. "When the rivers have overflowed we will fight them again. When the rains and the fevers have come. But now—let us wait for them to weaken. These new soldiers who have just come in the ships make them too strong."

"You are wrong," Dessalines said. "We ought to hold out in the mountains until that time you talk about." His left hand tightened still harder on the snuffbox. Guiaou was surprised his fingers did not bleed. "Never, never betray ourselves to them."

"Give me that box," Toussaint rapped out. For a moment, Dessalines looked purely astonished. Guiaou thought for a moment he would refuse. And then? He shifted his weight slightly, so that his hand swung a little toward the handle of his *coutelas*. At the edge of his eyes he felt Bienvenu watching him. But Dessalines relaxed and sent the box spinning across the table toward Toussaint.

"You hate tobacco," Dessalines said.

"Yes," said Toussaint. He left the box where it had stopped; he did not touch it. "Maybe you are afraid that the Captain-General will hold you to account for everyone you massacred at Saint Marc and Port-au-Prince and Petite Rivière."

"I am not afraid of anything," Dessalines said, and then, as his eyes dropped away from Toussaint's, he added: "to do with the Captain-General."

Toussaint nodded to Riau, who went on reading: *As soon as the state of the troops commanded by Dessalines shall have reached me, I will make known my intentions as to the position they should occupy—*

And Toussaint raised his hand. "He will not pursue you for anything that you have done until this day," he said. "This I have arranged for you, though not without much trouble."

To this Dessalines gave a terribly twisted smile. He turned his face toward the shuttered doorways.

"And also this—he swears, before the eyes of the Supreme Being, to respect the liberty of all people of Saint Domingue."

"And you believe it," Dessalines said.

"He has sworn it," Toussaint said. But this time it was his eyes that skated away. He got up, soundlessly, and left the room. Placide and Monpoint rose and followed him. Riau and Guerrier and Guiaou remained. Dessalines was staring at the snuffbox; the lamplight gave it a coal-like glow. He seemed to constrict still more tightly upon himself.

"If I yield one hundred times," he muttered, "I will betray them one hundred times."

Then he too got up and left the room, pocketing the snuffbox as he passed.

Guiaou swallowed. No matter the water he had just drunk, his tongue was sticky and his throat dry. The departure of the generals did not lighten the weight he felt on his chest.

"Will you come with us?" Riau was speaking to Bienvenu. But Bienvenu, instead of answering, dropped himself into the chair where Dessalines had sat. He looked at the polished sheen of the tabletop intently, as if he could still see the reflection of Dessalines's snuffbox there.

"If I give myself up one hundred times," Bienvenu repeated, "I will betray them one hundred times." He raised his head. The lamplight made his eyes look yellow.

"With Toussaint it is the same," Riau told him. "Even if he did not say so."

Now Guiaou was watching Riau, who seemed to draw the confidence Guiaou had lost up through the ground beneath the floor, through the soles of his booted feet. In his heart Guiaou believed that he himself owned more of Toussaint's trust, but Riau, who had the secret of the words on paper, owned more of Toussaint's knowledge.

Bienvenu passed a hand across his face. "Is it true?" he said.

Riau turned to Guiaou, and raised a fingertip to trace the furrow of the old sword scar that slashed down from his temple across the flesh of his cheek. This was strange, for Riau and Guiaou had not touched one another with their hands since the time long ago when they had tried to kill one another over Merbillay. They were friends now. They claimed the same children. But they did not touch. Riau moved his finger carefully, as he might have traced a line of words over paper, and Guiaou felt blood spreading under his skin, along the edges of the scar.

"It's true," Riau said. He dropped his hand, inhaled once deeply, and left the room through the door Toussaint and Dessalines had used. After a moment, the other two men followed him.

At dusk, when Doctor Hébert returned to the Cigny house, he found Zabeth and Michau crouched in the foyer, scrubbing blood from the floor with hard-bristled brushes.

"What has happened?" he said, though by the seizure of his throat he thought he knew. Zabeth gave him a stricken look.

"Madamn Elise endispozé," she said. Madame Elise has fainted.

The house felt cold, though it was not. "Where is she?" he said.

"Maman Maig' has taken her." Zabeth lowered her head over her scrub brush.

He hurried through the darkening streets. Some people were already carrying torches, and that unnerved the doctor slightly, much as he told himself the town was secure. What was to stop them setting it afire again? Maybe it had never really stopped burning.

He found Isabelle wringing her hands on the steps of the shell of the church atop the hill. Claudine stood beside the three wooden crosses, her brittle hair loosed in the wind and streaming out behind her.

The doctor stopped wordless before Isabelle. "I can't go down there," she said, twisting her head toward the trail that wrapped around the church. "It frightens me—I can't."

"It's all right," the doctor said. "I am here. You must go home."

He went to Claudine and touched her elbow. "Please take her to her house," he said. Claudine placed his hand between both of hers. For a moment he felt the stub of her missing finger pressing a vein on the back of his hand. She nodded to him, without speaking.

The way down from the church to the *lakou* was a goat path, and as he hurried through the dark the doctor lost footing on the shale and slid the remaining distance on the seat of his pants. Moustique appeared at his side to help him up. Someone shifted one of the palm panels to admit them to the *hûnfor*.

Four candles burned around the central post with its rainbow twining. The candles made a yellow orb within the bluer starlight that rained down from the sky. In the shadow behind it, some twenty feet away, was a low, squat cross with short, heavy arms. It must have always been there, the doctor supposed, but he did not remember it. It was not the cross of Christ, of that much he was certain. As he turned from it, he felt something of the fear that Isabelle had mentioned.

At the opposite end of the line the cross and central post defined, more candles had been lit around an open doorway. Hesitantly the doctor approached. The cold pressure of that dark cross lay on the back of his neck. Moustique dropped a pace behind him. Within the shelter, his sister lay on a bed of freshly cut green boughs, her eyes closed, and still as death. The doctor halted a few feet from the threshold. His breath stopped. It did not appear to him that Elise was breathing either. She was as frostily pale as the sheet that covered her.

"*Li pako mouri.*" The doctor turned his head toward the voice of Maman Maig' at his left. *She is not dead yet.* The massive figure of the *mambo* was barely distinguishable from the darkness in which she stood. He wanted to think it was all her doing, but he knew she had only done what Elise asked.

"I have the knowledge from slavery time," Maman Maig' said, as if responding to his thought. "In that time, many children were sent back, beneath the waters, before their eyes could open on the prison of their days."

The doctor could find no reply. Nanon had come up on his right side, and placed her hand on the small of his back. The warmth of her palm encouraged him. He stepped forward, knelt, and lifted Elise's limp wrist. Her pulse beat faintly, under the skin. She stirred and murmured but did not wake. He laid her arm down on the springy boughs. As he rose he saw that Fontelle and Paulette were watching him from beyond the candles.

"Do you have the knowledge to save her?" Maman Maig' said.

"No," said the doctor. "No, I don't."

"*Fok w priyé,*" Maman Maig' said. Then you must pray. After a pause she added, "We are all praying."

The doctor felt somehow calmed by this statement. He bowed to Maman Maig', brushed Nanon's cheek with his lips, and moved in the direction of the central post. Now it seemed to him that the cross on the other side of it must be the gateway of death itself, but yet it was not certain that Elise would pass through it.

Still in the dust beneath the candles was a shard of mirror he had left there long ago. He stopped to examine it, then started back. In the place where he'd expected his own features hung a star.

Placide left the mass at Marmelade, well before it had concluded— before the Act of Contrition and the Peace. Toussaint would be angry were he aware of his departure, but he was unlikely to notice from where he sat on the front bench, unfolding all the torment into his heart to the all-seeing eye of *BonDyé.* So many times in this campaign, Placide had seen Toussaint bring his remorse to the altar, like some animal he led to sacrifice, or his uncertainty, if ever he were uncertain. Toussaint emerged from these observances both salved and resolved. But lately, Placide found no balm in them. And today the decision had already been made. In an hour's time they would ride for Mornet, to make an official submission to the French.

He walked along the road that climbed from the upper edge of Marmelade in the direction of Dondon. On a high, tight turn he stopped and looked back over the town square, where still the sound of singing rose from the church, with the high chime of the priest's brass bell. It unsettled him, to the point of nausea, to be so far out of accord with his father. Though he knew his father must know better—certainly, he *must*—Placide would have followed Dessalines, to hold out in the mountains.

He took the red cloth from his pocket, shook it out in the cool dawn breeze, and bound it to his head. The band of pressure around his temples and the pressure of the knot at the base of his skull seemed to steady his focus. The irritable buzzing of his thoughts was not completely silenced, but grew quieter. It was a lesser version of the silent calm the cloth gave him for battle, a calm so deep sometimes that he would emerge on the other side of it with no memory of what had taken place or what he himself had done.

Above and below the road where he stood, many soldiers were camped in pockets on the slopes, and now Guiaou and Guerrier appeared from the mouth of a little ravine and came toward Placide— almost as if his assumption of the head cloth had called them. He smiled at the thought. He knew very well that Guiaou and Guerrier were apt to appear at his heels whenever he wandered alone from camp—it might have been at his father's order, but he thought it more likely to be their own initiative.

When they were near enough, he touched their hands and returned their smiles. Guerrier yawned and shivered slightly. It was early, the morning mist still lifting from the trees, and still a little chilly at this height. Somewhere in the jungle above the road a drum began to tap, then throb, and Placide turned his ear toward it; at the moment it had more of his sympathy than the doleful chanting still audible from the church. With the movement of his head he caught sight of Riau and Bienvenu coming up the road from town. The two of them must have also absconded from the mass.

"One day we will bring you to the drums," Guiaou said.

Placide did not answer, though his attention was well captured. A tingle ran from the back of his head down his spine. Riau had come close enough to hear that last sentence.

"His Papa will be angry if we bring him," Riau said.

"Poukisa?" said Guiaou. Why?

"He wants to give the boy's head to Jesus," Riau said.

Though they were talking past him, Placide did not mind it. Instead he found it strangely comforting.

"Do you think so?" Guiaou said. Pressing a palm against Placide's head cloth, he gave the smile turned hideous by his scars. "I don't think it was Jesus dancing in his head those times we fought the *blancs*." The smile faded. "But all that is under the eye of *BonDyé*, like everything."

"Sa," said Riau. It is so.

Behind him, Bienvenu was nodding. The edge of the sun just cleared the ridge, throwing a single beam toward the center of the square below them, and picking out an ornately garbed horseman now riding in, escorted by several drabber companions. Placide blinked and rubbed his eyes. Yes, it was his brother Isaac, wearing the dress uniform which Bonaparte had given him.

He wanted to run, but held himself in. There was a dignity to sustain, but still he strode along so quickly that a couple of times he stumbled on the gravelly descent. Isaac jumped down from his horse to embrace him, then pushed him to arm's length. Under Isaac's examination, Placide felt a certain pride that his uniform was worn and stained from his campaigning, while his brother's was pristine. Or maybe that was vanity.

"So it is finished," Isaac said. "There will be peace, after all your battles."

Placide dropped his arms, though Isaac still gripped him by the shoulders. He wasn't sure that it was meant to sting, but his brother's remark had stung him.

"And Maman?" he said, to cover his resentment.

"She is well, and sends her love to you," Isaac told him. "She stays now at Vincindière, till everything is settled, but then she will come back to Ennery."

Placide nodded. "I am glad to know that she is well, and to see you so," he said.

Isaac still gripped the points of his shoulders and searched his face, his eyes under the red band of the head cloth.

"You've changed," he said thoughtfully, and the sour bubble of Placide's ill-feeling burst into warmth.

"Yes," he said, and pulled his brother to him. "But you—you have not changed."

Then Toussaint was coming out of the church, surrounded by Monpoint and Gabart and Morisset and the others, and Isaac broke from Placide and ran to him. Placide stood aside from their embrace, thinking that after all it made some kind of sense that Isaac should somewhat resent how he'd been so much closer to their father since their return. Even if it was Isaac's own decision that had brought this difference about. *You will give in to the French, after all your battles*—well, Isaac had not phrased it quite that way. But Placide was struck by another, iron-hard thought: *Though I must bow my head to them, I will not give it.*

An hour before noon, Captain Daspir was summoned by General Hardy, who, with no explanation, led him to the stables behind the barracks on the Rue Espagnole. A pair of grooms was just leading out an enormous white stallion, who tossed his head and fought their close grip either side of the bit, eyes rolling.

"I've seen that you are something of a rider," Hardy said. "Do you suppose you can man that animal?"

"It would be my honor to try," Daspir said.

"Have at it, then," said Hardy. "Others have failed."

Daspir found it necessary to dry his palms on his trouser legs before he caught the stallion's mane and swung himself up. No sooner was he seated than the horse broke free of the hands on the bit rings and snapped his head up sharply, with a rear. Daspir had just time to turn his face aside, or his nose would surely have been broken. As it was he was half stunned by the impact, but maybe that saved him, for his first responses were all instinct; he could not spoil them by thinking. Bel

Argent bunched his legs and erupted in a great wriggling buck—Daspir felt the horse's spine worm under him like a dragon's. He held on with his knees, firm but not too tight. The reins were loose, and when the horse landed he decided to run. Daspir didn't fight him. As his head cleared, he took up some rein but put no pressure on the bit. The gate from the stableyard to the Champ de Mars was open and Bel Argent stampeded through it. A couple of sentries dove out of the way. Daspir's eyes were streaming. The hedge that bordered the parade ground was rushing up toward him and he knew that this horse could sail over it with no hesitation, but he didn't know what was on the other side, and it was time to exert some kind of control. He tightened the left rein slightly and the stallion turned and galloped more smoothly now, along the hedge.

Daspir resumed breathing. He let Bel Argent make two full-tilt circuits of the Champ de Mars, then brought him gradually to a canter, then a trot. *He was riding Toussaint's horse.* Delighted, he rode the stallion through the stable gate, still snorting and picking his feet up high, and reined him to a stop before General Hardy.

"Excellent," Hardy said. "Your abilities have not been exaggerated, Captain. You are to go with these gentlemen to Mornet—the Captain-General has a rendezvous there with Toussaint Louverture, but he is unable to be present." Hardy smiled, a little ironically. "We wanted to see you well mounted, as the distance is considerable, and the hour already late." He handed Daspir a sealed packet. "Here, take these dispatches; they are directed to Toussaint."

Guizot was a member of their party, riding a distinctly less spirited horse, and also a handsome young black colonel, Robillard. Two squadrons of cavalry provided them with a rather heavy escort—and would certainly slow their pace. Bel Argent led the procession; Daspir felt no more than a passenger, till he was inspired to divert them all from the Rue Espagnole to the Rue Vaudreuil. As he'd passionately hoped, Isabelle Cigny was taking the air on her balcony, and Daspir greeted her with a great flourish of his hat. Isabelle smiled with what appeared to be genuine amazement. She fluttered her handkerchief, and Daspir thought she might have blown him a kiss, but just then Major Maillart appeared beside her on the balcony.

He rode on, forbidding himself to look back, fingering the bullet hole in his hat. But still—it was a triumph to sit where he now sat. He remembered his first glimpse of the white stallion, with Toussaint's small, dark figure astride him, on the far side of the river at Limbé. And now— Daspir glanced at Guizot to see if he'd grasped the import of their situation. Guizot grinned back at him and even winked. Daspir replaced his hat, at a jaunty angle. Toussaint had come to terms with Leclerc, and now it looked very much as if they were going to bring him in.

. . .

In spite of everything, Placide felt his heart rising as they rode out of Marmelade, the guard almost its full two thousand strong and all their silver helmets gleaming in the rising sun. They held a brisk trot for most of the way, breaking the gait only when the grade up or down was too steep to sustain it. On the level ground on the plateau of Mornet, they broadened their line and swept into a canter, pennants streaming out behind them, then pulled up, none too sharply, before the pickets of the French advance guard there.

Leclerc was not present to receive them after all. In his place appeared General Fressinet, who made them much courtesy, inviting Toussaint and his officers to lunch in the *grand'case* of the *habitation* where he had made his camp, with a contingent of the Tenth Colonial Demibrigade and a smaller force of European soldiers. Placide sat on Toussaint's right hand, between Isaac and his father, listening to Fressinet explain how the French had made their way across the Spanish side of the island with scarcely a battle to fight. And Fressinet also had dispatches which showed that the peace between England and France had definitely been concluded. Toussaint said little to this news, but nodded and massaged his jaw, as if his old wound pained him there. On the same excuse he ate very little, taking only a glass of water and part of a soft, ripe mango which he'd peeled and cut himself.

Fressinet embraced Toussaint very warmly when the meal was finished, but when Toussaint returned to the horses, the senior officers clustered around to dissuade him from riding on to Le Cap. Morisset and Gabart, especially, feared that Leclerc's absence from the rendezvous forbode some treachery, and Gabart had sounded the men of the Tenth and thought that they might turn on the *blancs*, if given encouragement, and follow Toussaint back to the mountains of Marmelade.

Toussaint listened to their urgent whispers, still stroking his jaw and gazing past their worried faces, toward a pair of hawks circling the western edge of the plateau. One folded its wings to fall upon some prey—a smaller bird it must have been, which Placide's eye could not pick out at this distance—and then the two hawks flew away beyond the rim of the plateau, losing themselves in the green of the trees that covered the mountains. Placide shifted his eye to Isaac, who was watching Toussaint anxiously—afraid, Placide realized, that the surrender might be aborted.

"No," said Toussaint, when the others had gone silent. "With the treaty between the English and the French, there is nothing to stop more soldiers from coming here, and they will come." He smiled and wiped the smile away with his hand. "Besides, I have given my word to the Captain-General, and we must all trust to the word he has given to me."

So they rode on, descending the winding trail from the height of Mornet. The sun had reached its height by then, and the heat grew stronger as they moved onto the plain, man sweat mingling with the hot smell of the horses. Green fronds were sprouting everywhere from fields that had been burnt, though no one worked them, and some of the gateposts either side of the road were still smoke-stained. Placide and Isaac rode in a pocket formed by Riau and Bienvenu and Guiaou and Guerrier. A change of aspect in Guiaou was Placide's first signal that something was coming their way from the outskirts of Haut du Cap. A little thread of tension ran around their pocket, though no one spoke; only Isaac seemed unaware of it. When they'd ridden on another quarter-mile, Placide began to see the dust of another party of horsemen on the way out to intercept them. Someone at the fore of their column sounded a trumpet, joined by several conchs as their speed increased.

Daspir had the chance for a little more preening in the saddle of Bel Argent as they passed along the main street of Haut du Cap. Most of the soldiers of the Sixth Colonial Demibrigade stayed in barracks, though a couple of sentries appeared for a *pro forma* salute, but the women and children came in numbers almost enough to line the street, with the young girls pointing and giggling as the big white stallion passed, then hiding their embarrassment behind their hands.

At the edge of the town, Daspir's concentration tightened, because there was a big dust cloud rolling very quickly toward them down the road, long red pennants streaming above, and dots of silver gleaming within it. A brass horn sounded, then, more unnervingly, several of those squealing conchs. Mornet was still a long way off. Daspir stole a quick glance at Guizot, whose face reflected his own concern. Colonel Robillard faced strictly forward, his handsome features completely impassive.

Though there was no shock of battle contact, Toussaint's guard swept over their smaller party, reversing its direction back toward Haut du Cap. In the shifting movement, Daspir felt Bel Argent shuddering between his knees, and he slacked the rein and stroked the horse's withers. As the stallion settled, Daspir plucked out the bundle of dispatches and displayed them.

"General Louverture!" he called.

At that Bel Argent raised his head to whinny, and might have reared, but Daspir was ready and held him in. Toussaint was just a length away, but looking at his captured horse exclusively. When his eyes raised to Daspir, they were hot enough to have burned him out of the saddle. The bundle of dispatches fluttered in Daspir's hand, ignored. Toussaint, who rode no mean horse himself, turned his mount away and shouldered past. Robillard rode up then to meet him, and Daspir heard the colonel raise his voice.

"Governor, I am sent by General Christophe to say that he awaits your orders."

"I never want to hear that name," Toussaint rapped out. At the sound of his voice, Bel Argent bunched his legs and tried another buck that Daspir had more trouble containing. His tone was so sharp that Robillard's immovable expression buckled for a moment, but then Toussaint softened slightly: "I am glad to see you, Colonel Robillard," he said, "though I have no answer to give you on the subject of your mission."

Robillard's horse fell into step beside Toussaint's, and the two men continued toward Haut du Cap, talking in a tone too low for Daspir to make out what they said. They seemed to have assumed the head of the whole procession. Daspir looked back and saw a horseman with a red head cloth riding on him. Though it had almost completely healed since La Crête à Pierrot, his shoulder gave a painful throb. Daspir thought his flinch was only mental—was almost completely sure it did not show. And Placide was holding out an empty hand to him.

"*La paix*," Placide said. Peace.

Daspir put a quick, hard grip on the hand he'd offered, but Placide returned no pressure. This was the style of handclasp he'd lately learned from Guiaou and Guerrier and others like them. Let the Frenchman make of it what he would. In fact, Captain Daspir smiled at him quite warmly.

Then Isaac rode up and leaned half out of his saddle to give Daspir his full embrace. Placide watched the white hands settle either side of his brother's spine. Bel Argent's dark eye rolled toward him. That his father should see an enemy astride his favorite horse and not swipe his head off with his long sword—it was then Placide had realized the surrender was truly inevitable.

He pulled the red cloth from his head and folded it in a careful triangle and put it into his pocket for some other day—the future that Toussaint might still secretly be planning. The French tricolor he'd snatched from Daspir's hands at Gonaives still rode on its shortened stave in the holster by his boot, and beside the holster hung the silver helmet of the guard. Since Guiaou had given it to him, Placide had preferred the headcloth in every fight, for protection and for inspiration too. He would not look at Guiaou now, but loosened and raised the helmet and buried his whole head inside.

As they returned through Haut du Cap, the whole of the Sixth, with Clairvaux himself, turned out to salute them with cheers and musket shots and hats tossed in the air. Half an hour later, when they reached the gate of Le Cap itself, the same military honors were rendered them. There were even cannons firing salutes from a couple of the ships out in the harbor, quite as though Toussaint were entering in triumph.

In the second rank of the riders, Daspir could not help but feel a little disregarded. He caught Guizot's eye in hope of encouragement, but Guizot seemed to have suffered a similar drop in his own spirits. Only when he saw Paltre among the onlookers crowding the gateway did Daspir feel moved to some display of bravado.

"You see, we *have* brought him in at the last!" *Rag-headed Negro* . . . In fact, the yellow madras binding Toussaint's head was what led them through the gate. Daspir would have liked to flourish his sword, but settled for a big sweep of his hat. Paltre looked more flabbergasted than impressed. He stood with his mouth open, massaging the bridge of his twice-broken nose. Then, as if struck by some other thought, he twisted and ducked away through the thickening crowd.

Daspir shot another glance at Guizot, who did no more than shrug. Well, Paltre had been queer in recent days, ever since his quarrel with the doctor. Let it pass. And this entry *was* a triumph, never mind whose. Daspir pressed Bel Argent with his knees and urged him forward through the cheering crowd, moving just behind the head of the column, toward the center of town.

Leclerc had lunched aboard ship with the Vice-Admiral Magon; it was cooler there, and the fresh harbor breeze relieved the fevers that still plagued him. Also, this situation gave him respite from Pauline's plaintive interruptions. She was ever more discontent with the noise and dust of Le Cap under reconstruction and wished to return, if not to France, again to La Tortue (with of course a whole covey of lovers from the officer corps) or to Port-au-Prince, where she'd discovered a large plantation to her liking. And with Magon there was much to discuss: the dubious quality and insufficient quantity of supplies and reinforcement trickling out of France, the quite unreasonable demands of the Minister of Marine that several key vessels of Leclerc's fleet be returned to the home port . . .

They had moved to the afterdeck, for their digestion and discussion, when the shots began exploding around the lower gate of the town. Once the cannons began to bark from the ships deeper in the harbor, Leclerc felt a stirring of alarm; the cannonade was in the style of a salute, but who was being so honored?

Then his eye fell on a rowboat pulling rapidly to their ship from the shore, though it went against the tide. An officer stood precariously in the bow, gesticulating; when the boat came astern, Leclerc recognized Captain Paltre. He was shouting with such fervor that spittle flew out of his mouth to mingle with the sea foam, but the wind carried most of his words away.

"What?" said Leclerc, cupping his ear as he leaned over the rail, and now he made out the phrase, *Toussaint has come*. At once he swung his legs over the rail and scrambled down a knotted rope, rocking the boat so deeply that Paltre had to crouch and clutch the gunwales to stop from being catapulted into the water. Captain Cyprien came clambering down after him.

"Toussaint has come," Paltre repeated.

"To make his submission," Leclerc said, with much more confidence than he felt. Only that morning he had suddenly decided that the rendezvous at Mornet was not secure enough for his liking and that he would send instead another emissary—Daspir, whom he would not object to losing.

"Yes, so they claim." Paltre turned and pointed. "But he has come with two thousand horsemen, and the people are cheering him like a conqueror wherever he goes."

"You do well to tell me." Leclerc swallowed, and shouted up an order to Magon—that he should make the ships ready for an assault on the town if it were needed. Then he gestured to the oarsmen that they must return to the shore with all possible speed.

In the early morning Doctor Hébert had passed by Morne Calvaire to look in upon his sister, who lay still pale and feeble on her bed of boughs, though she did not look so moribund as before. Her bleeding had slowed, though not entirely stopped, the women told him. She had no strength and did not speak to him. How it would go with her was most uncertain, the doctor thought. Sophie had come with him on the morning visit, with Paul—they were both frequent visitors to the *lakou* anyway, but the infant Mireille had been kept away by Isabelle. Afterward the doctor had sent Sophie and Paul back to the Cigny house. Though Sophie had a whim to try her hand at nursing in the hospital, the doctor thought Elise would not have liked the risk, and besides, there was some party of pleasure being organized for the children with Dermide Leclerc and Saint-Jean Louverture.

Worry for Elise kept him from settling to any concentrated work. Though at first he'd been relieved by Tocquet's absence, now he very much wished he'd return. Before she—he wouldn't think that. But often he rose from whatever task and drifted to the hospital gate, looking through the ironwork as if he expected some arrival.

Midafternoon there was a tumult in the lower part of the town, punctured by salvoes of gunfire too orderly to be that of battle. Some parade exercise most likely, but what? At last he saw Captain Cyprien coming up toward the gate, his figure distorted by the shimmer of the afternoon heat.

"Have you any men fit enough to bear arms?"

"Very few," said the doctor, startled.

"Turn them out, whoever you have—the Captain-General's order." Cyprien looked over his shoulder. "Look to your own weapons too—it is a general muster—army, militia, everyone."

"Are we under attack?" The doctor unchained the gate for Cyprien to come in, and went to get his pistols from a bag that hung on a stob of a tree above his hammock.

"Toussaint has arrived," said Cyprien. "To surrender—they say—but he has brought a great many men with him for that purpose, and they seem to have invested the Government House."

The doctor canvassed the pick of his malaria and dysentery cases, and with this escort of unfortunate conscripts they went staggering through the blazing heat across Rue Espagnole. A stronger contingent of troops was filing down from the barracks higher on the hill. All halted below the gate of the Government, where the doctor found Tocquet and Arnaud waiting by the gate along with Major Maillart.

"Well met," said Tocquet. He pulled the doctor to him and kissed his cheeks. "We have not returned an hour from La Tortue, and what do we find? It looks like a double encirclement."

The doctor peered through the bars of the gate. What he saw made Tocquet's remark seem quite reasonable. Hundreds of Toussaint's guardsmen stood in ranks in the courtyard, holding their sabers bare. They stood in pairs by the smoke-stained trunk of every palm that lined the avenue and lined the stairway that rose to the main entrance of the building. The gathering French troops, meanwhile, were all without, and had filled every street on the square surrounding the Government compound.

"And Leclerc?" said the doctor.

"He has already gone in," Arnaud said.

"And let us follow," Tocquet said, with a glance at Maillart, who pushed the gate inward. No one opposed them. Cyprien followed them through, though he pushed the gate back against other French soldiers who might also have come in. They walked slowly up the avenue of palms. With every step the pistol butts scraped awkwardly under the doctor's loose shirt, and the stony eyes of Toussaint's guardsmen inclined him to hold his breath. The brilliant sunlight reflected on the edges of those naked blades. It was quiet, too quiet—even the crows in the high palm crowns had ceased all palaver. But on the steps the doctor recognized Riau and Guiaou, and they smiled and took his hands briefly when he offered them.

The Government building had been much restored, though it still smelled faintly of soot and smoke. But in the grand salon a number of attendants were laying long tables for a meal, and there the stronger smell was of spiced beef. They went on down the corridor to a doorway to the Governor's cabinet, where others had clustered. The hall was crowded but by standing tiptoe the doctor could see Leclerc's small form, puffed as full as a rooster's but overshadowed by the Generals Hardy and Debelle on either side of him. Leclerc inclined his blond head to the oath of loyalty to France that Toussaint was reciting to him in a low but quite clear tone.

"He's actually submitting," Tocquet breathed in the doctor's ear. "It astonishes me."

"Why?" the doctor whispered, without turning his head.

"He was winning," Tocquet said, then fell silent.

When Toussaint had finished his oration, Leclerc raised his voice to address him:

"General, one can only praise and admire when one has seen how well you have borne the burden of the government of Saint Domingue. Your presence in this city is proof of your magnanimity and your good faith.

Our reconciliation will make this island, of which you have been the restorer, flower again, and will consolidate the new institutions which are the fundamental basis for the liberty and happiness of all."

Toussaint passed a hand over his mouth and replied, "Since the people of Saint Domingue had just triumphed in a foreign war—both for France and for themselves—they did not think that they would ever have to resist the protective power of France. If some notification had preceded you in this island, the cannons would only have fired to honor the envoy of a great power, and you would only have been illuminated, upon your arrival, by fires of celebration and joy."

Tocquet laughed out loud at that remark, and several people in the hallway turned to stare at him, though he was unabashed. Toussaint went on in this vein for about five minutes, and Leclerc's response, though cordial, was a little tight-lipped: "Let us not cling to any memory of the past," he said; "everything will be repaired; let us rather rejoice, General, in our union."

He turned then, and beckoned everyone waiting in the hallway to crowd into the cabinet, where he repeated his declaration that all Toussaint's officers would be maintained in their grades as they were incorporated into the French army, and that the liberty of all citizens of Saint Domingue would be eternal.

As the echo of those fine phrases died, there was a fresh commotion in the corridor, and the doctor turned to see Isabelle and Pauline Leclerc approaching, with Nanon and many of the children of their household. Saint-Jean Louverture broke out of the pack and rushed to throw himself on his father—it was unclear who was lifting whom, since Toussaint was scarcely taller than the boy. Toussaint kissed him and rubbed his head hard, and Saint-Jean swung around to wrap his arms around both his elder brothers at once, while the French generals smiled at his enthusiasm. Leclerc, meanwhile, was urging them all toward the grand salon; the double doors had been opened and the aroma of peppered beef was stronger than before.

As they shuffled in, the doctor recalled the day before the town was burned, when he'd glimpsed Leclerc's envoy Lebrun dining in solitary splendor here, from an extravagant service of gold plate which must have since been looted, if not melted in the fire. An equally opulent service was laid before them now, just recently cast, so the rumor ran, from coin sent out to pay the troops.

Maillart tested the weight of a fork in his hand, and clicked it rather moodily against his plate, but he said nothing. Tocquet, with a somewhat cursory nod at Pauline Leclerc, bowed over Isabelle's hand and murmured some compliment, then, raising his eyes to her face, he said, "And my lady wife?"

"She is indisposed." Isabelle had colored slightly. "Of course she did not expect you or she would certainly have come."

The doctor turned his face away, but Tocquet said no more on the subject, perhaps distracted by the bowls of beef and rice that were being served, or more likely by some bottles of very presentable red wine. Toussaint, he noticed, took neither wine nor meat nor anything at all but a piece of bread from a whole loaf and a square of cheese carefully dissected from the center of the wheel. He gazed rather gloomily at an equestrian portrait of himself which had been hastily replaced at the far end of the salon once Leclerc got wind of his arrival, and seemed scarcely to attend to the blandishments of Pauline Leclerc, who had been seated to his right.

Placide saw that Daspir had come into the salon and taken a seat with Cyprien and Guizot and Paltre at the lower end of the table, where Christophe was also, with Robillard, but as far from Toussaint as might be. His father studiously avoided looking in that direction. Riau and Guiaou had joined Christophe and the other officers, and seemed to be speaking with Christophe civilly enough, though the group was too distant for Placide to make out what they said. He wondered if what Dessalines had claimed could be true—that Toussaint's hidden hand had moved Christophe to his surrender—and yet his father's coldness seemed so genuine. As they entered the salon, Toussaint had even snubbed his brother Paul, for yielding Santo Domingo City to the French without authority—"You ought to have been guided by my example," Toussaint had said, and turned his back—all this in spite of the tale of the false dispatches which Guiaou had brought.

Pauline Leclerc, feigning to be wounded at Toussaint's indifference to her, had turned her attention to the green parakeet that walked over her bare shoulders and her arms, leaving tiny pink claw marks on her delicate skin, and repeating in a monotone, "How beautiful you are." Then Isabelle Cigny leaned across the doctor and drew Pauline into some other conversation, commiserating with her homesickness for Paris, with its luxuries and entertainments, the sharper changes of its seasons . . .

Leclerc turned to Toussaint and said, "Tell me, General, if you had chosen to continue the struggle, how would you have procured your arms and ammunition?"

Toussaint turned and smiled more naturally than Placide had seen him do since he left the church at Marmelade that morning. "Why," he said. "I would have taken them from you."

At the far end of the table, Daspir was doing what he could, which was not much, to dissuade Paltre from a stupid jape he kept trying on Christophe. Paltre had filled Christophe's glass with wine, but the black general did not want it. As often as Christophe poured it back into the bottle, Paltre refilled the glass and, with a fixed grin, set it again before him. Paltre was already drunk, Daspir saw, and certainly on something stronger and rougher than this wine, and no one, least of all Christophe, was in any humor for this teasing. Robillard and the other black captains who sat with him, especially that one with the terrible scars, had all gone very silent and grave. But Paltre would not notice Daspir's nudging.

At the fifth reprise, Christophe crushed the balloon of the wine glass with a quick movement of his large hand, then held out his palm, full of wine and blood mingled, under Paltre's nose.

"You desire to see me drink?" he said, in a grating tone that carried from one end of the room to the other. "Before today, I have drunk blood from the skulls of little white men like you. Insist, and one day I will drink a toast from yours."

For one grisly instant the whole room fell silent; even the ringing of silverware stopped. Leclerc and the others at the head of the table must certainly have heard what Christophe had said, and yet they affected not to, until Pauline shrilled out some pleasantry which Isabelle took up and extended. Daspir yearned toward Isabelle, hopelessly since she was many places distant from him. Christophe wiped his palm clean with a napkin and squeezed it in his hand to stop the bleeding, lowering the balled cloth to his knees. With his left hand he spooned up a morsel of his food, and Robillard and the others started some semblance of conversation.

Only Paltre remained immobile, pale and staring, as if Christophe's words had transfixed him physically. A yellow sweat gathered on the fine hairs at his temple and in the creases of his broken nose. It had just occurred to Daspir that Paltre must really be unwell (not merely drunk as usual), when Paltre flopped out of his seat to the floor—as he fell, a great quantity of black vomit rolled out of his mouth as if poured from a bowl. Daspir started up and back before the vile-smelling stuff could reach his shoes—he looked for Doctor Hébert, who was already hurrying down toward them.

"What's the matter with him?" Guizot said uneasily.

The doctor looked up from where he'd squatted by Paltre's head, to take a pulse from his limp arm. "*Mal de Siam*," he said shortly. "The yellow fever. Come on, we've got to get him out of here."

Another pall of silence had fallen over the room. Daspir reached down to get a grip, but Guizot had already raised Paltre's shoulders and two of the black guardsmen, the scarred one and the one they called Riau, had taken his feet. Empty-handed and feeling quite useless, Daspir followed them toward the door. A servant had come to mop up the vomit. As they left the room, the babble of festivity was gradually renewed.

"*Fatigué?*" The little boy's voice held more curiosity than concern. Tired? And truly, Elise felt so exhausted she could scarcely turn her head to look at him. Little Dieufait—child of Marie-Noelle and Moustique. He looked at her round-eyed, pleasantly smiling.

"*Pa kè. Fatigué!*" he said, brightly and conclusively. No heart—tired!

With that matter decided, Dieufait skipped out of the door of Elise's chamber, singing a snatch of song as he capered.

Palé O, Palé O
La fanmi Asefi a palé O
Asefi ki jeté youn pitit sèt mwa . . .

A couple of the other children scampered around him, taking up the song, until the low rumble of Maman Maig' 's voice drove them out of the enclosure. Elise heard their voices spreading and fading over the steeper slopes above the *lakou*.

Asefi ki jeté youn pitit sèt mwa
Asefi ki jeté youn pitit sèt mwa
Pitit se byen O, palé O . . .

Dieufait did not mean to wound her; this she knew. The children scarcely knew the meaning of the words they sang. He had not even meant to call her heartless. It was only a Creole expression for exhaustion, which was all she felt. A light fever had come over her, though she thought it had little to do with her bleeding or the child she had thrown off. It was only a new visit from some old fever which had found its way to her again, now she was weak. The fever put her pain at a distance. It jumbled her memory and confused her waking with her sleep. She didn't know how long it had been since Maman Maig' had made the second effort between her legs with her long wooden spoon. She didn't know how much blood had poured out of the cavern the spoon had opened in her body.

But now a shadow blocked the doorway and Paulette came and knelt beside her and with her fingertips began to massage the area between her navel and her *fente*. Fontelle stood behind her, looking on.

"You must try it yourself," Fontelle said. "This rubbing is the only thing to close the hole the blood comes from."

But Elise had no heart for that effort either. She only submitted to the aching pressure of Paulette's fingers, and thanked her weakly when she had gone. Almost hourly, one of the women came to her with their hands, Paulette or Fontelle or Marie-Noelle or Nanon, and sometimes Maman Maig', though most often Maman Maig' only stood by to advise and instruct the others.

Paulette had let the white drape fall over the doorway when she left, to shield Elise from the lowering afternoon sun. She had raised Elise's feet, and Elise felt her head begin to swell, with the fever's rising. There was some unusual noise in the town below—regular volleys of gunfire, and cannons from the direction of the harbor, but it did not much interest or worry her, though it did disturb her sleep. In half-delirium she seemed to struggle through a viscous fluid, a ghostly underwater world where everything was floating and the seaweed-tendriled shapes near her were somehow presences. One of those fetal forms abruptly rolled and raised its head from the blood in which it had been drowned and opened a hole in its skull to grin at her.

She woke with a terrible start, but the scream that she'd heard was not her own. No sound in her chamber but the sick, quick beating of her heart. The white drape had been raised from her doorway and she could see out past the striped central post to the shadow of the squat low cross beyond it. It was full dark now; she saw by starlight and by the light of candles waxed to small stones here and there. Someone was drumming, but she could not see the drums. The figure of Claudine Arnaud stood by the center post: fixed, rigid, shuddering. It was not Claudine herself who had screamed, Elise understood. The scream had only come through her.

Then Claudine's body collapsed, as though the tendons that strung her limbs had melted, and Maman Maig' appeared to catch her and cradle her in the vast cushion of her body, till whatever it was that occupied Claudine shook itself free of the *mambo* and rose. Moustique came toward her, cautiously, not quite cringingly.

"*Maîtresse Erzulie!*" he whispered as he offered his gifts: a comb, a round hand mirror, bright beads, and a small bottle of perfume. But Claudine's hands dashed the offerings to the ground. The perfume bottle spilled into the dirt, releasing a weak musk. Claudine—it was not Claudine—seized up the mirror and crouched to beat it against a stone. Rising again, she curled her fingers into claws and raked two vertical slashes on her cheek.

"*Sé Ezili Jé Rouj li yé.*" Maman Maig' 's voice was calm, even detached. Moustique retreated, out of Elise's line of sight. Erzulie Jé Rouj was turning, marching straight toward her where she lay. As she approached, her figure blocked the shadow of the cross.

"*Ki moun ki rélé mwen?*" she said, her voice tight with fury. Who called me?

Elise's eyes fixed on the gleam of blood within the furrows of the nail cuts. She could not answer; it was as if a heavy chain lay across her tongue, but still she felt she was responsible—guilty, rather—for summoning the apparition.

"That was not your dream, white woman," Erzulie Jé Rouj pronounced. "You dreamed the dream of the *blanche*, Claudine Arnaud—it was *she* who cut the child unborn from the mother's belly, long ago and yesterday and always, and ever since the child has walked with her. Would you walk with them, white woman? Would you dream that dream, with them?"

I'd rather die, Elise was thinking, but still she could speak no word.

Ezili cocked her head toward the street below the *lakou*. The light of the candles around the doorway shimmered in the burning tears that filled her eyes. "Listen," she said. "Can you hear them there?"

Elise strained her ears but could hear nothing. Even the drums were silent now.

"Toussaint has come to give his head to the *blanc* general," Ezili said, and of a sudden she shrieked and tore at her hair, and tears spilled into the cuts along her cheek. "Do you know? We might all have saved each other. Toussaint carried that dream to the crossroads, but the *blancs* will not let it pass the gate. Now we have seen it die aborning. Now it must wait unborn four hundred years." She threw away the fistfuls of hair she had torn from her head and scratched up dirt from the ground to pound into her face.

Though she choked with terror, Elise was also inspired with a terrible pity for the being before her, though she knew it was much stronger than herself. All its power was for self-destruction. And she, herself, could not reach or comfort it. From the soles of her feet to the roof of her mouth she was frozen. She could neither speak nor weep.

From the shadows near the entrance of the *hûnfor*, the doctor and Tocquet watched as the figure of Claudine Arnaud rose from beside Elise's couch, turned, and swept toward them. It passed them blind, twin gashes shining red on its cheek, and went into the dark beyond the gateway. A rustle up the doctor's spine moved in the direction of its movement, like iron dust following a magnet.

"What is it?" he said—to Moustique, who had followed Claudine in the direction of the gate and now was hesitating near them.

"You might do better to ask the spirit that touched you," Moustique said. His gangling grasshopper's silhouette was very still in the weak blend of light from the stars and the candles. Though his voice was not exactly unfriendly, his usual ingratiating manner had dropped away from him.

The doctor glanced at Tocquet, who looked unastonished by anything that had happened since they had left the feast of Toussaint's surrender to come here. In truth, the doctor was not much astonished either. It all seemed strange but inevitable.

"That is Ezili Jé Rouj who has passed," Moustique said. "She come for one reason or another. Sometimes she comes to send back children who are not wanted here."

"And Madame Arnaud?" the doctor said.

"She is the spirit you have called out of your own need," Moustique said, but the doctor thought he was not yet speaking of Claudine, or not entirely of her. "She sees what you don't know you see, and says what you can't say." He paused, turning his large head in silhouette against the vague light of the harbor. "Madame Arnaud will return to herself," he said. "Now I will go to her." He lowered his head and went past them through the gate.

A wind came up and swirled around the *hûnfor*. The candles were all cunningly shielded with angled stones, so that their flames guttered but did not die. The shrouded figures of the women stood about the enclosure, bending slightly with the wind, like trees. The doctor thought that these were Paulette and Marie-Noelle and Fontelle, but he could not distinguish them one from another, except for Maman Maig', by her bulk. Four candles flickered around the doorway of Elise's chamber. She lay on the branches, still, but still living.

"So," Tocquet said, rocking back to his heels as the wind faded. "What is it that this spirit sees, that we can't say?"

The doctor said nothing. They had come here to visit Elise, but the descent of the spirit had held them back, and still an invisible membrane seemed to divide them from her. He had let Tocquet know that Elise had miscarried, but no more.

"*Pitit sé byen-o*," Tocquet whispered. Children are riches. There was just the ghost of a tune in his words. The doctor kept his silence. His mind ran to Paltre, borne to the hospital two hours before. Cases of the yellow fever were increasing day by day.

"Your sister and I have had fair days and foul ones," Tocquet said. "I think you have been by to see some of both. You must know that with all that has passed, I would never raise a hand to harm her, no matter what she did. Had done. Do you care to tell me any more?"

"No," said the doctor.

"Well," Tocquet said, and almost with an air of relief. "Perhaps it's better so."

Maman Maig' broke out of her stillness and moved toward the chamber where Elise lay. They watched her lower herself beside the couch of branches.

"I think we may as well leave them now," Tocquet said. "I will come again tomorrow."

"Yes," said the doctor, and Tocquet nodded.

As they turned to leave the *hûnfor*, Tocquet did something that struck the doctor as strange, though he had sometimes seen the black men do it. He took the doctor's hand in his own, and held it lightly for a pace or two, as they passed through the gate together, and then he let it go.

Maman Maig' 's smooth round face appeared in Elise's vision like the rising of a full black moon. For some time after Ezili had left her, she had been drifting blurrily on the tides of her fever. But now as her eyes opened, her mind was clear and the pain was nearer to her than it had been before.

"Where is the child?" she said.

"*Anba dlo*," Maman Maig' said. Beneath the waters. She touched Elise on the cheek with her blunt finger: the spot where Ezili's scars had been. "Don't be afraid," she said. "Yours is not alone. Many, many have been sent back. When it would have been worse for them to live."

Elise felt the sting as her tears spilled over the bone of her eye sockets. Maman Maig' nodded, content to see her cry.

"Bay'l dlo nan je'w," she said, encouraging. Give him water from your eyes. Her voice was gentler than Elise had ever heard it. "You are coming back to the world now." She held Elise's head between her hands. "There is no death," she said. "There's only change."

Isaac was troubled, Placide felt, when Captain Paltre toppled from his place at the table, and convulsed with his vomiting on the floor. Isaac might even have gone to assist him, but Placide touched his knee beneath the table to hold him back. He himself felt only an abstract interest. The illness of Daspir or Guizot would have touched him more.

Toussaint was watching, his attention pointed, as Doctor Hébert went down the table to direct Paltre's removal from the hall. He said no word and made no gesture, but Placide felt a phrase from long ago appear in his mind, as plainly as if his father had repeated it aloud. *Konpè Général Lafièvre . . .*

The banquet did not last much longer. When Toussaint had concluded his courtesies with Leclerc, all of them mounted and rode from the town. By midnight they had regained the camp of General Fressinet on the Mornet plateau, and there they halted for what remained of the night. Toussaint slept soundly, next to Isaac, surrounded by two thousand of his guard, but Placide volunteered for the watch. A very considerable guard had been posted, considering that all hostilities had officially ended. Placide stayed with Riau and Guiaou, who remained alert but completely silent, till the first roosters began to crow at dawn.

At first light they rode to Marmelade, and there Toussaint dismissed his guard, as he had agreed with Leclerc to do. For a quarter-hour he spoke to the men, praising their courage and their devotion, and finally recommending them all to the way of peace. When he had done, he embraced all of the officers, and many of the men came to embrace him too, and some could not stop themselves from crying. Placide felt himself begin to weaken, from the exhaustion of the last day and night and the longer, deeper weariness of the whole campaign, but he kept his eyes dry, distracting himself by changing into civilian clothes and packing away his uniform and helmet. The red cloth Guiaou had given him he kept folded in the pocket of his shirt.

Guiaou and Guerrier had vanished with the main body of the guard, which was meant to report back to Leclerc at Le Cap, but Riau and Bienvenu were riding with them still, part of the much smaller escort that accompanied them from Marmelade on the ascent of Pilboreau, divested of their uniforms, though carrying their arms. Only Isaac still wore the dress uniform of Bonaparte's gift, seemingly unaware of its incongruity.

On the height of Pilboreau, Dessalines awaited them, with a larger force than now rode with Toussaint. Both generals dismounted, to confer for half an hour's time. Toussaint let Dessalines know that although Leclerc was not willing to give him a military post immediately (as he had done with Christophe and most of the other generals), Dessalines's surrender had been accepted with Toussaint's, and he need not expect to be pursued. If Dessalines did not seem wholly content with this news, he did not voice any objection to it either. In silence, he rode away with his men toward Marchand, where he was supposed to retire to Habitation Georges.

Toussaint was bound to follow the same road, as far as Ennery, where he'd elected to retire on his plantations, but he lingered a little while on Pilboreau, so as not to follow too closely on the heels of Dessalines. The market at the crossroads was uncharacteristically silent; indeed no trading was taking place, and the women did not even cry their wares. All were silent at their places, but gradually more and more people began to filter out of the foggy trees on either side of the road, men and women and children alike, until the crowd of onlookers numbered some hundreds.

At last, as Toussaint climbed to his horse, a woman in a spotted head-cloth called to him.

"Papa Toussaint, have you abandoned us?"

Toussaint took off his hat and stared for a moment into the crown of it, then looked at the woman who had spoken, and swept his gaze over all the people who were there.

"No, my children," he said finally. "Your brothers are still under arms, and the officers are at their posts."

As they moved out, the crowd moved with them, but silently, and conserving a little distance—the people never came within hand's reach. When Placide had passed this way in their first return to Ennery, he'd felt the boundaries between himself and all the others wash away, and the bitterness of the difference between that day and this one was so large he had to struggle to swallow it. The others all rode with their heads bowed low, and even Isaac looked a little uncertain—not quite so happy as he had been earlier, to be restored to the bosom of France.

Gradually the crowd fell away behind them. A few children ran behind the horses, till their mothers called them back. And always, at every bend of the descending road, appeared a couple of people, four or five or half a dozen, to watch solemnly after them as they rode deeper into solitude.

39

When Elise's eyes opened, a shadow lay over her, hawk-beaked and dark. It blocked the brilliant light of the sun beyond the doorway, and so at first she was afraid, believing that the demon of that low black cross had come for her, but the words of Maman Maig' sounded in her head, *You are coming back to the world.* Two hands were holding one of her own and stroking it, down into the hollow of her wrist where her pulse beat closest under the skin. She saw Dieufait with one of the little girls of the *lakou,* watching from beyond the threshold: curious, tentative, half amused.

It was a little longer before the features of Xavier Tocquet came clear in the indoor shade, and as she recognized him, he let go her hand and traced a line from the corner of her eye down to her jaw below her ear. When his finger first indented her skin, she had to control an impulse to flinch, but his touch was gentle all along its track.

"You've had a bad time," he said. "But you've lived through it."

He shifted his head, and a blade of light struck through the doorway into her face. Her eyes were aching in her sockets. But before she could speak, he laid his forefinger across her lips.

"Don't say it." He paused. "I haven't told you everything. We can be better quit of this without a word."

He took away his finger, but Elise said nothing. She could see his eyes more plainly now; they looked distant to her, considering.

"Sometimes one has to live alone with what one knows," he said.

She nodded. It seemed to her that the cool sensation of his finger sealed her voice still. He lifted a bowl from the ground and gave her water. As she swallowed, the two children smiled and ducked their heads and skipped out of the doorway.

"Sophie is waiting," Tocquet said. "And Mireille. Will you come back?"

"I'm ready," Elise said.

The pain in her lower abdomen was duller than before when she struggled to sit up. Tocquet got an arm under her shoulders and helped her to her feet. As they stepped out together, he put his own straw hat on her head to shield her from the sun. The irregular circle of the *hûnfor* rocked around her for a second or two, then stabilized. Everyone who watched her emerge—Paulette, Fontelle, Marie-Noelle, and her husband's familiars Gros-Jean and Bazau—had shrunk to the palm panels of the perimeter to seek whatever shreds of shade could be found in the midday sun.

Tocquet released her and walked to where Maman Maig' stood motionless beside the striped *poteau mitan*. When he let go, Elise felt a reel, but it was only inward; she was standing solidly enough on her own two feet. The lank, dark rope of Tocquet's hair lay as always between his shoulder blades, secured with its thong, but when he lowered his head, she saw for the first time that the skin of his scalp showed indistinctly through the hair on top. He had taken both Maman Maig' 's hands in his and dropped his forehead to her breastbone, and in this gesture Elise saw that he really did value her own life and wanted for her to remain with him.

"Eh, Madame . . ." Bazau and Gros-Jean were both hurrying toward her, solicitous, for now she really had begun to swoon, the straw hat slipping sideways on her head as her knees began to dissolve. But Tocquet reached her first. He put one arm around her waist and the other hand under her elbow, and so, with Gros-Jean leading and Bazau following, supported her down the narrow twisting trail from the *lakou* to the corner of the street below, where a carriage waited.

General Pamphile de Lacroix, clothed in the finest dress uniform that campaigning in such a climate had left him, walked from the dockside up the slope toward the Government House, in the company of Major Maillart. The afternoon heat was beginning to abate, and people of every color and station were emerging from the afternoon siesta onto the streets, yet no one took any particular notice of the French general's passage—no more than to step just barely out of his way as he advanced. So far as Maillart could see, Lacroix did not take exception to this failure of respect. He was an amiable, practical man, far less attached to the protocols of his rank than most of the French general officers.

Then as they reached the Rue Espagnole, they crossed a rumor of the coming of General Dessalines, who was arriving to present his compli-

ments to Captain-General Leclerc for the first time since the peace.
When Dessalines did appear on the street, the people who lined the narrow walkway under the balconies, men and women and children alike,
of every color without distinction, prostrated themself before his passage, bowing so deeply that the dust of the street whitened their hair.
Only Isabelle Cigny and Claudine Arnaud, who happened to be standing
near the gate of the Government compound, took no special notice of
Dessalines's arrival. They remained upright, Isabelle willowy and Claudine somewhat rigidly so, under the parasol that Isabelle held to cover
both of them. Dessalines's eyes swept across the two women, though if
he had actually taken any notice of them was hard to discern. The gate to
the compound opened to him, with salutes and the sounding of a trumpet, and he strode up in the direction of the building.

"Madame Cigny, Madame Arnaud," Maillart said. "I present you the
General Pamphile de Lacroix—my commander at Port-au-Prince and
the battle of La Crête à Pierrot, and a very good soldier on behalf of us
all."

Isabelle smiled and dropped a courtsey. Claudine offered her left
hand; Maillart watched Lacroix subdue his start when the stump of her
missing finger bumped his palm.

"The General has come from Port-au-Prince," Maillart went on. "He
will remain here with us for a short time before going on to take up a
post in the Cibao Mountains."

"Ah," said Isabelle. "And how did you find the situation in the west?"

"I find that my departure is precipitate," said Lacroix. "Like that of the
General Boudet not long ago. The colonial troops of that region no
longer see before them the generals who led their last campaign, and so
their natural mistrust becomes more active."

"You are frank," Isabelle smiled, and tapped his cuff with the edge of
her fan. "I like that in a general."

"I like a lady who will not bow before that slaughterer who has just
passed," Lacroix said. "As I noticed you did not. When I think of the massacres at Verrettes and Petite Rivière and Saint Marc—"

"Indeed, one prefers not to think of them," Isabelle said, as if to arrest
his indiscretion. "As for the others—his power awes or terrifies them."

"Madame." Lacroix inclined his head. "Your perception of that matter
seems most clear."

"Thank you," said Isabelle. "I am at home this evening. Major Maillart
is most familiar with the way." With a smile she stroked his coat sleeve
with her light fingers, then put her hand on Claudine Arnaud's elbow and
led her, unblinking and apparently oblivious to anything that had
occurred, away along the busying street.

With Lacroix, Maillart walked into the Government compound, up
the stairs through the main door, and down the corridor. In the Captain-
General's anteroom, Dessalines turned toward Lacroix, though he

looked over his shoulder, at the newly plastered fire cracks in the wall, instead of meeting the French general's eyes.

"I am the General Dessalines," he said in a harsh voice. "In unhappy times I have heard much talk of you."

For a moment Lacroix did not reply; then Leclerc emerged from the inner cabinet to give him some brief and dismissive instruction, even as he walked Dessalines inside. Soon Maillart and Lacroix were retracing their steps, back along the corridor and down the steps toward the gate.

"He must feel himself very strong to strike that attitude," Lacroix muttered. Maillart turned toward him to catch, in a still lower voice, almost a whisper: "I don't suppose he will look so assured once chained in the hold of a brig bound for France."

"He is to be deported, then," Maillart said, scanning his eyes suspiciously over all the people streaming past him along the Rue Espagnole. "When Leclerc has just assigned him a new command?"

"That action is against the instruction of the First Consul," Lacroix said shortly, as they turned uphill toward the Champ de Mars. "He has ordered quite plainly that Leclerc must rid himself of all the leaders of the insurrection. Thus far he has failed to comply."

Maillart looked at him curiously. The reasons for Leclerc's reliance on black troops and their officers was no mystery; he'd heard Lacroix discuss it before. With so many of his European troops either slain or in hospital, Leclerc had scarcely any other force to rely on. But he made no comment, for the hospital was their destination and now its gate was visible, just at the end of the block.

As the afternoon sun declined behind the wall above the ravine, the doctor watched Madame Fortier watch Nanon, who crouched, beside the pallet of Captain Paltre, spooning a clear broth between his slack jaws. The other three captains leaned against the wall, also observing this procedure, scraping their shoulders on the rough-laid brick as they shifted their feet, but Madame Fortier did not spare them so much as an ironic glance. In recent days she had appointed herself in charge of the whole crew of nurses here, who accepted her authority without a murmur. What moved her the doctor couldn't have said, though he thought it could not be any special affection for the invading French soldiers.

Paltre choked and turned his head to one side, gagging, projecting a stream of black, foul-smelling vomit onto the ground beside his pallet. At the snap of Madame Fortier's fingers another of the nurses came forward to clean the vile stuff up. As Paltre subsided, weak and gasping, Madame Fortier scraped a little loose dirt over the residue of the vomit with the side of her shoe.

Paltre's eyes drifted shut. Nanon laid a hand on his forehead, turning an ear toward the ragged sound of his breathing. Then she withdrew her hand and stood up, smoothing her skirts and coolly returning the gaze of the three captains by the wall. When they had dropped their eyes, she turned from them and walked, with the slightest swing in her step, down the rows of other ailing men toward the hospital gate, where Maillart and General Pamphile de Lacroix were just arriving.

When she had gone, the three captains detached themselves from the wall and approached, but only Cyprien knelt beside Paltre's pallet, and even he lacked the courage to touch him. Whatever Cyprien might have murmured was thoroughly muffled by the scented handkerchief with which he shielded his nose and mouth. Paltre did not respond to anything he said, and presently Cyprien abandoned his effort and stood up. On his pallet, Paltre stirred and moaned in his delirium. With a horsetail whisk she held in her hand, Madame Fortier brushed off a fly that had settled on his nostrils.

"Will he recover?" Guizot said, looking at the doctor with his usual expression of devotion. He'd put this question day after day, since Paltre had first been stricken.

"I can't be certain," said the doctor, and then, when he saw that all three of the captains still seemed to be searching his face, "I have recovered from this disease myself, and have sometimes seen others survive it, so at least I can say that recovery is possible."

The captains nodded, mumbled, shuffled their feet, and turned away. A faint breeze stirred the leaves of the tall palms as they passed under them. The wall above the ravine had stretched its shadow across the first row of the moribund below it. The captains exchanged brief courtesies with Maillart and Pamphile de Lacroix, who stood with Nanon just within the gate. Madame Fortier watched, with her hand on her hip, until they'd moved outside beyond the gateposts. With a sniff and a shrug she moved along the rows of the sick and wounded, in the opposite direction from the doctor, who was going down to greet the newcomers.

"Tell me, how do you get on?" said General Lacroix.

"Neither well nor far," said the doctor, accepting the hand Lacroix had offered. "It's only the disease that progresses here."

"Truly," said Lacroix. "I have recommended to the Captain-General that our new arrivals be sent to the eastern mountains, where all this dangerous miasma is swept away by the wind, until they are better acclimated to this place. But as you see, our situation is such that they must all be hurled into the abyss at the moment they first debark, and perish before they can render any service."

The doctor glanced briefly at Maillart. The candor of General Lacroix was surprising, and yet the predicament was obvious enough, at least to anyone in his own position. He held Lacroix's gaze for a moment and then looked away, along the close-packed rows of the dying. Even in the open air the stench of their putrid humors was abominable. The scheme of transporting yellow fever patients to the height of La Vigie had not materialized—the rate of fresh infection was so staggering that it could not be achieved. In the weeks since Toussaint's submission to Leclerc, the doctor had seen a couple of thousand troops march straight from their ships into their graves, this hospital only a way station on their passage to La Fossette. Most expired within a day or two of their first symptoms—Paltre's long lingering was exceptional, and perhaps after all he would survive, though for many days he had seemed unable either to live or die.

"There is no cure," the doctor said, looking into Lacroix's amiable face, answering what he supposed to be the unspoken question behind his eyes. "Some do recover, but by a reason of their own fortitude which I cannot explain. We can do nothing, really, to save them here."

That evening at the Cigny house they dined on doves that the doctor had brought in the previous day from a hunt on the headland beyond Fort Picolet. His marksmanship was much praised at the table, along with the sauce Isabelle had organized out of oranges and cloves. Maillart ate half a dozen of the bite-sized birds and felt that he could have put away a few more, but afterward, when they'd repaired to the upstairs salon and he'd drunk half a glass of rum, he felt a pleasant glaze settle over him.

There was the usual company—the Arnauds, the doctor, Nanon, and Tocquet, who'd come alone, without Elise. Though much recovered from her miscarriage, she seldom stirred out in the evenings, but remained in her own half-reconstructed domicile, where she and Tocquet had set up temporary quarters in the room where the doctor stored his paraphernalia and herbs.

From downstairs, Maillart could hear Zabeth giggling, and Michau chaffing her in a lower, indistinguishable tone, as the two of them cleared spent dishes from the table. A few more callers trickled in, including Captain Daspir. He was without his usual companions tonight—Guizot and Cyprien had gone whoring, Maillart reckoned, to be more certain of their game. He himself was reasonably certain that Isabelle still entertained Daspir privately from time to time (and after all there really was some fiber in the boy), but tonight she was fully occupied by flirting with General Pamphile de Lacroix, who was enjoying himself tremendously, although with no notion of following through.

Maillart found that he rather enjoyed watching Isabelle practice her wiles on Lacroix. A few years back, he'd have fumed with jealousy, as Daspir was visibly doing now. But tonight he was content to loll in his chair and admire her work, as he half attended to the gossip circulating through the room around him. It was possible that the late Bertrand Cigny had sometimes felt the same—that thought startled Maillart, so much so that he made, surreptitiously, the sign of the cross.

He waited until the others had departed or retired to their rooms, till even Daspir, despairing of Isabelle's favor, had run his finger around his collar and somewhat sulkily made his *adieux*. But Isabelle took no notice of Maillart either. As Daspir's boots clomped down the stairs, she shrugged and sighed and strolled out onto the balcony. Maillart waited a moment before he followed.

The night was cool, and breezy enough to send away the mosquitoes. Below, they heard the door slap shut, and Daspir appeared in the middle of the street, turning his wistful face up to Isabelle, who affected not to notice him. She'd raised her own eyes to the moon, and held them there until Daspir had dropped his head and begun limping slowly back toward the barracks.

"You tease the boy terribly," Maillart observed.

"Ah." Isabelle laughed softly, deep in her throat. "But sometimes I reward him, too."

Strangely, Maillart was not piqued by this remark, but rather felt pleased by her confidence. He watched, admiring the lift of her breasts as she raised both arms to loosen her hair. From their moments of intimacy, he knew there were now a few white strands in the current of dark curls flowing loose of their ribbon, although the moonlight was not strong enough to betray them. The breeze swirled up and the salt air moved an excitement through him. He wanted to sink his finger into her hair, but something moved him to reach for her hand instead.

"Will you marry me?"

Isabelle shook back her hair and turned to him, eyes wide with the moon.

"No," she said. "I will not."

"It is better to marry than to burn," Maillart quoted.

Isabelle's fingers fluttered within his palm. She was looking at him with a distressingly distant curiosity.

"I didn't suspect you knew so much scripture," she finally said, then disengaged her hand from his and curled it over the warped iron railing. "Well. Perhaps I prefer to burn."

Maillart felt no need to say anything further. In fact he was more surprised by his own question than her answer.

"I am much sought after," Isabelle said brightly. "Captain Daspir made the same offer, and not long ago."

"The pup!" said Maillart. "I should spank him with the flat of my sword."

"He meant well by it," Isabelle said. She turned and looked up into his face.

"I don't want a husband," she said. "I want a friend."

"Yes," said Maillart. "I suppose I understand that."

She raised herself on her toes to kiss him very lightly on the cheek. "You've been a good friend to me," she said. "Don't stop."

A little before noon of the following day, Maillart was summoned by none other than Daspir to wait upon the Captain-General Leclerc. They walked together from the barracks of the Carénage, where Maillart was now billeted, up the slow rise to the gate of Government House. Maillart led them close along the house walls, to take advantage of whatever thin patches of shade could be found at that hour. Daspir stumped along behind him, uncharacteristically glum, and eyed Maillart with a certain suspicion whenever he thought the major was not looking.

Of course, Maillart thought, he supposes I will win the prize we have both missed. He grinned at Daspir and stepped toward the middle of the street, throwing back his shoulders and expanding his chest, letting the full sun pour all over him, and glancing back from time to time to see if Daspir was appreciating the implications of his display. But after all he found small pleasure in this teasing. The truth was he'd gone home alone himself last night, unsatisfied as the younger man, though he hadn't felt the sharpness of frustration that came steaming off of Daspir.

Maillart slackened his pace, letting Daspir overtake him, and dropped his hand on the captain's shoulder, giving it an amiable squeeze. Daspir recoiled at the gesture, at first. But his humor seemed to lighten as they walked on. The courtship of a woman such as Isabelle would render a man philosophical, Maillart thought, and that was what he wanted his attitude to convey, though he could not have phrased the words aloud.

When they had been admitted at the gate of the Government compound, Maillart saw the heavy, tight-knit figure of Dessalines preceding them along the avenue of scorched palm trunks. The black general climbed the steps, slapping his thigh with his plumed hat, and disappeared into the shadows of the doorway. Once they got into the corridor themselves, it was a little cooler, though not calm, for the hall echoed with the clattering of hammers of laborers still busy replacing sections of the roof. Dessalines went into the Governor's antechamber, and a moment later Christophe emerged, passing the two white officers with the barest flicker of acknowledgment. Maillart caught a wisp of his mustache in the corner of his mouth and chewed it as he pondered.

Dessalines had already been admitted to the inner chamber, and the door was shut. Daspir would have knocked to announce their arrival, but Maillart shook his head and motioned him to one of the chairs that lined the wall, under the long casements where shards of glass shattered in the fire still hung in the melted leading. Maillart had no desire to disturb Dessalines—would rather not cross his path at all, though that looked unavoidable. And surely there was no love lost between Christophe and Dessalines these days.

They waited. Daspir was restless, crossing and uncrossing his legs, leaning forward, leaning back. His movements kept him well heated, kept the sweat rolling from his plump cheeks to the hollow of his throat. Maillart, whose years in Saint Domingue had taught him better, kept perfectly still, except for his breath, not even troubling to wipe his face or forehead. He watched Dessalines's hat, which hung from a peg; every so often a faint hint of breeze passed through the broken casements and stirred the plume that ornamented it. With the breeze, a few small golden bees hummed in and out of the comb of crazed lead. Presently Maillart's sweat had dried and he was cool enough that it scarcely bothered him when Dessalines came glowering out.

The black general did not seem to notice the two white officers either. His face was knotted; one hand gripped his ornate snuffbox as if he meant to crush it. He turned and snarled into the inner chamber:

"Mwen di—depi nan Ginen, li magouyé."

There was no reply from within. Daspir was staring frankly when Dessalines swung forward and locked eyes with him until he quailed. Then he snatched his hat down from the peg and stalked out of the antechamber.

I say—since Africa, he has been a treacherous man.

Maillart weighed the statement in his mind. Toussaint had not come from Africa; he was born here, in Saint Domingue, but Maillart knew the expression was figurative, and had little doubt it was Toussaint that Dessalines meant so to denounce. Leclerc did not understand much Creole, though, and if he did not have a translator with him, Dessalines's parting shot would have been more on the order of a ritual curse.

Now Leclerc himself appeared in the doorway, gripping a sheet of paper in his hand.

"Gentlemen," he said. "I have mastered them. I have mastered them all, and Dessalines especially."

"All?" Maillart got up to shut the outer door of the anteroom, which Dessalines had left ajar, and which Leclerc had not at all seemed to notice.

"Christophe, Maurepas, Dessalines—they have each come to me separately to warn me of the threat Toussaint presents—to ask, as privately as they may, for his removal. So cunningly I have played them one against the other."

"But Toussaint has already been removed," Maillart said. "What threat can he offer, retired at Ennery?"

His reaction was a little too quick, he saw. It had, in fact, been spontaneous. Leclerc was looking at him a little sharply, and Maillart, remarking the glitter of his eyes, realized that at least a portion of his elevation came from fever.

"I wanted you, Major Maillart," he said, as if he had forgotten until now. "I sent for you—and you too—come in, Captain Daspir." He gestured with the paper in his hand, which he had crumpled to a fan shape.

Maillart went slowly into the inner room, which was small and narrow, windowless, mostly filled with a long chart table, lined with shelves whose blank lines were occasionally broken by this or that old wormholed book. Even during Toussaint's rule he had not much frequented this place, whose closeness, must, and darkness now oppressed him. The clatter of hammers on the roof was audible here, though distant.

"You see," Leclerc nodded to them both. "As I am placed . . . it is the only way . . ."

This would not be *yellow* fever, Maillart reflected, for that would have laid the Captain-General low immediately; it must be one of the lesser malaises, which might derange the senses no more than a glass too many of rum. Daspir, where he stood next to the door, looked quite uncomfortable, but maybe that was only the queer light of the oil lamp flickering on his face. After all, there was some sense in Leclerc's muttering. The black troops who'd lately submitted outnumbered the French by a factor Maillart didn't care to calculate. To play one leader against another might be the only feasible diplomacy. Maillart pictured Dessalines and Christophe and Maurepas sitting in this shadowed room, together or separately, with the oily yellow lamplight playing over the sweat-sheen of their indecipherable jet features. It was quite as likely that these three had got up a cabal to manipulate Leclerc as the other way around, and what would be their end? All three had reason to fret about Toussaint. Dessalines because he hoped to supplant him—because Dessalines had not been willing to suspend the fight. Maurepas and Christophe because their surrenders to the French would put them out of favor if Toussaint should ever return to any place of power. Maillart knew that Toussaint had refused Christophe's most recent overture, and he had even rebuked his own brother Paul, for surrendering Santo Domingo City on the strength of a false order Toussaint had composed himself as a ruse.

"You were close to Toussaint yourself at one time, I believe," Leclerc was saying.

Maillart stopped the windmill of his thoughts. Best to go carefully now, but he shouldn't take too long to reply. "*Faute de mieux!*" he said brightly. For want of anything better! He scratched his head, for the aspect of innocent puzzlement the gesture might convey, and then went on, "We were all brothers in arms for a time, as you know, when Toussaint left the Spanish to join Laveaux in ninety-four."

"I understand you," Leclerc said. "Do sit down." He took a seat himself, between the dusty shelves and the table. Apparently he was satisfied by Maillart's response, and Maillart himself felt pleased with it—true as far as it went, though it omitted that Maillart had commanded under Toussaint well before the latter had switched sides to the French. It was the sort of answer that Toussaint himself might have devised.

"And your friend Doctor Hébert—he has been very, very thick with Toussaint, I believe?"

"What?" said Maillart, now really alarmed—he remembered Pascal and Borghella and several other Frenchmen whom Leclerc had ordered deported to France as collaborators with the rebel regime. "In a way, but generally under duress—you know he survived at La Crête à Pierrot only because Dessalines wanted his services as a doctor, and from ninety-one on it has been the same. He met Toussaint as a prisoner in the camps of Grande Rivière." This reply was probably more in the doctor's interest than the one he would have given if he had been present to speak for himself. Leclerc was smiling, Maillart saw with some relief. The fever sweat shone on his forehead.

"No, no," he said, smoothing his damp hand over the dark mahogany surface of the table. "I mean no accusation. I only thought—" He looked up, his illness shining through his eyes. ". . . your friend might sound Toussaint for us. Discreetly. If he were to go down to Ennery, where I understand he has some connection."

"Of course, if you desire it," Maillart said automatically. "But is he not more urgently needed here, with the cases of fever increasing?"

"It seems no doctor can do any more than nurse our men along to their deaths," Leclerc snapped, then lowered his voice. "I am sure Doctor Hébert is more knowledgeable than most, yet it might be a greater service to France . . ."

"And do you believe Toussaint so dangerous?" Maillart said. "When he has so lately sworn his loyalty, and laid down his arms."

"No oath of his is worth the breath it takes to utter it," Leclerc said, pushing back and knocking his shoulders into the shelves in exasperation. "He would rejoin the battle again at the first opportunity—well, if you doubt it, read this." He pushed the sheet of paper toward Maillart, who hesitated for a moment, then spread it smooth. The letter was addressed to Adjutant-General Fontaine, not long since one of Toussaint's staff officers.

You don't give me enough news, citizen. Try to stay in Le Cap for as long as you can. At La Tortue they said that General Leclerc's health was poor, and you must take great care to keep me informed of it. We must look to North America for a . . .

Arms, the writer must have meant; though he had not written out the word, it was plain enough. Maillart read on, silently. The drumming of the distant hammers ceased a moment, then resumed.

I ask you if it might not be possible to win over someone close to the Captain-General, so as to set D . . . free—he would be most useful to me in North America. And get the message to Gengembre that he must not leave Borgne, where the field hands must not return to work. Write to me at Habitation Najac. Signed TOUSSAINT LOUVERTURE

"I don't recognize the hand," Maillart said eventually. He was thinking: that *D . . .* would likely refer to Dommage, the commander who'd surrendered Jérémie and was now a prisoner at Le Cap.

Leclerc sniffed. "Toussaint is unlettered, as is well enough known. He has no hand—his missives are the work of others."

But Toussaint was far from illiterate, as Maillart knew. On the contrary, he was widely and roundly read, though Leclerc was right that his correspondence was an amalgam of the styles of his several secretaries.

This letter, roughly written and uncertainly, phonetically spelled, might actually be the product of Toussaint's own hand—Toussaint deprived of his detachment of scribes. Or it might not. The signature looked much as it ought, with a curlicue of the final *e* returning to enclose the usual three dots below the name.

"I wonder," Maillart said. "If there are so many whose interest is against Toussaint, might not this letter be a forgery?"

"One might take you for one of his partisans still," said Leclerc.

"Not at all," Maillart said. "But surely, you must consider that any action against Toussaint would provoke all manner of popular disturbances."

"Of the sort that plague us even now, Major—the sort which Toussaint is covertly encouraging." Leclerc flicked the edge of the letter with the nail of his forefinger, then slid it across the table to Captain Daspir.

"Besides, another letter has been intercepted," Leclerc went on. Daspir looked up from the wrinkled sheet that had been passed to him.

"In the second letter," Leclerc said acidly, "Toussaint desires the citizen Fontaine to inform him how frequently the death carts go to La Fossette."

Maillart kept silent. In these last weeks, Le Cap had become a charnel house. Each night more bodies were stacked at the gates of the barracks and hospitals to be carted to the cemetery at dawn.

"I will speak to Doctor Hébert today," he said. "If it is your order."

Leclerc inclined his head, and Maillart rose from his seat. Daspir followed him, blinking, into the brilliant sunlight of the Government courtyard. Maillart turned to face the captain before he took his leave, though he was not quite sure what he wanted to say.

"There is a rumor that Leclerc's secret program, or that of the First Consul, is to arrest and deport all of the black officers one by one."

Daspir's eyes were steady on Maillart. There was sometimes a hardness in his eyes which the major would not have expected from the concupiscent contours of his face. The contrast would appeal to Isabelle, he thought.

"If so," said Daspir, "I have not been privy to it. For I was assigned at the beginning to escort Toussaint's sons. Quite likely the details of the First Consul's strategy were not opened either to me or my comrades in that duty. The reasons are obvious, I think."

"Fair enough," Maillart said. There was something more he might have added, but he could not articulate it. He offered Daspir his hand and, after a barely noticeable hesitation, the captain took it.

As he went off in search of the doctor, Maillart found himself thinking of Major O'Farrel, an Irish mercenary of the Regiment du Cap, who had at one time claimed a considerable share of Isabelle Cigny's affection. Maillart would have fought over her once. It seemed a long time ago.

O'Farrel had laughed him off, though in a friendly manner. He had made Maillart see that the game was not worth bloodshed. Maillart would have liked to do the same for Daspir. He felt a certain affection for the boy, because they shared an enthusiasm. That was the way O'Farrel had seen it. He wondered where O'Farrel was, if he were still alive. He had gone over to the English, along with many of his regiment, when the English invaded Saint Domingue in 1794, and no doubt had left the colony when the English abandoned it. At any rate, Maillart had heard nothing of him since then.

The doctor had only just left the hospital when Maillart arrived there, and he missed him again, though narrowly, at Morne Calvaire and at the Cigny house. At last in the evening he found the doctor drinking with Tocquet in the remains of Elise's garden. With a nod he accepted the glass of rum he was offered and sat down in one of the low caned chairs that had recently been furnished to the place.

"But why now?" The doctor was pursuing some previous thread. "The difficulties here are apparent enough, but I don't see it as an especially propitious time to travel down to Ennery."

Tocquet reached behind his shoulder and lifted the tail of his bound hair so that the evening breeze could reach the back of his neck. "Elise is fit enough to travel now, and I think she will recover more quickly in the country." He glanced to where she knelt with a trowel by the garden wall a few yards distant, and lowered his voice a little. "I would like to get her away from this latest outbreak of fever. And the children too, especially."

"Of course." The doctor polished his glasses and put them back on. "But that is not all you are thinking."

Tocquet turned his head to spit into the ash-strewn dust. Elise, who was returning from planting her row of flowers by the wall, frowned at this action, but Tocquet pretended to ignore her. He cleared his throat with a swallow of rum.

"Security," he said.

"What?" said Maillart. "How do you believe Ennery more secure than here?"

"At Thibodet we should be still under Toussaint's wing," Tocquet said.

Elise laughed. "Husband, how you have changed your tune."

"I am as the aeolian harp, my dear," Tocquet flashed her his crooked smile. "My melody is determined by the direction of the wind."

Elise stood beside him, her hip grazing his shoulder. She ruffled his hair and laughed again and walked into the reconstructed portion of the house, with a nod to Michau, who sat under the portico washing his upper body with a bucket of water and a rag.

"But Toussaint has no more force of arms," Maillart said. "He has dismissed his men, even the honor guard."

"Yes, and where are they?" Tocquet said. "They were meant to report to the Captain-General here at Le Cap, but do you see them? Not Morisset or Monpoint or Magny. Not Riau, or Guiaou, or any of that company."

"I see," the doctor said slowly. "Well, but I don't know. Somehow I feel I am more useful here."

"They don't want doctors here," Tocquet continued. "What they want is a burial detail. Leclerc has scarcely enough European troops here to throw up a screen around his own positions. Suppose Dessalines were to turn on him, or any of the others; he would be hard pressed. I wouldn't like our chances of getting onto a ship then, and the plain would be on fire from Grande Rivière—where Sans-Souci is still giving them a lot of trouble—all the way up to Limbé, if not further."

"But Ennery is still more remote," Maillart said. "Here at least the troops are concentrated." He didn't want to mention the likelihood that Leclerc might try to arrest Toussaint, and given what Tocquet had just said, how easy would that be?

"There are not troops enough to concentrate," Tocquet said. "Once you subtract the colonial troops. And Dessalines, especially, is quite likely to subtract himself. It can go wrong anywhere, I think, but if it goes wrong at Ennery we might try for a ship at Gonaives, or the passes through the Spanish mountains if that way looked better."

The doctor massaged the bridge of his nose, pushing up his glasses. The skin below his eyes had bagged from his days of fatigue.

"They don't want doctors here," Tocquet repeated. "They want gravediggers."

He pulled three cheroots from his shirt and offered them. Maillart accepted. The doctor shook his head.

"Have a care you don't dig your own grave," Tocquet said, and tucked the third cheroot back into his shirt.

Maillart bent toward the flame Tocquet had struck, then leaned back, exhaling a luxurious cloud of smoke and stretching his legs out before him from the low seat of his chair. He looked toward the far wall of the garden, where a couple of brown doves called in their round voices, perched among the shards of bottle glass mortared to the top of the masonry. If Leclerc were to inquire further, he could now say that the subject of going down to Ennery had been broached to the doctor, and he would be telling the truth.

When every course was so uncertain, sometimes no action was the best. It was not hesitation, but stillness, the only way to survive the extremes of heat. Maillart felt how Toussaint was still at Ennery. He found in himself no enthusiasm for proposing that the doctor go deliberately to spy upon him there.

Removing Toussaint would have no more effect than lopping a single head from a Hydra. How would Xavier Tocquet have reacted to what Leclerc had told Maillart this afternoon? But Tocquet was shrewd and thorough in his regard of all such matters, and probably would have already surmised much of what Leclerc had revealed.

Maillart slumped more deeply in his chair, whose short legs raised him barely a foot above the ground. He flicked a little ash from his cheroot to the ashes still scattered across the dirt around him. Already shoots of grass had begun to push up through the paste of earth and ash, and beside the wall the plumes of red ginger Elise had planted were trembling in the evening breeze. A few fronds sprouting from the burnt stump of the yellow *cocotier* were now big enough to cast their shadows. Maillart kept still and let the breeze drift over him. He felt cooler now, and empty even of desire.

Paltre had grown meager, wasted to his bones. The other three captains visited him daily, but now he seldom knew them when they came. Sometimes he took them for his brothers, or his parents, believing himself a child again in France. Sometimes he did not know that anyone was there at all. Guizot no longer asked the doctor if he would recover. Daspir wondered how it was he did not die.

His hands were palsied and often moved at random, weaving invisible threads in the air. All his joints had turned knobby, the flesh shrinking to the bone, tendons tightening beneath the desiccated skin. Patiently, Nanon held the soup bowl to his lips, while Paltre sipped or gulped or choked. With small, deft movements she avoided his sudden bursts of vomiting, while always remaining near enough to clean his face and soothe him. He did not know her either, but she could soothe him better than anyone, pressing her gold fingers to his wrist or brow.

She must be poisoning him, Cyprien sometimes accused. How could she mean him any good? But Daspir and Guizot hushed him whenever he began in that vein. To Daspir, only Madame Fortier seemed a little menacing, when sometimes she would stand tall and regally erect at the head of Paltre's mat, arms folded over her narrow chest, expecting his death with a consuming patience. Yesterday, Paltre had enjoyed a period of lucidity. He recognized his friends and professed himself to feel relieved of many of his pains. Guizot at least had been encouraged, but afterward Madame Fortier had let them know that such brief rallies were more often than not presage of the final end, and today Paltre was lapsed again into the fever.

Daspir did not like to look at his white lips on the soup bowl. He glanced at the sky, where the sun tilted westward. In an hour's time, when the heat had begun to fade, he would go to exercise Bel Argent. This had become his daily privilege. Few riders could manage the white stallion. Daspir would certainly plan a route that passed the Cigny house, and hope that Isabelle would appear on the balcony to receive the impression he meant to make on her. If she was there or if she was not, he would call on her that evening. She had not admitted him to any intimacy for more than ten days, and so in his vitals he felt she was bound to do it soon.

Sweat ran stinging into both his eyes, and the discomfort pried him out of this agreeable daydream. He took off his hat, wiped his forehead, and fanned himself with the brim, staring absently toward the gate, through which he'd very much like to be gone. A black nurse, trim in a blue dress and white headband, was working her way along the row of mats with a pail of water and a gourd dipper. The doctor walked behind her, his face in shadow under his straw hat, and when she'd given each man a drink, he stooped to take a pulse or exchange a word or two.

Then the nurse had dropped her pail and the doctor had pushed past her, was hurrying up toward the place where Daspir stood. The straw hat had flown off, but he did not notice it.

"C'est la crise," Madame Fortier said dispassionately. Her long shadow spread over Paltre's torso. It is the crisis. Paltre had convulsed and sat up sharply, his knees drawing tight to his chest. His mouth was crusted with a black rime, and blackened blood was running from his nose and even, Daspir saw with an awful fascination, from the corners of his eyes. He sucked for air without success and shuddered, and his eyelids sank shut with a heavy weight, but the balls still twitched beneath them. Nanon was trying to stretch him out, murmuring, pressing a hand to his chest, but Paltre fought her, struggling to hold up his head.

"She's stopping his breath," Cyprien hissed through the scented cloth he held over his mouth and nose. But anyone could see that it was the fever stopping Paltre's breath and not Nanon. Above the cloth, Cyprien's eyes darted frantically. Daspir could not bear to look and could not look away. Paltre bared his teeth in a terrible grin. The teeth were covered in yellow-white scum. On a front tooth, one of those fat black buzzing flies alighted. Madame Fortier dangled her horsetail whisk from under a folded elbow, but she did not trouble to flick the fly away. Nor could Daspir break his frozen posture to brush away the insect. Paltre arched his neck, and the fly hummed away of its own accord. Nanon cradled his head in her joined hands.

"Do something," Guizot grated out of his misery.

"Rien à faire," the doctor said. There is nothing to do. He'd dropped to one knee beside Nanon, and was trying to disengage her. Then all the muscles of Paltre's body slackened and he lay flat, and Nanon let go of his head and sat back on her heels. Paltre was motionless, save for a twitching around his eyes. His head lay again in the shadow of Madame Fortier's skirt. Then the twitching stopped, and Madame Fortier turned and walked away, leaving Paltre's grinning skull exposed to the sudden glare of the sun.

The captains were all avoiding each other's eyes. The doctor lifted Paltre's wrist, then laid it down. Daspir took note of the stiffness that had already set into the arm. Cyprien lowered his handkerchief.

"You let him die," Cyprien said. It was not clear whether he meant to address the doctor or Nanon or both of them together. "You—"

"Stop it," Guizot said. "Just be silent." And Cyprien stopped his mouth with the handkerchief.

"I'm sorry," said the doctor, blinking slowly through his dusty glasses. When no one spoke, he turned to call for help in moving the body.

"No, we'll do it," Guizot said, with a glance at Daspir. And Daspir stooped and lifted Paltre's body by his bare feet, while Guizot caught him underneath his emaciated shoulders. There was no weight to him. The rags of his ruined uniform dripped from his bones. Directed by the doctor, they carried him to the gate and let him down beside five or six bodies of other men who'd perished in the course of the day.

Cyprien overtook and passed them without a glance, walking stiff-legged toward the gate. Guizot took the doctor's hand and pressed it and turned wordlessly away. But Daspir was still looking at Paltre, the rictus of his death mask, the awful way the fingers hovered slightly off the ground, at the end of his plank-rigid arms. At last he took his eyes away and faced the doctor. It seemed that there was something he ought to have said, but in the end he was as speechless as Guizot had been; he bowed and took his leave.

They caught up with Cyprien a block below the hospital gate. "That yellow bitch," he began again. "You know she and her paramour had every reason to wish him dead—"

"Oh, be quiet about it," Guizot said. "They did all they could for him. He died the same as the others do. You could see plain enough for yourself there was nothing to be done."

Cyprien dropped his head and walked a little faster. In half a block more he muttered, "We ought to have buried him."

"Who'll bury us?" said Daspir, without knowing that he would.

"Don't say that," Guizot said. "It's unlucky."

Cyprien laughed bitterly. "What in this whole damned colony has ever brought good luck?"

"Maybe it was Christophe who cursed him," Daspir said. It was another image that took him by surprise—the moment at the banquet when Christophe, aggravated by Paltre's teasing with the wine, had finally threatened to drink blood from his skull . . . And just before that moment Paltre had seemed to be his usual irritable and irritating self. But all the other victims fell ill in the same dramatically sudden way.

"Ah, Christophe will be deported soon enough," said Guizot. "Along with every other black who's worn an epaulette."

"What do you mean?" Daspir said, skidding to a stop in the middle of the street.

"Rochambeau was boasting of it, when he was in drink. All the black generals are to be arrested and shipped off, one by one."

Daspir considered. Here was the point Maillart had brought to him a day or so before. The other two captains had stopped to wait for him. They were better placed to hear such rumors, he supposed, since they spent their nights carousing while he, Daspir, paid a politer court to Isabelle Cigny. Drink, whore, and be merry, for tomorrow we die. That watchword seemed to work very well on the looser women of the town, professional or not. The shadow of death that lay over all the garrison seemed to have its erotic aroma too. Daspir knew he might have succeeded as well as his friends if he'd chosen to follow them down that road, but somehow, if Isabelle sent him away, he preferred to sleep alone on his plank in the *caserne*.

"So much the better," Cyprien said at last. "Let all the black bastards rot on the hulks."

Daspir fell into step with the others again. He'd realized he was going in the wrong direction—Bel Argent was stabled at the *caserne* higher on the hill—but he was reluctant to part from the other two just now. Though he couldn't say he found their company altogether pleasant, the pall of Paltre's death would weigh more heavily on him once he was alone.

The doctor stayed in the hospital till well after dark and watched the curl of new moon rise above the wall. At sunset Nanon had gone back to the house, to pack and make the children ready for their journey to Ennery. Although he had not planned it so, the doctor found that Paltre's death released him from his sense of obligation here. He didn't need to attend all the other deaths that were sure to follow. And Maillart had intimated, though obscurely, that Leclerc would not object to his departure.

Madame Fortier had agreed to manage the hospital in his absence. In this predicament her skills were equal to his own, there being no cure for the yellow fever. Under the moon and a spangle of stars she helped him arrange the corpses by the gate for the cart that would collect them in the morning.

In the few hours since he had expired, Paltre's flesh had drizzled from him like melted tar. It was often so with the yellow fever—the bodies were half decomposed already by the time the doomed man drew his last breath. The doctor bore Paltre no resentment. Long before today, he'd ceased to be the person who had insulted him and Nanon. Cyprien's accusation was false and he thought that even Cyprien knew it. He bore Cyprien no resentment either. Every word and action and death seemed foreordained.

He barely noticed the smell any more, but once the bodies had been stacked and covered with a square of canvas, he was relieved to wash his hands in scalding water from the kettle under the palm. Madame Fortier passed him the towel she'd used to dry her own. She meant to stay a little longer, till her husband came to fetch her with their wagon.

"You know," the doctor said, "sometimes I wonder why you take such pains to nurse these men." He hung the towel over a branch near the fire. "It cannot very well be for love."

Madame Fortier smiled at him from her height. "Have you put that question to your wife?"

"No," the doctor admitted. He rubbed his chin and looked down at her feet.

"BonDyé desires us to forgive our enemies," Madame Fortier said. "It may well be that Nanon has the grace to do it."

"But not you." The doctor raised his eyes to her again.

"Oh no. Not me." Madame Fortier held out her strong, square hand and the doctor clasped it.

"Nanon has a greater heart than mine," she said. "You are fortunate, *blanc*, to have found a place there."

She kept her grip on his hand as she spoke, and the doctor reflected that tonight the appellation *blanc* on her tongue had lost the hostile edge it usually had and seemed, indeed, almost affectionate.

"I would not tell it to Nanon," she said, letting his hand drop at last. "But I'll tell you: it does content me to watch them die, when I know I have done all I could to save them."

40

Morning brought a rainbow up from the sun-spangled ravine east of *grand'case* of Descahaux. Placide, who had slept but poorly, looked on the colored band with pleasure. The ribbon ascended from the mist of the stream at the bottom of the gorge and, after a curve no greater than that of a saber's edge, disappeared into a cloud above. It seemed to give the day some unexpected promise.

His mother raised the coffeepot, but Placide shook his head. Isaac was oblivious as she refilled his cup, his nose sunk in a leather-bound volume of Ovid. Since their return to Ennery, Isaac had buried himself in the studies that had occupied their time at the Collège de la Marche, preferring the pages of whatever book to anything in his actual surroundings. Only the day before, he had returned from a mission to Le Cap bearing a letter from Leclerc to Toussaint, but he had little to say about that expedition—no more than a monosyllabic grunt. This morning he did not even notice Saint-Jean, though the boy sat on the edge of his chair, waiting for Isaac to look up.

Placide got to his feet and kissed his mother's cheek. He rubbed the head of his youngest brother and went from the gallery to find his horse. When he had mounted, he touched his thumb to the *mouchwa têt* he now kept folded in his shirt pocket, then turned his horse in the direction of Sancey, where crews were clearing the rubble of the buildings the French had burned.

Above, the rainbow had begun to fade and dissipate, its color dissolving into the vacant blue of the sky, and in spite of the bright sunshine Placide felt his mood begin to sink. There was a chattering in his head he could not seem to stop, a perpetual inner argument that would not let him sleep. The chattering cycled through a thousand questions: Where would new tiles be found to roof the Sancey *grand'case*? Why had his father given in to the French? And why had his generals seemed to betray him? Who would transport brown sugar to the port at Gonaives? And when would the struggle be rejoined? All in a random jumble of small issues with great ones. Why had so many French soldiers recently been sent to their vicinity, like a plague of grasshoppers devouring everything in the canton of Ennery?

The sunlight spilled on two men hacking at a hedgerow, just at the bend of the road ahead. Two ordinary laborers, they appeared to be, but one of them turned up a face that shone brilliantly through its maze of terrible scars, and saluted Placide with a *coutelas* whose spoon-shaped blade was almost unique to Guiaou. Placide returned the gesture automatically, and as he rode past he realized that the other man had been Guerrier—and by the time he reached the next turning in his road, he remembered that he'd seen Guerrier's old musket half hidden in the thorny branches of the hedge.

When had they come? But now Placide remembered that only yesterday he had seen Monpoint—he was now quite sure it had been Monpoint, though he was in civilian clothes and at some distance—commanding a work detail in the coffee trees of Sancey. And if some others in that *konbit* looked familiar, that was because they had lately been his comrades in Toussaint's honor guard.

They must have been filtering in for days, weeks even, now that Placide assembled his memories. Indeed, he didn't know how he'd failed to put them together before. He'd been oblivious as Isaac. But the guardsmen were here, metamorphosed into field hands, or so disguised; if they were not precisely under arms, Placide was suddenly quite convinced that they must all have their arms as ready to hand as Guiaou and Guerrier had theirs.

The flush of that excitement stayed with him through the day. For an hour or two he rode with his father from one field to another, and in the afternoon he made further rounds on his own—for Toussaint was giving him more responsibility these last few weeks, as Placide gained competence in the management of coffee and cane fields, the mills and drying barns. Wherever he went Placide now recognized more and more of his old companions of the guard. Half-consciously adopting his father's gesture, he'd cover his mouth with a hand whenever he met another one of them, to hide the smile of complicity.

At evening he felt calmer than usual at that hour, when often the chattering of his head would come to a disagreeable crescendo; he understood better now why some men tried to smash it down with rum. Instead of drinking, he walked into the fruit trees behind the Descahaux *grand'case*. Between that orchard and the house, some roses that Suzanne had planted had withered in the heat, but the hibiscus flowers were luxuriant and the scent of orange and lemon was strong and sweet. Among the citrus trees he came upon Guiaou as if by design; Guiaou took his hand and led him out of the far end of the grove onto a narrow trail where Guerrier, trailing his musket, fell into step behind them.

The way led down the hill to a low place where they crossed the stream at the bottom of the ravine on stepping stones. When they reached the other side, Guiaou asked Placide if he had his *mouchwa tèt* with him, then indicated he should put it on. Once Placide had tightened the knot at the base of his head, it seemed that the buzzing in his brain was almost completely compressed away. Since the surrender he had forgotten how it had always been so, when he fastened the cloth around his head before a battle.

The trail wound over the contours of two more *mornes*, passing under cover of dense trees, then emerging on a rising slope above the coffee trees of Habitation Thibodet. Placide stopped and turned into the wind, looking down toward the *grand'case*, where Saint-Jean sometimes went, with Riau's son Caco, to play with the white and colored children who lived there. Above the valley, the sky was fading into darkness, but toward the coast a great bloom of cloud was tinted by the setting sun, reminding Placide of the rainbow's morning promise.

On the crown of the hill above them, a small red flag flew square from a long bamboo whip, within a palisade of crooked sticks. Guiaou and Guerrier led Placide through the gate. Inside, Riau was waiting with Bienvenu, and Quamba and the woman Placide knew as Caco's mother, Merbillay. There were some others whom he did not recognize. His eyes were drawn to Merbillay, who was more finely dressed than usual and had her hair wound high in a red turban with shiny gold fringe, but he was not looking at her as a woman. She had the hieratic beauty of one of the stone carvings the Tainos had left in the caves underneath this land. All of the people stood as still as trees planted around the edges of the peristyle.

"W'ap vini," said Quamba. You have come. Now Placide remembered what Guiaou had said, on the road from Marmelade to Dondon, the day they rode to Le Cap to surrender. *One day we will take you to the drums.* Though the light was swiftly failing, he saw a tall drum leaning against the central post, hairy goatskin shrunken and straining around the pegs, but there were no drummers. The wind lifted and the flag whipped on its pole, and Placide felt a fluttering of the loose ends of cloth below the knot of his *mouchwa*.

Arms folded over his chest, Quamba stepped nearer, so he could look through Placide's eyes to the very bottom of his head. He was near enough to inhale Placide's breath. His own smelled faintly of cinnamon. Placide relaxed, as if salt water buoyed him.

"Well," said Quamba. "I will make a service to help you to receive the spirit."

He had not changed his posture or expression, but now there was a question in his eyes. Placide nodded. He had come for this, though without knowing that he knew it, and such a long, long way. The roll of the hilltop under his feet was like the swell of the waves under the ship that carried him from France.

Quamba unfolded his arms to discover a dry gourd strung with beads. When he moved it the seed inside and the beads outside combined in a sound like the rattle of a snake, and someone lit a candle and raised it to the four directions, and someone touched the head of the drum, though in no pattern: once, twice, three times the hollow note, and on the third beat the darkening air was shattered by a scream that rocked Placide to the bottom of his heels.

He stared: Bienvenu had fallen and was kicking and tearing at the dirt. Or he ripped his fingers into his scalp, weaving his head as if it had filled with a swarm of bees. The voice that came out of him was harsh and shrill and querulous, the voice of an angry woman. Guiaou and Merbillay and Guerrier had surrounded him—or her, for Bienvenu was only harboring this furious woman, Placide saw—they spoke to her in low, ingratiating voices, stroking her, soothing her. "No, no, Maîtresse," Guiaou was murmuring, "you have come before the hour . . . let us go now." He showed her something hidden in his palm, and Bienvenu's hand grabbed for it but Guiaou backed away, and the being that inhabited Bienvenu followed the lure, supported by Merbillay and Guerrier. Finally they passed through the gate outside. Placide had not turned to watch. His hair stood stiff on the back of his neck. Outside the enclosure there were sounds of some scuffle and then the harsh female laughter declining. Guiaou and Guerrier and Merbillay came back inside, Guiaou quietly turning to close the gate behind them.

A blanket-like darkness covered the *hûnfor*, so thick the stars could not penetrate. Placide's thoughts were scrambling up and down the inner wall of his skull like a pack of drunken monkeys bent on destruction. He did not know where to rest his eyes. But the candle was still lit, and in its aura he picked out the rainbow spiral on the central post where the drum had been propped, and that pattern closed with the rainbow he had seen that morning, restoring a wholeness. He calmed enough to understand Quamba's words.

"*Bay têt ou,*" Quamba said. Give up your head.

Placide unfastened his *mouchwa têt* and stuffed it into a trouser pocket. Loosening the string at the throat of his shirt, he stepped forward and knelt before the wide wooden bowl that had appeared on the ground before him. Hands came through darkness to peel the shirt back from his shoulders—Guiaou's and Merbillay's. Placide noticed the cool strength of her fingers.

"Make the sign of the cross," Quamba said, and Placide obeyed him. He lowered his head above the wooden *gamelle,* whose water released a pungent scent, colored with herbs and a trace of coffee beans. The monkeys scrabbled harder at the folds of his brain, so desperate to cling to that territory. Then Quamba raised a double scoop of water and began to wash from the hollow in the back of Placide's neck where the knot of his *mouchwa* had been fastened, up and over the top of his head, back into the warm pool of the *gamelle,* and again like that, until the monkey fists released their hold, and Placide's whole head was like a boil that had been lanced and rinsed and purged and healed, and the tears of his relief poured freely in the slowly cooling water. Now in the bottom of the bowl he found the stars.

When Riau walked with Placide home to Descahaux, Guiaou went to the *case* with Merbillay. He did not lie close beside her then (though the next night it would probably be Guiaou sleeping alone in the camp by Descahaux) but rested alone on a mat in a corner of the clay-packed walls, his head loosely wrapped in a white cotton cloth.

He was content with how the *lavé têt* had passed, Placide's head-washing, which Guiaou had wanted to aid and witness for a long time. Yet it puzzled him that Ezili Jé Rouj had chosen to appear. The master of Placide's head was meant to be Lasirène, Erzulie of the waters. Guiaou understood that better than Placide, whose mind was a little fogged by thoughts the *blancs* had tried to stuff in his head on the other side of the ocean (though less so than the mind of his brother Isaac). Lasirène was the woman of Agwé, Guiaou's *mêt' têt,* and that was why, from the beginning, there had been a natural harmony between Guiaou and Placide. It was certainly Lasirène who swam beside Placide through all the battles, parting the waters for him to pass through unharmed. Guiaou had wanted to help Lasirène to her rightful seat in Placide's head, and that was how it had gone in the end, no matter that Ezili Jé Rouj had wanted to interfere.

Guiaou matched his breathing to the breath of the children who slept on Merbillay's far side, and listened to the slight movement of a mouse in the palm thatch overhead, and to the whistle of a night bird in the trees outside. From the roof-tree, Riau's *banza* hung like a big gourd. Guiaou closed his eyes. He had served today, and served to good effect. It was Guiaou who distracted Ezili Jé Rouj and enticed her out of the peristyle, coaxing her with the hollow blue bird's egg he had been carrying to give to Marielle. Outside, Ezili had snatched the egg and crushed it, but it was worth the sacrifice. She had not spoiled the ceremony, after all.

It worried him a little still, why Ezili Jé Rouj had chosen to intrude. But that was a thought he would let go. Let Lasirène drown it in the waters. Merbillay snuffled in her sleep, turning on her side. Her hand strayed toward him, and Guiaou touched her wrist and caught the thread of her pulse and followed it into sleep.

Next morning there was no sign of a rainbow, but Placide felt as never before how the whole world was held together by a charm. He had slept deep and without thought or dream. All the dream power was outside him now, enforcing the charm, maintaining it as firm and fragile as an eggshell. His mother seemed to feel the radiance that had suffused him; her smile was special as she poured his coffee and spooned in the sugar and set before him four quarters of an orange. Even Saint-Jean abandoned trying to distract Isaac from Ovid, and came to press himself cat-like against Placide, though usually he preferred Isaac, since Isaac would sometimes beguile him with fantastic tales of France.

Inside the house, Toussaint was laughing. "Look at these *blancs*." His voice rose cheerfully. "They don't suspect anything—they think they know everything—but still they have to consult old Toussaint."

Placide felt warmed by his father's good humor. For the past few days, Toussaint's spirits had been occluded, especially since yesterday, when Isaac had returned from Le Cap. There was some hovering cloud of doubt, it seemed; Sylla was still resisting Leclerc in the mountains of Plaisance, as Sans-Souci was resisting at Grande Rivière, and the Captain-General had the idea that Toussaint might be encouraging either or both of these rebellions (and might be encouraged in this idea by Dessalines, so Isaac had reported). Then there were too many French troops quartered in the canton of Ennery, carelessly looting the fruits of all the fields, and the garrison in the town itself had turned surly, no longer rendering Toussaint the military honors due to him when he passed through.

How good if that cloud had been dissolved. But when Monpoint emerged from Toussaint's company, his face was dark. At his glance, Placide got up and followed him down the steps and around the corner of the house, into the blighted garden of tea roses.

"He says he will go to meet General Brunet at Habitation Georges," Monpoint said unhappily, pushing the dry dirt with the toe of his boot.

"Yes," Placide said vaguely; he was reluctant to have his sense of harmony in the day disrupted.

"But it cannot be wise for him to go," Monpoint said, turning to pace along the desiccated rose plants, then sharply turning back. "And there were two more ships landing many *blanc* soldiers at Gonaives only yesterday—"

The rising sun cleared the roof of the house, striking Monpoint harshly in the face. He and Placide moved away from the house wall into the shade of the citrus grove.

"Those soldiers are boasting they have come to arrest Toussaint," Monpoint said gloomily. "Let them come to take him here, if they have the heart to try it!" He raised one hand and closed it so tight that it trembled. Out of uniform and without his tall silver helmet, Monpoint looked a little smaller than Placide had thought him, but this gesture restored his full size. "But if he puts himself into their hands . . ." Monpoint dropped his hand and scuffed the turf between the roots of the lime trees.

"The soldiers have been boasting that way ever since the fleet sailed out of France," said Placide, who had overheard more of his guardians' rash talk during the voyage than any of the four captains ever suspected. "So far those boasts have come to nothing."

Monpoint glanced up, startled by a footfall. Isaac had appeared, one arm draped over a lime tree branch. For some reason he'd clothed himself today in the uniform of Bonaparte's gift, and even had strapped on the ornamental sword.

"And you, *monchè*?" Monpoint said. "Have you been near enough to the *blanc* General to breathe his spirit?"

Placide knew that Isaac often looked sullen when he was worried. That explained the sulkiness with which he plucked a small, lumpy lime and cut the skin with his thumbnail before he replied.

"It is Dessalines more than anyone who wants to hurt my father in the eyes of the Captain-General. Dessalines who whispers and insinuates. The Captain-General showed to me letters signed by Dessalines, which tell stories that are not true."

"What stories?" Monpoint said.

Isaac licked the flesh of his lime before he answered. "That our father is in league with Sylla at Plaisance and Sans-Souci at Grande Rivière. That he will use the battalion of Gonaives to start up the war all over again."

"The battalion of Gonaives!" Monpoint snorted. "No one could start a war against all those *blancs* with that. And Toussaint is not even at the head of it." He shook his head, looking down at the ground. "Well. I know the *blancs* are unhappy because they can't dig Sylla out of his place at Mapou. But they cannot prove that your father has anything to do with that."

No, thought Placide, it couldn't be proved, but the fort of Mapou was not far off from Ennery. In fact it was near enough that a fair number of the men who worked at Descahaux by day walked back to Mapou to sleep at night, and so everyone knew that Sylla was doing all he could to gather and stockpile provisions and materials for war.

"But maybe the Captain-General does not believe the lies of Dessalines," Isaac said. "He has written to my father very cordially."

"Maybe," said Monpoint, but without much verve. He had plucked another misshapen lime from another tree and was turning it over and over in his hands. "But why will Toussaint put his head in the lion's mouth? Vernet and I have warned him against it, and even his brother

Paul." Monpoint shrugged and let the lime drop on the ground. "But maybe he will listen better to his son."

Monpoint was looking at Placide when he uttered this last sentence, rather than at Isaac, who had taken a pace or two away from the grove and stood with his back to them. The long scabbard of his sword had cut a furrow in the dirt behind him. Placide reflected that neither he nor Isaac had ever used their swords. Placide had shot more than one French soldier with the fancy pistols Bonaparte had presented him, but he had adopted a shorter saber for the battles, handier to wield in the saddle, though not so short as Guiaou's *coutelas*.

Placide nodded to Monpoint and walked up toward the house. Suzanne and Saint-Jean had disappeared from the gallery and the breakfast dishes had been cleared away. Placide felt the weight of all Monpoint had told him, but it did not really oppress him yet. The aura of the *lavé têt* was around him still, so that everything seemed foreordained, even his own actions, even his words. He had soaked his *mouchwa* in the water of the *gamelle* before leaving the *hûnfor*, and it remained slightly fragrant where it lay folded and dry in his shirt pocket. He touched it with his thumb as he stopped on the threshold of Toussaint's small scriptorium.

"*Honneur,*" he said, the country greeting.

"*Respect,*" said Toussaint, completing the formula. He looked up with an unmasked smile from the three letters he'd been examining on his desk, and offered Placide his hand.

"They say you are going to visit General Brunet."

Toussaint released Placide's hand and covered his mouth. He glanced at the three letters fanned on the table before him, from Pesquidoux, Leclerc, and Brunet.

"Brunet has invited me." Toussaint passed one of the letters to Placide. "I may go if I choose."

Placide skimmed the page: *We have, my dear general, some arrangements to make together which cannot be dealt with by letter, but which a conference of one hour would complete. Were I not overcome by work and troublesome details, I'd be today the bearer of my own response, but as I am unable to leave these days, come to me yourself, and if you are recovered from your indisposition, let it be tomorrow. One must never delay when it is a question of doing good. You will not find, here at my country plantation, all the amenities I would wish to organize for your reeeption, but you will find there the frankness of a gallant man who has no other wish but for the prosperity of the colony and your own personal happiness . . .*

"They say it is a trap, this invitation." Placide swallowed, with some difficulty. His throat had gone dry, and his sense of certainty was beginning to fracture. He let the paper flutter to the tabletop.

"Do they say so?" Toussaint looked up, his eye bright and canny as a bird's under the line of the yellow madras cloth that bound his head. Placide returned him Brunet's letter and Toussaint secured it under the moss-colored vase with the white frieze depicting his victories over the English. Isaac had rescued the vase, miraculously unbroken, from the ashes of the Sancey *grand'case*, and also the small orary that sat on the opposite side of Toussaint's desk; he had diligently cleaned and polished both before returning them to his father.

"Where is it that you find the snare? As you may see from the letter which the Captain-General has sent, I have only to meet with General Brunet to settle the problem of the *blanc* soldiers at Plaisance who are marauding all over the plantations of this canton," Toussaint said. "And that is a problem which must be addressed." He proffered another folded sheet. Placide opened and scanned it.

Since you persist in thinking that the large number of troops now found at Plaisance are frightening the cultivators there, I have charged General Brunet to arrange the placement of a part of those troops with you . . . It did not strike Placide that the tone of these phrases was quite so cordial as what Isaac had described.

"Do we want more *blanc* soldiers here?" he said. "And even as he sends this letter, the Captain-General has sent two ships to Gonaives with a lot more soldiers, who are full of bad talk."

"Do they say so?" Toussaint repeated. "Well. Maybe it is a trap after all." He looked past Placide, who made a half-turn to see that Isaac had also come quietly into the room, and stood in the shadow left of the doorframe, the long scabbard of his sword propped out from him like a third leg or a tail.

"To take risks for my country is a sacred duty." He shrugged and smiled and looked at them both frankly. "To avoid risks to save my own life would be shameful."

"But who'll protect the country if not you?" Placide burst out.

"Another. There will be others always now. Charles Belair, or Dommage, Sylla, or Sans-Souci." He masked a smile as he stood up, and gathered the letters from the desktop. "Perhaps even Dessalines or Christophe." He folded the letters together and slipped them into an inner pocket, then smoothed down the front of his coat and took a step forward, toward Placide. "It might even be you. Or Riau, or Guiaou, or any of the others whose names we don't yet know." As Placide's knees weakened slightly, Toussaint kissed him and passed on. Isaac stepped forward and received his kiss. Toussaint turned back in the doorway.

"Where one is cut down, another will spring up," he said. "A dozen others. Always. You must remember that."

Placide followed him out onto the gallery. "Let me go with you."

Toussaint shook his head. "No," he said. "I want you to go down to Gonaives and have a look at those ships you mentioned. It is an order," he said, when Placide hesitated.

"*Oui, mon général.*" Placide pulled himself upright in a salute which Toussaint crisply returned. Behind him in the yard Riau and Guiaou and a dozen other riders waited, one holding a saddled horse for Toussaint, who softened slightly as he lowered his hand.

"*N'a wé,*" he said, looking closely at Placide. "*Si Dyé vlé.*"

Elise sat on the gallery at Thibodet, sipping coffee and watching the sunrise gild the grass around the pool in front of the house. The purple blooms of *bwa dlo* were just beginning to open to the morning's warmth. She took a spoonful of *soupe giraumon,* and rubbed her thumb along a vine of bougainvillea that was climbing the gallery rail. Ought it perhaps to be cut back? But the blacks all thought it had the virtue to keep bad spirits away from the house, and maybe they were right.

Sophie, her gown rumpled and her eyes blurry with sleep, was holding both Mireille's hands and helping her to walk, so carefully, down the steps toward the shining pool, while Zabeth's Bibiane managed on her own, backing down on all-fours, her head twisted over her shoulder to follow the progress of Mireille. Zabeth stood watching at the top of the steps, hands propped on her hips, until Michau, as he passed through the yard with a sack of charcoal, called some teasing remark to her. Zabeth whipped away, flaring out her skirt, but even as she spun her face turned back toward him, eyes and smile flashing. In this twist Elise saw the fabric of Zabeth's dress stretch over a belly rounder and harder than it had been the month before.

So. Elise allowed herself a smile, as if at the sunshine and the antics of the children; she could even share this smile with Zabeth, as she went into the house to fetch more bread. Not quite a year since Toussaint had commanded Zabeth's last man to blow his own brains out, but she had found a place in herself for new love and new life. Elise's eyes went swimming, so that her family and servants moved like bright reflections on wind-ruffled water. That was something like what Maman Maig' had said.

She grasped the vine and raised her head to let the tears run back, looking up at the notch between the *mornes* where the road toward Dondon lay, and beyond it Grande Rivière, where Sans-Souci would still be fighting, if he had not been captured or killed. She felt the dead place under her navel, the spot where Zabeth was now fertile and ripe. There would be no more children for Elise, and probably no more such adventures.

Tocquet's hands settled on her shoulders, lightly rolling tension from her back. Since her recovery, he was more attentive, almost solicitous. He kept closer to home. How often Isabelle must have known this sensation; the touch of one man with the thought of another.

"What is it?" Tocquet said.

A tear must have spilled onto her cheek. "It's nothing," Elise said, unclasping her hand from the bougainvillea. "I pricked my thumb."

Tocquet stooped to kiss away the brilliant dot of blood. Down the drive came the sound of horses, but Elise did not turn to look. She raised her face to her husband and said, "I'm lucky to be alive."

As they turned in at the Thibodet gate, Captain Daspir spurred up his horse, distancing himself from Guizot, Ferrari, and Aloyse, and overtaking Major Maillart at the head of the column. He leaned across, and Maillart bent his ear to him.

"It's true what you said," Daspir told him.

"What," said Maillart. "What did I say?"

"All the black generals are to be deported, in the end," Daspir said, lowering his voice as he leaned closer. "Once the disarmament is complete."

"The disarmament." Maillart snorted so vigorously his horse whickered in response. Leclerc's effort to disarm the populace had so far been a complete fiasco. Toussaint had taught them all too well that the musket was the physical embodiment of freedom.

"I had it from Guizot, some time ago," Daspir said. "About the deportations. Rochambeau speaks of it loosely, when he drinks. And I remembered that you wanted to know . . ."

"Well, thank you." Maillart looked him in the eye and touched his hat brim. Daspir nodded and fell back, as the Thibodet *grand'case* came into view around the curve of the drive. Good of the captain to have given him that news, Maillart supposed. It must mean no hard feelings over Isabelle. But in a way he'd rather not have known. He did not much care for his present mission either, though he could not have avoided it without casting his own loyalty in doubt. Soldier's luck and a soldier's pay, he thought in the jogging rhythm of his horse's trot. And of course for the younger officers it would be a great thing to be in at the kill.

"Hello the house," he called out heartily. "No fever here?"

"Fever? There is none," Nanon replied from the gallery. Behind her the doctor emerged barefoot, wiping his glasses on the shirt he carried wadded in one hand.

"You've come in force," Elise said, standing to survey the sixty horsemen of their detachment. "Let me send to find out what can be found from the kitchen—but you, Major, come up and take some soup."

"No, no." Maillart grinned and belted out his loudest voice. "We've only come to greet you—we can't stop. We must join General Brunet at Habitation Georges."

"I'll ride with you that far," the doctor said. "Let me get my boots."

"Oh no," said Maillart, "I don't think, really—"

"I won't be a moment," the doctor said, shrugging into his shirt, and then Guizot was chiming in: "Of course you must come—it will be a grand outing."

In five more minutes the whole cavalcade had reversed direction and was moving back the way it had come, with the children gamboling after the horses toward the gate, and the doctor bringing up the rear, astride a mule, his rifle balanced across his knees, having professed the intention to bring back wild meat for the table.

"What did they come for if they won't stop?" Elise directed the question toward Nanon, but it was Tocquet who responded.

"I don't know," he said musingly. "But they seem to have left us a good dozen sentries."

Elise stood up and shaded her eyes. It was true; four dragoons were lingering at the lower end of the drive, and several more had circled behind the house and the cane mill and were fanning out across the rising terraces of coffee.

"Whatever for?" Elise said lightly. Tocquet was lighting one of his cheroots, though it was a little early in the day for him to begin to smoke.

"A kindness of the major, I suspect," he said. "To see us safe." He turned toward her, his whole face crooked. "I think they must be going to arrest Toussaint."

Isaac had unbelted his sword, for it was uncomfortable to sit and read with the hilt of it sticking into his side. He'd hung scabbard and belt and all over a waist-high post of the gallery rail and propped back his chair against the wall as he delved the story of Paris and Syrinx out of the Latin, how the nymph escaped by changing herself into a reed which the satyr then harvested to trim into a flute. It was a slow pleasure, won with difficulty, but Isaac gave it all his patience, knowing that while Toussaint prized a fluency in Latin, he did not really understand the language as *blancs* did, but could only scatter a few phrases he had picked up from church liturgy. If Placide had made himself a warrior for their father, Isaac might evolve into a scholar, and so, in the peace which was now begun, might prove of equal value to his brother, if not greater.

He was so well drowned in the depths of this reading that he was slow to notice the noise of shooting from the direction of the road. By the time he had laid down the book and risen, his mother had come out to stand at the head of the stairs, the blue headcloth tight above her eyes, gazing through and beyond the line of French grenadiers who, bayonets lowered, had flushed a crowd of skirmishing field hands out of the woods around the lane. Saint-Jean had pressed himself against her, and Suzanne held him under her crossed hands, in front of her, both of them facing the soldiers as they advanced.

Guerrier and Bienvenu ran up the steps, well ahead of the others in retreat, Guerrier clasping his right arm to his side. Blood came trickling through his fingers. Bienvenu snatched Isaac's sword from the post and thrust it toward him, as Guerrier said between his gritted teeth, "Hurry, there is still time to get away, a horse is waiting in the stable yard—"

But Isaac's feet were rooted to the floor. "If they have already killed my father—" he began. His whole face was numb, not only his tongue. "There is no reason for me to save myself."

There was a racket from within; they had broken into the back of the house. Sound of a slap and a woman's shriek, then one of Isaac's girl cousins raced with her hands over her face and cowered against Suzanne Louverture. A *blanc* soldier appeared in the doorway, and Bienvenu dropped Isaac's sword to draw a pistol, but there was only a dead click when he fired, for the weapon had already been discharged. Bienvenu howled his disappointment as he vaulted over the rail, rolled, and ran after Guerrier, who had already taken the same way to the ravine.

The soldier raised his bayonet as Isaac approached him, but Isaac shouldered past him and went to his father's scriptorium. One officer was scattering paper from the desk; he kicked the orary which Isaac had salvaged from Sancey against the wall, bending the mechanism. Captain Cyprien was doing his best to stuff the vase depicting Toussaint's triumphs into the pocket of his coat, though it was too large to fit.

"Captain," Isaac said. "I did not take you for a thief. That is my father's property."

At once another grenadier backed him to the wall with a bayonet to his throat, and one of General Brunet's aides-de-camp turned from the mantel to sneer, "Your father has no property."

"Why," said Isaac, outraged, "you have stolen my plume." In fact the aide-de-camp had taken the fine feather from the hat which completed Isaac's dress uniform, and which had been hanging in the scriptorium, and placed it in the band of his own hat. In one hand he also held Isaac's ornamental spurs.

"Let the prisoner be silent," smirked the aide-de-camp, and then as he turned back to the mantel he addressed the room at large: "Can you imagine the effrontery, to clothe the Madonna in this gaudiness?"

On the mantel stood a foot-high image of the Virgin, a gift to Toussaint from General Clairvaux. The aide-de-camp pulled the gold coronet from her head and snapped off the hand that wore a ruby ring and broke loose her china ears to get the pearls in them. As he dropped this loot into his pocket, Isaac lunged out from the wall to stop him, but the grenadier smacked him in the ribs with his gun stock, then chivvied him out onto the gallery, prodding him in the kidneys with the bayonet. The battalion commander Pesquidoux had appeared in the yard, and was handing the women up into a wagon, where Saint-Jean had already found a seat.

Cyprien approached him again, standing near enough that Isaac could smell rum and rot on his breath. "Where is your brother?"

"I don't know," said Isaac. "I thought that he had started for Gonaives."

Cyprien cursed and turned from him. "If we have let him slip away . . ." he said to Brunet's aide-de-camp, who was just coming out of the house. "This one's no worry, but the other will fight."

Cyprien bent to scoop Isaac's sword belt from the floor and handed it to him. "Go on," he said shortly. "Get into the wagon."

Isaac's face burned as he buckled on the sword. That aide-de-camp was grinning at him, and the bayonet was gouging him in the back again, and all of them knew that his weapon was no more dangerous to them than a loaf of bread. Slowly he clambered into the wagon, his ribs paining him with every breath, and took a place among the others, facing backward. The sobbing of his cousin hurt his head. His mother and brother were silent, and there was no sound except the creaking of the wagon as the mules began to pull; speechless, they all watched the *grand'case* of Descahaux shrink away from them.

From the moment they rode out of Habitation Thibodet, everything ran contrary to the progress of Maillart's detachment. Huge *gommiers* had blown down across a section of the road, making it impassable. A normally negligible stream had somehow risen to a flood, so that they must work their way nearly two miles down the bank before finding a place that horses could cross.

Worst of all was the doctor, who had no understanding of their errand (Maillart had not wanted him to understand it) and so behaved as if the whole journey were a hunting expedition—whenever he was not straying from the trail to harvest herbs. At last he deployed his long American rifle to bring down a wild goat from a crag some five hundred yards distant, so that the half of the detachment who'd bet on his success shouted their enthusiasm, while even the losers groaned a grudging admiration. Maillart collected from both Daspir and Aloyse, but whatever pleasure he took in his winnings was tempered by knowing that now there was nothing for it but they must recover the carcass from the inaccessible crevice into which it had dropped, and then it must be bled and gutted and dressed . . . The doctor's mule was inured to carrying butchered game, but the blood smell panicked the horses.

It was dusk when finally they came to Habitation Georges, and Brunet's sentries were seething with impatience.

"My Christ," one of them hissed. "Where have you been?"

"No use telling it," Maillart sighed, squinting at the house. "Is he here?"

"He has been here for some time." The sentry looked over his shoulder. "He's in the house—but he's impatient. He brought more guards than we expected—take your positions quickly, will you?"

Maillart nodded and looked back the way they had come. The doctor had not yet materialized—he was trailing the others by a couple of hundred yards, to keep his blood stench away from the horses. Maillart gave a few quick orders, and as his men dispersed to their duties he walked up toward the *grand'case* with Guizot and Daspir and Aloyse, toward a couple of Toussaint's guards who were talking quietly below a tall hedge that covered them from the house. Young Captain Ferrari had already gone inside, with a couple of Brunet's people.

As Maillart drew near enough to pick out the faces of Toussaint's men, he let out a quick breath of dismay.

"What is it?" Daspir said, bumping his shoulder.

"Nothing," Maillart whispered. "Only—that one with the scars is a fanatic. We'll take Toussaint over his dead body." But it was Riau whose presence really troubled him—if only Riau, above all, had not been there.

Half a mile north of Morne Saint Juste, Placide pulled up his horse. César, one of his father's men who had been riding with him, reined up too and looked at him. Placide turned his face across the wind that blew in steadily from the coast. The low plain was empty except for scrubs of *raket* and *baroron* and the blowing white dust. The shaly white eminence of Morne Saint Juste was the only feature west of the road, round and white as a church dome. On the summit Placide could just make out the faces of a few people who were standing there; their bodies were mostly indistinguishable because they were all dressed in white. The wind was blowing at their backs. In spite of the distance he felt that possibly they saw him too.

"Come on," he said and turned his horse. A long way south down the road, below Morne Saint Juste, bloomed a cloud of dust that concealed other riders.

"Koté n'alé?" César said. Where are we going? But he didn't seem surprised or troubled when Placide did not answer.

They held a trot going up the hill down which they had just come. A file of market women passed them, going down to Gonaives, and one of them looked up, smiling, and returned her head to the way before her. Placide felt how the eggshell closed around him. It still possessed the harmony he'd felt that morning, but it was no longer working in his favor. When the ground leveled they rode in a smooth canter toward the crossroads of Ennery. The red *mouchwa têt*, folded in Placide's shirt pocket, felt warm over his heart, and he thought of stopping to tie it on his head, but then thought better of that, or worse.

A strange silence covered the mango sellers at the Ennery *kalfou*, though the *marchandes* had been jovial when they passed that way an hour before. A French cavalry squadron was galloping down the road ahead, and now foot soldiers swarmed up from the river, overrunning the women with their baskets full of mangoes. Placide wheeled, to see that the other squadron, the one they'd seen below Morne Saint Juste, was coming up to cut off that retreat.

César produced an enormous dragoon pistol, but Placide checked him with a hand on his arm.

"Don't," he said. "There's no hope in it." And César seemed to accept what he had said. Mutely he shifted his hand from the grip to the barrel, ready to give up the gun to the approaching *blancs*. Placide supposed he would do the same with his own weapons.

The moment was whole, though inauspicious. *We'll see each other*, Toussaint had said, *if God wills*. But apparently God willed otherwise.

A couple of middle-sized boys trotted alongside the doctor's mule as he rode up the drive of Habitation Georges, smiling appreciatively at the butchered goat. One of them reached out shyly to touch a dangling hoof. It would be agreeable, the doctor thought, to cut off a shoulder for their mothers' cookpots. But if he started on that course he wouldn't have a scrap of meat to offer back at Thibodet.

He dismounted a good distance from the others' horses and pegged the mule on a long tether so it could graze. The goat was still strapped behind the saddle and the rifle tilted crazily before it. In the thickening dusk he could just make out the shadowy figures of Maillart's men as they spread along the pathways that spiraled in back of the house and into the fields, encountering others of Brunet's corps, and also some of Toussaint's guards, he now realized. It was peculiarly quiet, the air damp and heavy, as before rain. Though he could see the direction of movement of the clouds in the dark, the stars above him were closing off one by one. On an impulse he checked the pistols on his belt, and looked back once to where his mule grazed calmly, secure on its tether.

As he turned forward, he recognized the group beneath the hedge: his friends, Maillart and Guiaou and Riau, with Daspir and Guizot. His vision rushed out from him to the distant point where these men stood, as it had done that afternoon when he picked the goat off the crag. Though he had never known why this gift was his, to see a target at any distance was the same as touching it with a bullet from his gun.

When he reached the little group below the hedge, one of his pistols had climbed into his hand, and he knew the others most certainly were aware of it, though none of them looked at it directly, and no one spoke. The sound of thunder shuddered over the mountain east of the *grand'case*. Now the doctor knew why Maillart had been so reluctant for him to come here; he saw it as clearly as the place behind the shoulder of the goat where he had known his rifle would surely send its bullet. But there was no action he would take. He could not choose between Maillart or Riau or any of the other men who stood before him. The pistol dropped from his slackening hand and discharged as it hit the ground, the bullet digging a furrow in the turf.

Guizot barked his surprise and skipped aside, though the shot had not come near him. The doctor turned away from the group before anyone else could react or speak to him. He walked in a hasty, stumbling stride, passing the mule and turning toward the low ground where brush and small trees sprouted from a branching ditch. A little stream ran through it, and the doctor crouched on the bank, pulling his knees to his chin and wrapping his hands around his head, thinking: It could have all been different. It should have all been different, but it wasn't going to be.

Toussaint turned his head toward the open window through which they'd heard the shot.

"What was that?" he said, though his tone barely made it a question.

"The thunder," Brunet said with an uneasy smile. The two of them were alone in a pleasant rectangular room with generous windows on three sides, though now the glass had darkened as the rain settled in with the night. The table between them was spread with maps and lists of the disposition of French troops in the region, but little progress had been made on the matter at hand. Since Toussaint's arrival, Brunet had filled most of the time by pressing him to stay the night and wondering why he had not brought his wife and sons with him and professing to be awaiting another officer who would come with more current information about the quartering of the troops.

"A gunshot." Toussaint turned his head and touched the knot of his yellow headcloth with a fingertip. "A pistol, I would say."

"Surely not. Look, there is the rain." Brunet raised his chin. Beyond the window the first raindrops were splattering onto the hedge that enclosed the house.

"But pardon me," Brunet said. "I will investigate."

Toussaint could discern the faintest tremor in the *blanc* general's fingers as he rose. Brunet bowed out of the room and drew the door carefully shut behind him. The door latch clicked. Beyond was the sound of whispering. Toussaint got up and walked slowly along the three walls of windows, cocking up the hilt of his sword so that the scabbard would not drag the floor. The windows were slick with rain, and several of them were ajar, so that rain blew in on the east side of the room to dampen the carpet, but Toussaint did not trouble to close them. The lamp on the table behind him returned his reflection, his face fractured and multiplied across the glossy black panes. The rainfall muffled the quiet movements of men outside, shuffling invisibly beyond the hedge. Toussaint returned to his seat, his long sword twitching behind him like the tail of a stalking cat.

When he had settled in his chair, General Brunet entered and stood with one hand on the doorknob behind him.

"It is nothing," he said. "A misfire—the soldier has been reprimanded. But pardon me only a moment more. The man is just now coming with our information."

Again the door latch clicked, and Toussaint relaxed, flattening his hands on the tabletop. He let his eyes sink almost shut and listened to the sound of scuffling feet outside, half covered by the growing roar of rain.

Though he had been warned and in any case knew what was likely to happen, Daspir was quite unprepared when, just as the first raindrops scattered over them, Maillart flung himself on Riau and carried him bodily to the ground. Maillart was much the larger of the two, and he covered Riau so entirely that it was not clear whether he meant to attack or somehow to shield him. Guizot looked frozen in his tracks, and even the veteran Aloyse was taken unaware, wiping rain from the barrel of his musket with a worn-out sock. Guiaou moved first, his *coutelas* rising to strike at Maillart's back, but Daspir, with a strength and speed he didn't know he possessed, swung his saber with a force that made a fresh tear in his injured shoulder and sent Guiaou's severed head tumbling to a stop against the hedge. Guizot and Aloyse stared open-mouthed as the headless body took two steps forward, past the white man and the black one entwined on the muddy ground, and then as though its intention had changed, stabbed the *coutelas* deep into the earth as it collapsed.

Someone hissed from the next corner of the hedge: "Is it done?" And Daspir heard his own voice answer, "Yes, we are all secure."

This other man gestured him urgently toward the house. Daspir had unconsciously been stripping blood from his blade with his fingers; now when he saw his bloody hand he held out the palm for the rain to cleanse it. Guizot nudged him, and Daspir began to walk toward the house, with Guizot a pace behind. He nudged him once more when they reached the steps, and Daspir remembered to return the saber to its sheath.

Riau only struggled a moment when Maillart flattened him to the ground, for Maillart pressed his lips to his ear as if he would kiss it and hissed, "Lie still, if you want to live. Lie still." Then Riau went completely limp, pressed down into the damp earth by Maillart's weight and so completely covered that no one could reach him.

When Daspir and Guizot had gone, Riau began to speak in a low voice, almost indistinguishable in the rain. "Tell me, my captain." He had the rank wrong, and yet it was right. Maillart had been Riau's captain at the start; that had been their first relation.

"My captain, you mean to betray us all to slavery."

Maillart turned his face to the side and found himself looking at Guiaou's head, upright on its stump against the hedge, the eyes still open and holding the false gleam of the rain. Nearby were the toes of Aloyse's boots, and Maillart felt the weight of the sergeant's unhappiness settling on him like shame, but Aloyse was soldier to the bone; he would not deviate from orders.

"Captain, you don't look at me," Riau still whispered. "You don't answer, my captain. That is because you do not want to lie."

Rainwater poured from Guiaou's open eyes, filled the deep furrows of his scarred face, and carried the blood of his death into the ground.

Maillart was choking uncontrollably, spilling fat salty tears into the cup of Riau's collarbone, so bitter to him was the sum of his own actions. He did not remember any time when he had wept before, though he supposed he must have done so when a child. Riau wriggled to disengage one arm and laid it over Maillart's back. Aloyse's feet shifted as he trained his musket, but it was clear enough that Riau only meant to hold Maillart a little closer to him.

"So?" Brunet whispered when Daspir and Guizot entered the hall. The general's face was pale and speckled with cold sweat.

"His guards are in our hands," said Daspir, as that seemed to be the reply expected.

"It's well it was done quietly," Brunet said. A dozen more officers were with Ferrari in the foyer, and the salon opposite was full of bristling grenadiers.

"Let us get on with it," Brunet said. But it was clear that the general himself did not mean to enter the room where Toussaint waited. And so for that moment there was no leader. Daspir saw in a flash that he and Guizot might very well take command in this vacuum, and make the capture they had wagered to make. But he no longer desired the prize, and he saw from a glance at Guizot's face that Guizot didn't either.

In the end it was Ferrari who took them through the door. Since Paltre's death, Ferrari had completed the quartet of captains. He was a more agreeable fellow than Paltre, though because they had shared less, the other three did not feel as close to him. And Cyprien was absent, off on some other mission; Daspir felt how queer it was to be distracted by that thought now, as they all pressed into the room where the little black general was waiting.

At first Toussaint seemed completely unaware of them, so deep was his stillness behind the table, but in the next moment he was on his feet, the table overturned between him and the officers, and Toussaint had put his back into a corner where he could not be reached from either window, where any man moving toward him would tangle with the table legs. His sword was half out of the sheath, and his hip was cocked to complete the draw.

"General," said Ferrari. His voice was careful, but warm at the same time; Daspir thought it was just the right note to have struck.

"We don't intend any attempt on your days," Ferrari said. "But you must know that the house is surrounded, and all your men have been disarmed."

Toussaint made no reply to that. The grenadiers were jostling in behind Daspir, but they were pressing for a look, not to attack. The invisible half-circle between Toussaint and the soldiers remained inviolate, and Daspir knew he did not have the will to break the barrier, and he doubted if anyone else among them did. Then Toussaint settled on his heels, and sheathed his sword.

Dessounen:
Fort de Joux, France

April 1803

The flagstones on the floor were frozen. Each step fired a bolt of cold from the arch of Toussaint's foot to the top of his head. He crept to the hearth, curling his shoulders around the pain of his heartbeat and his ragged breath. His left arm was a dead weight in its sling. One-handed, crouching at the edge of the fireplace, he slowly teased a coal free of the ash and blew it to flame, then added tinder till the fire began to grow.

For some little time he rested, squatting on his heels, then pushed himself up and went to the table where his provisions were laid. He put a measure of oats and a measure of water into an iron pot and covered it and set it on the fire. A few beads of water sizzled dry on the outside surface of the iron. With his one good arm he dragged his chair to a spot almost within the hearth and sat.

As often, it seemed that the heat could not reach him. Though the flames were bright and lively, they felt cold as the snow outside the fort. There was a draft behind him, a current of cold air running from the grate that closed the far end of the cell to the crack beneath the iron-bound door. Behind him too was another figure which Toussaint saw in his mind's eye, black-garbed and crouching like a cricket, twitching the bones of its fingers to make a rattling sound. The tall black hat slouched down to cover the dark left socket of the toothy skull.

Baron was here. In the bones of his left hand, he held the filigreed iron cross. Toussaint knew, in part, that the rattle came from his own labored breathing, but truly it belonged to Baron Samedi, who waited just a pace behind him, raising his cross high above the cemetery gate. But this time he was not afraid, though Baron owned his breath. On the cemetery ground stood Guiaou and also the one-eyed Moyse, and between them Quamba, the *hûngan* of Thibodet. Strangely, the earth of the cemetery had all been covered over with cement, and Quamba was explaining to the other two that it was done to stop *bokors* from stealing corpses and raising them to work as slaves.

But all this masonry had no strength. Quamba stooped and showed how it would shatter in his hand, crumbling as easily as any dried-earth clod. Then Moyse and Guiaou fell to work with the tools they carried with them, Moyse a pointed spade and Guiaou his *coutelas*. Together they began to open the earth. Toussaint recognized with a shock and a thrill that the hard carapace of the Fort de Joux was breaking apart at the touch of their blades. If he had known sooner, if he could have known how easily the stones of the fort would disintegrate, he would have been gone a long time before now.

He sagged in the chair, resting the swollen side of his face against the stones around the fireplace, and let his right hand trail down to the floor. The cold of the paving stone made no impression on him now. In fact it was warm, as warm as himself, but the heat did not come from the fire. The source of the warmth was the great light above and behind him, a luminescence clearer than the sun. He saw his twin shadows moving on the timbers of the door, the dark shadow dancing within the flicker of the pale one. In the hollow at the base of his head he felt the fluttering of his own *mêt' têt*, Attibon Legba, the master of changes, moving like a moth about to fly.

Then the two shadows parted as the door opened between them, and from the highest point of the vault he looked down to see Franz and Amiot walk in. Amiot called the name, *Toussaint*. When no reply came the commandant crossed the cell and brusquely shook the body slumped in the chair. The cold face skated against the wall, and the dangling arm jerked stiffly; Amiot recoiled as if he'd reached for a human hand and touched a snake instead.

The abandoned pot foamed a scum of oatmeal onto the fire. Franz stooped to move it from the heat, then knelt beside the chair. He lifted the dangling hand and held it for a moment between his, stroking the wrist for the absent pulse and looking up toward the top of the vault as if, perhaps, he had recognized something, but Toussaint was already gone.

Amiot held the wax stick to his tilted candle's flame. A red blob dripped to the fold of his last letter, and he impressed it with the seal carved on his ring. Outside, the castle bell began to clang, but Amiot was too distracted to count the strokes. It was night and dark and bitter cold. The wax hardened quickly on the edges of the paper where he'd inscribed his request to be relieved of command of the Fort de Joux. Bonaparte's trust was surely a valuable prize, but Amiot had begun to curse the aspect of fate that had made him a jailer.

At his left hand the other documents were signed and stamped and sealed as required. There was the report of the autopsy conducted by Doctor Gresset and the surgeon Pajot: *A little mucus mixed with blood in the mouth and on the lips . . . Bloody swelling of the right lung and of the corresponding pleura. Mass of purulent matter in that organ. A small fatty polyp in the right ventricle of the heart, of which the rest was in its normal condition . . . In consequence we conclude that apoplexy and pleural pneumonia are the causes of the death of Toussaint Louverture.*

There too was a report of Toussaint's effects which had been sold at auction in the town of Pontarlier; commencing with *a suit of calmouk rayé, half-worn-out, sold for nine francs after several bids to the counselor Faivre, bookseller of Pontarlier* and concluding with *six blue quadrille kerchiefs sold after several bids to the citizen Jenat, merchant of Pontarlier, for nine francs.* Between, the other items auctioned consisted mostly of personal linen, with one riding coat and two religious tracts. In a separate document Amiot had reported other articles which had been confiscated and were in his own possession before Toussaint's demise: *one gold collar button, one watch with a gold case accompanied by a chain and a key of perfectly convincing imitation gold, one pair of silver spurs, one uniform in bad condition, decorated with a light gold braid, with yellow leather buttons and two epaulettes, one used hat decorated in gold, and one case with a razor.* These items remained in Amiot's charge because he did not know what to do with them. Perhaps they might be returned to Toussaint's survivors; there was supposed to be some family, though he didn't know much about it and did not wish to know more.

To the Minister of Marine Amiot had reported the date and hour of Toussaint Louverture's death, at eleven o'clock on the seventh of April; that he had sent a special messenger to notify the general in chief commanding the sixth military division of the event, and that he had caused Toussaint's body to be buried by a priest of the commune by the old chapel of the Fort de Joux, where in former times soldiers of the garrison had been interred. *I believe,* he concluded, *that in taking these precautions I have fulfilled the wishes of the Government.* He had taken the further precaution of leaving Toussaint's grave unmarked, lest it should somehow become a shrine, this action too, in his belief, fulfilling a wish of the Government. As if the savage blacks who had been his fanatics could travel round half the curve of the earth to bring their furies here.

And so he came to his last letter, which he lifted and placed on top of the stack. Let the reply come soon and be favorable. Amiot felt confidently justified in requesting his relief, because he had accomplished his mission, which had been—had always been, as he certainly knew—to see Toussaint Louverture dead.

Already he was anxious to be gone, though he knew he must endure some days of waiting, he hoped not weeks. What a joy it would be to depart from this place. He had begun to think that there really was something about it which deranged people. Toussaint was far from the only person to have suffered and died in the fort's oubliettes, but Amiot, as a rational man, refused to believe that the place could be haunted. More likely the air at this altitude was simply too thin, or the cold impeded circulation of the blood, so that the brain, starved of its nourishment, produced these peculiarly plaguing fantasies.

The guardsman Franz was already gone. Amiot would have liked to punish him, but could find no legitimate pretext. So he had simply given him a two-weeks leave to visit his family hovel across the Swiss border. With any luck, he himself would have departed by the time the old soldier returned. He had proposed that Franz needed a leave to rest and recover, on the evidence of the mad thing he had uttered when he and Amiot had discovered Toussaint dead in his cell.

The very sight of Franz had become odious to Amiot, with his deep-set eyes and his war-weary face and the outmoded pigtail he persisted in wearing to remind everyone that he had served the First Consul in a former avatar, when Bonaparte had been a liberator. Even now, when it was late and his office tasks were at last concluded, he was reluctant to lie down and close his eyes, lest the image of Franz should appear before him, kneeling, holding Toussaint's stiff hand between his, parting his lips to pronounce his queer sentence. It was nonsensical, but Amiot could not elude the phrase. It invaded his head in the night when he woke and could not sleep again, or wormed into moments of the day when he believed his mind was empty: *The prisoner has escaped.*

Weté Mò anba Dlo
Haiti
April 1825

Since Quamba died at Vertières, I, Riau, I keep the *hûnfor* on the hill at Thibodet. Quamba did not go to the fighting before, but he carried Guiaou's *coutelas* to Vertières, and the last of the French *blanc* soldiers were defeated there, though Quamba was killed too, with others of our people. I, Riau, before that time, had gone to Grande Rivière to fight with Sans-Souci. When Toussaint was taken, I got up from the mud where Maillart's weight had pressed me, and I turned my back on the *blancs* forever.

Since Guiaou has gone beneath the waters, Riau does not wander any longer, but stays with Merbillay in the *case* behind the *hûnfor* where Quamba lived before. Caco is a man now, and lives with his woman and the children she has given him in the *case* that once was Merbillay's, where Riau's *banza* still hangs from the roof pole. I, Riau, go there sometimes to play the *banza*, and see the little children dance and laugh. The letterbox is left there too in Merbillay's old *case*, that box where Toussaint hid the tokens of his *blanche* lovers. I put new paper in the box, and quills with a knife to sharpen them, but no one calls Riau to copy letters now.

Yet sometimes I will open the box and smooth the paper and sharpen the quill and mix water with the dust of the old ink. I write the names of my children and Guiaou's, and Caco's children, and the names of the children Yoyo and Marielle will begin to bring. I do not often think of anything more to write when those names have been written. Nothing comes to me any more, to make the words march up and down the page like soldiers, as Riau sometimes used to do. Toussaint showed me how the mind of a *blanc* could climb through the words to come into my head and move with me as a spirit moves. This I still know, and sometimes I go walking with that spirit for a little way, but I give it no more service than the rows of names, which I place in the secret part of the box, where Toussaint's souvenirs were hidden.

Merbillay still cooks for the *grand'case*, though all the *blancs* are gone. Only the doctor stays there now, with Nanon and Paul, who is a man now too, married to one of Fontelle's younger daughters. And Fontelle stays there, and Zabeth and the children she made with Bouquart and Michau, and I have written their names too and put them into the box, where no one ever reads them but Riau.

Only the *blanc* gunrunner Tocquet seemed to understand what was certain to happen when Dessalines called all the *grand blancs* to come back to the country and make sugar and coffee again on their planta-tions, the same way that Toussaint had done before. Only Tocquet saw how different was Dessalines's spirit from the spirit that once had walked with Toussaint. Those *blancs* made a reunion in the Cigny house at Le Cap and I, Riau, stood with Bazau and Gros-Jean in the next room, so I heard some of what they said. I heard Madame Isabelle Cigny stamp her foot and cry, "It cannot happen again. It will not!" Then Tocquet said in a low voice, "But it will," and Isabelle demanded, "Why?" Tocquet did not often raise his voice, though he was always ready to slit a throat, but I could hear his anger when he answered, "It will happen again. It will never stop happening. Because the people who rule don't know history."

Then Tocquet took Elise and Sophie and Mireille across the border at Ouanaminthe, with Bazau and Gros-Jean and their women and children and a few others who wanted to go with them. None of the other *blancs* would go, however Elise begged. They all still wanted to believe in the world Toussaint meant to make, where he had saved a place for them. All but Tocquet's people. From Santo Domingo they took a ship to North America, and sometimes even now the doctor has a letter from his sister in the place called Louisiana where they stay, but those people will never come back any more.

There are no more *blancs* in Haiti. At Thibodet, no one grows cane, but only coffee, and not much of that. The doctor treats the sick of all the canton of Ennery, and so the people in the *grand'case* live, though usually he does not ask for pay.

Sometimes I put names of *blancs* in the box, though I do not know for certain why I do it. I have written, *Isabelle Cigny, Robert Cigny, Héloïse Cigny. Michel Arnaud,* and *Claudine Arnaud. Monsieur Cigny* I have writ-ten too, though now I can't remember any longer if his name was *Bernard* or *Bertrand*, and besides he was killed before the others and in a different place. It was not long after Tocquet took his family across the border that Dessalines hunted all the *blancs* of Le Cap out of their houses and herded them into the Place d'Armes. Some of these *blancs* tried to pretend they really were *gens de couleur,* but then the soldiers made them sing—

> *Nanon pralé chaché dlo*
> *krich-li casé . . .*

Anyone who sang French words instead of Creole was known to be a *blanc.*

> *Nanon's going to look for water*
> *her jug is broken . . .*

They were all caught, whose names Riau has written, and the doctor was taken with them. The doctor could have sung that song very well, but he would not do it. His own Nanon and Paul were not taken, since it was plain Nanon and Paul had the blood of Guinée. When he walked before the *blancs* who were herded together in the Place d'Armes, Dessalines stopped to look at the doctor for a long time, but the doctor never dropped his eyes, and finally Dessalines moved his snuffbox to his right hand and said, *Li nèg*—and the soldiers let the doctor walk away. He is black, Dessalines had said. The doctor's back was straight and he held his head up with his beard's point sticking out, and the only thing that showed of his feeling was a small tremble in his finger ends. He did not stop to look back at the people he was leaving behind him.

Then Dessalines's band played "La Carmagnole" and the soldiers marched all the *blancs* to La Fossette and killed them there, the men, the women, and the children, all, but I, Riau, I did not follow to that killing ground. I ran away for the last time into *marronage,* because I did not want to kill any more people whether they were *blancs* or not. Later on I heard that at first the other soldiers did not want to start the killing either, until Clervaux caught a *blanc* baby by its legs and smashed its brains out on a rock, and so the rest of them were able to begin.

I knew that when Toussaint had asked the *grand blancs* back to live in peace and freedom, they betrayed him and sent him away to die alone in France. Boisrond Tonnerre gave the words to Dessalines: *For our declaration of independence we must have the skin of a blanc for parchment, his skull for an inkwell, his blood for ink, and a bayonet for pen.* I knew the reason Dessalines acted as he did, but still I did not want to join in that action. At first I went to Grande Rivière, though Sans-Souci was already dead by that time. Christophe had tricked Sans-Souci to a meeting at the foot of Morne la Ferrière and killed him there. Later on, when Dessalines was killed too, Riau came home to Ennery.

There was nothing I could do to save my captain Maillart.

People say that when the soldiers came back with their bloody hands from La Fossette, the band did not play any music at all, but I, Riau, I was not there to hear them if they played or not. Before that day, Dessalines had already gone down to Arcahaye, where he tore the white band from the middle of the French flag, and Catherine Flon sewed the red and the blue cloth together. Since then there are no more *blancs* in Haiti. Even the doctor is *nèg*.

Sometimes when the day is ending, I sit and drink rum with the doctor on the gallery of the *grand'case* at Thibodet. During those times we do not talk much, but only listen to the voices of the doves finding their nests under the eaves, and the hum of the bees who go in and out of the holes they have bored in the wood of the gallery. When the sky darkens I feel that the doctor is thinking how everything might have ended differently if Toussaint had not gone to meet Brunet that day, or if some other small thing had been other than it was. Maybe it could have been, but it is not.

Depi nan Ginen, nèg rayi nèg, the old people say. Since Africa, people have hated one another. I see it is not the only truth, but there is much to prove it. I see that Christophe killed Sans-Souci because neither he nor Dessalines could bear to know that Sans-Souci began the last fight against the *blancs* before them, and they could not bear that others knew it too. I see that Dessalines and Christophe and even Maurepas did work of the left hand against Toussaint for the same reason, and for that same reason Dessalines killed Charles Belair. Now Dessalines is dead himself, his body torn to pieces where they killed him at Pont Rouge, and Christophe after him is dead, killed by a bullet of his own gun in the midst of another rising.

I, Riau, will live to grow old. Already I have made more than half my journey. In the letterbox I keep the names of many who have gone beneath the waters or will go, *Macandal, Boukman, Moyse, Toussaint, Sans-Souci, Charles Belair, Maurepas, Dessalines, Christophe, Charlemagne Peralte, Benoît Batraville, Sonson Pasquet, Riquet Pepignard, Phito Dominique, Jean Chenet, Jacques Alexis, Richard Brisson, Gerald Brisson, Gusle Villedrouin, Roger Rigaud, Réginal Jourdan, Louis Drouin, Marcel Numa, Georges Izmery, Antoine Izmery, Père Jean-Marie Vincent, Guy Malary, Amos Jeannot, Brignol Lindor, Jean Dominique* . . . There are worms who come into the box to feed on the paper where the names are written. Those worms are too small for the eye to see, and they do not hurt the wood of the box, but they make holes through all the papers, till the paper is like lace. No one reads the names Riau has written but the worms.

When the time was right, I, Riau, I made the *Weté Mò anba Dlo*, and called the spirit of Toussaint to the *canari* where still it rests, at one with Attibon Legba, in the *kay mystè* high on our hill above Ennery. There was no one better than Riau to make that service. The sons of Toussaint's wife never came out of France again, and Toussaint's bones were scattered a long way off in the land of the *blancs,* but his spirit is still waiting here, amidst all *sa nou pa wé yo.* There is more of *what we don't see* than what we do. Sometimes the spirit of Toussaint will walk a little way with one whose name Riau has written in the box, if it is one who has already died or one who has not yet been born.

Now my eyes don't see the things of this world as clearly as they used to do. My eyes turn toward *les Invisibles, les Morts et les Mystères.* I see that day which is long ago now, when Riau called Toussaint's spirit back from beneath the waters, to sigh in the jar where still it waits for a name strong enough to carry it all the way to the end of its road. There were no clouds and no wind on that day, and the air was so clear that one who stood with Riau on the hilltop could see beyond Ennery all the way to the coast. Away to the west the horizon curved up to meet the falling of the red sun, and the top of the ocean was like the skin of a drum stretched tight.

GLOSSARY

During the Haitian Revolution, Haitian Creole had no systematic orthography. The spellings of Creole words used in this book are modeled on those used by francophone writers of the period, and are not meant to be consistent with the orthography of Haitian Creole today.

À LA CHINOIS: in the Chinese manner.

ABOLITION DU FOUET: abolition of the use of whips on field slaves; a negotiating point before and during the rebellion.

ABUELITA: grandmother.

ACAJOU: mahogany.

AFFRANCHI: a person of color whose freedom was officially recognized; most affranchis were of mixed blood but some were full-blood Africans.

AGOUTI: groundhog sized animal, edible.

LES AMIS DES NOIRS: an abolitionist society in France interested in improving the conditions and ultimately in liberating the slaves of the French colonies.

AJOUPA: a temporary hut made of sticks and leaves.

ALLÉE: a lane or drive lined with trees.

ANCIEN RÉGIME: old order of pre-Revolutionary France.

ANBA DLO: beneath the waters—the Vodou afterworld.

ARISTOCRATES DE LA PEAU: aristocrats of the skin. Many of Sonthonax's policies and proclamations were founded on the argument that white supremacy in Saint

Domingue was analogous to the tyranny of the hereditary French nobility and must therefore be overthrown in its turn by revolution.

ARMOISE: medicinal herb for fever.

ASOTO: large drum.

ASSON: a rattle made from a gourd, an instrument in Vodou ceremonies, and the hûngan's badge of authority.

ATELIER: idiomatically used to mean work gangs or the whole body of slaves on a given plantation.

AU GRAND SEIGNEUR: in a proprietary manner.

BAGUETTE: bread loaf.

BAMBOCHE: celebratory dance party.

BANANE TI-MALICE: small sweet banana.

BANANE LOUP-GAROU: large plantain-like banana.

BANZA: African instrument with strings stretched over a skinhead; forerunner of the banjo.

BAGASSE: remnants of sugar cane whose juice has been extracted in the mill—a dry, fast-burning fuel.

BARON SAMEDI: Vodou deity closely associated with Ghede and the dead, sometimes considered an aspect of Ghede.

BARON CIMETIÈRE: Vodou deity associated with the dead, an aspect of Ghede.

BÂTON: stick, rod. A martial art called *l'art du bâton*, combining elements of African stick-fighting with elements of European swordsmanship, persists in Haiti to this day.

BATTERIE: drum orchestra.

BEAU-PÈRE: father-in-law.

BÊTE DE CORNES: domestic animal with horns.

BIENFAISANCE: philosophical proposition that all things work together for good.

BLANC: white man.

BLANCHE: white woman.

BOIS BANDER: tree whose bark was thought to be an aphrodisiac.

BOIS CHANDEL: candlewood—a pitchy wood suitable for torches.

BOKOR: Vodou magician of evil intent.

BOSSALE: a newly imported slave, fresh off the boat, ignorant of the plantation ways and of the Creole dialect.

BOUCANIERS: piratical drifters who settled Tortuga and parts of Haiti as Spanish rule there weakened. They derived their name from the word *boucan*—their manner of barbecuing hog meat.

BOULETS ROUGES: red-hot shot.

BOUNDA: rectum.

BOURRACHE: curative herb.

BOURG: town.

BOURIK: donkey.

BWA DLO: flowering aquatic plant.

BWA FOUYÉ: dugout canoe.

BWA KANPECH: canapeche tree.

CACHOT: dungeon cell.

CACIQUES: Amerindian chieftains of precolonial Haiti.

CALLALOO: stew with an okra base; gumbo.

CALENDA: a slave celebration distinguished by dancing. Calendas frequently had covert Vodou significance, but white masters who permitted them managed to regard them as secular.

CANAILLE: mob, rabble.

CANZO: intermediate level of initiation and commitment in Vodou.

CARABINIER: rifleman; also a popular dance admired by Dessalines.

CARMAGNOLES: derogatory expression of the English military for the French Revolutionaries.

CARRÉ: square, unit of measurement for cane fields and city blocks.

CASERNES: barracks.

CASQUES: feral dogs.

CAY (CASE): rudimentary one-room house.

LES CITOYENS DU QUATRE AVRIL: denoting persons of color awarded full political rights by the April Fourth Decree, this phrase was either a legal formalism or a sneering euphemism, depending on the speaker.

CHAUDIÈRE: cookpot.

CHICA: bawdy dance.

CLAIRIN: cane rum.

COCOTIER: coconut palm.

COCOTTE: girlfriend, but one in a subordinate role.

COLON: colonist.

COMMANDEUR: overseer or work gang leader on a plantation, usually himself a slave.

COMMERÇANT: businessman.

CONCITOYEN: fellow citizen.

CONGÉ: time off work.

CONGO: African tribal designation. Thought to adapt well to many functions of slavery and more common than others in Saint Domingue.

CORDON DE L'EST: Eastern cordon, a fortified line in the mountains organized by whites to prevent the northern insurrection from breaking through to other departments of the colony.

CORDON DE L'OUEST: Western cordon, as above.

CORPS-CADAVRE: in Vodou, the physical body, the flesh.

COUI: bowl made from a gourd.

COUP POUDRÉ: a Vodou attack requiring a material drug, as opposed to the *coup à l'air*, which needs only spiritual force.

COUTELAS: broad-bladed cane knife or machete.

CREOLE: any person born in the colony whether white, black or colored, whether slave or free. A dialect combining a primarily French vocabulary with primarily African syntax is also called Creole; this patois was not only the means of communication between whites and blacks, but was often the sole common language among Africans of different tribal origins. Creole is still spoken in Haiti today.

CRÊTE: ridge or peak.

DAMBALLAH: Vodou deity associated with snakes, one of the great *loa*.

DEBAKMEN: Debarkation, landing.

DEMOISELLE: Miss, damsel.

DÉSHABILLÉ: a house dress, apt in colonial Saint Domingue to be very revealing; white Creole women were famous for their daring in this regard.

DESSOUNEN: the separation of the *loa mêt' têt*–spirit master of the head—from a person undergoing the transformation of death.

DEVOIR: duty, chore.

DIVERTISSEMENT: diversion.

DJAB: demon.

DOKTÈ-FEY: leaf-doctor, expert in herbal medicine.

DOUCEMENT (DOUSMAN): colloquially, "take it easy."

DOUCEMENT (DOUSMAN) ALLÉ LOIN: "The softest way goes furthest"; a famously favorite proverb of Toussaint Louverture.

ÉBÉNISTE: woodworker.

ÉMIGRÉ: emigrant. In context of the time *émigré* labeled fugitives from the French Revolution, suspected of royalism and support of the *ancien régime* if they returned to French territory, and often subject to legal penalty.

ERZULIE (EZILI): one of the great *loa*, a Vodou goddess roughly parallel to Aphrodite. As Erzulie-Jé-rouge she is maddened by suffering and grief.

ENCEINTE: pregnant.

ESPRIT: spirit; in Vodou it is, so to speak, fungible.

FAÏENCE: crockery.

FAIT ACCOMPLI: done deal.

FAROUCHE: wild, unconventional.

FATRAS: litter, garbage.

FATRAS-BÂTON: thrashing stick. Toussaint bore this stable name in youth because of his skinniness.

FEMME DE CONFIANCE: a lady's quasi-professional female companion.

FEMME DE COULEUR: woman of mixed blood.

FERS: irons.

FILLE DE JOIE: prostitute.

FLEUR DE LYS: stylistically rendered flower and a royalist emblem in France.

FLIBUSTIER: pirate evolved from the wartime practice of privateering.

GAMELLE: large wooden bowl.

GARDE-CORPS: charm, for bodily protection.

GENS DE COULEUR: people of color, a reasonably polite designation for persons of mixed blood in Saint Domingue.

GÉRANT: plantation manager or overseer.

GHEDE: One of the great *loa*, the principal Vodou god of the underworld and of the dead.

GILET: waistcoat.

GIROUMON (JOUMON): squash.

GOMMIER: gum tree.

GOVI: clay vessels which may contain the spirits of the dead.

GRAND BOIS: Vodou deity, aspect of Legba more closely associated with the world of the dead.

GRAND BLANC: member of Saint Domingue's white landed gentry, who were owners of large plantations and large numbers of slaves. The *grand blancs* were
politically conservative and apt to align with royalist counterrevolutionary
movements.

GRAND'CASE: the "big house," residence of white owners or overseers on a plantation; these houses were often rather primitive despite the grandiose title.

GRAND CHEMIN: the big road or main road; in Vodou the term refers to the pathway
opened between the human world and the world of the *loa*.

GRANN: old woman, grandmother.

GRÂCE, LA MISÉRICORDE (GRÂS LAMISERIKÒD): the liturgical phrase Have grace, have
mercy.

GRENOUILLE: frog.

GRIFFE: term for a particular combination of African and European blood; a *griffe*
would result from the congress of a full-blood black with a *mulâttresse* or a
marabou.

GRIFFONNE: female *griffe*.

GRIOT: fried pork.

GROS-BON-ANGE: literally, the "big good angel," an aspect of the Vodou soul. The *gros-
bon-ange* is "the life force that all sentient beings share; it inters the individual
at conception and functions only to keep the body alive. At clinical death, it
returns immediately to God and becomes part of the great reservoir of energy
that supports all life."[1]

GROSSESSE: pregnancy.

GUINÉE EN BAS DE L'EAU: "Africa beneath the waters," the Vodou afterlife.

GUÉRIR-TROP-VITE: medicinal herb used in plasters to speed healing of wounds.

HABITANT: plantation owner.

HABITATION: plantation.

HATTE: terrain for raising horses and livestock, a ranch with a crude dwelling.

HERBE À CORNETTE: medicinal herb used in mixtures for coughing.

HERBE À PIQUE: medicinal herb against fever.

HOMME DE COULEUR: man of mixed blood; see *gens de couleur*.

HÙNFOR: Vodou temple, often arranged in open air.

HÙNGAN: Vodou priest.

HÙNSI: Vodou acolytes.

INTENDANT: the highest civil authority in colonial Saint Domingue, as opposed to
the Governor, who was the highest military authority. These conflicting and
competing posts were deliberately arranged by the home government to make
rebellion against the authority of the metropole less likely.

IBO: African tribal designation. Ibo slaves were thought to be especially prone to
suicide, believing that through death they would return to Africa. Some masters discouraged this practice by lopping the ears and noses of slaves who had
killed themselves, since presumably the suicides would not wish to be resur-
rected with these signs of dishonor.

[1] Wade Davis, *The Serpent and the Rainbow* (New York: Simon and Schuster, 1985),
p. 181.

JOUISSANCE: pleasure.

JOURNAL: newspaper.

KALFOU: crossroads.

KONESANS: spiritual knowledge.

L'AFFAIRE GALBAUD: armed conflict which occurred at the northern port Le Cap, in 1794, between French royalists and Republicans, as a result of which the royalist party, along with the remaining large property and slave owners, fled the colony.

LAMBI: conch shell, used as a horn among maroons and rebel slaves. Also, the meat of the conch, a popular dish.

LANCE À FEU: fire spear.

LA-PLACE: Vodou celebrant with specific ritual functions second to that of the hûngan.

LATANA: medicinal herb against colds.

LAVÉ TÊT: head-washing, initial step of Vodou initiation.

LEGBA: Vodou god of crossroads and of change, vaguely analogous to Hermes of the Greek pantheon. Because Legba controls the crossroads between the material and spiritual worlds, he must be invoked at the beginning of all ceremonies.

LES INVISIBLES: members of the world of the dead, roughly synonymous with Les Morts et les Mystères.

LESPRI GINEN: spirit of Ginen.

LOUP-GAROU: a shape-changing, blood-sucking supernatural entity.

ISLAND BELOW SEA: Vodou belief construes that the souls of the dead inhabit a world beneath the ocean which reflects the living world above. Passage through this realm is the slave's route of return to Africa.

LOA (LWA): general term for a Vodou deity.

LOI DU QUATRE AVRIL: decree of April Fourth from the French National Assembly, granting full political rights to people of color in Saint Domingue.

LOUP-GAROU: in Vodou, a sinister supernatural entity, something like a werewolf.

LIBERTÉ DE SAVANE: freedom, for a slave, to come and go at will within the borders of a plantation or some other defined area, sometimes the privilege of senior *commandeurs*.

LWA BOSSALE: an uninstructed spirit, who may disrupt the decorum of ceremonies.

MACANDAL: a charm, usually worn round the neck.

MACOUTE: a straw sack used to carry food or goods.

MAGOUYÉ: devious person, trickster, cheat.

MAIN-D'OEUVRE: work force.

MAÏS MOULIN: cornmeal mush.

MAÎT' KALFOU: Vodou deity closely associated with Ghede and the dead, sometimes considered an aspect of Ghede.

MAÎT' TÊTE (MÊT TÊT): literally, "master of the head." The particular *loa* to whom the Vodou observer is devoted, by whom he is usually possessed (though the worshipper may sometimes be possessed by other gods as well).

MAL DE MÂCHOIRE: lockjaw.

MAL DE MER: seasickness.

MAL DE SIAM: yellow fever.

MALFINI: chicken hawk.

MALNOMMÉE: medicinal herb used in tea against diarrhea.

MAMBO: Vodou priestess.

MANCHINEEL: jungle tree with an extremely toxic sap.

MANDINGUE: African tribal designation. Mandingue slaves had a reputation for cruelty and for a strong character difficult to subject to servitude.

MANGUIER: mango tree.

MANICOU: Caribbean possum.

MAPOU: sacred tree in Vodou, considered the habitation of Damballah.

MARABOU: term for a particular combination of African and European blood; a marabou would result from the congress of a full-blood black with a *quarteronné*.

MARAIS: swamp.

MARASSA: twins, often the sacred twin deities of Vodou.

MARCHANDE: market woman.

MARCHÉ DES NÈGRES: Negro market.

MARÉCHAL DE CAMP: field marshal.

MARÉCHAUSSÉE: paramilitary groups organized to recapture runaway slaves.

MAROON: a runaway slave. There were numerous communities of maroons in the mountains of Saint Domingue and in some cases they won battles with whites and negotiated treaties which recognized their freedom and their territory.

MARRONAGE: the state of being a maroon; maroon culture in general.

MATANT: aunt.

MAUVAIS SUJET: bad guy, criminal.

MÉNAGÈRE: housekeeper.

MITRAILLE: grapeshot.

MONCHÈ: from the French *mon cher,* literally "my dear," a casual form of address among friends.

MONPÈ: Father—the Creole address to a Catholic priest.

MORNE: mountain.

LES MORTS ET LES MYSTÈRES: The aggregate of dead souls in Vodou, running the spectrum from personal ancestors to the great *loa.*

MOUCHWA TÊT: head scarf.

MOULIN DE BÊTES: mill powered by animals, as opposed to a water mill.

MULATTO: person of mixed European and African blood, whether slave or free. Tables existed to define sixty-four different possible admixtures, with a specific name and social standing assigned to each.

NABOT: weighted leg iron used to restrain a runaway slave.

NÈG: black person (from the French *nègre*).

NÉGOCIANT: businessman or broker involved in the export of plantation goods to France.

NÈGRE CHASSEUR: slave trained as a huntsman.

NÉGRILLON: small black child (c.f. pickaninny).

NOBLESSE DE L'ÉPÉE: French aristocracy deriving its status from the feudal military system, as opposed to newer bureaucratic orders of rank.

OBUSIER: mortar.

OGÛN: one of the great *loa*, the Haitian god of war. Ogûn-Feraille is his most aggressive aspect.

ORDONNATEUR: accountant.

OUANGA: a charm, magical talisman.

PAILLASSE: a sleeping pallet, straw mattress.

PARRAIN: godfather. In slave communities, the *parrain* was responsible for teaching a newly imported slave the appropriate ways of the new situation.

PARIADE: the wholesale rape of slave women by sailors on slave ships; the *pariade* had something of the status of a ritual. Any pregnancies that resulted were assumed to increase the value of the slave women to their eventual purchasers.

PATOIS: dialect.

PAVÉ: paving stone.

PAYSANNE: peasant woman.

PETIT BLANC: member of Saint Domingue's white artisan class, a group which mostly lived in the coastal cities, and which was not necessarily French in origin. The *petit blancs* sometimes owned small numbers of slaves but seldom owned land; most of them were aligned with French Revolutionary politics.

PETITE CERCLE: intimate group.

PETIT MARRON: a runaway slave or maroon who intended to remain absent for only a short period—these escapees often returned to their owners of their own accord.

LA PETITE VÉROLE: smallpox.

PETRO: a particular set of Vodou rituals with some different deities—angry and more violent than *rada*.

PIERRE TONNERRE: thunderstone. Believed by Vodouisants to be formed by lightning striking in the earth—in reality ancient Indian ax heads, pestles, and the like.

PINCE-NEZ: eyeglasses secured by a nose-clip spring.

POMPONS BLANCS: members of the royalist faction in post-1789 Saint Domingue; their name derives from the white cockade they wore to declare their political sentiments. The majority of *grand blancs* inclined in this direction.

POMPONS ROUGES: members of the revolutionary faction in post-1789 Saint Domingue, so called for the red cockades they wore to identify themselves. Most of the colony's *petit blancs* inclined in this direction.

POSSÉDÉ: believer possessed by his god.

POTEAU MITAN: central post in a Vodou *hûnfor,* the metaphysical route of passage for the entrance of the *loa* into the human world.

PRÊTRE SAVANNE: bush priest.

PWA ROUJ: red beans.

PWEN: a focal point of spiritual energy with the power to do magical work. A *pwen* may be an object or even a word or a phrase.

QUARTERONNÉ: a particular combination of African and European blood: the result, for instance, of combining a full-blood white with a mamelouque.

QUARTIER-GÉNÉRAL: headquarters.

RADA: the more pacific rite of Vodou, as opposed to *petro*.

RADA BATTERIE: ensemble of drums for Vodou ceremony.

RAMIER: wood pigeon.

RAQUETTE: mesquite-sized tree sprouting cactus-like paddles in place of leaves.

RATOONS: second-growth cane from plants already cut.

REDINGOTE: a fashionable frock coat.

REQUIN: shark.

RIZ AK PWA: rice and beans.

RIZIÈ: rice paddy.

ROMANIÈRE: curative herb.

SACATRA: a particular combination of African and European blood: the result, for instance, of combining a full-blood black with a *griffe* or *griffonne*.

SAGE-FEMME: wise woman, midwife.

SALLE DE BAINS: washroom.

SANG-MÊLÉ: a particular combination of African and European blood: the result, for instance, of combining a full-blood white with a *quarteronné*.

SANS-CULOTTE: French Revolutionary freedom fighter.

SEREIN: evening breeze.

SERVITEUR: Vodou observer, one who serves the *loa*.

SI DYÉ VLÉ: If God so wills.

SIFFLEUR MONTAGNE: literally mountain whistler, a night-singing bird.

SONGE: dream, vision.

SONNETTE: medicinal herb.

SOULÈVEMENT: popular uprising, rebellion.

SOUPE GIRAUMON: squash soup, also known as *soupe joumoun*.

TABAC À JACQUOT: medicinal herb.

TAFIA: rum.

TAMBOU: drum.

THYM À MANGER: medicinal herb believed to cause miscarriage.

TI BON ANGE: literally, the "little good angel," an aspect of the Vodou soul. "The *ti bon ange* is that part of the soul directly associated with the individual . . . It is one's aura, and the source of all personality, character and willpower."[2]

TONNELLE: brush arbor.

TREMBLEMENT DE TERRE: earthquake.

VÉVÉ: diagram symbolizing and invoking a particular *loa*.

VINGT-ET-UN: card game, a version of blackjack.

VIVRES: life stuff—roots and essential starchy foods.

VODÛN: generic term for a god, also denotes the whole Haitian religion.

YO DI: they say.

Z'ÉTOILE: aspect of the Vodou soul. "The *z'étoile* is the one spiritual component that

[2] Wade Davis, *The Serpent and the Rainbow,* p. 181.

resides not in the body but in the sky. It is the individual's star of destiny, and is viewed as a calabash that carries one's hope and all the many ordered events for the next life of the soul. . . ."[3]

ZAMAN: almond.

ZOMBI: either the soul *(zombi astrale)* or the body *(zombi cadavre)* of a dead person enslaved to a Vodou magician.

ZORAY: ears.

[3] Wade Davis, *The Serpent and the Rainbow*, p. 181.

CHRONOLOGY OF
HISTORICAL EVENTS

1789

JANUARY: In the political context of the unfolding French Revolution, *les gens de couleur*, the mulatto people of the colony, petition for full rights in Saint Domingue.

JULY 7: The French Assembly votes admission of six deputies from Saint Domingue. The colonial deputies begin to sense that it will no longer be possible to keep Saint Domingue out of the Revolution, as the conservatives had always designed.

JULY 14: When news of the storming of the Bastille reaches Saint Domingue, conflict breaks out between the *petit blancs* (lower-class whites of colonial society) and the land- and slave-owning *grand blancs*. The former ally themselves with the Revolution, the latter with the French monarchy.

AUGUST 26: The Declaration of the Rights of Man causes utter panic among all colonists in France.

OCTOBER 5: The Paris mob brings King and Assembly to Paris from Versailles. The power of the radical minority becomes more apparent.

OCTOBER 14: A royal officer at Fort Dauphin in Saint Domingue reports unrest among the slaves in his district, who are responding to news of the Revolution leaking in. There follows an increase in nocturnal slave gatherings and in the activity of the slave-policing *maréchaussée*.

OCTOBER 22:   Les Amis des Noirs (a group of French sympathizers with African slaves in the colonies) collaborate with the wealthy mulatto community of Paris, organized as the society of Colons Américains. Mulattoes claim Rights of Man before the French Assembly. Abbé Grégoire and others support them. Deputies from French commercial towns trading with the colony oppose them.

DECEMBER 3:   The French National Assembly rejects the demands of mulattoes presented on October 22.

1790

OCTOBER 28:   The mulatto leader Ogé, who has reached Saint Domingue from Paris by way of England, aided by the British abolitionist society, raises a rebellion in the northern mountains near the border, with a force of three hundred men, assisted by another mulatto, Chavannes. Several days later an expedition from Le Cap defeats him, and he is taken prisoner along with other leaders inside Spanish territory. This rising is answered by parallel insurgencies in the west which are quickly put down. The ease of putting down the rebellion convinces the colonists that it is safe to pursue their internal dissensions. . . . Ogé and Chavannes are tortured to death in a public square at Le Cap.

1791

APRIL: News of Ogé's execution turns French national sentiments against the colonists. Ogé is made a hero in the theater, a martyr to liberty. Planters living in Paris are endangered, often attacked on the streets.

MAY 15:   The French Assembly grants full political rights to mulattoes born of free parents, in an amendment accepted as a compromise by the exhausted legislators.

MAY 16:   Outraged over the May 15 decree, colonial deputies withdraw from the National Assembly.

JUNE 30:   News of the May 15 decree reaches Le Cap. Although only four hundred mulattoes meet the description set forth in this legislation, the symbolism of the decree is inflammatory. Furthermore the documentation of the decree causes the colonists to fear that the mother country may not maintain slavery.

JULY 3:   Blanchelande, governor of Saint Domingue, writes to warn the Minister of Marine that he has no power to enforce the May 15 decree. His letter tells of the presence of an English fleet and hints that factions of the colony may seek English intervention. The general colonial mood has swung completely toward secession at this point.

Throughout the north and the west, unrest among the slaves is observed. News of the French Revolution in some form or other is being circulated through the Vodou congregations. Small armed rebellions pop up in the west and are put down by the *maréchaussée*.

AUGUST 11:   A slave rising at Limbé is put down by the *maréchaussée*.

AUGUST 14:   A large meeting of slaves occurs at the Lenormand Plantation at Morne Rouge on the edge of the Bois Cayman forest. A plan for a colony-wide insurrection is laid. The *hûngan* Boukman emerges as the major slave leader at this point. The meeting at Bois Cayman is a delegates convention attended by slaves from each plantation at Limbé, Port-Margot, Acul, Petite Anse, Limonade, Plaine du Nord, Quartier Morin, Morne Rouge and others. The presence of Toussaint Bréda is asserted by some accounts and denied by others.

In the following days, black prisoners taken after the Limbé uprising give news of the meeting at Bois Cayman, but will not reveal the name of any delegate even under torture.

AUGUST 22:   The great slave rising in the north begins, led by Boukman and Jeannot. Whites are killed with all sorts of rape and atrocity; the standard of an infant impaled on a bayonet is raised. The entire Plaine du Nord is set on fire.

There follows a war of extermination with unconscionable cruelties on both sides. Le Cap is covered with scaffolds on which captured blacks are tortured. There are many executions on the wheel. During the first two months of the revolt, two thousand whites are killed, one hundred eighty sugar plantations, and nine hundred smaller operations (coffee, indigo, cotton) are burnt, with twelve hundred families dispossessed. Ten thousand rebel slaves are supposed to have been killed.

During the initial six weeks of the slave revolt, Toussaint remains at Bréda, keeping order among the slaves there and showing no sign of any connection to the slave revolt.

In mid-August, news of the general rebellion in Saint Domingue reaches France. Atrocities against whites produce a backlash of sympathy for the colonial conservatives, and the colonial faction begins to lobby for the repeal of the May 15 decree.

SEPTEMBER 24:   The National Assembly in France reverses itself again and passes the Decree of September 24, which revokes mulatto rights and once again hands the question of the "status of persons" over to colonial assemblies. This decree is declared "an unalterable article of the French Constitution."

OCTOBER: Expeditions begin to set out from Le Cap against the blacks, but illness kills as many as the enemy, so the rebel slaves gain ground.

In France this month, radicals in the French Assembly suggest that the slave insurrection is a trick organized by *émigrés* to create a royalist haven in Saint Domingue. The arrival of refugees from Saint Domingue in France over the next few months does little to change this position.

NOVEMBER: Early in the month, news of the decree of September 24 (repealing mulatto rights) arrives in Saint Domingue, confirming the suspicions of the mulattoes.

Toussaint rides to join the rebels, at Biassou's camp on Grande Rivière. For the next few months he functions as the "general doctor" to the rebel slaves, carrying no other military rank, although he does organize special fortifications at Grand Boucan and La Tannerie. Jeannot, Jean-François, and Biassou emerge as the principal leaders of the rebel slaves on the northern plain—all established in adjacent camps in the same area.

NOVEMBER 21: A massacre of mulattoes by *petit blancs* in Port-au-Prince begins over a referendum about the September 24 decree. Polling ends in a riot, followed by a battle. The mulatto troops are driven out, and part of the city is burned.

For the remainder of the fall, the mulattoes range around the western countryside, outdoing the slaves of the north in atrocity. They make white cockades from the ears of the slain, rip open pregnant women and force the husbands to eat the embryos, and throw infants to the hogs. In Port-au-Prince, the *petit blancs* are meanwhile conducting a version of the French Terror. The city remains under siege by the mulatto forces through December. As at Le Cap, the occupants answer the atrocities of the besiegers with their own, with the mob frequently breaking into the jails to murder mulatto prisoners.

In the south, a mulatto rising drives the whites into Les Cayes, but the whites of the Grande Anse are able to hold the peninsula, expel the mulattoes, arm their slaves and lead them against the mulattoes.

NOVEMBER 29: The first Civil Commission, consisting of Mirbeck, Roume, and Saint Léger, arrives at Le Cap to represent the French revolutionary government.

DECEMBER 10: Negotiations are opened with Jean-François and Biassou, principal slave leaders in the north, who write to the Commission a letter hoping for peace. The rebel leaders' proposal only asks liberty for themselves and a couple of hundred followers, in exchange for which they promise to return the other rebels to slavery.

DECEMBER 21: An interview between the commissioners and Jean-François takes place at Saint Michel Plantation, on the plain a short distance from Le Cap.

Toussaint appears as an adviser of Jean-François during these negotiations, and represents the black leaders in subsequent unsuccessful meetings at Le Cap, following the release of white prisoners. But although the commissioners are delighted with the peace proposition, the colonists want to hold out for total submission. Invoking the September 24 decree, the colonists undercut the authority of the Commission with the rebels and negotiations are broken off.

1792

MARCH 30: Mirbeck, despairing of the situation in Le Cap and fearing assassination, embarks for France, his fellow-commissioner Roume agreeing to follow three days later. But Roume gets news of a royalist counterrevolution brewing in Le Cap and decides to remain, hoping he can keep Blanchelande loyal to the Republic.

APRIL 4: In France occurs the signature of a new decree by the National Assembly which gives full rights of citizenship to mulattoes and free blacks, calls for new elections on that basis, and establishes a new three-man Commission to enforce the decree, with dictatorial powers and an army to back them.

APRIL 9: With the Department of the West reduced to anarchy again, Saint Léger escapes on a warship sailing to France.

MAY: War is declared between French and Spanish Saint Domingue.

MAY 11: News of the April 4 decree arrives in Saint Domingue. Given the nastiness of the race war and the atrocities committed against whites by mulatto leaders, this decree is considered an outrage by the whites. By this time, the whites (except on the Grande Anse) have all been crammed into the ports and have given up the interior of the country, for all practical purposes. The Colonial Assembly accepts the decree, having little choice for the moment, and no ability to resist the promised army.

AUGUST 10: Storming of the Tuileries by Jacobin-led mob, virtual deposition of the King, call for a Convention in France.

SEPTEMBER 18: Three new commissioners arrive at Le Cap to enforce the April 4 decree. Sonthonax, Polverel, and Ailhaud are all Jacobins. Colonists immediately suspect a plan to emancipate the slaves. The commissioners are accompanied by two thousand troops of the line and four thousand National Guards, under the command of General Desparbés. But the commissioners distrust the general and get on poorly with him because of their tendency to trespass on his authority. Soon the commissioners deport Blanchelande to France.

OCTOBER: In the aftermath of a conflict between his troops and the *petit blanc* Jacobins of Le Cap, General Desparbés is deported by the commissioners to France as a prisoner, along with many other royalist officers. This event virtually destroys the northern royalist faction.

OCTOBER 24: The Commission led by Sonthonax begins to fill official posts with mulattoes, now commonly called "citizens of April 4." By this tendency Sonthonax begins alienating the *petit blanc* Jacobins of Le Cap by creating a bureaucracy of mulattoes at their expense. In the end, Sonthonax closes the Jacobin club and deports its leaders.

The Regiment Le Cap's remaining officers refuse to accept the mulattoes Sonthonax has appointed to fill vacancies left by royalists who have either been arrested or had resigned.

DECEMBER: Young Colonel Etienne Laveaux mounts an attack on the rebel slaves at Grande Rivière. By this time, Toussaint has his own body of troops under his direct command, and has been using the skills of white prisoners and deserters to train them. He also has gathered some of the black officers who will be significant later in the revolution, including Dessalines, Moyse, and Charles Belair.

Toussaint fights battles with Laveaux's forces at Morne Pélé and La Tannerie, covering the retreat of the larger black force under Biassou and Jean-François, then retreats into the Cibao Mountains himself.

DECEMBER 1: Laveaux is sent to try to recall the disaffected Le Cap officers to the fold, but his efforts are ineffective.

DECEMBER 2: The Regiment Le Cap meets the new mulatto companies on parade in the Champ de Mars. Fighting breaks out between the two halves of the regiment and the white mob. The mulattoes leave the town and capture the fortifications at the entrance to the plain, and the threat of an assault from the black rebels forces the whites of the town to capitulate.

In the aftermath, Sonthonax deports the Regiment Le Cap en masse and rules the town with mulatto troops. He sets up a revolutionary tribunal and redoubles his deportations.

DECEMBER 8: Sonthonax writes to the French Convention of the necessity of ameliorating the lot of the slaves in some way—as a logical consequence of the law of April 4.

1793

JANUARY 21: Louis XVI is executed in France.

FEBRUARY: France goes to war against England and Spain.

Toussaint, Biassou, and Jean-François formally join the Spanish forces at Saint Raphael. At this point Toussaint has six hundred men under his own control and reports directly to the Spanish general. He embarks on an invasion of French territory.

MARCH 8: News of the King's execution reaches Le Cap.

MARCH 18: News of the war with England reaches Le Cap, further destabilizing the situation there.

APRIL: Blanchelande is executed in France by guillotine.

MAY: Early in the month, minor skirmishes begin along the Spanish border, as Toussaint, Jean-François, and Biassou begin advancing into French territory.

MAY 7: Galbaud arrives at Le Cap as the new Governor-General, dispatched by the French National Convention, which sees that war with England and Spain endangers the colony and wants a strong military commander in place. Galbaud is supposed to obey the Commission in all political matters but to have absolute authority over the troops (the same instructions given Desparbès). Because Galbaud's wife is a Creole, and he owns property in Saint Domingue, many colonists hope for support from him.

MAY 29: Sonthonax and Polverel, after unsatisfactory correspondence with Galbaud, write to announce their return to Le Cap.

JUNE 10: The commissioners reach Le Cap with the remains of the mulatto army used in operations around Port-au-Prince. Sonthonax declares Galbaud's credentials invalid and puts him on shipboard for return to France. Sonthonax begins to pack the harbor for a massive deportation of political enemies. Conflicts develop between Sonthonax's mulatto troops and the white civilians and three thousand-odd sailors in Le Cap.

JUNE 20–22: The sailors, drafting Galbaud to lead them, organize for an assault on the town. Galbaud lands with two thousand sailors. The regular troops of the garrison go over to him immediately, but the National Guards and the mulatto troops fight for Sonthonax and the Commission. A general riot breaks out, with the *petit blancs* of the town fighting for Galbaud and the mulattoes and town blacks fighting for the Commission. By the end of the first night of fighting, the Galbaud faction has driven the commissioners to the fortified lines at the entrance to the plain. But during the night, Sonthonax deals with the rebels on the plain, offering them liberty and pillage in exchange for their support. During the next day the rebels sack the town and drive Galbaud's forces back to the harbor forts by nightfall. The rebels burn the city. Galbaud empties the harbor and sails for Baltimore with ten thousand refugees in his fleet.

In aftermath of the burning of Le Cap, a great many French regular army officers desert to the Spanish. Toussaint recruits from these, and uses them as officers to train his bands.

AUGUST 29:   Sonthonax proclaims emancipation of all the slaves of the north.

This same day, Toussaint issues a proclamation of his own from Camp Turel, assuming for the first time the name Louverture.

SEPTEMBER 3:   Sonthonax writes to notify Polverel of his proclamation of emancipation. Polverel, though angry at this step having been taken without consultation among the commissioners, bows and makes similar proclamations in the south and west.

On the same day, the Confederation of the Grande Anse signs a treaty with the governor of Jamaica transferring allegiance to the British crown.

SEPTEMBER 19:   The British invasion begins with the landing of nine hundred soldiers at Jérémie. The surrounding area goes over to the British, but the eastern districts and Les Cayes are still held by mulatto General Rigaud for the French Republic.

SEPTEMBER 22:   Major O'Farrel, of the Irish Dillon regiment, turns over the fortress of Le Môle with a thousand men, including five hundred National Guards, to a single British ship. The peninsula goes over to the British as far as Port-au-Paix.

OCTOBER: A thousand more British soldiers land in the south, the mulattoes of the Artibonite revolt, and a new confederation of whites and mulattoes invites the English into the west. Similar events at Léogane mean that Polverel and Port-au-Prince are surrounded by the British invaders. From Le Cap, Sonthonax reacts by advising Polverel and Laveaux to burn the coast towns and retreat to the mountains, but they refuse.

OCTOBER 4:   Laveaux, walled up with a small garrison at Port-de-Paix, is being encroached upon by the Spanish from the east and the English from Le Môle, with his forces crippled by illness and fewer than seven hundred men fit for service. He writes to complain to Sonthonax of insubordination of the black troops.

Laveaux has left Le Cap under command of the mulatto Villatte, who established control of the town after the rebels of the plain had exhausted the plain and left it. Le Cap becomes the mulatto center of the north during the next several months.

DECEMBER: At the end of the month, Sonthonax joins Polverel at Port-au-Prince. Toussaint, fighting for the Spanish, occupies central Haiti after a series of victories.

1794

FEBRUARY 3:   A delegation sent by Sonthonax, led by the black Bellay, is seated in the French Convention. Next day, the French Convention abolishes slavery, following an address from Bellay, in a vote without discussion.

FEBRUARY 9: Halaou, African-born leader of ten thousand maroons and newly freed slaves on the Cul-de-Sac plain, parleys with Sonthonax at Port-au-Prince.

MARCH: Halaou is assassinated by mulatto officers during a meeting with the mulatto General Beauvais. Leadership of Halaou's men is assumed by Dieudonné.

Intrigue by Biassou and Jean-François weakens Toussaint's credit with his Spanish superiors. Toussaint removes his wife and children from the Spanish to the French side of the island. Biassou lays an ambush for Toussaint en route to Camp Barade in the parish of Limbé. Toussaint escapes but his brother Jean-Pierre is killed.

MARCH 4: In France, Robespierre, chief of the French Terror, is arrested and subsequently executed.

APRIL: Toussaint, who now commands about four thousand troops, the best armed and disciplined black corps of the Spanish army, contacts Laveaux to open negotiations for changing sides.

MAY 6: Toussaint joins the French with his four thousand soldiers, first massacring the Spanish troops under his command. He conducts a lightning campaign through the mountains from Dondon to Gonaives, gaining control of the numerous posts he earlier established on behalf of the Spanish.

MAY 18: Toussaint writes to Laveaux, explaining the error of his alliance to the Spanish and announcing that he now controls Gonaives, Gros Morne, Ennery, Plaisance, Marmelade, Dondon, Acul, and Limbé on behalf of the French Republic. The Cordon de l'Ouest, a military line exploiting the mountain range which divides the Northern and Western Departments of Saint Domingue, is under his command.

MAY 30: The British and their French colonial allies attack Port-au-Prince. Commissioners Sonthonax and Polverel retreat to Rigaud's position in the south.

After their victory, the English ranks are decimated by an outbreak of yellow fever, which kills seven hundred men during the next two months and leaves many more incapacitated.

JUNE: An offensive led by British Major Brisbane fails to break Toussaint's Cordon de l'Ouest. Toussaint tries unsuccessfully to capture Brisbane through a ruse.

JUNE 9: Sonthonax and Polverel are served with a recall order from the French Convention; they sail to France to face charges derived from the many disasters which have taken place under their administration, including the sack and burning of Le Cap. Before his departure, Sonthonax gives his commissioner's medal to the maroon leader Dieudonné and invests Dieudonné with his commissioner's authority.

JULY 7: Jean-François, having lost various engagements with Toussaint's force on the eastern end of the Cordon de l'Ouest, falls back on Fort Liberté, where he massacres a thousand recently returned French colonists, with the apparent collusion of the Spanish garrison.

OCTOBER: Brisbane begins an offensive in the Artibonite Valley, disputing the natural boundary of the Artibonite River with Toussaint, supported by a Spanish offensive in the east. Toussaint uses guerrilla tactics against Brisbane, drives the Spanish auxiliaries from Saint Michel and Saint Raphael, and razes those two towns.

OCTOBER 5:   Toussaint attacks Saint Marc, capturing the outlying Fort Belair, and establishing a battery on Morne Diamant above the town. His fingers are crushed by a falling cannon. The British drive him from his new positions and he retreats to Gonaives.

NOVEMBER: Many of Toussaint's junior officers (including Moyse, Dessalines, Christophe, and Maurepas) are formally promoted by Laveaux. Laveaux tours the Cordon de l'Ouest and reports that fifteen thousand cultivators have returned to work in this region under Toussaint's control, and that many white colonists have returned to their properties in safety.

DECEMBER: Rigaud attacks the British at Port-au-Prince unsuccessfully, but succeeds in holding Léogane, the first important town to the south.

DECEMBER 27:   Toussaint leads five columns to engage Spanish auxiliaries in the valley of Grande Rivière.

1795

JANUARY: Toussaint drives Brisbane from the town of Petite Rivière and leads a successful cavalry charge against British artillery at Grande Saline. Mulatto officer Blanc Cassenave continues work on fortifications begun by the British at La Crête à Pierrot, a mountain above the town of Petite Rivière and the Artibonite River.

FEBRUARY 6:   Blanc Cassenave, arrested by Toussaint for a mutinous conspiracy with Le Cap commandant Villatte, dies in prison.

MARCH 2:   Brisbane dies of a throat wound he suffered during an ambush. Toussaint besieges Saint Marc once again.

MARCH 25:   Laveaux informs the French Convention that he has promoted Toussaint to colonel and commander of the Cordon de l'Ouest.

JUNE: Joseph Flaville, in a rebellion against Toussaint supposedly sponsored by Villatte, is defeated by Toussaint at Marmelade.

JULY 23:   The French Convention names Laveaux Governor-General. Toussaint, Villatte, Rigaud, and Beauvais are promoted to the rank of brigadier general.

AUGUST 22:   In France, the Constitution establishing the Directoire as national governing body specifies that the colonies are integral parts of the French Republic and are to be governed by the same laws.

OCTOBER 13:   News of the Treaty of Basel reaches Saint Domingue. By this treaty, Spain cedes its portion of the island to France, deferring transfer "until the Republic should be in a position to defend its new territory from attack." Jean-François retires to Spain. Most of his troops join Toussaint's army.

OCTOBER 25:   In France, after a lengthy trial, Sonthonax is formally cleared of all charges concerning his conduct in Saint Domingue.

1796

JANUARY: Having moved the seat of government from Port-de-Paix to Le Cap, Laveaux finds his relationship with Villatte deteriorating and begins to suspect the latter of plotting for independence. The mulattoes of the north are roused to further insubordination by the activities of Pinchinat, sent to Le Cap from the south by Rigaud.

FEBRUARY 12: Toussaint sends a delegation to Dieudonné with a letter meant to persuade him to join the French Republican forces. Dieudonné is overthrown by his subordinate Laplume, who turns him over to Rigaud as a prisoner. Laplume brings Dieudonné's men to join Toussaint.

MARCH 20: Villatte attempts a coup against Laveaux, who is imprisoned at Le Cap. Officers loyal to Toussaint engineer his release.

MARCH 27: Toussaint enters Le Cap with ten thousand men. Villatte and his remaining supporters flee the town.

MARCH 31: Laveaux, describing Toussaint as the "Black Spartacus" predicted by Raynal, installs him as Lieutenant-Governor of Saint Domingue. On the same day, Dieudonné dies a prisoner in Saint Louis du Sud, suffocated by a weight of chains.

MAY 11: Emissaries of the French Directoire arrive in Le Cap: the Third Commission, led by a politically rehabilitated Sonthonax and including the colored commissioner Raimond and whites Roume, Giraud, and Leblanc. The new Commission brings thirty thousand muskets to arm the colonial troops, but only nine hundred European soldiers, under command of Generals Rochambeau and Desfourneaux.

MAY 19: The Third Commission proclaims that colonists absent from Saint Domingue and residing elsewhere than France itself are to be considered *émigrés* disloyal to the French Republic, their property subject to sequestration.

JUNE 30: Sonthonax proclaims it a crime to publicly state that the freedom of the blacks is not irrevocable or that one man can own another.

JULY 5: Toussaint's elder sons, Placide and Isaac Louverture, embark for France on the French warship *Wattigny*.

JULY 18: Unable for want of European troops to take possession of the Spanish part of the island, Rochambeau is stripped of his rank and deported to France.

AUGUST 17: Toussaint writes to Laveaux concerning his wish that the latter stand for election as a delegate to the French legislature, representing the colony.

AUGUST 27: Emissaries sent by Sonthonax to Rigaud and other mulatto leaders of the south create such ill will that a riot breaks out in Les Cayes, in which many whites are killed. Rigaud parades Sonthonax's proclamations through the streets of the town, tied to the tail of a donkey.

SEPTEMBER: Sonthonax and Laveaux are elected, among others, as representatives from Saint Domingue to the French legislature.

OCTOBER 6: Members of the Third Commission write to the Directoire about their concern over the single-minded personal loyalty shown by the black troops toward particular leaders, especially Toussaint.

OCTOBER 14: With further encouragement from Toussaint, Laveaux departs from Saint Domingue to assume his position in the French legislature.

1797

MARCH: In France, royalists, reactionaries, and proslavery colonists make significant gains in new elections.

APRIL: Toussaint successfully recaptures Mirebalais and the surrounding area and uses the region as the base of an offensive against the British in Port-au-Prince. British General Simcoe defends the coast town successfully and attacks Mirebalais in force. Toussaint burns Mirebalais and makes a rapid drive toward Saint Marc, forcing Simcoe to retreat to defend the latter town. This campaign is the last British challenge to Toussaint's control of the interior.

MAY 1:   Sonthonax arrests General Desfourneaux, leaving Toussaint as the highest-ranking officer in the colony.

MAY 8:   Sonthonax names Toussaint commander-in-chief of the French republican army in Saint Domingue.

MAY 20:   The newly elected French legislature convenes, with the proslavery colonial point of view energetically represented by Vaublanc.

AUGUST 20:   Toussaint writes to Sonthonax, urging him to assume his elected post in the French legislature.

AUGUST 23:   Sonthonax consents to depart, in his words "to avoid bloodshed."

SEPTEMBER 4:   In France, royalist and colonial elements are purged from the government; the Vaublanc faction loses its influence.

OCTOBER 21:   Toussaint informs the French Directoire that, after successful negotiation with Rigaud, the Southern Department has been reunited with the rest of the colony.

1798

MARCH 27:   General Hédouville arrives from France as agent of the French Directoire to Saint Domingue. His orders include the deportation of Rigaud. He lands in Spanish Santo Domingo, to confer with Roume, a survivor of the Third Commission stationed in the Spanish town.

APRIL 23:   British General Maitland begins to negotiate with Toussaint the terms for a British withdrawal.

MAY 2:   A treaty is signed by Toussaint and Maitland. British will evacuate Port-au-Prince and their other western posts, in return for which Toussaint promises amnesty to all their partisans, a condition which violates French laws against the *émigrés*.

MAY 8:   Hédouville arrives at Le Cap and summons both Toussaint and Rigaud to appear before him there.

MAY 15:   Following the British evacuation, Toussaint and his army make a triumphal entry into Port-au-Prince.

JUNE: Following his first encounter with Hédouville, Toussaint indignantly refuses to obey the order to arrest Rigaud.

JULY: During interviews with Toussaint and Rigaud at Le Cap, Hédouville seeks to weaken the power of both generals by turning them against each other.

JULY 24:   Hédouville proclaims that plantation workers must contract themselves for three-year periods, arousing suspicion that he plans to restore slavery.

AUGUST 31:   Toussaint signs a secret agreement with Maitland, stipulating among other points that the British navy will leave the ports of Saint Domingue open to commercial shipping of all nations.

OCTOBER 1:   Môle Saint Nicolas, the port of the northwest peninsula, is formally surrendered by Maitland to Toussaint. Following the transfer, Toussaint dismisses a number of his troops from the army and returns them to plantation work.

OCTOBER 16:   Instigated by Moyse and Toussaint, the plantation workers of the north rise against Hédouville's supposed intention to restore slavery.

OCTOBER 23:   Under pressure from the rising in the north, Hédouville departs from Saint Domingue, leaving final instructions which release Rigaud from Toussaint's authority. Commissioner Raimond, previously elected to the French legislature, accompanies Hédouville to France.

OCTOBER 31:   Toussaint invites Roume to return from Spanish Santo Domingo to assume the duties of French agent in the colony.

NOVEMBER 15:   Toussaint announces that plantation work will henceforward be enforced by the military.

1799

FEBRUARY 4:   Roume brings Toussaint and Rigaud together at Port-au-Prince for a celebration of the abolition of slavery, hoping for a reconciliation between them. But Rigaud leaves the meeting in anger when asked to cede to Toussaint control of the posts he'd won from the British in the Western Department (Grand et Petit Goâve, Léogane).

FEBRUARY 21:   In an address at the Port-au-Prince cathedral, Toussaint protests the insubordination of Rigaud and warns the mulatto community against rebellion.

JUNE 15:   Rigaud makes public Hédouville's letter releasing him from obedience to Toussaint.

JUNE 18:   Rigaud opens rebellion against Toussaint; his troops seize Petit and Grand Goâve, driving Laplume back from this area.

   In the following days, the mulatto commanders at Léogane, Pétion, and Boyer defect to Rigaud's party. Mulatto rebellions break out at Le Cap, Le Môle, and in the Artibonite. Toussaint rides rapidly from point to point to suppress them, placing Moyse and Dessalines in command at Léogane and Christophe in charge of Le Cap. At Pont d'Ester, members of his entourage are killed in a night ambush.

JULY 8:   Toussaint dispatches an army of forty-five thousand men to the south to combat Rigaud and his supporters.

JULY 25:   Toussaint breaks the siege of Port-de-Paix, where his officer Maurepas was under attack from the Rigaudins.

AUGUST 4:   Fifty conspirators at Le Cap are executed after a failed attempt to take over the town for the Rigaudins.

AUGUST 31:   In the midst of suppressing rebellion on the northwest peninsula, Toussaint narrowly escapes assassination near Jean Rabel. Returning in the direction of Port-au-Prince, he is ambushed, again unsuccessfully, at Sources Puantes.

SEPTEMBER 23:   Beauvais, mulatto commander of Jacmel, who had attempted to maintain neutrality in the Toussaint-Rigaud conflict, sails for Saint Thomas with his family.

NOVEMBER: Dessalines's offensive retakes Petit and Grand Goâve from Rigaud.

NOVEMBER 9:   In France, Napoleon Bonaparte assumes power as First Consul of the French Republic.

NOVEMBER 22:   Jacmel, key to the defense of the southern peninsula, is besieged by Toussaint's troops.

DECEMBER 13:   In France, the new Constitution establishing the French Consulate states that the colonies will be governed by "special laws."

1800

JANUARY 18:   Toussaint requests Roume's permission to occupy Spanish Santo Domingo according to the terms of the Treaty of Basel, citing the urgency of stopping the slave trade which continued to some extent on Spanish territory. Roume denies the request.

JANUARY 19:   Pétion assumes command of Jacmel, entering the besieged town by stealth.

MARCH 11:   Pétion leads the survivors of the siege on a desperate sortie from Jacmel and manages to rejoin Rigaud with the shreds of his force, abandoning Jacmel to Toussaint. Rigaud retreats onto the Grande Anse, leaving scorched earth behind him.

APRIL 27:   Under pressure from Toussaint, Roume signs an order to take possession of the Spanish side of the island.

MAY 22:   Agé, a white general loyal to Toussaint, arrives in Santo Domingo with a symbolic force and is resisted by the population.

JUNE: A new group of emissaries from the French Consulate debarks in Spanish Santo Domingo, including General Michel, Raimond, and Colonel Vincent (the latter a white officer close to Toussaint). Their instructions are to keep the two halves of the island separate and to bring the black/mulatto war to a close— while at the same time conciliating Toussaint. Both Michel and Vincent are arrested briefly by Toussaint's troops, on their way into the French part of the island.

JUNE 16:   Roume rescinds his order of April 27, 1800, in the face of Agé's failure.

JUNE 24:   Colonel Vincent meets with Toussaint for the first time since his arrival, and informs him of the Consulate's intention to maintain him as General-in-Chief.

JULY 7:   Rigaud is decisively defeated by Dessalines at Aquin—last of a series of lost battles.

AUGUST 1:   Toussaint enters Les Cayes, Rigaud's hometown and the last center of mulatto resistance. Rigaud flees to France by way of Guadeloupe. Toussaint proclaims a general amnesty for the mulatto combatants. But Dessalines, left in charge of the south, conducts extremely severe reprisals.

OCTOBER 12:   Toussaint proclaims forced labor on the plantations, to be enforced by two captain-generals: Dessalines in the south and west and Moyse in the north.

NOVEMBER 4:   French Minister of Marine Forfait instructs Toussaint *not* to take possession of the Spanish portion of the island.

NOVEMBER 26:   Roume, blamed by Toussaint for Agé's failed expedition to Santo Domingo, is arrested by Moyse and imprisoned at Dondon.

1801

JANUARY: Toussaint sends two columns into Spanish Santo Domingo, one from Ouanaminthe under command of Moyse and the other from Mirebalais under his own command.

JANUARY 28:   Toussaint enters Santo Domingo City, accepts the Spanish capitulation from Don García, and proclaims the abolition of slavery.

FEBRUARY 4:   Toussaint organizes an assembly to create a constitution for Saint Domingue.

JULY 3:   Toussaint proclaims the new constitution, whose terms make him governor for life.

JULY 16:   Toussaint dispatches a reluctant Vincent to present his constitution to Napoleon Bonaparte and the Consulate in France.

OCTOBER 1:   The Peace of Amiens ends the war between England and France. Napoleon begins to prepare an expedition, led by his brother-in-law General Leclerc, to restore white power in Saint Domingue.

OCTOBER 16:   An insurrection led by Moyse against Toussaint's forced labor policy begins on the northern plain and, in the coming weeks, is suppressed with extreme severity by Toussaint and Dessalines.

NOVEMBER 24:   Moyse is executed at Port-de-Paix.

NOVEMBER 25:   Toussaint proclaims a military dictatorship.

DECEMBER 14:   The Leclerc expedition sails from Brest, with the fleet commanded by Villaret-Joyeuse.

1802

JANUARY 29:   The first ships of Leclerc's expeditionary fleet make a landfall off Cape Samana on the Spanish side of the island.

Toussaint observes the fleet from the heights. He commands at this point 20,000 regular troops in three divisions: 5,000 in the north under Christophe at Le Cap (with a smaller division under Maurepas at Port-de-Paix); 11,000 under Dessalines in the south and west; and 4,000 in Spanish Santo Domingo under Clervaux and Paul Louverture. By this time most of the cultivators have also been armed.

JANUARY 30:   Leclerc's fleet regroups. Two ships with 450 troops commanded by General Kerverseau sail for Santo Domingo City, while the rest of the fleet divides into three: Latouche-Treville takes 3,000 men commanded by General Boudet to Port-au-Prince; Magon takes 1,800 men commanded by Rochambeau to

Fort Liberté; Villaret-Joyeuse takes 4,000 men commanded by Leclerc to Le Cap.

FEBRUARY 2: Leclerc's squadron appears outside Le Cap harbor. Civilians in the town beg Christophe to submit. A storm drives the French fleet offshore.

Rochambeau demolishes the forts of Fort Liberté and executes the defenders.

FEBRUARY 3: Leclerc sends Lebrun ashore at Le Cap with a written demand for Christophe's submission.

When the French squadron appears at Santo Domingo City, the white population rises against the black garrison. In Saint Yago, Clervaux submits to French authority.

General Boudet arrives at Port-au-Prince, which refuses to surrender.

FEBRUARY 4: Rochambeau secures Fort Liberté and advances into the Plaine du Nord.

At Le Cap, Lebrun returns to Leclerc's flagship with the news that Christophe has asked for a forty-eight-hour delay so as to receive orders from Toussaint. During the day, the French fleet loads men on lighter boats to seek a landing elsewhere on the coast. Under pressure from Rochambeau's advance, armed blacks fall back on the town from the northern plain. During the evening, the whites and civilians of the town seek refuge on the heights of Morne la Vigie.

At nightfall the firing of a cannon at a ship approaching Fort Picolet signals the burning of the town. Overnight, Le Cap is reduced to ashes.

At Port-au-Prince, General Agé interviews emissaries from Boudet and says he must wait for orders from Dessalines (then at Saint Marc). Covertly, Agé lets Boudet's men know that he is not really in control and that his subordinate Lamartinière and other officers are determined to burn the city if there is a landing. Boudet's emissaries, Gimont and Sabès, are held prisoner.

FEBRUARY 5: Leclerc leads a force ashore at Limbé. On the road to Le Cap he meets opposition commanded (according to a note by General Hardy) by Toussaint Louverture himself.

Following Toussaint's orders, Christophe retreats from the ruins of Le Cap. Villaret-Joyeuse lands men and fire pumps in Le Cap and assumes control.

Boudet lands at a point south of Léogane and advances north toward Port-au-Prince. Fort Bizoton surrenders to Boudet and Fort Piémont is taken by a French assault. Lamartinière, who apparently believed he could defend Port-au-Prince without burning it, is forced to retreat, leaving the town intact, after a massacre of white civilians on the Savane Valembrun.

Laplume, commander of Toussaint's forces south of Port-au-Prince, offers to side with the French.

FEBRUARY 6: Leclerc's columns advancing from Limbé join with one of Rochambeau's columns from Fort Liberté to establish control of the Northern Plain.

FEBRUARY 7: Leclerc takes possession of the ruins of Le Cap, and dispatches Toussaint's sons Isaac and Placide with messages for Toussaint.

Toussaint writes orders to Dessalines to sack and burn Port-au-Prince at the first opportunity.

FEBRUARY 8:   At night, Toussaint meets his sons at Ennery. An exchange of letters between Toussaint and Leclerc begins.

Laplume's forces swear allegiance to France.

FEBRUARY 9:   Dessalines, having previously joined Lamartinière at Croix des Bouquets, retreats before Boudet's advance, burning the country behind him and taking hostages in the direction of Mirebalais.

Toussaint writes to Dommage at Jérémie, instructing him to scorch the earth behind him as he retreats toward the mountains of the interior.

FEBRUARY 11:   Dessalines circles Port-au-Prince to burn Léogane, but is forced to fall back before one of Boudet's columns. The French achieve secure communication with Laplume.

FEBRUARY 12:   Humbert lands with 1,200 troops at Port-de-Paix, where Maurepas with 2,000 regulars burns the town and retreats. Maurepas regroups in the hills with several thousand irregulars and counterattacks successfully. The French are barely able to hold the town with the help of the shipboard guns.

Leclerc writes to Toussaint requesting that he come to meet with him, and offers a four-day cease-fire.

FEBRUARY 14:   Reinforcements from the missing portion of Leclerc's fleet arrive at Le Cap.

FEBRUARY 17:   Leclerc outlaws Toussaint and Christophe as rebels—Toussaint having failed to respond to his letter of February 12. Leclerc orders a blockade of the coast to cut off Toussaint's resupply links to the United States, and swears not to take his boots off until he has captured Toussaint.

Some 1,500 men sail from Le Cap to reinforce Humbert at Port-de-Paix, while other ships go to Môle Saint Nicolas, which surrenders without a struggle.

FEBRUARY 19:   Leclerc launches a three-pronged attack on Toussaint in the Cordon de l'Ouest: Rochambeau moving from Fort Liberté, Hardy from Le Cap, and Desfourneaux from Limbé. The strategy is to force Toussaint out of the mountains and onto the coastal plain near Gonaïves.

Reinforcements reach Humbert, who attacks Maurepas and is defeated with heavy losses.

FEBRUARY 20:   The French advance in the Cordon de l'Ouest is delayed by heavy rain.

In Santo Domingo City, Paul Louverture, whose instructions from Toussaint have been intercepted, submits to Kerverseau.

FEBRUARY 21:   Boudet, held down at Port-au-Prince by Dessalines until today, sends a column north to contribute to the convergence on Toussaint in the Cordon de l'Ouest. Plaisance submits to Desfourneaux, and Hardy takes Marmelade from Christophe, who retreats toward Ennery, delaying Hardy's advance with ambushes. Rochambeau wins a battle at Mare à la Roche to reach Saint Michel. The French noose appears to be tightening on Toussaint at Ennery.

FEBRUARY 22:   Rochambeau presses south as far as Saint Raphael, intending if possible to capture Toussaint's family at Habitation Lacroix, near Ennery. Toussaint's youngest son, Saint-Jean, is captured by Hardy's men during the family's flight from Ennery. That night Rochambeau occupies the heights of

Morne Barade at the same time Toussaint arrives at the top of Ravine à Couleuvre, and battle begins.

FEBRUARY 23:   Driven from Ravine à Couleuvre by Rochambeau's troops, Toussaint breaks Rochambeau's advance with a cavalry charge on Habitation Périsse and forces the surviving French back to the ravine.

The troops of Hardy and Desfourneaux, now united under Leclerc, enter Gonaives after resistance by Vernet, who burns the town before retreating. Toussaint, now ill with fever, retreats south to Pont d'Ester, joined by his family.

FEBRUARY 24: Dessalines massacres the whites of Saint Marc, then burns and evacuates the town.

FEBRUARY 25:   Boudet, delayed by terrain and harried by Dessalines, finally reaches Saint Marc to find scorched earth and a few hundred corpses of white prisoners. By an intercepted letter from Toussaint he learns that Dessalines, whose army vanished from view, is attempting again to destroy Port-au-Prince.

FEBRUARY 26:   By night, profiting from the absence of Boudet, Dessalines attacks the lightly garrisoned Port-au-Prince, but is repelled by Pamphile de Lacroix, supported by maroon bands of Lamour Dérance and Lafortune, who have abruptly switched sides to the French. Dérance and Lafortune ambush the 8th Demibrigade (which had attacked Port-au-Prince in concert with Dessalines) and capture the commander, Pierre Louis Diane. Dessalines retreats across the Cul-de-Sac plain, leaving scorched earth behind him.

Leclerc, leading Desfourneaux's division and 1,500 of Hardy's men from Gonaives, advances north to Gros Morne to attack Maurepas. Meanwhile, Lubin Golart, a former commander of Maurepas's 9th Demibrigade, attacks Maurepas from Jean Rabel. Surrounded and misinformed that Toussaint was completely defeated at Ravine à Couleuvre, Maurepas surrenders to the French.

FEBRUARY 28:   Dessalines moves toward Mirebalais, seeking to rejoin Toussaint. He finds Toussaint at Petite Rivière and begins repairing the fort of La Crête à Pierrot on the heights above the town and the Artibonite River.

MARCH 1:   After Toussaint's departure, Dessalines massacres the white population of Petite Rivière, along with numerous white prisoners he has herded there during his previous movements.

MARCH 2:   Learning that he has been outlawed by Leclerc, Toussaint proclaims Leclerc outlaw. He threatens Gonaives with a feint, burns the town of Ennery, and begins to circle from Ennery through Saint Michel, Saint Raphael, Dondon, and Marmelade, raising resistance as he goes.

Rochambeau, who believes that he is pursuing Toussaint from the banks of Artibonite into the Grand Cahos Mountains, captures a pack train carrying treasuries from the coastal towns.

Leclerc orders a convergence on Toussaint's supposed position in the mountains above Petite Rivière.

MARCH 4:   With 2,000 men, General Debelle attacks Lamartinière's garrison of 300 outside the fort of La Crête à Pierrot. His men are decimated when the defenders jump into the ditches recently dug around the fort, and Debelle himself is severely wounded.

D'Henin, detached from Boudet's division, finds Mirebalais burned by Dessalines.

MARCH 5: Toussaint takes Bidouret, an outpost above Plaisance, planning to attack Desfourneaux at Plaisance and then proceed to Port-de-Paix to join Maurepas.

MARCH 6: Toussaint loses an engagement to Desfourneaux in the Plaisance area, confronts soldiers of the 9th Demibrigade, now led by Lubin Golart, and so learns for certain that Maurepas has surrendered at Port-de-Paix. He turns south toward La Crête à Pierrot with the idea of capturing Leclerc by a movement of double encirclement.

MARCH 9: Boudet's division unites at Verrettes and discovers 800 whites massacred there by Dessalines.

MARCH 11: Harassed by Charles Belair, Boudet's division crosses the Artibonite and reaches La Crête à Pierrot.

MARCH 12: Recently returned to La Crête à Pierrot, Dessalines declares he will blow up the fort if it is penetrated by the French. Boudet is lured into the same trap as Debelle on March 4, with heavy losses. In the late morning, Leclerc arrives to support Boudet, but the French attacks are confounded by the entrenchments and by cavalry charges by Toussaint's honor guard, out of the nearby woods. By the end of the day, Leclerc and Boudet are both wounded. Pamphile de Lacroix (the only uninjured general on the scene) moves the troops to a position northwest of the fort. Leclerc determines to lay siege while waiting for the arrival of Hardy and Rochambeau.

MARCH 13: Dessalines arranges for fortification of a second redoubt above La Crête à Pierrot, and leads a sortie to get gunpowder from the Plassac depot, which Boudet has already blown up on his march from Verrettes. At the approach of Hardy, the honor guard cavalry evacuates the area, trying to rejoin Toussaint or Dessalines.

Rochambeau occupies the destroyed town of Mirebalais, repelling Dessalines from the Cahos onto the Central Plateau and cutting him off from the besieged fort.

MARCH 22: Rochambeau arrives on the right bank of the Artibonite, completing the encirclement of La Crête à Pierrot. Rochambeau demolishes the redoubt recently established outside the main fort. Lamartinière, commanding in Dessalines's absence, raises red flags of no surrender, no quarter at La Crête à Pierrot. The French begin three days of bombardment of the main fort, with the artillery corps commanded by Pétion.

In the north, meanwhile, Christophe raises rebellion against the French around the Northern Plain.

MARCH 24: An order to evacuate is smuggled into the fort of La Crête à Pierrot, from Dessalines to Lamartinière, who manages against all odds to cut his way through the French lines by night and escape with about half of the 900 men Dessalines left there. The March battles around the fort have cost the French 2,000 casualties. Toussaint joins Dessalines at Morne Calvaire and learns that the fort has surrendered. He is too late to execute the plan to capture Leclerc.

MARCH 25: Rochambeau's soldiers enter the fort at La Crête à Pierrot and murder all the wounded who remain there. In Europe a treaty is signed to ratify the Peace of Amiens.

MARCH 28: Toussaint meets the French emissaries Sabès and Gimont at Chassérieux, his Grand Cahos headquarters, and sends them to Boudet with a letter to Napoleon. Hardy raids Toussaint's property at La Coupe a l'Inde, and captures Toussaint's warhorse, Bel Argent.

MARCH 29: Toussaint, pursuing Hardy, fights an engagement with him at Dondon. Christophe attacks from one side, Toussaint from the other. Though Christophe is nearly taken prisoner, Hardy is chased down the road to Le Cap.

APRIL: Yellow fever breaks out in Le Cap. Toussaint learns of the signing of the treaty confirming the Peace of Amiens.

APRIL 1: Leclerc writes to Napoleon that he has 7,000 active men and 5,000 in the hospital—omitting to say that another 5,000 are dead. He also has 7,000 "colonial troops" of variable reliability, including many black soldiers brought over by turncoat leaders.

APRIL 2: Following the battle at Dondon, Christophe pursues Hardy to the gates of Le Cap. At this point, Toussaint's forces have retaken Saint Michel, Marmelade, Saint Raphael, and Limbé, and have isolated Mirebalais. Leclerc returns to Le Cap to support Hardy.

APRIL 3: The Havre Flushing Squadron arrives with 2,500 fresh troops for Leclerc.

APRIL 26: On a promise of retaining his rank in French service, Christophe arranges his submission to Leclerc in a meeting at Haut du Cap, and turns over 1,200 troops to the French. But Toussaint still holds the northern mountains with 4,000 regular troops and a larger number of irregulars. Leclerc writes to the Minister of Marine that he needs a total of 25,000 European troops to secure the island—i.e., reinforcements of 14,000.

MAY 1: Toussaint and Dessalines offer to submit to Leclerc's authority on similar terms as Christophe.

MAY 6: Toussaint makes a formal submission to Leclerc at Le Cap. Leclerc's position is still too weak for him to obey Napoleon's secret order to deport the black leaders immediately. While Toussaint retires to Gonaives, with the 2,000 men of his honor guard converting themselves to cultivators there, Dessalines remains on active duty. Leclerc frets that their submission may be feigned.

In May, the generals Hardy and Debelle die of exhaustion and their wounds. At Port-au-Prince and Le Cap, surviving French troops suffer heavy losses to the yellow fever epidemic.

JUNE: By the first week of this month, Leclerc has lost 3,000 men to fever. Both Le Cap and Port-au-Prince have become plague zones, with corpses laid out in the barracks yards to be carried to lime pits outside the town. Deaths are proportionately higher among the officers and civilians of high rank. Sailors in the fleet are also dying by the thousands.

JUNE 6: Leclerc notifies Napoleon that he has ordered Toussaint's arrest.

JUNE 7: Lured away from Gonaives to a meeting with General Brunet, Toussaint is made prisoner.

JUNE 15: Toussaint, with his family, is deported for France aboard the ship *Le Héros*.

JUNE 11:　Leclerc writes to the Minister of Marine that he suspects his army will die out from under him—citing his own illness (he had overcome a bout of malaria soon after his arrival), he asks for recall. This letter also contains the recommendation that Toussaint be imprisoned in the heart of inland France.

In the third week of June, Leclerc begins the tricky project of disarming the cultivators—under authority of the black generals who have submitted to him.

JUNE 22:　Toussaint writes a letter of protest to Napoleon from his ship, which is now docked in Brest.

JULY 6:　Leclerc writes to the Minister of Marine that he is losing 160 men per day. However, this same report states that he is effectively destroying the influence of the black generals.

News of the restoration of slavery in Guadeloupe arrives in Saint Domingue in the last days of the month. The north rises instantly, the west shortly afterward, and black soldiers begin to desert their generals.

AUGUST 6:　Leclerc reports the continued prevalence of yellow fever, the failure to complete the disarmament, and the growth of rebellion. The major black generals have stayed in his camp, but the petty officers are deserting in droves and taking their troops with them.

AUGUST 24:　Toussaint is imprisoned at the Fort de Joux, in France near the Swiss border.

AUGUST 25:　Leclerc writes: "To have been rid of Toussaint is not enough; there are two thousand more leaders to get rid of as well."

AUGUST/SEPTEMBER:　In his cell at Fort de Joux, Toussaint composes a report of his conduct during Leclerc's invasion, intended to justify himself to the First Consul, Bonaparte.

SEPTEMBER 13:　The expected abatement of the yellow fever at the approach of the autumnal equinox fails to occur. The reinforcements arriving die as fast as they are put into the country, and Leclerc has to deploy them as soon as they get off the boat. Leclerc asks for 10,000 men to be immediately sent. He is losing territory in the interior and his black generals are beginning to waver, though he still is confident of his ability to manipulate them.

As of this date, a total of 28,000 men have been sent from France, and Leclerc estimates that 10,500 are still alive, but only 4,500 are fit for duty. Five thousand sailors have also died, bringing the total loss to 29,000.

SEPTEMBER 15:　General Caffarelli, agent of Napoleon Bonaparte, arrives at the Fort de Joux for the first of seven interrogations of Toussaint.

OCTOBER 7:　Leclerc: "We must destroy all the mountain Negroes, men and women, sparing only children under twelve years of age. We must destroy half the Negroes of the plains, and not allow in the colony a single man who has ever worn an epaulette. Without these measures the colony will never be at peace. . . ."

OCTOBER 10:　Mulatto General Clervaux revolts, with all his troops, upon the news of Napoleon's restoration of the mulatto discriminations of the *ancien régime*. Le Cap had been mostly garrisoned by mulattoes.

OCTOBER 13:　Christophe and the other black generals in the north join Clervaux's rebellion. On this news, Dessalines raises revolt in the west.

NOVEMBER 2:   Leclerc dies of yellow fever. Command is assumed by Rochambeau.

By the end of the month the fever finally begins to abate, and acclimated survivors, now immune, begin to return to service. In France, Napoleon has outfitted 10,000 reinforcements.

1803

MARCH: At the beginning of the month, Rochambeau has 11,000 troops and only 4,000 in hospital, indicating that the worst of the disease threat has passed. He is ready to conduct a war of extermination against the blacks, and brings man-eating dogs from Cuba to replace his lost soldiery. He makes slow headway against Dessalines in March and April, while Napoleon plans to send 30,000 reinforcements in two installments in the coming year.

APRIL 7:   Toussaint Louverture dies a prisoner in Fort de Joux.

MAY 12:   New declaration of war between England and France.

JUNE: By month's end, Saint Domingue is completely blockaded by the English. With English aid, Dessalines smashes into the coast towns.

OCTOBER: Early in the month, Les Cayes falls to the blacks. At month's end, so does Port-au-Prince.

NOVEMBER 10:   Rochambeau flees Le Cap and surrenders to the English fleet.

NOVEMBER 28:   The French are forced to evacuate their last garrison at Le Môle. Dessalines promises protection to all whites who choose to remain, following Toussaint's earlier policy. During the first year of his rule he will continue encouraging white planters to return and manage their property, and many who trusted Toussaint will do so.

DECEMBER 31:   Declaration of Haitian independence.

1804

OCTOBER: Dessalines, having overcome all rivals, crowns himself emperor. A term of his constitution defines all citizens of Haiti as *nèg* (blacks) and all noncitizens of Haiti as *blanc* (whites)—regardless of skin color in both cases.

1805

JANUARY: Dessalines begins the massacre of all the whites (according to the redefinition in the Constitution of 1804) remaining in Haiti.

ORIGINAL LETTERS
AND DOCUMENTS

Quotations which appear italicized in the main text derive from the historical record, and are reproduced here in their original versions.

FROM FRANCE, FORT DE JOUX, OCTOBER 1802, PAGES 5–7:

Puisque vous persistez à penser que le grand nombre des troupes qui se trouve à Plaisance effraye les cultivateurs de cette paroisse, je charge le général Brunet de se concerter avec vous pour le placement d'une partie de ces troupes. . . .[1]

Voici le moment, citoyen général, de faire connaître d'une manière incontestable au général en chef que ceux qui peuvent le tromper sur votre bonne foi, sont des malheureux calomniateurs, et que vos sentiments ne tendent qu'à ramener l'ordre et la tranquillité dans le quartier que vous habitez. Il faut me seconder. Nous avons, mon cher général, des arrangements à prendre ensemble qu'il est impossible de traiter en lettres, mais qu'une conférence d'une heure terminera. Si je n'étais pas excédé du travail et de tracas minutieux, j'aurais été aujourd'hui le porteur de ma réponse, mais ne pouvant ces jours-ci sortir, venez vous-même, et si vous êtes rétabli de votre indisposition, que

[1] Colonel Alfred Nemours, *Histoire de la Captivité et de la Mort de Toussaint Louverture* (Paris: Editions Berger Levrault, 1929), p. 31.

ce soit demain. Quand il s'agit de faire le bien on ne doit jamais retarder. Vous ne trou-
verez pas dans mon habitation champêtre tous les agréments que je désirais y réunir
pour vous recevoir, mais vous y trouverez la franchise d'un galant homme qui ne fait
d'autres voeux que pour la prospérité de la colonie et votre bonheur personnel. . . .[2]

The letters from Toussaint Louverture quoted on pages 6 and 7 appear in Général
Alfred Nemours, *Toussaint Louverture Fond à Saint-Domingue La Liberté et l'Égalité*
(Port-au-Prince: Editions Fardin, 1945), pp. 91–2.

FROM CHAPTER 2, PAGE 37

Votre père est un grand homme, il a rendu des services éminents à la France. Vous lui
direz que moi, premier magistrat, je lui promets protection, gloire et honneur. Ne
croyez pas que la France ait l'intention de porter la guerre à Saint-Domingue: l'armée
qu'elle y envoie est destinée, non à combattre les troupes du pays mais à augmenter
leurs forces. Voici le général Leclerc, mon beau-frère, que j'ai nommé capitaine-
général, et qui commandera cette armée. Des ordres sont donnés afin que vous soyez
quinze jours d'avance à Saint-Domingue, pour annoncer à votre père la venue de
l'expédition.[3]

FROM CHAPTER 6, PAGES 87–8

J'apprends avec indignation, citoyen général, que vous refusez de recevoir l'escadre et
l'armée française que je commande, sous le prétexte que vous n'avez pas d'ordre du
général Toussaint. La France a fait la paix avec l'Angleterre, et le gouvernement envoie
à St-Domingue des forces capables de soumettre les rebelles, si toutefois on devait en
trouver à St-Domingue. Quant à vous, citoyen général, je vous avoue qu'il m'en
coûterait de vous compter parmi les rebelles. Je vous préviens que si aujourd'hui vous
ne m'avez pas fait remettre les forts Picolet et Bélair et toutes les autres batteries de la
côte, demain à pointe de jour, quinze mille hommes seront débarqués. Quatre mille
débarquent en ce moment au Fort-Liberté; huit mille au Port-Républicain; vous trou-
verez ci-jointe ma proclamation; elle exprime les intentions du gouvernement français;
mais rappelez-vous que quelque estime particulière que votre conduite dans la colonie
m'ait inspiré, je vous rends responsable de tout ce qui arrivera.

Le général en chef de l'armée de St-Domingue, et capitaine-général de la colonie.

Signé: LECLERC[4]

---

[2] Nemours, p. 31.

[3] Antoine Métral, *Histoire de l'Expédition des Français à Saint-Domingue* (Paris: Éditions Karthala, 1985), p. 230.

[4] Thomas Madiou, *Histoire d'Haïti* (Port-au-Prince: Éditions Henri Deschamps, 1989), vol. II, p. 171.

Le premier consul aux habitants de Saint-Domingue

Quelles que soient votre origine et votre couleur, vous êtes tous libres et égaux devant Dieu et devant les hommes.

La France a été, comme Saint-Domingue, en proie des factions et déchirée par la guerre civile et par la guerre étrangère; mais tout a changé: tous les peuples ont embrassé les Français, et leur ont juré la paix et l'amitié; tous les Français se sont embrassés aussi, et ont juré d'être tous des amis et des frères; venez aussi embrasser les Français, et vous réjouir de revoir vos amis et vos frères d'Europe.

Le gouvernement vous envoie le capitaine général Leclerc, il amène avec lui de grandes forces pour vous protéger contre vos ennemis et les ennemies de la République. Si l'on vous dit: Ces forces sont destinées à vous ravir la liberté, répondez, La République ne souffrira qu'elle nous soit enlevée.

Ralliez-vous autour du capitaine général; il vous apporte l'abondance et la paix; ralliez-vous autour de lui. Qui osera se séparer du capitaine général sera un traître à la patrie, et la colère de la République le dévorera comme le feu dévore vos cannes desséchées.

Donné à Paris, au palais du gouvernement, le 17 brumaire an 10 de la République française.

Le premier consul,
Signé Bonaparte[5]

Au quartier général du Cap, le 13 Pluviôse an 10.
Henri Christophe, général de brigade commandant l'arrondissement du Cap au général en chef LECLERC.

Votre aide-de-camp, général, m'a remis votre lettre de ce jour. J'ai eu l'honneur de vous faire savoir que je ne pouvais pas vous livrer les forts et la place confiés à mon commandement qu'au préalablement j'ai reçu les ordres du gouverneur Toussaint Louverture, mon chef immédiat, de qui je tiens les pouvoirs dont je suis revêtu. Je veux bien croire que j'ai affaire à des Français, et que vous êtes le chef de l'armée appelée expéditionnaire, mais j'attends les ordres du gouverneur, à qui j'ai dépêché un de mes aides-de-camp, pour lui annoncer votre arrivée et celle de l'armée française; et jusqu'à ce que sa réponse me soit parvenue, je ne puis vous permettre de débarquer. Si vous avez la force dont vous me menacez, je vous prêterai toute la résistance qui caractérise un général; et si le sort des armes vous est favorable, vous n'entrerez dans la ville du Cap que lorsqu'elle sera réduite en cendres, et même dans cet endroit, je vous combattrai encore.[6]

[5] Madiou, vol. II, p. 173.
[6] Madiou, vol. II, p. 172.

FROM CHAPTER 8, PAGE 128

N'oubliez pas qu'en attendant la saison des pluies, qui doit nous débarrasser de nos ennemis, nous n'avons pour ressource que la destruction et le feu. Songez qu'il ne faut pas que la terre baignée de nos sueurs puisse fournir à nos ennemis le moindre aliment. Carabinez les chemins, faites jeter des cadavres et des chevaux dans tous les sources; faites tout anéantir et tout brûler, pour que ceux qui viennent nous remettre en esclavage rencontrent toujours devant eux l'image de l'enfer qu'ils méritent.[7]

FROM FRANCE, PORT DE JOUX OCTOBER 1802, PAGE 163

Voici mon opinion sur ce pays. Il faut détruire tous les nègres des montagnes, hommes et femmes, ne garder que les enfants au-dessous de 12 ans, détruire moitié de ceux de la plaine et ne pas laisser dans la colonie un seul homme de couleur qui ait porté l'épaulette. Sans cela jamais la colonie ne sera tranquille et au commencement de chaque année, surtout après les saisons meurtrières comme celle-ci, vous aurez une guerre civile qui compromettra la possession du pays.[8]

FROM CHAPTER 15, PAGES 223–5

Au citoyen Toussaint Louverture, général en chef de l'armée de Saint Domingue.
Citoyen Général,
    La paix avec l'Angleterre et toutes les puissances de l'Europe qui vient d'asseoir la République au premier degré de puissance et de grandeur, met à même temps le gouvernement de s'occuper de la colonie de Saint-Domingue. Nous y envoyons le citoyen général Leclerc, notre beau-frère, en qualité de capitaine-général comme premier magistrat de la colonie. Il est accompagné de forces convenables pour faire respecter la souveraineté du peuple français. C'est dans ces circonstances que nous nous plaisons à espérer que vous allez nous prouver, et à la France entière, la sincérité des sentiments que vous avez constamment exprimés dans tous les lettres que vous nous avez écrites. Nous avons conçu pour vous de l'estime, et nous nous plaisons à reconnaître et à proclamer les grands services que vous avez rendus au peuple français; si son pavillon flotte sur St-Domingue, c'est à vous et aux braves noirs qu'il le doit.
    Appelé par vos talents et la force des circonstances au premier commandement, vous avez détruit la guerre civile, mis un frein à la persécution de quelques hommes féroces, remis en honneur la religion et le culte de Dieu de qui tout émane.
    La constitution que vous avez faite, en renfermant beaucoup de bonnes choses, en contient qui sont contraires à la souveraineté du peuple français. Les circonstances où vous vous êtes trouvé, environné de tous côtés d'ennemis, sans que la Métropole puisse ni vous secourir, ni vous alimenter, ont rendu légitimes les articles de cette con-

[7] Pierre Pluchon, *Toussaint Louverture* (Paris: Fayard, 1989), p. 481.
[8] Paul Roussier, ed., *Lettres du Général Leclerc* (Paris: Société de l'Histoire des Colonies Françaises et Librairie Ernest Leroux, 1937), p. 256.

stitution qui pourraient ne pas l'être; mais aujourd'hui que les circonstances sont si heureusement changées, vous serez le premier à rendre hommage à la souveraineté de la nation qui vous compte au nombre de ses plus illustres citoyens, par les services que vous lui avez rendus, et par les talents et la force de caractère dont la nature vous a doué. Une conduite contraire serait inconciliable avec l'idée que nous avons conçue de vous. Elle vous ferait perdre vos droits nombreux à la reconnaissance de la République, et creuserait sous vos pas un précipice qui en vous engloutissant, pourrait contribuer au malheur de ces braves noirs dont nous aimons le courage, et dont nous nous verrions avec peine obligés de punir la rebellion. Nous avons fait connaître à vos enfants et à leur précepteur les sentiments qui nous animaient, et nous vous les renvoyons. Assistez de vos conseils, de votre influence et de vos talents le capitaine-général. Que pouvez vous désirer? La liberté des noirs? Vous savez que nous dans tous les pays où nous avons été, nous l'avons donné aux peuples que ne l'avaient pas. De la considération, des honneurs, de la fortune! Ce n'est pas après les services que vous avez rendus, que vous rendrez encore dans cette circontance, avec les sentiments particuliers que nous avons pour vous, que vous devez être incertain sur votre considération, votre fortune et les honneurs qui vous attendent.

Faites connaître aux peuples de St-Domingue que la sollicitude que la France a toujours portée à leur bonheur a été souvent impuissante par les circonstances impérieuses de la guerre; que les hommes venus du continent pour l'agiter et alimenter les factions était le produit des factions qui elles-mêmes déchiraient la patrie; que désormais la paix et la force du gouvernement assurent leur prospérité et leur liberté. Dites que si la liberté est pour eux le premier des biens, ils ne peuvent en jouir qu'avec le titre de citoyens français, et que tout acte contraire aux intérêts de la patrie, à l'obéissance qu'ils doivent au gouvernement et au capitaine-général qui en est le délégué, serait un crime contre la souveraineté nationale qu'éclipserait leurs services et rendrait Saint-Domingue le théâtre d'une guerre malheureuse où des pères et des enfants s'entregorgeraient. Et vous, général, songez que si vous êtes le premier de votre couleur qui soit arrivé à une si grande puissance et qui se soit distingué par sa bravoure et ses talents militaires, vous êtes aussi devant Dieu et nous le principal responsable de leur conduite.

S'il était des malveillants qui disent aux individus qui ont joué le premier rôle dans les troubles de Saint-Domingue, que nous venons pour rechercher ce qu'ils ont fait dans des temps d'anarchie, assurez les que nous ne nous informerons que de leur conduite dans cette dernière circonstance, et que nous ne rechercherons le passé que pour connaître les traits qui les auraient distingués dans la guerre qu'ils ont soutenue contre les Espagnols et les Anglais qui ont été nos ennemis.

Comptez sans reserve dans notre estime, et conduisez-vous comme doit le faire un des principaux citoyens de la plus grande nation du monde.

Paris, le 27 Brumaire an 10 (18 novembre 1801)
Le Premier Consul (signé) BONAPARTE[9]

---

[9] Madiou, vol. II, pp. 209ff.

FROM CHAPTER 15, PAGE 230

Il déclarait que ces droits lui imposaient des devoirs au-dessus de ceux de la nature; qu'il était prêt à faire à sa couleur le sacrifice de ses enfants; qu'il les renvoyait pour qu'on ne le crût pas lié par leur présence. Il finissait par dire que, plus défiant que jamais, il lui fallait du temps pour se décider au parti qui lui restait à prendre.[10]

FROM CHAPTER 15, PAGE 238

Les Blancs de France et de la colonie réunis ensemble veulent ôter la liberté . . . Méfiez-vous des Blancs, ils vous trahiront s'ils le peuvent. Leur désire bien manifeste est le retour à l'esclavage. . . . Je donne l'ordre au général Laplume de brûler la ville des Cayes et les autres villes, et toutes les plaines, dans le cas qu'il ne pourrait pas résister à la force de l'ennemi.[11]

FROM CHAPTER 17, PAGES 255–6

*Au quartier général du Cap, le 28 Pluviôse
an X (17 fevrier, 1802)*

HABITANTS DE SAINT-DOMINGUE,

Le général Toussaint m'avait renvoyé ses enfants, avec une lettre dans laquelle il assurait qu'il était prêt d'obéir à tous les ordres que je lui donnerais. Je lui ai ordonné de se rendre auprès de moi, je lui ai donné ma parole de l'employer comme mon lieutenant général. Il n'a répondu à cet ordre que par des phrases, il ne cherche qu'à gagner du temps. J'entre en campagne et je vais apprendre à ce rebelle quelle est la force du gouvernement français. Dès ce moment il ne doit plus être aux yeux de tous les bons Français qu'un monstre insensé.

J'ai promis aux habitants de Saint Domingue de la liberté, je saurai les en fair jouir. J'ordonne ce qui suit:

ARTICLE PREMIER.—Le général Toussaint et le général Christophe sont mis hors la loi; il est ordonné à tout citoyen de leur courir sus. . . .

ARTICLE 3—Les cultivateurs qui one été induits en erreur et qui auraient pris les armes seront traités comme des enfants égarés et renvoyés à la culture.

ARTICLE 4—Les soldats qui abandonneront l'armée de Toussaint feront partie de l'armée française . . .[12]

[10] Général Pamphile de Lacroix, *La Révolution d'Haïti* (Paris: Editions Karthala, 1995), p. 313.

[11] Pluchon, p. 481.

[12] Victor Schoelcher, *Vie de Toussaint Louverture* (Paris: Éditions Karthala, 1982), p. 127.

Ministre de Marine au commandant du Fort de Joux
Paris 5 brumaire an X

Je reçois votre lettre de 26 vendémiaire, relative au prisonnier d'Etat, Toussaint-Louverture. Le Premier Consul m'a chargé de vous faire connaître que vous répondez de sa personne sur votre tête. Toussaint Louverture n'a droit à d'autres égards qu'à ceux que commande l'humanité. L'hypocrisie est un vice qui lui est aussi familier que l'honneur et la loyauté vous le sont à vous-même, citoyen commandant. La conduite qu'il a tenue depuis sa détention est faite pour fixer vos opinions sur ce qu'on doit attendre de lui, vous vous êtes aperçu vous-même qu'il cherchait à vous tromper et vous l'avez été effectivement par l'admission près de lui d'un de ses satellites déguisé en médecin.

Vous ne devez pas vous en tenir à la démarche que vous avez faite, pour vous assurer s'il n'a ni argent, ni bijoux. Vous devez faire fouiller partout pour vous en assurer et examiner s'il n'en aura ni caché ni enterré dans sa prison. Retirez-lui sa montre; si son usage lui est agréable, on peut y suppléer en établissant dans sa chambre une de ces horloges de bois, du plus vil prix, qui servent assez pour indiquer le cours du temps. S'il est malade, l'officier de santé le plus connu de vous, doit seul lui donner des soins et le voir; mais seulement quand il est nécessaire et en votre présence, et avec les précautions les plus grandes pour que ces visites ne sortent sous aucun rapport du cercle de ce qui est indispensable.

Le seule moyen qu'aurait eu Toussaint de voir son sort amélioré eût été de déposer sa dissimulation. Son intérêt personnel, les sentiments religieux dont il devrait être pénétré pour expier tout le mal qu'il a fait, lui imposaient le devoir de la vérité; mais il est bien éloigné de le remplir et par sa dissimulation continuelle il appro che ceux qui l'approchent de tout intérêt sur son sort. Vous pouvez lui dire d'être tranquil sur le sort de sa famille, son existence est commise à mes soins et rien ne lui manque.

Je présume que vous avez éloigné de lui tout ce qui peut avoir quelque rapport avec un uniforme. Toussaint est son nom, c'est la seule dénomination qui doit lui être donnée. Un habillement chaud, gris ou brun, très large et commode, et un chapeau rond, doivent être son vêtement. Quand il se vante d'avoir été général, il ne faut que rappeler ses crimes, sa conduite hideuse et sa tyrannie sur les Européens. Il ne mérite alors que le plus profond mépris pour son orgueil ridicule.

Je vous salue.[13]

Rien n'est plus fort que l'humiliation que j'ai reçue de vous aujourd'hui. Vous m'avez dépouillé de fond en comble pour me fouiller et voir si je n'avais pas de l'argent, vous avez enfin tout bouleversé, tout mon linge et fouillé jusque dans ma paillasse.

[13] Schoelcher, p. 352.

Heureusement que vous n'avez rien trouvé: les dix quadruples que je vous ai remis sont à moi, et c'est moi qui vous l'ai déclaré. Vous m'avez ôté ma montre et quinze et sept sols que j'avez dans la poche, vous m'avez pris jusqu'à mon éperon; je vous préviens que tous les objets sont à moi, et vous devez m'en tenir compte le jour qu'on m'enverra au supplice. Vous remettrez le tout à mon épouse et à mes enfants; quand un homme est déjà malheureux on ne doit pas chercher à l'humilier et vexer sans humanité ni la charité, sans aucune considération pour lui comme un serviteur de la République, et on a pris toutes les précautions et les machinations contre moi comme si j'étais un grand criminel. Je vous ai déjà dit, et je vous le répète encore, je suis honnête homme et si je n'avais pas l'honneur, je n'aurais pas servi ma patrie fidèlement comme je l'ai servie, et je serais pas non plus ici par ordre de mon gouvernement. Je vous salue.[14]

FROM FORT DE JOUX, FRANCE, MARCH 1803, PAGE 502

28 janvier: Toussaint souffre de douleurs dans différentes parties du corps qu'accompagnent deux petits accès de fièvre. Il a une toux très sèche.

9 février: Louverture, dont la santé s'était améliorée pendant quelques jours, se plaint de l'estomac et ne mange pas comme à son ordinaire.

19 février: le prisonnier a été pris plusieurs fois de vomissements que l'on soulage. Cependant, il a la figure enflée.

4 mars: le détenu est toujours dans la même état d'indisposition. Il a la figure enflée, se plaint sans cesse de maux d'estomac, et a une toux très forte.

19 mars: La situation de Toussaint est toujours la même. Il se plaint continuellement des douleurs de l'estomac et a une toux continuelle. Il tient son bras gauche en écharpe depuis quelques jours pour cause de douleurs. Je m'aperçois depuis trois jours que sa voix est bien changée. Il ne m'a jamais demandé de médecin.[15]

FROM FORT DE JOUX, FRANCE, MARCH 1803, PAGES 502–3

. . . il devait être enchaîné vivant à un poteau, exposé dans une voierie, pour que les corbeaux et les vautours, chargés de la vengeance des colons, vinssent dévorer chaque jour non pas le coeur, car il n'en eut jamais, mais le foie renaissant de ce nouveaux Promothée.[16]

FROM CHAPTER 32, PAGE 528

Vous êtes un officier de marine, Monsieur, eh bien! si vous commandiez un vais-seaude l'Etat, et que, sans vous donner avis, un autre officier vînt vous remplacer à

[14] Pluchon, p. 533.
[15] Pluchon, p. 535.
[16] Pluchon, p. 538.

l'abordage par le gaillard d'avant, avec un équipage double du vôtre, pourriez-vous être blamé de chercher à vous defendre sur le gaillard de l'arrière?[17]

FROM CHAPTER 32, PAGE 528

Le droit des gens, qui les met à l'abri de toute arrestation, ne me donne pas celui de les considérer comme prisonniers. Je désire que vous agissiez de même à l'égard de mon neveu et aide-de-camp, le chef de bataillon Chancy, qui est au Port-au-Prince.[18]

FROM CHAPTER 32, PAGE 533

Vous me proposez, citoyen général, de vous fournir les moyens de vous assurer du général Toussaint: ce serait de ma part une perfidie, une trahison, et cette proposition, dégradante pour moi, est à mes yeux une marque de l'invincible répugnance que vous éprouvez à me croire [in]susceptible des moindres sentiments de délicatesse et d'honneur. Il est mon chef et mon ami. L'amitié, citoyen général, est-elle compatible avec une aussi monstrueuse lâcheté?[19]

FROM CHAPTER 34, PAGE 557

Au Quartier Général de la Crête à Pierrot, le 4 Germinal (25 mars 1802)
    Le Général en Chef au Premier Consul

  Citoyen Consul,

J'ai l'honneur de vous envoyer mon frère qui vous rendra un compte exact de ma situation à Saint Domingue. J'ai fait une des campagnes les plus pénibles qu'il soit possible à faire et c'est à la rapidité de mon mouvement que je dois la position dans laquelle je me trouve.

  Je suis un peu indisposé par la fatigue. Quand j'aurai rétabli l'ordre ici, je vous demanderai à rentrer en France, car ma santé est bien altérée.

  Agréez l'assurance de mon repectueux attachement, Citoyen Consul.

LECLERC[20]

---

[17] Saint-Rémy, *Mémoires du Général Toussaint Louverture, Écrits par Lui-Même, Pouvant Sevir à l'Histoire de Sa Vie* (Paris: Libraire-éditeur, 1859), p. 64.

[18] Métral, p. 263.

[19] Madiou, vol. II, p. 300.

[20] Roussier, p. 116.

FROM CHAPTER 34, PAGE 566

Au Quartier Général au Port-au-Prince, le 11 Germinal (1er Avril 1802)

Le Général en Chef au Ministre de la Marine et des Colonies.

   Citoyen Ministre,

Immédiatement après la prise de la Crête à Pierrot, j'ai fait un détachement sur le Mirebalais, que j'occupais faiblement. J'ai coupé la retraite à l'ennemi sur les Grands Bois. Le détachement de cent cinquante hommes que j'y avais a été culbuté par Dessalines. Ce poste s'était reployé sur Trianon, qu'il avait conservé. L'arrivée de quatre cents hommes de la 56e légère, que j'ai envoyés, en a débusqué Dessalines, qui nous a cédé le Mirebalais et s'est rejeté sur les Cahos. Je vais établir un fortin sur ce point qui est un des plus importants de la colonie.

J'ai fait remettre en état la Crête à Pierrot. Je la fais approvisionner pour cent cinquante hommes. Ce point me gardera la plaine de l'Artibonite et le débouché des Cahos.

Le général Hardy en s'en allant dans le nord aura nécessairement rencontré et battu le général Toussaint. Ce qui vous fera juger la position difficile dans laquelle se trouve ce général, c'est que lors du débarquement du général Boudet au Port Républicain, ce général avait envoyé un de ses aides de camp et un officier de marine porter une lettre au commandant de cette place pour l'engager à lui rendre la place.

Ces deux officiers ont été arrêtés comme prisonniers et depuis emmenés par les rebelles. Vingt fois ils ont étés menacés de la mort. Ils ont été témoins de tous les massacres qui ont été faits et, le huit, le général Toussaint les a fait venir. Après avoir beaucoup parlé avec le citoyen Sabès, aide-de-camp du général Boudet, en se plaignant de l'ingratitude du Goveurnement français à son égard et des mesures que j'avais prises, qui avait dévasté la colonie, le général Toussaint lui a dit que, si je voulais, on pouvait avant deux ans rétablir toute la colonie. Ensuite il l'a chargé de remettre une lettre au général Boudet et une autre adressée au général Bonaparte.

Dans la lettre au général Boudet, il se plaint amèrement de la conduite que j'ai tenue à son égard. Dans celle au Premier Consul, il m'accuse d'être l'auteur de tous les maux de la colonie et proteste de son obéissance à la République, si on veut lui envoyer un autre homme que moi. Cette démarche de sa part me donne le secret de sa faiblesse. J'ai ordonné au général Boudet de lui renvoyer un de ces neveux, qui est son aide de camp, que avait été pris portant ses dépêches. Je lui ai ordonné de lui écrire une lettre assez vague, qui le mît à même de faire des ouvertures, s'il avait envie de se rendre; quoiqu'il n'aie sous ses ordres en tout plus de deux mille deux cents soldats, non compris deux milliers de cultivateurs, il peut encore nous faire beaucoup de mal. En conséquence je suis disposé à faire des sacrifices pour m'en débarrasser.

Toussaint n'est point un homme ordinaire. Il a de la force de caractère et la tête large. Et s'il eût été comme nous témoin des événements qui se sont passés en Europe depuis dix ans, s'il n'eût pas été gâté par les succès qu'il a obtenus sur les Anglais et qu'il eût eu une idée de la puissance de la France, ce pays était perdu pour nous sans retour.

Envoyez-moi promptement les forces que je vous ai demandées.
J'ai l'honneur de vous saluer.

LECLERC[21]

FROM CHAPTER 34, PAGE 567

. . . Je vais m'occuper de remettre un peu d'ordre ici; car jusqu'à présent nous avons marché dans le cahos et au milieu de décombres. . . .[22]

FROM CHAPTER 36, PAGE 606

. . . quelles que fût les ressources de l'armée française, il serait toujours assez fort et assez puissant, pour brûler, ravager, et vendre chèrement une vie qui avait aussi été quelquefois utile à la mère patrie.[23]

FROM CHAPTER 38, PAGE 631

Je vois avec plaisir, citoyen général, le parti que vous prenez de vous soumettre aux armes de la République. Ceux qui ont cherché à vous tromper sur les véritables intentions du gouvernement français sont bien coupables. Aujourd'hui, il ne faut plus nous occuper à revoir les maux passés. Je ne m'occupe que des moyens de rendre, le plus promptement possible, la colonie à son ancienne splendeur. Vous, les généraux et les troupes sous vos ordres, ainsi que les habitants de cette colonie, ne craignez point que je recherche personne sur sa conduite passée. Je jette la voile de l'oubli sur tout ce qui a eu lieu à St-Domingue avant mon arrivée. J'imite en cela l'exemple que le Premier Consul a donné à la France, après le 18 Brumaire.

Tout ceux que sont ici ont une nouvelle carrière à parcourir, et à l'avenir je ne connaîtrai que de bons et de mauvais citoyens. Vos généraux et vos troupes seront employés et traités come le reste de mon armée. Quant à vous, vous désirez du repos; le repos vous est dû; quand on a supporté pendant plusieurs années, le gouvernement de Saint Domingue, je conçois qu'on en ait besoin. Je vous laisse maître de vous retirer sur celles de vos habitations qui vous conviendra le mieux. Je compte assez sur l'attachement que vous portez à la colonie de St-Domingue, pour croire que vous emploierez les moments de loisir que vous aurez dans votre retraite, à me communiquer vos vues sur les moyens propres à faire refleurir dans ce pays, le commerce et l'agriculture.

Aussitôt que l'état de situation des troupes aux ordres du général Dessalines me sera parvenu, je ferai connaître mes intentions sur la position qu'elles doivent occuper.

---

[21] Roussier, p. 118.
[22] Roussier, p. 126.
[23] Madiou, vol. II, p. 303.

Vous trouverez à la suite de cette lettre l'arrêté que j'ai pris pour détruire les disposi-tions de celle du 23 Pluviôse (17 février) qui vous était personnel.

(Signé) LECLERC[24]

FROM CHAPTER 39, PAGE 664

Au Quartier Louverture, an 10

Vous ne me donnez pas des nouvelles, citoyen. Tâchez de rester au Cap, le plus longtemps que vous pourrez. On dit la santé du général Leclerc mauvaise, à la Tortue, donc il faut avoir grand soin de m'instruire. Il faudrait voir pour des a . . . de la Nou-velle. Quant à la farine dont il en faudrait comme de cette dernière, on ne l'enverrait pas sans avoir passé à la Saône, pour connaître le point où on pourrait en sûreté les mettre.

Si vous voyez le général en chef, dites-lui que les cultivateurs ne veulent plus m'obéïr, on voudrait faire travailler à Héricourt, dont le gérant ne doit pas le faire. Je vous demand si on peut gagner quelqu'un près du général en chef, afin de rendre D . . . libre. Il me serait bien utile à la Nouvelle, par son crédit et ailleurs. Faites dire à Gengembre qu'il ne doit pas quitter le Borgne, où il ne faut pas que les cultivateurs tra-vaillent. Ecrivez-moi à l'habitation Najac.

(Signé) TOUSSAINT LOUVERTURE[25]

FROM FORT DE JOUX, FRANCE, APRIL 1803, PAGE 695

Un peu de mucus mêlé de sang dans la bouche et sur les lèvres. Le sinus latéral gauche, les vaisseaux de la pie-mère gorgés du sang; épanchement sérieux dans la ven-tricule latérale, même côté. Le plexus choroïde infiltré et parsemé de petites hydatides. La plèvre adhérente en grande partie à la substance des poumons. Engorgement san-guin du poumon droit, de la plèvre y correspondant. Amas de matière purulente dans ce viscère. Un petit polype graisseux dans ventricule droit du coeur qui, au reste, était dans son état normal. Amaigrissement de l'épiploon, état pathologique de cette mem-brane pareil à ce qui se rencontre après une longue maladie.

L'estomac, les intestins, le foie, la rate, les reins, la vessie n'ont offert aucune altération.

En conséquence, nous estimons que l'apoplexie, la pleuropéripneumonie sont les causes de mort de Toussaint Louverture.[26]

Un habit de calmouk rayé mi-usé, après plusiers criées, a été adjugé pour neuf francs au conseiller Faivre, libraire à Pontarlier. . . . Six mouchoirs bleus quadrillésad-jugés après plusieurs criées au citoyen Jenat, marchand de Pontarlier, pour neuf francs.[27]

[24] Madiou, vol. II, p. 305.
[25] Madiou, vol. II, p. 324.
[26] Pluchon, p. 536.
[27] Nemours, p. 275.

Une boucle de col en or, une montre à boîte d'or unie qu'accompagnaient une chaîne et une clé imitant l'or assez parfaitement, une paire d'éperons d'argent, un mauvais uniforme, garni d'un léger galon, à boutons de cuivre jaune, et deux épaulettes à gros grain au dessous à frange, un chapeau usé galonné d'or et un étui avec un rasoir.[28]

Au château de Joux, ce 19 germinal an XI (9 avril 1803) de la République française.

Amiot, chef de bataillon, commandant d'armes, au citoyen Ministre de la Marine et des Colonies.

Citoyen Ministre,

J'ai eu l'honneur de vous rendre compte par ma lettre de 16 germinal de la situation de Toussaint. Le dix-sept à onze heures et demi du matin lui portant des vivres, je l'ai trouvé mort assis dans une chaise auprès de son feu. Vous trouverez ci-joint, Citoyen Ministre, les formalités que j'ai cru devoir prendre à son égard. J'ai fait partir un courier extraordinaire qui a devancé la poste pour annoncer sa mort au général en chef commandant la 6e division militaire. Je l'ai fait enterré par un prêtre de la commune dans le cavet sous l'ancienne chapelle côté au fort de Joux où autrefois on enterrait les militaires de la garnison.

J'ai cru en prenant ces précautions remplir les voeux du Gouvernement.

Salut et Respect
SIGNÉ: Amiot[29]

[28] Pluchon, p. 536.
[29] Nemours, p. 270.

PERMISSIONS ACKNOWLEDGMENTS

Grateful acknowledgment is made to the following for permission to reprint previously published material:

Mimerose Beaubrun: "Ogou o Wa De Zanj" by Mimerose Beaubrun. Copyright © 1998 by Mimerose Beaubrun. Reprinted by permission of the author.

Elizabeth McAlister: "Rara La Belle Fraicheur de l'Anglade" from *Rara! Vodou, Power, and Performance in Haiti and Its Diaspora* by Elizabeth McAlister (Berkeley and Los Angeles, CA, 2002). Reprinted by permission of the author.

ALSO BY MADISON SMARTT BELL

ALL SOULS' RISING

In this first installment of his epic Haitian trilogy, Madison Smartt Bell brings to life a decisive moment in the history of race, class, and colonialism. The slave uprising in Haiti was a momentous contribution to the tide of revolution that swept over the Western world at the end of the 1700s. A brutal rebellion that strove to overturn a vicious system of slavery, the uprising successfully transformed Haiti from a European colony to the world's first Black republic. From the center of this horrific maelstrom, the heroic figure of Toussaint Louverture—a loyal, literate slave and both a devout Catholic and Vodouisant—emerges as the man who will take the merciless fires of violence and vengeance and forge a revolutionary war fueled by liberty and equality.

Fiction/1-4000-7653-6

MASTER OF THE CROSSROADS

Continuing the trilogy of the Haitian slave uprising, *Master of the Crossroads* delivers a stunning portrayal of Toussaint Louverture, former slave, military genius, and liberator of Haiti, and his struggle against the great European powers to free his people in the only successful slave revolution in history. At the outset, Toussaint is a second-tier general in the Spanish army, which is supporting the rebel slaves' fight against the French. But when Toussaint is betrayed by his former allies and the commanders of the Spanish army, he reunites his army with the French, wresting vital territories and manpower from Spanish control. With his army one among several coalitions, Toussaint eventually rises as the ultimate victor as he wards off his enemies to take control of the French colony and establish a new constitution.

Fiction/1-4000-7838-5

VINTAGE BOOKS
Available at your local bookstore, or call toll-free to order:
1-800-793-2665 (credit cards only).